The Untethered

S.W. Southwick

The Untethered
S.W. Southwick

Roble Arrow Publishing Ink
RobleArrowInk@gmail.com
First printing, February 2017.

Part 1:
Jet Black Eyes

Chapter 1

"The density times the material derivative is equal to…" Roble Santos mouthed as he read the book slumped across his lap.

A newspaper across the aisle stole his attention and he glanced up.

Two large hands held the paper amid a row of US Airmen. Half the uniformed men and women looked asleep; the other half dazed from the constant droning inside the windowless aircraft.

What is that? Roble leaned forward, pushing against his shoulder restraints, peering at the photo of a jet on the newspaper. *Its shape is so…* He frowned. *It's probably just concept art from a movie or something.*

He sat back, dropping his eyes to his coverless textbook, feeling the airplane vibrate his calloused hands. He tried to concentrate on the Navier-Stokes equation, but it was impossible with that jet's image prostituting itself across the aisle.

Closing the book and wedging it between his seat and his neighbor's, he unhooked his restraints and dropped to his knees. At eye level with the paper, he pushed back his hair and studied the image.

The jet's gloss-black fuselage splayed across the page in front of him. Its slender nosecone began a gracious line that followed under a long neck. The line continued back until it met two sensually curved air intakes that stretched into lengthy engine encasements. The jet's tail arched subtly upward then thrust vertically into a soaring fin with horizontal winglets. Its swept-back wings flared thick and muscled at their bases but tapered out into dainty tips. Along its top, a sleek, clear canopy extended almost from nose to tailfin, revealing just a hint of the cockpit inside.

Roble's chest expanded. *That's the sexiest jet I've ever seen.*

The image sank toward the aircraft's floor. He followed it down.

"Can I help you, Airman?" a hard voice said in his ear.

Roble looked up, surprised to be kneeling on the floor and even more so to be staring at the sergeant holding the paper. Several airmen seated nearby laughed.

The sergeant shook his head, frowning.

"May I read your paper when you're finished?" Roble asked.

He dropped it on Roble. "Put your damn restraints back on."

Paper in hand, Roble sat back in his seat, fastened his restraints, and read the headline below the picture: *Supersonic, but at what cost?* His eyes returned to the image.

"That Patra chick, she's hot." A young airman sitting next to Roble jabbed his finger into the side of the newspaper, his chapped lips cracking a smile.

Roble ignored the comment, focusing on the photo of the jet.

"Did you catch her wearing that swimsuit in *Sportsman Quarterly*'s charity edition?" the airman asked. "Now *that's* how you raise money for a good cause. I even read the article, at least the highlighted parts."

Why haven't I seen this jet before? Roble began to read the editorial.

His talkative neighbor slapped his shoulder. "Can you believe she's in charge of saving Nevada's homeless kids? Plus, she's like the commander of her own charity. And get this—they want her to run for governor. Look at her," he said, gawking at the newspaper. "That's the complete package—uh, what's your name?"

"Roble."

"That's the complete package, Ronald. I don't care if she's thirty-five; I'm looking her up when we land."

Roble folded down the top of the paper and gazed at Ms. Patra's picture. *Alexandria Patra Taking Nevada's Public/Private Partnership National* splashed across the page above her. He stared at her smiling lips and frowning eyes. *She was unusual. And what a day that had been. How long ago was that?* He rubbed his chin.

Almost six years ago…

State truancy officers had captured him a few days after running away from the Sands family. Taken to Ms. Patra's state office building, Roble sat in a chair leaning against her secretary's desk, passing the time by watching a truancy officer munch potato chips and sip a soda the size of his head. The building smelled like the last middle school he'd been forced to attend— the scent of fresh vomit covered with janitorial cat litter. Luckily, they'd expelled him.

"She's ready for you," the secretary said. The truancy officer gestured at Ms. Patra's door with his soda. Roble rose, took one final glance at the potato chip shrapnel littering the floor, and entered the office.

Alexandria Patra stood behind her desk, poised like an Egyptian queen. She wore a crisp white blouse and long black skirt, a silver wrist cuff her only adornment. Her toughness looked honest, and he liked the thought of trusting an adult for the first time.

Yet the longer he stared, the gentler and more accepting her pose became. At first, he thought her hair appeared straight but he was mistaken—it coiled into supple black curls. Her eyes looked like impenetrable black onyx, but they softened as he approached. Her kind veneer forced him to raise his guard, knowing from experience it must hold an unknown danger. Even so, her appearance intrigued him.

Ms. Patra sat down and motioned for Roble to follow her example.

He obeyed, before bolting back up, frowning at his response to her command.

She watched him without speaking.

Roble paced the room, its single window unable to offset the harsh fluorescent lighting. Awards from politicians, CEOs, and private foundations covered three walls, along with dozens of photos that displayed Ms. Patra standing among groups of smiling children.

Two framed posters hung on the wall opposite the desk. Roble stopped before them.

One pictured a group of people, their arms interlocked at the elbows, staring down into the center of a circle. Their smiling faces appeared convinced and complacent. The word *Unity* was written at the center. The other poster displayed a barren mountain peak with the word *Sacrifice* printed below.

Roble gazed back and forth between the two posters, then at Ms. Patra. *Uh-huh*.

"Hey." The chapped-lipped airman snapped his fingers, laughing.

Roble looked up from Ms. Patra's picture in the paper.

"Don't stare too long or you'll go blind. Plus, I already called dibs."

Roble felt the aircraft climbing, the engines vibrating his hands.

"Ever been to Vegas?" the airman grinned.

"Born...and raised," Roble said, glancing back at Ms. Patra's grainy picture.

Alexandria Patra, balancing on high heels, took a step down the boarding ramp in line with the prospective passengers. "Hello, Preton," she said, the phone to her ear.

"Where are you?" Preton Moore asked, his voice exuberant.

"Still in Vegas, at McCarran."

"Well congratulations, my dear. I'm sorry I was out of town, but you pulled off quite a launch."

"Thank you, but it's not my victory." She switched the phone to her other ear. "It's the children's."

"Simply remarkable. Have you looked online? The president and six governors have already endorsed your partnership."

Alexandria exhaled. "Please don't try to flatter me. When—" Alexandria lowered the phone and held it against her tailored suit as a young girl with red hair whirled by. She turned cartwheels down the ramp, her untied shoelaces whipping like tassels in front of embarking passengers. Alexandria glimpsed a smile as she spun away.

A bony-shouldered woman with thick blue eyeliner ran after and caught the young acrobat by the arm. She dragged the girl back up the pathway, offering apologetic looks to everyone she passed. Beneath the captured girl's freckled scowl shined an unmistakable spark of satisfaction.

Alexandria turned away from the girl's gaze, feeling an unwanted sense of loss which tightened her empty stomach. She waited a moment before peeking up the ramp. The bobbing red hair disappeared into the crowd.

Hearing the distant squawking of Nevada's lieutenant

governor, Alexandria raised the phone to her ear. "Preton, my flight is leaving. I'll call you from DC."

Jet fumes and cheery-faced attendants greeted Alexandria as she queued into the hissing aluminum tube. Slipping between passengers, she plopped into her seat by the window. She felt relieved and a bit guilty to be tucked away out of the limelight.

A flight attendant reached out, lowered Alexandria's food tray, and set down a newspaper and a plastic flute with champagne. "Congratulations, Ms. Patra," she said.

Alexandria pressed her lips into a smile. *Is this what success feels like?* The numerous congratulations she'd heard today blared like car horns in her mind. *It must be.* She yanked the newspaper from the tray, hiding it in her lap. *I'm doing all the right things.*

Lifting the champagne to her lips, she sank the liquid in one smooth swallow, then closed her eyes, trying to feel some semblance of happiness. The cartwheeling girl's smiling face spun across her mind, and she cringed.

"We are sorry for the inconvenience," the loudspeaker said, *"but this flight is delayed due to inclement weather at our destination. We hope to have an update within half an hour."*

Alexandria moaned, rubbing her forehead. *I don't have time for this.* She thought about all the traveling she would be doing. *There has to be a more efficient way to travel.*

Two hours later, she peered out the oval window at the distant vein of a passing canyon.

The newspaper crunched under her elbow, reminding her she hadn't read the article—her article. She picked it up and studied the smiling image below her name, bemused to see herself looking happy. The thought of others seeing her appear happy gave an odd sense of peace, reaching so deep, she shivered. She pulled the blanket higher over her lap.

As long as I'm in charge, no child shall lose her dream.

Her eyes zeroed in on her own quotation sandwiched somewhere within the article, but looked away. She didn't know why she'd misspoken; she'd never said that phrase before. "No child will be lost from the arms of society," had been her quick correction to the reporter, but he obviously hadn't used it.

Of course children *were* lost from her state foster care—becoming runaways, locked up in juvenile detention, or worse. That's why she cofounded the nationally acclaimed charity

Children for Universal Hope, known as the CUH. It promoted group activities that encouraged children to feel comfortable belonging to something greater than themselves, thereby discouraging dangerous antisocial behavior.

With the guidance of Preton Moore, she'd designed the new public/private partnership between Nevada state foster care and the CUH to address finally and fully all the accepted risk factors causing children to fall through the cracks of both programs. She had announced the partnership's launch to great fanfare this morning in downtown Las Vegas.

Alexandria sighed, knowing that even if the public/private partnership became highly successful, some good kids would still be lost without explanation. She hated that reality. At least the children labeled as *high risk* could be explained.

Running a finger around the rim of her champagne flute, she tried to relax, but she knew not every kid could be easily cataloged by the state's accepted risk categories, even though nobody she knew would admit it. She didn't like to admit it herself, but she had the proof. Those painful, unexplained losses sat stuffed inside the bottom drawer of a filing cabinet in her state office.

That drawer haunted her.

She'd heard people retroactively try to diagnose those lost kids with sophisticated-sounding names, but she'd met most of them, and those labels hadn't explained anything. According to the state child-welfare manuals, *that* type of uncharacterized kid shouldn't even exist.

At the rear of that drawer, one dense file, pale blue with red *Delinquency* stamps emblazoned on it in the shape of a launching rocket, troubled her the most. She thought about it often. *How long has it been?* Reading the date on the newspaper, she realized almost six years had passed.

Roble Santos had entered her office wearing a grease-stained jacket plastered with motorcycle and skateboard patches. His straight black hair hung over his ears and forehead, drawing attention to his scarred, ruddy-tanned chin. His body looked thin and wiry, like that of a starving street kid, except his steps held a controlled energy that reminded her of a long-shot racehorse walking to a starting gate.

"Roble," she began with a smile, after he sat down on his second attempt, "it's nice to meet you."

Maintaining eye contact, Roble slid down in his seat, leaning his head against the back of the chair.

"If you would tell me what is going on, I can help."

Roble watched her without blinking. She stared back.

After a moment, he jerked his thumb at the door. "That hungry dude and another guy, who doesn't use deodorant, dragged me from my home."

"You were living in a pirate ship in front of a casino." She lifted her palms.

"No, I wasn't."

"No?"

He sat up. "I was living in the *HMS Dauntless*. The pirate ship sits too close to the tourists and its captain's quarters are actually a pump house."

She locked her fingers together. "What about before you ran away? Would you like to tell me what happened?"

Roble shook his head.

Opening his file, Alexandria glanced at the first page. "You've been through a lot of foster families for a twelve-year-old."

He shrugged.

"My office had hoped the Sands family would click with you. Donald is a well-respected, faith-based youth counselor and he's known as a supportive, athletic-type of father. They have a boy, Danny, your age…and even motorcycles, I hear." She looked at Roble's jacket. "They've hosted many foster children without any issues." Tapping the file, she asked, "So why did you run away?"

Roble lowered his face, bangs shielding his eyes. "You *really* want to know?"

Alexandria's eyes narrowed. She'd heard coworkers describing Roble as an inexplicably hopeless case ever since he was five. She glanced at the bottom filing cabinet drawer. "Roble, I *really* would like to know."

"I don't like what happened to me today." He brushed the hair from his eyes. "So I might sound mean. Everyone always says I'm mean." He rubbed his nose. "And this building stinks."

She caressed the worn cardstock of his file. "Go on. I'm listening."

"The Sands weren't the usual family taking me for the state's money. With that kind, all you gotta do is cost less than they get and they're happy. I figured out how to give all of *them* a big loss so they'd kick me out. I'll pay you back someday, if that's what you want."

Alexandria opened her mouth to speak, but Roble continued without pause. "The Sands also weren't the kind who talked all nice and stuff, trying to bribe me into doing things. With that kind, all you gotta do is what they say and they're happy. I never did, so *those* all kicked me out."

She leaned forward, surprised at the contrast between his gentle voice and his rebellious words.

"But Donald Sands? He was a real true-believing, hands-on type of guy." Roble touched his scarred chin. "He taught me the same lessons as all the blabbers, only he was better at it. I took it for a while, but it got boring." He dropped his hand to his lap. "He wouldn't kick me out like everyone else—so I left."

Oh no. Alexandria stared at his scar and stiffened. *This might explain his behavior.* "Roble, are you saying you were abused?" She opened a drawer and pulled out a multi-layered form. Clicking the back of a pen, she looked up.

He said nothing.

"Roble, I would like for you to explain what happened. Or would you prefer to speak to a counselor?"

"You want names?"

She pressed the pen to the form. "You don't need to be afraid; you will be protected."

"Okay. Write down the Bensons, the Everetts, the Cruisers, the Wards, the Marxes, the Lees, the Villafanas—"

Her thumb released the pen's button. "What are you doing?"

"I'm listing all the parents who should stop teaching kids anything. And don't forget the Costens. You can start with those, but I have more."

"You implied Donald Sands abused you."

"I said Donald was better at teaching the same lessons than all the others." Roble pressed his feet against the top edge of the desk, tilting his chair back.

Alexandria shot to her feet, crossing her arms.

The sudden movement startled Roble, sending his chair flipping backward, his arms flailing in the air for balance. His shoulders hit the floor as his feet followed over the top.

Lying on his stomach, he pressed himself off the floor with his palms, lifting his head to stare at Ms. Patra. A black arrowhead attached to a shoelace around his neck had fallen out from under his shirt.

Alexandria's arms fell to her sides. "Are you all right?"

Roble stood, wobbling on his feet. He tucked the arrowhead under his shirt and glanced behind him at the two large posters, then back at her. He seemed both troubled and impressed.

"If you are uninjured, please take a seat, Mr. Santos." She sat and returned the unused form to the drawer.

He lifted the chair back to its feet and sat down.

"You will *not* bring accusations against my families if you can't provide evidence." She closed the drawer with a gentle push. "And you will *not* lean back in my chair again."

His shoulders straightened.

"Now, let's start again, shall we?" She smoothed out the pages of his open file. "I am well aware that not every family and child is a match, but what they teach you is for *your* benefit."

She flipped a few pages into the public school section of Roble's file. He had never been disciplined for drug use, violence, or stealing, but he'd been expelled from every school he'd ever attended for disobedience and refusal to cooperate with other children. No apparent reason accounted for his behavior beyond plain, purposeful insubordination. *And why had Roble made the effort to get perfect grades in some classes while not lifting a finger in others before being expelled?*

Alexandria looked up, her brows bent. "Roble, you could excel in school if you wanted to. Why not just follow instructions?"

"What for?"

"It's for your—" she stopped. He was sitting up straight, seemingly obedient. "Look, Roble," she said, hand waving at the pictures on the walls, "don't you at least see the benefit in getting along with other boys your age?"

He looked at the pictures and shrugged. "I do stuff with kids I like. I listen to adults when they make sense. Everyone tells me I'm a problem, but I don't see how."

"Roble…" She paused and flipped back to the summary page of his file. "You've burned through eleven families and six schools. You might not like what I'm going to say, but when everyone else—and I mean *everyone*, without exception—says *you* are the problem, you might want to consider the possibility."

"Why should I care what they think?"

She blinked at the question, feeling a flash of pain somewhere deep inside.

"Ms. Patra," he said, gripping the armrests, "I want to be let go."

Alexandria stared at him, the tendons in her neck tensing to stop herself from glancing at the bottom filing cabinet drawer. "You are a child. You can't be let go."

"That's what I want."

She tapped a finger against the desk. "Roble, I'm here to help you."

He dropped his head and let it hang limp.

"Look, I get it. You're young and confused—"

"Half right." He rubbed a motorcycle patch on his arm.

She spread her palms on the desk, trying to remember how she'd been taught to understand as a child, but froze mid-thought, not liking the memory. She flipped distractedly though his file. Leaning over a page, she followed a lengthy description with a finger. He'd been sent to juvenile detention many times for this, but it might be a way to convince him.

"Your host families say you spent a lot of time inventing contraptions, rockets in particular." Alexandria didn't mention his arrests for using dangerous fuels and explosive materials to construct them. "Don't you want to go to college someday and learn to build real rockets?"

Roble lifted his head, eyes widening a bit.

"With the proper guidance, you could accomplish great things for society, but in order to learn you'll need to adapt to the right environments. The first step is to follow the rules at home and at school."

Roble's arm fell off the side of the chair and dangled.

Sweat formed on the nape of Alexandria's neck. "You can't legally work, you have no money for rent or food, by law you must go to school, and you need a loving support group. I can think of a thousand things worse than letting others help you."

"Like what?"

She closed the file and massaged her forehead. *No, I will not lose this one.* She rose to her feet, lifting his file and glanced at all the *Delinquency* stamps. With a flick of her wrist, the file dropped, thumping against the desk.

His arm returned to the armrest.

"I run the CUH." She shot him a cold glance. "Don't look at me that way. I'm not suggesting you enter a group program."

He sat attentive.

"For the last three years, Nancy Tatum, my CUH program director, has hosted a foster son, a physics genius. He reminds me of you in some ways. Nobody thought he could get along with anyone. Well, he just graduated from high school with honors and moved to South America to help homeless children full time."

She leaned over the desk, resting on her fists. "Now, Nancy is looking to host another gifted child. Beyond encouraging her children to excel in their respective fields of interest, she assigns them life goals and instills in them a sense of purpose by having them serve the community."

Alexandria sat down. "Roble, I think this opportunity could save your life." In a lowered voice, she added, "I was fortunate to have parents who raised me in a similar way…" She stared out the window, thinking back.

Regaining her focus, she concluded, "Please consider it carefully. Most kids with your track record would never get a chance to be a part of a family like this."

Roble stared at the blaze of red ink on his file.

"Ms. Patra," he said, their eyes meeting above the file. "I don't want to sound mean, but I don't want anyone to assign me goals or tell me what to do."

Alexandria's shoulders sank.

Lifting her arms, she said, "All right, Roble, I can place you in a monitored boys' home or detention. If you were in my shoes, what would you do?"

"I'd quit."

Her eyes shot to the posters of the mountain and the group standing together in a circle, searching for support. She drew in a breath and exhaled slowly. "Roble, I'm not doing this job for my sake."

"I know." His tone somehow sounded both accusatory and grateful.

She wrung her hands, not liking the sensation of being attacked or understanding why he seemed appreciative. "I don't want this outcome, and you know it."

Roble stood up, pointing a finger at his file. "You could throw me out like all the schools, churches, and most of the families did."

"You need help," she snapped.

Roble lowered his arms and gazed out the window.

Alexandria saw her hands trembling and hid them in her lap. "I'm sorry, Roble. I didn't mean to raise my voice. It's just that…I really do care."

He fell back onto his chair. "If that were true, you would've asked me what *I* needed, and would've returned what *you've* stolen." His voice rang soft, but clear.

She counted her shallow breaths. "Roble, what…what is it you need?"

He pulled his arrowhead out from his shirt and rubbed it. "I don't need to hear how scary the world is and how I shouldn't try anything. I don't need to know how much suffering there is out there," he pointed out the window, "or how bad I should feel about it. What I *need*…" he looked up, his grey eyes pleading, "…is to see someone who is still happy after growing up."

Lowering his head, he added, "I need to see *living*, Ms. Patra, because I actually want to live."

Alexandria tried to breathe. She searched the pictures on the walls, focusing on her own frozen smiles, but she couldn't feel them.

"You said…" She smoothed out her long sleeves. "Roble, what is it you think I took from you?"

"No matter how many fancy words you say, you stole my freedom. I want it back."

She nodded unconsciously, feeling strangely guilty. Swiveling in her chair, she stared at the bottom filing cabinet drawer. *What if everyone refused my help like Roble?* Her fingers ran along the coarse fabric of her skirt. *To what end will I have lived?* She turned back to him and stared, forgetting she should speak.

Roble squirmed under her gaze, looking uncomfortable for the first time.

Reaching up, Alexandria pulled her hair in front of one shoulder, wrapped it with both hands and stretched it out until straight.

"Ms. Patra," he said, "you're different from the other adults. I almost want to like you."

She released the hair, and it expanded back into curls.

"Not because I think you're trying to help me," Roble continued. "Maybe you're not allowed to admit it, but I think you understand me. It's in your eyes." His voice lowered. "So please—just let me go."

Without breaking eye contact, Alexandria slipped off her wrist cuff and held it in her hand. She watched as the shields before Roble's eyes slid away, making him look vulnerable for the first time. She could now see he was not angry, or even rebellious—but hurting.

An internal storm churned within her, a vortex blurring her thoughts with spinning memories. She tried desperately not to look too closely, not to remember, fearing that to linger would put her life's sacrifice at risk.

She closed her eyes to avoid the images, but instead of relief, she envisioned a young girl springing from her own chair and leaping over the desk with energetic gaiety, one leg kicked out straight, the other bent beneath her body. The girl landed on her toes and grabbed Roble by the arm, yanking him to his feet. With his hand in hers, she ran from the office, her hair streaming behind, whipping against Roble's chest. Alexandria heard the girl laughing as they ran along a sandy lagoon toward a sailing ship anchored in a harbor.

The sound of her own laughter snapped Alexandria from the vision. She glanced away from Roble's stare and slipped her wrist cuff back on. She stood and focused on the posters hanging above Roble's head—*Unity and Sacrifice*. A sense of uneasy relief washed over her.

Then she caught Roble's gentle gaze and trembled on her feet, feeling a wave of regret, but knowing somehow it didn't involve him. Her face flushed. Then, as if a circuit cut off in her mind, her chin dropped, followed by her eyes, and her hand pointed at the door. "This meeting is over."

Roble rose slowly.

"The truancy officer will take you to the boys' home," she said, unable to look him in the eyes.

As he walked through the doorway, she glanced at him, and wondered why *she* was the one who felt betrayed.

A few days later, with the file still on her desk, she learned Roble had run away again and hadn't been recovered. Swiftly and painfully, she had buried it in the bottom file drawer.

A flight attendant placed another champagne flute on the tray table, waking Alexandria from her memory. She turned and peered out the lofty porthole at the fields rolling away beneath her along the Missouri River, wondering what it might have been like to grow up in a different place or in a different time.

She picked up the champagne, leaned back, and poured it between her lips. The newspaper slid off her lap to the floor. Her smiling picture landed face down.

Chapter 2

A low rumble stirred the air, vibrating the gravel on top of Lou's Gas & Lube. Tattered fronds on a nearby palm tree rustled. The rumble increased into a driving whine like a field of windmills, enveloping the gas station and rippling its flat gravel roof into a blurry brown sea.

Several customers filling their cars looked up.

A shadow preceded a military transport with massive wings, its four engines hauling a long, green fuselage. Its tailfin looked like it would clip Lou's roof as it descended toward the western runway of Nellis Air Force Base.

Directly below the roof of Lou's Gas & Lube sat an empty attic—Roble's former home. Starting at age fifteen, he had lived there alone for three years, working in Lou's garage in exchange for rent and the store's expired food.

Its roof used to serve as a bed when the attic grew too hot, and as an observatory—not for stars, but for jets. Caressing the gravel at his sides, Roble had studied every detail of each passing aircraft. And a few times he stood tall, reaching up, grasping for their landing gear, wishing to be taken away.

Sketches plastered his attic's unpainted walls. An open laptop always sat upon art pads piled atop plastic bins. Model aircraft and rockets hung from strings stapled to the ceiling. Aviation magazines and books lay scattered across the uneven floorboards while paper and pencils buried his sleeping bag.

On those curling papers and dim computer screens, Roble drew every aircraft he'd ever seen, but never as they actually were—only as he thought they should've been.

The military transport dropped near the runway, three hundred meters from the abandoned attic.

Inside the aircraft, Roble's eyes narrowed when he felt the tires bark against the tarmac. The heads of all the airmen nodded from the jolt. He imagined puffs of smoke coming off the landing gear—a sight at Nellis he'd only seen from the other side of the fence.

Gazing across the faces around him, he noted their indifference to this particular landing, this milestone. *He* had finally flown over Lou's.

With his nosy, chapped-lipped neighbor distracted by listening to music with ear buds, Roble lifted the newspaper and finally read the editorial about the mystery jet.

> *This week, Libby Industries of Las Vegas unveiled their latest private jet, the Libby III, nicknamed the* Succubus. *Ms. Elizabeth (Libby) Dodge claims it will reach Mach 2, twice the speed of sound, which is a daring increase over the Libby II,* Wyvern. *It incorporates thrust-vectoring maneuverability and advanced avionics rivaling many fighter jets, but as it only carries four passengers and a list price of $60 million (the equivalent of a hundred-seat passenger jet), this* Succubus' *desire to draw blood seems more than just fantasy.*
>
> *In a bulletin issued yesterday, the FAA reiterated that supersonic speed in private aircraft is not allowed over the continental US, and over international waters only by special permit.*
>
> *Frederick Compros, the CEO of Defense Contractors United (DCU), explained: "It's dangerous to allow private citizens to own such a fast plane. The risk our supersonic military jets take is for the good of all, not just the indulgence of a privileged few. And while DCU must make some profits, we prioritize our values by giving back to nonprofit organizations. [Ms. Dodge] happily flings all her profits at developing toys for the rich when she's not too busy blasting her new luxury home into the side of an environmentally sensitive cliff. If it were up to me, I'd outlaw her jets."*
>
> *When asked why she chose to expend resources on such an exclusive, highly engineered piece of eye candy, Ms. Dodge said, "Because I could."*
>
> *It can be assumed that posters of the aptly named* Succubus *will be pinned to walls in teen boys' bedrooms, like pictures of all impractical supercars and supermodels, but in this day and age, perhaps society should prioritize its resources to accomplish the greatest good for the greatest many. The* Succubus *may be fast, but who is going to be left with the cost?*

That jet is real! Roble wanted to yell and run down the aisle high-fiving everyone. He looked around, but they all seemed oblivious to his discovery. He caressed the pictured jet. *A woman named Libby Dodge actually built that.*

Opening his backpack, he pulled out a pencil and sketchpad. A line flared across the page. His hand danced, leaving controlled dots, dashes, and arcs on the sheet, forming a tightly interconnected pattern. Dabbing the graphite with his thumb, he held the paper out in front of him. His eyes widened when he glanced back to the newspaper photo. His drawing possessed the fewest artistic modifications to a jet he had ever made.

He pulled a crumpled paper from his pants pocket, smoothed it on his knee, and made a single mark on it. Slipping it back into his pocket, he inadvertently knocked the newspaper to the floor with his elbow. The picture of Alexandria Patra landed face up.

When the transport stopped, Roble pulled on a jacket riddled with jet and rocket patches and stuffed his belongings into a backpack. Against the line of starched blue uniforms and buzzed scalps, Roble's short hair and unruly jacket stuck out; he hardly noticed.

Reaching the rear exit ramp, he gazed beyond the runway and through the distant barbed wire fence at the white rectangle of Lou's Gas & Lube. The exiting servicemen pushed him forward, complaining at the delay.

He descended the ramp, feeling the crumpled paper inside his pocket. Of all the hundreds of drawings from his former attic, this was one of only *two* he'd kept. The others he'd memorized and tossed in a dumpster when he entered the Air Force. But *this* one in his pocket was different because it wasn't finished. It was only an idea; no, an *idea* of an idea—a puzzle needing to be unraveled. He knew he would unravel it someday.

Eagerly sucking in jet fumes, Roble jogged down the ramp until the tarmac seared against his boots. He walked toward a row of khaki-colored buildings, in step with the mass of eager young men and women, many of them graduating mechanics who would soon disperse around the world.

A fighter jet roared by overhead, its circular exhaust palpitating bright amber flames. Roble forced his lips not to smile, but his eyes sparkled in defiance.

He veered away from the others and skirted the terminal

building alone. Squeezing through a loose gate in a chain-link fence, he entered a parking garage full of military vehicles.

Tucked in a corner near a stack of large tires, a dusty tarp lay over a ridged object. Roble peeled back the canvas, revealing a café racer motorcycle he'd built from scratch. From its thin seat, to its aerodynamic tank, to its low handlebars, the motorcycle sat flush to the ground as if begging to slice the road like a razor blade.

Roble ripped off his jacket and airman's shirt, leaving his obsidian necklace exposed on a fitted grey tee. He tossed the clothes under the bike's seat and jumped on, but before he could turn the ignition, his phone buzzed with a message: *Are you back yet? Meet at RR at noon. Danny.*

He stared at the message. *Danny Sands.*

Danny Sands sat on a German-built motorcycle, a backpack fastened over his shoulders. His football player body pressed into the seat, his athletic sneakers planted on the curb of the Road Runner Motorcycle Shop.

Peering out from his helmet visor, he gazed along a line of dried weeds above a gutter littered with syringes, dirty gauze, and crushed glass bongs.

Tilting his head, he envisioned drawing this place as a backdrop in a comic strip. *The contrast between the shade and the sun's direct angle really brings this disgusting stuff to life.* He looked away when he noticed huddled bodies sitting in cinderblock shadows on either side of the shop.

He'd never liked this place, but Roble often hung out here, bartering work with tattooed mechanics for spare parts. Danny didn't want to see him today—but he *needed* to. He'd needed to see him several weeks ago, almost as much as he needed to breathe.

Exhaling, he relaxed, knowing Roble would always meet him here.

Roble's café-racer motorcycle rumbled to a stop next to him.

Removing his helmet, Danny smoothed out his blond hair. His droopy eyes fell on Roble's face, which was reminiscent of a Native American warrior in a western movie or a hard rock drummer. "Already tossed the Army duds?"

"Hey, Danny."

"You never mentioned you were joining grunts when we camped last fall. Afraid to admit you were joining something respectable?"

"That was a good trip."

"Good? You hardly said a word." Danny reached out and patted Roble's back. "When did you enroll, a few weeks ago?"

"Four months ago."

Danny stared. "Are you serious? Why not join a social networking site or something so people can track you? You're like a freaking ghost."

"And it's the Air Force."

"The… Oh, right, that's what I meant, the Air Force—all your airplane sketches." Danny squinted at Roble's short but longer-than-expected hair. "You lasted longer than I would have guessed."

"How'd you know I was back?"

Danny frowned. "I worry about all my friends. I don't just ignore people. The Army's website—I mean the *Air Force's* website—said you were shipping back to Vegas today."

Roble raised an eyebrow.

Danny covered his mouth to hide his annoyance. "Don't take everything so literal. I got some phone numbers from their website and made a few calls to Nellis and Sheppard. And considering what I learned, I thought maybe you'd need someone to talk to."

Leaning back in his seat, Danny bit his dry lips waiting for Roble to spill the details of his discharge. *If Roble would just admit what it felt like to fail, just once, to be shot off his dreamy perch—it would make it much easier to say what I need to say.*

After an awkward silence, Roble asked, "So, what's going on, Danny?"

"What do you mean?" Danny wiped the sweat from his brow. "Things are going well. Really well." He gulped and coughed to clear his throat. "I guess you wouldn't know, but the California Military Institute accepted me."

"Congratulations."

Danny straightened up, nodding his head. "They train the best. It's the fast track to a Marine officer commission. I'm taking on real responsibilities."

"Okay, Danny."

Danny glanced down, frowning. *Why can't he at least act impressed?* He tapped the gas tank, feeling sick to his stomach. "You think I'm doing it because of my father, don't you?" He swallowed and looked back at Roble.

"I never said that." Roble rubbed his nose. "It's just I remember you wanting to go to art school is all."

"Art school?" Danny scoffed. "Being a Marine officer is more important than doodling. Everyone knows that. A Marine officer impacts real lives by serving and leading others," he said, his gut tightening.

"Is Jenny going with you?"

Oh God, Roble already knows. Danny's shoulders slumped as he thought of Jenny, her disheveled blonde hair and unrestrained boyish laugh, the way she'd always been since that first year in middle school.

He'd watched her in their introduction to art class, thinking he would never dare speak to her. Then Roble arrived at his parents' home as a foster child. He and Roble made so many childish bets against each other. Danny lost a big one over something he couldn't even remember now, for more money than he could've earned in a year, and Roble settled for forcing him to ask Jenny on a date to the Princess Fun Zone.

He would've killed Roble if he could've gotten away with it to avoid asking her out, especially to a place as unbearably uncool as that. But he'd been almost inseparable from Jenny ever since.

Roble turned off his engine.

"Did you call her?" Danny winced. "Is that how you know?"

"Know what?"

Danny's face reddened, always fearing Roble might try to steal her away. *And why wouldn't he try? Girls love bad boys.* But Jenny never left him, not even for the most popular guys in high school. She could have been popular, but instead of going out for cheerleading like all his football teammates' girlfriends, she worked at a casino food court at night and modeled for catalogs on weekends. She used the money to buy necessities for her little sister and alcoholic mother, keeping the rest hidden in a hole in the drywall behind a concert poster. "So when did you last talk to her?"

"Not since I saw you both on Fremont Street over a year ago. What's going on?"

Danny moaned as if slugged in the gut.

Roble lifted his palms.

"I was *accepted* into the CMI." Danny's fist pressed against his leg. "My parents announced it to everyone. I'd never seen my dad so proud of me before. Do you have any idea how that felt?"

"I haven't a clue," Roble said, his voice low and cautious.

Danny gripped his handlebars, rubbing them. "I've been planning to go ever since…well…I've always known I had to go. Everyone expects it. My *dad…*" his voice trailed off.

Roble looked down.

Sucking in a breath, Danny said, "But Jenny is pregnant." His words dropped to the ground like lead bricks.

Roble glanced up, eyes wide.

Danny turned away, shoulders heaving from labored breaths. His parents had never approved of Jenny because of her divorced parents, wrong religion, wrong neighborhood, immodest clothing—the list seemed endless. They forced him to break up with her many times, but the breakups never lasted. His mother often repeated, with great concern, "I just have a bad feeling about her, Danny."

His father threatened to kick him out of the house if he didn't break up with Jenny last year. Danny tried his best to avoid her, tried like hell, but it was their senior year and it had been impossible. He snuck out of the house at night to see her and met her at school without his parents' knowledge.

Danny and Jenny celebrated their graduation with a bottle of her mother's gin. He'd never physically gone all the way with Jenny before that night because he knew his father would literally kill him if he ever found out, and more than that, he couldn't risk Jenny getting pregnant because the CMI wouldn't admit anyone legally supporting a child and his father wouldn't pay the tuition to anywhere besides his alma mater.

Jenny asked Danny about wearing protection that night, but in his intoxicated state and feeling newly liberated from school, he didn't want to care what his father or everyone else expected of him. He had to be with Jenny without any restrictions. And she hadn't insisted otherwise.

They lay on a blanket on a moonlit lawn in a closed public

park. Jenny's wispy hair caressed her smiling lips as she nestled against his shoulder. He told her "I love you" for the first time and meant it. Their heated act felt like the best moment of his life.

The next morning Danny cried, teeth gritted together, consumed with guilt, remembering his parents' wishes and that he'd put the CMI at risk. He felt resentment toward Jenny for not stopping him and woke her, pleading she do whatever necessary not to be pregnant. He couldn't believe the betrayal when she revealed her pregnancy a few weeks ago.

"I'm happy for both of you," Roble said, his voice lowered.

Danny picked at the rubber grips, face contorted. "My parents don't know about it. Once everyone finds out, the CMI is gone. Everything I've worked for—gone. My life is ruined, Roble." He slumped over the handlebars, damp hair falling in a curtain of resignation.

Looking to the sky, Roble started his engine and revved it. It crackled, explosively alive.

Danny peeked through his hair as if the motorcycle's vibrations could wash away everyone else in the world.

Roble gripped the low handlebars and turned to Danny. "I'm riding to the Calico Basin." He pressed his body down and his eyes into slits. The racer ripped away as though catapulted from an aircraft carrier.

Danny blinked, donned his helmet, kicked his bike into gear, and tore after him.

West of the city, on the turnoff to the Calico Basin, a group of protestors with placards stood partially blocking the road. Danny watched as Roble stayed centered in his lane, head low, on track to barely miss the signs.

Seeing the approaching rider's apparent indifference to their cause, the demonstrators stuck their signboards in Roble's path. Danny swung into the oncoming lane to avoid the conflict. Roble lifted his boot and kicked two of the placards out of his way. His front wheel mowed down a third sign as he cut through.

Danny slowed down and read the flattened posters as he passed. *SAVE THE CLIFFS! RETURN THE LAND TO*

THE NATIVES! STOP LIBBY DODGE! Voices shrieked at him. He accelerated.

Near the base of a plateau on the western edge of the Calico Basin, along a rocky road, they pulled their motorcycles to a juddering stop.

"What the hell, Roble? You could have swerved around them," Danny said, watching Roble dismount and head off through crusty sand spiked with Joshua trees.

Danny ran after him. "Didn't you read those signs you blew through?"

"I can't read things stuffed in my face," Roble said as he continued through the desert.

"Some of them are fighting to give this land back to the Native Americans." Danny lifted his hands. "You're half Indian, right?"

"What's your point?"

Roble hasn't changed a bit. Danny shook his head, glad to have something to think about besides his father.

It felt like old times as they continued toward the plateau without speaking. After close to a mile they wound through a cluster of massive red boulders, some split down their center as though sliced by a giant sword. They scrambled up an incline, seeking traction along exposed sandstone. Above a series of jagged ledges, they reached the summit.

The hazy, crisscrossing veins of Vegas spread out in the distance. A line of casinos like a concave spinal column marked the valley's center.

Roble gazed north at a tall crane about half a mile away placing a red-hued window in front of a cavity in the cliff face. He pointed it out to Danny.

"No kidding," Danny said. "That's who's upsetting everyone."

Roble stared at the glass sparkling against the rock.

Danny frowned and opened his backpack, extracting beer cans, handing one to Roble. "I wish life were like this." He cracked one open.

"Like what?"

"*This.* Open. Free. You know—wide open." He gestured out with his can.

"Isn't it?"

Danny took a swig and shook his head.

Roble gazed at the distant slashes of the Nellis runways across the valley and sat down on the cliff's gritty edge.

Emptying his can, Danny sat next to him. "By the way, how did you get into the Air Force? You never even went to high school."

"That's what the recruiter said when I listed Glenn Curtiss, William Boeing, Howard Hughes, and a couple others on the application as my educators."

Roble pressed the cool can to his forehead. "So I had to waste a day passing both the GED and the Air Force entrance exam."

Danny picked up another beer. "You're just lucky your juvie stints didn't go on your permanent record."

"Am I?" Roble asked, watching a plume of ice crystals expanding behind an airliner.

"What do you mean—'Am I?' You worked for a drug lord. You're lucky to have escaped with your life."

"I didn't escape. And Stock's not a criminal, not if that word has any meaning." Roble looked at Danny. "Let's just leave it at that."

"What are you talking about? Just because Stock's gotten away with bribing every politician in town doesn't change the fact he's the greediest criminal in Las Vegas."

Roble handed back the unopened beer and rose to leave.

"Whoa. Hey," Danny said. "Everyone says it, not just my dad."

Roble began walking away.

"I take it back, all right? Don't leave."

Roble stopped.

"I'm sorry. It's all rumors anyway, right?" Danny held out the beer.

Roble turned and studied him for a moment. Danny lifted the beer higher. Taking the can, Roble sat down.

Danny touched Roble's shoulder with his beer. "Listen, I meant to say earlier, it's too bad what happened to you."

"What?"

"You know…" Danny gestured at Roble's non-military length hair.

Roble furrowed his brows.

"All right, I'll *say* it then. When I called Sheppard Air Force

Base, a guy mentioned you hadn't completed your mechanic's training. There, now it's out there. I'm sorry."

"Oh, that." Roble pushed back his hair. "Yeah, Sheppard got rid of me early. My instructor, Sergeant Peterson, said I broke just about every maintenance procedure. I guess it's possible, since I made up my own after learning everything they could teach me. And I don't think he liked me making my own parts and modifying the aircraft."

"Jesus. Well, it serves you right. There are some rules that just need to be followed."

"So I've been told."

"It sucks growing up, right? Now look at us. We're both screwed." Danny laughed, too loudly, and for too long.

Roble looked away.

Danny tossed up a hand. "Now what? Moving back to that attic?"

"I wasn't kicked out of the Air Force."

Danny dropped his beer. It rolled, spraying foamy blotches along the rock until it fell off the edge.

Roble set down his own beer and lowered himself over the ledge. Out of view, he said, "Last week, Peterson took me into his office, smacking shit off his desk with my rolled-up test scores." The can flew back onto the rock next to Danny. "I'd aced all their final exams halfway through training." His head popped back up over the rim. "I guess that took away Peterson's easy way to get rid of me. He cursed about the pain-in-the-ass procedures required for my involuntary discharge. He actually ordered me to quit to save him the trouble." He pulled himself back up onto the summit.

"And?" Danny prompted, his eyes wide.

"I told him you shouldn't expect others to give you what you want."

Danny's jaw dropped. "What'd he do?"

Roble tossed his unopened beer in the air, spinning it. "Maybe he actually liked my work, or just hated paperwork." He caught it. "Who knows, but he gave me my certificate early and transferred me as far away as possible."

"No way! Nobody else could get away with that shit." Danny turned and rummaged through his pack. Finding another beer, he popped it open, releasing fizz over his hand. He chugged it. "Why am I never lucky?" He leaned back on his elbows.

"Lucky like your father?"

Danny sat up, back stiff. "My dad never failed at anything." He lined up the empty cans along the rock. "Not as a Marine, not as a counselor, not with his reputation, not with disciplining his other foster kids—nothing." He lifted his legs and smashed the cans with his shoes. "But he failed to tame you, and he took that out on my hide. That was the only year he ever laid a hand on me."

"He shouldn't have." Roble winced. "But at least we learned something from it."

"From having the livin' hell beat out of us?"

"It left no illusions about what he was after. When he stops swinging fists and starts talking about love and sacrificing for others, that's when you should pucker up for the real punch, because you can't avoid your own fist if you've been convinced you deserve it."

"Huh?"

"When the message is demanding you give up the only things you care about, what's more offensive? A punch to the face or the kindest sounding words in the dictionary?"

Danny lay back onto the rock, staring at the sky. "I think I prefer more kind words and less hitting."

Roble rose to his feet. "Maybe that's why you feel unlucky."

Danny watched, thinking Roble might leap off the edge and soar away like a fighter jet. Roble always knew what he wanted. He wondered why *he'd* never really known.

He squinted, blurring his vision, and imagined Roble's outline transforming into himself. He liked visualizing standing like that, so bold, not caring about anyone—as cold as a killer. He envisioned himself kicking high into the air like a perfectly drawn cartoon ninja. *In another life I would have become an anime artist, but Father hated "foreign art," as he called it.*

"Why can't you at least draw something respectable, like Robin Hood?" his father, Donald, asked once before adding that, "All cartoons are childish." Donald used a Robin Hood logo for his youth counseling business. But Danny never drew anything his father mentioned, keeping his art as his only uncompromised activity.

His mother threw away his drawings, anime videos, and manga books, saying, "You have to grow up and get serious about life." His father told him to focus on playing football because it taught teamwork and would allow him to represent the whole community, not just himself.

Danny had represented Green Valley High as a wide receiver. He practiced harder than anyone on the team, his father driving him on. But whenever Danny ran for the long catches in the big games, he never saw the football, only his dad's face—the face Danny wanted to see beaming with pride at his success. When he caught the ball, he never felt a sliver of joy, only relief. And when he dropped it, he never felt a twinge of disappointment, only guilt.

Roble cracked open his first beer, tipping it toward the sky before sipping off the foam.

Danny rubbed his face, sat up, and peered over the edge. *One yard out, and it drops the distance of a football field. Touchdown.* He exhaled. "Sometimes, I wish I'd run away with you."

Roble set down his beer.

Danny lobbed a rock off the edge and watched it shatter below. "Remember that day my dad stood on the roof fixing shingles and you launched your rocket next to the house?" He coughed and wiped his eye. "He screamed like a girl in full view of Mr. Zindal. I'd never, *ever* seen my dad embarrassed before. I honestly thought you were a dead man."

"He should've just taken it out on me."

"I'm glad you did it—all of it. I'm pretty sure that was the best year of my life." Danny's shoulders relaxed as though a weight momentarily lifted.

Roble pulled his knees to his chest. "I'm flying out to Okinawa, Japan, next week."

Danny's shoulders tightened. "Transferred out of the country?"

"I'm going to work on fighter jets." He rested a hand on his pants pocket. "I might not be back for a while."

Danny looked away, the lump in his throat pinching off air. He didn't know it would hurt so much to hear that. After a moment, he said, "I'm glad you weren't scared of my father. You were the only one."

"I'm pretty sure there were *two* 'little shits' as your mother called us."

Danny nodded, almost smiling, then frowned. "But my dad was wrong about one thing—I got myself into more trouble without you."

"You'll figure it out."

Danny shook his head. "It's not just up to me."

Roble exhaled and pushed against the stone to rise. "I need to go find a place to stay until I ship out."

"Roble…" Danny looked over the edge, heart thumping in his ears, remembering he'd needed to see Roble weeks ago when he found out about Jenny. "I don't know how to make it all work—how to reconcile what everyone wants of me. Sometimes," he sighed, releasing a heavy breath that hung like smoke, "sometimes I can't see a way forward, can't see how to meet everyone's expectations of me. And I wonder if…" he stared at the ground far below, "…if there is a painless way out."

Danny held still, focusing on the boulders below, boulders that had fallen off this cliff and cracked. *Pebbles, a meaningless pile of pebbles.*

Glancing at Roble's boots, he thought how ironic it was that Roble brought him to this fatal ledge. He didn't know what he wanted Roble to do—beg him to stop so he could face his father, or walk away and let him jump. Somehow both choices seemed as indistinguishable as those pebbles.

Roble lowered himself to the rock and gripped the arrowhead hanging from his neck. Danny slumped forward. A warm breeze ran across their bodies, through the backs of their hair.

"You can end your world any time you choose," Roble said. "Nobody can stop you."

Danny sat up and opened his mouth to protest, then closed it and looked off the cliff again. He slid back a bit.

"It's a choice."

Danny blinked, unconvinced.

"I don't pretend to know how the world looks from your eyes," Roble said. "But whatever it is that's inside you, whatever was inside you back then…" he released the arrowhead, "…it belongs only to you."

Danny listened, hoping Roble would continue.

"If *you* decide your world is worth living in," Roble said in a voice as resolute as his grey eyes, "don't let it go."

Danny's palm gripped into a fist.

They faced the distant city as it dissolved beneath the deepening mountain shadow. When the sun eclipsed the jagged bands behind them, Las Vegas ignited into a golden sea of fire.

Chapter 3

L ibby Dodge gazed down on a parched, honeycombed desert stretching between desolate mountain ranges.

Brushing the control stick with her palm, she rolled the gloss-black *Succubus* wings vertical to the horizon. She pushed it further and the aircraft inverted. Her neck-length, russet hair hung toward the glass canopy.

Closing her eyes, she relaxed and released the stick. The *Succubus* fell in an uncontrolled arc, spiraling toward a barren plateau. Her hair swayed with the movement.

"*Auto recovery engaged,*" a mechanical voice said from a cockpit speaker. The jet rotated upright, lifting into the sky, pressing Libby against her seat.

She gripped the stick, thrust it forward, and held it there.

"*Auto recovery disengaged,*" the speaker said. The *Succubus* nosedived toward the ground.

Libby nudged open the throttles, accelerating the jet's speed, its engine exhausts pulsing bloodred.

"*Danger! Altitude warning! Control override. Auto recovery engaged,*" the speaker said.

Even as Libby pressed against the stick, the jet's nose pulled up. The throttle controls retracted against her hand, slowing the *Succubus'* speed. It entered a wide circular pattern.

"*Auto distress signal will initiate in three seconds unless disengaged. Three...two...*"

Libby disengaged the signal, placed an elbow against the canopy and rested her chin on her fist. *Nice work, Siggy.*

"*Ms. Dodge?*" a woman said from the cockpit speaker. "*Your 2:30 appointment is here.*"

"Hey Amanda. Who is it?"

"*The Commissioner.*"

"The what?"

"*Mr. Wright.*"

"Oh, him. Reschedule."

"This is the third reschedule. You told me not to let you push him off again."

"I did? What time is it?"

"2:28."

"On my way."

Libby slammed the control stick to the right. Her left foot lifted while her right foot hammered down. The jet spun on its belly, flipping directions. She opened the throttles wide. The air behind the *Succubus* combusted into flame, launching the sleek projectile across the sky.

By the time it ripped past Mach 2, the Las Vegas skyline broke into view. She cut the throttles, slowing below the sound barrier.

Gliding over a sea of tract homes, she opened a radio channel. "Hey Mackie, this is *Succubus*-zero-zero…oh never mind, it's me, Libby. I'm going to land on runway two from the north. Is that a problem?"

"Affirmative, that is a problem, Ms. Dodge. We have a Cessna one minute from final approach."

The *Succubus* roared over Libby Industries' expansive single-level structure adjacent to the North Las Vegas municipal airport. "I'll be in the hangar before the Cessna touches down. Libby out."

"That's another violation. I'll have to report it this time, Ms. Dodge. Do you copy?"

Zooming past the airport tower, the *Succubus* lined up with runway two, touched down, and sprinted along the tarmac.

The canopy opened as the jet rolled into the private hangar. A woman in beige overalls directed Libby with batons into an open slot. When the wheels stopped, Libby climbed from the cockpit and dropped to the ground. She sprinted to the bridge leading to her manufacturing building.

"Where is he?" Libby ran past Amanda at her desk.

"He's…" Amanda pointed at a chair in the reception area.

Libby stopped and turned.

Chris Wright jumped from his seat and took Libby's hand into his sweaty palms. "I'm so glad we could meet today, Ms. Dodge." His jowls drooped below his smile. "I think you'll like what we at the Federal Aviation Administration have for you."

Libby slipped her hand free, wiped it on her flight shirt,

and led him into her office. "All right, Commissioner. What's happenin'?" She motioned for him to sit and sat at her desk.

"As you know," Mr. Wright licked his lips, "there are some who disagreed with the certification of the *Succu*...the Libby III, but I was always in favor of approval, which is why it was certified." He bobbed his head. "Mach speed is a marvelous feat for a private jet, from a purely scientific point of view of course. However, there are many other important things to consider." He bobbed his head again, eyes searching for agreement.

Libby scratched her forehead.

Mr. Wright rubbed his arms. "Selling your jets to Asian billionaires is one thing, but the *Succu*...the Libby III is... How many have you sold now? Five?"

"Eight. Four in the US."

"Well you only sold five Libby II *Wyverns* and the Libby III just launched. There could be dozens in the sky soon. You know the rules about Mach speed over land. Most on the commission never thought it would actually sell when they voted for approval. But now, seeing the evidence, I fear they might be tempted to reconsider."

Libby drummed her fingers against the desk. "What evidence?"

"With so many Libby IIIs in the air, how do you expect us to monitor and cite them for speeding?"

Libby laughed hard, wiping a tear from an eye. "Good one."

Mr. Wright frowned. "Let's keep this civil, shall we?"

"Oh, you were serious."

"Look, Ms. Dodge, one must adapt to the concerns of safety and order. Aerospace manufacturing can be a very difficult business for those who don't cooperate, especially for small nontraditional outfits. Lord knows many have failed."

"If you're proposing to stop regulating me so I don't become another casualty, I accept." Libby stood. "I'm glad you stopped by. If you have a moment, come with me. I want to show you something really astounding."

Mr. Wright held up a palm. "You miss my point, Ms. Dodge. But you are right, *I am* on your side, and there are practical solutions to every problem. Here's where the good news comes in."

He leaned forward, bristling eyebrows leading the way.

"Frederick Compros has been looking to expand into the small civilian jet market for a while now. Defense Contractors United, as you know, is well organized to follow necessary rules and regulations. Model corporate citizens, DCU." He smiled, nodding his head. "Mr. Compros has 'unofficially,' just as a friendly courtesy, offered to buy Libby Industries."

Whipping a paper from a shirt pocket, he slid it across the desk. "It's a *very* generous offer."

Libby stared at Mr. Wright's bobbing head.

He dabbed his forehead with his tie. After a moment, he stood up. "Take your time. Of course this is a big decision, but one which I think is best for everyone." He turned and walked to the door.

Libby crumpled the unread paper and flicked it. It rolled after Mr. Wright's feet as he slipped from the office.

Shrugging, Libby pulled a report from a desk basket and studied it. Reaching the third bullet point, she dashed from the office.

"Ms. Dodge, your next appointment..." Amanda said as Libby flew by.

At the end of a hallway, Libby jogged around Mr. Wright and entered a wide doorway.

Shrieks of metal bending, lathing, and fusing echoed through the manufacturing floor. Libby grinned at the smell of grease and solid rocket engines as she veered around stainless steel tables surrounded with workers assembling toy rockets and jets. Passing a slow moving assembly line of aerodynamic jet-bikes, she saluted a woman ratcheting a black carbon wheel to a frame's front forks.

Near the far end of the building, she crossed behind a row of red manufacturing robots with *Bekken* written across them. She slowed to watch the robotic arms twisting and rotating along a *Succubus* wing like competing lovers kissing up the arm of a mistress.

Arriving behind a curtain, Libby stared wide-eyed at a partially assembled grey-blue aircraft surrounded by engineers.

She approached a tall man in a white overcoat. "Siggy." Libby gripped his shoulder. "You did it. I knew you could solve the electrical system issues."

Sigmund Evert nodded.

"But," Libby said, studying the fuselage, "what about the metallurgical complications, the dual mode ramjet's computational fluid dynamic issues, and the bugs in the primary quantum computational avionics system? Have we cleaned those up yet?"

The sedate-looking head engineer held up three fingers, one at a time. "Your job—sort of—and mostly."

"Keep up the good work." Libby leaped toward the cockpit.

Sigmund reached out and held her back with his lanky arm. "We're in the middle of some tests, and I *know* you don't want to slow us down."

Libby rolled her eyes. "Fine, I'll check out the engines."

Sigmund strode toward the engine testing area. She smiled and caught up.

"How did the new emergency back-up software perform in the *Succubus*?" Sigmund asked, his voice flat, scientific.

"That?" She shrugged. "Well, if our customers want to be bored to death—it works great."

They stopped before a massive metallic cylinder teeming with pipes and valves. Sigmund's brows lifted. "I heard you were scheduled to meet with the FAA today."

"Yes. It went fine." Libby poked and prodded the side of the turbine.

"The last time you said that the FAA made us rerun all our flight tests for the *Wyvern*. We need the Commissioner on our side if we want to have any chance of getting the Libby IV flight-certified."

"Stop worrying, Siggy. Once they see what we're making, they'll be blown away. I'm sure of it."

Sigmund turned, looking behind him. "Ahem." When Libby didn't respond, he tapped her shoulder.

"What?" Libby turned around.

Amanda stood, tapping her toe and pointing at her watch.

"Another meeting?" Libby asked.

"Mr. Victor Lafayette in the Calico Basin in one hour," Amanda said, frowning, and then winked at Sigmund.

"Victor? Why didn't you tell me?" Libby smiled. "That's today?" She tore away, yelling, "Call Halvern Black. Have him meet me at the stable."

Hooves hammered rhythmically against loose soil as Libby Dodge and Halvern Black rode horses around barrel cacti and creosote bushes. Dirt spit into the air when they flanked a flat-faced boulder below a cliff. Reining to a stop, both of their cowboy hats tipped upward.

Libby squinted against sunlight bouncing off sheer glass near the top of the plateau. The cliff house looked like an Anasazi dwelling, fused within the top of an art-deco skyscraper, perched atop a wall of sheer rock. An orchestra of uniquely spaced windows played reflective notes, some ringing dull from sunken crevices, others sniping bright bursts from exposed corners, and a few thundering bass salutes from wide red panes.

Cut-stone walkways connected glass to dark rectangular openings. A crane hoisted a girder up past the three completed lower levels to workers swarming through cavernous holes filled with rock pillars and steel beams below a natural rock roof.

"I love it," Libby said, rubbing her purebred Arabian's mane.

Halvern's white hat remained steady, angled up.

"Are we on schedule?" Libby asked with the excitement of a young girl awaiting ice cream.

He focused on the crane's cargo, then glanced at a mobile device in his hand. He moved three-dimensional renderings around with his thick fingers and grunted, almost mimicking his mustang.

"It's turning out better than I imagined," she said, patting her horse. "Just look at it, girl."

Slipping the device into his shirt pocket, Halvern faced her, revealing a gruff, black face, his frown wedged below grey-haired temples. "I'm building into a goddamn fractured cliff," his voice boomed from a barreled chest. "I anticipated obstacles, but, god almighty. The down shafts needed bracing through unstable formations. Natural springs are coursing through everything I want to keep dry. Our battery supplier can't figure out how to run the cabling, and they underestimated our solar window electricity generation by a factor of six."

"And?"

He wiped his chin and glared at the construction. "I need to get up there and sort things out. I'll meet your friend another time."

"So is it on schedule?"

"Goddammit, Libby. The EPA has sued for a temporary injunction to halt construction while they conduct environmental tests. The County Building Inspector wants to retract his approvals after taking heat from reporters. The protestors are harassing my workers and suppliers. Nonprofit groups are cluttering my desk with 'letters of ecological concern.' Lieutenant Governor Moore even called me, screaming that this land should've been appropriated into a state park. He'd probably send in the National Guard to shut this down if I wasn't designing a project on the Strip he wants to highlight in his gubernatorial bid."

Libby tilted her head. "So it *won't* be done on time."

"You're like a child who thinks life is supposed to be a fun day in the sandbox."

Libby furrowed her brows.

Leaning back in his squeaky saddle, Halvern's scowl transformed into a low chuckle. "And *that's* why I bought your *Wyvern*, relocated my business here from Hong Kong, and why I'm building you this house. Because I enjoy seeing a grown woman having so much goddamn fun. No, your house won't be done on time. It'll be done two weeks early."

Libby beamed at the house, stroking her Arabian's neck.

Halvern scanned the desert behind them. "When is your French aristocrat supposed to arrive? I don't have time to babysit you." He stared a moment too long, causing Libby to look back as well. A trail of dust blazed away from Libby's stable a half mile to the east.

"Victor's taking the long way," Libby said. "He must've misunderstood Guardo's instructions."

Halvern pulled out binoculars. "What the hell? Is he wearing some kind of medieval armor?" He glanced over the binoculars before looking through the lenses again. "Goddamn French."

Libby smirked as she watched Halvern.

"Oh, great," Halvern said, wincing and shifting in the saddle. "He's riding right into your trespassers."

Victor Lafayette, wearing a full suit of curvaceous matte-white armor, sat atop a prancing black Percheron. He seemed drawn to the protesters like metal to lodestone.

Pulling to a stop at the mob's edge, he flipped open his visor, revealing narrow indigo-blue eyes and a few strands of platinum hair stuck to his face. He read the signs, pausing on one that said, *Take back our lands!* In a thick French accent, he said, "Good morning, my American compatriots."

The twenty or so protestors stared, confused. A few backed away. One freckle-faced man wearing a t-shirt depicting a dragon yelled, "All right."

Victor raised a gauntleted fist in the air as though rallying troops into battle, exposing gunmetal chainmail at his joints. A cheer erupted from the crowd. Victor's thin lips pursed. *"Viva la liberté!"*

He repeated the cheer. Many protestors joined in.

"Son of a brass buttress," Halvern whispered. He handed the binoculars to Libby.

Libby peered through the lenses, her gut shaking with laughter.

Victor fed the group's growing energy with French slogans. They followed along.

The apparent leader of the protest, a bearded man in a tweed jacket, yelled, "This is what I've been talking about."

Removing his helm, Victor exposed neck-length hair and an angelic bone structure. Several young women and a middle-aged man jostled forward trying to get in a better position to see the Frenchman.

A doe-eyed brunette pushed past the competitors, placing her hands on Victor's armored leg. He reached down and pulled her onto the front of his saddle, seating her sideways. She stared into his eyes only long enough for Victor to press his lips against hers. The crowd roared in communal romantic triumph.

"Please tell me, beautiful," Victor whispered in her ear, "where may I find my friend, *Madame* Dodge?"

She shook her head. "I...ah...I... You're Libby Dodge's friend?"

"You're looking for Libby Dodge?" the bearded man asked.

Tension rippled through the crowd.

"Naturally. *Madame* Dodge invited me here. Were you not invited to be on her land as well?"

"What?" several people yelled in unison.

The brunette passenger fidgeted.

"I'm here to engage in a morning ride with the *Madame*. I hear she is crafting a *château* in these parts. By chance have you seen it?"

Several picketers looked north at the clearly visible cliff house. "He's a traitor," shouted a plum-faced woman.

Victor lowered the young woman from his steed. "You have chosen a lovely day to celebrate. Carry on." His fingers flicked in the air.

The protestors shrieked and bounced signs. One threw a rock. It deflected off Victor's chest plate. Donning his helm, Victor tweaked the reins, spurring the Percheron toward the Libby House. A placard flew after him.

Libby lowered the binoculars as the white knight on a black horse pranced up to them.

"Ahh, found you." Victor removed his helm in one motion and set it on the saddle horn.

Halvern spit on the ground. Victor squinted up at the Libby House, his face glowing in the sunlight.

"Ahem." Libby pointed at Victor. "Halvern, this is Victor Lafayette, the brain behind Bekken Advanced Robotics in Germany, among other things." She motioned toward Halvern. "Victor, this is my architect, Halvern Black."

Victor bowed low from his steed, extending a gauntleted hand to Halvern.

Halvern scowled, turning to Libby.

"My architectural compliments, *Monsieur* Black," Victor said, looking back at the house.

"I suppose he jousts too?" Halvern asked.

"I brought Victor here because of his many talents."

"Is kissing your dissenters one of them?"

"There was a real beauty over there," Victor said, looking back.

"Victor missed his time slot to be born during the Renaissance," Libby said, smiling. "But he's an expert in robotics, plasma tools, and solid state lasers."

"A jack of all trades and a knight? Pardon my French but—"

"His plasma tools can melt high volumes of sandstone into tempered glass," Libby said, not wanting to discover the breadth of Halvern's French vocabulary.

"Can you cut out ten thousand square meters of manufacturing space from under our feet and have the roof be self-supporting?" Halvern asked, spitting again.

"Of course," Victor grinned, "*Monsieur* Black."

"He excavated many caverns in Africa while in the Legion's Mountain Commando Group. Let him see the blueprints."

"Does he plan to hire those screaming protestors to help him dig it?" Halvern pulled the blueprints from a saddlebag and tossed them at Victor's face.

Victor snatched them from the air, flicking them open.

Leaning forward, Halvern gripped his side and winced. He straightened up, snapped the reins, and spurred his mustang toward the construction crane.

"Thanks, Halvern," Libby yelled.

Victor studied the plans and then scanned across the desert. He pointed north. "Who owns the land over there?"

"Believe it or not, Halvern bought it six months ago, even before he learned to ride a horse."

"May I send an underground passage across a corner of his land? It would be more efficient."

"You can ask him when we get back. Just ignore his grumpiness."

"Grumpiness? Didn't notice." Victor smiled at the complex diagrams in his hand.

"By the way," Libby glanced back at the picketers, "that was some show you put on out there. Do they teach protesting in French grade schools or something?"

Victor laid the blueprints against the horse's neck, removed a gauntlet, pulled a smartphone from his saddle, and typed calculations. "Don't worry about protestors, my friend. If I dig the cavern, nobody will know it. My plasma gougers don't produce roll-off waste."

"Can you complete the cavern during that month you Europeans call a holiday?"

"Certainly. I was going to use that time to upgrade your manufacturing robots, but that can wait." He nudged his horse around to see the desert from a different angle and looked back at his calculations.

"Now hold on there," she said, moving her Arabian next to Victor. "I need my robots upgraded as soon as possible. I can't wait until next year."

"That is what you Americans call 'wanting to eat your cake and keep it too.' No?"

"No, it's called figuring out a way to make lots of cool stuff super-fast."

Victor raised an eyebrow.

"Look, just quit Bekken and work for me full time. I need you to dig the cave *and* upgrade my robots."

Victor tapped his smartphone screen and lifted it to his ear.

"What are you doing?" Libby scratched up under her hat.

"Der Udo Bekken?" Victor said. "Please excuse the late hour, but I respectfully resign my position." His expression revealed nothing as sharp German grunts reached all the way to Libby's surprised face. "I appreciate the offer, but I must respectfully decline. And once again, please excuse the improper hour." He hung up the phone, sniffed, and looked at Libby.

"Uhmm… You always quit like that?"

"No." Victor pushed the phone into the saddle pocket.

"I haven't hired you yet."

"No." He folded the blueprints and wedged them under the saddle.

She stared, searching for even a trace of fear on Victor's face. Seeing none, she said, "All right then, in addition to upgrading my robots, I want new ones installed in the cavern once you're finished excavating. That sound like a good job description?"

"No." Victor pulled on his gauntlet.

"Money? Fine, I'll give you twice what Bekken was paying."

He yawned.

Libby winced. "Two and a half times?"

"Start a fourth manufacturing line at your facility."

"Start a…" She scrunched her brows. "That's your condition to working for me? What in the blazes do you want to manufacture?"

"Body armor." Victor lifted his helm with both hands. "Your aerospace grade alloys combined with nanotube fibers and ceramic plates should allow for impenetrability and deflect-ability against almost any hardened round, perhaps even against depleted uranium." He gazed across the desert as if surveying a new world. "My friend, the day of the knights in shining armor may come again."

Libby followed his gaze. "You just got me kinda excited." She slapped Victor's plated shoulder. "Make whatever you want; just get everything else done first."

Victor slid the helm back over his head. "And I'll take three times my Bekken salary." He spurred the Percheron away.

Libby shook her head, grinning.

Chapter 4

Sun-drops sifted through pine branches, sprinkling blond diamonds on Stock Brant's spiky hair. He stood erect, clad in black, drawing back a sword.

A young pinyon tree reached to the sky in front of him. He thrust the blade into its bark, twisted, and withdrew it.

Stock held out the concaved, alloy blade, its serrated edges sharper than a razor. Inhaling the scent of the tree's core, his shoulders relaxed and his eyes narrowed.

He scraped the sample into a testing device, pegged the sword into the ground, and leaned against the pinyon. When the device chirped, he studied the results, and slid his hand off the bark.

Reaching up to an enormous pinecone, he plucked out a truffle-sized pine nut. He carried it between two fingers, his boots crunching across the mulch. He removed his leather jacket and tossed it like a blanket over a fallen bristlecone trunk. Lying down, he gazed up at his creations—a pinyon variety existing nowhere else on earth.

He dropped the nut into his mouth. Spitting out the shell, the remaining flesh melted like edible gold. Pleasure coursed through his body.

His eyelids drew closed. *This is how the world should have been.*

Hours later, as the shadow of Mt. Charleston fell across his trees, Stock veered his dust-covered motorcycle onto the Las Vegas Strip forty miles away. Tourists meandering along sidewalks turned toward the whirling rumble. A cone of fire pulsed from a center exhaust behind his matte-black jet-bike, as sleek and daring as a hound from hell.

Wind rustled Stock's hair. Sunglasses, like dark voids, clasped his hard cheeks and stubby nose. His jacket and jeans looked fitted over living granite. His military-style boots were scuffed yet tailored and sat on the jet-bike's platinum foot pegs.

Stock didn't appear forty; he made one forget about age because he looked indestructible.

The Sin's black stone façade rose in the distance like a gothic cathedral turned skyscraper, replete with gargoyles and medieval saints, but also adorned with modern concrete balconies and glass railings.

It wasn't the largest hotel and casino in the city, but certainly the most expensive. Some local authorities suspected Stock Brant owned it, yet it couldn't be proven. Corporate entities encased within special interest vehicles wrapped within other corporate entities legally controlled it. Not even its cash flows could be traced to its ultimate owner since the flows were negative and nobody knew how it made up the losses.

Some rumors asserted that *The Sin's* penthouse replicated the interior of the Chartres Cathedral, but no verified accounts from hotel guests existed. A few former employees claimed Stock lived there, but their stories contradicted one another, which only increased the seductiveness of the rumors.

Ted Hollings, the manager of *The Sin*, never answered questions about Stock Brant, and it was said he'd fired every employee who had.

The Sin's marquee, a poised silhouette of a naked woman, stood three stories high. Stock gazed at her as he rode near. He'd had it designed after a woman he first saw in the news. Four years ago, before *The Sin's* construction was complete, he made an exception to attend a public function, *her* function. And that single view of her body had convinced him to make her the undisclosed model of the marquee.

People complained that the marquee looked vulgar—and they were right, Stock thought—not because it stood naked, but because it shone too beautifully for his own depraved eyes to behold.

The public also accused the marquee of being unrealistic—and they were right, Stock thought—not because the body displayed flawless proportions, but because he'd hidden its eyes in shadow. He had seen her real eyes, and they apologized for, and thus imprisoned her body, just as he knew society's laws apologized for, and thus prohibited his unapproved genetic creations.

Therefore, *The Sin's* marquee represented the impossible, the unrealistic, the mere silhouette of a world Stock knew could never exist: a world allowing him to create without being evil and allowing him to look upon her body without hating her eyes.

But the model of the marquee *did* exist, and both her body and eyes were real, as was the world. And that reality brought Stock to this intolerable state between pain and desire, this state he'd endured so unbearably long. And as he'd risked the price of touching the soul of forbidden genetics, so now he would risk the price of touching her forbidden body.

The Sin's shadow wafted across Stock as it spread out over the Strip and the corner of McCarran International Airport. He thought of his phone call one week ago to Lieutenant Governor Moore, relaying an offer to his living marquee in exchange for a benign request. Stock shivered, knowing it wasn't benign, but an insufferable snare for his siren.

Stock received no answer from her at first, the silence screeching more cruelly than any response. After waiting a day, he walked into one of her charity events unannounced, but she was not there—her first absence in an immaculate career.

After that night, he attended every one of her scheduled public functions. He forced himself to attend, to mingle, and to be photographed the way a man forces himself to saw off an arm when pinned under a boulder.

At the end of each event, as the manicured guests faded away, Stock drank himself into the solace of knowing he'd caused her absence, but still wished in those moments for just one more untouchable glance.

Lifting his head, he spotted the penthouse atop *The Sin* and pictured the note Ted Hollings delivered early this morning. *I'll be there at 7 tonight.* Stock recalled the bold lettering, softened to look grateful, just as he once studied her bold body with eyes tempered to look obedient.

An airliner flew out of McCarran International over Stock's head. His Hell Hound accelerated, roaring against the whining jet turbines above. He touched the pocket containing the note, and for just one moment wished he hadn't made that call or that she hadn't accepted, for he understood that with sirens—as with death—there could be no half measures.

He stared at his marquee. *I will see her eyes tonight.*

The jet-bike growled past *The Sin's* main entrance, swinging into a narrow alleyway. Beyond a lone dumpster, a rusty gate rolled out of Stock's way, allowing entrance in to an abandoned parking structure. He parked in a dark alcove.

Loose concrete crunched underfoot as he walked through the windowless garage. A locked metal door marked the entrance to a former motel, known now by its clandestine inhabitants as *The Hole*. Instead of being razed to the ground, *The Hole* had been secretly swallowed up, cocooned by the many levels of *The Sin's* new parking structure during construction.

Stock wound through *The Hole's* stale, cigarette-reeking halls, home to many of his unofficial employees. Several clusters of scruffy-looking men cleared the path as he progressed. A couple of tattooed men walked by. Nobody looked directly at Stock.

He glanced behind him and thought his employees looked older, somehow different from what he remembered. *There are so many now.*

Shaking his head, he entered a stairwell, the metal treads clanging under his heavy footfalls. Beyond a reinforced door, concrete steps led beneath the Strip. He passed doors, tunnels, and more employees along the way, ignoring them all.

At the bottom, a row of lit bulbs dangled from wires, casting shadows down a shrinking passage. The walls absorbed his scuffing steps, soaking up the evidence of his life.

Reaching an oversized wooden door, he stopped and gazed further down the hallway—to a white door near its end. It led to his pharmaceutical lab, a place where he had developed his last three genetically engineered biologics; none submitted for government approval, but each a cure to a terminal disease thought to have no hope for a cure.

He looked away and opened the wooden door before him, releasing a wave of humid light. A domed cavern dripping with lamps spread out the distance like a Midwestern farm and its bright sky had sunk down to the center of the earth. His nostrils flared wide, drawing in the aroma of soil and vegetation—the smell of home.

At the far end of the cavern, Kat Lister glanced over oat stalks, revealing pale eyes beneath sandy hair. She was twenty years old and Stock's only remaining genetic research assistant. She joined him when she was just fourteen, at a time when Stock still employed a dozen runaway youths to perform his biologic research procedures with a meticulous eye.

Kat was also his special delivery girl. Every few months, she used craft and ingenuity to anonymously distribute packets of raw diamonds to many local politicians and appointed government leaders. The packets contained nothing else—no requests, no demands, no hint of their origin.

Since many recipients turned the diamonds over to the state or donated them to charity, news stations across Nevada publicized the mysterious payments. But because Stock left out no political party or interest group, and revealed no purpose for the loot, nobody understood who should be upset, though everyone claimed to be. Committees formed and investigations were launched, but nothing was discovered except the mistrust of every politician against every other, and the mistrust between politicians and investigators.

Some rumors claimed the diamonds came from Stock, but people discounted these like all rumors about him—except for those people who secretly kept Stock's diamonds, and *they* publicly claimed to be the most doubtful of all.

Stock walked along a row of wheat, noting each nuance of the spikelets, sheaths, and leaf blades. He stopped and tore off a floret, fondling it.

A slim, black-haired young man with a friendly face slipped into the cavern like a summer shadow, leaving the entrance door ajar. He stopped a few steps behind Stock.

"Shut the door, Jesus," Stock said without turning, and bit down on a wheat kernel, separating out its germ.

Jesus "Jessy" Gorronza walked back and closed the door, standing for a moment to appraise Stock's crops.

Stock moved the germ against his teeth, detecting traces of magnesium and zinc, but a disappointing lack of leucine.

"Our monthly report is ready," Jessy said as he returned.

"Give me the genetic sales numbers."

"Yes, of course, but before we get to genetics," Jessy said, his voice smooth, "we should discuss our latest distribution success."

Stock breathed in, mixing the air's nitrogen with the wheat's phytic acid. *It could use more water.* "Which is what?"

"Desomorphine." He opened his arms wide. "It has flooded the valley with such ease we should…celebrate."

Stock spit out the germ, staring at the wheat in his hand. "A synthetic street chemical? You wish to celebrate our customers' deaths?"

"Not their *deaths*, Stock…" he lowered his arms, "…their *desire* to free themselves from society and its corrupt laws."

"The laws are *not* corrupt." Stock lowered his head and crushed the wheat in his hand. "I'm headed to hell and our customers will meet me there."

A grin spread across Jessy's lips.

"The next time you feel the need to free someone from something," Stock continued, "just liberate yourself and leave me."

Jessy bowed. "We are only here to serve and protect you."

Stock sifted the pulverized wheat through his fingers, his boot burying the chaff with a swipe of soil. "How much of this month's filthy lucre came from my genetics?"

"Stock," he placed a hand to his chest, "the more *elevated* principles of our endeavors shouldn't be measured with mere profits."

"Don't try to explain elevated principles, Jesus." He spun on his heel. "I only understand dirt and drugs." Marching away, he pressed through rows of crops, stopping to inspect a line of barley.

Jessy followed behind. "We sold fifteen metric tons of genetically modified seed, which is down only about ten percent. And biologic Ds and Ks are selling…fine. But," he lowered his voice, "as you already know, almost all profits now come from street drugs."

Stock exhaled and ripped golden flower heads off a stem. "If that's all you have to report, you may go." Biting off a floret, he measured its resistance to pressure while tasting its earthy, nutty flavor. *A hint of unusual bitterness. What is off?*

Jessy paced behind him like an attorney preparing an argument. "However, we do have a slight distribution issue. The price of powder is declining due to an unfortunate oversupply. As a purely defensive measure, perhaps it is time to…consolidate competitors in the Spring Valley."

Stock gnashed the floret with his molars, his arms stiffening.

Jessy stopped in his tracks. "Stock, if we consider the good of the entire valley's drug industry, it becomes clear it needs organizing, and that should be done by us. Even you've said our competitors are unprincipled and violent, so why not use a little proactive muscle against them?"

Stock winced, having no answer for why he wouldn't allow it. "The powder you've been selling is compost, and almost as bad as the synthetics. The customers were right to pay less."

Jessy frowned.

Stock touched his jaw. *Maybe it's not a macro that is off. The acid balance?* He moved his tongue, tasting the barley mesh. Looking at the flower heads in his hand, he noticed Jessy's shadow below him and spit out the mesh. "If you're going to sell street drugs, then at least sell *good* street drugs. The Columbians' coca methods became lax after the rebels surrendered to their new government. Everyone in Vegas is importing their refuse. Change to Bolivian sources, the ones willing to grow Erythroxylum at high elevations and not harvest until after twenty months. Then raise the price."

Jessy shrugged in defeat, but smiled in acceptance of Stock's expertise. "We will make the changes right away." He turned to leave.

Stock picked up a dirt clump, crushing it in his palm. He moved the granules around with his other hand.

"Oh," Jessy turned back to him, "there is one more unpleasant detail to report. L523s…"

Dirt rained from Stock's hands. "How many did we sell?"

"Two doses." Jessy narrowed his eyes at more than just the low number.

Stock lifted his head, the ceiling lamps brightening his face as he recalled how he'd discovered a way to make biologic L523 using a technique nobody else in the world had dared to contemplate.

"We sold one to a late-stage pancreatic cancer victim…"

Stock brushed his hands clean. "Who else would buy it?"

"It ended up," Jessy cleared his throat, "he worked undercover for both the FDA and the DEA. We tested him for the correct cancer before we sold it, so we thought we were safe. Two of our men were lost in the sting."

Stock's neck tensed. "Why did you wait to tell me this?" He squinted against the brightness. "And what happened to the customer?"

"The feds confiscated the dose as evidence, so he will die, as society's justice demands," Jessy said, averting his gaze.

Stock closed his eyes, unwilling to grimace for relief.

"We will be more careful next time," Jessy said.

"I want customers screened properly. The feds will never get another dose. *Ever*. And triple the price of L523. If a customer wants to be cured, he'll have to pay for the sin of using my biologic."

"That is wise," Jessy said, "to reduce demand for genetics. The feds have been diverting resources to stop unapproved biologics and GMOs. It's that news story: the father robbed and stabbed to death downtown while seeking to buy one of your doses for his daughter. Without it, the girl died in her hospital bed on live TV while onlookers prayed for her health and politicians demanded an end to illegal drugs. The public blames the existence of the biologic for both deaths."

"The public is right," Stock said, his voice heavy, face sinking into shade.

Jessy stared with satisfaction in his eyes. "The feds' new drive against genetics is reducing the risk of selling street chemicals and drugs, but it's also making it easier for our competitors, which is why we might—"

Stock's shoulders tightened.

"Why we might wish to consider other options," Jessy finished, his shadow slicing across Stock's back. "If physical consolidation is out of the question, perhaps we could direct a portion of your diamonds in, shall we say, a more politically friendly manner? We have men to make the deliveries."

Stock gripped his hands into fists. "My bribes are not to entice others to help us. I give them as recompense for my crimes." Exhaling, he whispered, "I am begging."

Jessy took a step back, his boot catching a young barley stock, breaking its fibrous backbone. "Someday society might forgive you for your sins against them."

"You are an optimist, Jesus," Stock said, his voice tired, "but it is wasted."

"Serving you is an honor."

From across the cavern Kat's eyes lifted and glared at Jessy. Her pupils seemed to expand and contract with each measured breath.

"Have you hired more runaways?" Stock asked, his voice deflated as he again walked away. He knew they were becoming less useful as the empire expanded toward street drugs. But in the early days, those kids were sharp and eager to help produce his genetic creations and sell them like hungry Victorian street peddlers. His favorites had all been runaways, and three had been brighter than all the rest. Two were in this cavern. He stopped at the edge of an apple orchard near a cavern wall, his boots digging into loose soil.

Jessy caught up, stopping several paces behind. "Those types of ex-foster kids don't come around like they used to."

Stock smoothed over his boot craters, his face pulled tight, contradicting his easy movement.

"We had another kid deserter last month: Jack Noonan." Jessy's voice hung tentative as though seeking and fearing a reaction.

Where are the best kids going, and why? Stock exhaled, his shoulders falling limp.

Jessy nodded at the lack of response. "We've ramped up the recruiting of more mature and tractable candidates. Don't worry about foster whiz kids—we don't need them anymore."

Stock whirled around, his stare twin beams of blue flame searing Jessy's face until he turned away.

"You're an ex-foster kid." Stock's voice became hoarse. "Roble was an…" He turned and clasped his hands against an apple tree.

"Ah yes…Roble." Jessy blinked with pleasure. "If only treachery did not cut so deep. We'll keep looking for replacements, as always."

Stock ripped a massive, green-speckled apple from the tree. Roble had been his most favored runaway. Yet unlike the others, he didn't work on genetic production or distribution. Instead, he spent his time souping up Stock's motorcycles in *The Hole's* garage or tinkering with Stock's private jet in the hangar. He reminded Stock of a fledgling monk, describing all things mechanical with a religious reverence.

In the rare daytime hours when grease didn't cover Roble or he didn't hold a socket wrench, he stood at Stock's side in the labs asking questions with childlike wonder about the creation process and about which principles could be applied to other fields.

At night, they sometimes talked for hours in the hangar, or in the air in Stock's jet, about what was yet possible for mankind. It was like they spoke a language nobody else understood or cared about.

Stock's sunglasses fell back over his eyes.

Just days before Roble left, Stock offered Jessy the position of second-in-command of his empire, but Jessy refused, insisting Roble be given the position in his place. Jessy told Stock that Roble confided in him that he was leaving to seek fortune on his own, and suggested that giving Roble a position of power and riches was the only way to make him stay. Stock didn't understand Jessy's selfless rejection or why Roble would want to leave him, but he couldn't bear the thought of losing him.

So even though Roble was only fifteen at the time, seven years Jessy's junior, Stock announced his surprise promotion in front of everyone. To his immediate relief, Roble didn't refuse—he didn't say a word.

Stock pressed the apple to his heart, trying to replace something ripped out. *Why did you still abandon me?* He shook his head.

It seemed impossible to comprehend, but only in retrospect did he realize he hadn't felt like a criminal for the three years Roble worked for him. *How did you make me feel that way?* He lowered the apple to his side.

Gritting his teeth, a swell of betrayal and anger washed over him. He threw the apple. It arced across the cavern below the lights like a sparkling sunstone. *Roble, I don't understand.* The apple smashed against a cavern wall with a sickening pop.

Jessy strolled out of the growing chamber.

Stock plodded through the crops, his head lowered. He stopped and peered over Kat Lister's shoulder at her mobile computer screen.

Kat glanced at his face and winced. "Did the new sword work this morning?" she forced out, trying to sound hopeful.

"Just give me the results."

Kat studied her device, her short hair creating two sharp points before her face, her nimble fingers scrolling through graphs. "The J87 oats are using eighty-one percent less water, have double the soluble fiber, and so far I'm finding them sweeter than J86s."

Stock noticed the time on Kat's display: 6:12 PM.

"Want to see if we can increase the omega 3s?" Kat raised her head.

Stock walked away without answering, his boots thumping against the dirt, in sync with his heart.

It is time to see her eyes.

Chapter 5

Alexandria Patra entered the only open lobby elevator at *The Sin*, glancing at the thin-mustached operator in a black buttoned-up suit with a gothic hood resting on his back. "Penthouse," she said.

The man studied her, then opened a mahogany panel, inserted a key, and pressed a sequence on a pad. His wristwatch flashed 6:59 PM.

As the cab rose, Alexandria almost gagged at the thought of the hotel patrons frolicking in the lobby's pompous display. The décor, a mix of royal furnishings replicated from eras ranging from Charlemagne's court to the later European Renaissance palaces, was smeared together with a heavy spill of purple velvet, shellacked with gold leaf, and left guarded by marble gargoyles. Everything appeared fabricated with ancient forms of hand craftsmanship using the costliest imported materials—which was particularly offensive considering the talk at her state office that *The Sin* somehow dodged paying taxes. Alexandria attended social functions in every hotel in the city but by her own will, *never* this hotel.

She watched the Roman numerals lighting up as they ascended. *We're passing the tenth floor already?* She wasn't ready to see Stock Brant again so soon, even though it had been four years since their only encounter.

That long-ago night she hadn't known what he looked like; she hadn't wanted to know. She'd just assumed anyone with such an unlawful reputation would be monstrous, an image involving a single strand of greasy hair, two sweaty chins, and three gold necklaces.

From across the vaulted ballroom, she'd observed a man enter. His short, unkempt hair wisped like flame atop charcoaled roots. A tailored black suit emphasized his impeccable frame, which ended in mud-caked biker boots. His hard face insulted the dignified guests seemingly without their notice as he passed them.

He stopped and stood alone, receiving two fingers of whiskey from a waiter in lieu of the champagne flutes everyone else held. As the manicured herd forced conversation upon him, it was his uninterested expression, not his boots, which seemed to kick mud across their freshly dry-cleaned outfits. One by one, each peeled away with an indignant frown, only to be replaced by eager new guests.

Alexandria's eyes remained riveted on him, the most rugged yet poised man she'd ever seen. She stared so long a group of donors she was entertaining walked off, offended by her inattentiveness.

When he returned her gaze without even the decency of discretion, she blushed. His piercing blue eyes held an obscene intelligence and a scorn that seemed both personal and ferocious. His lips pressed together as though holding back even the pretense of conversation—or hunger. She turned away.

Standing alone, she knew his gaze must be on her neck, her shoulders, her legs. Her mind buzzed, feeling aware of the gown stretched against her body. Her breathing quickened, becoming shallow, and she felt guilty for liking the sensation.

Lieutenant Governor Preton Moore caught her by the arm and she jumped. His brilliant white grin apologized as he said, "Don't look now, but Stock Brant crashed our event. I'm not sure if it's a compliment or an affront."

She swung her head around, searching the ballroom entrance, shocked she hadn't seen that slimy criminal enter. Then Preton pointed in the direction she hadn't dared look again. She had clenched her fists for she'd stared like one of Stock's rumored concubines. Downing her drink, she had fanned her cheeks with a cocktail napkin before walking away to find her lost donor guests.

Twentieth floor of The Sin; *halfway there. The floors are counting by too quickly.* Alexandria raised a finger, contemplating pressing the elevator's emergency stop button. But the finger recoiled as she remembered walking into Preton's state office a week ago.

He often called her in to plan events and to give advice, but this get-together was something unprecedented. He suggested she meet privately with Stock Brant to accept an 'anonymous' donation. The subtle lines of Preton's face implied the unthinkable purpose for Stock's request.

She'd stood without answering, remembering Stock's ballroom glance four years earlier. When she imagined meeting alone with Stock, she felt heat flash down her body.

Staring at Preton's calm face, she felt her redness become fueled by anger. Crossing her arms, she told Preton that Stock should be locked up in jail, not indulged by law-abiding citizens trying to help others.

Oddly, Preton hadn't insisted. He simply revealed the size of the donation awaiting the CUH. He enunciated an amount so large her last eight years of squeezing money from vodka-and-chive-breathed donors seemed laughable.

Alexandria knew no matter how much money Stock offered, it was dirty and its acquisition must have hurt innocent people. But she swallowed her anger when she remembered she had no personal line of comfort that couldn't be crossed if done in the service of those in need. How could she enforce society's sense of justice on Stock by refusing him, when it would come at the expense of helping hundreds of underprivileged children?

Without reply, she left Preton's office, and went home for the day, the first time she'd ever left work early in her life. When she didn't return to her office or go to her charity fundraiser the next day, she told herself she felt physically ill, or needed to attend to personal issues, or just needed her first vacation—the justifications morphed by the hour.

She filled the time working on the phone and computer—working harder than if she'd gone to the office. But she wouldn't leave and risk an encounter with Stock, as seemingly impossible as it sounded, for fear some inappropriate, selfish desire within her would make her forget her reasons for wanting to avoid the proposed meeting.

When she heard from her assistant that Stock was attending her scheduled public functions that week, Alexandria glanced out the window, knowing a decision must be made. She walked toward the phone to call Preton, but veered away and sat atop her bed, just to rest for a moment. She didn't wake up until the next morning.

As the days passed, not even the actual sickness in her stomach made her isolation feel justified. At night she turned the air conditioner as cold as it could go, but sleep still fled as she twisted under sweaty sheets, trying not to envision what Stock wanted when he stared at her from across that ballroom, while her mind repeated he was an insensitive, society-loathing criminal.

After a week of seclusion, an embarrassingly obvious solution came to her. She felt relieved that it would fulfill her duty to the children without giving Stock what he did not deserve. His offer demanded nothing but her presence and that is all he would get. Everything could be gained and nothing lost. The plan sounded so solid, especially late at night when she'd concocted it.

"As I've often said, when it comes to the greater good," Preton had told her when she called yesterday to surrender, "the end always justifies the means, or else what are we sacrificing for?" She had set the phone down, her fingers releasing one at a time, and walked away.

Thirty-fifth floor; almost there. Pressing her back against the elevator wall, Alexandria searched along the ridged panels for an escape hatch, yet she felt secret relief there wasn't one. "This is an official meeting on the future of Nevada's children," she whispered. *This certainly isn't a date.* She checked her hair as the elevator doors opened directly into the penthouse.

Stock stood before her, his bloodshot eyes meeting her widening stare. His hair was spiked wet as though he'd just stepped from a shower. Wearing a white tee, cargo pants, and sandals, he should have looked sloppy, yet the simple clothing seemed becoming on his solid frame.

Her intent had been to understate her dress as a reproach to *The Sin's* gaudiness, but looking at Stock, she realized she'd failed miserably.

His gaze left her eyes, and dipped to her platinum choker, making her feel as if it burned like ice across her neck. When he followed her glistening curls down to her white dress, which clung to her curves, she snapped her chin up, averting her gaze, not daring to see his reaction.

She took a breath and stepped from the elevator, wishing he would step back. He didn't. His body smelled of freshly tanned leather splashed with desert rain.

"Thank you for coming, Ms. Patra." His voice rang low and raspy.

"Of course, Mr. Brant," she said, feeling too exposed and forcing a smile. "You've offered to become a valuable patron of the CUH charity. As such, I'm here to discuss the needs of the children."

"Mm," he narrowed his eyes.

Alexandria glanced beyond his shoulders at the penthouse. It didn't seem possible it was in the same building as the lobby. It looked open and minimalist, slashed with clean edges of black and silver across white surfaces. Floor-to-ceiling windows absorbed the colorful city lights, accenting the penthouse's single integrated style more convincing than any material decoration. It felt like they floated above the earth as if it were mankind's natural state to live in the sky. She'd never beheld a more beautiful home.

He took her hand so easily she didn't believe it had actually happened, and he led her to the balcony. Loving the feel of his rough skin on her palm, she followed. But in a flash of disgust, she ripped her hand free, or at least she thought she did. She looked down—his fingers still held hers. She commanded her hand to pull away, but before she could, he released her and leaned against the glass rail.

Alexandria turned away, feeling both indignant and disappointed, gazing instead at the rambling gothic roof far below. She exhaled, silently cursing Preton for expecting her to be here. Her eyes panned back to his chiseled profile. "Why name this place *The Sin*?"

"Don't think it fits?" His eyes held the city.

"Too well, I think."

"Not well enough. It's much worse."

"What's worse than *sin*?"

His gaze shifted to her darkened state office building in the distance. "You should approve of *The Sin*. It has the state's consent to operate."

She opened her mouth to protest, but stopped and thought for a moment. "I think you made it despicable on purpose to blame society for your own faults."

His jaw tensed.

She smiled, liking his show of discomfort. Then she frowned, knowing it was improper to revel in it. Remembering this was a philanthropic meeting, she decided to wait politely for him to speak again, but instead said, "I've heard it's the only casino in the world that somehow loses money on gaming."

"What of it?"

"If you're running at a loss purposely to avoid taxes, the city would be better off if *The Sin* were sent back to hell."

"That is true," he whispered.

Her brows furrowed.

"Nobody will ever profit by *The Sin*," Stock said. "Not even I."

"But that's a complete waste of…everything." She motioned a hand across his penthouse. "So instead, you purposely make *all* your money through crime?"

"Not all of us have dreams that are good."

She pressed against the railing, glimpsing a memory of her dream, feeling sick. Her gaze caught the shadow of *The Sin's* marquee, and her disgust made her forget. Straightening up, she said, "That doesn't make sense. You actually *want* to be a criminal?"

"Want? We don't get to choose what is called right and wrong."

But… Alexandria glanced from his chest to his eyes. She swallowed, which pressed her beating neck against her choker.

"Mr. Brant," her voice came out husky, "there must be some good in you. You're offering to make a contribution to the CUH so large…I'm…" She stopped, looking away to avoid seeing the sudden scorn in his eyes attached to the thought of his generous donation, and not wanting to consider whether she found it repulsive or irresistible. "The Lieutenant Governor appreciates your donation. He told me so, which is why—"

"Which is why you prostituted yourself here."

She whirled around, slapping him across the jaw. The blow echoed off the glass walls and hung in the air. Her own violence stunned her, stealing away the anger, and left her feeling guilty for hurting him—and even guiltier for having enjoyed it. She pressed her stinging hand against her hip.

"Did Preton send that as well?" He felt the welt on his chin.

Her eyes glared, but her mind reeled.

"I didn't think so. He wouldn't risk my donation. But I'm sure you already knew that."

His eyes moved down the length of her body like hands.

Alexandria pressed her thighs together. A flash of unwanted

heat rushed through her, melting her wall of denial that had masked her naïve scheme to come here. She knew he wouldn't give his donation unless she slept with him—she'd always known it. And her own desire to do so now slapped her in the face with guilt. *No.* She winced. *What I want is irrelevant.*

Then her gut tightened as she remembered her duty to the children. "You think this is a game?" She curled her throbbing hand into a fist. "You think I enjoy coming here to watch your immature act?"

He watched her, his lips hard.

Her fingernails dug into the palm of her fist. "We had an agreement. If you had any honor, you would keep it. I've already done my part by coming here. Now you do yours by paying." Her heart raced, wishing her words could dissolve this impossible conflict before her.

Stock's gaze mirrored that in the ballroom four years ago, only more so.

Her breath escaped her. *I can't make this choice!* Curling her other hand into a fist, she stepped back, lowering her forehead as though readying for battle. A tingling of eagerness and fear shot through her.

"My payment will be made as promised," he said. "You may leave."

She felt her body falling as from the balcony, but her feet hadn't moved. She stared at his hands. *That much money for just… this? Why does my relief feel like my worst defeat?* Her fists unraveled. Stepping forward, she searched his eyes for an explanation, but they escaped her scrutiny.

He pointed at the elevator. She rubbed her still stinging palm against her thigh.

"That is all, Ms. Patra. You've done your duty."

"God damn you, Mr. Brant."

Stock turned away. "He already has."

"But—"

"Don't forget to smile in the photograph with my check."

Her chest rose and fell with barely controlled breaths. "I guess we are done here." Alexandria strode toward the elevator, feeling lightheaded.

"Wait."

He said it so softly she wasn't certain if it had been his voice or just her own thought. She stopped midway across the floor. *Don't…* She glanced at her feet.

He walked past her. Stopping next to a liquor cabinet, he pulled out a bottle with a hand-drawn label: two crossed six-shooters with *Wayne Smoke* written across them.

She flushed. *No, I can't. He is what he is. I have no further purpose here.* "Save it for one of your sluts." Her heels clicked along the floor to the elevator.

"You are right to leave," he said, not turning around.

She reached for the elevator call button, but instead of pressing it, glanced over her shoulder at his back moving beneath the white cotton as he filled two glasses.

"I've never invited anyone here before," he said.

Before she could turn away, her eyes absorbed the motion of his approach. A tanned forearm held out the smoky liquid.

He'd already returned to the balcony before she realized she held the drink. It smelled of hickory-charred corn, earthy and clean. *Why did I take it?*

Stock leaned against the rail, holding his glass.

Without taking a sip, Alexandria walked to the liquor cabinet, her hair sweeping behind her dress. The bourbon splashed over the rim as she stamped the glass on the counter. Holding still for a moment, she rubbed her bourbon-drenched hand across her lips, tasting its unusual bittersweet flavor. She wanted desperately to drink it.

No. Brushing the tumbler away from her, she faced him across the room. "You hate society but donate large sums to it. You insult everything I stand for, but invite me for a drink in your penthouse?" She lifted her palms and then forced them back to her sides, demanding an explanation.

He set the Wayne Smoke down on the railing. "Why are you still here?"

Alexandria's brows angled into Egyptian daggers. With elongated steps, she went to him. "I'm trying to do what is right. But with you, everything is an act of rebellion—even this meeting. You're cynical to the point that nothing virtuous matters." She waved toward *The Sin's* marquee below. "But I guess you have it all figured out. You must be really happy with the results."

"No," he whispered, "I'm not happy." His eyes held hers without defense.

She glanced behind her at his penthouse, then back at his face. She trembled. *Who could be so honest and evil, so beautiful and ugly, all at the same time?* It broke her heart he wasn't happy, but somehow it also gave her hidden comfort. She wanted to be happy, but she'd concluded long ago that the loss of happiness was the price for being good—but for Stock, how could his loss also be the price for being evil? Were they both guided by something similar yet unseen? Gripping her elbows, she tried to refocus her thoughts. *That can't be. Everyone agrees I'm doing the right things—not Stock. Be strong.*

She extended her arm. "You don't have to be this way."

"You're wrong." His tone rang dense, as if many layers of pain had long ago compacted together.

Alexandria rubbed her lips together as she studied his face, his indestructible veneer, but she saw torture in his eyes, like he'd been the victim of some long-past cruelty. Her years of working with troubled children rushed through her mind. She grasped the railing. *Someone abused him.* She hoped to be wrong, but she knew what she saw.

"Let me help you," she said. "I know it may be hard to talk about. But the effects of…some experiences…can be reversed. They don't need to determine your course."

He downed his drink, eyes aflame.

Alexandria waited, hoping and fearing he would speak.

He turned away. "This was a mistake."

She reached for him but pulled back and studied her fingers.

"Stock…I'm still here because I want to be," she whispered.

He didn't move for a long time. "It's funny I guess." He shook his head and looked off in the distance. "Growing up on a farm, I received nothing but what you would consider love. You wouldn't have recognized me. I obeyed my parents, my church leaders, my community leaders—everyone. You should have seen how proud they all were. My first grade teacher once declared in front of the entire class," he gestured at his casino, "'Stock Brant, why can't everyone be just like you?'"

How could that be? Alexandria cringed at the anguish in his voice.

"But that was before I developed a flaw…"

She gripped tighter to the rail.

"…a reality affliction. I couldn't see the same world everyone claimed existed. And it made me ask—*why?*"

She furrowed her brows, wondering what he had questioned. Her heart beat faster, thinking of the answer.

"I finally needed to know the reason for every command, for every burden and prohibition demanded of me. I was giving up my life to obey them, and all I needed to understand was, *Why?*"

Alexandria sensed something dark bubbling up, but not inside Stock. Her eyes darted to the elevator, but immediately returned to him.

"Do you know what answer I received? Every single time and from everyone I asked?"

She shook her head, not wanting to hear it.

"*Because—I—said—so.*"

Her body tensed to flee at his words, but she held still.

"The priest, the university, the politician, the FDA panel, *the majority*—said so."

Her throat felt so dry she couldn't swallow.

"Are they driven by love? Concern for others? Righteousness? Higher ideals?" He faced her, their eyes meeting. "Yes."

He lowered his head. "It must be all of those things. Therefore, they are morally right."

Alexandria recoiled, shocked his words hadn't filled her with a sense of vindication or at least relief. She felt nauseous.

"I know why seeds grow. I understand the genetic code—it is knowable and unchanging." Stock's chin continued to lower until it nearly touched his chest. "But with morality, there are no rational answers. I cannot understand it."

A warm breeze blew across Alexandria's body, sending wisps of hair over her lashes.

"I finally could not be good any longer, because I could not obey what I could not comprehend. Their beliefs made me evil. I hate them. I rebel against them. But I must accept them, just as I must accept the genetic code. I do not control truth."

Alexandria stepped forward, his words drawing her closer—so tragic, yet so familiar.

"Why is the world this way?" he asked.

Reaching out, she touched his hand to feel his warmth, his desire to understand. At her touch, he closed his eyes.

"Can you tell me why it had to be so?" he whispered. "Alexandria, I don't know the answer."

Why did Stock have the courage to admit his uncertainty when she dared not? And how could they both be at the mercy of the same mystery which had stolen their ability to be happy? She could think of no answers, but his honesty and his question shot an unwanted spark of mutiny through her. It ignited and burned a small hole through a vault she'd created to conceal all she'd feared to ever see again: her childhood questions, her abandoned dream. She could feel them spreading through her like an intangible dark threat and knew they were evil because they would neither help nor obey anyone. She'd always had the strength to suppress them, to hold them back. Her strength faded now, even as she knew she must keep the darkness inside. It churned within her, neither suppressed nor released. The sensation tingled dangerous and enticing—like sin.

Alexandria felt rebellious and without shame that Stock might now glimpse her darkness, even if she dared not look at it herself, and the thought of Stock seeing it made her want him, because it made her desire herself.

Her fingertips pressed against his sides, causing him to look up. With the uplift of her chin, she revealed her eyes and whatever lay concealed beneath.

Stock stared, focusing deep inside her, as if seeing the impossible. His hands moved to her body, but stopped. She pulled his hands to her waist. They both froze, sensing the reality of this moment.

Alexandria felt a dangerous loss of strength, blood pumping through her veins, his fingertips on her. *You wanted my body, Stock. That's why you asked me here. I'm offering it to you.*

Stock's hands traveled up her sides; hers remained atop his, urging his movement.

He ripped his hands away and staggered back, staring at his hands as though they'd just committed a crime.

Stepping forward, Alexandria brushed his hands out of the way and laid hers on his heaving chest. They moved along the fabric, tracing his muscles.

Stock seized her wrists, gripping tight, until she winced. Throwing her hands away, he said, "I was wrong to ask you to stay, and I can't throw you out. So please," he looked away, "leave."

Slipping her hands under his shirt, she touched his skin; it felt so hot. She could smell his desire and her own, like summer rain on sage.

"Alexandria," he breathed, as if begging for her to both save and take his life, "I don't understand how or why your eyes have changed, but I can't look at them because if the world hasn't," he gasped, "if the world hasn't changed also and you asked me again to give up my crimes, what *I am*, I—"

"Don't say anything." Alexandria pressed her body against her own hands beneath his shirt, peering at him. *I can't explain it, but this, right now, is me. Look at me, Stock.*

His eyes returned to hers.

Alexandria saw the scorn vanish from his eyes as they raged with hunger. *Would you rebel against the darkness within me? Would you accept a command if it was only my soul that said so?*

Stock shuddered.

Take. Me.

Stock seized her shoulders. Her body held rigid, her face unrepentant. He forced her against his chest. Her mouth found his, inhaling his kiss. Her hands slid down his back, digging her fingernails into his skin, wanting him to feel her.

She gasped when he yanked the platinum band from her neck and bit the skin underneath. Gripping her dress, Stock pulled it over her head, throwing it to the floor.

Alexandria stepped back, extending an arm to stop his advance.

Stock stood still, chest heaving, watching her.

With deliberate slowness, she unfastened her bra, but left it on. Her fingers slipped below it. Her other hand dropped to her panties. She watched his eyes as they followed her movements. Seeing what torture she inflicted on him made her dizzy with pleasure. Her breathing synced with his.

When she felt her body trembling, Stock's arms enveloped her, lifting her off her feet. She floated across the sparkling city skyline and fell onto his bed. Her mouth and hands went to him, Stock's pulse driving a musical rhythm in her mind.

He spun her body away from him, bending her arms in against her chest, her face pressed against the mattress. She fought him, pulling against the sheets, wanting to break free—and loving the strength that wouldn't let her go.

The thought of Stock doing this to her, giving her these sensations, sent her over the edge, falling, only to climb again. He would not stop—she wished he would never stop.

At the end of the ascent, she felt the detonation of his agony and pleasure fused with her own. They collapsed, Stock pressing her flat on her stomach, numb to everything but the beating of two hearts.

Kaleidoscopes danced on the ceiling, lights disconnected from their sources beyond the window. Alexandria closed her eyes, drifting off to sleep.

When she awoke to the hint of sunrise, she watched Stock sleeping. His face looked so calm, and he breathed with a serenity she had never seen.

She rose and walked to the window, feeling beautiful, her body glowing. Pulling on a curl of her hair with both hands, she straightened it out, and gazed through the sheet of glass.

Her gaze stopped on the CUH center and her state office building. Glancing behind her, she noticed her shadow cutting across Stock's body. She released the hair, and it contracted back into a curl. *I'm not disconnected from those outside.* Her body fell limp against the pane, her strength gone.

Alexandria pushed herself away from the glass, crossing her arms over her nakedness. Walking across the room, she found her dress and slipped it on. She stood with her back to Stock, her platinum choker hanging off two fingers.

Placing the collar back to her neck, she felt her strength return, and it pressed down the darkness that had threatened her. A dull aching peace ran through her, which she wiped from her eyes with the back of a quivering hand.

She left Stock, knowing she must never return, because she must never again see her own darkness and feel this much pain.

Stock awoke to the sound of Alexandria's soft steps and watched her silhouette fade across the floor. He felt surprised that his siren had refused to demand his life in exchange for what he'd desperately wanted and received. His heartbeat slowed in agonizing relief because she'd not sacrificed her goodness by staying.

Moving to the window, he beheld his marquee below and knew the world he'd glimpsed last night, the world he'd so desperately wanted, was not and never could be real, and therefore his unbearable pain now didn't matter.

"It was just a bribe," he whispered, "a necessary penance to all those who understand what I cannot obey."

He stepped back and fell on the bed, wishing to be comforted by that familiar blanket of hatred toward mankind. But instead, he saw a long strand of Alexandria's hair on the pillow. He fondled it between his fingers and pictured her forbidden eyes, the ones more impossibly beautiful than his marquee's body.

Chapter 6

"I put my life in your hands every time I'm up there," an officer in a flight suit and pilot's cap said, pointing at the sky, "and every time I'm called to go up, I will protect yours. Act accordingly. Dismissed."

Those words comprised Major Gavin Sircor's entire speech to his 67th squadron maintenance crew four months ago—a week after Roble arrived at Kadena Air Force Base in Okinawa.

Roble had heard many speeches since entering the Air Force, most of them quotes from famous generals and presidents, but he only remembered Sircor's because Roble felt certain he meant it. That same night, out of respect for Sircor, he buzzed off his hair, something his sergeant, Jason Perry, had been screaming at him to do since arriving on base.

The shade under the open-walled hangar couldn't ease the afternoon's humid oppression as Roble knelt atop an F-15 Strike Eagle's wing.

He scanned its skin for stress-fissures using an ultrasound device. Sliding his hand along the grey surface, he felt each nuance of its texture and temperature, wondering how much torque and friction it could withstand before disintegrating.

Lifting his head, he watched Major Sircor's F-35 Lightning II taxiing out on the southern runway, leading a formation of three other intensely angled fighter jets.

From speaking with other airmen, Roble learned that Sircor had spent two years in the renowned *Thunderbird* aerobatic flight team, served a stint as the youngest experimental test pilot at Edwards Air Force Base, and flew the air-superiority F-22 Raptors at Elmendorf Air Force Base in Alaska. He received his first command, over the mixed F-15/F-35 fighter squadron, the 67th, two years ago at Kadena.

Everyone in the Air Force knew the 67th was, without debate, the best squadron in the Pacific theater. Those in its maintenance crew spoke often of duty and excellence; the two ideals Major Sircor referred to when explaining orders to Sergeant Perry.

Roble peered back into the scanner and tilted his head. *Is there really a gap down inside there?* He looked again. *Must be a disjointed strut.* Reaching into his pocket, he pulled out a fabric tape measure and stretched it across the wing in different directions while taking notes in a small pad. *I need to look inside the wing.*

The rumble from Sircor's F-35 afterburner forced Roble to sit up and watch the Lightning II streak away from the runway. It cut to the west over the East China Sea like it owned the sky. A second F-35 followed behind, rolling its wings back and forth.

"Santos," a voice growled from below. "Get the hell down from there and perform that engine test. I scheduled it for this morning."

Roble finished writing his notes before sliding off the wing and landing with a thud on his feet. Standing at attention, he said, "Sergeant, I finished the engine test last night. It needed a turbine blade realignment." He slipped the notepad into his pocket. "I completed the realignment at 0500."

Perry glared with eyes sitting too high on his narrow face. Looking around to see if anyone stood nearby, he said, "In my office now, Airman."

As they walked into an enclosed hangar to an oversized tool chest used as a desk, Roble said, "I want to check the wing struts inside Captain Meek's F-15."

"Why in the hell would you want to check those?" Perry shook his head. "You were testing for micro stress-fissures."

"I saw a disjointed strut below the alloy."

Perry rounded his desk and sat down. He flicked his cheek with a finger, creating a watery *bop*. "Read the manual again. You don't check struts with ultrasound through the surface; those are examined by hand and are not scheduled to be checked for another six months."

"That's what I saw."

Bop. Perry flicked his cheek again. "You weren't even supposed to be stress-testing the alloy today." He flicked his same finger into a straight line, pointing at a whiteboard on the wall. "You are supposed to follow the schedule. There is no leeway as to when you can do things, Airman." He rubbed his face. "Or leeway in *how* you do them."

Roble turned to the schedule. "So right now you want me to be at the engine testing area?"

"No, I don't want you to go over there—now." Perry exhaled. "You already did the blade realignment."

Roble squinted at the schedule.

Bouncing his knuckle against the desk, Perry scanned the hangar.

Roble shifted his glance to another whiteboard next to the schedule that contained the 67th maintenance crew's quality-check scores. Only his own column displayed a flawless record and no late assignments. He looked back at Perry, waiting.

Perry pointed at an airman adjusting the controller on a missile-bay door. "Grab Wynn over there and have him help you check the wing struts on Captain Meek's F-15. That's an order. Do it now."

"Yes, Sergeant." As Roble walked away, he heard a watery *bop* behind him.

Airman Wynn threw a screwdriver into a toolbox when Roble relayed Perry's orders. "That's not on the schedule." The black rings under Wynn's eyes stretched tight. "*This* needs to be done today."

"I'll do the wing examination myself," Roble said.

"Yeah, right. It's an order, asshole. I have to do it." Wynn stormed away to Meek's F-15.

Roble shrugged and followed.

Unfastening the first underwing panel, Wynn said, "If you don't follow *this* procedure by the book, I'm going straight to Perry."

Roble had already marked a spot underneath the wing and removed two panels.

"You're probably too dense to notice," he stopped, and glared at Roble, "but nobody likes you. You don't belong. Think you're too good to eat lunch with us? When we go out for drinks, where are you? Probably in your barracks crying to Mommy on the phone."

Roble removed a fourth panel as Wynn continued talking. "When it's break time, you'd better quit so I don't look bad. And don't talk to me unless I ask you to."

"Yep, there it is," Roble said atop a stepladder, his head inside the wing.

The next day, Sergeant Perry selected Roble for cross-training duty with the Japanese 204th located at nearby Naha Air Base. Most US mechanics loathed the assignment because they considered the Japanese cross-training protocols to be too strict, the hours too long, and the Japanese too boring.

Roble grinned. *This is a chance to see different types of jets.*

Arriving at Naha a week later and two hours early, he followed Japanese Maintenance Airman Toki Kozumi on an inspection of the Japanese F-15Js and F-15DJs, known as Peace Eagles.

As Roble eyed the rows of smooth-bodied, twin-engine fighters, his gaze froze on one parked at the end. Its variable flaps atop the air intakes appeared unusually angled and the tailfin rudders larger and more curved than normal.

He walked over for a closer examination; his Japanese counterpart stayed back. Unlike the other Japanese F-15DJs, the decals on the twin tailfins didn't display a landing bald eagle with the word *Hyakuri* underneath. This one had an ominous skeletal eagle with extended talons transposed over crossed air-to-air missiles.

Rounding a wing to look at the tailfin rudders, Roble stopped when he noticed tiny vertical fins directly in front of the wings' ailerons. *What in the world?* He reached up and touched one, his mind in furious thought. Yanking out a piece of paper from his pocket, he sketched the aircraft and its modifications.

As he walked back to the aircraft's nose he almost tripped, seeing a young officer standing rigid as a board under the nosecone. The man's hair was bleached with lines like the youths Roble saw in the city, but never on anyone wearing a Japanese uniform. The officer's eyes shot focused rage.

Roble bowed, knowing this was the pilot, the unofficial owner of this modified machine.

The pilot didn't flinch, his face expressing impending murder. Roble slipped his drawing into his pocket and departed.

Returning to his Japanese counterpart, Roble asked. "How do you say 'fighter pilot' in Japanese?"

"Jieitai-no-pairotto."

"Who is that jetta…i…no…parrot…o?" Roble pointed at the officer near the jet he would now call the *Skeleton Eagle*.

Airman Kozumi cringed and bowed.

"I probably didn't say the word right, but who is he?" Roble asked, still pointing.

"Hai," Airman Kozumi said, bowing again.

"Who?"

Kozumi's eyes darted back and forth. "Captain Takinato. You are not to talk to him. And stay away from his jet."

Captain Takinato… Roble rubbed his chin, then pulled out his sketch of the *Skeleton Eagle* and studied the strange modifications.

He spent the rest of the day going over maintenance procedures with the Japanese mechanics, but his mind remained focused on the *Skeleton Eagle* and Captain Takinato. Before he returned to Kadena Air Base, he stood near the Naha runway, straining his eyes to examine the modified fighter jet one more time.

At his Kadena barracks, he sat in his tiny living room buried in maintenance manuals and pecking at a laptop keyboard. He researched variable intake flaps, aileron rudders, and wing configurations, trying to determine the purpose of Captain Takinato's modifications. He also studied the types of advanced materials comprising the Japanese F-15s.

Within weeks, the two wooden crates Roble used as a coffee table disappeared under research notes, his laptop's hard drive filled to capacity with three-dimensional renderings of Peace Eagles.

He often stayed late at Naha after cross-training, sketching additional versions of the *Skeleton Eagle* from afar. At his barracks, he redrew the unusual fighter and all its modified parts on artboards in exacting detail, but not as they were—as he thought they could be.

Standing alone in his living room in the middle of the night, he examined his finished work. He pulled out his crumpled, unfinished dream from his pocket and studied it. He made a single mark near the edge.

On his next visit to Naha Air Base, he brought his completed drawings. He scanned for Captain Takinato, asked about him, but Takinato couldn't be found. *Where is that* Jieitai-no-pairotto? He took his drawings home, disappointed.

After failing to find Takinato on his next visit to Naha, Roble approached the forbidden *Skeleton Eagle* with his drawings in hand.

Instead of waiting by the tailfins as he'd planned, he found a wooden wheel chock and stood on it. He felt across the surface of an intake flap, examining its texture and color and comparing its radiant heat from the sun to the alloys used in the surrounding fuselage. Once satisfied, he stepped down and moved to the rear of the jet and waited in the tailfin's shade.

The hair on his neck spiked when eyes bored into him.

Keeping his gaze lowered, Roble walked toward the jet's nose. He placed the artboards on the ground before Takinato's flight boots, turned, and left.

Roble spent more workdays at Naha than allowed, but neither Sergeant Perry nor any of the 67th maintenance crew complained. He stared often at the *Skeleton Eagle* but never glimpsed Takinato.

At night, he thought about his drawings and wondered if Takinato had looked at them. *Just tell me what you think about my ideas.* Roble pictured him ripping them to shreds.

Two weeks after he left his drawings at Takinato's feet, Roble strolled by the *Skeleton Eagle*, daring its owner to appear. But even this impertinence didn't summon him. His absence made Roble uneasy. *Regardless of what he thinks of my ideas, why would he avoid me?* Roble glanced again at the *Skeleton Eagle* and exhaled.

Later that night, having no reason to go home even though the weekend started, Roble loitered alone in a Japanese maintenance hangar at Naha, reconstructing the fan on a jet turbine. He mumbled to himself, trying to memorize the part names in Japanese.

As he knelt on the floor, a shadow crossed his body. He looked up.

Takinato stood above him, his face pulled tight. "Come with me," he said in crisp staccato English.

Feeling his heart skip a beat, Roble dropped his plyers. They clanked to the ground.

Takinato marched from the hangar to a nearby parking lot. Roble followed behind, feeling apprehensive but more than curious. Takinato disappeared into an unlit area with only the faint outline of a vehicle near a fence.

Roble slowed his pace, trying to adjust his eyes to the darkness.

From the glint of a distant street lamp, he could see that Takinato stood next to a muscle car. By its wide tires, wired-down hood, and oversized exhaust pipes, the car was obviously modified for racing.

Takinato climbed in and fired up the engine. Roble's eyes widened at the guttural roar, before focusing on the red hood as the headlights flipped on. The window rolled down.

"Get in," Takinato ordered.

Roble jumped into the passenger seat and glanced at Takinato, but Takinato stared forward. Looking around, Roble noted the austere interior, bare metal on hard black surfaces.

Pumping the pedal, Takinato sent the high-pressured valves screaming in steady swells. Caramelized gas fumes filled Roble's nostrils. He breathed deep, trying to absorb not only the smell, but also the vibrations.

Takinato slammed the gearshift into first. The car rocketed forward. They sped to the old Naha downtown, drifting through corners and breaking every convention of orderly driving. Yet despite the speed and aggressiveness, his control of the car felt comforting.

They screeched to a stop in an alleyway covered in graffiti and smelling of greasy restaurant trash. A garage door rolled up, and they pulled in to the narrow space.

Squeezing himself out of the car, Roble glanced up through beams of overhead lights at a system of suspended chains and pulleys holding a motorcycle next to an elevated loft.

Takinato climbed a ladder and Roble followed. They exited onto a grated metal floor overlooking the garage. Above them hung an even higher loft. Tools and parts from cars, jets, and unidentifiable machines filled workbenches and wall-mounted shelves. Manuals and magazines stuck out from the objects.

Walking past Takinato, Roble stood in front of his *Skeleton Eagle* sketches hanging between shelves on a wall.

"Want to know what I think of them?" Takinato lit a cigarette and moved next to him.

Roble stared at his artboards displayed in meticulous rows, and swallowed. "I think you've already told me."

He bowed. "I am Takinato, Kazuki."

"Roble Santos."

"Can you make the parts you have drawn?"

Roble shook his head. "I don't have the advanced materials or the machine tools for them. It's not like modifying a cargo plane."

Takinato moved closer to the drawings, blowing a cone of smoke across them. "What kind of performance will they give me?"

"Well," Roble rubbed up and down his arms, "if I could reinforce the wing structure to withstand the additional Gs, my rudders and ailerons can give you three degrees more turning angle. But a simple vectoring capability would really make a difference for turning."

"Could that be retro-fitted?"

"I think so. I've been toying with the idea, but I haven't finished my analysis."

Takinato thumped a finger against a drawing. "Your variable intake flaps are different from what I'm using."

"Mine would give you another five percent thrust during supersonic flight." Roble scratched his head. "You had the right idea, but if your flaps are made primarily of aerospace grade aluminum, as they appear, I'd reattach the original parts; they won't be strong enough to withstand the heat for too long." He slapped his forearm against a drawing. "If I could widen the intake by just a centimeter right here, I could get you an additional two to three percent thrust in both sub and supersonic speeds." His arm dropped. "But then you'd have to fortify the turbine blades to handle the pressure."

"How did you learn all this?"

"How'd you learn to modify that car?" Roble pointed down.

"*Hai*," Takinato said, flaring the tip of his cigarette bright gold.

Roble reached out, lifted the corner of one of his drawings, and glanced at Takinato. Removing the artboard, his eyes absorbed the uncovered tease of power and grace.

Takinato raised an eyebrow.

Setting his drawing on the nearby workbench, Roble went back for more. As each artboard came down, he came closer to something unexpected and exhilarating. With the last piece of the puzzle removed, he stepped back. There lay a huge, glossy photo of a pitch-black *Succubus* Jet. "How old are you, Captain Takinato?"

"Why?"

"Something I read a while back was almost right."

Takinato frowned, blowing out a line of smoke.

"Maybe you're not a teenager and maybe this isn't your bedroom wall, but the *Succubus* is certainly impractical," Roble said. "So impractical it makes me feel like anything's possible."

"You wish to see one?"

"That's what I'm doing."

"No," Takinato said, his voice cutting. "Do you want to *see* one?"

Roble turned.

"At the Misawa Air Show next month. My friends and I are flying there. Come along."

Roble looked back at the *Succubus*, a thin smile on his lips.

Chapter 7

Libby's face glowed blue.

She slid her elbows forward on her desk and scrolled through diagrams on a handheld screen. Outside the window, an airliner's headlights bathed the office before it dissolved back into darkness.

"*Gary Sanders is here to see you, Ms. Dodge,*" Amanda said over a loudspeaker.

"So late?" Libby glanced out the window at the illuminated airport hangars beyond the fence.

"*He wanted to catch you when you weren't so busy.*"

"What are you still doing here at this hour?" Libby asked.

"*I waited so I could remind you of your test flight in the morning on your way out.*"

"Send him in. And you, go home."

Gary opened the office door, stopping at the dark threshold. Libby blinked when the lights flipped on, but her eyes remained on the screen.

"Oh, I…Amanda told me to come in." Gary carried a stack of files under an arm and sat in a chair, his thin hair arched in one direction across his round head.

Libby glanced up. "More government lawsuits?"

"Worse." Gary pulled out a sheet of paper and tossed it on the desk. "DCU is crucifying you in the media. The first round of defense will be this press release explaining our side of things."

"Our side of what?" Libby brushed the sheet away.

"They're turning the public against us, making you sound like an insensitive money-grabbing capitalist." He jiggled the files in his hands.

"Well," Libby smiled, "what if I am?"

"Just read our response. Our best people plus McCormick and Clapton worked on it."

Libby picked up the sheet, held it between the two of them

and ripped it down the center, revealing Gary's shocked face on the other side.

Wadding up each piece, she tossed them, one after another across the room, sinking them both in a wastebasket. "Anything else?"

"For goodness' sake, Ms. Dodge. Haven't you read any news recently?" Gary removed several newspaper clippings and shuffled through them, shaking his head. "Mr. Compros said, and I quote: '*Especially disappointing to me, Libby Industries uses robots for a majority of its labor, thereby stealing high-paying American jobs. We at DCU use robotics only when absolutely necessary because we care about our workers.*'"

"Did they at least show a decent picture of my robots? Victor made one that looks like those cool toys that change into things. You know the ones I'm talking about, right?"

Gary pushed his hair to the wrong side of his head, spiking it in the air, and continued reading, "'*All of DCU's facilities are EPA certified while Libby Dodge jackhammers the face off a pristine cliff.*'" He glanced up. "Want me to continue?"

"Not really."

"Ms. Dodge, it goes on and on, and not just from Frederick Compros. You are being accused of destroying the environment, coddling the rich, thumbing your nose at the government, turning a blind eye to the dangers of your supersonic jets, and—don't kill the messenger—being a sociopath."

"Spare me the compliments, Gary."

"They are not... Look, you hired me to protect you. So let me do my job." Jabbing his finger at the trash can, he added, "Starting with that press release."

"You are supposed to protect me from lawsuits, not hot air. You got the judge to deny the temporary injunction against the cliff house, right? Just keep doing legal things like that."

"We may have won *that* legal skirmish, but the war isn't over. You're upsetting powerful people, Ms. Dodge. The EPA is still going ahead with their environmental testing of your cliff. One foreign government and many nonprofit groups are assisting them. Even if the EPA can't submit their final results to the judge until after your cliff house is complete, you could still lose the case and receive environmental fines."

"It's my house, on my land, right? I'm sure the court will see it the same way."

Gary shook his head with a groan. "And there's something else that worries me, but I can't quite put my finger on why." He swallowed. "The Department of the Interior subpoenaed your purchase documentation of the cliff, and I have it from reliable sources they've also ordered the title work. I'm not sure what they're up to, but I don't like it one bit."

"That sounds like legal stuff. You're a lawyer—fix it." Libby looked back at her screen and scrolled through some technical drawings.

"I'll do what I can," he smoothed out his tie, "but you need to get the public on your side, otherwise people will try to stop you."

"It's a free country, Gary." She leaned back in her chair, threw her socked feet onto her desk, and wiggled her toes.

He smoothed his hair back to the correct side. "You must defend yourself."

Libby stared at his smooth arching hair, and then back at her screen, contemplating the aerodynamics of her new jet canopy.

"Ahem." Gary shuffled the files, crinkling the paper.

Libby blinked. "Oh, you said defend myself?" She dropped the handheld device onto her elevated legs. "Isn't that what I'm paying taxes for? To be protected by my government? Stop worrying."

"Taxes? Ms. Dodge, I can't even get you to file a tax return." He rubbed his cheeks and squished the sweat between his fingertips. "*Libby Tax Dodge* was a front page headline last year."

"The IRS calls me every year sounding upset I didn't file," she yawned, "and I tell them which government functions I want to donate to and for how much, but they never listen. They just send over a bunch of dreary suits to audit me." She scrunched her brows in thought. "If I remember correctly, they took over forty million dollars from my bank account last time and I have no idea what they spent it on. But certainly it was enough money for them to protect me from whatever it is you're talking about, right?"

"But…you don't understand," he sputtered, shifting in his seat. "People have the perception you don't care about anything but yourself." Throwing both hands in the air for emphasis, his files dumped to the floor. He bent over, picking them up. "But I think we can spin that back around with a few well-placed ads."

"Will media spin design me a hypersonic aircraft or manufacture a single jet engine?"

He sighed, his head still below the desk.

"I'm glad you agree." Libby wiggled her toes. "Oh, and next time, don't print out all that garbage. It cuts down too many trees for no good reason."

Gary raised his head and grinned with a look of pain.

———

Four workers, all in reflective heat-resistant suits and holding rifle-like barrels, shot streams of red plasma against sandstone walls, melting them into lava.

A woman, using an elevated robotic arm, pressed a string of carbon-encased lightbulbs into the molten rock along the top. Two other workers sent streams of high-pressured freezing gas from nozzles into the lava flow, blowing it back up the walls and onto the ceilings in smooth waves. The new walls hardened into tempered glass.

When a worker collapsed, hitting his head on the cave floor, the other workers quickly extinguished the flames and freezing gas.

Somebody lifted him into a seated position and pulled the heat shield from his head, revealing the unconscious and sweat-drenched face of Victor Lafayette. A drip from his hair sizzled into a puff of steam against his reflective chest. A bruise swelled on the side of his forehead.

"Get some water!" someone yelled.

Victor's eyes flicked open and glanced around. He sprang to his feet, standing tall.

"Are you all right, sir?" a man in a heat suit asked.

"Nothing like a refreshing nap, my fine *travailleur*." Victor patted the man's shoulder and walked to a scaffold holding brilliant work lights. He rotated the intense beam away from the excavation point and across the cavern. A shimmering glass cavity spread out in the distance, translucent columns supporting its vaulted thirty-foot ceiling.

Victor ripped off the rest of his heat suit, leaving only sweaty long johns, and strode west toward the passage running from the cavern to beneath the Libby cliff house. Along the way, he stopped to mark the floor with a handheld etching laser.

A man ran down the ramp from Libby's horse stable into the eastern end of the cave, whistled and then yelled, "Victor! Libby needs to see you immediately."

Thirty minutes later, Victor sprinted into the Libby Industries' airport hangar. Libby Dodge and Sigmund Evert stood in front of two tarp-covered jets.

"Victor!" Libby motioned him over. "What took you so long?"

"What is the emergency, *Madame*?" Victor asked, looking around.

"We completed the Libby IV's fifth test flight this morning," Sigmund said, his voice flat, his eyes sedate. "Let's just say we're very happy with the results."

"*Monsieur* Evert, are you feeling well?" Victor flicked his fingers in the air. "I've never seen you this excited."

"And I've never seen you sans armor." Sigmund stared without expression at Victor's still sweat-soaked pajamas. "I guess we're both going ape nuts."

Libby bounced on her toes, grinning. "How soon can you get the manufacturing in the Calico Cave up and running?"

Victor raised an eyebrow.

"We took it up to speed," her grin widened.

Victor glanced at the covered jets. "The Libby IV? Up to... *speed*?"

Sigmund leaned against a covered jet, still no expression on his face.

"It must have been glorious," Victor whispered. "Does that mean we could be selling them within a year?"

Libby tapped Victor's shoulder three times. "Sold. Three. Today."

"Certainly you jest?"

"Halvern brought over a few of his Asian architectural clients to observe the speed test. He mistakenly told them it's nicknamed the *Skyscraper*." Libby rolled her eyes with a smirk. "But whatever, they put down deposits and want the—*Sovereigns*—as soon as possible."

Sigmund pushed himself off the tarp. "We'll bypass FAA

certification on the initial lot since we're selling to private citizens in Singapore. And we'll make room to assemble the first few here—"

"But," Libby interrupted, "I want Calico ramped up so we can hit efficient volume—" She blinked her eyes and gripped Victor's shoulders, staring at his bruised forehead. "What the hell happened to you?"

"I took a nap."

"I thought that's why you wore armor?"

"You must see the cavern, *Madame* Dodge. It is…" Victor kissed his fingers like a satisfied chef. "And nobody knows it is there."

"I want to see it right now," Libby's eyes sparkled. "But I'm flying out in a few minutes to meet a supplier. I'll take you up in a *Sovereign* tomorrow when I get back. You're going to soil your little French PJs when you see what will emerge from your cave." She glanced at the covered jets, stepped back, and wiped an eye.

Sigmund walked away.

"This," Victor patted Libby's back, "is a stupendous day, my friend."

From behind a mirrored canopy, Libby gazed at the shimmering horizon below a sinking ball of fire.

A string of green blotches floated atop the ocean miles below. Her knuckle hit a brushed-alloy switch on the console, dropping two empty fuel tanks like bombs from beneath the grey-blue jet.

Red letters blinked across a screen: *Ramjet ignition.*

The vibrations from the turbofans faded and Libby's body compressed against the seat, leaving only the serene sensation of unimpeded speed. The sun held steady before her, unable to escape into its watery bed.

"*Ms. Dodge,*" a woman said over a speaker, "*I have Frederick Compros from DCU on the line.*"

"Really?" Libby pushed a hand through her hair. "All right, patch him through, Amanda."

"*Libby,*" a silky, drawn-out voice said. "*How are you? It seems like forever, doesn't it?*"

"What's up? Something bothering you?"

"What makes you think…?" Frederick asked. *"No. No. Don't be ridiculous. Where are you?"*

"Hawaii."

"Oh great, love the place. Martha and I have a wonderful spread on Maui. Sometimes a little R&R is just what one needs—that's what my grandfather used to say."

Libby glanced at the Machmeter and whistled softly.

"Ahem, well," Frederick grunted. *"I called to congratulate you for starting your new prototype. It sounds very interesting, very interesting indeed. I think you will learn, as I have, to respect the complexity of attempting hypersonic speed."*

Libby watched the jet's nose piercing the air, searching for signs of the heat lapping against the alloy. It appeared as cold as ice.

"Libby? Did our call drop? Amanda, did my call drop?"

"I'm here," Libby said, "what do you want?"

"Oh, look Libby, we've known each other for a long time. In fact you've always reminded me of myself in a lot of ways. Maybe that's because I trained you well at DCU—too well, perhaps." He chuckled until he coughed. *"I just wanted to say it's a damn shame what the FAA did to your jets. Lord knows we've all had our share of headaches. But don't worry, I understand the thinking over there, and I have it on good authority that if you were to allow DCU to represent you, in say, an ownership position, I could guarantee this little regulatory misunderstanding would be cleared up."*

The faint pulse of the ramjets vibrated the controls, tickling her fingertips.

"Are you there?" Frederick blurted.

"I think you were saying something about how you convinced the FAA to withdraw their flight certification from the *Succubus* and limit the approved speed of the *Wyvern*. Or were you reminiscing about the day you fired me from DCU?"

"What? I never mentioned… Don't you…" He cleared his throat. *"Look Libby, the bottom line is DCU can help you."*

"Don't you have a tee time you're late for or something?"

"Be practical for once in your life. The government will not lift their flight ban on the Succubus *without feeling completely confident in its safety. Many, many people are concerned. There are questions, new questions people have asked; additional flight tests won't be enough. It will take a lot of compromise on your end to get her back up in the air. If you don't, the Libby IV, if you ever figure out how to make it, will never be certified."*

"I've already sold three."

"I'm not saying you didn't sell some Succubuses…Succubusans… Libby IIIs before decertification. I'm just saying—"

"I sold three Libby IV *Sovereigns.*"

"Libby IVs? That design isn't even really possible with current technology. Is it?"

Libby tweaked the flight stick, cutting the *Sovereign* to the southwest. The glowing, blue band at the atmosphere's edge rolled over her.

"Libby. Even if you found a way to make it, it's not approved to sell."

"True, but approvals don't make it fly."

"You might find a few nefarious foreign buyers for your jets, but you'll never sell them in sufficient volume. You'll never make money selling so few."

"I'm going to lose a ton of money on them because of the FAA's decision." She glanced down at the green outline of Japan to her right.

"See. That's the first sensible thing you've said. Don't throw good money after bad—that's what my grandfather used to say. I want to help you meet regulatory compliance and help us both make money. Just sell me fifty-one percent of Libby Industries and you'll be shipping a dozen Succubuses… Succubi…jets…a quarter. I'll let you run DCU's entire research and development team. You'd report only to me, just like old times." He stopped, wheezing over the speaker. *"But don't answer me until you hear this—two point one billion dollars. Huh? How does that sound? That's twice what any other competitor would pay. My board will push back, but I'm certain I can push it through."*

Libby rolled the *Sovereign* upside down. She hung, hair drooping toward the canopy, her eyes laughing at the distant strait between the Philippines and Taiwan. "Nah."

"You don't need more enemies. I could bleed your company dry dragging you through lawsuits. Who knows, the State Department might get nervous about American technology falling into the wrong hands overseas. Don't you dare think exporting gives you a free pass around federal regulations."

"I have no doubt you could convince the State Department to prohibit my international sales." She rolled the jet upright and pushed the stick forward. "And you could probably sue me until my business goes bankrupt—but you *can't* have it."

"What? We could work as a team. I'm your friend."

"Ah, friends."

Silence.

"Changi Tower," Libby said into her mouthpiece, "this is flight Sam-Zero-Zero-Three requesting permission to land, over."

"*Permission granted Sam-Zero-Zero-Three. Please wait for instructions.*"

"*Changi?*" Frederick asked. "*I thought you said you were in Hawaii?*"

"Was. Now I'm in Singapore."

"*But it's been less than an hour. You'd have to be flying close to… That's hypersonic!*"

"Indeed-a-roo."

Chapter 8

A firestorm of public protest twisted high into the Las Vegas sky, its heat focused on the construction of the Calico Basin cliff house and Libby Dodge the woman who intended to make it her home. And the closer it came to completion, the higher the temperature rose. The outrage seemed so unanimous almost no one thought she would dare to occupy it.

On the day the cliff house construction was completed, protestors set record attendance. They arrayed themselves along the Calico Basin Road and across Libby's desert land, equipped with tents, signs, and food coolers. Shouts ignited by a bullhorn boomeranged in waves from within the mass of bodies.

A lone construction worker walked over to the vocal mob from the cliff house and tapped a sign into the ground, which read: *Private Property. Visitors welcome to hike trails.*

He taped a piece of white cardboard below it that added: *Open House Today.* A half-eaten peach flew over his head as he strode away.

Within an hour, more cars parked along the already crowded road. These new arrivals trekked along a dirt trail to the Libby House, enduring occasional flying food and raucous shouts. "Don't justify a crime!" "You're murdering a dying planet!" "Public lands in public hands!"

As the morning wore on and the number of visitors increased, the voice behind the bullhorn intensified.

Several foot trails crossed Libby's land, leading to sandstone peaks, hidden canyons, and desert valleys. The most popular led up the cliff's face to the left side of the Libby House by way of carved sandstone switchbacks. It connected to the cliff home's exterior walkways and continued up to the top of the plateau.

The visitors who entered the lower floors of the home found a mix of multi-shaded slick rock rooms and winding hallways, some drilled deep into the cliff's heart. Some windows framed views of distant Las Vegas casinos while others sat secluded within shadowy canyon crevices. Thin waterfalls cascaded into narrow rock troughs imbedded in the floors, and water poured along suspended aqueducts in the walls, wiping away the noise from the outside world. The air inside felt cool, smelling like a mossy mountain stream.

Visitors' children ran wild through the lower catacombs of halls and chambers, playing an animated game of hide-and-seek. To their delight, some discovered secret doors and hidden passages. Parents spent hours trying to locate missing children, while children spent hours maneuvering between secret hideouts.

The upper levels of the cliff house became ever more grand and open. From the top floor, made of white stone, and akin to a grand ballroom, guests looked out a towering, uninterrupted pane of glass. At the rear, two stone, floating spiral staircases led up to the home's plateau roof.

The roof offered panoramic views beneath a flawless blue sky. Pathways led guests around cacti and trickling streams to areas with stone benches and white cushioned daybeds. An open stone kitchen sat in the center. Chefs barbecued pork, rainbow trout, and mushrooms, the smoke wafting across starving guests. Wine glasses filled with pomegranate seeds and diced cactus fruit decorated rock slabs. By late afternoon, over four hundred visitors mingled atop the deck.

As some visitors returned to their cars, they glanced at the picketers' signs displaying slogans that denounced what they'd just seen. A few protestors merged with exiting visitors, asking questions. Other picketers hiked to the house, a place they had witnessed from its birth, through its growing pains, and to its ultimate realization.

The bullhorn of the protest leader continued to yelp as his army melted away, leaving a sea of rubble and trash on the trampled desert.

One protestor, a woman with short hair and a child slung across her chest, found Libby as she stood on her third floor office balcony. Wearing her cowboy hat, Libby explained to several visitors how the inversion of airflow would cool the house on summer days. Her hand swept out from her body as she spoke, highlighting the fact the balcony had no railing.

One of the guests said, "It looks so natural."

The woman protestor stepped forward and countered, "But it *isn't* natural, is it?"

Libby turned and smiled at the woman's baby. "Hello, I'm Libby Dodge."

The protestor shifted on her feet. "This is Jack." She watched Libby ogling her baby. Reforming her stern expression, she added, "I'm Maggie. Why would you destroy nature like this?"

"Maggie," Libby looked up from the baby, "this house is as natural as I am."

"You made it with jackhammers and dynamite. How can you say that?"

The other visitors cringed and stepped away.

Libby twinkled her fingers at Jack. "Aren't humans natural beings? And isn't it their nature to create things such as this?" She pointed at the water pouring from spouts in the stone walls.

"But don't you think the earth should be protected?"

"From whom?"

"Those who would destroy it. You."

Libby dipped her toes, sticking out from a hiking sandal, into a water trough in the floor. "Isn't this great? I hope nobody would destroy it. It's really hard for me to express how excited I am today, Maggie. This is the first home I've ever built."

Maggie looked at Libby, her face attempting to contract into a frown, but failing. She patted Jack's chest. "This home might *appear* beautiful, Ms. Dodge, but I feel what you did here is wrong. I really worry that humans are changing the environment."

"Oh," Libby said. "Humans are most certainly changing the environment. Do you happen to know of another way to survive other than to control the elements?" She stuck her finger into Jack's reaching hand.

"We can be smart about how we treat the environment. We all live together on this planet."

Libby nodded. "I love hearing smart ideas. If you'd like to share some, I'd like to hear them."

Maggie's nose scrunched. "Really?"

"It is a bit hectic today, but come back when it's not so busy, and please, let's talk." Libby wiggled Jack's hand. "We might or might not agree, but I won't ever force anything on you, as I would hope you wouldn't on me."

Maggie exhaled, shoulders relaxing.

"If you're hungry," Libby said, "go upstairs to the deck. There is plenty of food, and the iced tea is my own special recipe. I got the idea from distilling jet fuel."

Maggie frowned. Jack chirped at Libby's blinking eyes.

"Just try it." Libby laughed. "Tell the chefs to dig up whatever Jack wants. He eats, doesn't he?"

"You will really let people hike on your land? Every day?"

"And all night." Libby slipped her finger from Jack's hand and peered off the balcony. "I love owning this land. You should see how it feels hiking with the coyotes howling and the glow of the city on the rim of a starry sky."

Maggie stood silent for a moment. "I do have some ideas. How can I contact you?"

Libby pulled a business card from her pocket and handed it to Jack's outstretched hand.

"Okay," Maggie said, "I'll go try your iced tea."

As the sun set and the radiance of the distant city became backdrop to the leaving visitors, a local news reporter approached Libby near the rooftop's ledge. One of the most vocal critics of the cliff house's construction, he came to compile evidence of the environment's destruction. Still holding his pen and notebook, he asked, "Why didn't you listen to anyone's concerns?"

Libby turned to him. "I listened to every rational argument made, all two of them. This house is better because of them, and I'm grateful."

"*Which* ideas did you listen to?"

"One, the solar windows and batteries provide all the home's power. And two, the shape of the openings and the tunnels provide passive cooling." Libby rubbed her chin. "Oh, I guess I actually received three good ideas—the natural seepage through the cliff is used for all of our water. The house is off the utility grid and indefinitely sustainable, all because of rational suggestions I received. Do you think I should have listened to anything else?"

"No matter what excuses you make, the community has strong feelings about what you did to this cliff, Ms. Dodge," the reporter said behind a strained jaw. "Doesn't that matter to you?"

Libby sipped her iced tea and turned back toward the city lights.

The reporter glanced across the rooftop deck, down along the carved balconies and walkways below, the trickle of water flowing over the edge as a backdrop. Looking up to Libby's undisturbed profile and the golden city in the distance, he dropped his notebook to his side, nodded, and walked away.

His news story the next day said in part: *Now that the cliff house is built, however unfortunate that may be, it should be considered a local landmark and preserved for future generations.*

The national and international news media declared: *Destruction! How did we let this happen? Shouldn't somebody do something?*

Nonprofit groups, business executives, politicians, housewives and househusbands from around the country demanded the deconstruction of the cliff house, that Libby Dodge be fined and jailed, and that local permitting authorities be investigated for corruption.

But while the collective winds of protest swirled in distant bands gaining strength—inside the storm's eye an accepting calm emerged. Most of those who had visited the house spoke about it in private, frequently, and in awe.

By the next week, no local protestors gathered below the cliff, just admirers and a steady flow of hikers and climbers. A consensus seemed to seep through the residents of Las Vegas that the Libby House *should* exist on that cliff, and that it somehow belonged to them—just as a city skyline belongs to all those who raise their upturned glance.

Chapter 9

Roble and Takinato strode onto Misawa Airfield following behind four ladies whose legs moved in rhythm below tailored skirts. The group of six directed their eyes forward as though nothing in their periphery existed.

They passed the airshow's presentations, pomp, and crowds, zeroing in on a *Succubus* sitting beyond the end of a runway.

The group spread out in a line several feet in front of the sleek temptress.

Roble stepped closer.

The tallest woman, Sugemi, with immaculate black hair and sharp eyes, reached out and ran her fingernails down the back of Roble's arm. He shivered and slid a hand along the smooth *Succubus*.

Watching him caress the jet, Sugemi withdrew her hand and fondled the arrowhead hanging around her neck. Roble pressed a cheek against the black alloy, looking down its lines.

"Don't do anything indecent with her in public," Sugemi said. "We're going to see the U-2 *Dragon Lady*."

Roble glanced behind as the four ladies marched away, their elbows touching. "Thanks for the lift," he said.

Sugemi lifted a hand in the air as she walked away.

Takinato stood watching the exchange, an eyebrow raised.

Roble exhaled, feeling lightheaded. After a moment, he pulled a sketchpad from his backpack, stepped back from the *Succubus*, and drew a long sensual line.

"Whose body are you drawing? The *Succubus*', or Sugemi's?" Takinato asked.

"I figured your friends would be pilots. But you never mentioned they were all women," Roble said, not looking away from his sketch.

"You never mentioned you were interested in anything but jets."

Roble stopped his pencil mid-stroke on a curve of a *Succubus* wing, thinking of the flight here. He'd sat in the cockpit next to Sugemi, the owner and pilot of the private jet.

After takeoff, he kept glancing at her refined poise and black-lined eyes, highlighted against the sophisticated jet. *What kind of woman is this?*

Not saying a word, she kept her attention on the horizon, hands moving with precision at the controls.

She looks ruthless.

"See something you like?" she asked after minutes of silence.

Roble turned away, cringing. "Uhmm…I was just admiring… your jet."

"What do you like about it?"

He glanced down her body to her short skirt. "It must have a thrust rating above two thousand pounds."

"Over twenty-five hundred if I use the performance reserve," she said.

"A five-minute reserve?"

"Eight."

"No way." Roble shook his head.

Sugemi punched a button and cranked the throttles to maximum. The jet accelerated, the turbines whining under the pressure. Roble watched the clock. After five and a half minutes the turbines downshifted.

Roble grinned.

Tapping a dial, she said, "You were right, but I pulled almost three thousand pounds of thrust. That's more than some early fighter jets."

"You don't say," Roble said, aroused by the sound of her voice talking about jets. "How much thrust did the first fighter jet have?"

"The first operational one? The Messerschmitt Me 262 first took off under its own jet power with a twenty-two hundred pound thrust engine."

Roble tried to hide his surprise by rubbing his forehead. "Yeah, but that was their version three. How much thrust did their version one have?"

After an hour of debate about the development of jet aviation, the topic shifted to the greatest aviators in history. When they disagreed on who was the first woman to circumnavigate the globe in an airplane, Sugemi said, "Want to bet?"

"I never lose bets, Sugemi. Keep your thousand yen for cotton candy at the airshow."

"You can have my jet if I lose."

Roble blinked. After a moment he chuckled. "I own some crinkled magazine pictures of private jets. Your wager is a *little* out of my price range."

"Your necklace," she said.

His heart thumped in his chest as he touched his necklace—the only possession his real parents had left him. Lifting it, he studied the diagonal crystalline lines sparkling within the obsidian. He'd never let anyone even hold it before. "You would risk your jet for a necklace?"

"Would you risk your necklace for a jet?" she asked, her sharp eyes watching the sky.

Roble peered out at the aircraft's glossy nosecone, then at Sugemi's confident profile. Breathing in, he rubbed his hands together and pressed his fingers against the pocket containing his crumpled dream. *This is too good to be true. This jet could fund my idea.* "Are you sure you really want to do this?"

She turned her head and looked him up and down, stopping on his eyes. He shivered, a wave of icy sensuality penetrating him.

"Are you?" She narrowed her eyes.

Damn. Why do I feel drunk? He removed his necklace and held it in both hands. Clearing his throat, he took a breath. "All right," he said, and in broken Japanese added, "You're on. But I apologize in advance for winning."

She spread her knees creating a V out from her skirt. Roble tried to keep his gaze from dropping.

"Takinato," she looked back into the passenger cabin, "please look up the first woman to circumnavigate the globe in an airplane."

When Takinato yelled the correct answer, Roble winced, reached over and dropped his necklace between Sugemi's legs. It slid under her skirt, into the V of her lap.

A rush of heat poured over Roble, his eyes losing their focus. He knew he should feel beyond devastated at the loss, but a strange excitement swirled in his gut.

Sugemi had closed her legs, leaving his arrowhead there the rest of the flight.

Roble grinned at the memory, inhaling the scent of jet fumes. Looking up at the *Succubus,* he moved his pencil again, completing the long curve.

Takinato walked around the *Succubus* examining every inch of it, a cigarette limp between his lips.

When Roble finished sketching, he slipped the drawings into his backpack and scanned the airfield. Without a word, Takinato headed toward an F-22 Raptor and a MiG 35 Fulcrum parked side-by-side. Roble caught up.

"Thrust vectoring," Takinato walked behind the fighter jets, "the real deal."

Roble knelt behind the fighters and sketched a new version of Takinato's *Skeleton Eagle.*

Later, as they stood near a concession booth eating bowls of soba noodles, Takinato said, "I will be honest, I have never met anyone who likes jets more than me."

Roble wiped his messy attempt at slurping soba noodles off his scarred chin.

"How did you get interested in jets?" Takinato asked.

He looked at Takinato, realizing no one had ever asked him that. "Want the long or short version?"

"The true one," Takinato said in Japanese, pointing at a curb where they could sit.

Roble sat, placed his noodles to the side and exhaled. "When I ran away, I was pretty young. I had no idea how hard it was going to be on my own without a home." He shook his head. "But I was determined to be free of everyone who wanted to control me.

"Those first few months I found ways to earn a bit of money on the streets, but it wasn't enough. Maybe that's because my only skills were building toy rockets, disassembling go-kart engines, and reading aviation magazines.

"I ended up eating out of trash cans because I wouldn't beg." Roble swallowed, pushing his noodle bowl away. "Street kids roughed me up a couple times, breaking my jaw and my arm because I wouldn't join their gang and swindle tourists."

Roble glanced at the sun. "The Vegas heat blistered my skin like you wouldn't believe. No matter how much water I drank, I couldn't stay hydrated." He licked his lips. "Each day a hunger knot grew tighter in my stomach." He touched his belly, watching Takinato eat noodles. "I used to call it 'the nugget of pain.'"

Takinato set his bowl down.

"I don't like to think about it, but," Roble rubbed his nose, "there were moments I thought I was going to die. And what's worse, I thought the world itself was an evil place and I was glad to leave it."

Takinato massaged his chin, his head drifting from side to side.

"One day," Roble said, "this tough-looking dude in biker boots walked by and asked me some questions—odd ones, logic and science stuff like on a test or something. I told him to get lost." He rubbed his brow. "I saw him again several weeks later outside a casino, but he didn't acknowledge me. I don't know if I was just curious about him or bothered that he ignored me, but I walked up and answered the questions he'd asked weeks before. He just stared at me, looking kinda angry. I thought maybe he was going to hit me."

Takinato narrowed his eyes.

"When I was about to walk away, he asked me two more questions." He tapped two fingers against his knee. "'What's the ratio of dark matter to dark energy in the universe, and why do galaxies rotate seemingly against the laws of gravity?'" He retracted his fingers.

Takinato dipped his head, waiting.

"I answered both, and he offered me a job."

"Doing what?"

"Selling illegal drugs."

Takinato leaned back, his cheeks pressing up into his eyes. "He was a criminal, like the Yakuza?"

"More of a gardener of sorts, really. I took the job so I could eat, but I was terrible at it." Roble clasped his knees. "I'm pretty sure I didn't do what he wanted me to. I didn't sell anything for him. I just spent my time improving anything he owned that had an engine, and he had some amazing stuff. He probably should have fired me."

Takinato pushed a hand through his striped hair. "What kind of drug lord lets you do what you want without firing you, if not cap you in the knees or bury you in the desert?"

"He didn't talk or act like any adult I'd ever met." He shook his head, thinking back. "He created new plants and drugs seemingly out of nothing, as if somehow that's just what people did. From watching him I learned more about how the physical world worked than from every lesson I was taught in school put together—times a million."

Takinato glanced at the artboard leaning against Roble's leg, the new sketch of the *Skeleton Eagle*.

"I stayed with him for three years, and I would have remained longer," Roble said with a deep exhale.

"I'd just turned fifteen and was walking along the Las Vegas Strip gazing up above the casinos, probably searching for jet contrails or just daydreaming—I don't remember. From out of nowhere," he looked up, squinting, "a strange hum and a shadow blew through me, stopping me in my tracks." He shivered. "A long, slender B1 bomber, like a titanium war lance thrown from the hand of a god, roared over my head, not far above the casino roofs. I have no idea why it flew over or why so low. Its four engines crackled, ripping apart the very atoms in the sky." He touched his own chest as though it were still vibrating, catching his breath.

"It was the most incredible thing I'd ever seen or felt," Roble said, still looking up. "Somebody not only imagined, but figured out how to create that jet. It was real, right there above me. For the first time I felt grateful somebody was brave enough to show me in material form what was possible. I looked around at the buildings and the people and knew the world was a wonderful place because I finally knew what *I* wanted to do."

Roble felt along his front pocket. "I went to the hangar where my boss kept his private jet and sat on the floor with a blank piece of paper. I stared at that sheet, knowing someday it would contain the completed design of an aircraft, one that would fly like how I felt in my heart. That day, I made my first mark.

"I knew it would take years to figure out," he continued. "I thought I'd found a place I could design and create it without anyone stopping me. But that same day, my boss announced I was to become his second-in-command and oversee his entire distribution network."

Roble pressed a knuckle to his forehead. "He didn't ask—he ordered me to take the position. It was the first direct command he'd ever given me, and I knew all the responsibilities and duties it would require. He explained how I would become rich, learn to be just like him, and we'd fight against the entire world together."

"Why didn't you explain your idea to him?" Takinato raised his hands. "Ask him to change his mind?"

"He never made false gestures or backed down from orders he gave anyone, ever. I knew he meant it, even though I still don't understand why he did it." Roble rubbed an eye.

Takinato started to speak but hesitated.

"Because of everything he did for me, I considered taking the promotion. He had given me the only real home I'd ever had and he protected me. And that's why it hurt so much." Roble lowered his head. "There was nothing I could say to change his order, and I would not compromise my dream." He rubbed along his pocket. "That night, I left him without a word."

Takinato held still.

"You asked how I became interested in jets." Roble lifted his chin, his eyes wet. "It is about more than jets to me." In heavily accented Japanese, he added, "It is about choosing who I am."

Takinato bowed.

They picked up their noodles and finished eating in silence.

When they walked back to the center of the airfield, Takinato asked, "What do you think of Sugemi?"

"She's the first girl who can kick my ass with her mind. What's not to like?"

"Sugemi is the twenty-two-year-old daughter of a Japanese industrial legacy. Her family, the emperor, and the whole country have expectations for her life."

Roble swallowed.

"But she is also the kind of girl who knows what she wants," Takinato added. "She turned a sleepy back-office division of her father's company into the fastest growing consulting business in Japan, and she did it even before her father knew she started running it."

"Well," Roble said, "I guess all of that should probably scare me."

"Yes, it should, because I want her for myself." Takinato grinned. "We need to catch up with them. Her jet leaves in half an hour."

Roble looked around at the parked jets. "I'll catch up with you. I want to see if I've missed anything."

"All right, but she said she cannot be delayed."

"If Sugemi is the type of girl I could respect," Roble said, walking away, "she'll leave me if I'm late."

Roble wandered the airfield like a child at his first amusement park.

As he approached the red, white, and blue US Air Force *Thunderbirds*, something caught his eye. Squeezing between the fighter jets, he rose onto his toes, and looked beyond the chain-link fence. He saw an angled tailfin, the abrupt curve of an air intake, and above all else—a brazen poise.

He ran to the edge of the airfield, gripped the fence, and peered into a private aircraft lot. Behind a business jet sat the half-concealed shape of a dark-skinned, unidentified fighter. "What in the world?"

Seeing no openings along the fence, he tossed his backpack over, removed his jacket, and threw it over the fence's razor wire. Moments later he stood on the other side.

As he neared the private aircraft hiding his target, his heart raced. Ducking below its wing, he caught the full view of the unidentified jet. Colors flashed before his eyes as blood drained from his head. Crouching to his knees, he lowered his head to maintain balance. After a few seconds, he looked back up.

If the *Succubus* embodied an irresistible, dark, and dangerous paramour, then this was her heroic, unconquerable lover. Its lines cut more boldly, its angles harder. Its engines flexed like massive quadriceps dominating its rear haunch, yet they integrated seamlessly into the grey-blue body.

Roble rounded the jet. The engine exhausts contained two layers, an inner core and an outer ring. "Dual mode?" he whispered, having seen nothing like it.

Above the curved engine encasements, two horizontal tailfins splayed out below two thick vertical fins that reached high and tilted outward. Its deltoid wings flowed like the watery arc of a swimmer's back stroke. The air intake on its chest opened wide as though it could inhale the entire sky. Its nosecone resembled the broad chin of an ancient warrior. The passenger canopy reflected like a bluish-silver mirror. "*Sovereign*" inscribed a tailfin in black letters.

Roble rubbed his arms. "Oh…Libby Dodge!"

He walked around it many times, touching it, sketching it, but he couldn't leave it. He *had* to see it fly. When the sky darkened into night, he looked up, surprised at the time.

Hours later, he curled up next to the landing gear, pulled out his crumpled dream from his pocket and added a few delicate marks.

He still held it when the sunlight woke him the next morning. His hand slid across the tires to confirm the jet hadn't disappeared. Ignoring hunger and dehydration, he waited.

Around noon, a small group of Asians in business suits approached. Their pilot prepared the *Sovereign* for flight.

"Excuse me," Roble said to the pilot in broken Japanese. "May I ask you some questions about this jet in English?"

The man crossed his arms over his chest. One of the businessmen lashed Roble in an unfamiliar language, obviously not Japanese. Roble stood back and watched the passengers board the jet.

Knowing what he was about to witness, Roble smiled, not paying attention to the shuffling of footsteps behind him.

Men gripped his arms.

"Wait!" Roble looked back at the security guards.

They loaded him in a vehicle and dumped him on the curb outside the terminal.

He ran around the outskirts of the airfield, running faster than he ever had in his life. He didn't care about the constricted pain in his lungs, the metallic taste of exhaustion in his dry mouth, or the hedges and concrete barriers he'd leapt over—only that he moved toward the end of that runway. He had to get there in time; nothing else mattered.

Gasping for breath somewhere beyond the airport fence, he stood below the flight line.

Within seconds, he felt a low rumble massaging his aching lungs. The thunder increased until he saw it—the majestic body lifting off the ground, barreling toward him. "Oh…" He lost his breath.

He reached up as the landing gear on the *Sovereign* disappeared into its fuselage above him. He spun around as the jet passed overhead. It roared like a dragon's breath, his body quaking in its blasting wake. The outer ring of its engine exhausts flared first yellow and then hot white.

Roble gripped his chest, his mouth open. *That's the greatest aircraft I've ever seen.* He shook his head, straining his eyes as it shrank in the sky.

When it disappeared and he could no longer hear its engines, he looked around, shocked to be standing on the center dividing lines of a busy highway near the airport fence. Car horns beeped at him from both directions. He waved at the cars as he crossed the road, heading back to the airport terminal.

Back at Kadena Air Base a day late, Sergeant Perry reprimanded him for tardiness and ordered him to work double shifts for a week.

Late that night, Roble sat in his barracks surveying his airshow drawings of the *Sovereign* and *Succubus*.

He pulled the new *Skeleton Eagle* sketch onto his lap and wrote every detail of every modification he'd envisioned for it while referencing his laptop renderings and research notes. Once completed, he pulled out a paper and penned a letter asking for a price quote on the engineered parts necessary to complete the modifications. He addressed a large envelope to Libby Dodge at her company's listed North Las Vegas facility.

Before sealing the envelope, he inserted his two artistic drawings of the *Succubus* and the *Sovereign*.

The next day he mailed it from a Japanese post office outside the airbase.

Chapter 10

Danny Sands lay motionless on his bed. Snow fell into the window well, burying the basement bedroom in darkness.

Last week, his parents had relocated to Pocatello, Idaho, and had lugged him along like a wounded soldier.

Gripping the bedsheet at his sides, Danny recalled the conversation outside Jenny's apartment months ago and the words that took him down like a bullet.

"I'm pregnant," Jenny said. "And I'm going to keep it because I wouldn't change what we did that night for anything." Touching his hands, she added, "I know your parents will be upset because you can't go to the CMI, but we can make this work. It might take a little longer, but you could still be an artist, and we would be together." Her voice had lowered. "But if you don't want to be involved, I'll raise the baby on my own. You don't have to marry me." Unable to speak, Danny had walked away.

Staring up into the bedroom darkness he moaned, thinking of the day he told his father about Jenny's pregnancy. He had prepared himself for a fight or at least a beating, but instead received something more painful—silence.

The days without his father's response simmered in his gut, filling him with resentment, not for his father—but for Jenny, because she'd ruined his chance to make his father proud.

Danny punched his pillow and curled into a ball remembering how his father's silent mourning morphed into something far worse still—his mother's plans for his wedding.

He'd always wanted to ask Jenny to marry him, right up to the day his mother decided for him. He never actually proposed to her, he'd just told her, "We're getting married. We have no choice." Jenny had stared at him without response.

With the wedding date marked on his mother's kitchen

calendar and the preparations begun, his father broke his silence, saying: "Now you'll finally learn the meaning of responsibility."

Pressing his face to the pillow to soak up the tears, Danny thought of Jenny, the Jenny he knew before it all went so wrong—that burst of blonde energy, always happy to be alive no matter how tough life became. He remembered her laugh, rough and contagious, the laugh that tumbled from her lips even with his lame attempts at jokes. And she loved his anime drawings, encouraging him to chase his dream, despite his parents.

My drawings... Danny jumped from the bed and flung open a clothes chest. Throwing old football uniforms and pads to the floor, he searched for his remaining art pieces he'd hidden from his mother. His fingers scraped the bare wood at the bottom—all his childhood drawings had vanished.

He bent over, unable to breathe. Staggering back, he fell on the bed and stared at the ceiling. *It's just as well.*

A hesitant knock on the door broke the silence. He knew his mother wanted to feed him his favorite soup and read him stories to cheer him up, like she used to when his father grounded him as a child—and had tried every day this past week.

"Go away," he mumbled. He shook his head, knowing his mother was right; he was miserable. And the misery worsened one month into the wedding preparations when Jenny revealed her miscarriage.

Danny hadn't realized how much the loss would hurt, because before that moment he'd never accepted Jenny's pregnancy as something concrete, only an abstract guilt. He cried alone after he found out, imagining that they would have had a girl. He could almost feel her tiny hands in his as he swung her in a circle, her face beaming. *She would have been as beautiful as Jenny. I would've drawn her a hundred times.*

Seeing that the wedding calendar had been removed from the fridge, Danny asked, "Where is it?"

"We're moving out of state and you're coming with us," his mother said.

"Why? You canceled the wedding?"

"Danny, you're his only son. Your father gave speeches upholding you as the example to the youth. Your irresponsible actions tainted his reputation as a faith-based counselor. We're going to Pocatello to live by your grandparents."

"What?"

"Or just stay here with that *girl*," she'd said. "Why should you care what I think is best? I'm just your mother. I've only sacrificed everything for you."

Danny rolled onto his stomach and rubbed his hands against the sheets. The Idaho basement felt so cold, so quiet, so dark. The day after arriving in Pocatello, he'd felt the urge to ride his motorcycle back to Las Vegas and ask Jenny to marry him anyway. But he didn't, knowing that without her, gaining admission into the CMI and his father's forgiveness were now possible. He decided to call her instead, just to talk, like they used to in high school. It seemed harmless, and he couldn't stop himself.

The anticipation of hearing her voice as the phone rang reminded him of the day he called to ask her on that first date to the Princess Fun Zone. He smiled, feeling excited and nervous all over again.

When she answered, her voice hummed so hoarse and lovely it felt as if her fingertips caressed his ear. He only managed, "Hey."

"Why are you calling me?"

He choked, unable to speak.

"How are you?" she asked, her voice softened.

He winced. "Really good," he forced out, "and stuff."

"I needed you after…after it happened." She sniffed. "Why did you move away even after I asked you to stay?"

"I didn't want to. It's complicated, you know how it is with my—"

"I don't care what your family thinks!"

He gulped.

"I'm so hurt, but I still…" Her voice fell close to whisper. "Just tell me how you really feel about me."

Danny almost hyperventilated and held the phone away, thinking of his father and how this call put everything at risk again.

"Jenny," he gasped, "I…we can't see each other again." He felt surprised by his own words, then an unbelievable sense of relief, like when he'd caught the football in a big game with his father watching. In the next second, he felt his heart constricting in sharp clutches, wishing he could take back his words.

"If that's how you really feel…" she said.

Danny squeezed his eyes closed. *Jenny…*

"Goodbye," she hung up.

The phone remained in Danny's hand, his chest tight. Pressure built along his spine until he bent over, a weight crushing his shoulders toward the floor.

I did the right thing, my duty. He inhaled, rising back up. Then, like all the mysterious events he'd experienced in life, he buried this moment deep inside so he wouldn't have to think about it, and therefore never feel its pain again.

He dialed the CMI Admissions Office and asked if he was eligible to re-enroll due to a change in paternity circumstance. He waited, expecting the worst. When they said he could enroll next semester, it wasn't joy he felt pour through him, but mud, oozing into the raw void where happiness should've been.

Dropping the phone, he ran to the garage to tell his father. Donald turned and faced him without expression. As Danny finished explaining, he searched his father's face for a sign of acceptance. But what he saw made him nauseous—the narrow-eyed look of resentment his father always wore after Danny had disappointed him. Danny looked away.

When he found his mother in the kitchen washing dishes, he told her about the CMI's decision. She sobbed.

"What's wrong? Mom?" he'd asked, trembling. "Attending the CMI is what you both wanted, isn't it?"

"Your father spent *that* money to move us to Idaho and start his new counseling business." With the sink still running, she'd hurried from the kitchen, crying, "Why didn't you just listen to us?"

Danny's own cry roused him from the cold bed, or had it been something else? He looked up, squinting through the darkness at the light pouring under the bedroom door. A glossy rectangle lay illuminated in the beam.

He rolled off the mattress and picked it up: a recruitment pamphlet for enlisting in the Marine Corp, enlisting as a simple grunt. He read it several times breathing in shaky gasps, uncertain if the emotion choking him resembled more guilt or anger.

Blinking his eyes, he noticed a picture of a Marine base in Okinawa, Japan, with fighter jets soaring in front of the blazing sun. He ripped the picture out of the pamphlet.

As he studied it, the light from the photo leaked into the room, pushing back the darkness like a glimmer of hope. *Roble.*

Sitting in the Marines recruitment office the next day, Danny grinned as he filled out the application's education section, imagining Roble writing aerospace inventors on the high school line.

An hour later, he stood and turned to leave, but spotted a cartoon poster on the wall. One of the characters, a Marine, rode a horse under heavy gunfire. It reminded him of his favorite childhood anime drawing—the one he once planned to base an animation series on when he grew up. He clutched his stomach, feeling sick.

"Congratulations Marine," the recruiter said.

Danny spun around, eyes wide, uncertain if he should salute or run outside and vomit.

On the day to ship out to Camp Pendleton, he entered the living room and set his suitcase before his parents. His mother looked up from the TV and cried. His father said, "Now you'll finally learn the meaning of duty and honor."

Chapter 11

Alexandria Patra peered through her SUV's windshield. In the sky above, two jet contrails streamed toward one another. *Everything had lined up perfectly.* And it seemed so appropriate—because today was her thirty-sixth birthday.

The contrails collided, forming a giant X over the jagged red cliffs ahead. And Alexandria directed the SUV toward the treasure she knew lay below that mark.

She grinned, thinking of this meeting she'd kept a secret from the public/private partnership's board, the results of which would accelerate the rollout of the partnership between the CUH and state governments. The idea for today's meeting developed several weeks ago after speaking with a man named Bill Jerrgin.

Bill Jerrgin recently inherited the largest homebuilding company in Las Vegas from his father after never having worked a day in his life. And as his first act of repentance for the unwanted wealth, he donated generously and publicly to the CUH. For his second act, he purchased a Libby II *Wyvern,* the very one his father insensitively withheld from Bill's sensitive soul.

After the CUH donation, Bill invited Alexandria to solicit his potential donor friends in Aspen, Colorado. She didn't have the time and hated the idea of flying commercial so often, but she accepted, squeezing it into her schedule on a red-eye flight. Bill surprised her the night of the departure by taking her in his *Wyvern.*

It was the first time she'd flown in a Libby jet. The white fuselage resembled a stylized version of a retro-futuristic 1950s fighter jet, boldly round with an air intake in its nose.

Sitting in its cockpit under the transparent canopy, she didn't feel cramped as though stuffed into the belly of a submarine like all the other jets she'd flown in. She beamed like a child on takeoff until she saw Bill's puffy cheeks grinning at her in response. Pressing her hands to her lap, she lowered her eyes, concentrating on the higher purpose of the trip.

Once in the air, the *Wyvern* actually *felt* like flying—not *it* flying, but *her*, soaring weightless and free like a jet-powered trapeze artist.

After landing in Aspen, Bill didn't immediately open the canopy so they could exit. Instead, he whipped out a glossy brochure from under his seat and flashed it at her, like a compulsive teenager unable to keep porn to himself. The idea of Bill flashing anything at her made her want to gag, but then her gaze caught the photo—a Libby III *Succubus*. She couldn't look away.

"Have you flown in one?" she asked, before biting her tongue for encouraging him.

"I was this close to buying it." He held up a pudgy thumb and forefinger. "I really was, but it's illegal and I've never broken a law in my life, unlike my greedy father."

Alexandria nodded, forcing a smile to hide the disappointment that she wouldn't learn more about the jet.

"By the way," he said, "it just occurred to me that Libby Dodge is another one of my good friends who might donate to your cause, unless she already has, of course."

Alexandria parted her lips, suddenly feeling fortunate to be trapped under the canopy with Bill. "Are you being serious? I've never met Ms. Dodge." She leaned closer. "She's never accepted an invitation to my charity functions or anyone else's, as far as I know."

The cocktail of Bill's sweat and cologne made her recline back. Touching her nose, she added, "But I haven't lost much sleep over it. She's so controversial with that irreverent house, not to mention everything else."

Bill laughed. "Libby made my father so mad when she didn't choose *him* to build that cliff house. But it sure as hell served Dad right; he only cared about making money. I guess I'm one of the few enlightened aficionados who really appreciates the Libby House for what it really stands for.

"Libby and I are like twins," he pressed two fingers together with the help of his other hand, "you know, misunderstood by society regardless of how much we have to offer. I'm almost certain she'll be your biggest donor if you can just get in front of her. I'll set up the meeting if you want."

"That's amazing, Bill. I've never run into anyone with connections to her."

He grinned, rocking in his seat.

"Do you think she would donate something substantial to the CUH and its partnership, like a *Wyvern* or…or that, that one in the picture you showed me?" Alexandria asked, trying not to sound too interested. "Perhaps the Libby III isn't illegal to fly for government or nonprofit use?"

"Don't be silly," he snorted. "It's an FAA issue. Plus, do you want your cause to be associated with something called a *Succubus*? Libby probably made it just to upset her own father, that's all. We're like twins—did I mention that?"

Alexandria forced another smile.

"Go ahead," Bill said, "ask her to donate a *Wyvern*. It might be too much to expect but who knows, I wouldn't put it past her. And Lord knows she could use all the positive press she can get."

"Could you set up the meeting at her cliff house? Large donations always seem smaller when requested in the presence of something very expensive, and…selfish." Alexandria winced. "No offense, of course."

"None taken—I hate rich people. I'm just a victim of my father's fortune. And with Libby, that type of pressure won't even be necessary, but I'll set up the meeting at her cliff house if that's what you want."

The *Wyvern's* canopy opened, sucking in a gust of fresh air. Before Alexandria could jump out, Bill had added, "Be sure to tell her hello for me."

"Thank you, Bill," she'd said, her mind buzzing with anticipation.

Alexandria shifted in her SUV seat as the white X of contrails above the Calico Basin cliffs dissolved into haze. Craning her neck, she searched the top of the canyon wall. Her eyes widened. The Libby House looked vast and enormously expensive.

She tried to calm her enthusiasm, envisioning Preton's face this evening when she revealed her triumph of a donated *Wyvern*. It would allow the thirty million dollars already approved for a private jet to be spent accelerating the partnership's nationwide rollout.

This donation will mark a symbolic capstone of my life's work—my success. A sense of peace washed over her, but the jostling on the gravel road seemed to keep it from settling too deep. "It will make everything worth it," she whispered.

The SUV rolled to a stop in the plateau's shadow.

She glanced at the clock on the dashboard: 5:55 PM. *Five minutes early.* Smiling, she stepped from the vehicle. Her high heels sunk into loose stones. *No sidewalk?*

Straightening her suit, she walked in perfect balance across the unstable rocks to a redwood door embedded in the canyon wall. She knocked, but the surface swallowed the thumps almost without sound.

A stone placard next to the door read: *Utility elevator only. Please use path to the south.*

Stepping back, she searched for another door, but saw only sheer rock. *How could there not be a residential elevator?* She exhaled, hating to be late.

Striding south along the primitive trail, her pumps sank and filled with sand with every step.

When she reached the base of the vertical stone switchbacks, she watched two hikers with walking sticks jaunt down past her, gawking at her suit and heels. Shaking her head, she began her ascent.

Halfway up she gasped for breath but pushed on, accelerating her pace around every turn, sweat dripping down her back. Her exhausted legs reminded her that duty had come before personal exercise. She slipped off her shoes and continued climbing.

Reaching the first gate to the house, she tried to unlatch it. *Locked.*

She glanced up at a gate atop the next switchback and sighed. Leaning against a rock alcove, she pulled her long hair off her sweaty neck. *Now I'm late. What type of person builds an entrance like this?*

A brass bell on a string tinkled in the breeze in the alcove behind her. Shrugging, she pulled the string. The pure tone echoed across the canyon. *A perfect C.* She cracked an involuntary smile.

A woman with neck-length brown hair in a hiking outfit exited from an opening beyond the gate like an archeologist emerging from a lost world.

That's Libby Dodge? She looks different than in her pictures. Sweat fell from Alexandria's temple as she slipped on her heels. Looking up, she watched Libby approach. *I know she's my age but she appears so young. I almost thought she would look like a man, since that's how everyone talks about her. But she certainly does not.* Alexandria swept the hair back over her own shoulders. *She's…beautiful.*

Libby swung open the gate, her sparkling emerald eyes contrasting against her tanned skin. "You're late," she said with a pleasant chuckle.

Alexandria frowned.

"But you probably set a record marching up the switchbacks." Libby glanced at Alexandria's calves.

Taking a breath, she smiled and extended a hand. "Alexa Patra, Director of the Public/Private Partnership between the states and the Children for Universal Hope. Thank you for meeting with me today, Ms. Dodge."

Libby clasped her hand. "I'm happy to finally meet you, Ms. Patra."

Alexandria opened her mouth to continue the niceties, but Libby turned and trekked away, waving for her to follow. Alexandria strode after her, exerting to keep up as Libby wound along exterior walkways and interior corridors and up two more levels. Alexandria had no time to wonder where they were going or to examine the interior of the house.

Libby entered a stone doorway and slowed her pace. Alexandria followed her in and stopped, her sweat-stinging eyes relaxing enough to absorb the surroundings.

Bookshelves notched the wall behind a desk carved from the same red stone as the floor. Water fell from slits on each side of the door, pouring in to flush floor troughs leading to a balcony. Glass panels, pushed into slots in the exterior walls, opened up the office like a cave. A redwood table and chairs sat near the unprotected ledge of a high-perched balcony.

Libby stopped on the balcony near the table and motioned for her to sit.

Alexandria's balanced steps clicked to the balcony's edge. A breeze cooled her face, caressing her long curls. Glancing down, she watched the streams cascading over the edge into a suspended rock pool. Several seconds passed before she realized Libby had taken a seat. She wiped her cheeks and sat down.

The susurrus of the water and breeze weighed on Alexandria's eyelids. Straightening up with effort, she said, "This is a unique home, Ms. Dodge. You are quite fortunate."

"I like seeing you in it, Ms. Patra. It suits you. If you have time later, I'll show you my ballroom."

I was hoping for a sliver of guilt, but I'll take...flirting? Alexandria smiled.

Libby smiled back.

"Bill Jerrgin speaks highly of you." Alexandria placed her hands together atop the table. "As you probably know, he's a big supporter of the CUH. I think he understands that helping children requires the combined efforts of everyone. And it's clear Bill thinks you feel the same way."

Libby leaned back in her chair.

"I speak with the more privileged in society every day," Alexandria said, "and the one thing they usually tell me is they *want* to give back." She paused, expecting the customary response.

Libby said nothing, still smiling at her.

That's odd. Alexandria cleared her throat. "Ms. Dodge, with the proper support, the partnership will convince every state's foster care program to join together with the CUH, thus reaching a point where no child will be lost." She leaned forward. "You have a unique opportunity to be a part of the solution."

Alexandria studied her. Libby wasn't acting like any potential donor she'd ever met. She hadn't given a single nod of agreement, shown an expression of mutual concern, volunteered an altruistic anecdote, shifted her eyes in guilt because of her wealth, or even revealed the faintest fearful dilation of pupils due to her expected civic duty. Libby just seemed pleased to see her, like an old friend.

"As the partnership's director, I travel extensively," Alexandria continued, spreading her fingers on the table. "Flying commercial is needlessly taking away time I could use to expand the organization and fundraise. A private aircraft is required for this essential work." She stared at Libby's smile. *Why won't she react to my hints of a private jet?*

"I've done research," Alexandria swallowed, "including flying with your friend Bill in his *Wyvern*, and I am convinced *your* jet would be perfect for our cause." She paused, hoping to see at least some reaction. Failing, she added, "That being said, every dime we can save avoiding large capital expenditures will enable us to more quickly achieve our goal of helping children."

Libby leaned forward, peering into Alexandria's eyes.

What's she doing? Alexandria shifted in her seat, wanting to close her eyes to the scrutiny. She was about to look away when Libby blinked, startling her.

"It is my greatest hope," Libby said, "that every child achieve her own dreams in this life."

Alexandria knew she should feel pleased at Libby's implied desire to help, but instead her heart rate quickened. Touching her own beating neck, Alexandria said, "That's why I'm here, Ms. Dodge, to ask you to donate a jet to help the children."

"No," Libby said so easily, it sounded as if she'd actually said *yes.*

Alexandria's brows furrowed. *No?* Her face tightened with determination. "Ms. Dodge, a donated jet would be viewed as the symbol of our great cause, giving you positive publicity and goodwill, possibly erasing much of the bad press you've received in the past. Libby Industries could claim it generated profits with a purpose. My other donors, including Bill, love that slogan. Surely you want to give something back?"

"What have I taken?"

Alexandria brushed a strand of hair from her cheek. *What's going on?* "Ms. Dodge, this cause is too important for any misunderstandings." She turned up her palms. "Allow me to rephrase. Would you please consider generously donating a jet to the children's partnership?"

"Which child would I be helping?"

Which...one? "Not *a* child...the entire shared need of—" she stopped when Libby placed her hands on the table to rise. Alexandria lifted an open palm, pleading with her to remain seated. *There is too much at stake to be off my game!* Her mind raced. *What signal did I miss? What did I say wrong?*

Libby stared at Alexandria's hand in the air as it swayed like a ballerina.

"Ms. Dodge, I thought you wanted to help." Alexandria leaned over the table, her hopeful expression returning. "I'd very much like to facilitate you in doing so."

"I said," Libby slid a hand across the table, stopping just before Alexandria's elbow, "it is my greatest hope, that every child achieves her own dreams in this life."

Alexandria sat back, pulling her arm away. "Yes, that is what you said. I think the partnership is designed to allow children to get…to that point. But first, we must make sure they don't fall through the cracks of—" she paused, watching Libby's eyes focused on her fingertips drumming the edge of the table. Clearing her throat, Alexandria stopped her hand.

Libby looked up.

"I must admit Bill mentioned a jet might be too much to ask," Alexandria's shoulders sank, "but I always start with the highest of hopes when it comes to potential donations. However, let me be clear, the partnership would be very grateful for any offer. If we were to purchase your jet and we still gave you the publicity, would you consider donating just the gross profits?"

Watching Libby's gaze return to her fingers, Alexandria realized they'd started tapping again and pressed them still against the table.

Libby again looked back to her eyes.

Alexandria held her breath, waiting for the answer.

"No," Libby said.

Alexandria flushed. *I don't understand. Just—no? Couldn't she at least make a counteroffer? If she doesn't wish to help children at all, why allow me to come here?* "Ms. Dodge, as a member of society, isn't there some level of civic duty—"

"Oh, I'm not a member," she cut her off, her lips smiling.

"You're not a…?" Alexandria stared in confusion and then frowned. *The negative news about her was much too generous.*

Alexandria's gaze drifted from Libby's untroubled face to the darkening firmament beyond the balcony. An airliner caught the last spark of the sun, reminding her of how she'd felt flying in the *Wyvern*.

Could this woman, who wouldn't help children, really have created something that made me feel like a child again?

The electric fires of Las Vegas ignited along the horizon. *There are children out there who would benefit if the partnership had a private jet. The board already approved the money. I'd just hoped…* Alexandria deflated.

"You picked a perfect evening to visit, Ms. Patra."

Alexandria sucked in a breath and held it, wishing she could discover some way to convince Libby to make a donation. When her oxygen expired, she lowered her eyes. "All right, I'll *buy* your *Wyvern*. I'll pay you cold hard cash, which is the only language you seem to understand." Her stomach sickened at her own weakness.

Libby's face displayed something resembling remorse.

So now *she feels guilty. Well, it serves her right.* Alexandria inhaled, feeling redeemed by Libby's display of emotional self-justice. *So she is just another miserable rich person after all, what of it? It won't stop me. I'll recoup the partnership's payment for her jet by working harder.* Alexandria exhaled, accepting the disappointing outcome of the meeting.

"My answer is still no."

Color drained from Alexandria's hands as she pressed them against the table. "You are refusing to sell me a jet at full price?"

Libby nodded.

"You...you're not allowed to do that. You are much, much worse than your friend, Bill Jerrgin. He at least has a conscience."

"I don't recall ever meeting Bill Jerrgin. If I did, it was wholly unmemorable. I liked his father though." She smiled. "Ms. Patra, if your organization wishes to purchase a *Wyvern*, have them call my office tomorrow. *They* will be able to buy one."

"What?" Alexandria jumped to her feet. "You are refusing to sell a jet to *me* personally? Why did you agree to see me?"

"I was curious to see what you were like up close."

Alexandria bit her lip and her fingers pinched the ends of her hair, twisting them into tight curls. "And...?" The worry in her voice cloaked her anger.

"I found out what I wanted to know, which is why I'm making an exception and not selling you a jet."

Releasing her hair, Alexandria leaned over the table, her eyes hardening. "Listen, Ms. Dodge, I don't know what you think you're doing, but the jet isn't for my personal use. I'm sacrificing to serve others, unlike—*you*."

"Yes, your choice is very clear."

Alexandria's heart thumped in her temples. *Choice? It isn't a* choice... The pounding continued until it pumped away her anger, leaving her exposed to an unwanted regret. She pulled away from the table and turned to leave.

"Not that it would have changed my mind," Libby said, "but you also asked to buy the wrong jet."

Alexandria cringed, remembering Bill's brochure. *How did she...? I can't believe this meeting. What an inexplicable disaster.*

With a sigh, she took a step to leave, but the exhaustion from the long day pulled at her body, stopping her movement. The cascading waterfalls soothed her, drawing closed her heavy eyelids. She reached up and touched her own cheek.

Libby stood. "It was truly a pleasure to meet you, Ms. Patra." She pointed at the exit. "Please use the utility elevator on the way out. And by the way, I wanted to say earlier," she looked at Alexandria's feet, "you carry yourself with an elegance I haven't seen...in a long time. You must have been *quite* a performer."

Alexandria glanced at her own feet, using all her remaining strength not to cry. "Good day, Ms. Dodge." Straightening out her suit, she marched from the office.

Stopping to remove her high heels, Alexandria strode through the house and down the switchbacks. Every time her body begged to stop, she pushed it harder until she collapsed against her SUV.

She glanced up at the distant waterfalls marking Libby's office balcony and jerked open the SUV door. Exhaling, she slid into the seat, and slammed the door tight, hoping to seal herself off from the unwelcome emotions she'd just felt.

Her hands gripped the steering wheel; her face lowered to her hands; tears and sweat trickled down her arms.

Why do I feel this way?

Chapter 12

The Libby House slept, the chill of morning darkness holding the air.

Twenty meters away, Libby dropped onto a narrow outcropping partway down the cliff face. Her headlamp washed over the red stone and Victor's armored body far above. Holding an anchor rope steady, she motioned for Victor to follow.

He pranced down the rock wall, his metallic plates clanging a hypnotic rhythm. Four other climbers descended ropes to their right, unaware they rappelled next to the owner of the cliff.

The morning's first sunray ignited a rock spire atop the plateau, brightening the cliff. Libby turned off her headlamp and smiled. *What a beautiful start to the day.*

Halfway down to her, Victor held up a gauntleted fist.

Libby scrunched her brows and snapped the rope taut, stopping his descent. *What's wrong?* Hearing a swelling rumble, she peered at the valley below. Seven black sport utility vehicles rolled along the gravel toward the cliff house. *Who is that?*

Victor ran back and forth along the cliff face, creating a giant pendulum, gaining momentum.

Really, Victor?

He flew feet first across a deep canyon, his body reaching horizontal at the arc's peak.

Okay... Libby released the anchor rope as Victor swung for the Libby House.

His armored shins caught the inside of a stone ledge along a pathway. Hanging upside down, he released the rope, swinging it back to Libby. He waved for her to follow.

If you insist. She gripped the rope and climbed about five meters. *Here goes nothing.* Taking a breath, she ran side to side along the cliff, mimicking Victor's swing. Even without the burden of armor, she needed twice the time to get enough momentum to reach the house.

Victor reached out, gripped her by the arms, and pulled her up to the path. The four other climbers gawked at the display.

"What's going on, Victor?" Libby gasped, bending over, hands on her knees.

"I knew it felt too quiet, *Madame*." He faced the desert basin, flipped up his alloy visor and slid down a transparent green one. "I assume they were not invited?"

Libby shook her head and removed her headlamp. "Who are they?"

Victor knelt down before the stone railing, studying the SUVs through his visor. "Federal agents—marshals. I know their typical armament."

Reaching down to his sides, he pulled two stainless steel objects from his waist belt and screwed them together. After extending out a shoulder rest for the curved weapon, he held it below the rail. "I could probably take them all, my friend, if events spiral out of control." His jovial voice vanished under the iron veneer of a former French Foreign Legion officer.

"Uhh…" Libby tugged on his arm. "I don't think that will be necessary. But thanks for the offer…I guess. I'll go see what they want."

Victor jumped to his feet. "I shall seal the down shafts, lock all nondisclosed doors, and secure the manufacturing cavern. I'll await you at the ranch stable, in case you require a place to go."

Libby blinked. "We don't even know what they want. Aren't you overreacting?"

"I pray so, *Madame*." He touched her shoulder and sprinted through a stone entrance into the house.

With a shrug, Libby descended to the valley in the utility elevator. As the doors slid open, she saw a dozen armed, helmeted officers in black forming a line at the base of the switchbacks. Three of them carried a battering ram.

Another group of people, some wearing suits, conversed near the vehicles. One, a thin woman with hair in a bun, spotted Libby and motioned for those around her to follow. They marched to the elevator.

"Libby Dodge?" the woman asked, her tone official. Her composed face wore no makeup.

"Yep." Libby glanced at the holstered guns on two of the men in marshal jackets.

"I'm Diane Curtis, Western Regional Administrator of the EPA. This," she pointed at a large man with skinny arms wearing a sweater vest, "is Dr. Walter Hughbner, the Southwest Director of the Bureau of Land Management. We are accompanied by the head of the Nevada State Park Service and our assistants."

Dr. Hughbner, who had yet to look up from the ground, bent down, picked up a clump of dirt, and mumbled something inaudible.

"You chose the right day to hike my trails. Simply amazing weather, isn't it?" Libby smiled. "But don't go shooting at my wild burros with those popguns; they're harmless enough."

"We have a federal search warrant." Diane handed a creased paper to Libby.

Libby took it and read. "I don't get it." She handed it back.

With his head still lowered, Dr. Hughbner stepped forward, his belly almost touching Libby. "Some of this ecosystem will never recover from being disturbed."

Leaning over, Libby examined the crusty dirt in his hand, her mouth inches from his ear. "Huh."

Dr. Hughbner dropped the clump, and it burst into dust on Libby's climbing shoes. "Oh, dear," he waddled back.

"Please step aside," Diane flicked out her wrist.

"And if I refuse?" Libby shook the dirt off her shoes.

Dr. Hughbner lifted his head and looked at Diane, his eyes blinking.

Diane frowned. "We are authorized to use force to gain access." She motioned for the two marshals to enter the elevator.

"Force?" Libby winked at Dr. Hughbner. "Well, by *all* means, come in."

Dr. Hughbner averted his gaze. All thirteen bodies squished inside the elevator.

When they reached the lowest floor of the house, Libby waited as everyone shuffled out. One of the suited assistants let out a low whistle.

"See what you're searching for yet?" Libby asked.

"Don't make light of this, Ms. Dodge," Diane Curtis said. "Several decades ago this land was under federal control. It was transferred, in what we now believe was an inappropriate land swap with a rancher. We are certain the transfer wouldn't meet today's standards. It is a problem that should be corrected in short order."

"The *problem*, as you call it," Libby scrunched her brows, "is mine. I bought it two years ago."

"Perhaps," Diane waved a hand at the cut stone walls, "if you wouldn't have caused such reckless destruction to this land, nobody would have looked into the original land swap. Over the past year, we've been inundated with complaints from concerned citizens and elected leaders from around the country, and even from foreign diplomats."

Libby glanced out a window, noting the absence of protestors.

"My office, as well as Dr. Hughbner's, sent numerous letters to you expressing our concerns about your actions. We asked you to stop construction while environmental studies took place. We even tried to slow you down with a temporary injunction." She pressed her hands against her suited hips. "But no matter how much we tried, you refused to cooperate. So as you can see, our offices had no choice but to take appropriate action."

"Oh yeah," Libby said, "I remember all those letters. I used them as fire starter in my forge so those trees wouldn't die in vain."

"Don't *you* accuse *me* of harming the environment," Diane said.

Libby winked again at Dr. Hughbner. He wiped his dirty hands across his vest.

"Yesterday," Diane said, "we completed our preliminary environmental study on this cliff, and our official conclusion is in agreement with multiple parallel studies done by nonprofit organizations. We have unanimously determined that you irreparably altered the environment."

Libby scratched her head. "Well, I could have told you that for free."

"A judge accepted our preliminary finding last night." Diane removed a thick document from a folder. "He has granted us an emergency injunction to—"

Libby turned and strode away. Over her shoulder, she said, "I made a pot of coffee earlier. I'm going to get some."

"I'm not done explaining, Ms. Dodge," Diane said, "and believe me, you will want to listen." She walked after Libby, followed by a motley assembly.

Libby wound through passages, rooms, and up five different stone stairways before reaching the rooftop deck. In the outside kitchen she poured several cups of coffee, took one, and sat on a white cushioned couch facing a table near the cliff's edge. The morning sunlight absorbed into the cool rock around her.

Diane and Dr. Hughbner's assistant, breathing with effort, reached the roof ahead of the others and rested against the outdoor bar. After a moment, they picked up coffees, walked over, and sat across from Libby. Two federal marshals emerged onto the roof but stood at a distance.

"Who did you say you worked for, Ms. Curtis?" Libby leaned against the seat cushion.

Diane set her coffee on the table and straightened up. "The Environmental Protection Agency."

"So you are here to protect my environment." Libby took a long sip. "That's good. I like that."

"I'm here to protect *the* environment, Ms. Dodge. I have the full backing of the federal government on my side, a court order, and the encouragement of Nevada's Governor. Lieutenant Governor Moore even told me how you refused to help homeless children while sitting perched up here like a queen."

Libby laughed, spitting coffee down her hiking pants. "I had no idea my exception would be taken so brilliantly."

"Excuse me?"

"No, *thank you*—for relaying that information. Priceless." She glanced at her bare wrist. "Well, I don't know about you, but I already feel protected. How about we wrap this up?"

The assistant glanced at Diane.

Diane shifted in her seat, holding the emergency injunction above the coffee table. "The actions we are taking today came from a unanimous decision among many agencies and a federal court; no *one* person is responsible."

"I have no idea what you just said."

"All right, I'll lay it out for you." Diane leaned forward. "This court order requires that you cease occupancy and all activities on this land until such time as we have conducted additional studies for discovery in building our case." She dropped the documents to the table with a thud. "And once we win in court, Ms. Dodge, we will argue for fines and jail time for your actions."

Libby glared at Diane, her shoulders tightening.

"Now that your jokes are over and I have your attention, Ms. Dodge," she took a sip of coffee, "I want to present you with an offer—a mutually beneficial compromise." Her voice softened. "We are going to give you a chance to donate this land to us. You can even participate in a joint press conference and take credit for the idea. It's a win-win compromise that will allow people to forgive you for your actions against the environment and will prevent them from ignorantly accusing us of using a heavy hand. In exchange for your cooperation," she set down her coffee and turned up her palms, "we will not prosecute you for your environmental crimes."

This cannot be real. Libby focused on breathing.

Diane reached for her coffee again. "Now, people in my organization, as well as many in outside nonprofit groups, will be upset you got off so easily, but compromise takes courage. If I were you, I'd show some—and take this offer."

Libby cleared her throat. "Do you own a house, Ms. Curtis?"

"Don't go there. This is not the same thing. I live in the city where there's nothing left to preserve. And the government never owned my land."

"So you're grateful the Bureau of Land Management and the EPA didn't exist when your city was built?"

"Don't make this ugly, Ms. Dodge."

"Ugly?" Libby's eyes narrowed.

"This is not just about you," Diane pointed at a red-rock spire. "It's about the big picture, the needs of the country as a whole, and perhaps the very survival of the human race."

"And the guns you brought into *my* home," Libby glanced at the federal marshals, "those are necessary to enact this beautiful vision?"

"That's not what's happening here," Diane snapped, the sharpness in her voice startling the assistant at her side. She returned the coffee cup to the table and took a breath. "Be reasonable. We want to negotiate with you, Ms. Dodge."

"I paid for this land with money I *earned*." Libby pointed at the ground. "What's there to negotiate?"

Diane frowned. The young assistant gritted his teeth as the marshals approached.

"There are a lot of government agencies rummaging through

my home supposedly trying to protect something," Libby said. "Which one is here to protect *me*?"

The marshals stopped near the couches, hands on their weapons. They looked to Diane Curtis. The assistant's eyes widened.

"By leaving voluntarily," Diane brushed red dust off her suit, "you will be able to make the donation announcement and take the credit."

Libby sipped her coffee, placed it back on a coaster, and stood up.

Diane followed suit. "Wise decision, Ms. Dodge."

Libby crossed her arms. "I'm *not* volunteering. Get…out."

Diane's face drained white, and she stepped back. "We have a court-ordered occupancy of this land for legal discovery." She motioned for the marshals. "You will be escorted from it for your own safety while we conduct additional tests."

"You know, Ms. Curtis," Libby said as the lawmen neared, "I just realized something from a conversation I had the other day." She gripped her biceps. "There really is a way you can survive on this planet without changing the environment."

Diane glanced at the marshals, then back to Libby.

"You can just loot the people who already have."

Dr. Hughbner arrived and pressed his legs against a couch, sweat dripping from his chin. "Oh dear, look at this place," he mumbled, and glanced at Diane. "Did you tell her about the compromise we've offered?"

The assistant placed a hand over his forehead. Diane nodded at the marshals.

"Don't touch me!" Libby shouted, glaring at the marshals. "I'm calling my lawyer." She picked up the emergency injunction from the table, pulled a phone from her pocket, and called Gary Sanders.

The federal marshals took a step back. The assistant stared wide-eyed at everyone.

After reading the first two pages of the injunction to Gary over the phone, he said, "Libby stop, that's enough information. You have to vacate the property or they'll throw you in jail. I'll contact the judge right now and get our outside lawyers working on this at once. Call me when you get to the office."

Libby tried to breathe to avoid fainting. Throwing the court order at Diane, she darted past the marshals and to the stairs. Descending through the house, her mind swirled in an incomprehensible daze.

She stopped at her office and saw people in suits holding clipboards standing on the balcony. They turned and stared at her.

"May we help you, Miss?" one asked.

Libby's body shook. Covering her mouth, she spun away and continued through the house until exiting onto the switchbacks.

Near the bottom, she approached the marshals in body armor lined up along the path still holding the battering ram. They lowered their eyes as she passed.

"Mission accomplished," Libby said, wiping her mouth.

In the graveled lot by the black SUVs, she untied her Arabian horse and rubbed its shiny, chiseled body. Its high-carried tail swished in response.

"Come on, girl." She mounted and rode to the base of the cliff.

I just can't... She gazed up at the house and stroked the horse's mane. *How could anyone do this?* Shaking her head, she clicked the reins and galloped east to her stable.

Inside, her ranch hand, Guardo, drove a forklift away from an old cattle truck, having placed a glossy manufacturing robot next to three others.

Victor leaned from the truck window, his helm off. "I'm sorry to see you have come, *Madame*. We've taken the finest robots out of the cavern, just in case. Want them transported to the main facility?"

Libby climbed down and patted the horse's nose. Turning away, she said, "Do whatever you want."

She mounted her jet-powered motorcycle and flared the turbine enough to roll from the stable. It glided with a dull hum down the dirt road leading to the highway.

When she arrived at her North Las Vegas facility, Amanda handed her two envelopes.

"Are you feeling all right, Ms. Dodge?" she asked.

"Have Gary Sanders call me," Libby muttered and entered her office.

Standing by her chair, she dropped the envelopes on the desk.

When the phone rang, she picked it up. "Gary, what the hell is going on?"

"Ms. Dodge, the judge who signed the emergency injunction won't return my calls. Unfortunately, I have spoken with the county title office, the Governor's office, and the EPA." Gary exhaled. "This is a legal nightmare, Ms. Dodge. The environmental case the feds are gathering evidence for may already be moot—because they have filed a separate action claiming you are not even the owner of the property."

"What?"

"Since the federal government claims the land never 'properly' transferred into private hands in the original land swap, they are seeking to have your deed declared void. And the county title office, under the direction of Lieutenant Governor Moore, is cooperating with the feds to facilitate the 'correction.'"

"That is my home!"

"Look, we will fight this in court, believe me. But I'm afraid it may be near impossible to force the federal government to vacate land they physically possess *and* claim is theirs."

"Then why did you tell me to leave my house with them in it?"

"They had a federal court order, Ms. Dodge. You would've been hauled off in handcuffs."

Libby gripped her gut. "How could the federal government and Nevada not protect the private property of one of its residents? Did you ask them that?"

"You've been so villainized in the national media even if some sympathetic local bureaucrat or a judge had wanted to help you, they didn't dare."

She shook her head. "I just don't understand."

"If only you would have let me spin your side of things in the national media. Maybe none of this would've…" His voice lowered. "I'm sorry, Ms. Dodge."

Libby released the phone and slumped into her chair, staring at the envelopes. One had an official seal from the US Department of State, the other—a much larger one—had a handwritten address from Japan.

She ripped open the official letter and read.

To Libby Industries and all employees thereof;

The Department of State, in conjunction with the Department of

Defense, have determined all Libby IV Sovereign *sales and associated parts are hereby considered advanced military capable technologies and are therefore banned for export from the United States. Department of Defense inspections will commence at Libby Industries at random intervals to verify compliance.*

Louise Johnson, Deputy Secretary of State

General Robertson, Chairman of the Joint Chiefs of Staff

Libby tossed it to the floor and stood up. *Breathe. Just breathe.* Brushing the other letter off the desk, she left the office.

Inside the company's airport hangar, she approached the *Sovereign* at the far end, the last one built. *This can not be happening.* She stood before it, eyes on the ground.

At a press conference the next day, Diane Curtis and Dr. Walter Hughbner stood flanked by Nevada state officials and members of several nonprofit organizations. A large banner hanging behind the group read: *Your Public Lands.*

The hum of reporters and spectators filled the crowded room.

With her face stern, Diane began. "I am here to announce that we have enacted the necessary steps to preserve our western lands for future generations. The tract containing what was formerly known as the Libby House has been liberated back into the surrounding public lands."

The shutter from a single camera highlighted the silence in the room.

"Actions are being taken," Diane continued, "to hold to account those responsible for inappropriately occupying this land and causing harm to the environment. Once we complete a remediation study of the offending structure, we will sue for damages necessary to return the land as close to its natural state as possible. In the meantime, the appropriate government agencies will jointly manage the land. Let me just say we are pleased with this outcome. Are there any questions?"

Hands flew into the air.

"Did Ms. Dodge donate the house or was it confiscated?" a local news reporter asked, pulling his tie loose.

"Appropriate…actions were taken to recover the land to the satisfaction of the government."

"Will the hiking trails remain open?" a young, ponytailed man asked.

Dr. Hughbner shuffled to the microphone, not looking up. "In order to revegetate the disturbed areas, all hiking and climbing will be temporarily suspended."

"Do you have to deconstruct the house?" a voice shouted from the rear of the room. Everyone looked back at the young woman with a baby slung across her chest. "Wouldn't it be a better idea to preserve it?"

Diane Curtis retook the microphone. "As always, we will act in the best interest of the public. That's all the time we have. Thank you all for coming."

Protests began the next day near the edge of a newly built fence surrounding the former Libby House. Maggie, with baby on her chest, became their unofficial leader.

Signs outside the barbed-wire enclosure, read: *PRESERVE THE CLIFF HOUSE! OPEN THE TRAILS! PUBLIC LANDS IN PUBLIC HANDS!*

Two federal park rangers stood guard behind the fence to keep the unauthorized demonstration at what they called "a safe and appropriate distance" from the cliff house.

After two weeks of protests, the Environmental Protection Agency in conjunction with the Bureau of Land Management announced that preserving the cliff house as a museum and a field office for state and federal government officials would be less damaging to the environment than demolition.

Halvern Black stomped through a dirt lot, *The Sin's* black façade towering into the hazy sky across the Strip.

"One hundred," he mumbled as he walked, "one hundred and one—" His phone rang, cutting off his measurement.

"What?" he growled at the phone.

"Mr. Black?" a man asked.

"I said, 'What?'"

"Oh. Ahhh…The Bureau of Land Management would like to hire Halvern Black Architects."

Halvern winced and gripped his gut.

The caller cleared his throat and continued, "We need you to convert the former Libby House into field offices and a museum."

"Not interested," he rasped, hanging up the phone.

Dust puffed over his cowboy boot as he stamped it forward. "One hundred and two—"

Ring. Ring.

Halvern jabbed the phone screen and lifted it.

"Mr. Black, please listen. You are our first choice for this job. No one else understands how to construct inside that cliff. We will compensate your firm based on a preferred government code sheet, which I think you'll find more than lucrative."

Halvern rolled his eyes, shaking his head. "Stop wasting my goddamn time."

"If you refuse to do the conversion," the man sniffed, "you will be forced to give the original blueprints to Bill Jerrgin so his company can do the project."

"Tell Bill Jerrgin to go to that buttress-ugly county inspector's office and get the plans himself."

"Don't make this unpleasant, Mr. Black. We've seen the blueprints on file at the county office, and they are incomplete, which is a clear violation of law on your part."

"If you don't like the goddamn plans on file, create your own."

"We will subpoena the original blueprints and even ask the city to seek criminal charges against you if we must. Do you understand the conse—"

Halvern hung up the phone and dialed his office. "Give me Macht."

"One moment, Mr. Black."

"This is Macht."

"Destroy *every* hard and soft copy of the Libby House plans. No exceptions."

"Every copy?"

Silence.

"Yes, sir," Macht said.

Halvern stuffed the phone into his pocket and stepped forward. "One hundred and three…"

Chapter 13

Libby hadn't shown up for work since losing her cliff home. She sat inside a tiny, mid-twentieth century house that had never been updated. The one-acre property, located in one of the most rundown neighborhoods in Las Vegas, also contained two large metal sheds—the birthplace of Libby Industries.

Amanda brought Libby her office mail each day. It lay in an unopened pile along with dirty dishes on the dining table.

Libby gazed out the dining room window at the swath of unkempt grass and the gnarled trunk of a cottonwood tree. Glancing back at the cluttered table, she noted several official government letters. *No...* She doubled over in pain and slumped to the floor from her chair.

Her shoulders shook, but she made no sound. *By what right did they do it?* Shadows from the chair legs stretched across her body like bars on a cage. She reached out to grab one, but her hand slipped through the air. Her body shriveled into the fetal position.

When she looked up, the corner of an upside-down envelope with a Japanese postmark hung over the table's edge. She pulled the oversized packet to her lap and studied the handwriting. Reaching back up to the table, she found a knife with dried jam on it, and used it to rip open the envelope. Its contents scattered across the floor.

She pushed the table and chair out of her way and knelt on hands and knees above the papers. Unfolding two large drawings, she smoothed them out atop the tile floor: a *Succubus* and a *Sovereign,* drawn as she'd never seen them—more audacious, striking, and proportioned than she had made them. She rubbed her eyes.

Shooting to her feet, she found adhesive tape, hung the two art pieces on the dining room wall, and stood back.

When the room darkened into twilight, she looked again out the window at the untamed lawn below the tree, then back at the two drawings on the wall, noting their exacting, purposeful lines. *Purposeful thought, leading to purposeful...* Again she looked at the lawn.

The walk to one of her sheds seemed unreal as if her motion and body were somehow separate. Pulling an old lawnmower to the edge of the grass seemed just as surreal like her action might somehow be undone by an unseen force.

When the mower started with a stiff pull, she gripped the handle, absorbing the vibrations. She pushed it across the grass in planes, forming complex patterns. She reformed the designs over and over again until the mower ran out of fuel.

In the hushed landscape below the glowing night sky, Libby lifted her hands before her face. Lowering them, she studied the lawn's angled arrays. Closing her eyes, she inhaled the scent of tamed earth.

Returning to the dining room, she flipped on the lights, picked up the remaining envelope contents from the floor in one hand, and brushed the dirty dishes and other mail off the table with the other, sending them crashing to the floor.

With the letter from Japan and its contents atop the table, she wiped her hands clean with the edge of the tablecloth and read everything. A signature marked the sketch of a proposed *Skelton Eagle* project and its accompanying letter, a name she'd never heard of.

"Roble Santos," she whispered.

Victor's phone buzzed. "*Excusez-moi,*" he said to a blacksmith at his side pouring alloy into a plate armor mold. Lifting the phone to his ear, he asked, "*Madame* Dodge, are you all right?" He smiled before he heard any words, the buoyant energy reaching him ahead of the voice.

"Drop everything, Victor," Libby said. "Drive that cattle truck with my robots to my house downtown. Wake up Siggy and bring him with you. We're going to redesign a fighter jet."

Kat Lister noted the *L* with a dot above it painted on the glass door as she entered Libby Industries' North Las Vegas facility.

Deliverymen scurried about in the reception area. Shipping boxes and pallets surrounded a single desk at the rear. A redheaded young woman sat at the desk signing delivery receipts, a phone pressed to an ear.

Kat approached the desk, her tiny frame making her look like a teenager.

"Hello, may I help you?" the receptionist asked, not looking up, still holding the phone and writing.

Kat sighed. "I'm here to buy a jet."

The receptionist whipped out a catalog and handed it to her. "Please call in your order or use the internet."

Kat strummed the colorful pages of toy rockets and jets with a single brush of a thumb, before tossing it onto the desk.

"Thank you for choosing Libby Industries, and have a nice day." The receptionist hung up the phone and placed a hand on the discarded catalog. "Is there something else I can help you with?"

"I'm here to buy a *jet aircraft.*"

"You have thirty million dollars on you?" She smirked, picking up the phone again.

"I left it in the car."

"Cute."

"Is Sigmund Evert available?"

The receptionist scrunched her forehead and set the phone down. "You know him?"

"Yeah, I know 'im."

"You know our head of aeronautical engineering? And you want to buy…a jet aircraft?" She ignored the ringing phone and the deliveryman waiting for a signature.

Kat sighed again.

"What's your name?" the receptionist asked.

"Kat Lister." She extended a hand.

"Courtney." She shook Kat's hand, picked up the phone, and pushed a button. "I have a Kat Lister here to see Mr. Evert at the front desk." Lowering the phone, she said, "This is a bit unusual. We sell tons of toys and jet motorcycles, but we don't sell many aircraft anymore. You look so young, I just thought… If you don't mind me asking, how can you afford a Libby Jet?"

"It's for Stock Brant."

"Oh. Oh, wow." Her eyes widened and she glanced around, still ignoring the ringing phone and the deliveryman. "What's he like?"

Kat leaned close. "He's very dangerous…and loves redheads."

Courtney blushed, signed the delivery receipt, and placed the phone back to her ear. "Libby Industries," she breathed, "how may I help you?"

Sigmund Evert entered the reception area from the rear and approached wearing a white lab coat. "Follow me," he said, turned, and walked back to the door he'd entered.

Kat followed him through the manufacturing facility. As they climbed the footbridge leading to the North Las Vegas airport hangar, she asked, "Did the dose work?"

Sigmund stopped. "My mother reached stage four."

Kat breathed in. "On how much of the lung's surface?"

"There's no trace of the cancer left." His head jerked up and down in small movements. "Thank you." After a moment he asked, "Did the sword function as you expected?"

"What do you think?"

"Libby made it for me as a huge favor. You asked for an odd shape, but with the alloys used, it's probably the strongest and sharpest blade ever forged. I could never have afforded the doses otherwise."

"Now we're even." Kat headed toward the hangar. "Like I mentioned last time, Stock doesn't like his old jet anymore, but he loves his Libby jet-bike. Let's see if we can make a deal."

Inside the domed hangar sat three jets, plus a large object under a tarp near the far wall.

Pointing at the white jet, Sigmund said, "The Libby II, *Wyvern*. It's the only jet we sell that's legal to fly anywhere in the world. It outperforms anything on the market, even with its maximum speed restricted by the FAA to Mach 0.9. The tandem cockpit holds three, and it costs thirty million dollars."

Kat pulled out a mobile device and typed notes. "*Can* it hit Mach speed?"

"We're not allowed to remove the throttle regulator. But if you removed it yourself, it will go supersonic."

Kat walked around the *Wyvern* and climbed the cockpit ladder. She sat inside inspecting the retro brushed-alloy controls. After a moment, her gaze drifted to the two, larger black jets parked nearby. "What about those?" She pointed.

"Libby III, *Succubae*. Unfortunately, unless your boss wants to keep it out of the country, he'd be wasting his money. It's not FAA-certified anymore to fly within the US."

Kat walked to the nearest *Succubus* and ran a hand along a wing. "Top speed?"

"She'll push Mach 2, on a bad day."

Kat climbed into the cockpit, noting the tight, black leather interior. "This is the one Stock would want. How much?"

"Sixty million dollars. But like I said, it's not certified."

Kat descended to the hangar floor. "Just answer me this—is she the best you've got?"

Sigmund rubbed his arms. "She's the best I can sell."

"That's not what I asked."

Sigmund glanced at the tarp. Kat followed his eyes.

"*That*," Sigmund said, "will never be FAA-certified and is illegal to export outside the US. It's only good as an expensive museum piece. And with the money we spent on production we're going to take a huge loss since we only made four."

"Who was stupid enough to make a jet that can't be sold?"

"You're looking at one of the stupids."

Kat grinned. "By its shape, it must have some big engines. What's it called?"

"It's probably the last *Sovereign* we'll ever manufacture."

"How fast is it?"

"Look, Kat," he lowered his voice, "it's not practical to buy jets that can't legally be flown. If I were you, I'd buy Stock the *Wyvern*."

Kat's pale eyes hardened like ice. "If I wanted something practical, I'd go to your competitors and buy whatever their mommies allowed them to make. Is that the best aircraft you have?"

Sigmund exhaled, rubbing his head. "There's *nothing* like it in the world."

"How much do I owe you?"

"Kat, I can't in good conscience sell it to you."

"You probably know rocket science, but *this* purchase only requires second grade flash cards."

"We sold the first three for an average price of eighty million dollars."

"Sold."

"You haven't even seen it."

"I've seen Libby's work. I'd be willing to stake my life on its integrity. In fact, that's just what I'm doing."

Sigmund stared at her.

"Have someone fly it to Stock's private hangar at McCarran. I'm sure you can figure out how to get it there, regardless of the rules. I'll go get the money."

In the parking lot, Kat popped the trunk on an old, rusted-out car, and removed a steel suitcase. She laid it on Courtney's desk and asked her to summon a security guard.

Flipping open the lid, Kat counted out eighty million dollars in unregistered Swiss bearer bonds. "I'll need a receipt."

Chapter 14

Why haven't I purchased a jet for the partnership since meeting with Ms. Dodge? Alexandria slashed black eyeliner out from the corners of her eyes.

Flowery acidic perfume, the kind she always wore to important events, spritzed across her beating neck. Rubbing her nose, she realized she hated the scent. The crystal bottle rolled off her fingertips and clanked into a trash can.

That night, Alexandria strolled through the formal Children for Universal Hope fundraising gala, smiling to herself, knowing that she'd mixed the biggest atheist donors with the most generous religious donors, and that the direct contact always stoked each group's competitive desire to out-give the other and prove the truthfulness of their causes through overt displays of altruism.

Gliding past two men she knew well, Alexandria heard one mention "Stock Brant." She stopped with her back turned, surprised at her resentment when hearing his name in public, as though it were her own private possession.

"Illegal drugs are taking over the city, driven no doubt by Stock Brant," Randal Graph, the most popular pastor in the Las Vegas Valley, said. He wore a blue tuxedo, his hair swept back in waves. "The youth are the victims. The temptation to use the devil's poison is too great."

"You're old fashioned, Pastor," Jacque Milne, a self-proclaimed humanitarian, wearing a shiny coffee-colored suit over a frail frame, said. "Drugs are a legitimate form of escape, like your religion, from this materialistic world these kids were born into." His milky eyes bulged outward, seemingly without lids. "It's the profit seeking and the violence of Stock's gang that are immoral and must be stopped."

"You are wrong about most things, but you *are* right about the drug violence. Although…" Randal gripped Jacque's bony elbow. "Wasn't your nephew cured of pancreatic cancer by one of Stock's biologics?"

Jacques slipped his elbow free. "You of all people should be outraged by Stock's attempt at playing God. What if he creates a genetic mutation that wipes out life on earth? Plus," he whispered, his eyeballs nearing Randal's necktie, "my nephew has parents who believe in your church's hocus pocus—to your probable delight—and they claim *prayer* healed him."

"Ah," Randal nodded. "Your nephew's recovery *was* a miracle indeed. Stock be damned."

Alexandria forced herself not to snap her champagne flute's stem in two and brought the rim to her lips.

Gripping Jacque's elbow again, Randal added, "See? Who says you and I can't agree on anything?"

"We are in agreement on Stock, if nothing else." Jacque pulled his elbow free yet again.

"Good evening gentlemen." Alexandria slid in between them. "It's delightful to see you two getting along so well."

"Why hello, my Egyptian princess." Jacque cracked a delicate smile. "I was just in Somalia with your father last month. He's the best UN envoy to Africa they've ever had."

"You were helping to feed the underprivileged, I assume?" Alexandria asked.

"I assisted your father on a most critical mission. We organized the renaturalization of the Somali Hobyo Desert. Rogue desert-tolerant oats have sprouted everywhere, planted by naïve villagers using genetically modified seeds. It's a scourge, and quite embarrassing for me personally since those seeds are believed to be coming from my own backyard—from Stock Brant."

Alexandria grimaced behind an upraised hand at Stock's name leaking out from Jacque's sinewy lips. "I thought the Somalis were starving to death?" she asked, knowing she shouldn't question his good intentions, but added anyway, "It sounds like they found a way to feed themselves. Why is that a scourge?"

"Those seeds are illegal," Randal blurted.

"Nature must be protected from mankind," Jacque droned. "The deserts of Africa are some of the last untouched lands, not to be used for agriculture, especially when the food is genetically modified and could be harmful to the Somalis' health."

Alexandria knew she should agree, but instead said, "So what do you expect them to eat?"

"Your father and I are attempting to enlist the regional warlords to force the villagers to uproot the rogue oats, in exchange for a tripling of UN relief supplies." Jacque smiled, sipping his champagne.

"We are sending food as well. Don't take all the credit," Randal said.

"Oh," Alexandria said, swallowing hard with guilt, "that... that is very humanitarian of both of you."

Jacque lowered his eyelids in lieu of a bow. Randal nodded, his cheeks beaming.

"I'm looking forward to working with your father on this project," Jacque added. "We promised our European colleagues if we ever verifiably trace those illegal GMOs back to Stock, we will try him in an international court of law."

Alexandria turned away to hide her frown.

"I don't believe in all that international bureaucratic nonsense," Randal scoffed. "Just throw him in the county jail—he'll talk. I don't know why everyone is always tiptoeing around *Stock Brant*."

Unable to stop herself, Alexandria faced them, her smile etched cold, feeling blinded by some unwanted anger. "It would be tragic if one man discovered a way to allow everyone else in the world to grow their own food. You would both have to find new careers, and I wouldn't like that, because I enjoy having you at my charity galas."

Both men stared at her, then laughed.

"What a witty joke. You've always thrown the best events in town," Jacque said. "You take right after your mother."

"One more joke perhaps," Alexandria said, curling a hand into a fist. "If Stock's genetic creations were not illegal, would there be any violent street gangs to blame on him? Or would those street kids be wearing name tags and working at the corner drug store selling cancer-curing biologics, cocaine-flavored ice cream, and hemp diapers?" She smirked at their shocked faces.

After a moment, Randal burst out laughing. "I had no idea you could be so delightfully playful and fun, Ms. Patra." His soft hands lifted to show his mirthful gratitude.

"Stock deserves to be laughed at, right before he is hung,"

Jacque said, staring at Alexandria, his protruding eyes taking on a glossy sheen. "There is no place for him in modern society."

Randal dropped his hands, his cheeks pulling downward in sympathy with Jacque's loss of amusement.

"Stock is indeed an awful man," Alexandria looked at Jacque, raising her champagne, "which really is the only kind, since mankind *is* what is wrong with the world, right Mr. Milne?" She turned to Randal. "And Stock is indeed going to hell because he dares to play God—I quite agree, Pastor Graph. Perhaps we shouldn't say his name anymore so as not to taint ourselves." She curtsied. "Thank you both for coming."

They looked at her dumbfounded, having expected no one to agree with them so completely or so crudely. She handed her half-drunk champagne to Jacque and walked away.

After losing herself in the crowd, Alexandria stopped, and pressed the back of a hand to her forehead. *What did I just say?* She took several deep breaths and dropped her hand to her side. *I'll have to apologize later.*

Shaking out her wrists, she looked up, surveying her guests, and gulped at the sight of Jessy Gorronza. "Why did you invite *him*, Preton?" she whispered, already forgetting the prior conversation.

Her gown flowed across the room as she passed chatting groups, determined to remain one step ahead of Jessy's purposeful, meandering approach. He was the only child Alexandria didn't regret losing from foster care after he disappeared ten years ago. She'd always felt guilty for not missing him, since he was the kindest-speaking, most obedience-loving child she'd ever met.

Two weeks ago she unexpectedly bumped into the long-lost Jessy at a golf course fundraiser. When she heard his older, yet still humble voice, she recalled all the reasons she hadn't missed him. Jessy had applied his foster parents' views of obedience on his foster siblings so skillfully they minded him at the expense of their own parents. One set of foster parents filed for divorce because the wife obeyed Jessy like a submissive spouse. And every family returned the sweet-faced child to her office with speechless horror painted on their faces.

"Why, Ms. Patra, how wonderful to see you again," Jessy had said as she stood near a golf green two weeks ago. "In gratitude for your efforts, it is only fair that those whom you've helped give something back. Would you please accept an offer to host a series of your CUH group activities? Teaching children obedience is a higher calling, dear to many like us."

Alexandria had never turned down an offer to help the children before, but she couldn't ignore the wave of revulsion washing over her. "Thank you for the generous proposal, Mr. Gorronza," she'd replied, watching a golf cart roll by. "I'm pleased to see that you've turned into a positive contributor to society, but I'm afraid we have more than enough volunteers at the moment."

"Please," he'd oozed, adjusting the collar on his mauve golf shirt, "if the children—or you—ever need assistance in *any* way…"

Alexandria shuddered at the memory and spied over her shoulder at the formal gala, trying to spot, and thus avoid, the newly resurrected Jessy.

She gasped as Preton Moore captured her body between prim tuxedoed arms.

He led her from the crowd, his photogenic face pressing close. "Have you bought the jet? The governor of Illinois wants to discuss the partnership in person this week."

"I'll book a flight to Springfield tonight."

"Just buy a jet for heaven's sake. The partnership's board approved your request six months ago." His breath smacked of mint drowned in stale grapes. "You could be making twice as many visits, and nobody is nearly as good as you at representing the cause."

She guided his arms away from her. "I'll have the partnership buy a jet this week, Preton."

"By the way, I'm glad you told me how uncooperative Libby Dodge was toward the partnership. I gave my *full* support to the federal government for any necessary action within our state, including my assistance in 'correcting' county title documents, before they made their brave decision to liberate the Libby House." He winked.

"You told them about my meeting," her voice cracked, "with Ms. Dodge?"

"She deserved it." Preton smiled so broadly Alexandria saw her own shocked reflection on his teeth.

"That's why they stole her house?"

"Stole? Don't use silly words, my dear," Preton said. "As you know, society is the rightful owner of all property. And when it is not used for the greater good it is our duty to reallocate its possession. Whether we correct a property title mistake or impose a one hundred percent tax makes no difference. We must always find a way to uphold our higher ideals."

Alexandria swallowed, taking away Preton's champagne flute. She'd also heard about the government prohibiting Ms. Dodge's international jet sales. *Did she deserve that too?* She took a large sip. *Why did Libby refuse to sell me a Wyvern?* Her next gulp emptied the flute. *Would she still be so prideful now? Perhaps the world looks different when you need help, Ms. Dodge.* Her shoulders relaxed and she attempted another sip, but found the glass empty.

"I'm glad you're enjoying the evening," Preton said. "I brought you a fresh donor. He's been asking about you."

Her shoulders tightened.

"Mr. Jesus Gorronza is such a polite and earnest young man." Preton's smile almost blinded her.

"He goes by Jessy."

"Well, he's newly wealthy and willing, and hinting at contributing in a big way to my next campaign, but he wanted to discuss donating to the CUH with you first." Preton raised a finger. "Something tells me he has the right stuff for a future political career."

Alexandria shivered and rubbed her bare arms. Her eyes searched Preton's; they looked like those of a selfless saint—or a power monger. "How did he get his money?"

"He's some kind of hotshot, rising star at *The Sin*."

She gripped Preton's sleeve to steady herself. *He works for Stock? How? Why?* Her eyes darted around the room fearing or hoping to see Stock's hard face insulting her guests. An improper tingling ran through her body.

"Is something wrong?"

Concealing her relieved disappointment, she turned back to him. "No…no. I'll speak with Jessy." She smiled. "The children can use all the support they can get. Thank you for inviting him."

"That's what I love about you, my dear." Preton straightened his bow tie and dabbed the sides of his gelled hair. "I know you will always do the right thing at the right time." He stepped away, clasping the jiggling arm of a concerned-faced woman dripping with encrusted rubies as she walked by.

Alexandria ambled across the ballroom, head lowered, thinking of Stock. Hearing someone breathing near her made her stop and swallow. Glancing up, she found herself eye level with Jessy's perfectly combed hair. She touched her stomach. *Oh, no. How close is the bathroom?*

Returning his smile with effort, she said, "I'm so pleased to run into you here, Mr. Gorronza. You were saying the other day?"

Jessy nodded and offered his ideas for more closely monitored after-school programs. "It's the antiquated idea that free time is good for children that has led to the disaster we see in the world today. If only there were more like us who cared about instilling the comfort of order upon them."

"Uh-huh." Alexandria coughed, trying not to gag at the ripeness of his sweet tone. "Has *The Sin*…or Stock…set up any private programs to help out in that regard?"

Jessy leaned in, causing Alexandria to cover her chest with a hand. "Stock?" he whispered. "We don't associate with anyone like that, of course. But there are rumors. Far from helping after-school children, he's acquired a new toy, a Libby jet. One of those banned *Sovereigns*, no less."

A Libby jet? Alexandria's stomach tightened. "Please excuse me, I need to…" She held a hand to her mouth and strode away.

Returning from the ladies' room, Alexandria stood gnawing a celery stick behind the hors d'oeuvre table. She nodded as a lanky bald man droned on about his abstract art while munching a handful of organic cashews.

How did Ms. Dodge justify selling a private jet to Stock and not me? She dropped the half-eaten celery on a napkin.

Turning her head, she said, "The meaning of your art sounds reassuring. What's your favorite piece?" She did not listen to the answer.

Sitting in her office the next day, Alexandria called her assistant, "Janice, please set up an appointment with Libby Dodge."

Chapter 15

After work, Alexandria drove to a downtown neighborhood mixed with pawnshops and rundown apartments.

Pulling the SUV to a stop in front of a metal fence and gate, she rechecked the address on her map. *This area has the highest murder rate in the city. Libby wants to meet here?*

She glanced up as the gate slid open one side at a time, pushed by Libby Dodge. Libby's hair stuck to her cheeks, her bare arms glistening against a soaked t-shirt beneath denim overalls. *She looks like a member of a chain gang? What is this place?*

Driving onto the cracked asphalt driveway, she watched Libby walk away and peg an axe into a cut log near two metal buildings. A small house sat to the left. *Wait…she lives here?*

Alexandria stepped down from the SUV, shocked at Libby's gritty surroundings.

"Welcome." Libby waved at her.

Alexandria hesitated in returning the wave, feeling a bit guilty and more than a bit overdressed. Raising her voice she said, "Thank you for—"

"Come." Libby wiped sweat from her brow and strolled to the house.

Following her, Alexandria stared at the back of Libby's overalls covered in wood-dust and grease. *I can't believe how humbled she looks.*

Libby led her through a sunken living area and to a dining room. Sunlight poured in from the window overlooking a cut lawn and an old cottonwood tree. A white bowl with bark-colored miniature eggs sat at the center of a dining table. The air smelled of fresh pine.

Alexandria liked the minimalist-retro feel of the house, but it seemed ridiculously modest compared to the cliff house. As they sat down, her eyelids lowered as she recalled the cliff house balcony and its waterfalls.

"You wanted to see me?" Libby wiped her hands on her pant legs.

"I'm sorry to hear about your cliff house," Alexandria softened her eyes, "and about your jet sale prohibitions. We can all find ourselves in situations of unexpected need at times."

Libby pushed a hand through her own hair, releasing sawdust to her shoulders and the table.

"Ms. Dodge," she clasped her hands together atop the table, "I've received a lot of pressure to purchase a competitor's jet, but I didn't, because I know that thirty million dollars can make a big difference to a small firm when times are tough. Your *Wyvern* is the right jet for the cause, and I'm still willing to pay you full price."

"I really appreciate your offer, Ms. Patra." Libby brushed sawdust off the table.

Her shoulders relaxed. "Please, call me Alexa."

"I've never needed money more desperately in my life, Alexa." She rubbed her throat.

Alexandria nodded in understanding, holding back her reassured smile.

"However, I won't sell *you* a jet," Libby said. "You should've sent somebody else."

"But…" Alexandria blinked and glanced around at the house. "You *need* this sale."

"I'm not stopping you from owning a jet. Purchase one from somebody else or have your organization call my office and order one."

"What do you have against me personally?" Her arms crossed her chest. "Do you actually think I'm doing something wrong?"

Libby shook the sawdust from her shoulders.

"Well, do you?"

"Only you can answer that."

"I know what I'm doing is *right*." Alexandria's arms fell to the table.

Libby gazed at Alexandria's fingers.

Alexandria studied her own hands as they tapped the table. *I've sacrificed so much for what I believe to be true.* When she glimpsed in her mind *what* she had sacrificed, her hands froze and her heart raced. Clearing her throat, she asked, "Libby, don't you believe there is a higher law, a path in life more important than what we each want?"

Libby looked up, raising an eyebrow.

Alexandria spread her fingers upon the table, studying them. Taking a breath, she said, "May I ask you a personal question?"

Libby waited.

"Were you not taught altruistic and humanitarian values growing up?"

Picking up a brown egg from the bowl, Libby held it under her nose, breathing in.

Alexandria frowned. "Well, don't you at least think that children should learn those values?"

"I think," Libby replaced the egg in the bowl, "teaching values that lead to a child's own happiness is the most significant responsibility a parent has."

Pressing her fingers to her eyes, Alexandria thought of the result of what her parents taught her. *Coming here was a mistake. The partnership will buy a different jet, and everything will continue as normal.* She stood to leave.

"It was a pleasure to see you again, Alexa." Libby stood as well. "Please don't be offended by me saying this, but your body movement is so fluid, it's like watching air flowing off a jet's wingtip."

Alexandria held still, conscious of her body, and remembered the last thing Libby said to her at the cliff house. *Why had she mentioned that?* Brushing a strand of hair behind an ear, she stared at Libby.

"Here," Libby held up the bowl of dark eggs, "please take a pine nut with you."

Pine nut? She stared at them. *Those are much too large to be...* A waft of roasted, salty pine caressed her nose. She breathed in. It reminded her of something which made her gut tingle. "Where did you get them?"

"On the corner right outside the fence." Libby pointed out the window. "From a young drug peddler. They sat exposed in a box and made me curious. It's the most expensive food I've ever bought."

They smell so delicious. Alexandria touched one. *I wonder what they taste like.* "You always buy contraband from criminals?"

"I'd never thought of buying anything from a drug dealer before." Libby smirked. "I guess I made an exception."

Alexandria fell back into her seat and shook her head. *An exception? Why did Libby make an exception not to sell* me *a jet? There must be something evil in the answer.*

Libby returned the bowl to the table and sat back down.

Turning to the window, Alexandria watched the grass blades shifting in the wind like a field of grain. She wondered what Stock would've looked like standing on his farm as a young boy. Her eyes shot back to Libby. "Why did you sell Stock Brant a jet and not…" She stopped herself.

"Why did you come here?"

Alexandria's heart raced. She lifted a hand before her face and asked the question she feared and had come here to ask, "Why won't you sell *me* a jet?" Her hand swayed in the silence, fingertips shifting in a delicate motion.

"Alexa, I won't act against you."

"Won't act against," her eyes lifted, "*me?*"

Libby's expression looked strange, like a display of kindness, only it wasn't anything she'd ever seen.

"What do you see in me?" Alexandria pulled on a strand of hair until it straightened and gleamed like flint.

"Just a girl with a dream."

Alexandria's eyes dilated.

"The exception I made for you," Libby said, "is a greedy plea from deep inside me."

"A plea? For what?"

"To not abandon what *you* want—because *I* want to see it."

*Not to abandon what…*I *want.* Alexandria's uplifted hand trembled. She thought she should feel embarrassed at Libby's presumption; she wanted to be angry, but she felt something else. "You actually know what I've given up?"

Libby didn't answer.

"I've always wanted to be good," Alexandria whispered.

The touch of skin felt so comforting when Libby's hand lowered Alexandria's to the table.

"I'm ashamed to say it," Alexandria swallowed, "but I'm miserable. Everyone says I shouldn't be, but I am. I've never told anyone before."

Libby held her gaze.

"I'm not like everyone else," Alexandria continued, "like those who can seek balance or split themselves into pieces of different sizes and shades. For me it is one or the other. All or nothing. Good or selfish." She exhaled. "And I made my choice long ago."

"I like that about you," Libby said. "It shows your strength and desire to shape your soul into a single unified style."

Sliding her hand out from under Libby's, Alexandria watched her own fingers shifting to the music flowing through her mind. The melody enveloped her body like a steam bath, opening every pore in response. A selfish, dark ember burned deep inside her.

As she looked up, her eyes watered, like the wet polishing of pure onyx. "You're not at all what I expected, Libby Dodge."

Libby stood and pushed back her hair. "Now if you'll excuse me, I have some chores to finish."

"You're kicking me out?" Alexandria wiped her eyes, looking at the black smears on her hands.

Libby waited.

"May I use your washroom?" Alexandria asked.

She led Alexandria to a small bathroom with a worn black and white tile floor.

Standing before the tarnished mirror, Alexandria saw somebody she hadn't wanted to recognize in a long time.

Walking back through the living room, she asked, "How did you know I was once—" She heard the muffled thumps of Libby chopping wood outside. "…a performer?" The thuds ticked by like a large metronome.

She approached the kitchen table. Leaning over, she took a giant pine nut and smelled it. Her heart fluttered. *Stock.*

Blades of grass shimmered beyond the window. She again tried to envision Stock on his childhood farm, but instead she saw the expansive front lawn of her own childhood home. Her eyes squeezed shut and her body trembled. *What am I doing? I can't go back in time.*

Exiting the house, she passed Libby without looking. She jumped in her SUV and drove away, feeling the rapidity of her breath and the pine nut clenched in her fist.

The next morning, Alexandria visited Emma Rosland, a Nevada State Department head she respected. After some banter about the new office coffee maker, Alexandria asked, "Did you choose this job because it's what you really wanted to do, or for some…higher reason?"

Emma scrunched her face until it focused at the tip of her nose, as if that question should never be asked.

Alexandria widened her eyes, wondering if that would've been her own reaction to that question. "It was a bad joke, Emma." She laughed, clearing her throat. "Let me buy you brunch."

At a panoramic rooftop casino restaurant, Alexandria spent lavishly on Emma. Alexandria forced herself to smile a lot, hoping everything would return to normal.

Returning her credit card to her handbag, Alexandria touched something smooth. She removed the large pine nut and placed it on the tablecloth while Emma spoke about the need for higher license plate fees.

With a butter knife, Alexandria cracked the shell along its center, pried it open, and took the golden flesh into the palm of her hand. Emma continued speaking, but her words melted into a piney scent until Alexandria heard nothing more.

When Alexandria placed the nut in her mouth, she stood and walked to a window. She bit into it and moaned deep in her throat. The flavor and texture couldn't be explained—only felt. Touching the glass, she covered the view of *The Sin*, held fast by the swirling within her. She could no longer tell if it was an evil sensation or if she cared what anyone else would call it. Her long-held truce with the world began to disintegrate—and she liked the sensation.

"Are you all right?" Emma asked, standing next to her.

Alexandria turned, trying to remember who Emma was. "Oh, yes," she said. "Thank you for asking." She felt so light. "I'm fine." She smiled, still tasting the pine essence in her mouth. "Are you ready to go back to work?"

"A silhouette," Stock Brant whispered.

He stood gazing from his penthouse balcony at his marquee,

his hands caressing the rail, remembering the smoothness of Alexandria's skin. *Those eyes are not allowed to exist...not in this world.*

As he glanced at the city, his vision blurred. Colorful objects moved before him like living, carbon-based cells, splitting and growing. Their movement slowed, rearranging themselves at the command of his thoughts forming into the vision of his first biologic breakthrough while in graduate school.

He'd broken the accepted rules of genetic engineering protocols to come up with a solution—a cure for color blindness. The dean of science expelled him for his unethical methods weeks before he would've graduated. When the biologic, legally owned by the university, became a sales blockbuster, they built a new science facility, named after the dean of science, and funded hundreds of student scholarships.

The living cells before Stock morphed into complex patterns, the double helix of the genetic code twisting in the background— the memory of his second biologic. He developed it over five long years at a struggling, disreputable pharmaceutical company, the only one that would hire him without a graduate degree and overlook his research methods.

The cells before his eyes multiplied out of control like the esophageal cancer his biologic would have cured. His heart pounded as the unstoppable cells crushed his body. Rubbing his eyes, Stock escaped the vision, but there had been no escape for the biologic; the FDA rejected it without comment. The pharma company abandoned the research and fired Stock the day of the announcement.

He closed his eyes. *A shadow, covering the whole earth.*

Gripping the rail, breathing with effort, Stock opened his eyes, focusing on the people gathering in a tumbleweed-strewn lot across the Strip. He blinked, remembering why he'd come to the balcony.

He'd read about the controversial skyscraper proposal. Critics argued it would be too disruptive to current hotel owners and to scenic views, too tall for air traffic and earthquakes, too dangerous in case of a fire or terrorist attacks, and too antagonistic to countries without skyscrapers or even some with them.

"You are all right," he whispered, "the world doesn't deserve it."

Stock watched a large black man cut through the crowd, climb atop a stage, and stand behind a podium. A plaque below the man's hands read: *Halvern Black Architects.* Well-groomed politicians gathered before a line of cameras near the stage.

A procession of suited architects filed onto the lot, following the path taken by Halvern. They flanked behind him like an impenetrable wall.

Halvern leaned into the microphone and pointed at the ground, his growl echoing off the adjacent casinos. "Some have argued against building this skyscraper. *They* don't need to build it."

He walked off the stage, picked up a handful of dirt, and returned to the podium. Wincing with his fist outstretched, he dumped the dirt on the stage in front of the news cameras. "Consider this ground broken. Are there any questions about *The Spirit of Man* structure?"

Spectators glanced around, shocked at the brevity of the ceremony anticipated for months in the news. Many already missed the speech as they straggled onto the lot.

"Which consortium funded the construction, and how much taxpayer money was used for loan guarantees?" a reporter asked, his wiry hair blowing in the wind.

"It is none of your business who is funding it."

"We have a right to know," a voice from somewhere in the crowd yelled.

"Next question."

"Are you trying to send a message to the world by using a minority architectural team?" a bearded, pale-skinned man wearing a checkered sports coat asked.

"I will answer questions regarding the *structure.*"

"Why did you refuse to negotiate with the workers' unions?" a woman reporter, with beehive-shaped hair, asked.

Halvern narrowed his eyes and gripped the podium. "Since nobody seems capable of asking a question about the structure, I'm going back to work."

"Mr. Black!" Hands from the press spiked into the air. "Mr. Black!"

Halvern gripped his side and walked from the platform, pushing his way through the babbling crowd.

"You naïve fool." Stock leaned back from the railing. "They will never allow you to build it as you designed it."

Halvern's staff followed him out a chain-link gate in the construction fence. Politicians fought each other for the microphone. Lieutenant Governor Preton Moore spoke first, taking credit for the future economic benefit of the project.

Stock entered his penthouse and slammed the glass door. Two hours later, he still heard the muffled speaking of politicians outside.

Chapter 16

The moon raced alongside Roble on wet asphalt as he rode his motorcycle onto Kadena Air Base. He couldn't believe how the three months since the Misawa Air Show had incinerated like a flash in a combustion chamber.

With his bike parked, he walked to the rear of his barracks. Entering through the patio gate, he stopped in a puddle, staring at a huge crate blocking the back door. "What the hell?"

Red arrows pointed up the sides of the wooden box. On its top, a barcode sticker under plastic listed *Las Vegas, Nevada, USA,* as its point of origin, but nothing else. *Could this be…?* He rubbed his chin. *I didn't even send her any money.*

Rising on his toes, he scanned over the patio fence making sure no one was around. He pressed a boot tip against the crate but it wouldn't budge. He tried to push it through the doorway but it was too heavy. *How did this get here?*

Jumping over the crate, he entered his barracks and retrieved a tire chalk, four sofa coasters, two blankets, and a hammer. He hammered the chalk under each corner and inserted the sofa coasters for wheels. Using the blankets, he pulled the box in through his kitchen, and slid it into the living room.

He stood back, hands on his hips, heart pounding in his chest. *Oh, please don't let this be a practical joke.* Prying off the lid with the hammer, he found a letter sitting atop packing-foam. It read:

Dear Mr. Roble Santos,

Thank you for sending me your drawings and design requests. Enclosed is the first batch of improvement parts for the F-15DJ. Installation instructions are in the enclosed laptop, along with my first version of avionics software. Please designate a secure off-base location for future deliveries, as I had to make special arrangements to get this to you undetected. Respond to me only by private carrier at the listed mailbox. Once the project is complete, please destroy

151

this and all correspondence, including the laptop. Your payment to me will be the successful modification of the fighter jet. If the improvements prove effective, I intend to sell the upgrade package to the Japanese Self-Defense Force.
Highest regards,
Libby Dodge.

Roble dropped to his knees and plucked a few parts from the crate. He felt their texture and studied their color under a lamp light. *Oh, these are the real deal. Ultralight, high strength alloy inner wing ribs, struts, and spar reinforcements to replace the aluminum ones.* "Hah… it'll be able to take so much G-force."

Out came the laptop. As it powered up, Roble's mind raced in sync with the humming microprocessor. Three-dimensional renderings of the F-15DJ improvement phases flashed across the screen, one after another. His eyes absorbed the pixels like activated carbon soaking up gem dust.

The modification plans were extensive, their scope beyond what Roble had requested. He paused on one rendering of a complete jet turbine rebuild. "Holy…" he squinted, his face drawn to the screen. "That's…" He shook his head at the shape of the turbine blades and the alloys she used, which he knew would significantly increase the jet thrust.

After throwing the demolished crate into an alleyway dumpster, he placed all the shiny parts in rows along the living room floor in relation to where he thought he would install them. Sitting on the couch, he admired his orchestration. *I can't wait to tell Takinato.*

Captain Takinato pulled the *Skeleton Eagle* out of service and assigned Airman Toki Kozumi to take exclusive charge of the deep maintenance procedures. He ordered Kozumi to follow Roble's instructions and say nothing to anyone on base.

Every night, Takinato, Kozumi, and Roble took over an older, seldom used Naha Air Base hangar and worked on the unauthorized modifications.

Roble overnighted letters to Libby—asking for clarifications, offering further design ideas, and explaining issues he'd run into;

Libby would respond promptly in turn. The crates arrived at Takinato's home loft every few days.

By the end of that first month, they had installed all the new internal fuselage and wing supports. Captain Takinato put the *Skeleton Eagle* back into service, but the nighttime modifications had only just begun.

Standing in the humid air near the start of Naha's runway lights, Roble scanned the moonlit sky. A second month of alterations on the *Skeleton Eagle* had passed, and the new thrust vectoring systems installed.

A distant light grew until the F-15DJ roared over his head, its engines pulsing, flaps and vectors snapping in different directions with hydraulic whines. The fighter dropped to the center line of the runway and hit with a welcoming screech. A skeleton talon on its tailfin flashed by a runway light. Goosebumps shot along Roble's arms as he ran to the hangar to greet Takinato.

The *Skeleton Eagle* rolled into the hangar and fell silent, its canopy closed. Roble waited, squirming with impatience. Takinato's helmet pointed straight ahead as if he were still in flight.

Stepping back, Roble glimpsed Takinato's glazed-over eyes and wet cheeks. Realizing the personal nature of this victory, he walked away and jumped on his motorcycle.

He zipped toward Kadena, leaning in to the turns. The world zoomed at him and he pierced through it, boring a tunnel of streaking lights.

In his barracks, he showered off and pulled on pajama bottoms and an old t-shirt. Exhausted, he collapsed on the worn couch, placing his hands behind his head, relishing his greatest triumph yet. But he knew he wouldn't be able to sleep, his mind replaying every modification he'd done to the *Skeleton Eagle* over and over again.

After a couple of hours, he pulled an English and Japanese version of his favorite novel—about an aspiring architect—onto his chest and read. Since starting his cross-training at Naha, he'd studied constantly to improve his Japanese, but reading had come much more slowly than speaking. Tonight, the meticulous translation process relaxed his churning mind.

A soft knock roused his attention. Glancing across the room, he read the clock—3:15 AM.

He rose and opened the door, expecting to see a lost, drunk airman.

Sugemi stood in a tight silver dress, a lit cigarette between two fingers. Her eyes ignited into embers as she drew on the rolled tobacco.

Roble's gaze dropped to his arrowhead between her small breasts, continued to her flat stomach, to her bare legs, stopping on the diamond anklet cuffed above a thin-strapped sandal.

As Sugemi lifted the necklace, he glanced up, watching it sparkle in the porch light. She exhaled a lick of smoke which curled up around her wrist and caressed the arrowhead. The heat from her breath burned like a lit fuse down his body.

"How did you get on base?" he asked in Japanese, his voice hoarse.

Dropping the arrowhead back to her chest, she stepped into him, blowing smoke against his ear. "I know lots of things... remember?"

He swallowed. "Did you forget that I'm just a mechanic? Dirty hands and all."

"Make them touch me." Her lips brushed his ear, accelerating the burn inside him.

Roble's hands slid around her waist, clasping the small of her back.

Wrapping an arm around his neck, Sugemi sucked in another drag from her cigarette, and flicked it behind her. Her thighs pressed to his.

Roble swung the door closed and ran a hand through the back of her satin hair. His other hand cupped the front of her neck. Her skin felt so smooth under his calluses, and he squeezed. She exhaled from her nose, the smoke caressing down his arm. His palm slid down, pulling her dress with it, stopping between her breasts.

"Tonight is a night to celebrate, isn't it?" she asked in Japanese, pressing harder against his legs.

"How do you know that?" His words sounded muffled in his own head.

Her eyes narrowed as her fingernails raked the back of his neck. "Maybe I felt the vibrations in the air."

Roble pulled her head back and ran his nose along the curve of her neck. "How long are you staying?" He slid both hands down her back, under her thighs, lifting her up and against him.

She wrapped her legs around him. "How many minutes can you spare?"

He pushed her dress up, squeezing as he moved. "More than the thirty you gave me on your last two refueling layovers."

Sugemi brought her forehead down to his. "You wasted time touching my jet more than me. That's your fault."

Curling his fingertips inward between her legs, Roble found the smooth strip of fabric.

Sugemi gasped and pulled his shirt over his head. "Come visit me in Tokyo." Her hands gripped his bare shoulders. "I promise to make two whole hours for you." She kissed him.

"Tokyo?" he mumbled against her lips, pulling away. His hands slid her dress up farther. "Sure, no problem. I'll just tell my team of assistants to cover for me while I fly up there in my private jet."

"You talk too much." She slipped a hand down between her legs and into his pajama bottoms.

He sucked in a breath.

Her mouth went back to his lips. "Roble," she moaned, as he pressed her body against the door.

The next morning, Roble awoke to the buzzing of his alarm clock.

His eyes didn't want to open, but he smelled something salty and arousing. Rolling over, he saw Sugemi, the arrowhead resting against the edge of her nipple.

He touched the necklace and glided his hand down her body. She stretched like a cat.

Snuggling his nose below her ear, he inhaled.

"You like my scent," she said. "Want me for breakfast?"

He groaned and forced himself out of the bed. "I'm going to Naha."

"Awww. I rearranged my schedule to have breakfast here."

"Make yourself at home." He walked away naked, pointing at

the kitchen. "Corn flakes are on the counter, protein milk in the fridge. I have stuff to do."

"You really like jets more than girls?"

"Yes," he stopped at the closet. "Much more."

"Stay, and I'll talk dirty jets with you."

"Too dangerous." He reached for an airman's shirt. "I'm running out of things to bet with."

"You don't want a chance to win it back?"

Roble glanced down at his bare chest.

"This time if I win," she said, "you will service my jet for a year."

Roble laughed. "Nice try." Pulling on the shirt, he added, "You really think you can have my body just because you're smart?"

"Takinato told me all the naughty things you're doing to his fighter. If I didn't know better, I'd think you were using him just to touch it."

"Jealous?" he asked in Japanese.

"Very."

Glancing back, he watched her pressing his arrowhead to her lips, her eyes closed, lower back arched subtly off the bed.

Oh, you're cruel. He walked to the bed and straddled her stomach.

Her eyes opened and she slid her hands up his legs. "Not in a hurry anymore, mechanic?"

"You don't even care a little that I'll get in trouble for being la—" He sucked in his breath as Sugemi's fingers moved higher.

"Don't worry," she said in Japanese. "I know what you need." Pushing him back on the bed, she reached over and lifted two greasy jet cup-links off the floor.

Roble's eyes widened.

She grinned and threaded the cup-links with the F-15 electrical cables sticking out from under his bed.

"Oh…" Roble swallowed, body squirming.

"Hold still," she said, cuffing his wrists and tying the cables to the bedframe. "There. Now you're touching a jet." Her hands ran across his abs and continued down. "Yep, I thought so," she laughed.

Roble swung open his Naha maintenance locker and immediately slammed it shut. *Wrong one. I need more sleep.* He frowned when he noted it *was* the correct locker number before him.

Shaking his head, he opened it again. A Japanese fighter pilot flight suit and helmet hung inside. "What…?" He glanced around the alcove at the rear of the hangar.

Captain Takinato stood behind him in full flight gear. "You are late," he said, eyes narrowing.

Roble waited, feeling uncertain about Takinato's harsh tone.

"Do you have any idea what you have done?" Takinato asked.

Roble's gut sank, thinking of how he must have screwed up the *Skeleton Eagle*, then he thought of Sugemi lying in his bed.

"Put on that flight suit," Takinato said.

Feeling uneasy, Roble obeyed. Once in gear, he approached the *Skeleton Eagle*. Takinato sat in the front pilot seat with the canopy open and the boarding ladder waiting.

Roble walked around the fighter jet, touching it, thinking of all the effort he'd put into it, of everything it should be capable of. He studied the thrust vectoring system. *It looks fine. So was Takinato talking about Sugemi?*

Takinato cleared his throat.

Roble glanced at the cockpit.

Takinato pointed at the seat behind him.

Oh… Roble swallowed.

As he climbed the ladder, he tried to suppress the tingling in his gut, having never flown in a fighter jet before. Lowering himself into the navigator seat, his heart raced. He pulled on his helmet as the canopy closed. When it sealed shut, he touched the inside of the glass, looking out, trying to recall how to execute the hick maneuver which he'd read about—a technique necessary to overcome extreme gravitational forces and stay conscious. He squeezed his legs and abdominal muscles in anticipation.

Takinato ignited the jet's twin turbines. Roble's fingers vibrated, and he curled them inward. He couldn't believe how intoxicating the jet fumes smelled.

As the modified Peace Eagle taxied from the hangar onto the runway, Roble reached for his necklace, but gripped only air; he pressed his hands against the sides of the cockpit instead. Takinato radioed the tower.

"*Reaper, you are cleared for takeoff,*" the tower controller said over the helmet speaker.

Gravitational force slammed Roble into his seat, stealing his breath. The roar of the afterburners consumed his mind. The lines on the runway ticked by then screamed into blur.

Takinato kicked the elevators, flaps, and vectors downward, pitching the fighter vertical. They launched like a rocket.

Blood rushed to the back of Roble's head, his eyes trying to focus on the clouds approaching in rapid waves. He thought he might have screamed but couldn't hear himself.

"*Now,* you will see what you have done." Takinato cut the fighter hard right, slamming Roble against his restraints.

Roble tried to smile, but his face drew tight as the horizon held perpendicular. One wingtip stretched down as if to slice the ocean; the other reached up to incise the sky.

"Hold on." Takinato inverted the *Skeleton Eagle.*

Roble reached above his head toward the glimmering sea, gasping for breath.

They plunged down in an inverted loop, accelerating in full afterburner. "Uhhh…" Roble grunted, trying not to pass out, his arms pulling tight to his chest.

Shooting back up into the sky, Takinato asked, "Want me to stop?"

"No," Roble rasped in Japanese. "Not ever."

The fighter leveled out, shooting across the sky. Their speed decelerated and Roble thought he heard Takinato laugh, but he wasn't certain. The *Skeleton Eagle's* nose popped up from the torque of the vectored thrust. The jet flipped over backward, completing a somersault in mid-air.

"Oh," Roble moaned, his gut raging with joyous pain.

Takinato laughed; Roble was certain of it this time. They dove again. The maneuvers became bolder, Roble's grimaces broader.

When the *Skeleton Eagle* planed out, cruising high above the endless sea, Takinato asked, "You still back there?"

"I think so," Roble said, feeling so exultant that the fighter jet could've ejected him into the ocean to be eaten by sharks and he would not have complained.

"Take the stick."

Roble looked down and seized it, knowing exactly what he'd always wanted to do. He pressed it to the left and held. The fighter jet rolled over and over again, faster and faster, as if boring a hole into the fabric of the sky.

"*Uwa!*" Takinato retook the stick, bringing the jet back under control. After several breaths, he said, "My fault. I will give you lessons on how not to try to kill us next time."

On Roble's next day off, Captain Takinato took him back up in the *Skeleton Eagle*, unofficially starting Roble's fighter jet training.

While in the air, they spoke only in Japanese and of nothing but the modified Eagle and fighter jet tactics.

During the next six months, Roble, Kozumi, and Takinato implemented the remaining *Skeleton Eagle* modifications. Libby's avionic computers and software tied the enhancements together. She also provided radar jamming equipment to be installed behind the nosecone to create radar stealth capabilities.

As the final step, they rebuilt two F-15DJ turbine engines using reinforced shafts with broad, widely spaced blades made of titanium and cobalt. With the modified engines and the lighter fuselage parts installed, nothing in the Japanese Air Self-Defense Force came close to matching its performance.

In celebration of the completed *Skeleton Eagle*, Takinato invited Roble to his downtown Naha loft.

They hauled a metal barrel and empty wood crates up to the roof of the three-story building. Takinato lit a stack of Libby's used correspondence envelopes on fire and tossed it into the barrel. Between shots of sake, they took turns throwing Libby's modification notes and wood crate slats into the blaze. Takinato smashed Libby's laptop with a heavy wrench and flung it in.

Roble held his original artistic drawings of the *Skeleton Eagle* over the edge of the can, the ones taken off Takinato's loft wall. With a wince, he let them slip into the smoky flames.

"You made it real, Roble Santos-san." Takinato raised a shot glass.

"To Kazuki Takinato-san." Roble clanked his glass to Takinato's.

Filling their last shots, they downed them, then threw the

glasses in the fire. They stood watching the yellow wisps rolling with sparks into the dark sky.

"How do you feel about your Japanese?" Takinato asked in Japanese.

"Better when I'm not drunk," Roble said in near perfect Japanese.

"It better be. I do not want to get booted from the JSDF."

Roble lifted his hands, staring at him.

"Once your hangover wears off," Takinato slurred, "you are taking the *Skeleton* up solo, without permission."

Roble stood still, face reverent in the fire's glow.

Takinato bowed, then grappled Roble's neck and held him down laughing. "Just do not crash it, you wild Indian."

The next afternoon, Roble wore Takinato's flight gear with a mirrored helmet visor. He spoke in a mix of Japanese and Japanese-accented English as necessary to the ground crew while he boarded the *Skeleton Eagle*.

As the canopy sealed him in the cockpit, he flipped open his helmet visor and glanced around at the complex array of controls. *Wow, here I am.* He toggled on the auxiliary power, the whine of the hydraulic systems making him shiver. Staring at the ignition button, he swallowed, thinking of the seventy-three thousand pounds of thrust in the rebuilt engines.

His gloved fingertip hovered over the ignition button as he glanced at the sky. He inhaled and pressed it. The turbines whirled into a vibrating whisper, then accelerated into a quaking roar.

Closing his helmet visor, Roble turned on his radio. After receiving the correct commands from the control tower, he taxied to the start of the runway.

When he heard, *"Reaper, you are cleared for takeoff,"* he held the brake and punched the throttles forward. The fighter jet rumbled, streaks of fire bellowing out from behind, but the modified F-15DJ sat still.

Releasing the brake, the *Skeleton Eagle* catapulted forward. With his back plastered to the seat, his vision shaking, the world zoomed past him.

Lifting into the air, Roble switched off his helmet microphone, sucked in a breath and yelled, "Yeah!"

Takinato advised him to stay below Mach 1 for his first run. It sounded like sage advice on the ground, but in a plunging corkscrew down from sixty thousand feet, Roble glimpsed the Machmeter pegged at 2.7. "Oh...shit," escaped his lips.

He pulled into a steep climb, grunting against the oppressive G-forces, enjoying the ride. "I'll slow down next time," he whispered.

Before his final descent, Roble gazed upon the blue expanse of the earth, its cottony clouds far below. He remembered the first rocket he built from toilet paper rolls at age seven, the one he sent blazing up into an overcast sky from a foster parents' backyard.

He had waited, pacing the dry lawn for it to reappear with its hamburger wrapper parachute. After an hour, he lay on the ground and watched the clouds until they darkened into night. He'd always hoped the lost rocket had continued upward and still flew to this day, never touching the earth again.

Roble's eyes lifted from the clouds and followed the path his rocket might have traveled. The *Skeleton Eagle* lifted higher, its nose angled up. Listening to the rumbling engines, he stared at the glowing barrier at the edge of the sky.

When he touched down on the runway, he realized—this was the best day of his life.

He pulled a pencil and crumpled paper from his flight suit, smoothed the drawing on his knee, and made a few careful marks near the center. Stuffing his dream back in his pocket, he smiled.

Chapter 17

Roble walked along a damp sidewalk, the broad Kadena lawns bathed in morning dew.

What in the world? He turned his head.

"Oh…" His boots stopped as he waited for what he heard coming.

A black B1 bomber—its retractable wings extended for additional lift—descended several hundred yards away on a runway, retrofiring its engines. The reverberation of its four turbines caressed Roble's eyes into a smile, making him forget his destination.

Two officers marched around him on the concrete strip. "Snap to it, Airman," one said as he passed.

Shaking his head, Roble remembered his meeting and jogged to a flat, whitewashed building with paneled windows. He removed his airman's cap, slipped it under an arm, and entered.

A lieutenant sitting in a cubicle glanced at Roble's nametag, pointed at a door, and returned to her paperwork.

The plaque on the door read: *Major Gavin Sircor.*

In his fifteen months at Kadena, Roble had never met with the 67th Fighter Squadron Commander and there had been no reason to think he ever would. Checking his freshly ironed uniform, he entered the office.

Sircor sat behind a desk topped with two fighter jet models, a cup with two pens, and a neat stack of papers. He held one of the papers in his athletic hands, studying it, his gold maple leaves glinting atop squared shoulders. He appeared out of place in an office like a cruise missile sitting in the middle of a library.

Roble snapped to attention and saluted.

Without lowering the paper, Major Sircor said, "Airman Santos, I don't like hard decisions. Unfortunately for both of us, I have to make one today." He looked up, his face hard as titanium.

Roble swallowed.

Replacing the paper atop the pile, Sircor said. "I do not tolerate insubordination." The words hung like a noose in the air.

Roble tried to swallow again but his throat felt too tight.

"For some reason Sergeant Perry hasn't requested formal disciplinary action against you." Sircor leaned back in his chair. "Please enlighten me, Airman, as to why my maintenance sergeant would put his career on the line to protect a disliked insubordinate?"

"That is," Roble cleared this throat, "unknowable to me, sir."

"I called your instructor back at Sheppard this morning, Sergeant Peterson."

Roble blinked.

"He said you learned how to maintain every 'heavy' in the fleet faster than anyone he'd ever seen and that you'd requested to work on fighter jets on your first day." The tendons in his neck tensed. "But he also admitted you modified aircraft against procedures and his direct orders."

Roble stood motionless.

"I am certain from my conversation that he wanted to discharge you, but he obviously didn't. Instead," Sircor's jaw tightened, "he transferred you here—into *my* squadron." He leaned forward. "Do you know what I think of that?"

"No, sir."

"Sergeant Peterson is a fucking coward."

Roble itched his nose.

"He also accused you of being antisocial. Are you anti-social, Santos?"

"I don't know, sir."

His fist slammed the desk. "I don't give a flying cock about your social behavior." His fingers spread flat against the surface. "But I do care about your sense of duty."

"And sense of excellence," Roble whispered.

"What's that?" Sircor gripped a piece of paper and compressed it into a ball.

"I…inferred from the speech you gave when I arrived, and from how you run your fighter squadron, you care about both duty and excellence, sir."

Sircor narrowed his eyes, his fist squeezing the wadded paper.

He looked like he might spring over the desk and kill Roble with his bare hands.

Releasing the paper, Sircor turned and looked out the window. "My pilots tell me you've made unauthorized 'tweaks' to my fighter jets. Is that so?"

"Are you dissatisfied with the aircraft's performances, sir?"

The air inside the room thickened.

"No, I'm not," Sircor said, his voice softening. "I can't figure it out. My entire squadron maintenance team hates you. You don't follow approved procedures. Yet my always duty-abiding sergeant hasn't recommended *any* disciplinary action against you. Why is that?"

Roble pressed his boots together. "I couldn't know that, sir."

Sircor picked up an F-35 fighter jet model from the desk. "Does it have something to do with the fact my F-35s are in the best condition of any aircraft I've ever seen in my twelve years in the force? Sergeant Perry has no explanation as to why *that* is." He jabbed the model at Roble. "Do you?"

Roble scratched his head. "I've tightened up a few loose bolts here and there."

"Do you have an advanced degree in aerospace mechanics?"

"No, sir."

"Last week I executed a high yo-yo maneuver while in pursuit and hit the steepest pitched turn I've ever experienced. I've been in the same jet for two years. How is that possible?"

"If your target implemented a full-burn, unloaded extension," Roble brought one hand up in front of his face and pointed it down like a diving fighter jet, and used his other hand to intersect it like a chasing attacker, "it's helpful to have your thrust vectors modified to rotate and hold a one percent more acute angle, as long as your flaps have also been improved to compensate for the additional yaw. That should've allowed you to achieve a steeper pitch and maintain tail angle on the bandit."

Sircor pushed his chair back, his eyes wide. "Are you a pilot, Santos?"

"Not officially."

"What've you flown?"

"I'd prefer not to say."

Scooting his chair back to the desk, Sircor scratched his

forehead with the F-35 model. "I'm told you spend a lot of time with the JSDF at Naha."

Roble nodded.

"I hear the Japanese have an unusual Peace Eagle. The past few months it has gone up against some of our squadron in training—and it *won* dogfights. We never lose to the Japanese, not in our F-35s, not even in our F-15s." His eyes held Roble, "Do you know anything about that Japanese fighter?"

"Yes, sir."

"What is it?"

"A modified F-15DJ."

"Modified by Mitsubishi and DCU?"

"I'd prefer not to say."

Sircor pressed the nosecone of the model against his temple. "My pilots tell me it must have a ten percent higher thrust-to-weight ratio than our F-15s and close to that of our F-35s."

Roble stood thinking for a moment. "Over twenty percent more than your F-15s and five percent more than your F-35s."

Major Sircor stroked the model. Roble counted the clock ticking above his head.

"Who in the hell are you?" Sircor asked.

Roble brushed a hand over his nametag, saying nothing.

Sircor glanced at the cockpit of the model in his hand. "I also heard a rumor, which at the time I didn't waste my precious time considering," he shook his head, grinning with tense cheek muscles, "that an unidentified American pilot was seen flying that Japanese Peace Eagle. Does that seem strange to you?" He looked up.

"The way you put it… Yes, yes it does, sir." He shifted his cap from under one arm to the other. "Would you like to fly it?"

Sircor slapped the base of the model against the desk and stood up. "God…*dammit*, Santos." His chest heaved and he slumped into his chair. Turning away, he mumbled, "Duty… *or* excellence." He stared at the pictures of himself standing at attention in front of the red, white, and blue *Thunderbirds*.

Roble waited.

"Yes, I want to fly it," Sircor whispered.

Captain Takinato waded through heavy fog, a gloved hand trailing along the *Skeleton Eagle's* fuselage to keep it from dissolving into mist. He grinned when his finger touched the Paiute arrow painted on the side of an air intake.

Walking to the unseen cockpit ladder, he shook his head, knowing he couldn't have glimpsed a phantom. He stopped, eyes straining to pierce the fog until the outline of a short, rigid body took shape in front of him. Two black points for eyes flashed into view and then vanished in the vapor. Takinato peered more intently and shivered at the sight of three silver stars glinting atop the shoulder of a flight suit. Snapping to attention, he saluted the general.

"Captain Takinato," a low, guttural voice said, "you did not have permission to modify this fighter."

Takinato's stomach sank as he beheld the renowned General Yamatomo, commander of the 83rd Air Group. *I knew the risk of modifying this jet.* He lowered his eyes. *Now I must pay the price.*

Yamatomo's face held solemn, as if he were about to send Takinato to his death on a kamikaze mission.

It's strange, how facing the end focuses the mind and makes each act important...sacred even. Takinato swallowed. "I will turn in my wings, General," he bowed low, holding back a tear.

The general turned and climbed the flight ladder. Taking the rear seat of the cockpit, he donned a helmet.

Takinato blinked and stared at the open cockpit. Bowing to the mist, he scaled the steps. Waves of uncertainty and determination washed through him as he took the pilot's seat, sensing the general's eyes on the back of his shoulders. He toggled switches as the canopy sealed them inside. Twin burning circles punched flaming trails through the fog from behind the *Skeleton Eagle*.

Once in the air, Takinato began his scheduled exercises, executing each maneuver better than he'd ever done in his life. General Yamatomo grimaced and grunted at the enhanced cuts and acceleration produced by the *Skeleton Eagle's* modifications.

On their final descent, Takinato noted he'd set a Japanese speed record in a jet turbine aircraft. The General never spoke during the flight.

As they touched down, the sun robbed the fog of its last breath. The canopy sparkled as it opened. General Yamatomo removed his helmet and climbed to the tarmac.

Takinato joined him on the ground, standing at attention. He reached up to unpin the silver wings from his chest.

The general bowed. "I have tried to upgrade these fighter jets in my air group for a decade. You have brought *great* honor to our country."

Takinato dropped his hand. He felt his body lift off the ground and soar into the stratosphere. His boot scraped the tarmac to connect with reality. He bowed, unable to speak.

"Deliver to me," General Yamatomo ordered, "the details of what you have done, where you obtained the parts, and an estimate of the costs to implement. That is all...*Major* Takinato." He saluted the promoted pilot and walked away.

———

"Get me the State Department on the phone. Now!" It wasn't so much a demand as an animal scream howling from behind a gleaming, glass-walled corner office at DCU headquarters in Long Beach, California.

Frederick Compros paced across the Italian Carrara marble floor, his pudgy legs jumping a few times. "My phone is not ringing!"

When the phone on his desk buzzed, he snatched it and yelled, "Libby Industries is *not* authorized as a defense contractor." He stumbled around his office, his head lowered, knocking things off the desk with a flailing hand. "How did this happen?"

"Calm down Frederick, darling," the Deputy Secretary of State, Louise Johnson, said through the speaker. "Any foreign country can *place* a military-related order, but all defense sales must be approved by my office and the Pentagon."

"How do you know Libby Dodge hasn't already sold the parts to the Japanese without asking? And how did they *get* a Libby Industries prototype in the first place?"

"I'll have General Robertson look into that. Don't get too worked up, Frederick. The Japanese always back down when we make an issue of our disagreement."

"You better be right." His chest heaved. "The economy within this congressional district will suffer if DCU loses this order for Japanese F-15 modifications. And I've spent a lot of money funding your boss's campaigns." Frederick's voice rose to a whine, "I want to speak with that impertinent Japanese general who made the request. He needs to know who he's dealing with."

"I'll have General Robertson's office give you the contact information. I have to go. I'll see you at the Children for Universal Hope gala in DC next month. Kisses."

"Frederick Compros of DCU is on the line, sir," a voice said from a speaker sitting atop an austere desk.

"Colonel Aki…" Yamatomo said, staring at the speaker.

"My sincere apologies, General," Colonel Aki said. *"This time Commanding General Imamura's office in Tokyo transferred the call at the request of…US Chairman of the Joint Chiefs, General Robertson."*

Yamatomo's eyes narrowed. Raising the phone to his grey sideburn, he waited.

"General Yamatomo?" Frederick's shrill voice asked over the phone.

"Hai."

"I understand you submitted a purchase request for F-15 modifications from Libby Industries. Is that correct?"

"Hai."

"Let me remind you, General, your air self-defense force depends on DCU for the bulk of its aircraft and replacement parts. You can't afford to make a mistake of this magnitude."

"I do not recall seeing a DCU prototype."

"We have been working overtime to perfect the design."

"For six years?"

"Our top people are working on it," Frederick said. "We've spent over a billion dollars in development costs so far. Libby Industries can't match that."

"Spare me your embarrassment."

"Your…" Heavy panting muffled the line. "Your purchase order with Libby Industries will not happen, General. The US Government will not—I repeat—will *not* recommend it for approval."

Yamatomo studied a wall map of China, Russia, and North Korea, noting the different shapes representing fighter/bomber bases and medium-range missile silos. "We shall see."

"You have no idea who you're dealing with, you order-taking

peon. DCU has connections to the top levels of the JSDF and the Pentagon. We've produced world-class aircraft for decades. Libby Industries is untested and dangerous. Ask the FAA. Would you really risk your pilots' lives in unproven fighters?"

"Risk?" Yamatomo's fist pressed against the desk. "My entire country is at risk because my enemies can now produce a superior fighter aircraft. If excuses could shoot down fifth-generation fighters and stealth drones, you would be the first person I would call."

Something breaking near Frederick's phone echoed over the line. "I'm sending a DCU team to Naha. They will take possession of your Libby Industries prototype. It contains prohibited transfers of American military technology. If you refuse to surrender it, I'll go straight to the top of joint command and have them force you to turn it over."

Silence.

"That's right," Frederick added. "Don't you ever cross me again."

Yamatomo's low voice cut through the phone line. "Come to Naha personally, Mr. Compros, so I can throw you in my brig for attempting to steal my fighter jet. I will let you call joint command from your jail cell." *Click.*

Two days later, General Yamatomo gazed from his window at three DCU employees being hauled away in handcuffs and secured inside a Japanese military vehicle.

"What do we do with them, General?" Colonel Aki asked, standing on the opposite side of Yamatomo's desk.

Yamatomo said nothing.

"Imamura will not approve of any American detentions," Aki said. "Mr. Compros has already placed some calls. Sir, joint command canceled the F-15 modification order with Libby Industries. Nothing we do here will change that."

"Throw them in the brig."

"Sir?"

"Tomorrow, drop them off at the gates of Kadena. They will be charged with attempted theft if they ever enter Japanese territory again."

Victor Lafayette stood on a red rock balcony, his white plate-armored toes hanging over the edge, a breeze blowing through his platinum hair.

In a gauntleted hand he held an article from the Las Vegas Desert News. He already knew what it would say before he read it—federal marshals, with the assistance of certain unnamed aerospace industry experts, raided Libby Industries' North Las Vegas facility. They confiscated all aerospace manufacturing equipment, citing suspicion of exporting unauthorized military technology to a foreign government.

Victor flicked the paper away. It dropped twenty feet, landing on a messy redwood table on a balcony below. "You found no trace of Japanese F-15 parts or design plans—did you, my power-hungry étrangers."

Chapter 18

A mixture of excitement and anxiety tingled Danny's spine as he stepped from the transport plane onto Marine Corps Air Station, Futenma.

He gazed across the grass separating the airstrip from the flat military buildings buried in leafy mangroves. A few lanky palm trees rustled against the Ginowan city, Okinawa skyline. *So this is Japan.*

A wide-eyed recruit exiting the transport with Danny stopped to observe a pair of F/A-18 Super Hornets circling the base. Outranking the young man, Danny knew it was his duty to command him to move along, but instead Danny touched his shoulder. The private saluted, swiveled on his heels, and marched away.

Danny shook his head, exhaling. When they promoted him to group leader at Miramar, California, a few months ago—placing him in command of four Marines in fighter jet maintenance—he discovered he hated giving orders to others and wasn't strict enough because of it.

The constant pressure to command his subordinates made him uneasy, worrying they might secretly wish to be doing something else. And when they obeyed him, which they always did, he felt responsible for hijacking their time, time he knew they'd never get back.

Lugging his body-sized duffel bag away from the airstrip to his barracks, Danny peered at the low-hanging clouds to the north, knowing what lay below them, or rather, who.

On his first leave day, he e-mailed his father, as he did every week, informing him that he'd arrived in Japan and that he was upholding his duties in the Marines with honor. After sending the message, he took a bus north to Kadena Air Base.

Walking along a row of stucco barracks, hands twitching with nerves, he stopped in front of a window with drawn curtains. *I can't believe it's been over a year.*

He gulped and stared at the reflection of a Marine in full dress, looking like a dapper cropped-blond actor from an old war movie. *You look successful, stop worrying.* Taking a reassured breath, he shuffled a few feet to his left and raised a fist in front of a door. *Just knock already.* He knocked, the brass buttons on his sleeve clinking in the sun.

Roble answered wearing an untucked Air Force mechanic's shirt, hydraulic-lubricant stained pants, and Japanese flight boots. He tilted his head. "Danny? How did you get here?" He squinted at Danny's uniform. "The Marines?"

Danny raised his arms in victory and peeked over Roble's shoulder. "I thought you joined the military, not a sorority. They give you 'blue-suiters' living rooms?"

"Come in." Roble removed stacks of sketches and flight manuals off the old couch. He piled them on the coffee table crates, atop assorted jet parts and other sketches. Blueprints and jet-fighter combat maneuver posters draped the walls.

"Nice haircut," Danny said, grinning as he sat down, making himself more comfortable than he intended. "Two stripes after being in the Air Force this long?" Danny patted his own shoulder displaying three yellow stripes.

"I didn't know you'd enlisted." Roble pulled over a stool and sat down. "Where are you stationed?"

"Futenma. What a coincidence, huh? I'm maintaining F/A-18 Hornets. They're really cool…really…cool. Marine pilots are the best in the world. What have you been doing…here in Japan?"

Roble leaned forward. "F/A-18s are awesome. I had no idea you wanted to work on jets."

"There are a lot of things you don't know about me. I've always loved jets…and stuff." Danny tried to hold a confident smile.

Roble sat attentive.

"Yes, a lot's changed since Vegas," Danny said. "Things have worked out pretty well, pretty well. I broke up with her. You know how girls can be. Who needs 'em, right?" He laughed, but it rang a bit too hollow. "Don't worry; the baby thing didn't work out." He covered his mouth and coughed, blinking his watery eyes.

Roble rubbed along his pants legs.

Tossing a hand in the air, Danny cleared this throat and said, "I told my dad he could stick the CMI where the sun don't shine and I was joining the real Marines, not that soft CMI officer shit. So here I am, livin' the life." He forced a smile.

Roble raised his brows.

Danny's smile sagged as he realized Roble bought no part of his act—no, worse than that—Roble didn't even *acknowledge* his acting. He wanted to scream, "Coming here had nothing to do with you, and everything I just said is true!" But instead, he swallowed.

"I didn't know about Jenny or the… If you want to talk about it or anything, you know…"

Jenny… Danny deflated and wiped an eye. "Sometimes things just happen for a reason, a higher reason we can't comprehend." He shook his head. "Don't pretend you don't know what I'm talking about."

Roble placed his hands in his lap.

Danny shifted on the cushion, unable to stop the inexplicable agony seeping from his heart. "You're still messing around with this…kid stuff?" He pointed at the papers plastered throughout the room, not liking his own words.

Roble scratched his head, watching him.

"Why can't you ever drop the act, Roble. You're not this untouchable badass you want everyone to see. You're just a two-striped airman following orders like the rest of us."

Roble turned up his palms.

"Being a Marine gives me purpose," Danny said. "Just admit that the Air Force does the same for you."

Roble's eyes narrowed.

"You must know it, or you wouldn't still be here." Danny rubbed his forehead, and whispered, "You're no different than me."

Roble brushed his chin with the back of a hand. "I'm not criticizing you."

Danny eyes widened. "Why *don't you* criticize me?" He thumped a hand against his chest, jangling the uniform's buttons. "Or let others have input into what you do?"

Roble gazed across his drawings.

Danny couldn't believe his own words, but he had a blind,

insatiable desire to see Roble crack. He slapped a pile of drawings. "Why be so full of yourself?"

Roble looked up, eyes hardening into steel. "I *am* myself," he said, his breath slashing like a blade before Danny's face.

Danny froze, knowing he'd succeeded, and with a sinking feeling, wishing he hadn't. He fell back against the couch and rubbed the back of his neck. "I didn't mean to…" His head lowered. "I don't know why I said all that."

Danny's mind drifted, thinking back to when Roble set him up on his first date with Jenny, and how in the end Jenny ruined everything with his father. *I miss her.* He moaned, placing his elbows on his knees and his face in his hands. *Roble knew my parents wouldn't like Jenny. Why does he always have to ignore everyone?*

He tried to breathe, but his chest constricted. *Why is there always conflict between what I want and what everyone expects? Why can't there be just a single answer or a single path in life? A path nobody could question?* He glanced at Roble, as if realizing something, "Don't you ever wonder if there is a God?"

"Where is this coming from?" Roble shook his head. "It wouldn't matter to me one way or the other."

"What do you mean? How…" He scratched his wrist. "How wouldn't it matter?"

"Just that. It wouldn't matter to me."

"But what if there *was* a God, and he had all the answers, and he appeared before you and told you what to do? What then?" Danny breathed with anticipation, knowing Roble's submission would make his own sacrifices seem less important. He leaned in, trying to envision Roble bowing down before the Almighty.

"I'd fight him," Roble said.

"You would…? What?"

"Look," Roble said, "if God existed and I obeyed him instead of doing what I wanted, he would do what? Put me in heaven where I would live under his absolute rule forever and ever with no possibility of escape? No thanks."

Danny blinked, feeling surprised that he *could* feel surprised by any display of Roble's defiance. "I never knew you were an atheist." His hands sank to his lap.

"I'm not."

"You just said you don't believe in God."

"I don't, but I also don't need to belong to anything to know what I believe."

Danny laughed, looking away. "Well God is one thing, and you won't know for sure until you're dead, right? But other people are real. You can't deny that. What if others know something you don't?"

"What if?"

Danny gripped his hair. "You can't just decide what you want to know. Everyone has to try to agree on what's true. That's why we all go to school, join organizations…and stuff. That way we all know what we're supposed to do."

"Agreement doesn't make truth, Danny—reality does. Only by understanding what's real will I be able to achieve," he touched his front pocket, "…this."

"What?"

Roble pulled a crumpled paper from his pocket and stared at it. "An idea for an aircraft."

"Have you ever considered if love is more important than material things?" Danny asked, pointing at the paper. "Unlike you, I have a family. You can't blame me for accepting what they believe. You can't understand what that kind of love feels like."

"Danny—" he stopped and pressed the paper back into his pocket. "I have things to do before my next shift." He stood up. "You can stick around if you want."

Danny looked at his own limp hands, then the brass cufflinks on his uniform, and cringed.

Walking to the kitchen, Roble said, "I was making bad pork and noodles when you knocked."

After a minute, he brought back two bowls and balanced one atop a stack of notepads. He sat on the stool, holding the other.

Danny lowered his head.

"I never knew my parents," Roble said.

Danny looked up. Roble had never talked to him about his parents.

"I'm grateful to them for giving me life. It's the absolute highest gift possible. But I don't owe them anything. I didn't choose to be born—that was *their* choice." His eyes held Danny's. "If they were still alive, I would never have lived for them…and I would not have respected them if they'd asked me to."

Danny rubbed his eyes. "I can't choose not to love my parents. Haven't you ever loved anyone?"

Roble reached for his own chest, grasping only air, and turned away. "Why ask anyone what you *should* feel, or for whom you *should* feel it?" he whispered.

Danny inhaled. *What I feel...* He exhaled, remembering the first time he snuck from his house at night and met Jenny at a playground by her apartment. They sat on swings wondering aloud what they would do when they grew up. Jenny said she wanted to model for some fancy agency, one in New York or Paris, and buy a big house with a pool where she wouldn't hear neighbors fighting and yelling. Danny said in a different life he would illustrate anime movies. The expression on Jenny's face as he explained his idea for a storyboard was the most beautiful thing he'd ever seen.

He studied the cluttered apartment, then Roble's serene face. Loosening his uniform collar, he relaxed for maybe the first time in over a year. He picked up a bowl of noodles and they ate in silence.

When Danny finished, he asked, "Do you remember my drawings?"

Roble stood and left the room.

What did I say? Danny rubbed his forehead. After a couple of minutes he rose to leave. *I guess I deserved that for everything I said earlier.*

Roble returned holding a folded piece of paper and tossed it to him.

Danny's eyes widened as he unfolded it, unable to look away. The anime style drawing displayed a young man in ragged prison clothing riding a horse. One arrow whizzed by each side of his head. A third arrow embedded itself in his left shoulder, appearing less like an enemy weapon and more like a fellow escapee joining along for the ride. The youth's face didn't reveal pain or fear but the determination of an explorer gazing across an untouched horizon. "Where did you get this?"

"That's the first animation cell you drew when I arrived at your house."

"You stole it?" Danny looked up. "And kept it all these years?"

"I used to stay up nights looking through your animation sequences, amazed at how you made the world come to life."

Roble sat down and laced up his boots. "I guess I never told you, but your art—"

"You stole this?" Danny asked again, shaking the colorful page.

"Yes," Roble lowered his eyes. "I saw how your mother threw away your drawings, thinking she was protecting you from Donald, and I just couldn't stand for *that* one to go too. When I ran away, I took it with me for the same reason. I was wrong to take it and I should've given it back sooner." He looked up. "I'm sorry, Danny."

Danny's fingertips caressed his anime rider. He grinned, eyes misting, and fell back against the couch cushion. "Never thought…I'd see any of it again. I haven't drawn anything in years."

Roble gathered up the empty bowls. "I hear there is an anime artist in Naha who gives discounted lessons to US military. You know…if you wanted to brush up or something." He carried the dishes to the kitchen.

Folding the animation cell, Danny slipped it into a pocket. He picked up one of Roble's jet sketches and noted some parts labeled in Japanese. When Roble returned, Danny tossed it to the table. "What do you think of me animating a story like… Robin Hood?" he asked, wincing. "But in anime style and based in Japan?"

"What do you think of it?" Roble asked.

"Oh…I mean, it would still be anime, but the story would be something *people* could relate to. You know…normal, respectable."

Roble rubbed his nose. "You're the artist."

"It was just an idea, is all." Danny glanced at his watch. "Do you need to go to your shift? I don't want to make you late."

"I usually go early, but it's fine if I just get there on time."

Danny smiled. "Have you met anyone we know from Las Vegas out here?"

Roble shook his head.

"I ran into Brandon Sheffield at Miramar," Danny said, his voice light and unwound. "You remember that skating maniac from middle school? You wouldn't recognize 'im now—super big and completely bald. He brought up that stunt you pulled on our principal, the one in his office while he interviewed with the local TV station. Brandon wanted to know how you did it. I didn't know because you never talked about it. What was our principal's name? Ran…Radmall. Ah, I bet everyone still remembers that day."

"Seriously?" Roble smirked. "I've already admitted to stealing your art, how many youthful indiscretions do you want me to confess to?" He leaned back on the stool. "Believe it or not, I actually sent Radmall my first Air Force paycheck to pay for his old suit and toupee."

"Wow, you're generous. He looked better without them." Danny grinned. "And the toupee wasn't technically your fault."

"I was always surprised they forced me to go to school, but even more so to discover how simple it was to get expelled."

"Simple? I don't think you understand what that means." Danny hunched forward. "How'd you do it?"

"Too easily. First of all," Roble looked up the wall, "who's the genius who built the auditorium stage pulleys on the other side of Radmall's office wall, anyway? And the wheels on that massive lunchroom slop bucket? The easy-to-open air vent above his desk chair was a no-brainer. From there, it was just a matter of physics and logistics."

"I still can't believe it. You dumped it on his desk the moment he raised a fist to the camera and said, 'This is one principal who will not tolerate any—' and *Blam!*" Danny slapped his own chest with his palms and wiped them down his body to his knees, laughing, almost happily. "The best part," he couldn't breathe for a second, "when Radmall ripped off his toupee, he slammed it into the muck, splashing the reporter."

Roble looked away, staring at the clutter atop the coffee table crates. Danny followed his gaze to an artistic drawing of an F-22 Raptor.

"Physics and logistics," Roble said, barely above a whisper.

Chapter 19

On Danny's next day off, he visited downtown Naha.

In a shiny glass building, he found an anime art studio advertising discounts to US military. Pressing his hands to the window, he watched US service personnel sitting at tables drawing action figures that had been positioned on a pedestal. A white-haired professor paced the classroom reading out of a manual.

Danny's gut churned. *Something about this place feels fake, like high school.* He couldn't stand the thought of sitting in a fluorescent-lit classroom jockeying with everyone for grades again, especially in something as personal as art. Shaking his head, he walked away.

Rounding a city corner, he entered the older part of downtown filled with grey-stained wood-slat buildings and some dingy concrete buildings all on narrow streets. He stopped in front of a dilapidated wooden door with something in Japanese scrawled above it. In faded lettering mixed into the Japanese symbols, he read: *Yuki Manga Shop.*

A bell tinkled as he entered the dim shop. It smelled of moldy paper and fresh ink, a scent he hoped existed in heaven. He browsed the manga comics as a young man with blue hair sitting at the cashier counter spied on him. Two Japanese teens ignored Danny when he pushed his large body past them through a tight aisle.

The rear of the shop contained the adventurous type of manga he loved to escape into as a kid. He didn't care if he couldn't read the dialog—the art itself said everything.

With a handful of books ready to buy, he turned to the checkout counter, but stopped when he heard voices coming from a door squeezed between two bookshelves. He peered through the tiny window in the door.

Beyond the glass, a young lady in a karate outfit with one side of her long pink hair shaved stood before a small group of

Japanese teenagers. The teens sat on the floor drawing on wide parchments using ink and quills.

Whoa. Danny pressed his face against the glass. Even from a distance he could tell they drew detailed manga scenes. *Real manga art lessons.*

He tossed the handful of manga books he was holding onto a shelf and opened the door, waiting for the teacher to say something. No one in the art room looked up, but the teacher pointed at a spot on the floor.

Danny sat in the middle of the group, feeling out of place with his broad football player shoulders, green t-shirt, camo pants, and blond hair next to the scrawny students wearing black clothes and colorful sneakers.

The teacher placed a blank parchment, a quill pen, and an ink jar in front of Danny, saying something in Japanese. He glanced around, noting that each teen drew something different. Scratching his head, he figured he might as well attempt his long delayed anime series with the boy escaping on the horse.

The teacher picked up a pot with a miniature bonsai tree and placed it in front of him.

"You want me to draw this plant?" Danny asked.

The teacher said something in Japanese and a few of the teens smirked.

"Okay," Danny mumbled, shaking his head. He studied the light hitting the bonsai tree from the skylights above. Dipping the quill in the ink, he began to draw.

When the class stood in unison and handed their art to the teacher, so did Danny.

She studied his drawing, her pink hair not much higher than Danny's bellybutton. Her expression remained unrevealing, eyes narrow. Picking up a quill with red ink, she wrote in Japanese with lines pointing to different parts of his drawing. When finished, his bonsai tree rendition lay buried in red. Turning the parchment over, she wrote *C* and handed it back.

"Uhmmm," Danny mumbled. "Is this like my grade…or something?" He winced.

She spoke a few words in Japanese and walked away.

With brows scrunched, he carried his drawing into the shop, found his stack of manga books, and purchased them. The guy behind the counter glanced at Danny's red-drenched bonsai sketch and asked for the Yen equivalent of one hundred dollars.

"Is that the price of the art lesson?"

"*Hai. Sensei Nishiko.*"

"Sensei Nishiko," Danny repeated, and paid the young man. He knew from his childhood English version manga books that *sensei* meant master or teacher.

On the bus ride back to Futenma Marine Air Station, he tried to discern the Japanese symbols on his drawing, but he hadn't a clue. *Did I really get a C grade? Father would freak if he knew.*

Remembering he'd seen Japanese writing on Roble's jet diagrams, he jumped off the bus at the next stop and transferred to Kadena Air Base, hoping Roble could translate.

Danny watched Roble sitting on the frayed couch, holding the marked-up drawing of his bonsai tree.

"The place that gives discounted lessons to US military wrote their notes in Japanese?" Roble asked.

"A girl with pink hair in a karate outfit wrote it," Danny bit his lip. "What do you think of the drawing?"

"I can hardly see it, there's so much writing." He turned it over and looked at the *C*.

"Just ignore that; it isn't a grade or anything," Danny said.

Roble pulled out his Japanese translation books and wrote on a notepad. After a while he handed his notes to Danny. "These translations aren't exact, and some I couldn't figure out. But from what I can tell she talks about light. Each comment makes a specific point about angle and brightness. It's like she didn't look at your tree, only how the light reflected off of it."

Danny read Roble's notes, looking back and forth between his drawing and what Roble wrote. *Sensei Nishiko is so right. I mean not just right, but…*right. Jumping to his feet, he walked to the front door. "Thanks, Roble," he said, leaving.

The next week Danny spent every spare moment drawing objects, focusing on how the light touched them. He drew aircraft parts, spoons, bricks, plants—anything. He no longer saw objects around him, just reflections of light.

Before bed one night, he opened his laptop and saw a message from his mother asking if he was okay. *What day is it? Damn, I'm a day late in sending Father his e-mail.* He typed a message apologizing for the delay, explaining how his jet maintenance crew had been forced to work overtime preparing for a critical war simulation. And then he added that his performance evaluations exceeded most of his peers. His art class didn't make it into the e-mail for the same reason he never mentioned that Roble lived in Okinawa.

On the same day and time as the week before, Danny took the bus from Futenma to the Yuki Manga Shop. He entered the small room in the back and sat with the Japanese students. He couldn't wait to show Sensei Nishiko how well he now under-stood light.

Once again, Nishiko placed a blank parchment and ink quill in front of Danny.

"Can I draw what I want this time?" Danny looked around at the others sketching manga scenes.

Nishiko placed the same bonsai tree in front of him.

"Okay," Danny sighed. This time, he drew the bonsai tree only as the light fell on it. When the class ended, he stood up holding the sketch.

Taking Danny's drawing, Nishiko narrowed her eyes. She whipped out the red quill and wrote more than last time, reducing the size of her symbols to fit all the comments. The bonsai tree disappeared into a sea of red. Flipping over the parchment, she wrote, *C-*.

What? Danny's eyes widened. "Is this a grade?"

Nishiko said something in Japanese, turned, and walked away. *A C-? Oh my God, I suck at this.*

The blue-haired young man at the shop's cash register said something in Japanese as Danny slunk past the counter. Danny stopped and looked at him. The man held out an open palm.

"Oh, for the class," Danny said. "All right." He pulled out a one-hundred-dollar bill.

The man shook his head, pointing up with his thumb.

Scrunching his brows, already feeling embarrassed because of the low grade, he handed him fifty more dollars. The cashier closed his fist and Danny left.

Danny found the first express bus to Kadena Air Base, but Roble wasn't at his barracks and he didn't respond to his text messages. He waited on Roble's front step, holding his marked-up drawing with anticipation as the sun set.

As the hours passed, he sat and stared at Nishiko's writing, listening to the crickets gaining strength as though powered by the rising moon. Roble didn't show up until after midnight.

"What were you doing so late?" Danny asked, his backside sore from sitting on the concrete step.

"Fixing up jets." Roble brushed his hands down his grease-stained uniform. "How's it going on the F/A-18s?"

Danny handed his drawing to him. "What do you think of this?"

Roble took the drawing and stared at it. He entered his barracks, sat down, and translated the Japanese onto a notepad. "She's still talking about light or lack thereof." Pointing at a red arrow leading to a branch, he added, "See how she highlighted this top branch and this pebble below the tree? She's comparing your interpretation of how the light falls on each with each material's ability to absorb or reflect light in different ways."

Taking back his drawing along with Roble's translation, Danny studied them. *I see what Sensei Nishiko is saying. It's so obvious.* "Thanks," Danny said, leaving Roble's barracks.

All that night Danny drew objects in his small kitchen, observing how each material absorbed or reflected light. Over the next week, he studied different materials as he worked on jets.

When he missed his weekly e-mail to his father again, his mother shot him a message chastising him. Danny apologized and made an excuse for the tardiness. His father wrote back asking about his rank and how many Marines he now led.

Danny answered that he would receive a promotion to squad leader soon, which would double the size of his command to eight Marines. His gut ached as he hit the send button.

"Why not transfer to a combat unit?" his father replied. "More high-profile leadership opportunities lie in combat units. Never hide when you can show honor."

Danny stared at his father's e-mail and exhaled.

At the Yuki Manga Shop the next week, Danny arrived early to have more time to perfect his bonsai tree drawing. After class, he couldn't wait for Nishiko to see what he'd drawn using his new skills at understanding light.

Nishiko cleared her throat and scrawled on his drawing, somehow fitting more writing over it than before. When she turned it over, Danny swallowed hard.

She wrote: *D+*.

What did I do so wrong? He shook his head. "Am I really that bad at art?"

Nishiko walked away without comment.

Head lowered, Danny shuffled to the exit of the shop. *Maybe I should quit.* A coin tapped against the counter, catching his attention. The cashier held out a hand. Danny approached and pulled a hundred and fifty dollars from his pocket.

The blue-haired cashier waited for more.

Really? "Why does the price go up every lesson?" Receiving no answer, Danny handed him an additional fifty dollars.

The man stuffed the money in the register, and said, "Your address." He pointed at an open notebook and handed him a pencil.

Danny shook his head, wrote down his address on base, and left.

On the bus back to Futenma, Danny almost ripped his drawing to shreds, but he couldn't bear the thought of not knowing what Nishiko wrote. He changed buses and headed to Kadena Air Base. Once again Roble wasn't home.

When Roble arrived well past midnight, he held out his hand for the art. Danny rubbed his tired eyes and handed it over, not bothering to ask what Roble thought of it this time.

Roble stared at the drawing buried beneath the writing before translating the Japanese. "She talks a lot about integrating your interpretations of light into a concise whole. It's like she wants the person seeing your art to understand every detail you've drawn, yet not focus on any of the individual parts, just absorb the *feeling* of the result."

Danny read the comments, staring back and forth at this drawing. *Wow. I didn't realize there was so much to learn. I totally see what she's saying.*

"Later, Danny," Roble said, as Danny left with his art.

Danny drew during every spare moment, art consuming his mind. Yet he fulfilled his Marine leadership and jet maintenance duties by the book, never letting his art get in the way. In his weekly e-mail to his parents, he emphasized his dedication to the Marines, always leaving out anything he thought they wouldn't respect.

When Danny received a *D* from Nishiko at his next lesson, it was almost too much to take. To add insult to injury, the price of the lessons rose yet again. The indignation from both overwhelmed him, but Roble's translations of Nishiko's comments inspired him to try harder.

After three months of lessons, Danny felt like he'd mastered every quality of the bonsai tree. He drew it from memory, every detail of light and shadow, nuanced for each specific material, and integrated into a whole, like a story of a bonsai tree more meaningful than the tree itself.

This time, with his art finished, Danny took it to Roble the night before class and before any red marks. Roble gripped it with both hands and sat down. His eyes transfixed.

"What do you thi—" Danny asked.

Roble held up a hand cutting him off. "Can I have this?"

Danny's eyes widened. He knew since childhood Roble rarely liked anyone's art.

"Uhmm…well," Danny said, "I want to show Nishiko first."

"She'll mark it up," Roble raised the parchment into the light. "I want this as is."

Grinning, Danny knew he'd succeeded. "This one's going to Nishiko. Sorry."

Before class started, Danny handed the drawing to Nishiko. She studied it without pulling out her red ink quill.

"Do you think I could try a manga storyboard today, like the other students?" Danny asked. "I have some ideas for a series I could animate."

She pulled out the quill and rained blood upon his bonsai tree. Danny wobbled on his feet, squinting in horror. The comments and the lines connected into a spider web of tightly packed symbols. Turning the drawing over, Nishiko wrote *F* and handed it back.

Danny sank to the floor, head between his knees. *That was the best damn drawing of a bonsai tree I've ever seen. Roble even thought so.* He wadded up the drawing with his fists. *An F? Father would disown me if he knew I failed this horribly at anything.*

Nishiko placed a blank parchment and an ink quill before Danny and pointed at the bonsai tree.

I won't draw that again. Gripping his crumpled failure, Danny shot to his feet and stormed from the art room. He passed the shop's cashier without paying for the lesson.

At his barracks, he stuffed the wadded-up drawing in a sock drawer and pulled out his laptop. He typed an e-mail to his father that said in part: *I'll be promoted to squad leader soon. Duty and honor, Danny.* Wiping the sweat off his lip, his gut churning, he hit the send button.

He made it happen by working overtime, following the rules down the line, and commanding his subordinates more severely. Within three weeks, his superiors promoted him to a leadership position over eight maintenance Marines.

Chapter 20

Do I really want to be on Preton's gubernatorial ticket? Alexandria Patra waded naked through a swirling sea of disheveled gowns on her closet floor.

"You must accept, my dear," Preton told her in his office last week. "Just think of all the good we'll accomplish together. You may not realize it, but I've been training you to be my lieutenant governor for ten years. Who else can I trust?" He'd smiled and added, "Allow me to deliver the news to your parents. I just know how much they'll appreciate hearing it."

She'd imagined her parents' expressions, exhaled, and nodded.

Glancing at the few dresses still hanging in her closet, her neck artery throbbed. *But why must you announce my nomination at* The Sin, *Preton? S*he seized a gown from a rack. *I've purposely not gone back there since…* Heat shot down her exposed skin. She lifted the buttery-silk dress into the sheen of light, and let it fall to the floor with the others.

Facing the wardrobe mirror, she imagined Stock's glare of scorn and desire on her body. She rose onto her toes, sucked in a breath, and held her own stare. Her eyes cut down along the supple curves of her skin. "Thirty-seven years old, Alexa." *Thirty-seven.*

Dropping back to her heels, she looked away. *Was it worth it? Did I make the right decision?* Her palms pressed against her temples.

She reached for an old t-shirt and held it to her chest with a defiant grin, then frowned and snatched her most expensive evening gown instead, black and strapless. She slipped it on, followed by the finest jewelry she'd never worn: a platinum blue sapphire necklace, wrist cuff, and matching earrings—gifts from the prime minister of Egypt to her mother, later given to her.

Turning back to the mirror, she studied the woman she knew everyone respected, admired, and even lusted after. *Who are you?* She closed her eyes.

The limo sent by Preton brought her to the entrance of *The Sin*, below its marquee. She peered out the window at the swarming news cameras. *I've never seen such a frenzy.*

The strobe-lit paparazzi trailed her from the car. A throng of guests in black ties and gowns smiled at her as she entered the grand lobby.

"Congratulations, Ms. Patra. You have our full support to do what needs to be done," a wafer-thin woman said in a tone of angry righteousness. She held the arm of a delicate-faced man wearing a tuxedo and pink neck scarf who winked at Alexandria, twice.

Support for…?

"You won't get my vote," a voice boomed from behind.

She turned.

"But you would if I lived in Nevada," chuckled an elderly man in a tuxedo wearing gold-rimmed glasses.

She remembered him from her childhood in Beverly Hills. "What are you doing here, Reverend Cromwell?"

"I'm here to give moral and monetary support to your bid for lieutenant governor, of course. I always told your parents they needed to instill a little spirituality in you, but I stand most humbly and embarrassingly corrected. You've made everyone I know very proud." He patted her hand. "Have you seen your parents?"

She shook her head.

"Maybe they've already gone to the ballroom. You look so lovely. Take care, child." He nodded and ambled away.

Alexandria smiled to hide her panic. *Am I* really *going to run for lieutenant governor?* The guests continued to congratulate her as she moved toward the ballroom.

She floated into the current of people, like driftwood to a waterfall. Looking around, she searched for a rock or a branch to grab on to.

An elevator opened across the wide hall, a strip of dry beach before the rocky plunge. She swam for it, pressing across the flow of bodies. People spoke to her, their voices lapping across her ears. Gasping for breath, she lunged into the elevator.

The doors snapped shut, creating an abrupt silence, exposing her labored breathing.

She glimpsed the tips of two black shoes to her right. Startled not to be alone, she glanced up. The same thin-mustached elevator operator who'd taken her to see Stock almost two years ago stood next to her.

He nodded. Alexandria stepped back.

"Penthouse again, Madam?"

Her eyes widened, her fingertips touching beneath her necklace. "Is he…? I…"

"He is home. Would you like to go up?"

She swallowed, unable to speak.

"Or would you like me to open the doors and let you out?"

She glanced at the closed doors.

"It is far from my place to say, Madam, but he changed after you left. Became sadder, yet …" he touched his chin, "more *hopeful* perhaps?"

She blinked, awakening from her thoughts, and frowned. "I thought employees were not supposed to talk about Stock."

"Quite right, they aren't. I've fired many good ones because of it."

"You…? Fired?" She brushed a strand of hair off her lashes, staring at his proper frame. "Who are you?"

He bowed, a forearm pressed to his waist. "Ted Hollings, manager of *The Sin*."

"Working as a bell hop?"

"When I'm aware you will be visiting. All of two times. Stock asked me to be here the first time, but today, I am here only because I hoped you would come up."

"Why would…?"

"Forgive me, Madam. I've disregarded my place." He turned and faced the control box.

She ran a hand along the mahogany paneling, her other touched her lips remembering the taste of Stock's Wayne Smoke bourbon and…

The elevator moved upward. She watched the Roman numerals increasing, knowing she shouldn't be doing this, and also that she didn't want the elevator to stop. Her breathing turned shallow as she recalled how Stock led her by the hand to his balcony. She could still see his hand clutched in pain at his longing to understand morality. Thinking of where his hand had later touched, her back arched slightly.

Winding a strand of hair on a finger, she winced at the

memory of standing alone at the window that next morning. Her eyelids dropped, trying to forget why she'd left. Most of all, she couldn't forget Stock's broken eyes. "Why is Stock so sad?" she asked herself, not realizing she'd spoken aloud.

"Perhaps, Ms. Patra, because like all of us, he deserves exactly what he believes."

She glanced at him. "What does he believe?" she asked, breathless.

"That others know what is right for him—not his own mind and the reality of the world he understands and loves. And because of his belief, Madam, I think he is losing the will to differentiate between what others call evil—and what might actually be."

Her heartbeat accelerated like a runaway clock. "But if that's true," she shook her head, "why haven't you just told him to stop believing…and hating…what others say is right?"

He stared at her. "What an interesting thing to say, Ms. Patra."

She glanced away.

"However," he opened a hand, "do you think someone can be saved from their own beliefs? Think a person can change their deepest axioms after hearing a lecture, or after enduring a million well-claimed assertions? Perhaps instead, Madam, he must be—"

"Shown?" Alexandria cut him off.

"Who on this planet…" he raised his brows, "could possibly catch his attention, *and* show him what he will not see?"

She pulled a handful of hair straight, causing the sapphire on her wrist cuff to flash across her eyes. "Stock doesn't realize that rebelling against what others believe is…"

Mr. Hollings tilted his head.

"Do you think that rebelling," she released her hair back into curls, "is just the flip side of the same coin…as obeying?"

He touched his chin.

Is that why they are both equally miserable? She watched her own hands swaying to the music in her mind.

"Ms. Patra, I am pleased you decided to visit the penthouse this evening, but permit me to say this…" He cleared his throat. "Even *if* Stock someday saw an example he admired, changed his beliefs, and became the happiest man on earth because of it… there is something I'm not sure you understand."

Numerals counted away above her head. She stepped toward him, her face attentive, almost pleading.

"What would happen," Mr. Hollings asked, "if Stock only made what he loved, forgot everyone considered him a criminal, and operated in the open like the bravest inventors of the Dark Ages?"

What? She scrunched her brows.

He slid a hood from the back of his medieval-styled suit over his head. "Would your friends not lock him up based on their beliefs, under the auspices of public safety or moral righteousness? Can you imagine the injustice of imprisoning a man who creates with his mind and forces nothing upon others? I'd rather see the earth blasted to dust than see it." He pointed to the elevator doors, "That, Ms. Patra, is why I try to protect him."

Alexandria glanced up. *Thirty-eighth floor.* "Stop the car."

The elevator stopped on the thirty-ninth floor, one below the penthouse.

"Take me back to the lobby." Her voice cut like the edge of a gem.

"Madam?"

"The lobby, Mr. Hollings."

He nodded. The car descended in silence.

When the doors opened, Alexandria touched him on the arm and strode from the elevator with her eyes narrowed and head lifted.

Stepping into the packed, gothic-domed ballroom, her hearing exploded into a pensive silence.

Atop the stage at the far end, Preton Moore spoke into a microphone, his voice registering only as irritation against her eyelashes. The crowd of polished people on both sides of the wide aisle smeared by as she glided to the stage.

Moore/Patra for a United Nevada read a banner hanging from the ceiling.

Preton concluded Alexandria's introduction and moved to assist her onto the stage. As she touched his hand, his speech computed within her mind. He'd listed all her selfless, public achievements over the past decade.

Swiveling around, Alexandria gazed across the applauding audience—a monolith of confident, complacent noise, like a collective demand. The medieval ceiling transformed the chanting into reverberations of bouncing pitchforks. She glanced at Preton's smile reflecting back at the sea of faces. Her parents seated in the front row beamed as though she'd achieved all their dreams.

Taking Alexandria by the arm, Preton directed her to the microphone and announced, "Ladies and gentlemen, the next lieutenant governor of the great state of Nevada, Alexandria Patra."

The applause, and the demand, intensified. Preton raised Alexandria's hand above his head and then stepped back.

Alexandria stood alone at the podium.

The applause melted into hushed anticipation. She drew in a breath and looked again at her parents and everyone congregated behind them. *What do they expect me to do? Do for whom? To whom?* She shuddered. *Which of their beliefs do they wish me to force on Libby Dodge, Stock Brant—or anyone else?*

The spotlight radiated off Alexandria's skin, casting black shadows under her sharp features. Her eyes sliced back and forth along the rows of faces until she had seen them all.

In the prolonged silence, the audience shifted in their seats as if Alexandria washed away their shared confidence, leaving each alone with their own thoughts.

She lifted her palms in front of her chest, observing the thin lines leading to her fingers. *Do these people know they would be justifying others to force their beliefs on them as well?*

Preton stepped forward and whispered in her ear, "This is the moment we've worked for. Now, tell them what *we* believe."

Glancing up at the awaiting audience, Alexandria leaned into the microphone. Everyone in the hall pulled toward her, like boats without oars drawn to the promise of effortless motion— or into the propeller of a giant ship.

"If you vote for us…" the vibration of her voice pierced through all, "you will *deserve* exactly what you believe."

The crowd cheered with relief. Alexandria backed away from the podium into darkness. Preton grabbed the microphone.

As Preton spoke, Alexandria walked off the rear of the stage, found an emergency exit and escaped into the cool night air. At the end of an alleyway, she emerged onto the Las Vegas Strip and lifted a hand, flagging down a taxi.

In the back seat of the cab, she watched the blurred tunnel of lights rush by, as had the passage of her life.

Chapter 21

Adarkened state office building greeted Alexandria as she stepped onto the curb. She entered and walked through its echoing halls that smelled of worn vinyl and polished dust.

Flipping on the lights to her office seemed to deaden, rather than illuminate, the still air. She stepped around the room, gazing at the pictures of herself smiling with children, and stopped in front of the two posters. *Unity* and *Sacrifice*.

Turning away, she moved behind her desk. The filing cabinet stood before her—the one she had feared and hated for so long.

Thumping. She felt each ventricle in her heart compressing and releasing in clunky spasms, shaking her body.

Bending down, she ripped out the bottom drawer. It crashed to the floor, scattering blue files.

She gathered up the folders and stacked them along the back of her desk. An air vent hissed in the background as she sat down.

It is time to understand—why. With the first file pulled between her arms, she began to read.

As the hint of morning seeped through the window, she slid the last file before her, on it a blaze of red *Delinquency* stamps formed a launching rocket.

Her eyes lifted to the chair in front of the desk. Roble Santos no longer sat there—but it wasn't empty. There sat the memory of a young girl, a toddler, with feet dangling over the edge.

The girl smiled at her parents who spoke with a man in a white jacket…

"She can't seem to hear our instructions," the mother said, her petite nose twitching.

"It's true, she rarely responds to anything anyone asks of her," the father said, his sharp-featured face pulled long.

The doctor lifted the girl's straight black hair over her ears and probed them with a penlight. The girl giggled, tapping her fingers along his arm. "Now Alexa, I want you to push these buttons based on what you hear. Do you understand?"

Alexandria poked the doctor's nose, her feet bouncing off his knee.

"I'm so sorry," her mother, Thema, said, brushing back blonde locks with dark roots which matched her long lashes.

The doctor slid headphones over Alexandria's ears and started the hearing test. After a while he switched it off. Her parents waited for the inevitable.

"Hold on a moment." He plugged the headphones into a different computer and placed a colorful keyboard across her lap. Pushing a button, he stepped back.

Alexandria hammered the keys with energy, seemingly at random. When the doctor disconnected the earphones, Alexandria's mother released a quiet sob.

"Can it be fixed with surgery?" her father, Darius, asked, adjusting his tie. "We'll pay for anything to improve her hearing."

The doctor stroked his chin, studying the computer screen. "You are probably not going to believe this."

Darius slumped into a chair. "Just say it."

"Your daughter's hearing is not only beyond extraordinary, she has perfect pitch. I've never observed hearing ability this acute. You should probably train her in something musical if she hasn't already begun herself."

Alexandria—still wearing the large headphones—hummed her voice, drumming her fingers against the keyboard, watching her parents' faces. She didn't see expressions of relief, but something she didn't understand.

The sky stretched clear as Alexandria skipped along a sidewalk outside a Beverly Hills kindergarten two years later. She wore a prim, checkered uniform smothered with dirt, one of her socks missing. In her hand she held a teacher's note explaining every instance that day in which she'd disregarded instructions, refused to join group activities, or hadn't shared personal items with others.

Numerous parent/teacher conferences followed the notes. "Beyond not sitting still and humming through lessons, she requests frequent trips to the bathroom," the teacher said, looking at Alexandria. "When we allow her to go, she disrupts other classes by dancing down the hallway. Once *in* the bathroom, she locks the toilet stall and sings with such volume the teachers in adjacent classrooms are forced to call the janitor to drag her out."

"I'm so sorry." Thema fidgeted with her pearl necklace.

The teacher removed her glasses. "Have you considered special needs counseling or medication?"

"We will try anything. It's very important she fits in. Thank you for meeting with us." Darius stood up.

"Yes, well…" The teacher frowned. "Unfortunately I've not covered everything."

Darius sat back down.

"On Friday we discovered that she'd been sneaking over the fence to the third grade playground, learning karate from boys in exchange for kisses. We only found out after Alexa sent one of them to the nurse's office with injuries."

She pulled out a paper with signatures. "I wanted to tell you this in person so you would understand why we suspended Alexa's recess privileges. The next time she exhibits this type of inappropriate behavior, she will be expelled."

Everyone turned to Alexandria, who chopped the edges of her palms against her knees in rhythm to some unheard melody.

The Patras hired a private assistant to sit with Alexandria in school. The assistant interrupted her humming and took her by the arm, forcing her to join group activities. Alexandria didn't complain, or stop her behavior.

The assistant also had standing orders to give one of Alexandria's toys from home to the class each time she refused to share personal items with others. Halfway through the school year, she had no more toys.

Over the next few years, Thema and Darius tried numerous techniques to reform Alexandria, including grounding her until she learned to obey. But every time they sequestered her to her bedroom, regrettably positioned over their own bedroom, she sang and danced with such raucousness they felt no choice but to extract her from her blissful detention, only to find she'd locked and blocked her door with furniture.

Once, Alexandria held out behind a barricade for an entire day before the gardener scaled the home, entered through a window, and cleared the debris.

Thema tried to rectify Alexandria's conduct by directing her energy into what she called "respectable activities for a young lady of distinguished background." These consisted of after-school opera and ballet classes.

To Thema's initial surprise, Alexandria excelled at both. But after a few months, they reprimanded Alexandria in ballet for trying unrecognized moves, and in opera for morphing the Italian lyrics into punk rock songs she'd heard older boys playing at school.

Alexandria began skipping both classes, signing herself up for gymnastics and karate. When her parents received the bill for the unapproved lessons and called to cancel, the teachers of the rogue classes perplexed them by saying she was a model pupil.

As punishment for Alexandria's deception, Darius made her volunteer at a city foodbank after school. "You can take those other lessons once you learn to think of others first and listen to authority," he said.

Within a week, the foodbank politely asked the Patras not to bring Alexandria back, because her "rowdy and chaotic presence" disrupted those trying to eat in quiet dignity.

Despite the ongoing conflict between Alexandria and most every adult, by the time she turned nine years old, performance directors across Southern California recognized her as a singing and dancing prodigy. The parents of the competing ballet and opera students referred to her disparagingly as "Little Miss Alexa Donna."

Soon after turning ten, Alexandria performed the lead role in a professional child-adapted musical based on the novel *Anna Karenina*. Unlike Thema, Darius didn't like the play's popularity but wholeheartedly approved of Alexandria's role, explaining that the character of Anna demonstrated that one should never go after one's passions if it's against the will of society, as it only leads to personal suffering and tragedy.

Alexandria smiled at her father's advice and said, "I like jumping in front of the train at the end. Did you see how far I jumped last night and how loud I screamed when it ran me over?"

For the grand finale of the musical's run, it left Southern California for three consecutive daily matinées in Las Vegas. After the last performance, Alexandria's parents hosted several attending United Nations dignitaries at their five-star hotel's restaurant. Left in the hotel room, Alexandria convinced Thema's assistant to take her out on the Strip for some fresh air.

Spotting a casino with a clown's face and three colored balls for a marquee, Alexandria said, "I'm starving," and pulled the assistant by the hand inside. Finding a food court across from a circus ring, they ordered salads and sat at a table. Alexandria didn't touch her food as she ogled the circus acrobats twirling on ropes.

It took some begging, but the assistant agreed to let Alexandria attend the next show if she ate her salad. Taking a seat in the front row, Alexandria watched the first act with rapt attention, running her favorite gymnastics moves through her head. Studying the layout of the ring, she grinned and waited for her chance.

During a pause between the aerial hoop dancers and the announced Russian contortionists, Alexandria excused herself to use the bathroom. She slipped under a security rope, snuck around the back side of the circus ring, and untied her ponytail. Before anyone backstage knew what was happening, she was climbing the trapeze ladder.

Spectators murmured, pointing at the girl high above the ring. Thema's assistant jumped to her feet, clasping her mouth.

A spotlight hit Alexandria as she launched across the top of the arena, hanging below a swing, her loose hair streaming behind. She let go at the swing's pinnacle, to the gasps of the audience, spun into a somersault with a twist, and flew toward the stationary swing on the other side. Feeling weightless, she knew *this* was the best moment of her life.

With hands outstretched and determined, she missed the swing—short by ten feet. The crowd screamed in horror. Alexandria plunged, flipping head over feet once, arms flailing to regain balance and form. After a couple of elongated and noisy seconds, her feet sunk deep into the safety net.

It shot her back in the air. The audience drew in an audible breath. At the height of Alexandria's ascent, a spotlight sparked off her smile, hair floating above her head. Tucking into a ball, she rotated into a triple-roll, her hair wrapping her body in a liquid, black stream.

Her legs extended down and she stuck the landing, bouncing

like a firing piston as the net slowed to a stop under the onslaught of the spotlights and cheers.

Several acrobats climbed atop the net and escorted her down to the ring. A squat ringmaster took her by the hand and led her to the front of the stage. Covering his microphone, he whispered in her ear with an exotic accent, "My little flying squirrel, what is your name?"

"Alexa Patra from Beverley Hills," she beamed. "I can sing too, if you want."

He turned to the audience, pointed at Alexandria, and announced, "Ladies and gentlemen, please give it up one more time for our very own acrobat in training, Alexa Patra!"

The crowd roared.

As the applause dissipated, the ringmaster whisked her away to his backstage office where Thema's frantic assistant waited.

That night, upon learning what had happened, Alexandria's parents fired the assistant, grounded Alexandria to her room for a week, and prohibited her from performing outside of L.A. ever again.

Several months later, while performing in a Beverly Hills ballet, Alexandria stayed after each performance, telling her parents she needed additional practice. She soon achieved a black belt in Isshin-Ryu Karate from a young sensei named Hisoka who worked part-time as a stagehand.

When Thema discovered Alexandria's violent training, she confiscated her karate gear and told her to expect to suffer real consequences this time.

The next morning, her parents sat her at the breakfast counter. "Sweetheart," Darius began, "you're eleven years old, and must learn you're not the only person on this earth. Selfishness is a very ugly thing."

Thema frowned. "We've been too lenient, Alexa, honey. To help you learn respect, we are instituting a zero tolerance policy for disobedience."

"Sometime this week," Darius lifted a hand, "we expect you to choose half your favorite possessions to donate to needy children. Your practice time will be cut in half so you can spend time teaching underprivileged children to sing and dance."

"This is for your own good, princess," her mother said. "If you refuse to cooperate," Thema swallowed, "*all* of your things will be given away, and we will have no choice but to pull you from *all* practice sessions and performances."

Alexandria ate her breakfast without a word. After going upstairs to get ready for school, she tossed possessions out her bedroom door.

Her parents climbed the spiral staircase and stared at the mountain of items piling up on the open landing. Alexandria stuffed her mattress out the door last, sending other things crashing over the ebony railing and into the living room.

"I don't want to give up half my practice time," Alexandria said, "so take it all, I guess."

A month into the performance and practice prohibition, the Patra's chef prepared waffles with pine nut sprinkles for breakfast, Alexandria's favorite.

"Sweetheart," her father said, standing in the kitchen, "we want you to know we are not giving in to what you want. We've arrived at a consensus after discussing our situation with many others." He poured Alexandria a glass of juice. "For the good of the local community, we might be willing to let you perform again, but only if you start teaching other children as well. Do you understand the compromise we are offering?"

"No."

"*No,* you don't understand? Or *no,* you won't do it?" Thema crossed her arms over her vicuna wool suit.

"Both." Alexandria pushed the waffle away.

A few days later, after school in the car, Alexandria asked, "Mom, can I get a job so I can pay for my own classes?"

"You're missing the point, honey. It's not about money; it's about principles." The luxury car turned onto Rodeo Drive. "If you would just donate *some* of your time to help others and at least *act* like you cared about our rules, we would let you perform again."

"I don't like teaching those kids." Alexandria looked out the rear side window.

Thema squeezed the steering wheel. "Don't you ever say that around anyone your father and I know."

"I don't like anyone you know."

"Alexandria Patra!" The car screeched to a stop in front of a glistening boutique. Thema turned to the back seat. "I want you to think about how your attitude makes others feel. Do you think it's fair you can do things so easily when other children have such a hard time at them? Because of your talents, you owe it to others to give something back."

Alexandria fell silent, shocked by her mother's words, never realizing she'd stolen something from other children. She couldn't stand the thought. "So I've actually taken from others by being better than them?"

"You've been unfair to them, honey. That's what we've been trying to tell you. Being selfish is like taking from those you could've helped."

"Well," Alexandria's fingers moved along the seat, her head bowed, "how much have I stolen, and how much do I owe?"

"My darling princess," her mother smiled in triumph, "why don't we drive over to the children's center right now and work with those kids. Once you're done, I'll sign you up for some performance lessons. How does that sound?"

Alexandria scrunched her nose, not looking up. "Necessary, I guess."

Over the next several months, Alexandria tried not to complain about helping other kids, but she hated spending her time on anything other than improving her own skills. When she couldn't take it any longer, she spoke with her favorite performance director, a thin Ukrainian triple-gold-medaled gymnast.

"Mrs. Dodopolov, do you think it's my duty to help those kids?"

"Alexa," Mrs. Dodopolov whipped back her silver ponytail, "what you and I do is just a performance. The important thing is to help people in the real world. Your parents are right and you should obey them."

"But why isn't *this* a part of the real world?" Alexandria pointed at the uneven bars. "Why isn't what I want important? And why does what I do hurt people, and how much do I owe everyone if it does?"

"Oh, Alexa," Mrs. Dodopolov shook her head, amused. "Don't think of being talented as hurting others, but as an opportunity to find joy by sacrificing for them." She placed her hands on Alexandria's shoulders, leaning in. "You will know in your heart when you've given enough."

Alexandria pressed her lips together, trying to understand what her heart knew. Despite receiving no response, she looked up, a spark of hope in her voice. "Maybe I just need more time to think about it."

"Some things can't be understood by thinking, Alexa, only by feeling and believing." Mrs. Dodopolov hugged her. "I'm glad you came to me; these are very important life lessons. Now let's get back to work."

The next day, Alexandria spent two hours helping kids learn basic tumbles. She thought maybe she felt something inside, but wasn't sure. Each day thereafter, she tried harder to feel it.

By age twelve, talent scouts attended Alexandria's increasingly exceptional performances. Many job offers arrived to her parents, some from international dance companies and Broadway musicals. Two record labels wanted to sign contracts, each promising to make her a pop star. Her parents didn't tell her about any of the offers.

Alexandria found out about some of the opportunities through her performance directors. They each encouraged her to petition her parents to accept the best offer in their respective fields. But as exciting as the prospects sounded, Alexandria hesitated, uncertain if it might be wrong to seek after what she wanted. She knew her parents must have hidden the offers for a reason—perhaps for a higher reason she wasn't yet old enough to understand, so she never asked her parents about them.

Months later, eating cereal alone in her kitchen after a dance recital, she noticed a stack of mail on the counter. A clown's face and three colored balls covered the top corner of a letter addressed from the same circus-themed Las Vegas casino where she had spontaneously performed at two years ago.

Tearing it open, she dumped out the single sheet of paper. It contained an invitation to be either a flying acrobat in training, or a singer—her choice, at their circus.

Alexandria ran to her room, leaping four steps at a time, and dove onto the bed. She read the letter over and over again. Smiling, she envisioned springing into the air, untethered by gravity like a musical note, her voice holding a lyric on a perfect F5 above the staff. *I want to be a singer* and *a flying acrobat—at the same time!*

She forgot how to sleep that night, but dozed off just as the morning light filtered through the blinds.

Awaking minutes later to her alarm clock, she froze in a cold sweat, remembering how her parents reacted the last time she performed at that circus. *I can't disobey my parents, or hurt anyone else by being selfish.*

Sitting up, she found the letter and ripped it to pieces. She cried until her mother's assistant knocked on the door. Hiding the scraps in her backpack, she rushed to get dressed for school.

During second period class, Alexandria dumped the shredded letter across her desk. By lunchtime, she'd taped it back together.

In between afternoon classes, she called her mother telling her that she'd accepted an offer at a circus. Thema scolded her for the joke, and Alexandria hung up.

A highway patrol officer drove Alexandria home that evening. He'd found her alongside a freeway almost a mile from school, hitchhiking to Las Vegas. Her parents looked pale, their voices hoarse. Alexandria tried to apologize, but they wouldn't listen. They hired a guard to monitor her twenty-four hours a day.

Over the next three days, Alexandria refused to attend any performance practices, eat, or speak to anyone. Lying on her bed wearing headphones, eyes shut, she wondered if the world was a bad place and if she was the cause.

Her parents dismissed the guard by her bedroom door, entered, and sat on the edge of the bed. Alexandria opened her eyes, blinking a few times at their unfamiliar demeanor. She considered sitting up but felt too weak from lack of food.

"Alexa, sweetheart," her father said, "since we can't safeguard you every second, and because you seem determined to make your own decisions, we feel our only recourse is to allow you to make an important one in our presence so we'll know what you will do." Her parents touched hands.

Alexandria set aside her headphones.

"Princess, before we give you the choice," her mother wiped a cheek, "please remember the principles and values that we've taught you."

Alexandria pressed herself up against the headboard, listening.

"Here is the choice." Darius breathed deep. "You can disregard everything we believe and move to Las Vegas to take that circus job; we would make the arrangements. Or you can remain with us, have our guidance to lean upon, and grow up to be a virtuous young woman."

He straightened the cuffs on his dress shirt. "It is up to you."

Alexandria rubbed her eyes, stunned, speechless. Her parents had never given her a life-determining choice before, or shown her so much respect. She hadn't realized so much was at stake for her life or for the lives of those who loved her. And she hadn't fully seen the conflict between her own desires and her parents' higher ideals so clearly—as irreparably opposing paths.

Running her hands through her straight hair, she twisted it into curls.

Her parents waited, but Alexandria had already forgotten about them. After a while they sighed and left the room.

Alexandria didn't sleep that night; the terrible hunger in her stomach felt irrelevant. With the seriousness of the world weighing on her young shoulders, she asked: *Do I want to be good as everyone has taught me—or be selfish? Do I want my life to be a symbol of obedience and virtue—or of weakness?*

She stared at the hair twisted tight around her wrist like a comforting moral restraint. *I only have one life, one chance, and I will never be able to go back in time.*

With the repose of a morning after a great battle, Alexandria lay still on her bed. *It seems so obvious now—how did I not feel it before?*

Last night she had pushed down and locked away her childish dream in a vault deep inside herself. Once sealed, she'd felt the most surprising wave of tranquility pour over her—a stillness so deep it ached. *This must be my reward for choosing to be good.* "I will never be selfishly weak again. Not in any way."

At the breakfast table, Alexandria made her announcement. "Mom, Dad," she looked them in the eyes, "I am going to be good."

The intensity of her soft voice made them laugh as they poured their coffees. By the time the toast popped, they stared at her with eyes wide.

"What exactly does that mean to you, Alexa, to be *good?*" The coffee cup trembled in Thema's hand.

"You know what it means," she smiled. "You taught it to me," her voice held only youthful certainty.

Darius cleared his throat. "I knew you would make the appropriate choice."

Thema tried to sip her coffee but it shook too much. Instead, she mumbled, "That's wonderful, princess."

Alexandria snatched toast from the table and skipped from

the house. Taking a bite, she twirled on the manicured lawn next to an effervescing fountain, breathing in the air with a sense of a higher beginning, and the start of a long hard road.

She informed her performance directors that she'd adopted a higher purpose in life, and therefore must resign from all her self-centered activities.

Mrs. Dodopolov cringed. "What do you mean?"

"You said sacrificing for others was the right thing to do." Alexandria smiled. "I *feel* it now."

Mrs. Dodopolov raised a hand, sputtering.

Alexandria hugged her. "Thank you for having the courage to teach me values."

Walking away, Alexandria felt at peace with the world and a burning pain in her heart—and just like her former physical workouts, she knew the more it burned, the more her sacrifice would pay off.

She curled her naturally straight hair to make herself appear more accepting of others. And she formed two different after-school clubs, both dedicated to assisting those in need. Teachers sent notes to her parents congratulating them on Alexandria's miraculous new attitude.

After graduating from high school, Alexandria entered a Los Angeles university, working toward a degree in sociology. This was partly at Darius' urging, but mostly because she wanted to learn in detail what society expected of her. The professors taught her that only by acting in unison could something meaningful be accomplished, and that truth could only be understood by studying the ubiquitous fabric of the masses.

She studied hard and tried to understand everything, but couldn't quite figure out how she could learn the material if she wasn't supposed to comprehend truth within her own mind, or why it was theoretically impossible to make a difference on her own. After that first semester, in a flash of bewilderment, she switched majors.

Despite disliking biology, blood, and all physical ailments, she transferred to nursing, figuring she would at least be able to make a difference using her own hands.

Due to her stunning looks and friendliness, she became extremely popular on campus. Many boys, and a few girls, wanted to date her—more than she had time to spare—so she prioritized by going out with those she found least likely to be accepted by others.

After each of her dates, she felt as she did after bestowing any act of charity—at peace with the world. But late at night, while she lay in the humidity of her sheets, she thought of some other boys she'd glimpsed on campus, feeling an unwanted sense of darkness and forbidden pleasure.

On graduation day, she told her parents she'd received a residency in a children's ward at the Beverly Hills Hospital. Darius trumped her by revealing an available nonprofit nursing opportunity helping children in a Venezuelan jungle.

"That's amazing," Alexandria said. "Really?"

Darius nodded.

"Once you have enough experience, honey," Thema added, "your father can recommend a social services position at the United Nations."

"Why?" Alexandria asked.

"Government service," Thema answered, "like what your father does, allows for *everyone* to help those in need, not just the *few* who volunteer."

"Unity and sacrifice," Darius gripped his fingers together, "is a social imperative, sweetheart."

Alexandria stopped her hands from dancing at her sides and nodded.

The conditions in the jungle involved mud floors, dripping-wet heat, and countless insects. Her hair developed bald patches, and she cried herself to sleep many nights. And as she'd feared, she abhorred nursing; yet she never missed a day of work.

On the rare days she ran out of children to assist, and her thoughts turned to herself, she noticed her deteriorating body and wondered about her long-ago decision. It was in those moments she almost *hoped* to find more misery around her so she could sacrifice and forget what lay locked deep inside. But the idea of *needing* misery in others left her feeling empty and made her question if the world really was an evil place.

At the end of her second year in the jungle, on a day she found time between nursing appointments, she walked to a river and watched children swinging on a tree rope. One longhaired girl let go and somersaulted with a half twist, diving into the river. With a flash of nausea, Alexandria ran to her hut and knelt on the floor.

Reaching under her cot, she pulled out an empty suitcase, unzipped the lining, and removed a taped-together letter. She couldn't produce tears as she thought of the offer made to her twelve years ago—she could only walk to the remote airstrip.

Before she let herself admit what she was doing, an airline pilot announced their arrival in Las Vegas.

Still in a nurse outfit, she took a taxi to a parking lot along the Strip. She stood, gazing at a clown's face and three colored balls perched above a casino entrance. Pulling a strand of her hair straight, she felt something dark and selfish swirling inside. She bounced on her toes, thinking she might leap in the air.

Glancing at her uniform, she shook her head. *What am I doing?* Inhaling, she pulled the hair across her neck. *I made my decision long ago.* She released the hair back into curls. *Be strong.*

With a sense of panicked desperation, she looked around and spotted two homeless teenage boys sitting near a parking structure. Removing the taped-together letter from her pocket, she compressed it in her fist. *I must never be this selfishly weak again.* She tossed it in a trashcan and approached the teens.

"Hello," she said. "Do your parents know that you're here?"

"Forget parents, I need a nurse." The one with the longest hair roamed his eyes up her outfit. "My lips hurt."

The short-haired teen placed a hand on his friend's knee. "Hey, I thought I was your nurse."

"I'm Alexa." She knelt down. "What are your names?"

"Ferris," the longhaired one said, picking up a worn guitar at his side.

The short-haired one shook his head. "You're the nosiest prostitute I've ever met."

She glared at him.

Looking away, he mumbled, "Go bother somebody who's interested in girls."

"Look," she sighed, "I'd like to help you two. Where do your parents live?"

Ferris strummed a cord. "I only have a devoted nanny named Preton Moore."

Alexandria scrunched her brows.

"He's the head of crybaby care services," the shorter-haired teen said. "He keeps sticking us with families, and we keep running away." He scratched his head. "We're what they call *hopelessly non-conforming*."

Leaning over his guitar, Ferris hammered his fingers across the guitar frets, blazing through scales in rapid succession.

Alexandria forced her fingers to stop dancing to his music.

Ferris lowered his guitar, looking at her. "If you don't believe us, ask my nanny. He has the files to prove how bad we are."

"Aren't you scared to be out on the streets?" She stood up and glanced around, her gaze purposely avoiding the circus marquee. "Why run away from families who care about you?"

The short-haired one scoffed. "You sound *just* like Moore."

Ferris lifted his guitar by its neck. "All I want to do is to cut this six-stringed axe through a packed stadium like a twirling blade." He ran his fingers along the high note frets, shredding out a solo.

She placed her hands on her hips to keep them from reacting to his intricately harmonized notes. "You may not realize it, but those in authority can help you, and they can provide valuable direction. Believe me; I've been there." Softening her eyes, she asked, "This Preton Moore—where's his office?"

The short-haired one gestured north. "In the building that smells like asshole."

"Nevada Social Services," Ferris said. "But don't waste your time telling on us."

She pulled out her phone and took their picture, but not before the short-haired teen sprung his middle finger. "Someday you'll understand I'm doing this for your own good," she said, before walking away.

Locating the Nevada Social Services building, Alexandria asked to meet with Preton Moore.

He invited her into his office, smiling broadly. "How may I assist you?"

Leaning over his desk, she showed him the picture of the boys. "These two need our help."

"*Our*?" He rolled his chair back and removed two red-stamped files from a cabinet. "Does that mean you want a job here?"

"I'm…" she thought of her parents' advice, and also that she never wanted to be a nurse again, "…interested in public service."

"Do you have a four-year degree?"

She nodded.

He filled out a form. "Give this to the truancy officers down the hall and lead them to those delinquents. If you can get them back into state care, you're hired."

Days later, Alexandria hung a *Unity* and a *Sacrifice* poster in her new foster care office.

Less than a year into her career, Ferris ran away— her first unexplainable, permanent loss. The thick blue folder slid into her bottom filing cabinet drawer becoming its initial inhabitant. She wanted to quit that day, but instead, with Preton's encouragement she redoubled her efforts.

Preton advanced her through the department ranks at a rapid pace. When he became lieutenant governor after her fifth year, he promoted her to Director of Nevada Foster Care Services. Many in the office with more seniority were upset, but nobody argued the genius of his decision.

Once Alexandria settled in as the director, Preton asked her to start a children's charity outside of work. She jumped at the challenge to do more, forming the Children for Universal Hope.

Years later, when she asked Preton if there was anything else she could do to stop children from falling through the cracks of society, he recommended she place the CUH into a partnership with the government.

"But what's the benefit of partnering a private charity with the government?"

"Not everyone is as virtuous as you, my dear, or as willing to give up what they want most to help others. It's time you learn that when the highest virtues of mankind cannot be accomplished fully through voluntary actions, the greater good demands that the government compel people to do them. That is, after all, the only moral purpose of a government. It would be unfair to society if anyone were allowed to refuse to sacrifice their self for the collective dream of peace, unity, and equality."

She had looked at her hands under Preton's office lights, and for just a second wanted to move them only to the music in her mind...before nodding obediently.

As the memory faded, Alexandria stared at the empty chair

beyond her desk. The air vent hissed above her head. *What have I believed?*

Glancing at the stacks of blue folders, she slipped off her wrist cuff, earrings, and necklace. *What have I done?*

The flicker of office light grated across her limp hands as they sat on Roble's file. *He asked to see someone pursuing happiness—I told him to obey others. He asked for his freedom—I locked him up.*

Raking her eyes across the red-stamped files, she no longer saw problems to be solved and losses to be feared—only children who'd refused to give up what must never be taken or surrendered in this life.

She rose to her feet, head lowered, hair falling over her face.

The sun's first beam blazed through the window, igniting the sapphire jewelry on the desk, detonating an azure brilliance that swept away the deceased fluorescence of the office.

Her chin lifted. Her eyes, like jet-black diamonds, absorbed the dawn's new birth.

Alexandria Patra stood alone.

Chapter 22

"You can't go in there. Ms. Patra is not in yet this morning," Janice said. Her voice stopped the shaggy-haired courier heading toward Alexandria's office.

Alexandria Patra flung open her office door and strode out, her face projecting placid certainty.

The courier staggered back. Janice's eyes widened behind her glasses. Both stared at Alexandria's strapless black dress and hair lashed in a knot at the back of her head.

"You're right on time, Rex." Alexandria tossed a packet from the stack in her hand to the courier.

Rex caught the envelope, blinking.

"Deliver that to the Nevada State Board of Elections without delay," she said.

"Ms. Patra, I didn't realize you were in your office," Janice stammered. "You look...different."

Alexandria dropped a folder on Janice's desk. "Please submit this resignation to the Board of Directors of the Children for Universal Hope." She flung down another. "Submit this resignation to the Directors of the Nevada Public/Private Partnership." Flopping down a third, along with a set of car keys, she said, "Once you've submitted the other two, deliver my resignation to the head of Nevada Social Services."

"But, Ms. Patra, what...?" Her mouth hung open.

Alexandria retrieved more envelopes and a handful of sparkling jewelry from her office, and turned to leave. "I wish you the best."

"Oh, but wait," Janice said. "The Lieutenant Governor called this morning wanting to see you. Should I still set up the appointment?"

"That won't be necessary." Alexandria almost floated on her high heels away from the reception area.

Passing the departing courier in the adjacent hallway, she stopped him. "Mr. Rex Livingston."

"Yes ma'am?"

"I've always thought you seemed trustworthy, Rex. That's why I called for you," she said. "Please decline the job I'm about to offer if you have any doubts as to whether you are willing or able to do it."

His eyes widened.

Alexandria held out nine letter-sized envelopes. "These must be hand delivered, and only to their intended recipients. Four are to go to foster children and must be given without their foster parents' knowledge. The other five will go to ex-foster children, but I don't know where they are, and I need you to locate them. Nobody is to know who sent the letters."

"That sounds difficult. Without their parents' knowledge? Is that even legal?"

"One more thing," Alexandria dropped the envelopes in his hand. She opened her other hand, revealing a platinum and sapphire necklace, earrings, and wrist cuff. "Sell these to Star Jewelry in Summerlin. The owner quoted me a price this morning; I'll tell him you're coming. You will keep five percent of the proceeds as your fee if you are successful in all the deliveries. Place the remaining cash in nine equal shares in each of these envelopes along with the enclosed letters."

She held out the jewelry. "It's a difficult job in exchange for a lot of money. If you accept and fail—you'll wish you hadn't." She paused, narrowing her eyes. "Do you understand what I'm proposing, Rex Livingston?"

He nodded.

She waited.

He stood taller. "Yes, Ms. Patra. You can trust me. I'll do it."

The jewelry dropped into his palm.

"Get moving," Alexandria said. "Deliver the election package first and immediately."

Rex turned and ran down the hall.

Alexandria's heels clicked in rhythm along the vinyl tiles to the State of Nevada's Las Vegas executive branch offices. Heading to Preton Moore's door, she passed his secretary without comment.

"Oh, Ms. Patra. You haven't set up an—" the secretary blurted.

Alexandria swung open the office door and slammed it shut behind her.

Preton fumbled fingernail clippers off his desk and swept the pile of nails from the gleaming surface.

"Alexa. Where did you go last night?" He rose, his bronzed face contrasting against a tailored blue suit. He stared at her evening gown from last night. "What happened?"

"I had some files to catch up on." She stepped to the center of the office, her shoulders relaxed.

"Files? You left in the middle of our big night for *files*? Aren't you excited about the nomination?"

"Thank you, Preton," she said, "for placing me on your ticket."

"All right," he scrunched his forehead. "Well, don't fret too much about your misstatement last night. I covered for you, but you need to get out in front of the cameras right away and make a proper speech."

"I'm not worried about it."

"You're not? Well…." He straightened his tie. "Well good. That's what I like to hear. You always find ways to overcome obstacles; that's why I put you on the ticket. Just don't scare me like that again." He touched his head as if remembering something. "By the way, you should call your parents; they were worried about you last night."

"Anything else?"

"You'll be in Sacramento this afternoon, right? Showcasing the public/private partnership with the Governor of California is a great publicity opportunity. And with the new Citron jet I had the partnership buy, it should be an easy trip."

"I'm not going."

"What do you mean?" Preton placed both fists on the desk, leaning forward. "Did that bastard cancel on us?" He swung an arm as if tossing something off the smooth surface.

"I quit the partnership."

"You…what?" He stumbled back, gripping the desk chair for balance.

"I also quit my job and resigned from the CUH."

"Who in the hell told you to quit?" He released the chair, leaving it spinning in circles.

Her face remained statuesque.

"Your high profile duties were part of the campaign plan." He motioned his hands out wide. "I should have coached you about this before the announcement, but I had no idea you'd do something so rash without my permission. You already quit everything this morning?"

"Yes."

"Reverse it," he ordered.

Alexandria watched him, her breathing calm.

He whipped a phone out from his suit and tapped the screen. "I'll call the boards and have them refuse your resignations. We'll tell them it was an office snafu. That's it. It will work."

"I'm done, Preton."

"You're done with…?" He shook the phone at a framed poster displaying a woman who embraced several children with the words *Unconditional Love* written underneath.

"I failed a child I could have helped," Alexandria said.

"You failed…" The phone lowered to his side. "So *that* explains last night." His face relaxed. "Now don't go quitting just because we lost one more child. I know how emotional you get about runaways, but you know very well we can't prevent them all."

"She didn't get away."

"Well, whatever," Preton snapped. "You don't quit just because something happened to *one* child. We are going to save the *entire* state of Nevada."

"Preton, I've said what I came to say. I'm leaving."

"Fine," he waved the phone, "take a day off to pull yourself together. Then we'll get you in front of the cameras."

She smirked.

Preton studied her for a moment, then a grin squeezed across his lips. "You had me scared for a moment. Ha! Randal Graph told me several months ago you'd acquired a sense of humor, but I didn't believe him."

"He's right. I see a lot of things as funny now."

Preton cupped a hand to his forehead and paced behind his desk. "You know, you might be right. No—you're a genius, Alexa. All right, I take it all back. You were right to quit. You are the most admired woman in Nevada and we weren't going to take full advantage of you on the campaign trail. Now we can. I'll get on the horn with James." He swiped the phone screen, his feet shuffling on the carpet. "My dear, why didn't I think of this earlier?"

"I'm not going to campaign, Preton."

He froze, his smile still plastered on his face. The phone slipped into his pocket and he leaned forward, his hands pressing against the gleaming desk. "'If you vote for us, you will deserve exactly what you believe?'" His smile drained from his face. "That's what you said last night." He stood up straight, his fingertips massaging his chin. "You *meant* it."

Alexandria folded her arms.

"So you've switched sides," he said.

"Which side would that be, Preton?"

Still massaging his chin, he asked, "Did Stock Brant convince you to throw it all away?"

"Seriously?" Alexandria laughed. "Stock rebels against you more loyally than your wife. And you understand perfectly well the leash he thinks he has on you is just a noose he's fastened to his own neck. Who else *willingly* bribes you just for the privilege to breathe?"

"Who have you been speaking with?" He moved to the front of the desk, his steps cautious.

"Afraid of something?" She took a step forward, causing him to press back against the desk.

He shook a finger at her. "I wonder if you really know what you're doing." He slid around to the side of the desk and gripped it for balance.

"Do you?" she asked.

He held still like a cornered animal.

"Preton, I'm thirty-seven years old," she opened her arms. "The prime of my body is almost over. I regret it…I regret it so much."

"What is this?" He shook his head, standing tall. "A mid-life crisis? Pull yourself together."

"I gave up *my* dream—for what, Preton? A 'higher' purpose?" She lowered her arms to her sides and breathed in. "But that's not even the worst of it, is it? Want me to say it? Want me to confess what makes me an actual felon and reserves me a choice spot in hell?"

"Please, Alexandria Patra," he said, "tell me all your regrets."

Her eyes narrowed. "I taught *children* to surrender their

developing minds to concepts like the greater good or the good of society which can't exist in any form in this world without actual kids being trampled underneath their untouchable banners."

Pointing at her own chest, she added, "*I* taught children that in order to live up to those 'higher' ideals they must be obedient—to others, must sacrifice their dreams—to the needs of others. I taught them it was more important to be a part of a group than to stand on their own judgment. I told the non-conforming kids they should feel guilty for wanting to live on their own terms."

Alexandria swept a hand forward, pointing it at Preton. "I then delivered every ego-stripped, dream-crushed child to the power mongers of the world like you, who will use this universally accepted mirage of morality to control them."

Preton lowered his forehead, sinking the hollows of his cheeks into shadow. His eyes, like colorless orbs, remained locked on her. "Well, this is quite a sad story. You've acquired an antisocial disorder, and so late in life. What a rare and pitiful event, considering I spent so much of my effort enlightening you. You are done, Alexa. Done and gone."

She watched him without movement.

He grinned. "Since I hadn't yet submitted your application to the election board, perhaps your friend, Jesus Gorronza, will take your place. Voters just love underdog stories. Wouldn't you vote for a humble, underprivileged orphan who became rich only to serve society?" Snickering, he pulled out his phone and dialed a number.

"I agree, Jessy is perfect for you, Preton. A match made in heaven."

"Get out!"

"Even though I will not be campaigning, I filed my election board paperwork this morning," Alexandria said, "*accepting* your nomination."

Preton's head snapped to attention, his expression that of a man about to be run down by a speeding train.

"So," she continued, "unless *you* wish to withdraw from the governor's race, we're married on this ticket."

Preton dropped the phone; it thumped to the floor. A distant "*Hello?*" sounded at his feet.

Alexandria stepped closer. He stepped back.

Raising a finger, she said, "I could destroy any chance we

have of winning this election by opening my mouth, just like you tasted last night, but that isn't what I want."

"What...what do you want?" He continued backward, pressing against a bookshelf behind the desk.

"To be lieutenant governor," she said, following him.

"Why?"

"Because I no longer deserve what you or anyone else believes."

He attempted a laugh but managed only a cough. "You're naïve. The lieutenant governor has no power."

"Then why look so scared?"

Preton wiped his upper lip, glancing around the room. "You will really stay out of sight and not campaign while on my ticket?"

"You won't see or hear me." She smiled. "Nor I, you." She pointed at the poster labeled *Unconditional Love*. "Go ahead and trumpet my pristine record of service if you want. I paid dearly enough for it. And it would almost be a shame if nobody used it to gain power."

"What will you do during the campaign?"

"That," she said, "is none of your business."

"And once *in* office?" His words fell from his lips one syllable at a time.

"The same."

"I don't understand."

"Of course not."

Preton slumped into the desk chair. Alexandria's toe spun it around until he faced her. He pressed his hands to his glistening forehead, his cheeks turning pale.

"You should work on your tan, Preton. I need you to look good for the TV cameras if we're going to win." Striding from the office, she said, "I'll see you in nine months, at our victory party."

Like the final page of a ghostwritten book, the state office building's glass door whispered closed behind her.

Chapter 23

Feeling buoyant, Alexandria walked along a dozen downtown blocks until she arrived at a tall, corrugated fence set back from the street.

She knocked on its gate. As she waited, her feet shuffled beer cans and tumbleweeds.

Several men across the street sat on apartment steps, watching.

Receiving no answer, Alexandria searched the perimeter of the fence, dodging rusted oil barrels and shrub brush. Finding no other entrance, she pressed her hands to her hips and estimated the height of the fence—about twice her height.

Perpendicular to a cottonwood tree on the other side of the fence, she stacked stray cinder blocks around an upright oil barrel, constructing a tiered pedestal.

Two men from the apartment shuffled to the far edge of the street, ogling her as she worked in her strapless gown. One whistled.

Alexandria removed her heels, held them in one hand, and stepped back to the middle of the street. The cracked asphalt felt liberating under her bare toes. She smiled to herself, feeling like a young girl.

The two men approached from behind. One, with a torn shirt and an oversized beer can, reached for her with off-balance steps, mumbling incoherently.

Alexandria stepped back, passing him, barely avoiding his grasp. She almost burst out laughing at the thought of jumping the fence. She'd not attempted even a low vault in decades.

"Hey, pretty lady," the other, more rancid-smelling man slurred from behind, and touched her bare shoulder.

Shrugging him off, she focused on the makeshift ramp. She reached down and ripped her dress at the bottom to give her legs leeway to run.

The man wrapped his arms around her shoulders. "You're coming home with me."

Alexandria slammed her elbow into his gut. Whirling around, she leaned a shoulder low to the asphalt, and unloaded a thrust-kick to his chest. He staggered back and fell to the ground.

She turned and sprinted to the fence, bouncing off the road in long strides, already forgetting everyone behind her.

One foot landed midway up the stacked cinderblocks and launched her higher. With her knees bent, both feet found the top of the ramp and sprung her upward in a line. Her toes pushed off the top of the fence and propelled her toward the cottonwood tree.

Wind swept across her skin. With a sense of childlike fascination, she realized she'd cleared the fence with too much velocity.

One arm caught an outstretched branch as leaves whipped her face, her opposite hand still clutching her high heels. Her grip on the branch failed, and she flew beyond the trunk, careening to the ground. Her feet slammed into the grass and she rolled hard, knocking the breath from her lungs.

When she stopped, she lay flat on her back, bare arms and legs spread wide atop the grass, shoes still in one hand. Adrenaline pumped through her veins like liquid fire.

Gazing through a mess of undone hair, she smiled at the leafy canopy and petted the soft blades beneath her body like a childhood blanket. Sitting up, she looked at her legs, then at the tall barrier she'd overcome.

I'm free.

She jumped to her feet, ran across the lawn, and circled the house to the front door. As she stood on the step, awaiting an answer, she heard the crunch of footsteps and dropped her heels, spinning around.

Libby stopped several yards away, wearing a one-piece white uniform like a surgeon turned mechanic.

With disheveled hair dancing in the breeze, Alexandria glanced at her own leaf-covered and grass-stained black dress, while her toes brushed playfully against the concrete.

Libby pushed back her hair and tilted her head to the side.

Alexandria ran forward and wrapped her arms around Libby's waist, her bare toes standing atop Libby's work boots.

Libby gripped her shoulders, and coaxed her back, searching her eyes. Alexandria felt tears streaming down her cheeks, unsure if they came from laughing, crying, or both.

Taking her by the hand, Libby led her inside the house, sat her on a sofa, and walked to the kitchen.

Alexandria dried her eyes and caressed her scratches and bruises, thinking they felt wonderful.

Returning with two glasses of iced tea, Libby placed them on the coffee table and sat across from her, resting her hands on her knees.

Alexandria brushed away a wild strand of hair sticking to her face and smiled.

Libby smiled back.

"Not going to ask me why I'm here?" Alexandria wiped a blade of grass from her gown.

"Nope." Libby picked up a tea and relaxed against the sofa.

"I think you should know that I'm…" Alexandria's eyebrows scrunched with concern, "…that I'm running for lieutenant governor on Preton Moore's ticket."

Libby spit tea down her white clothes, laughing.

"You're not upset?"

"About what?" Libby dabbed her chin.

"I thought you'd hate it. I'm sorry for what's been done to you—to your jets, and your cliff home. I probably made it worse."

Libby reached out, setting her glass on the coffee table.

Alexandria leaned forward and clasped Libby's wrist, gazing at her through her hanging hair. "The things you make, they say a lot about you—maybe everything." She shook her hair to reveal more of her face. "I know this might sound strange, but…thank you for actually loving what you do and for not apologizing for it."

Letting go of Libby, Alexandria stepped onto the coffee table and stood above her looking down. She breathed with such ease.

Libby's gaze moved up her body, stopping on her hands.

Alexandria's hands swayed to music in her own mind. "I know this must seem forward…" she leapt down atop Libby, her legs kneeling on either side of her hips, "…and I'm actually in love with a man," her palms pressed to Libby's ribcage, "but this is how I feel about the exception you made for me." Alexandria kissed her, the softest kiss she'd ever given.

Libby didn't respond to the kiss.

Alexandria drew back, staring into her eyes.

"Alexa, you don't—"

She covered Libby's lips with her fingers. "I know. You don't need to say it." Her fingers dropped away. "I owe you nothing and you would never ask me to give up anything."

"You don't know me at all." Libby's emerald eyes twinkled. "I was going to say—you don't know how hot you look in that dress."

"Don't mess with me. I've already kicked a man to the ground today for trying to grope me, and I'm not afraid to hit a girl."

Libby grinned. "Okay, you're right. That's pretty much what I was going to say to you." Her hands touched Alexandria's back. "I really am glad you came to visit me. For any reason you choose."

Alexandria blinked her smiling eyes and relaxed against Libby, face nuzzling into her neck. Within moments, the night without sleep overtook her.

When Alexandria awoke, she breathed in, smelling something dreamy like the distant smoke of a campfire in the woods. Opening her eyes, she saw the line of Libby's neck and noticed the lighting in the room had dimmed to a subtle blue. She whispered, "Libby, today is real, isn't it?"

Libby caressed the back of Alexandria's dress.

Rubbing her nose on Libby's shoulder, Alexandria exhaled. "Show me your workshop. I want to watch you making something."

Libby stood up, Alexandria's body still clinging to her. "Come along then."

Alexandria dropped to her feet and followed her outside.

The building they entered looked like an inventor's workshop at the dawn of the industrial revolution. Its ceiling reached twenty-five feet high, a chimney poking up through the center. Racks of metallic body armor, manufacturing robots, drafting tables, jet engines on blocks, and mechanical parts on shelves filled the space. Blinking computer servers spread out against a wall.

Alexandria wandered through the workshop, tracing her fingers along everything she passed, enjoying the feel of Libby's world. As she neared a drafting table, her eyes caught a name inscribed on a sketch. She leaned over the table, scrutinizing the drawing—a fighter jet with aggressive sweptback lines. She spun around, her voice breathless, "You know Roble Santos?"

"I do," Libby said.

Alexandria touched her own hair, undoing the partially tied knot.

"Maybe I should ask you the same question," Libby said.

"Oh," Alexandria glanced back at the drawing, her hand brushing through her hair. "It was a long time ago."

Libby raised an eyebrow.

"How is he, Libby?" She studied Roble's signature. "Where is he?"

"I don't even know what Roble looks like. He sent me a really nice letter not quite a year ago. So naturally I'm helping him get into all sorts of unspeakable trouble on the other side of the globe."

Alexandria turned to her, smiling. "I'm glad he's okay…and that he knows you."

Libby waved a hand for her to follow. "I was making something for him when you fell into my backyard." She walked to a domed, ceramic forge, its shimmering fumes wafting from its glowing mouth.

A cord of freshly cut pine logs lay stacked nearby, the same type Alexandria once saw her chopping outside. Libby rolled her sleeves above the elbows and bellowed the dying embers until they burned white. Using tongs, she pulled an ingot from the forge and placed it upon an anvil. She struck the metal with a hammer. Silver sparks showered to the floor with each hit.

Alexandria darted her gaze between Libby's focused eyes and her swinging arm and started humming in sync with the hot pulse of the rhythmic pounding. After a minute, Alexandria strolled away in song, meandering through the manufacturing shed, studying the layout.

Returning to Libby, she said, "I like this place."

Libby plunged the glowing billet into a vat, causing it to shriek for mercy.

"How much spare manufacturing space do you have?" Alexandria asked.

Setting down the tongs, Libby placed her fists on her hips.

"I'd like to rent some of it," Alexandria said.

"Rent?"

Alexandria smiled.

"Nope." Libby removed the hardened alloy from the vat and stuck it back into the forge. "Don't have any extra space."

"Hmm…" Alexandria walked away, continuing to look around.

On a drafting table, Alexandria found a piece of paper and a pencil and wrote notes, glancing up at the building's arrangement. After a few minutes she walked back and handed the paper to Libby.

"What's this?" Libby studied the sheet in the fire's cracking glow.

"A proposal to rearrange your layout."

Raising an eyebrow, Libby gazed around the shop.

"I think it would free up about a thousand square feet in that corner," Alexandria pointed, "without much impact to your workflow. How much rent do you want for that space?"

Rubbing her chin, Libby studied her. "What in the world do you want to make?"

"Me."

Libby's gaze moved from Alexandria's eyes to her heels as if appraising a hypersonic prototype. Breathing in, she said, "This is primo space. I'd have to charge triple the average manufacturing rent per square foot in Las Vegas."

"You're ruthless, Ms. Dodge." She stared as though sizing up an opponent.

Libby stepped back an inch.

Alexandria moved closer, bringing their faces together. "This," she said, "is my first and only offer, Ms. Dodge. I will pay one percent above the average Vegas rent and you will throw in a *Succubus* flight."

A few seconds passed before Libby's face broke into a grin.

"See, that wasn't so hard." Alexandria lifted her chin.

Libby turned away, pulled the bluish-silver alloy from the forge, and hammered it.

Looking around at the aerospace materials, Alexandria thought back to her flight in the *Wyvern* and her conversation with Bill Jerrgin. Her eyes stopped on Libby. "What do your parents think of the *Succubus*?"

Libby laughed. "They absolutely love it. They've never understood me, but they are the most supportive parents in the world."

She smiled, picturing Libby as a young girl making things in a big backyard. "I'd like to meet your parents some time. Do they live in Vegas?"

"Upper east side." Libby continued pounding the alloy.

"Near Sunrise Mountain?"

"No, not Las Vegas—Manhattan. That's where I was raised."

"I would not have guessed it," she said as Libby smashed the metal.

"I was twelve when my parents brought me to Las Vegas on vacation," Libby said. "It was on that trip I decided I would make things that fly."

Alexandria's eyes followed the line of the hammer, along Libby's bare forearm, to the skin just above her elbow. Alexandria wanted to reach out and touch that skin—so she did. Libby continued hammering as if she didn't notice. Alexandria's fingers glided across the sweaty, hard ridge on the back of Libby's upper arm and then felt the round muscle in the front. It tensed under her touch.

She let go, happy Libby hadn't stopped or pulled away. Touching her wet fingers against her own soft upper arm, Alexandria asked, "May I use your phone? I need a taxi."

"I can give you a ride." Libby's eyes remained on the sparking metal.

"No thanks." She lowered her voice to mimic Libby's and added, "This is a primo body. It needs to be taxied by a professional driver."

Libby stopped the hammer on the anvil and turned. "Of course, Ms. Patra." She inclined her head toward a phone on a table, feigning a frown.

Speaking on the phone, Alexandria watched Libby caress along the arm where she'd touched. When Alexandria hung up, Libby picked up the hammer and continued her work.

I feel so young. Alexandria stretched out on her silky white sheets, toes curling and releasing, enjoying the morning's embrace.

Entering her closet, she smiled at the thought of wearing

whatever she wanted. Inside storage boxes, she found a worn t-shirt and slipped it on. Beneath old tattered jeans she spotted a baseball cap someone had probably given to her at a fundraiser. Picking it up, she froze. *The Sin* was stitched in gold thread across its front. *Stock...*

Kneeling down, she slid a hand across her shirt, feeling her breasts, remembering. Her nipples tightened into painful ridges; her breathing turned fluid; her face hot.

She slipped on the hat. Bowing her head, she traced the stitching with her fingertips, seeing Stock's bloodshot eyes. *I know I can't make you understand.* Alexandria stood up. *But I can eventually show you.*

Flexing her fingers, she felt the control over her body. *And if you somehow survive your accepted beliefs, I will protect you.*

She pulled on the tattered jeans and walked to the kitchen. Swiping a finger across her phone screen, she waited as it rang.

"Carl Morgenson," a voice said over the line.

"Hi, Carl."

"What can I help you with, Ms. Patra?"

"Please list my house for sale today."

"That's great news. I'll be over first thing tomorrow."

Shaking her head, she said, "No, today. I want cash buyers and I want it closed in less than two weeks."

Carl coughed. "I obviously can't guarantee it will sell in two weeks; you know that. The market is the market."

She glanced at a stack of copper-engraved fundraiser invitations on the counter. "Then list it at a discount. I can't wait."

"Do you need me to show you new homes as well? What are you looking for?"

"No, I'm going to rent." She brushed the invitations over the edge and into a trashcan.

"Then do you need me to assist you with finding a rental?"

"No, thank you."

"I don't understand."

"Just get it sold. Thanks, Carl."

Wearing sunglasses below her hat, Alexandria drove to a pirate-themed casino. She gazed at its pirate ship and the *HMS Dauntless* sitting in a drained sea adjacent to the Las Vegas Strip.

Construction workers crawled around the ships using assorted equipment.

Jumping the rope fence, Alexandria slid into the dry seabed, strode by several workers, and climbed a ladder hanging from the side of the *HMS Dauntless*.

"Hey. Are you supposed to be here?" a leather-skinned man wearing a hardhat asked.

Alexandria plucked the worker's hardhat off his head and placed it atop her baseball cap. "Yes," her obdurate voice and eyes left no room for doubt.

Locating the captain's quarters, she gazed at the plaster barrels, the table holding a plastic map, and the washed-out polyester tapestries. Below a row of multi-colored windowpanes, she lay down on a bench with her knees bent.

Her eyelashes fluttered when she read the three words engraved on the ceiling. *Roble is free.*

Leaping to her feet, she touched the scratch marks. Then, finding an unfastened screw, she used it to make her own inscription. *So is Alexa.*

She exited the cabin and stood behind the knobbed wheel at the helm. Closing her eyes, she washed away the construction ruckus and nearby tourists, imagining an open sea.

After a while, she tossed the hardhat to a workman and left.

Walking north along the Strip, she reached an old hotel and casino. Red, green, and yellow balls framed a clown's face above the entrance. The inside smelled of stale cigarettes, burnt popcorn, and over-vacuumed carpet, the most delightful aroma she could ever recall.

Beyond the bleeping slot machines lay the entry to a dimly lit pavilion. An elevated boardwalk with carnival games surrounded a circus ring. The walls of the curved entrance displayed faded frescos of elephants, lions, and costumed ladies. Alexandria ran a hand along the wall, tracing the flying trapeze artists.

When the circus performance began, she sat on the top row of the sparsely populated stands and clasped her hands to her lips, fearing her smile might erupt into laughter. The soaring performers sent shivers down her spine—the first acrobatic show she had seen since performing on this very stage twenty-seven years ago.

The trapeze artists twisted high in the air, gripping onto

one another, somersaulting, always finding the next swing. Alexandria's hands ran along the goosebumps and scrapes on her arms as butterflies swirled in her stomach. A melody rushed through her mind, encouraging the entertainers on.

When a woman dismounted by falling into the net and bouncing, Alexandria felt the rush of air as if she were flying.

As the performances recurred throughout the day, she moved down the rows to the front. She waited between shows, replaying every detail of each routine in her mind, remembering all the moves she practiced so long ago. By midnight, she'd seen eight shows and loved them all.

Walking from the casino into the warm night air, she felt no desire to go home. She perused the Strip until spotting a crowd of young people filing into a windowless bar near a casino parking lot.

As she neared the bar, a muffled beat vibrated her hair. Following them inside, she plunged herself into a rock concert, her first ever, featuring a local underground band.

After a few minutes she recognized the lead guitar player, but he didn't see her. *Hello again, Ferris.*

She sang along in the absorbing void of music and lights, placing her own words atop the unfamiliar lyrics, her body dancing to the determined rhythm and astounding guitar riffs. As her voice warmed up, it roared from a place deep within, as if it had waited for its dormant conductor to awaken.

Exiting the bar at the break of dawn, she'd never felt so intoxicated, yet she hadn't touched a drink.

Each day that followed, Alexandria visited different casino shows and concerts, wearing *The Sin* hat and sunglasses, making detailed mental notes of the best performers.

When her house sold, she pawned off her household belongings in bulk to a secondhand store. At her bank she withdrew the proceeds from her house, liquidated all her accounts, and cashed out her retirement plan with penalties.

With the money stuffed inside a large shoulder bag, she drove to a car dealership and sold her sedan for cash. From the dealership she walked to a nearby hair salon and costume shop. The purple neon sign out front read: *Super Starz.*

Five hours later, out strolled a woman with straight, bloodred hair and molten silver irises.

She purchased a prepaid smart phone at a convenience store, searched for a specific Isshin-Ryu dojo phone number in Los Angeles, and called it.

"Sensei Hisoka?" she said, "This is…Alexa. Do you remember me from the ballet in Beverly Hills?"

After a long pause he said, "*Hei.*"

"I'd like to restart my lessons. I'll pay for you to commute to Las Vegas."

In the weeks that followed, she visited backstage at shows along the Strip, meeting one-on-one with the best performers.

With her final handshake and cash deposit to a petite Russian acrobat, she hailed a taxi and disappeared.

Chapter 24

Libby answered the unexpected knock on her front door and stared into glowing metallic eyes.

The woman visitor stood there with straight, fiery hair ablaze in the porch-light, poised like a mannequin behind glass. She wore a white, zip-up, long-sleeved top and black leggings. A backpack hung behind her shoulders.

Libby peeled her eyes away to note the gate to her compound remained closed. *Could this be…?* She leaned closer. "A…Alexa?"

"Sitra," she said, her glossy black lips contrasting against white teeth.

"My god," Libby's hand ran through her own hair. "Your… everything…is so different. You look—"

"I know it is short notice," Sitra interrupted, "but may I also rent a bedroom in your house?"

Stepping forward, Libby closed the door behind her. "So you really *have* given up everything."

"Haven't given up a thing." Sitra grinned, her red brows pressing down.

Libby laughed. "I'll clean out my hobby room for you tomorrow."

Sitra pressed into her, wrapping her arms behind her neck.

"Uhmm…" Libby's eyes widened.

"I'm so happy." Sitra's lashes fluttered against Libby's cheek. "Uhmm…"

Sitra moved her lips close to hers. "I feel so alive."

Libby's hands moved around to rest against Sitra's backpack. "Are you sure you're really in love with somebody else? A man, did you say?"

"Yes." Sitra kissed her.

This time, Libby returned the kiss.

"Mmmm," Sitra breathed.

"Uh-huh," Libby answered.

As their lips parted, Libby raised her brows, tasting her black-smudged lips. "Sitra…is it?"

"For now."

"May I ask what's in the pack?"

"The next year of my life," Sitra said, stepping back. "I'll pay the rent for the bedroom and the manufacturing space tonight. My equipment arrives Tuesday and my first trainer starts Wednesday. We'll be starting very early each morning."

Libby blinked.

"I don't think I'll bother you too much," Sitra added.

"Bother? I'm looking forward to it. I hope you can tolerate my industrial ruckus all day long."

Sitra lifted her nose. "Oh, something smells delicious." She touched her stomach. "I think I forgot to eat today."

"We just finished dinner, but come in." Libby reached for the doorknob. "There's some left."

"Who's here?"

Libby paused. "Halvern and Victor."

"Your architect, Halvern Black? The cliff house?"

"Yep."

"And your…?"

"Frenchman."

She touched Libby's arm. "It's important nobody I distrust discovers who I am, or that I'm staying here. I'll come back when your guests have left."

Libby gripped her hand. "Don't worry about these two rascals. I only trust them with my life."

Sitra glanced at the fence before her gaze returned to Libby.

"Just come in." Libby smiled.

She nodded.

Libby led her inside. Halvern and Victor rose from the dining table.

Victor, wearing dark grey chainmail, approached and bowed his feathery blond head. "*Bonsoir, Madame.* I am Victor Lafayette." He turned to Libby. "Who is this god*dess* who graces you?"

"This…is Sitra. Sitra, meet Halvern Black," Libby said, as Halvern approached, "and well…you already heard Victor's introduction."

"Mr. Black," Sitra said, "I've seen some of your work. It's a pleasure to meet you."

Halvern's face remained stoic.

Turning to Victor, Sitra asked, "Mr. Lafayette, are you certain we haven't crossed paths before?"

Victor touched his chin. "I am *most* certain I would remember if I had."

Sitra smiled. "What do you do, Mr. Lafayette? When you aren't being the dashing French knight, I mean."

"We don't have enough time this evening to list it all," Libby interjected, "but the robots and the armor you saw in the shed? Victor designed all of it. And there is no need to call anyone around here mister. Don't let 'em fool you." She tapped Victor's armored chest. "These guys are ruffians."

"And you, my lovely Sitra," Victor said, with a grin, "what is your vocation?"

"I just changed what I do."

Victor narrowed his indigo eyes. Halvern crossed his arms and looked at Libby. Libby wiped her black-smeared lips and shrugged.

"I need to hire someone to help position my arriving equipment in Libby's manufacturing shed," Sitra said. "Would either of you be interested?"

"But of course, *Madame*," Victor said.

Halvern cleared his throat and pressed a hand against his upper abdomen, his face wincing.

Sitra stared at Halvern's midsection and then at his face.

"What will you be doing in the facility?" Victor asked.

"Training," Sitra said, still looking at Halvern.

Victor glanced at Libby. Libby shrugged again.

"I have things to do," Halvern said, his voice gruff. He held out his large, black hand.

Sitra slipped her hand into his.

Libby watched them eye each other for a moment before Halvern withdrew his hand. "Halvern," Libby touched his shoulder, "at least join Sitra for one glass of iced tea. Plus, you've lost so much weight lately you could certainly eat more."

Halvern grumbled but let Libby lead him to the dining room. Victor bowed with a lowered hand for Sitra to proceed ahead of him.

Sitra sat at the table and ate left over noodles and braised pork while everyone else drank and talked. The topics meandered from Victor's African war stories and vision for impenetrable body armor, to Libby's rare element alloys and their potential to increase the speed of aircraft, to Halvern's ideas of ever taller skyscrapers and their eventual use on other planets.

They drained a full pitcher of Libby's iced tea, three times, and Victor finished the bottle of wine.

After saying little, Sitra swayed her fingers next to her smiling lips. "I can tell you each believe in your dreams."

They turned and stared at her.

"I rarely see it," Sitra said, her fingers still dancing. "Do you ever wonder why people stop chasing them?"

"You seem to have reflected upon it, *Madame*," Victor said, tilting his head.

"Yes," Sitra touched the bowl of giant pine nuts at the center of the table, "I've begun to."

"Perhaps we are going to require more iced tea and wine." Victor raised his empty glass.

Libby smiled and left for the kitchen. Returning with a tray of drinks, she asked, "What will be the theme of your performance art…Sitra?"

"I've learned that words can deceive," she touched her black lips, "but not actions. That's why you'll eventually see my performance and decide for yourself."

"Hmm," Libby sipped her tea.

"I breathlessly await your physical feats, *Madame*." Victor tipped his wine glass.

Halvern rolled his eyes.

Sitra stared at Halvern. "You prefer to express yourself through the art of architecture instead of words. Am I correct?"

Halvern frowned.

Sitra slid her empty glass toward the iced tea pitcher. Libby grazed Sitra's fingers as she filled the glass.

"I'm partial to art from The Age of Enlightenment." Victor gestured through the air as if indicating a different place and time.

Halvern coughed and looked at his watch.

"In that brief period following the Renaissance," Victor continued, "reason, the rights of man, and art were thought of in unison by many, as an inseparable whole—an idea which seems to have gone on holiday as of late."

"Do you wish you could go back in time, Mr. Lafayette?" Sitra asked. "I can almost picture it."

"No, *Madame*. I've never desired to go back in time, except perhaps to compare fire-baked croissants." He licked his lips. "But I would that the enlightenment be brought forward into men's minds."

Libby smirked, staring at Victor's armor. "You sure you don't secretly wish, just a little," she pinched two fingertips together, "to travel back and be a knight?"

"Not once, *Madame* Dodge. However, I will impart this…" he said, his chainmail shining lustrous under the dining room light. "As it is a constant battle to survive on this planet, and as all *Messieurs* and *Mesdames* are modern knights of one shade or another," he sipped his wine, "I wish I could live under a warrior's code, upheld by a government of the highest order."

"And what is this 'warrior's code' you think you deserve?" Sitra asked.

"It contains only one rule." He laid an open hand upon the table. "Do *not* initiate force against *anyone* else."

Sitra scrunched her nose. "And how is that a 'warrior's' code if you don't believe in war?"

"What do you think marks an honorable warrior? His moral aim is to put an end to aggression if others commence it." He flicked his fingers into the air. "What more, what less, is requisite for *la liberté et la justice*?"

"Victor loves to wax poetic," Libby said, taking a drink of tea, "when he's not melting caves into glass or winding up cool robots."

"His views on art and laws are unassuming…if not romantic." Sitra turned to Halvern. "What about you, Mr. Black? What type of 'warrior's code' do you deserve to live under?"

"You were correct," Halvern groused, "words can be worse than a waste of time—especially when the blathering is in French." He stood up, pressing a fist against his abdomen. "Like I said, it's late." He nodded at the table and strode away.

As he opened the front door, he barked over his shoulder, "Libby, I'll add that upper deck on your manufacturing shed once *The Spirit of Man* is complete. Good night."

"*Au revoir, Monsieur* Black," Victor said as the door slammed shut.

"You must pardon Halvern's crankiness." Libby refilled Sitra's glass with iced tea.

"Not at all." Sitra plucked a pine nut from the bowl and held it in her palm. "Mr. Black is endearing…in his own way."

"Most truly, he is," Victor said.

Libby shook her head, holding back a laugh.

"Mr. Lafayette," Sitra said, "tell me how you first met Libby. Does it also involve romance and poetry…or just unassuming robots?"

"All three, my lady." He lifted the wine glass to his lips.

Libby blushed and gulped her iced tea.

The three conversed for another hour before Sitra's eyelids drooped and Victor excused himself and departed.

Sitra strolled to a sofa and sat down, a pine nut in her palm. She held it under her nose, her eyes closing.

Libby watched her for a moment and walked to the back of the house. "I'll go make up a bed for you in the hobby room."

Returning, Libby said, "It's ready…" She stood, looking at Sitra asleep with her head resting on her backpack.

Retrieving a bed sheet from the hobby room, Libby laid it over her. After removing Sitra's shoes, she sat on the edge of the sofa and tucked her in, trying without success to overlook her inadvertent touch against Sitra's curves.

"I was in the crowd that day," Libby whispered. Her fingers brushed a strand of hair off Sitra's cheek. "I watched you fly."

She stood up. "Sweet dreams, Alexa."

Part 2:
Supersonic Dreams

Chapter 25

Roble felt a tap on his shoulder and withdrew the whirling drill bit from an alloy sheet. He turned and watched Sergeant Perry striding away with a finger in the air. The finger pointed forward in the direction he walked.

"Amazing. You've done it again, doofus," Airman Wynn said, sitting across the workbench from Roble. "I told you, you aren't supposed to be in here."

Roble set down the drill and protective lenses, shrugged, and walked from the maintenance shed.

Perry waited behind his makeshift desk at the back of a hangar, his mouth open, a finger cocked back ready to flick his own cheek.

Glancing at the schedule on the wall, Roble said, "I guess I'm still supposed to be in hangar three, inspecting—"

Bop. Perry released the finger against his cheek. "You're being taken off Japanese cross-training duty."

Roble blinked.

"And you will not go back to Naha Air Base." His finger straightened, pointing in the direction of the Kadena runways. "That's a direct order from Major Sircor."

"Sircor," he whispered, rubbing his nose. "But—"

Another *bop* from Perry's cheek cut him off. "Understand me, Santos?"

No. All Roble could think was—*no.*

"Dismissed," Perry said.

Roble staggered away, clasping his hat in his hands. *But...he said he wanted to fly it. It was set up for tomorrow.*

The sun blinded him as he exited the hangar, making him stop and realize he didn't know where he was going. He glanced at the maintenance shed where he left the drill, then at hangar three where he was scheduled to be.

No... He snapped his body around and jogged to the

administrative buildings, the smell of island vegetation somehow making him nauseous.

He entered a single story structure, skirted a row of cubicles, and barged into Sircor's office. "Permission to speak, sir," he said, expending the last of the air in his lungs. He raised a hand in salute, holding his cap under an arm.

Major Sircor just stared at the tablet screen on his desk.

Someone approached from behind and breathed on Roble's neck. "He just slipped past me, Major. Want me to call the MPs?" a woman asked.

Sircor lifted his eyes to Roble.

The woman waited a moment and then closed the door, leaving them alone.

Sircor rose, knuckles planted on the desk, his face chiseled like ice. "There is zero tolerance in my squadron for disobeying rules. Do you know why that is, Santos?"

Something in Sircor's eyes looked very dangerous yet delicate, like the metallic glean of a hairpin trigger, as if a dropped feather could unleash it. Roble remained still, not lowering salute.

"We have adversaries at our doorstep." Sircor pointed at the window. "The North Koreans could launch missiles on Tokyo at any moment. The Chinese could send stealth fighters across this very strip of beach." He made a fist. "Do you have any idea what keeps them at bay, Airman?"

"Yes, sir."

Sircor slammed the desk with his fist. "You have no fucking clue!"

Roble lowered his salute.

"Those fighter jets do not belong to you," he jabbed his finger at Roble. "They are owned by taxpayers."

"I've paid some taxes," Roble said, his voice soft. "How much tax did the Air Force pay to be able to use them?"

The arteries on Sircor's neck flared. "Are you insane, Santos? Some kind of logical extremist?"

"Are those the same thing?"

Sircor's mouth fell open. "I'll give you this…" His face pulled into a sick grin. "You know how to go out with a bang."

Roble spread his boots, chest out, shoulders back, eyes at attention. "Sir, I know what keeps your adversaries at bay."

Sircor folded his arms, muscles flexing under his uniform.

Roble pointed at a picture of Sircor standing with a group of *Thunderbird* pilots. "Your piloting ability is real." He pointed at a model jet on the desk. "Your fighter jets and maintenance performance are real. That," he gestured out the window, "*Skeleton Eagle* sitting at Naha—is real. Those realities keep them at bay, sir."

Placing his cap on his head, Roble spun around. "I'm going back to work, so your jets will perform with excellence." He opened the door. "Kick me out if you must."

The next day Roble knelt below the *Skeleton Eagle* at Naha inspecting its landing gear.

Takinato jumped down from the flight ladder and walked past Roble mumbling, "*Uwa*," under his breath. "I'll handle this."

Roble stood and turned as Major Sircor entered the main hangar door. "No," Roble ran up to Takinato, "he's here for me. There's nothing you can do."

Takinato stared at Roble, his typically hard eyes now soft.

Ignoring Roble, Sircor saluted Takinato. "Afternoon, Major."

Takinato saluted back. "Major."

"I think we had an appointment." Sircor gazed at the *Skeleton Eagle*. "Permission to take her up?"

Takinato bowed. "Granted."

Sircor, holding a red helmet against his wrinkled grey flight suit, ducked under the nosecone. His gloved hand traced the fuselage as he rounded the fighter, inspecting it. As a fingertip slid across the flying arrow decal, his eyes darted to Roble.

Roble looked away and began walking to the exit.

Sircor climbed the flight ladder, taking the pilot's seat. "Where the hell do you think you're going, Airman?" he called from the cockpit.

Roble stopped.

"Get in," Sircor ordered.

The fighter jet taxied from the hangar, its tailfin's emblem gleaming in the sunlight like a war banner. It rounded a turn and aimed toward the East China Sea. The exhausts bellowed streaks of searing white, their growl shaking Roble's body.

"Ivanhoe, you are cleared for unrestricted climb," a speaker in their helmets said.

The *Skeleton Eagle* catapulted forward, depressing them into their seats.

"Holy shit," Sircor mumbled.

The F-15DJ roared off the ground, landing gear retracting, nose pulling up, exhausts scorching the departing tarmac.

They grunted, contracting their core muscles to maintain consciousness on the rapid ascent. Ripping above the clouds, Sircor cut the throttles and the jet stalled weightlessly. The nosecone tipped down into a horizontal plane. He punched the throttles, shooting them northward, accelerating until sound-waves tore mercilessly around them, crackling thunder upon the sea.

"This is unreal," Sircor said.

"You haven't even tried anything yet."

The fighter jet slowed. "Show me." Sircor released the stick.

Roble jammed the thrust vectors down, sending the fighter flipping nose over tail. When the *Skelton Eagle* finished its rotation, he ignited the afterburners, launching the jet through the sky. It twirled, boring a hole on a path out of the atmosphere.

"Son of a bitch," Sircor said.

Roble grinned, inverted the jet, and dove. The ocean below blurred as gravity pulled at his blood vessels, bulging his eyes like they might explode. He inhaled, holding his breath.

In the seemingly endless drop, the cockpit fell silent. He noted the Machmeter pegged at its max, unable to reveal how much past Mach 2.7 they pushed.

Near the bottom of the loop, blood drained from his head as though vacuumed into his legs. He contracted his core muscles, squeezing the blood back to his head, and then released his breath. Pulling the fighter up into the top of a completed loop, he leveled it out.

"You always fly like this?" Sircor asked. "Like it's your last day on earth?"

"Don't you?"

Sircor grabbed and pressed the stick hard right and forward, taking the jet into a steep spiraling dive.

Roble reached for his chest grasping for something, then placed his hands along the cockpit. "Have you ever," he groaned against the G-forces, "landed from the south onto Nellis Air Force Base? The Western runway?"

"Why?" Sircor rolled into a split S maneuver, flipping them upside down on the descent, and leveling out in the opposite direction.

"I just…" Roble sucked in a breath to equalize the pressure inside his body. "…wanted to thank you if you had."

Sircor tipped a wing down, accelerated, and turned sharp into a low yo-yo maneuver as if tracking a bandit. "I've flown that approach. Why?"

"I grew up watching that runway. I lived under the flight path."

"I flew over a kid standing on the gas station roof there a few times." Sircor maneuvered the fighter jet into tail alignment with the imaginary bandit. "That's an odd coincidence. Isn't it?"

"Yes, sir. Thank you, sir."

Sircor sent the modified F-15DJ into a barrel roll and opened up the cannons, sending yellow streaks across the sky.

"I'm glad you decided to come today, sir," Roble said.

Sircor toggled off the targeting controls.

Roble looked north at the distant dullness of land. "From what you said yesterday, I'm curious to know why North Korea is your adversary."

"Are you shitting me, Airman?"

"Not purposely."

"They don't believe in freedom," Sircor said. "Everyone knows that."

"What do they believe in?" Roble placed a hand on the canopy, studying the outline of his fingers against the sky.

"I dunno. Some call it forced brotherly love."

Roble removed his hand, leaving him staring at the distant outline of land. "Maybe I'll go there some day and see what that looks like."

"You're nuts, Santos."

The fuel gauge blinked *red*.

"Time flies when you're having afterburner," Roble said under his breath.

The *Skeleton Eagle* glided back to Naha.

Taxiing back on the ground, Sircor said, "You should go to college and apply to be a pilot. The Air Force needs more good pilots."

"Think college could teach me something?"

Sircor hesitated. "Enlisted airmen have no path to fighter pilot."

"Huh."

Sircor sighed.

The F-15DJ rolled into the hangar. Roble flipped switches, shutting down the fighter jet's systems.

Sircor descended from the cockpit and inspected the thrust vectoring fins. Roble followed behind. Takinato stayed back at a distance.

"How in the hell did you learn to do these modifications?" Sircor asked.

"I'm just human I guess."

"Most people say that derogatorily."

"Why's that?"

Sircor studied him, then the vectoring fins without answer.

"Someone taught me how to do most of it," Roble said.

"Major Takinato?"

"Also, yes."

"Who then?"

"A saint."

"Saint? I thought we were talking fighter jets. You religious, Airman?" Sircor held his helmet under one arm, waiting.

"I guess you could call me that. From my experience, it takes purity of thought to create something like this. The more complex the creation, the higher the level of morality needed. Like I said," Roble grazed a still-hot vector fin, "…a saint."

Sircor reached out and brushed his gloved fingertips across the same fin. "I'd love to debate that with you, but it would be like arguing with my ten-year-old daughter."

"Honored, I'm sure."

Sircor rolled his eyes. "Look, I'm impressed with what you've done here. I want to keep you in my squadron, I really do, so don't make it impossible for me. I'll let you keep your Naha cross-training duties, just do your *stuff*," he slapped the *Skeleton Eagle*, "over here with the Japanese. I want you to follow the rules at Kadena. Am I clear?"

Roble said nothing.

"I'll see you back on base, Airman." Sircor saluted Takinato and walked away.

What's this made of? Cardboard? Roble rarely donned his military dress uniform. The blue fabric itched. He pinned the silver double-striped insignia to his collar, denoting airman first class, and shrugged at the fact he had advanced slower than all his peers.

The bleachers at the Kadena Air Base auditorium filled to the rafters with the 18th Wing personnel, forming a cascading ocean glittering with brass, silver, and gold.

Major General Wissmark, grey-haired, gaunt, and stern-faced, took the podium. "In 1953, Howard Hughes inaugurated an award to commemorate the top fighter squadron in the world. The name of the award has changed, but its meaning is still the same. It comes from the innovators and creators of the firepower we use to protect our nation. To present the Defense Contractors United Annual Award, I'd like to introduce the president of DCU, Mr. Frederick Compros."

Applause greeted a squat man in a pinstriped suit as he took the microphone. His receding hairline made his cheeks and neck look too wide for his narrowly spaced eyes. "Ladies and gentlemen, this award showcases the selfless men and women who use our fighter jets to keep the peace. Our aircraft represent over five decades of developmental commitment from us, a selfless commitment."

He grinned. "My grandfather used to say our mission was to make the weapons that would win the next war, but," he raised a finger, "what he would say today is our profits should be donated to the underprivileged—for helping others *is* the next war. Let it never be said DCU doesn't care about its fellow man. That is the type of inspiration embodied in this award." He lifted the trophy.

Polite applause trickled down the bleachers.

"The DCU Annual Award this year goes to...the 67th Fighter Squadron, under the command of Major Gavin Sircor." Raucous cheers erupted. "Major Sircor?" He waved for Sircor to approach.

Sircor took the award, then the podium. He stood, shoulders squared, eyes alert. The crowd fell silent except for a single prolonged whistle from the top row.

"My fighter squadron," he began, "along with our ground and

maintenance personnel, accept this honor based on its history of recognizing duty and excellence. These men and women demonstrated the highest level of human performance. As long as we are provided with superior fighter aircraft, our country will remain free. If DCU aircraft are the best our country has to offer, we'll use them to their utmost capabilities. You deserve this night, 67th."

Roble stared at Sircor, pondering only one phrase—*superior fighter aircraft.*

The next day, Sircor entered General Wissmark's office.

"Excellent job on winning the DCU Annual Award, Major," General Wissmark said, holding a smoking pipe. "You were up against the top aces in the world."

"Thank you, sir."

"But goddammit. 'If DCU aircraft are the best our country has to offer?'" He smacked the pipe against the desk. "Keep your veiled commentary about the DCU's equipment performance to yourself next time."

"Yes, sir." Sircor flexed his jaw to hide his wince.

"I'm handing command of the 67th over to Captain Barnes. Do you have a problem with that, Major?"

Sircor contracted his core muscles as he would in a gravity pull maneuver, attempting to keep his mind straight. "Captain Barnes is the best pilot I have—had under me," he said. "I'm losing my command, sir?"

Wissmark brushed the spilled tobacco off his desk. "The Secretary of Defense is concerned with the evolving threats along the Pacific Rim. China and Russia are becoming more belligerent with island territorial disputes, and North Korea is threatening to test more long-range missiles over Japan's mainland. Therefore," he picked up a black folder, "the 302nd Fighter Squadron from Elmendorf, Alaska, is being redeployed to Kadena in two weeks."

Sircor swallowed, knowing his former F-22 Raptor squadron was the tip of the US military spear. He forced himself to stay calm. The general tossed the file to the desk and lifted a palm-sized blue box. Sircor eyed it, but his vision blurred.

"Congratulations, *Lieutenant Colonel* Sircor." Wissmark opened the box, revealing silver maple leaves. "I'm giving you command of the 302nd. Don't let me down." He placed the box in front of Sircor.

"Thank you, General." He saluted.

"That is all."

Roble stopped in front of the tool chest Sergeant Perry used as a desk to check the work schedule.

"Let's see, I'm supposed to be in...but I already—" He choked on his own spit seeing the bulletin pinned next to the whiteboard. He ripped it off the wall, holding it in both hands.

"What do you think you're doing?" Sergeant Perry leaned over his desk. "Put that back."

Roble read the bulletin several times. It announced the redeployment of the 302nd Raptor squadron maintenance crew to Kadena. And more importantly, their crew leader, Sergeant Nguyen, would take applications to fill a vacancy.

Roble looked up. "They're coming *here*?"

Sergeant Perry reclined in his chair, made a stiff oval with his lips, raised a hand to his cheek and flicked. *Bop.*

"Sir. I'd like to transfer to the 302nd." He stumbled on his words.

"You don't have enough experience to work on F-22s, Santos." Perry wiggled the now straight finger back and forth. "Not enough experience at all." He jabbed it at the whiteboard. "Pin that back up and go...go be where you're supposed to be."

"I've read every F-22 manual available since basic. I can do it, Sergeant."

"I am telling you," Perry pointed at the bulletin, "you *don't* have the qualifications."

Roble studied the bulletin again, and said, "I'll just interview with Sergeant Nguyen...and if he doesn't think I'm qualified—"

"I just spoke with Captain Barnes and we both agree; the 67th maintenance crew can't spare anyone."

"Just let me apply."

Perry shook his head and picked up the phone. "Get me Captain Barnes," he said into the receiver. "Hello, Captain. Our best mechanic is pleading to transfer to the 302nd. What are my orders?" Perry held a finger cocked near a cheek, waiting.

He silently flicked his own cheek while eyeing Roble. "That's what I thought, sir. Just wanted to keep you in the loop." He dropped the phone. "Just as I said, we can't spare anyone."

"'Your best mechanic?' I thought I wasn't qualified to apply?"

Bop. "Dismissed."

Sitting on a folding chair under an open-walled hangar, Roble stared at the sleek F-22 Raptors lined up in majestic rows before him. They looked as if in flight, slicing through liquefied air which poured over their titanium skin.

Beyond the studying mechanics waiting to be interviewed, Sergeant Nguyen stood next to an F-22, grilling a candidate. The candidate saluted Nguyen and strutted toward Roble. It was Airman Wynn.

"I got this in the bag, doofus." Wynn grinned. "I won't miss you at all, not one asshole bit."

"At least you were brave enough to go around Sergeant Perry to apply."

"Go around?" He laughed. "Perry begged me to apply. Said I'm eminently qualified." He saluted, ending his motion with a chop to Roble's forehead.

"Next," Sergeant Nguyen yelled, looking at a clipboard. "Santos, you're up."

Roble rose and moved next to Nguyen below the F-22's tailfins. Nguyen's eyes only came up to Roble's shoulders, and he appeared even shorter below the domineering jet. The sergeant's uniform was so wrinkle-free and clean he could've doubled as a collectible action figure.

Nguyen held out a hand without looking at Roble. "Give me your recommendation."

"Uhmm…" Roble itched at his nose. "Sergeant Perry still has it."

"First question," Nguyen said without pause, arm swiveling to indicate a spot on the Raptor. "How often do you replace the ten polyurethane O-rings in the fuel system?"

"I prefer to use carbon nanotube polytetrafluoroethylene O-rings," Roble said, stepping closer. "They can withstand at least twice the abrasion and more than a hundred degrees higher temperature. For only two dollars more per unit I think it makes a lot of sense, considering the cost of a failed O-ring."

"If you can't answer the question properly," Nguyen lifted his chin and eyed Roble, "get the hell out of my face."

"The manual says to change them every five hundred flight hours or every six months, whichever comes first." Roble swallowed. "But using only thermoplastic polyurethane, I'd change them sooner."

"If I wanted your opinion, I'd pull it out your ass. Next candidate." He looked back at the row of seated airmen.

"Oh," Roble said, "and there are not ten O-rings in the fuel system, there are twelve. Open up this panel." He pointed at the Raptor's fuselage. "And the one on the other side and I'll show you, or turn to page one hundred and forty in the service manual."

Nguyen jerked the manual open and flipped through it, frowning. "That's what I heard about you...a pain in the ass and hopelessly insubordinate."

Roble rubbed his nose.

"Airman Stark, you're up," Nguyen waved Roble away. "And stay the hell away from my jets," he barked after Roble.

Lieutenant Colonel Sircor descended the cockpit ladder, glad to have taken an F-22 into the sky again.

"Sergeant Nguyen," he said, walking over to his new maintenance chief. "Do you have a full crew yet?"

"I just selected a replacement mechanic today, sir." He saluted properly. "Airman Wynn will be joining us tomorrow."

"Airman Wynn, from the 67th?"

"Yes, sir."

Sircor bonked his helmet softly against his head. "If you're going to raid from the 67th, why not Airman Santos?"

"Ahhh, because he has a terrible reputation for starters. Wynn follows instructions down the line. A real straight shooter."

"This new mechanic needs to understand excellence, as well as duty, if he's going to work on my Raptors. Consider Santos."

Nguyen cringed and brushed a speck of lint off his sleeve.

"With all due respect, Wynn is the best choice for this particular assignment, sir. I've already approved it with Captain Barnes."

Sircor glanced at the F-22 Raptor. "Santos is your new mechanic." He saluted Nguyen. "Carry on."

Sergeant Nguyen returned salute, his face pulled tight.

During the first month of Roble's new assignment on the F-22s, he stayed after-hours dismantling and reassembling the jet to familiarize himself with each part, to understand how each one integrated into the whole.

Many nights he awoke in a sweat bothered by even minor issues such as a single strand of hydraulic tubing that seemed inefficient in its placement. He thought of ways to modify, improve, or eliminate parts and reorganize their assemblies. Before going to bed every night, he made detailed drawings of his ideas.

Chapter 26

rack, crack, crack. Libby thumped a hammer against a hot ingot at an even tempo.

Sitra hummed to the hammer's beat as she rolled in handsprings across a gymnastics mat beyond Libby's view. Libby lifted her chin, hair sticking to her face, and smiled at Sitra's music.

"Again! Higher! More spring! Back straight!" a distant woman's voice said with a Russian accent.

Libby set down the hammer and placed the smashed metal in a torsion machine. The glowing alloy twisted and stretched like taffy, revealing streaks of imbedded blue, grey, and silver. Once it stretched thin enough and cooled, she inserted it under an electron microscope.

She scrolled through a series of screens on a laptop, studying the alloy's atomic structure, hoping it would demonstrate improved strength over her prior fuselage material.

Amanda walked into the manufacturing shed and tossed a pile of mail next to Libby's microscope. "From the office, Ms. Dodge," she said before leaving.

Libby glanced at the mail without interest and returned to her analysis.

Snapping her head back around, she grabbed the large packet atop the pile, weighed it in her hands, and ran from the shed to her house, not bothering to close the front door.

Standing near the dining room window, she tore it open, dumping its contents onto the table. Her lips released a silent whistle as she shuffled through the drawings.

The largest diagram resembled a fighter jet she knew well. Yet this illustration wasn't of the aircraft DCU had assigned her to upgrade before they canceled the improvement project. This drawing depicted something far nobler and more beautiful. *This is how it* should *have been made.*

Shadows from cottonwood leaves rustled across the dining room. She dropped the diagram to the table and picked up the handwritten letter. "Uh-huh," she mumbled, pushing a hand through her hair. "Yep." She squinted. "Wow…that's…that's genius."

"All right Roble," she turned to the window framing the neatly cut lawn, "I hope you have a clean pair of underwear standing by."

Libby jogged back to the shed and chuckled as Sitra's bare feet flashed by in the air above the domed forge.

Reaching her workstation, she noticed the electron microscope still scanning the alloy. Leaning over the laptop screen, she coughed. *Whoa.* She whipped out a phone, and pressed a knight icon.

"*Allô?*"

"Victor, how's our body armor production line going?"

"Most spectac—"

"Sounds great," she cut him off. "Listen; put somebody else in charge of it for a few months."

"*Madame,* we just—"

"I know, Victor." She cut him off again. "I need you here for a special project. I need your robots reprogrammed, and more importantly, I need your mind. This will be a tricky one."

"The armor—"

"You can develop armor over here in your spare time."

"What are—"

"Modifying an F-22 Raptor."

"Indeed?"

"Indeed-a-roo. You have to see the plans." She looked again at the laptop screen. "And this alloy."

"I apologize, *Madame,* for asking this, but does Libby Industries have the resources at present?"

"Don't apologize. I'm using my personal savings. If we do this right, the Air Force will demand to have this jet. We could sell dozens of them."

"*Madame,* might I just say, if the same thing happens as with the F-15 modifications and they confiscate your remaining equipment over here, all your business lines will shut down, including body armor. You would be bankrupt."

"Victor, you scared?" Libby grinned, knowing he held no fear in his eyes. "I mean if you're worried—"

"When shall you require my services?"

"There's no rush but if you can be here within an hour that would be—"

"I've already departed, my lady."

Roble stood in Takinato's garage staring at a crate with a crowbar sitting on top. A long chain hung down from an overhead loft, swaying. Takinato drew on a cigarette, waiting.

Roble lunged forward, pried off the crate's top, and extracted the enclosed laptop. Sitting on the floor with legs crossed, he powered it up, impatiently tapping his fingertips. Takinato leaned over the crate, digging around the parts inside.

Three-dimensional F-22 modification plans rolled across the screen in front of Roble. "Oh... You didn't..." He rubbed his chin, grinning. "So *that's* the type of engine I saw on the *Sovereign*. I can't wait to meet you some day, you crazy son of a...daughter of a... I can't wait to meet you."

"How are you going to get these parts into Kadena?" Takinato crushed the cigarette under a boot.

Roble continued scanning the plans.

"You are going to need a car...and somebody who knows what they are doing to help you over there."

"Really?" Roble chuckled.

Takinato knelt by him. "There are airmen and some pilots, the best pilots by the way, at Naha who ask why you do not come around as often. They have a nickname for you."

"Oh, great." Roble rubbed his nose. "Maybe in Japanese it won't sound so harsh."

"*Kaze u~ōkā*," Takinato said. "General Yamatomo ordered the F-15 modifications from Libby Industries but the order failed. He knows you are the one who made the *Skeleton Eagle* happen. He gave you that name. *One who walks on wind.*"

Roble bowed and touched his chest.

"Do not get mushy." Takinato stood up. "Let us get to work."

Roble spliced wires inside an F-22's open panel, rerouting them against an interior spar. He itched his nose with his shoulder. *What's that smell?*

"What in the flying fuck are you doing, Santos? Sergeant Nguyen said, standing behind him in the auxiliary hangar. "To *my* jet, in *this* hangar, and," he glanced at his watch, "at *this* time of night?"

Without flinching or turning, Roble said, "I thought of a way to shorten the navigation and fire control wiring by about six inches and secure them with softer yet stronger fasteners."

"You what?"

"You see," Roble pulled out some cut wires, "since over the life of this Raptor a couple million vital signals will go through these lines, these six inches translate into over two hundred miles of excess length. Even at light speed that's fractions of a second of lost communication speed. And as you know, in the wrong situation that just might make the difference between success and catastrophe. Plus, the old fasteners had a higher chance of fraying the wires over time."

"Modifying the Raptor is *not* your job!"

Reconnecting the now shorter wires, Roble said, "It is my job to put this Raptor in top condition and that's what I'm doing."

"I don't care if you have political pull with the Lieutenant Colonel." Nguyen ripped Roble's hand away from the Raptor. "This behavior is way the hell out of line."

Roble rubbed his nose, grimacing. "Is that your cologne?"

"To your barracks, *now*, Airman," Nguyen ordered.

"Yes, Sergeant. Sircor will expect it to be ready by morning." Roble marched away.

The next morning, Nguyen waited for Sircor to return from a training mission.

As Sircor dismounted the fighter jet, Nguyen cut him off. "Sir, I need to discuss Airman Santos."

Sircor stood with his chest close to Nguyen's eyes, peering down. "Go on."

"He's implementing unauthorized maintenance on your F-22." Nguyen squirmed and straightened his sleeves. "This is what I was afraid of. I recommend an immediate discharge, sir."

"What's your opinion on the quality of his work?"

"It is not allowed; *that's* my opinion," Nguyen said, inadvertently misting spit across Sircor's flight suit. "I'll report this up the chain of command if you don't have him stopped, Colonel." He almost wiped Sircor's flight suit clean before gripping his hands into fists. "My ass is on the line."

Taking a breath, Sircor said, "I understand that you are following procedures, which is your duty. I also expect excellence, Sergeant. The mind, not the F-22, is the most powerful weapon our military possesses. Sometimes finding a balance between the two ideals is tough, but that's what I expect."

"Sir, but—"

"One more thing." Sircor lowered his face close to Nguyen's until his steely eyes pierced Nguyen's soul. "If you ever threaten to go over my head again…"

Nguyen gulped. "Sir, yes, sir."

Later that day Sircor sat in his office cleaning his flight helmet, waiting.

Roble entered, slouched into a wood chair, and glanced up.

Sircor leaned over his helmet. "Do I have to hold this meeting every time you join a new crew?"

"Apparently."

"In this case, I agree with Sergeant Nguyen. This isn't a case of being antisocial. This isn't even about improving older fighter aircraft. This is about messing with the best fighter jet in the world. You've no need to screw with it."

"Second best."

"What?"

"The F-22 is the second best fighter jet." It wasn't said as a challenge, but as one would deliver a boring fact.

"Oh really. Enlighten me, Santos, as to this mystery jet you refer to."

Roble straightened in his chair. "The Libby IV, also known as the *Sovereign,* is superior in every way."

"That's a playboy business jet." Sircor shook his head.

"Have you seen one?"

"It's not even FAA approved, if I remember right. Of course

I haven't seen one; nobody has. It's the most expensive flop in aviation history."

Roble scratched his arm, yawning.

"Not going to offer a defense for this supposed greatest fighter in the world?"

"You said you haven't seen one."

"You're wasting my time, Santos."

"I've seen it, Colonel." Roble stood. "If someone were to weaponize it, it would spank the F-22 like a crying baby."

Sircor chuckled. Roble remained sober.

"But…" Sircor picked up the F-22 desk model, "if that were the case, I'd know about it. Everyone would."

"I'd like to make the F-22 the best fighter aircraft in the world once again. Your life depends on flying the best. I have the people and the parts to make it so. All you have to do is not stop me."

Sircor stared incredulously. *Duty* and *excellence*. He had just lectured Sergeant Nguyen that he needed to balance the two, but what was his own answer? He had obtained his dream command. Would he really put it at risk for this young mechanic's impertinent ideas?

He studied the pictures and awards on the walls, reflecting on his meteoric rise in the Air Force. He glanced at the photos on his desk, one of his wife, Stephie, the other of his four young daughters. They depended on him to give material and spiritual support, but they also depended on him to defend their lives with the best fighter jets. *Duty* or *excellence*?

"Dismissed," Sircor said.

Sircor spent the next day examining Air Force files for information on the *Sovereign*, but found none. Searching the internet, he learned Libby Industries had only built a few and most of those were parked in private hangars in Singapore and Switzerland. The company's website contained several broad comments about the craft, impressive yet vague. "Hmm." He shrugged and wrote down the company's phone number.

That night as he sat at home unable to sleep, he picked up the phone and dialed the number.

"Thank you for calling Libby Industries. This is Courtney. How may I help you?"

"Hi. Uhmm…this is Lieutenant Colonel Gavin Sircor. I'd like to speak with someone about your *Sovereign*."

"Just a moment, sir," she said. "I'll transfer you to Sigmund Evert."

After a minute a dry voice said, "This is the head of aeronautical engineering. How my I assist you?"

"Hello. Well, this isn't an official Air Force call. I'm just hoping you could answer some questions regarding the *Sovereign's* capabilities."

"Its capabilities are not a secret," Evert said. "It's just that not many people care to learn about them since it's illegal to purchase, own, or fly anywhere in the world."

"I don't understand why it's illegal, but I'm listening."

Mr. Evert explained the flight test data and why various government agencies had not approved the jet, never once expressing an opinion or an emotion, only facts. The conversation lasted an hour.

"Thank you very much for your time, Mr. Evert," Sircor said, judging the engineer to be the most straightforward man he had ever spoken with.

"Colonel?"

Sircor waited.

"Thank you for defending our country. There's still much to be protected."

As Roble continued modifications on Sircor's F-22, Sergeant Nguyen detailed the evidence with pictures and testimony from other mechanics. Once he felt he had enough proof, he invited Sergeant Perry out for a drink.

"Santos? Yeah, complete trailer trash. I've no idea how he even got in the Air Force to begin with," Perry said.

"Why didn't you discharge him?"

Bop. Perry's finger flicked his own cheek in thought. "Oh, well, I never said he doesn't know his shit."

"He'll get *me* discharged, if not kill somebody. Will you back me up on his history of insubordination to procedures? I need to take action, and I don't think you'll want to be seen as having approved of his actions once it all goes down."

"Oh, I never said I liked him. It's just…" Perry sipped his beer. "The Colonel protects him, right? What can you do?"

Nguyen leaned in, eyebrows lifting. "I'm going over Sircor's head." He grinned. "And you're going to back me up."

Bop. Beer sprayed from Perry's lips, a foamy bead landing on Nguyen's cheek. "That's just as risky to your career…and mine."

Nguyen wiped his cheek, grimacing. "Pick your poison, Sergeant."

The meeting with the general three days later didn't go as well as Nguyen had hoped.

General Wissmark didn't let them finish their second sentence before yelling, "Follow the goddamn chain of command, Sergeants."

They marched from his office.

"Somebody shoot me," Perry moaned, pointing a finger at his own temple. With his other hand he flicked his cheek. *Bop.*

———

Sircor felt ill at ease walking into General Wissmark's office for the unscheduled meeting. He saluted and stood at attention. *Why does it feel so hot?*

General Wissmark pressed a fingertip to the desk, glaring at Sircor with watery eyes, like distant earths suspended in the dark void of his demeanor. "I'm almost speechless, Colonel. Explain to me why your current and former maintenance sergeants came to me to implicate one of your airmen?" His voice rose to a nasal pitch, "What's going on?"

Like jet fuel thrown into his face, Sircor burned with a dread he had hoped would not come, but somehow knew inevitable. *What's it going to be…duty or excellence?*

Silence thickened the air.

"Speak, Colonel."

"General Wissmark," he began, his heart pounding, "Airman Roble Santos—the man the sergeants referred to—he is, in my opinion, the best mechanic in your 18th Wing. I want to promote him to Technical Sergeant and place him in command of all maintenance of my 302nd Fighter Squadron. Sergeant Nguyen will be transferred. Do you have an issue with my plans, sir?"

General Wissmark reached for his pipe and stroked it. His

mouth cracked open, and like the pronouncement of a death sentence, said, "I support your command. That is all, Colonel."

The next morning, with Nguyen not present, Sircor made the announcement to the shocked 302nd maintenance crew, adding that if anyone disagreed with his decision, now was the time to transfer out of his squadron. No one did.

After Sircor left, Sergeant Roble Santos led his maintenance crew onto a runway.

"Your only job is to put the Raptors in the best possible condition for Lieutenant Colonel Sircor's pilots." He pointed at the tarmac. "Nothing but excellence will ever lift off this airstrip."

Pacing in front of them, he added, "As is my duty, I will never ask any of you to break the rules or procedures, but manuals and procedures are to teach, and are not ends in and of themselves. If you have questions—ask. If you have ideas—tell. Carry on."

Roble grew out his hair until it touched his brows; nobody said a word. His crew soon realized that even as their sergeant, he never spoke of anything but fighter jets, never asked anyone about their families or lovers, and was the most competent man they had ever worked for.

Without further interference, Roble accelerated the modifications on Sircor's F-22, working in deliberate phases, keeping the fighter in service with careful planning and an after-hours work schedule.

Takinato shuttled the arriving parts from his Naha garage into Kadena in the trunk of his car. He was Roble's only help with the modifications at first, but as time went on, more and more of Roble's maintenance crew volunteered in their spare time. Even Airman Kozumi from Naha Air Base came over during nights after cross-training duty.

The modifications had progressed for three months when Sircor entered the auxiliary hangar late one evening. Everyone except Roble slunk out the exits, knowing the Lieutenant Colonel had never barged in on their unauthorized work before.

Sircor stopped near the F-22, watching Roble sit on a wing tightening something inside.

Roble continued until finished, climbed down, picked up a

screwdriver sitting next to Sircor, and without a word, returned to the installation.

Sircor rolled his eyes. "Will it be flight-ready tomorrow?"

"Like always," Roble said, his voice muffled from inside the wing.

"I think you're missing one important aspect of this project."

Roble sat up and climbed down the ladder, screwdriver in hand. "What?"

"Flying an F-22," Sircor said, "is *not* like flying an F-15."

Roble furrowed his brows.

"Tomorrow morning," Sircor continued, "I want you in the Raptor flight simulator. You'll go through the series at your leisure so as not to interfere with your maintenance duties."

"Sir?"

"How can you make this the best fighter in the world if you don't know exactly how it flies?"

Chapter 27

Moonlight glowed against the wrinkled drawing in Danny's hands. *It's like a bonsai tree murder scene.* Exhaling, he knocked on Roble's barracks door.

Roble answered in a t-shirt and boxers with a grease smudge on his forehead and his hair disheveled. He yawned. "What time is it?"

Smoothing out the parchment on his uniformed chest, Danny asked, "Remember that bonsai drawing you wanted a while ago?"

"Whoa," Roble squinted. "What happened to it?" He motioned for Danny to come in.

Turning the drawing over, Danny revealed the *F*. "I never received lower than a *B* on anything in high school. I'm giving up on art." He handed the red-drenched sheet to Roble. "Keep it."

"Giving up?" Roble looked at the drawing. "Don't you want to know what she wrote?"

Danny winced and sat down.

Roble sat next to him, pulled out his Japanese translation books and wrote on a notepad. "Well, no remarks about light this time. But there are a lot regarding the bonsai tree's…soul."

"What?" Danny grimaced. "Soul?"

"Here, I'll let you read her comments. Sorry if the translation is choppy." Roble handed the drawing and notes to him. "You haven't been back to your class since you drew this?"

He shook his head and read Roble's notes. The comments referred to specific details of his drawing and how they revealed the tree's soul, as if the drawing were alive—a single living frame showing the viewer what this tree meant. Nishiko explained how Danny's drawing displayed a story and a soul that didn't correspond with each other, like a contradiction.

Story and soul? Contradiction? He gripped his hair. *It's just a tree. I can't do this.*

Danny tossed his drawing to Roble and walked to the front door. "Maybe I'll see you around."

Weeks later, Danny received a bill in the mail from the Yuki Manga Shop. He owed five hundred dollars for his final lesson and it was overdue. In handwritten English at the bottom it read: *If not paid within ten days, your superior officer will be notified.*

Damn...my superior officer? And five hundred dollars for one lesson? And a shitty lesson at that. Why did I ever go to that art class in the first place?

Walking into the Yuki Manga Shop on his next day off, Danny pulled out a painful wad of one-hundred-dollar bills. The cashier pointed at the backroom door without taking the money.

Not wanting to see Nishiko again, Danny tossed the money on the counter and turned to leave. He stopped when he heard the art studio door open.

Glancing back, he saw Nishiko approaching, a pink pigtail bobbing on the unshaved side of her head. She swiped the cash off the counter, stuffed it in her pocket, and headed to the shop exit.

He waited for her to leave, but she remained at the door staring at him. Shuffling to the exit, he said, "Look I know you never invited me to attend your class and I suck at art, but—"

"Shhhht," Nishiko hissed. She waved for him to follow and walked down the street.

Danny followed, eventually turning into a narrow alley. *What is this? The Yakuza going to kill me for drawing like shit?*

Nishiko stopped in front of a teakwood doorway below a painting of a Japanese water goddess who stood waist deep in the ocean with one fist raised and one palm lowered. A sea dragon swam around her and a dragon circled above her head. Three white stars lined the top of the painting.

"Did you paint that?" Danny noted the painting's quality, which exceeded anything he'd seen in art history books.

"*Hai.*"

"It's amazing." Danny stared at it, mouth open. "What is this place?"

"Come," Nishiko said, entering.

Danny blinked. "What the heck?" He walked after her. "You speak English?"

The door opened into an incense-filled karate dojo. Men and women in karate uniforms sat in a circle watching two combatants in the center trading blows.

Nishiko bowed.

A man in the center stopped fighting, raised a fist, and bowed to Nishiko before resuming his fight.

"This," Nishiko whispered to Danny, "is Isshin-Ryu. To be gentle like a mother, yet fierce in protecting all one values. Watch Sensei Kei." She pointed at the man who bowed. "Observe his motions, their purpose and their result."

"Why have you never spoken in English to me before?" Danny asked "And I thought you hated me."

"Watch how light reflects differently off human motion than anything else."

"You gave me an *F*. The harder I tried the worse my grades became."

"Just as light reflecting off a man in motion divulges his purpose, the way you draw light reflecting off an art character exposes his deepest premises."

Danny stared at Sensei Kei as he took down the other man. The fluidity of his movements revealed the certainty of control, yet as he pulled the other man back to his feet, an unmistakable respect for life.

"In order for you to capture a character's motions," Nishiko said, "you must first understand why he acts, how he exalts himself in life. But before you can see the inside of one of your manga characters, you must first understand what is in here." She touched Danny's chest.

He looked down at the calming hand on his heart.

"I do not grade my students against one another," Nishiko said. "That is done by those who live secondhand and have no self-respect. I grade art based on what I view as *your* potential."

"So the more you saw my art, the worse I got?"

"The greater I appraised your potential."

"My potential?"

She removed her hand from his heart. "One heart way."

"What?"

"In the Isshin-Ryu, just as in art, actions must be done

wholeheartedly. And all things great begin with *one* person. One heart way."

Danny bowed his head, thinking back over everything he'd drawn in class. "Why did you never write your comments in English?"

"You wish to master manga?"

Danny nodded. "I see."

"If you stop worrying about what everyone else thinks, you *might* see." Nishiko pointed at the Isshin-Ryu warriors. "This is where you will learn to draw manga."

Wow. What? Danny stared at the men and women warriors, watching light reflecting off their cotton uniforms as they moved. *I have so much to learn.* He swallowed. *I will learn it.* "One heart way," he whispered.

As his weeks of drawing in the dojo progressed, Danny filled his barracks' walls with completed artboards.

Each time he felt he'd drawn something especially well, he took it to Roble late at night. Roble never commented on the art, no matter how much Danny asked. But every once in a while, Roble studied one a bit longer and asked, "Can I have this?" Danny never gave those drawings to him, because those were the ones he hung on his own walls.

Once, Danny considered showing his father how professional his art had become, but decided against it, fearing his father would try to control the only thing he kept for himself.

His father continued sending advice on how to advance through the ranks and take on visible leadership roles. And since Danny didn't get promoted to maintenance sergeant of the entire squadron as he'd hoped, he agreed to his father's wish and transferred out of aircraft maintenance and into a combat unit at Futenma. *As long as I keep my art and Roble stays in Okinawa, I can do what Father wants.*

Staring at the art pinned to his walls, his thoughts drifted. *These are good times, so much like the year Roble lived with me in Vegas.* And as he did almost a decade ago, Danny thought of Jenny constantly, wanting to be with her. *If I could just see her looking at my art, like she used to, let her see how far I've come…*

He picked up his phone and scanned the contact list for

her number. *One touch and I'll hear her voice.* His fingertip hovered above the screen. *Things are going so well with Father.* He stared at her number until the screen faded into black. *I'll call her another time.*

The two Libby-Dodge-designed dual mode turbine/ramjets—the final stage in the F-22 modification—sat in emergent pieces at the far end of the auxiliary hangar. Volunteers swarmed over them every night. And always the last one to leave, Roble double-checked them for quality.

In celebration of the nearly complete Raptor modifications, Takinato invited the assisting mechanics to a victory party at his favorite downtown Naha bar. The place sat squeezed onto the second floor of what looked like a ramshackle pirate hideout. Its bartender, with long dreadlocked hair, actually looked like a pirate. The mechanics barely fit in the space, their shoulders almost touching.

Instead of the laser-focused mechanic, Roble conversed and laughed playfully. He even told stories about his upbringing in Las Vegas between rounds of rice beer. When the bartender slapped a vintage Singaporean pirate hat on Roble's head, he recounted the time at the age of sixteen when the owner of a single prop airplane at the North Las Vegas Airport let him take the plane for a test flight.

"I'd spent a week souping up his engine by over a hundred horsepower," Roble said, "and just wanted to see what it could do. I'll admit, I didn't really expect to be escorted back to the runway by shark-nosed F-16s." He rubbed his chin. "Apparently the Air Force monitors their bomb site airspace pretty well." Sipping a beer, he added, "Seeing those fighter jets maneuvering up close was incredible—probably the best day of my life 'til then. But," he tipped the pirate hat, "you should have seen the airplane owner's face. I don't think I mentioned that he was sitting in the co-pilot's chair."

Roble grinned, thinking back. "I wanted to offer him a free tune-up to calm him down, but by the smell in the cabin, I thought it more practical to reupholster his chair."

Beer splashed across the bar as everyone roared with laughter.

Takinato stole the hat and recounted flying his self-made ultra-light aircraft down the narrow streets of Harajuku, looking for cosplay girls. "I was seventeen, and thought I knew everything. I swear the one I picked up looked like a girl. He was crazy beautiful, and had the daintiest hands and sexiest pigtails I had ever seen."

Raucous shouts and beer ricocheted through the confined space.

At the end of the night Roble raised a toast. "I never asked any of you to assist me. I'm honored that you did. Thank you."

Afterwards, Takinato returned Roble to Kadena in his car, its engine shaking the air scoop and Roble's body. He drifted around a few corners along the way, but drove more subdued than usual. Roble never even saw the RPM gauge enter the red.

"I know you're a bit tipsy, but are you feeling all right?" Roble asked as they pulled up outside his barracks.

"I am glad we celebrated," Takinato said in Japanese. "You are one of the few people I have ever met who actually had something to celebrate. But I must warn you, I discharged one of my maintenance crew today. He sold detailed information about the *Skeleton Eagle* modifications to DCU. If DCU is bribing my men, they are probably doing the same to yours. Watch your back."

Roble winced, rubbing his nose.

"I apologize." Takinato lowered his bleach-streaked head. "I should have waited until the morning to tell you. Go home, Roble Santos-san."

As Roble rounded the corner of the barracks, he stopped.

Farther down the sidewalk, Sugemi leaned against his doorframe, her red cowboy boots crossed. His arrowhead necklace sparkled in the porch light atop her black leather jacket. A shadow from a military-style baseball cap hid her eyes.

Approaching her with measured steps, Roble said, "I didn't know you were in Okinawa."

"Takinato called me in Melbourne this morning, said you two had something to celebrate."

"Talk to him often?"

"Well, you're not much of a talker, are you?" She pushed herself off the doorframe.

"What do you want to talk about?"

"Hush." She took his hand, pulling him close.

Her fingers fished through his pockets, taking her time. He inhaled at the persistent contact. Eventually she slipped the keys from his pocket and unlocked the door.

Following him inside, she pushed him to the couch, closing the door with her heel. Roble leaned back, watching. She tossed her cap across the room, shook out her hair, and began stripping off one piece of clothing at a time.

Wearing only boots and thin white panties, she danced, her narrow eyes ravishing him.

When Roble tried to stand, she pressed him back with her boot. Her hips gyrated before him, torturing him. She parted his knees and turned around. Bending over, keeping her legs straight, she touched her ankles.

"Oh...my...G-force," Roble whispered.

"Glad I came to Kadena?" Sugemi teased, brushing down against him.

He reached around her, attempting to pull her onto him. "What's in Melbourne?"

She pushed his hands away as she continued her lap dance. "Business."

"Conquering the whole world or something?" he asked, laying back, abandoning any attempt at control.

"Mmhmm."

Turning around, she straddled his waist and pulled his shirt over his head. She snuggled into his neck as her hips moved, the arrowhead pressing between their sweaty bodies.

When Roble awoke, she was gone. His arrowhead necklace sat on the cluttered coffee table atop a note. He lifted the arrowhead, turning it over in his hand as he read the note.

Make it soar—Sugemi.

Chapter 28

The *Spirit of Man* stretched into the sky like a plume streaming behind a rocket. Then, as if the smoke had crystallized, four sheer white planes stood with unbroken bands of sparkling platinum forming the corners.

The 222nd—and top floor—presented views of the shimmering Lake Mead to the east; of the craters left from atomic bomb testing to the north; of the red, hazy peaks of the Sierra Nevada Mountains to the west; and of the searing lowlands of the Mojave Desert to the south.

Across the street, *The Sin,* with its black ornamented stone façade, looked like discarded costume jewelry compared to the clean-lined monolith five times its height.

Halvern Black, wearing a crisp dress shirt and jeans, limped onto the silver-draped stage, stopping before a podium, eyes focused above the gathered crowd. His architects lined up across the rear of the platform.

The skyscraper's shadow poured like water onto the hot, packed crowd.

"It is done," Halvern said, his voice gruff. "Well ahead of schedule, and under budget."

The audience applauded.

"I see before me many of the government, corporate, and nonprofit groups who erected road blocks, unfurled red tape, and filed lawsuits making this tower impossible to complete as I wished it to be. You owe yourselves a big hand for your efforts."

Uneasy glances boomeranged through the crowd.

"So, how *did I* complete this tower as I wished when you made it impossible?" Halvern pressed a palm against his side, suppressing a wince. "How did I not compromise its integrity by even a single bolt or weld?" He leaned against the podium, coughed, and lifted an arm. "I broke the law, and not just one, but countless laws and regulations that stood in my way."

The crowd murmured. One woman, with a plum-colored dress and a thin neck, screeched, "Somebody should do something!" She looked down when everyone stared at her in horror for saying aloud what they thought.

"This tower behind me now exists. I built it only on my terms." Halvern bared his wrists and held them out. "So now I stand before you waiting to be judged for my actions."

Attendees glanced at the well-groomed politicians and other leaders among them, pleading for help. The politicians and leaders glanced at their watches or their shoes.

Stock Brant stood at the back of the crowd, bloodshot eyes hidden behind sunglasses, scanning in vain for Alexandria. *How could she not be standing with her political friends?* He shook his head. *Where has she been the past eight months…and twenty-four days?*

He wished she could have felt Halvern's words shoved down her obedient throat and wished he could have observed her reproachful stance. Glancing at *The Sin*, at his penthouse, he wished to feel again the sting of her hand across his face, to look into those forbidden eyes, and to touch her skin. He trembled.

His gaze drifted back to Halvern, then up the length of the white tower until a sliver of sun burst out from behind, burning his eyes. *I don't deserve to be here.*

Halvern's voice boomed again, snapping heads back to attention. "This skyscraper is dedicated to those who've created everything good in this world. It stands as proof that mankind can achieve exaltation on earth. Ladies and gentlemen, I present to you—*The Spirit of Man*." He pointed to the sky, then gripped his abdomen and fell to his knees behind the podium.

An awkward silence engulfed the crowd standing under the tallest structure in the world. Two of Halvern's architects lifted him to his feet and helped him off the stage. No politicians stormed the microphone this time. It sat like a sonic barometer judging the crowd, shrieking a high-pitched line of reproach.

A concert band began to play, allowing the audience to emerge safely from their unease.

A young reporter, who covered commercial real estate stories, sat at a computer one floor above the Las Vegas Desert News' sign. She highlighted her news article and hit the delete key.

Frustrated, she walked to the city desk editor. "Do I print Halvern Black is an *alleged* criminal? Or an *admitted* criminal?"

Scratching his head with an envelope opener, the longhaired editor leaned back in his chair. "Has he been charged with a crime?"

"I called the state prosecutor's office and they won't comment during the investigation."

"If we label Mr. Black as a criminal before the election, it will reflect poorly on Moore's gubernatorial bid since Moore has personally taken credit for the economic benefits of *The Spirit of Man*. And we can't print anything damaging to Moore because this paper has endorsed his candidacy. We speak with one voice between these pages." He tapped the desk with the opener. "It's policy."

"So you want me to bury the story?"

"No, not at all. But I mean, how big of a crook could you be just for bolting together a skyscraper?"

"That's just it; there are thousands of rules to make a building like that, coming from dozens of agencies—local, state, and federal. Neither Halvern Black, nor his office, will comment further. The sole owner of the building apparently lives in Asia, and I can't find any contact information. Since Black publicly said he broke many laws, I kinda have to believe him."

"You know, some people are calling Black's speech a last-minute dirty ambush by Moore's political opposition." He pointed the opener at her nose. "Maybe look into that angle."

"You think Black is purposely tanking Moore at the risk of fines or worse? That would be a story, but I can't believe it."

"Look, you're overthinking this. Just fault Black for being prideful because of his own competence. That's the one sin the public won't forgive anyway. And it won't reflect poorly on Moore."

The young reporter opened her mouth to protest, snapped it shut, and strode away.

Halvern walked from *The Spirit of Man*, his footsteps short and unsteady, head covered with a hooded jacket, hands buried in his pockets and pressing against his sides.

He passed throngs of tourists as he entered the parking garage of *The Sin* across the street. Exiting out through a back alley, he turned north and continued toward downtown.

Along the way he rested at bus stops, hood lowered, before continuing on. At a gas station, he turned right and traveled several blocks east to a seedy downtown neighborhood, not far from Libby's compound.

A row of graffitied youth hostels stood among abandoned homes on litter-strewn lots. A freight train whistled in the background, reminding Halvern of the government projects in Atlanta, Georgia, where he grew up. When those passing trains had shaken his apartment, plaster dust rained on his sketches of skyscrapers and battleships. He recalled wishing his bedroom would crash down on his head because he thought the apartment lacked integrity, as did every building he had ever seen with his own eyes.

He removed his hood and entered a hostel, wandering through the cinderblock hallways, ignoring the awful architecture, but judging the faces he encountered as he had many times the past two years.

Many of the runaways begged him for money. Those who had tired of begging him hated him. The ones who had tired of hating him ignored him. The rare others no longer lived here. After an hour, Halvern left, disappointed.

On a bus stop bench on the way back, he sat and coughed wetly, horribly, his body hunching forward. Wiping his mouth with the back of his hand, he saw the blood.

He glanced up at the distant white tower and climbed to his feet, continuing his walk.

The next morning, Halvern poured pancake batter into expanding discs on a massive sizzling stovetop. The sunlight from the expansive window painted the griddle fumes orange as they sucked into the overhead vent. Several children and teens clustered around watching.

A boy ran from the kitchen at the sound of a buzzer.

"Mr. Black. Delivery," the boy yelled.

A courier waited at the elevator as Halvern approached. Snatching the letter with one hand while holding the spatula in the other, Halvern walked to the dining room to open it. A thin Asian woman plucked the spatula from his hand and herded several curious children back to the kitchen.

The letter was addressed from the US District Court, Nevada. It contained an injunction against the proprietorship of Halvern Black Architects. The court ordered the firm to cease all work until it could be proven to the satisfaction of a federal panel that it had not violated any safety or environmental regulations. They also ordered all relevant documents to be turned over.

Halvern slid the letter into his pocket and returned to the kitchen. He cracked eggs onto the hissing stovetop. "Who wants crushed pepper?"

After breakfast, he went upstairs to the only balcony in the skyscraper and called his attorney, setting up a meeting that afternoon. He also called his company accountant, directing him to wire all the firm's liquid assets within the United States to his accounts in Singapore by the end of the day.

He gazed west over the white glass railing. The far-off canyon containing the former Libby House caressed his eyes.

Looking down from a half a mile above the city, he wondered what the ancients must have envisioned when they created the concept of heaven. "They greatly underestimated its beauty."

He leaned against the railing, gripping it, the pain in his gut stealing the strength in his legs. A single drop of sweat fell from his brow, taken away by the cool desert air.

A federal judge pulled a letter from an envelope in his chambers and read: *Your honor, since you've ordered my company to cease operations, there is no reason to maintain the façade I still own it. I am, therefore, transferring to you Halvern Black Architects. You can now run it by whatever principles justified your injunction against me. Halvern Black.*

The other contents of the envelope consisted of deeds, legal descriptions, and the signatures necessary to transfer ownership to the judge.

Upon hearing about the transfer of Halvern Black Architects to a federal judge, all of Halvern's architects resigned.

The federal judge—demonstrating his unambiguous refusal to accept ownership—slapped Halvern Black Architects with a contempt of court ruling, but was forced to dismiss his own injunction upon learning that the firm no longer existed.

Three days after *The Spirit of Man* dedication, the Moore/Patra ticket swept into state office in a landslide.

Alexandria Patra, with black hair re-curled, stood behind Preton Moore on the balloon-drenched stage in *The Sin's* main ballroom. Governor-elect Moore made his first of many lengthy acceptance speeches with a pearly grin across a tanned face and tears in his eyes.

Stock watched Alexandria, mesmerized at how she could be more beautiful than before she disappeared, even more stunning than when he had made his marquee. *Where have you been all this time?*

He waited in the front row before the stage, unsure if he should throw the knowledge of his large contribution to her political ticket in her face, or if he should make an escape before he looked into her eyes.

Preton's speech ended and party music began.

Alexandria descended from the stage and walked toward Stock. He peered helplessly at her, but she didn't make eye contact as she passed, her profile serenely untroubled. He had no strength to speak or to follow. Glancing back, he watched her imperially gracious body glide from the ballroom. *Alexandria.*

As Preton began the first dance, kicking off the celebration, Alexandria crossed *The Sin's* lobby.

Ted Hollings stood below a grand crystal chandelier at the center of a circular tile mosaic near the entrance. He bowed as she approached, his wrist cuff sitting properly across his waist.

A tiny glass vial slid from his hand into hers as she strode by and exited out the main doors below the marquee.

On the other side of the Strip, Alexandria entered the massive lobby of *The Spirit of Man* and stepped behind a microphone. Her fingers caressed the vial.

Behind her stood a stone statue of a god-like naked man with narrow hips and broad shoulders, chest pressed out. Across the lobby stood a naked statue of a goddess, straight hair hanging down a slender arched back.

With only one young blog reporter and a few curious hotel guests present, Alexandria gave her acceptance speech. "I made no promises during this campaign. And I plan to keep them all."

She left the microphone, walked across the lobby and entered an elevator. As the doors closed she focused on the button at the bottom—*222*.

An elegant female voice flowed from the elevator speaker: *"Please swipe your card and enter your code."*

"I'm Alexa Patra." She stared into the flat-paneled camera near the speaker. "Halvern Black is expecting me."

After a moment, the *222* button illuminated and the car shot upward. She smiled at the rapid ascent. As the elevator decelerated near the top, she leaped in the air capturing a moment without gravity. When her high heels touched back to the floor, the doors zipped open. She wiped away her grin and brushed a hand down her suit.

Halvern stood before her, his typically large stature looking frail.

She nodded. "Mr. Black."

"Follow me." He limped away from the clean-lined lobby, and entered an office on the east side of the open floor.

She walked after him, staring out the floor-to-ceiling windows. The skyscraper's uninhibited height left her feeling weightless, as if floating above the whole world.

Halvern stopped near a desk and faced her. Alexandria strolled past him, and gazed down at *The Sin*, its black façade shrunk into a tiny toy model. The vial rolled back and forth in her palm.

"I would congratulate you on your political victory, Ms. Patra," Halvern said. "However, I neither donated to your ticket nor do I support it in any way. And if I could have donated less than zero to your political opponents, I would have done that as well. The only thing I appreciate is that you didn't annoy me by campaigning. So—" He coughed. "What do you want?"

"I want you to answer the question I asked nine months ago at Libby's house."

"Libby's house?" Halvern cleared his throat. "Not going to pretend you and Sitra are different people?"

"I could tell you knew who I was that night." She turned to him. "I don't know how, but you did."

"That's because," his eyes narrowed, "I don't judge buildings or people by their façades."

"And you didn't judge me worthy to hear your answer?"

"Why in God's name do you want to know what I think of," he shook his head, "a 'warrior's code' as Prince Charming put it?"

"I want to know what you think you deserve."

"Perhaps people deserve every law they've given themselves."

"Do *you* deserve to be punished for constructing this?" She swept a hand out, pointing across the floor.

He pressed a hand against his side, teeth gritted together.

She stared at his midsection, then lifted her eyes, studying the yellowing of his skin and eyes. The vial clenched tighter in her hand. "If you could use your mind to design a law instead of a skyscraper, by what rights and beliefs would you erect it?"

"If you want to understand rights," Halvern coughed into his hand, and leaned against the desk, "you must first understand the very fabric of reality. We don't live in an abstract world, Ms. Patra."

"Then school me, Mr. Black, on 'the very fabric of reality.'"

He pulled a handkerchief from a pocket and wiped his hand.

Alexandria fondled the vial between her fingers.

Halvern rounded the desk and slumped into his chair. "Since when do politicians care about reality?"

Alexandria placed the tiny vial on Halvern's desk, balancing it on one end.

Halvern glowered at it.

"Tell me what type of laws you deserve," she pointed at the vial, "and it's yours."

"Cough syrup won't help with what I have, Ms. Patra."

Alexandria drew in a breath. "You have pancreatic cancer. And you won't live to see your next skyscraper."

Halvern's eyes widened.

"Didn't think I could judge *you* correctly as well?" Alexandria asked.

"And I suppose that's a 'miracle cure?'" He nodded at the vial.

"This and five more doses."

He stared at the vial, at its label—*L523*. "And if it's *not?*"

"Then it's not." She picked it back up.

"That makes me suspect it is." His gaze followed the biologic dose as it swayed in her hand. "Which means it is an unapproved substance and therefore illegal."

"That seems to be the reality of it, Mr. Black."

"If you actually want to learn about reality, Ms. Patra, I will introduce you to my former high school math teacher."

"Math teacher?"

"Since everything that exists is real," Halvern said, "everything in reality can be understood with math."

"But how does that relate to your view of government laws?"

"All right…" He pressed his hands against his desk and swallowed with a prolonged grimace. "Here is a math problem. If only one person lived on this planet, what type of laws would she deserve?"

"Would she even need laws?"

"Need? Do the *principles* of reality change depending on how many people live on this planet?"

Alexandria glanced out the window, her brows furrowed.

"Tell me what laws *she* would deserve," Halvern demanded.

Alexandria shook her head. "I'm listening."

"Would she not perfectly deserve the results of *everything* she *did*—and *did not do*—with reality as her only judge?" He pressed against the desk, rising to his feet. "If you ever comprehend that equation, you will know what kind of laws *I* deserve."

Alexandria massaged her chin.

"So," he groused, "do you want to meet my math teacher or not?"

"Okay, Halvern, I do."

"Good, but don't hold your breath," he grumbled, "the man is very busy."

Alexandria laughed. "Has anyone ever accused you of being adorable?"

He scowled.

She rolled the vial across the desk to him. "I won't hold my breath, and you won't inject this biologic until you set up my lesson."

He picked it up. "When do you intend to start your show?"

"In five months." She lifted onto the points of her toes, her cheeks beaming. "I have a contract with a circus-themed casino."

He winced and indicated north using the vial as a pointer. "In that god-awful excuse for a building?"

"Don't think it will succeed there?"

Halvern coughed and twisted his neck. "I think I'd like an invitation to your opening night."

Chapter 29

Lieutenant Colonel Sircor walked below drooping palm trees charring red from the sunset, their checker-weaved trunks lining the path to General Wissmark's office building. He straightened his uniform, tugging it down with both hands, gazing at the pale office lights beyond the windows.

As he walked into the executive suites, a mustached adjunct opened the General's office door for him to enter. Sircor stared at the open doorway and loosened his collar, but his throat still felt constricted. With a dry swallow, he marched in.

The grey-haired general stood near a bookshelf, his back turned. "The Chairman of the Joint Chiefs of Staff, General Robertson, called me today."

Sircor wobbled on his feet, losing his breath.

"I didn't enjoy that conversation, Colonel." Wissmark turned around. "What is going on with my fighter aircraft?"

Sircor pressed a hand against a sweaty brow. "Sir," he cleared his throat, "our fighter jets are in top condition."

"Are maintenance procedures being followed?" Wissmark picked up a smoking pipe from a shelf and placed it between his lips.

"Our fighters are in combat ready posture, sir."

"Frederick Compros at DCU informed General Robertson that mandatory maintenance procedures are not being followed on my base." Wissmark lit a match. "I trust you will clear this up, Colonel. In doing so," he sucked on the pipe, stoking the tobacco, "I want involuntary discharge requests for those responsible on my desk tomorrow. If I'm not satisfied with your actions, I will request an investigation of my fighter squadron commanders. Do you understand me?" He blew a smoke ring. "Fighter Squadron Commander?"

Sircor coughed. "Yes, sir."

"That is all."

Back at his office, Sircor slumped into his chair in the darkness, chin falling to his chest.

He flicked on the desk lamp and pulled out an involuntary discharge form. His pen scribed forcefully across it. *Roble Santos.*

With the recommendation completed, he sealed it in an envelope and stood to leave, but stopped, holding the envelope over the trash can.

Shaking his head, he gripped it tight, left the office and traveled the dimly lit sidewalks to General Wissmark's now-dark office building.

The envelope slid through the inter-office mail slot but he held its end with his fingertips, unable to let go. *Duty*, he thought. *Duty…and… Duty.* He released it. A muffled thump. *It is done.*

Turning around, he noticed the night clouds formed an ominous crimson dome above Kadena. He marched to a hangar knowing it held the man he sought, yet didn't wish to see. He entered through the side door.

An F-22 Raptor crouched menacingly below beaming work lights, its shadow pressing across the polished floor. Sircor's gaze followed the dark shape until it met the lone man moving with purpose like a sculptor before a titanium masterpiece.

Sircor shuffled closer, his face sullen.

Roble ran forward, stopping below the Raptor's nose. He crossed his arms with a smile on his lips. "Come check out the installed dual mode ramjets." He jogged to the engines.

Sircor opened his mouth to speak, but instead, he followed. As he passed the Raptor, he thought it somehow appeared sleeker, bolder, and meaner than he remembered. Tracking Roble's stare, he peered inside a jet exhaust and noted two distinct layers. "What," Sircor coughed to clear his throat, "are they?"

Roble ran his fingers around the edges of an exhaust. "The outer chamber leads to the redesigned jet turbine, the inner to a ramjet. The turbines bring the Raptor to maximum blade-driven speed, then the ramjets compress the supersonic airflow and punch the craft hypersonic."

Sircor stepped closer.

"This," Roble pointed at the silhouetted beast, "is the completed Raptor *Super Kai*—the best fighter aircraft on Earth."

He ran over to the wall bringing back a large duffle bag and held out the handles to Sircor. "Your next flight suit. I have it from the manufacturer it will keep you conscious in maneuvers pulling well over ten Gs."

Sircor lowered his head and spoke barely above a whisper, wishing Roble couldn't hear his words, "I was ordered to stop all modifications…to undo them." He met Roble's gaze, and added, "I…I've requested your involuntary discharge. I have no doubt General Wissmark will sign it. There is no way out of this. I know it changes nothing, but I'll say it anyway—I'm sorry, Santos."

Roble hunched over and held both hands to his nose. Rising back up, he reached out and caressed the tailfin of the Raptor *Super Kai*. Sircor's gaze couldn't help but follow Roble's hand.

"Did you ever think," Roble rasped, swallowing hard, "something like this was possible?"

Sircor looked away.

"I really wanted to take her up." Roble closed his eyes. "I think it would've revealed the final piece of a puzzle I've been working on." He touched his pocket.

"I hope someday you'll understand…understand why it had to end this way."

"I knew the risk I took." Roble shuffled his feet. "You don't need to apologize."

Sircor exhaled, trying to keep his composure.

"Would you please discharge me here? I'd like to stay in Japan for a while."

Sircor walked away.

Nearing the exit, he glanced back and saw Roble reach for an electrical cord hanging from a row of work lamps. The Raptor *Super Kai* vanished into darkness.

Sircor fought back tears as he drove home, unable to shake the helplessness in his gut. A cough escaped, releasing tears at the memory of his remarkable *Skeleton Eagle* flight with Roble. He could hear him describing morality as evidenced in material form. *A saint.* "God…" He shook his head.

As he pulled into his home's driveway, he wiped his eyes.

Opening the front door, his four girls—all in colorful pajamas—pressed against his uniform with open arms yelling, "Daddy!" They began talking over one another.

Sircor moved his head in attentive consideration to each one, enjoying their excited voices.

Stephie stood in the open kitchen, smiling, the smell of

cinnamon rolls long ago eaten still in the air. "They wouldn't go to bed until they saw you. I didn't know you'd be so late."

"Go find me a book to read. I'll meet you in Jodee and Arikas' room," he said to the girls. "Make sure you've all brushed your teeth," he added as they ran away down the hall.

Stephie kissed him on the cheek. "Is everything all right, Gavin? You look tired."

He tried to smile.

She hugged him tight. "I love you. Whatever it is, I'm here for you."

He nodded, but couldn't stop a tear from rolling down his cheek.

Sircor peered from his office window at the auxiliary hangar he entered last night. Airmen and officers moved about the base as usual. Aircraft launched and landed as usual. Glancing at the clock, he realized he hadn't done anything for over an hour.

He left the office, telling himself he needed fresh air and that everything would soon be back to normal. He paced near the auxiliary hangar four times, pretending it wasn't there. On the fifth pass he turned and entered.

A flash of sunlight froze the Raptor's image in his mind before the door swung shut, sealing him inside.

He didn't know how long he spent in the hangar alone before he returned to his office, but the workday seemed half over. Looking at his desk pictures it felt strange that he'd arrived at this point in time, this point which split his life's efforts and ideals in two—like a contradiction.

A model Raptor sat on his desk near his hand. He picked it up and studied its shape and lines—not the fighter jet's—but those of his hand. Closing his eyes, he set it down. He could neither believe nor stop what he knew he would now do.

Sircor looked down, watching his own polished boots walking into General Wissmark's office building. He heard the echoing of his own voice pronounce the words necessary to request an impromptu meeting with General Wissmark.

"He is inaccessible," the general's adjunct said.

Sircor watched the airmen typing on keyboards and talking

on phones like nothing important was happening. He wished he were witnessing exploding fireballs and streams of black smoke—not this, not this calm indifference to how he felt.

The adjunct stared at Sircor for a while and picked up the phone. After a moment he said, "The General will see you, Colonel."

Gripping the doorknob, Sircor found himself focused on the finely lacquered wood door. As he pushed it inward, two eyes bored into him, snapping him from his daze. The General leaned over his desk supported by sharp elbows.

Sircor gave a hesitant salute and closed the door. "Sir, permission to speak."

Wissmark frowned.

"Sir," Sircor rasped, "you have my recommendation to discharge Airman Roble Santos under other than honorable conditions for his failure to follow maintenance procedures. I'm aware he will not challenge my basis for discharge."

Sircor drew a breath. "But sir, what I did not say in that report is that he is the one responsible for modifying the Peace Eagle at Naha, the most cutting-edge F-15 in the world. He's made similar improvements to our fighter aircraft here at Kadena. And I've known about his actions for some time."

General Wissmark's face tightened, his watery eyes boiling.

"But despite what DCU might have said, Airman Santos hasn't harmed us. He's given us a gift," Sircor continued, losing all trepidation. "If anyone has done something wrong, it is us and DCU for not seeing that something better was possible. His improvements are revolutionary and…I agree with every-thing he's done. Not only do I approve, I'm honored to fly in those aircraft. General, I made a mistake by recommending his discharge. Instead of booting him for not following a…" he pointed at a bookcase, "a procedural manual, let's reward him for improving the capabilities of your air wing. We need him, General, not the other way around."

He hadn't known what he was going to say when he entered the General's office, but he felt proud of his speech. He had fulfilled his duty—his duty to preserve his own integrity. *Duty* and *excellence*.

Standing at attention, Sircor knew everything he had worked for in the Air Force now hung on the General's next few words.

General Wissmark remained silent for what seemed like an eternity. Then he spoke.

"You disappoint me, Gavin. You dishonor the Air Force and your country."

The General opened Roble's file on the desk and signed the involuntary discharge. Tossing it to Sircor, he said, "You will resign as 302nd Fighter Squadron Commander. If you refuse, I'll also end your career as a pilot."

Sircor saw his own reflection in Wissmark's eyes—an ejected pilot ditched in a vast ocean, alone.

The General's voice rose. "Did I make myself clear?"

Sircor heard himself saying, "Yes, sir." He felt his arm salute, his hips turn, and his legs walk from the room.

———————

Three distinct knocks woke Roble. He answered his barracks' door, rubbing his eyes with a yawn, and stepped back in surprise.

Lieutenant Colonel Sircor stood in the doorway wearing a blue dress uniform. A large duffle bag hung in his right hand, a paper folder in his left. He handed the folder to Roble.

Roble kept his eyes squarely on Sircor.

"You've been officially discharged without," Sircor's voice choked, "honor, from the United States Air Force. As of this moment, you are a civilian. They will escort you off the base at 0800 hours."

He snapped his body around with military precision, facing away from Roble.

Beyond him, Roble noticed the morning dew glistening in beads along succulent petals and the ribbed glass of still-illuminated streetlights.

Sircor dropped the pilot flight bag. It hit the ground with a thud. "There's a flight approved for takeoff at 0700 in the... Raptor *Super Kai*, under the call sign Ivanhoe. Everything you need to get off the ground is in this bag."

The lieutenant colonel saluted into the morning air and marched away, dress boots rasping along the damp sidewalk.

Roble's body drew toward the doorway and he clenched his arrowhead. He bowed and then lifted his chin to the awaiting sky.

Chapter 30

Roble peered into the rolling fog, focusing on the hazy runway lights.

His gloved hand gripped the throttles and gently pressed forward. A faint rumble grew until it shook the cockpit with a deafening roar. Twin exhausts bellowed streaks of purple flame, melting into white behind the F-22 Raptor *Super Kai*.

It catapulted forward, sharp edges slicing through mist, vapor curling into vortices in its fiery wake. Off the tarmac with the landing gear rising, the fighter jet held inches above the ground, accelerating.

Roble's lips bent into a thin smile. *This is it.* His hand touched the pocket containing his crumbled dream. *Today, I will complete the puzzle.*

In the tower, Lead Air Controller Simkin peered through the marine layer at the unexpectedly fast launch. "Who's in that Raptor?"

"Ivanhoe," the assistant controller said.

"Mission?"

"Flight plan lists a solo training flight, with the mission tag: *Duty and Excellence.* Not sure what that means."

"When did he submit the plan?"

"Not until 2300 yesterday." The assistant tower controller hesitated, looking closer at the screen. "Whoa! I've lost his IFF transponder. And he's off raw radar."

"Hail him."

"Ivanhoe, this is Giant Samurai. How do you read?" The assistant narrowed his eyes, waiting. He turned to Simkin. "No response on the channels. Last known location is marked."

"Alert search and rescue." Simkin hadn't looked away from the unusually low flight path. His palms pressed against the window. "God *damn*, that was fast."

Two hundred miles north, the East China Sea glistened like

an endless glass sheet. The F-22 Raptor *Super Kai* flashed just above its surface, ripping twin aerated water plumes into the air.

A grey destroyer sat broadside in the water just ahead. Roble hurtled toward its bow without slowing.

Crossing above the ship, the jet's sonic shockwave rocked sailors to the deck as if Roble's soul had exploded through their bodies. Sea spray from the wake doused the ship's hull like an exclamation point.

"Pacific Command, this is the USS Zumwalt. We've just been buzzed by an unidentified supersonic aircraft heading northwest. Unable to track on Aegis. Requesting immediate AWACS scan of the East China Sea eighty nautical miles southwest of Korean peninsula."

Simkin, back at the Kadena air base tower, rubbed his stomach as he listened to the Navy's request. "What the hell? Was *that* Ivanhoe?" He picked up the mic. "Get me General Wissmark on the horn. Now!"

Water sparkled below Roble's canopy as he continued northward, golden sunrays warming his cheeks through the helmet's faceplate. He rolled the craft hard right, a wingtip reaching down as if to touch the ocean. A grunt escaped his lips as gravity compressed his body.

The wings leveled out, and the Raptor charged into the rising sun—and the coastline of North Korea.

Afterburners lit up, accelerating Roble like a bullet over crude fishing vessels, then treetops. He glanced down at the streaks of green, brown, and thatch. A few blurry faces atop hunched bodies caught his eye as they rushed by.

"Hmm…" The afterburners fell dark, slowing the craft. *Forced brotherly love looks peaceful.*

Burnt sheets of alloy vectored the jet's thrust, snapping the F-22's nose to the north.

Seconds later, dilapidated buildings on the outskirts of Pyongyang smeared by.

Roble sucked in a breath, the type one takes before plunging off a cliff. He pushed the stick forward, dropping the Raptor along the main thoroughfare of the city, its buildings reaching above the cockpit.

Languid bodies cowered under the deafening approach.

I've only seen more peace in a cemetery. The Raptor *Super Kai* sliced through the air.

He relaxed against the seat, hand toggling the throttles wide open. A sonic boom exploded between the canyon of wasted structures, shaking windows and brick.

With the central palace ahead, Roble jerked back on the stick and slammed his boots against the pedals. The Raptor's nose snapped upward, its erupting engines directed down, scorching the palace walls below.

The palace windows sucked inward from the change in air pressure, then shattered outward onto the great steps. Massive glass shards concussed against concrete followed by a continuing tinkle of chimes. A rumble rolled back down the quivering canyon. Then once again, there was peace.

Roble drove vertically into the heavens, eyes on the sky, his body compressing beyond anything he had ever felt.

Antiaircraft missiles fired from sites around Pyongyang, blazing upward. The Raptor continued climbing, accelerating, perfectly vertical, and untouched. Even with the immense pressure upon his body, Roble felt lighter than air.

The contrails of missiles below faded away as he watched the earth's horizon becoming clearer and darker. When the turbines wavered, he leveled out the fighter to the east.

A screen blinked: *Prepare for ramjet ignition.*

Tingles coursed through his body. *Here we go.* The turbine blades whirled to a stop.

The ramjets ignited, sucking him against the seat, pulling his face tight. He wanted to scream with elation but didn't want to risk waking himself if this was a dream.

After a while, the tranquil crackling of the exhaust made his eyelids droop. The F-22 wasn't designed to reach Mach 3; this one neared 5. *We did it Libby.*

He thought through all the ideas and procedures he'd used to modify this fighter jet. He listened to the engines and their hyper-sonic airflow. He studied the cockpit controls as he felt along his pocket.

Lifting his chin, his gaze followed the curvature of the earth until it found the seductive curves of the moon. *It's really not that far away.*

Looking down at the blue expanse, he spotted the distant island where he had modified this machine. *Sircor, I won't forget.*

He removed the wrinkled paper from his pocket, smoothed it over a knee, and studied it. Taking out a pencil, he connected all the dots and lines he'd drawn over the years. When he finished, he returned his completed idea—the unraveled puzzle—to his pocket.

His palm pressed against the canopy, blocking out the sun. It slid down the transparent surface until his face burned like the fire of exaltation.

The fuel gauge blinked *red.*

Pushing the stick forward, he plunged toward the main island of Japan. He dove for what seemed an eternity and he wished it had been, his gut tickling from the descent.

Structural tolerance warnings flashed across a screen as air resistance thickened in the lower atmosphere.

He pressed a button on the dashboard and the ramjets disengaged, throwing his body against the harness as the Raptor slowed. The turbine blades whirled back to life.

At ten thousand feet, he glanced at the aircraft tracking screens and identified three US and six Japanese fighter jets approaching rapidly from the west and the south.

He leveled out his flight path, turned on his radio for the first time, and typed on a handheld device connected to the central computer, reengaging the IFF signal.

Hectic voices vomited from his helmet speakers. *"Bandit Raptor, this is Widowmaker. You will divert to Misawa Air Base. Do you copy? Follow instructions or you will be shot down."*

"Widowmaker, this is Roble Santos aboard the Raptor *Super Kai.* I'm a civilian, and I alone am responsible for this flight. My intention is to fly over Tokyo and land at Yokota Air Base. I'm too low on fuel to reach Misawa."

The flurry of voices fell silent. Roble continued on course.

"Negative—Bandit Raptor. Land at Yokota immediately or you will be shot down. You do not have permission to enter farther into Tokyo airspace."

"Well, I guess shooting me down is your privilege since you have me out-gunned and out-fueled."

Silence.

"This is General Wissmark," a fainter signal sounded in Roble's

helmet. *"Airman, I know you must be upset, but this is not the answer. Land the Raptor, now."*

"Morning, General," Roble said.

Mount Fuji grew in his canopy, standing like a snowy-haired sentinel protecting Tokyo to its east.

"That's not your fighter. Don't waste it and your life. Don't be a fool," General Wissmark said.

"Only a fool would destroy it—so don't. I'm flying over Tokyo."

An empty static filled the radio waves.

Death is certain, living is not... The Raptor *Super Kai* stayed on course, Mount Fuji just ahead.

"Shoot him down," General Wissmark ordered. *"I repeat, shoot down the Bandit Raptor."*

Roble shrugged and forced the afterburners to life, leaving the escorting fighter jets behind. *...and danger is a fair price I'll pay for living.*

"Fox two...fox two...fox two!" Roble heard over the radio. Three air-to-air missile warning indicators flashed across a monitor.

His fuel warning flashed *Critical* as the afterburners sucked hard, choking on too little fuel mixing with too much air. He watched his Machmeter ticking down as he slowed. *What a shame.*

He placed his palms to the sides of the cockpit, to feel its gallant verve one last time.

Roble's eyes remained on the approaching Tokyo skyline, marveling at a city he had never visited, but which had produced someone as great as Sugemi.

"Evade. Evade. Incoming missiles," his helmet speaker bellowed.

The Raptor *Super Kai's* engines fell silent as the last of the fuel incinerated in the afterburners.

Roble spun the Raptor as it descended, toggling a switch to spit countermeasure flares from below the fuselage, flinging them in a wide-spiraling vortex. But it wasn't enough to thwart all three missiles, nor would it have mattered.

His last feeling was one of joy, for having flown the greatest fighter jet in history—a feeling no one could take away, and more importantly, a feeling no one could have given him.

He reached for the ejection handle and pulled.

The Raptor *Super Kai* exploded in the sky above the eastern edge of Mount Fuji. Burning pieces cascaded down in smoke trails.

Roble rocketed up into the freezing air, his hearing shattered in the silence of a monotone ringing concussion. His ejection chute opened, and he hung, legs dangling.

Fighter jets ripped past on all sides.

He floated down the eastern slope of Mount Fuji in full view of Tokyo. Cherry trees with white-spangled blossoms filled the ground below while the sky above streaked with contrails.

When his parachute snagged a tree branch, he swung forward then back again like a boy on a swing set, and reached out, picking a blossom.

He yanked the release on the parachute harness, dropping himself. His boots cratered into dark soil. Tossing his helmet to the ground, he trekked between the trees toward Tokyo, not looking back at the smoke wafting off the mountainside.

Entering a grass clearing, a thumping whirlwind from a helicopter whipped his hair into his eyes. He stopped and gazed at the tops of the Tokyo skyscrapers as armed Marines jumped from the landing helicopter.

He released the blossom into the wind and pulled the crumpled paper from his pocket. *It's everything I'd hoped to conceive.* Analyzing the paper one last time, he stuffed it in his mouth, and swallowed it.

Two Marines tackled him to the ground. With a knee smashing his gut and a boot stepping on his ear, pressing his face to the dirt, he thought of his completed idea, and grinned.

Chapter 31

High above the Las Vegas Strip, two teenage boys stood with their backs against a floor-to-ceiling window, pointing at a glass table. On the table lay a rectangular world map topped with colorful three-dimensional pieces.

Grins spread across the boys' faces as they stepped forward. One, with straight blond hair, checked his handheld computer and nodded. The other, with tight curly black hair, repositioned their naval, air, and ground forces on the board.

A younger brunette girl on the other side of the table bit her lip and looked up at Libby Dodge standing by her side.

Libby stared at Halvern Black who stood at the head of the table. "Have you gained some weight back, Halvern? You look great."

The girl rubbed her forehead at Libby's lack of attention to the game.

"Never felt better," Halvern said, somehow maintaining a scowl.

"And the pain?"

"Gone."

"How?"

Halvern motioned at the game. "You're about to lose North Africa and the South Pacific. It can wait."

The boys bumped shoulders and covered their smirks with their hands.

Libby smoothed out her hair and refocused on the playing pieces. She picked up a yellow fighter plane, twirled it between two fingers, and landed it on a northeastern territory in the Soviet Union.

The blond boy scoffed.

Squinting, Libby peered beyond the game board and out the window, catching the distant shape of a *Sovereign* taxiing along a runway at McCarran Airport.

Strange. It's painted white like a Wyvern. She massaged her chin. *The control tower won't allow takeoff of an unregistered jet.*

The brunette girl cleared her throat, bringing Libby's attention back to the board.

Libby leaned in and moved every unit of her yellow Japanese forces away from Pearl Harbor and the South Pacific and invaded them into eastern Russia.

"What?" the boys mouthed together.

"Your turn, Samantha," Libby said to her teammate. "And I wouldn't bother responding to the invasion of North Africa."

Samantha studied the board, eyes wide.

Rising on her toes, Libby watched the white *Sovereign* lift into the air and bank hard to the east. *Hmm.* She followed it until it dissolved into blue haze.

With her hand trembling, Samantha pushed every available German unit east toward Moscow, glancing at Libby for reassurance because she had left her western flank in Europe wide open and had not responded to the invasion of North Africa.

Libby winked.

The boys huddled, searching on handheld computers. They glanced back to the game several times. The blond whispered, "Those moves aren't listed online anywhere. How can they be so stupid to leave all their flanks vulnerable?"

After more discussion, they repositioned their supply lines to take advantage of the apparent folly.

One turn later, the Soviet Union collapsed under the pincer maneuver between Libby and Samantha's forces.

"That's not how the game was meant to be played," the black-haired boy said. "The highest probability move was for Japan to attack American Naval forces in the Pacific."

"Do you concede?" Samantha giggled.

"No."

Two turns later, Samantha and Libby possessed every key Asian, European, and African territory on the board.

"I have homework," the blond teen said.

"So you're admitting defeat at the hands of your little sister?" Libby asked with mock bewilderment, eyes sparkling in the sunlight.

The black-haired boy flicked the board, scattering pieces. "How did you know to do that?"

Halvern walked behind the boys, placing his large hands on their shoulders. "If you saw your opponents' actions as unexpected, ask yourself 'Why?' Those moves were set in place from the beginning, however improbable you thought they were."

The boys nodded, avoiding eye contact with each other and everyone else. Samantha beamed.

"Thanks, Libby, for teaching my two internet entrepreneurs a lesson in benevolent reality. Good judgment, Samantha."

"Excuse me for a moment," Libby said, feeling her phone vibrate.

She walked several steps from the table and touched the phone's blinking knight icon. "Victor?"

"*Madame* Dodge," Victor said, his voice uncharacteristically rushed. "An F-22 went down over Tokyo. I think it was your modification."

"What? My god…"

Halvern's eyes shot to Libby.

"Over Tokyo?" she asked.

"It gets worse, my friend," Victor said.

"*Roble*…" Libby whispered, closing her eyes.

"The media reported the pilot as lost in the crash."

Libby shook her head. "Are you sure it was him?"

"The Air Force is withholding the pilot's name. They assert mechanical failure; however, Japanese bloggers are reporting missiles fired. Tellingly, no Air Force pilots have been reported missing," Victor said. "They are covering something up, thus we should assume the worst. My utmost condolences."

Libby walked farther from the table and stood, neck crooked sideways, looking at the floor. *Roble*. "I…I don't want to believe it." She dropped the phone to her side and watched a passenger jet taking off from McCarran far below. Rubbing her eyes with the back of a hand, she put the phone back to her ear.

"*Madame*," Victor continued, "right now you must consider protecting Libby Industries, and posthaste. The fallout over this will be swift and severe, of that I have no doubt. Perhaps you assume your government will protect you and be just, but I won't stand by this time and watch you lose everything else. I already have a plan ready for this scenario."

"Victor?"

"Just give me the word, and *Monsieur* Evert will remove all the remaining aerospace research and development material from the North Las Vegas facility, as well as extract our best robots, all quantum software, and anything else you think we can't afford to lose."

Libby sucked in a breath and exhaled. "You really think that's necessary?"

Silence.

"Okay, Victor," she sighed.

"I'm proceeding to your house downtown with some men and we are going to remove everything we can from your manufacturing sheds, especially the design plans of the modified F-22."

"Where will it all go?"

"The cavern, naturally."

"Tell Sitra to vacate as well, at least for now," Libby whispered.

"Of course, my friend. And there is one more detail."

Libby leaned against the window.

"My family maintains a trust in Switzerland. If you wish, it will purchase your downtown property and the North Las Vegas facility. It will sell them back whenever you want. That would greatly complicate a government search warrant or seizure."

Libby shook her head. "I can't sell."

"I understand."

"No," Libby pulled on her hair until she felt pain. "You're right. Tell Gary Sanders to set it up."

"Take heart, *Madame*. It will all be done."

Libby slid the phone into her pocket and looked beyond the mountains. *Roble*.

Halvern walked up to Libby, his eyes respectfully avoiding hers. "Is everything all right?"

"No," she said.

"If you need anything…"

Libby held out a hand, palm up. "A dollar."

Halvern scowled. After a moment he reached into his pocket. "You parked at a meter or something?" He dumped fifty-five cents in her hand.

"You just bought my Calico Basin ranch stable and land. I'll have Gary send over the paperwork. Sell it back for whatever you think is reasonable once this is all over. I want to keep using the cavern underneath it. Is that okay?"

Halvern sank his fingers into Libby's shoulder. "Libby, whatever you need."

Stale fluorescent light poured over a long conference table at Kadena Air Base.

Three uniformed generals—Wissmark, Yamatomo, and Rho—sat in a line next to Frederick Compros, their backs facing a whiteboard. Across the table sat four younger men, two in unmarked, rugged khakis, and two captains in starched light blue uniforms.

"*The Chairman of the Joint Chiefs of Staff General Robertson will now commence this meeting,*" a woman said from a speakerphone at the center of the table.

"*Good evening,*" Robertson said from the speaker. "*Madam Deputy Secretary of State Louise Johnson is also on the line from Washington.*" He cleared his throat. "*It's been a tough week for us all. And now it's time to resolve the issue. I'd like to first go over the facts of the incident. Captains Davis and Lewis have the technical briefing. Please proceed.*"

The two captains at the table delineated the facts of the Raptor's flight, which they reconstructed from spy satellite data and the recovered onboard flight recorder.

"From our *own* analysis of the flight tracking data," Frederick Compros said, "we came to the conclusion that the data itself must be erroneous. No Raptor could have flown as high or as fast. As the manufacturer, we should know. The fact that the F-22 was illegally tampered with means it must have performed in a suboptimal way." He slapped the table. "And I'm outraged government sources reported mechanical failure as the cause of the crash. It unfairly tarnishes DCU's brand name. It should be admitted publicly that an airman went rogue due to lax discipline in the 18th Wing and that he purposely crashed the fighter."

"*The administration has already authorized payment to compensate DCU for being used as a cover for the incident,*" Secretary Louise Johnson said from the speaker. "*And don't worry, Frederick, everyone responsible in the 18th Wing will be punished.*"

General Wissmark's watery eyes drained, matching his parched face.

Frederick grinned, crossing one portly leg over the other.

"*General Rho, any update on the response from the North Koreans?*" General Robertson asked.

"Our sources indicate no material damage to Pyongyang," Rho said with a distinct Korean accent, his slick hair gleaming. "The leadership was obviously shaken by the incident; however, their response has been unexpected. They have turned silent instead of issuing their usual public threats. Troop and missile movements have stopped as if they do not dare move."

"*Should we contact them directly and apologize?*" Secretary Johnson asked.

Rho grimaced.

"*General Yamatomo, what is your position?*" General Robertson asked.

"A modified F-22 penetrated North Korean airspace without detection and almost scratched its ass on the dear leader's nose," Yamatomo said, standing up. "It did *in fact* reach altitudes and speeds it was never designed to reach. An *enlisted mechanic* not only modified it, but piloted it. The North Koreans could not shoot it down, but we somehow decided to. Why is that?"

General Wissmark rubbed his forehead and looked away.

"The North Koreans are humiliated," Yamatomo continued, "but why are we? The only thing I see as shameful is that a mechanic knew more about fighter aircraft than our defense contractors and trained pilots. Instead of apologizing to those who wish us destroyed, why don't we adopt these aircraft capabilities into our air forces? Are we more concerned with hurting the feelings of defense contractors and our enemies than defending ourselves?"

"*What we are dealing with,* General," Secretary Louise Johnson dragged out the title, "*is high diplomacy and critical political considerations. This isn't a debate on technology, principles, or any one person. This event has global significance that could destabilize the peace. Dialog and compromise—and perceptions—are of upmost importance. I wouldn't expect somebody with a straightforward duty such as yours to understand.*"

"*Madam Secretary, gentlemen,*" General Robertson said, "*I thank you for your input, but as long as the North Koreans do nothing, I'm inclined to act as if the violation of their airspace never happened. It seems the least risky course. Madam Secretary, will you concur?"*

"Fine," Secretary Johnson said, *"but I want to know what we're doing with this punk mechanic. General Wissmark, he did this under your nose."*

Wissmark's shoulder twitched. "He's not technically in the military any longer so we're holding him in detention as a foreign combatant even though he is a US citizen. I'm afraid the laws aren't supportive of what might need to be done." The smoking pipe in his hand trembled. "Lieutenant Colonel Sircor, his former superior officer, has been court-martialed for willful insubordination and misappropriation of public property. Five other Air Force personnel are under investigation for their roles."

"What about this loose cannon, Major Takinato, on the Japanese side? Is he the next Roble Santos?" Secretary Johnson demanded.

All eyes turned to General Yamatomo. Frederick leaned in with anticipation, his Italian suit shining.

"Major Takinato is not a topic for this meeting," Yamatomo said.

"I've been informed that Roble Santos spent a lot of time with this Takinato. I think that warrants an investigation. We can't afford to upset the North Koreans again, or anyone else for that matter," Secretary Johnson said.

"I promoted Major Takinato for his actions." Yamatomo glared at the blinking phone. "And Madam Secretary, I would like to thank you personally for thwarting my procurement order of Eagle *Super Kais* from Libby Industries. Maybe you could do me another favor and simply declare that my enemies cannot attack so I can just stop buying fighter jets altogether."

Frederick's shoe slipped to the floor.

General Robertson cleared his throat over the speaker. *"Those were interesting questions, Madam Secretary, and I thank the General for answering them, but I want to focus back on Roble Santos for this meeting. Operatives, please tell us what we know about him and what risk he poses."*

One of the men in khaki with cold eyes and a hard jaw, going by the name Ronin, placed an arrowhead necklace on the table. He slid it before General Wissmark. The general held it up, its brilliant dark crystals sparkling along angled fault lines.

"Roble wore that arrowhead when taken into custody last week," Ronin said. "His birth certificate lists his father only as a

Native American but the name field was left blank. His mother was a teen runaway from Brazil. She was murdered in Las Vegas when he was two. Roble joined a street gang at age twelve and served eight stints in juvenile detention for various offenses."

"*What a lowlife. How'd you let him in the Air Force, General Wissmark?*" Secretary Johnson snapped.

Wissmark dropped the arrowhead and his pipe.

"Figures," Frederick said.

Ronin slid the arrowhead along the table until it came to rest in front of Yamatomo.

The other operative, code named Hawkeye, added, "At age fifteen, Roble left the gang and lived alone. He skipped high school, working underage as a motorcycle and light aircraft mechanic. The FAA reprimanded him as a minor at least six times for flying light aircraft without a license."

"I've interrogated Roble," Ronin said, "using various *means*, but he hasn't revealed anything we don't already know. Based on our network and those of our allies, we are fairly certain he never contacted any known foreign agents. He received all his jet parts from the aerospace inventor Libby Dodge. We believe her motivation was to gain a sales contract with the US military similar to what she tried with Japanese F-15s."

"Now," Ronin looked at the speakerphone, "this supposedly uneducated, orphan 'lowlife' somehow redesigned the most advanced aircraft in the world and could've single-handedly eliminated the North Korean dictator on a whim, but chose not to. I don't know what type of twenty-one-year-olds you people are acquainted with, but this one astounds the hell out of me. And I'm in no way convinced he should be locked up as an enemy combatant." He leaned in. "In fact, if I were a woman, I'd want to fuck him."

"Excuse *me? Do you know who you're briefing?*" Secretary Louise Johnson said.

"File a complaint with the CIA director. I plagiarized my last line from him."

"*Roble is a terrorist!*" Secretary Johnson screamed.

"This is outrageous," Frederick whined, hitting the table with a fist. "The dirty Indian savage is dangerous and should be shot for treason, and Libby Dodge should be in jail as an accomplice. I'm warning you General Wissmark, and you too Yamatomo."

His fat finger shook at them. "If my jet designs are illegally modified again, I'll sue you each personally."

"That's quite enough, all of you," General Robertson said. *"Based on the evidence, here is my conclusion. I'll see to it Libby Dodge never makes another aircraft or part. Roble Santos will be held indefinitely as a probable terrorist. We can't risk the publicity of a trial, especially a civilian one if the North Koreans remain silent. Generals—no more anomalies with parts or personnel. This meeting and its contents are designated* top secret. *Do you concur with my decision, Madam Secretary?"*

"At least somebody is going to pay for this," she said. *"I'm glad you agree with me, General."*

"Meeting adjourned." The speaker beeped twice and the blinking green light turned red.

All in the conference room rose. Frederick scurried out first, followed by everyone except the men in khaki and General Yamatomo.

Yamatomo lifted the arrowhead and glanced at Ronin.

Ronin held his stare. "I think we're done here," he said to Hawkeye, leaving the arrowhead necklace with Yamatomo.

"Based on the military and federal personnel taking part in the raid, it seems plausible Libby Industries is being investigated for crimes of an international nature, possibly terrorism," a TV reporter said, standing near crisscrossing yellow tape fluttering in the wind.

Uniformed officers streamed in and out of the North Las Vegas facility. National Guard troops loaded office computers and manufacturing equipment into large trucks. Bewildered employees wandered to the parking lot, sent home without explanation.

Refusing to comply with the evacuation, Libby remained at her desk as they confiscated the contents of her office.

Government authorities also raided Libby's downtown compound.

The Swiss embassy, on behalf of the property-owning Swiss trust, demanded an explanation for the raids. No search warrants were cited as necessary since the raids were in regard to a classified national security threat, not a personal crime.

Frederick Compros, sitting on a velvet and gold-stitched sofa in an imperial suite at *The Sin*, dropped a handful of potato chips onto a napkin sitting on his suit pants and reached for the TV remote. He turned up the volume with delight, watching a reporter talk about the weeklong saga at Libby Industries.

When the reporter announced that Libby Dodge had canceled all customers' orders and laid off all her employees, Frederick jumped to his feet. Potato chips flew across the couch and floor. He paced excitedly, smashing oily wafers into the carpet and slapped the TV with a loose wrist as if patting a good friend on the back.

He plopped down on a clean sofa, enjoying its springs' feeble attempt at a rebound. A fingertip smudged across his mobile device screen, causing a phone to ring at Libby Industries.

"Hello," Libby mumbled.

"Libby. So good to hear your voice."

Silence.

"I'd like us to meet," Frederick said. "I have important business to discuss."

"Make an appointment with my secretary."

"But…you don't even have any employees left."

"Oh, yeah. Well, come over then. I'm here."

Frederick laughed. "Why don't we meet somewhere less controversial? Come to my hotel suite. I'll make you a drink."

Silence.

"All right," Frederick said, "wherever you want, Libby. When shall I come?"

"Now."

"But…" Frederick looked around at his comfortable, ornately decorated room, licking his oily fingers. "Fine."

Frederick ducked under the whipping yellow tape as his limo waited in the deserted Libby Industries parking lot. Entering the reception area, he gazed at the trash strewn everywhere.

A bored-looking police officer leaned against the reception desk. "You supposed to be in here, Bud?"

Frederick marched forward, polished shoes shuffling in haughty steps. "I'm Frederick Compros, goddammit." The officer shrugged as he passed by.

Entering the manufacturing space, Frederick froze. The facility lay stripped, silent, and dark. A flash of unidentified fear washed over him. He lunged ahead, scurrying through the manufacturing wasteland, his heart racing.

In a forced march, he reached Libby's office anteroom and stopped, heaving with exhaustion. He studied the ransacked secretary's desk and then stared out the window facing a chain-link fence wrapped in stray yellow tape. The place had the feeling of barbarism, like Rome after being pillaged by the Vandals.

He shuddered and rapped on Libby's office door, but opened it before anyone could answer. Entering, he glanced behind him as if being chased. He slammed the door, smiling with eyes wide, and dabbed his forehead with a silky cloth.

The lights were off, the blinds drawn. A faint sliver of light from a window above the door cut across Libby's hair as it hung over her face, her shoulders hunched forward. She sketched something on a paper. Two trash cans filled with debris sat next to her.

Frederick stared at the contrast between the calm woman and the plundered building. It made him feel both strangely reassured and angry—reassured because the Vandals weren't chasing him, but angry because Libby didn't look as desperate as he had hoped.

"May I sit?" Frederick asked, sitting down. He flipped a foot onto his opposing thigh and gestured around the room. "None of this was necessary."

Libby continued drawing.

"Look Libby, I'm actually a nice guy."

"Yes, you are, Frederick." She didn't lift her head.

"You really think so?" His lips turned up at the corners.

Libby set down the pencil and reclined in her chair. "You've only acted in a way you thought would cause others to like you."

Frederick smiled broadly. "Some people still want to prosecute you for your actions, but I told them you're a practical woman." Tapping a finger on his knee, he added, "I'll be your advocate. Just tell me where your research and development is and I'll get these people off your back."

"If it's all the same to you, I'll just wait until you find it and steal it."

Frederick's cheeks scrunched into greasy rolls. "Your game is up. Or haven't you noticed?"

"Then why come?"

"You always make these conversations so unnecessarily disagreeable," Frederick whined, plopping his shoe to the floor. "Okay, if you want to cut to the brass tacks, I'll lay it all out for you. There's enough evidence to charge you with bribing a US Air Force Airman as well as officers in the Japanese Self-Defense Force. Each charge could put you in jail for five years."

"I guess you'd know; you're the expert on bribes...or is it on charity? I can't remember."

"Jest all you want, but you gave material payment in the form of jet parts in exchange for influence to obtain military contracts. Witnesses will testify against you."

"Witnesses?" Libby's face brightened. "So Roble is alive?"

"Well, yes...I mean, I can't confirm or deny anything. That's not public information."

"I see." Libby looked out the window, a relieved smile stretched across her lips.

"Well? Will you let me help you?"

She tried to wipe away her grin, but failed. Turning back to him, she said, "Go ahead and tell your buddies to charge me and put Roble Santos on the stand to testify. Or don't they hold trials for the accused anymore?"

Frederick's finger shook at her. "If you don't cooperate, you'll never make another jet so long as you shall live."

"I'm glad we had this little chat. Now, if you'll excuse me, I'm busy." Libby lifted and studied her drawing, whistling a tune under her breath.

Frederick clenched his hands into doughy globs, eyes darting around the dark office.

"The door is right there behind you," Libby said.

Frederick stood up and opened his arms outward in surrender. "Look, with no business left, your research and development has no *value*. I could take it and achieve great things for all of society, just as you always wanted. Let DCU buy it for a lot of money; nobody else will pay for it now. Be selfish if you want. Name your price. Go retire on a tropical island and leave this mess behind. At least salvage something out of this."

Libby smoothed out the paper and finished drawing a fuselage.

After a moment Frederick sighed and shuffled to the exit. Just as the door closed behind him, Libby said, "Frederick?"

He swung the door back open, smacking it into the wall.

"Tell your friends to release Roble and bring back my property."

Frederick blinked a few times and stormed out.

A few weeks later, government authorities abandoned the raided facilities without charging Libby Dodge with a crime because the prosecution's main witness no longer officially existed and the Japanese officers refused to testify in a US court.

Chapter 32

Halvern Black walked over and sat on the bottom row of a bleacher near a Miami Beach tennis court.

Wiping sweat from his brow, he watched a ball popping like a champagne cork back and forth between a teenage boy and girl. Other teens practiced on adjacent courts. "Who in the hell plays in this much humidity, and on purpose?"

An elderly man standing on the sideline turned around. He wore a baseball cap over grey hair and clenched a clipboard in his hands like a scientist. "Oh, excellent. You're here."

"Dr. Thatcher," Halvern nodded. "I presume there is a reason you invited me to this mosquito infested swamp, other than to watch amateur tennis."

Renny Thatcher glanced at the players on the near court and made a note with a pencil. "Since the media reported that you retired, I thought maybe you'd want your first vacation. Welcome to the retirement state."

Halvern scowled. "*You* claimed to retire twenty years ago. That was the worst self-deception I've ever heard."

"I've always thought one person's retirement," Renny scratched the pencil behind his ear, "is another's new beginning."

"Now your 'new beginning' is as an amateur tennis coach? I didn't even know you played." Halvern squinted against the blazing sun. "When did your 'retirement' stop consisting of guest-lecturing at Ivy League schools and consulting for NASA?"

"Did I never tell you…" Renny asked, his voice thin and upbeat, while he scribed in the blotter, "…that I taught myself geometry on a tennis court at age six? There is something about the game." He glanced up, furrowing his grey brows at Halvern. "And you look healthier than I've seen in years. Pick up a sport yourself?"

Halvern's gaze followed a tennis ball as it launched back and forth on the court. "All right, I've been patient, Dr. Thatcher. Now, tell me why you really asked me here."

Renny nodded his visor at the blonde, ponytailed girl on court. "Look at her shot angles and precision. Have you ever seen anything as elegant as *that* in architecture?"

Halvern watched yellow dust burst off the girl's racket as she struck the ball. Her body twisted in a wide sinuous arc, following through a forehand swing. The ball shot over the net in a blur; midflight it swerved left, dropped, and nicked the sideline. Her practice partner had no chance of returning the ball.

"Did she create that cross-spin on purpose?" Halvern mumbled. "God Almighty."

Renny wrote in his notepad, his eyes glancing between the girl and his clipboard.

"So, she's also a math student of yours?" Halvern asked.

"You would notice that, of course. But she's not just *a* math student." He pointed his pencil at her.

Halvern studied the girl's large eyes. They narrowed into slits, scanning the far court like laser measuring beams. "She's mathematically calculating variables, isn't she."

Before the other player could complete his forehand swing, the girl leaped across the court. With her feet off the ground, she floated in the air as if pondering a decision, then drilled the ball before it could bounce and angled it short, spinning it to a line and out of reach.

"With all earned respect," Halvern shook his head, "is that level of math best utilized on a goddamn sport? Why not rocket science or something else important?"

"Why don't you go ask Nicolette if rocket science is more important than tennis?"

Halvern stopped his frown in mid-formation and exhaled. "Forgive my thoughtless question, Dr. Thatcher."

"I asked you to come to Miami, Halvern," he adjusted his baseball cap, "because knowing your history, and your interest in schooling youths, I imagined you'd appreciate observing a sixteen-year-old with such unusual potential."

Halvern stood up, his face dripping with sweat. "Where did you find her?"

"In your hometown. Only, instead of struggling to find

intelligent life in a crumbling inner city school like you, she suffered even more so at a country club."

Halvern slapped his arm, killing a bug.

Renny Thatcher smirked. "Come to the World Amateur Junior Championship final tomorrow. Miss Nicolette Popov will demonstrate on the court mathematics more complex than it took to build your skyscraper."

Halvern nodded and took a step to leave, but stopped. "By the way. Thank you for flying to Vegas to meet with…who you did. She…" he touched his abdomen, "*I*…appreciate it."

"The match starts at 10 AM, sharp." Renny turned back to the tennis court and made more notes.

"Yes, Dr. Thatcher," Halvern said, and continued off the court.

Nicolette Popov ripped a two-fisted backhand across her body, her knees bent low to ground. The ball skipped off the net's top-wire and skidded almost without a bounce on the back edge of the opposing baseline.

"Out," her partner yelled.

Nicolette ignored the incorrect call and returned to her baseline.

A baseball cap waved from the sideline, and Nicolette ran over to Coach Thatcher.

He replaced the cap and picked up his clipboard. "Your forehand error at 30-Love—explain it to me."

She dropped the racket, grabbed his blotter, and scrunched her small nose.

Sketching out equations, she considered the geometric inputs of the court, the ball, and her body. She rotated her wrist in thought before writing down the calculus of the shot's trajectory, acceleration, deceleration, and spin—adjusting for her estimates of wind and humidity. After integrating and completing the calculations, she circled the answer and marked the analogical spot on the court diagram.

She glanced at the actual court. "I think I missed by about three, maybe four millimeters to the duce court because my spin lacked about twenty RPMs, I likely overestimated the cross breeze, and I know my forearm tensed improperly," she said with a southern drawl, handing back the pad.

"Very close to correct. Just remember that humidity slows the ball's rotation. You under-spun your target RPMs by more than fifty. And always use your, or your opponent's, ball toss to calculate the cross breeze."

"Yes, Coach Thatcher." She nodded, returned to the court, and flicked the racket off the ground with her foot, landing it in her hand.

Her first shot marked a pixel in a butterfly pattern on the far side, using the ball's fuzz as yellow ink. The design turned out pretty well, but she wished she could've replaced a few errant impacts on its left wing. After completing it with a dot on the opposing baseline, she dropped the racket and walked around the net.

She paced her practice partner's baseline searching for something. Her partner glanced at his watch.

Renny met her on court. "Nice execution, Nicolette, but what are you—?"

Nicolette seized the blotter and wrote numbers and symbols atop a drawn tennis court. Renny folded his arms, the tiny metal rocket pin attached to his baseball cap glinting in the sun.

She slapped the pencil to the pad and handed it back.

Renny scanned her calculations. "Interesting. But what would you say if I told you to play the lines as drawn?"

"I'd say you're testing me. The proper tennis court dimensions are independent of how poorly somebody paints them."

"But these are the lines the judges will see."

"The judges aren't playing. I am, so I must identify all unknown variables."

"Except the court dimensions aren't supposed to be unknown variables."

"That's what makes measuring them so important, right?"

"How do you intend to win a match when you are right, but your shots are called out?"

"Stop testing me." She laughed. "I know what you taught me, and I know what I want, Coach Thatcher."

Renny smiled like a proud grandfather. "I'm calling it a day, Nicolette." He walked to the sideline and packed up his gear. "If you are so inclined, save your energy for tomorrow's final."

"Later." She ran over to recover her dropped racket. "I'll see you at Love."

She tossed the ball in the air and smashed it to her partner. In the middle of a volley, and her drawing of a yellow pixelated ladybug, she stopped play.

Her eyes locked on the dark-skinned Emilio Estrella arriving at the adjacent court. She'd seen him play before and knew he'd advanced to the boys' championship final tomorrow. He bounced on his muscled legs before his racket pounded the first practice ball across the court to his partner.

When Nicolette noticed her own partner packing up, she hit the ball at him; it bounced into his hand. He looked at it, then wearily at Nicolette, and returned to the court.

She practiced, watching Emilio with her peripheral vision. After a minute, she began calculating the mathematics of his shots as well as her own. She liked his shot angles and his shot strength even more so. Her stomach tingled every time he grunted.

Her practice partner lifted his racket in a sign she should quit for the day. She served the ball, forcing him to continue. As she played, her eyes kept darting to Emilio. He looked so untamed. Her thoughts surprised her because she'd never felt an interest in boys before, at least not like this.

She seemed to ignore a ball flying at her chest, and then casually deflected it to Emilio's far court, halting his play. Running onto their court, she stopped the ball with her foot. Conscious of her own body, she bent over to pick it up, slowing her movement so he would watch.

With ball in hand, Nicolette hit it to Emilio, ignoring his practice partner. Emilio returned it with a forehand stroke, obviously holding back his strength. She ran to the ball and spanked it with all her might to his backhand. He scrambled to get it back, his eyes wide. She returned it again, and they didn't stop playing. Emilio's practice partner shook his head and left the court.

Without a word, Nicolette started a match, wanting to feel his vibrations against her racket. She wondered if he could conquer her. She thought she wanted him to—and that's why she decided to win.

Spectators gathered along the fence. Emilio's speed and

strength pummeled Nicolette back behind the baseline, but she returned his shots, flinging them to the most difficult spots. Both played as if not caring to save their strength for tomorrow's finals.

Emilio only called out a few of her close line shots, acting chivalrous in his discretion. She knew he miscalled some of them but said nothing. According to Emilio's score, he won in three sets, with every set being won in a tiebreak.

Nicolette stood motionless on the baseline. Emilio's eyes raked over her body from across the court. She didn't shy away. Emilio averted his gaze and walked to the locker rooms.

She wrinkled her nose. "Huh."

After showering and changing into street clothes, Nicolette skipped from the tennis complex toward her parents' nearby hotel. Seeing Emilio standing outside the doors, she went to him in short purposeful steps, her eyes unapologetic in their intent.

Taking him by the hand, they walked to the boardwalk along the wide beach. He didn't speak English well, and even though she'd taken three years of Spanish, she felt no desire to talk much, not yet anyway. They didn't return to their parents' hotel rooms until early the next morning.

Nicolette attended the boys' championship final a few hours later, wanting to see Emilio again before her own match. She smiled in her mind at the phone number he'd given her—a long one with an international prefix.

Emilio lost his match in three embarrassingly easy sets. His coach and parents, sitting in the front row, scolded him in Spanish in front of the entire stadium. His father accused him of practicing too hard the day before. His mother cried that he stayed up too late with a shameless girl. His coach forbade him to do either behavior ever again. Emilio said nothing.

As Nicolette took the court, warming up for her match, the Estrellas remained in the bleachers, sitting near her own parents. She overheard Emilio's mother telling him, between quiet sobs, that she had sacrificed everything for his tennis career, and if he didn't make pro she would have to get a second job in Madrid. Nicolette stopped play and stared at him, but he wouldn't make eye contact.

Emilio knelt before his father, head lowered. "I am sorry," he said in Spanish. "Playing and leaving with that stupid girl was a horrible mistake. I will never do something like that again."

Nicolette turned away, brows furrowed, mouth pursed. *I don't understand. Maybe I didn't learn Spanish very well.*

Her match had been close, but her failed attempt at spelling of *EMILIO* on the far court in yellow ball dust cost her the third set, and therefore the match. Nicolette shook her opponent's hand and congratulated her on a fine match. From the faces of the two girls, it appeared as if Nicolette had won.

"How do you appraise your play?" Renny asked, his hand resting on the umpire's chair.

"I was a bit sleepy and made some miscalculations. I'll write them all out tonight so I can learn. But I'm happy with what I did."

Renny hugged her. "Someday the world isn't going to know what hit them." He waved Halvern over from the stands. "I want you to meet someone I've told you about."

Halvern clomped over in confident steps, his barreled chest and bothered, black face towering over Nicolette.

"This is Halvern Black. Halvern, Miss Nicolette Popov."

"Nice to meet you." Nicolette curtsied with a smirk on her lips.

Halvern stood unmoving, a scowl on his sweaty face.

"The way Coach Thatcher goes on about you," Nicolette said, "I kinda expected you to look bigger and a bit more sour-faced."

Halvern held out his large hand. "Impressive mathematical discernment on court, Miss Nicolette Popov." He leaned down to be eye level with her. "Keep learning from Renny and never abandon your blatant proclivity for fun."

She smiled and shook his hand, amazed at both its strength and gentleness. "I really want to see your skyscraper. It's so pretty in the pictures Coach Thatcher showed me. I bet they paid you a wad of cash to build it." Her nose scrunched. "But I would've painted it yellow."

Halvern turned to Renny and wiped his dripping forehead. "Now, Dr. Thatcher, if you'll excuse me, I'm flying back to the desert where the humidity is civilized."

"Cutting your inaugural vacation so short?" Renny asked.

"I'll have plenty of time for a sweaty vacation the day heaven won't take me."

Nicolette giggled, covering her mouth.

Halvern marched away.

Later, as Nicolette showered in the locker room, she felt a sense of excitement thinking about her match and adventure with Emilio the night before, ignoring what he could not have possibly meant when speaking to his father.

On the plane flight back to Atlanta, she glanced at her parents, remembering how they'd told her that life would be good. She smiled. *No, it's* way *better than that.*

Chapter 33

Danny held it in his hands, the first storyboard to his long dreamt of anime series based on his escaping horse rider. Glancing out the large window, he watched his bus pull up to the guard gate at Kadena Air Base.

He flashed his military ID and announced his visit to Airman Santos, as he'd always done. Only this time the guard said the strangest words, "Airman Santos no longer serves on base."

"What? He never said anything to me. Where is he?"

The guard looked at a screen and shook his head. "I can't help you."

Back at Futenma, Danny tried contacting Roble, but he didn't respond to this cell phone or e-mail, and the Air Force wouldn't provide a forwarding address. Roble had never joined any internet social networks, and internet searches of his name revealed nothing useful.

Danny sat on his bed, knees bouncing, hands holding his new storyboard. *I know he'd ask to keep it. I just know he would.*

Pinning the art to his wall, he stepped back. *Why haven't I named this character all these years?* He rubbed his chin, looking at the horse rider's face. *It would have to be something noble...or roguish. Maybe a name capturing both.*

He shook his head. *Roble, where the hell are you?*

As the weeks passed, Danny felt so alone at night without Roble to appraise his art. For the first time, Okinawa actually felt like an island, detached and isolated. *What happened, Roble? If you've run away from me on purpose I'll never forgive you, not twice.*

He drew fewer art pieces, skipping Nishiko's lessons occasionally—then more than occasionally—turning instead to the Marines to occupy his anxious thoughts.

"What is wrong Danny-san?" Nishiko asked, as they drew Isshin-Ryu warriors in motion at the dojo one day.

"Nothing." Danny exhaled. "I just have real stuff in my life taking up more time. That's all."

"Art shows us how real life should be."

Danny shrugged. "I'm just busy."

Roble lay on a prison cot tracing a finger across the bedsheet, his fingernail etching the lines of a three-dimensional jet assembly, his mind filling in the details. He studied it, smoothed it out and started another.

For the past three months, officers and operatives working in teams had grilled him. He told them everything they wanted to know, but they acted as if the straightforwardness of his answers only proved that he lied.

In many sessions he suffered waterboarding and sleep deprivation, but he didn't mind the intimidation and pain too much. It was his wasted time he found most painful.

One interrogator, however, wearing rugged civilian clothes, always met with him alone. He called himself Ronin.

Leaning against Roble's cell wall for his first interview, Ronin said, "I find certain individuals to be like obsidian," he crossed his arms, "those formed amidst the violence and heat of the world."

He pressed a boot heel against the wall. "It's the rapid change in temperature that defines obsidian and gives it its sharpness, just as some people define themselves by cutting through others' assumptions—and at times, the sky. So tell me, Mr. Santos..." he paused, his gaze dropping to Roble's prison shirt.

Roble reached for his arrowhead, but grasped only air.

"...what does the world look like peering out from heat-forged eyes?"

"You *really* want to know?"

Ronin tilted his head, waiting.

"Have you ever seen a world so amazing you wanted to inhale it?" Roble breathed in. "Like air sucking into a jet engine? And the more you inhaled, the faster you flew, until you knew, without having to ask anyone else, that you were living?"

Ronin touched his unshaven chin.

"That's what I see," Roble said, "and why I want to create things that fly."

Ronin massaged his chin. After a moment, he said, "Now that

you've revealed your soul to a complete stranger—do you have a question for me?"

Roble ran his fingers across the bedsheet. "How is Lieutenant Colonel Sircor?"

"Mr. Sircor is serving a sixteen-month sentence at Fort Leavenworth for misappropriation of public property and willful insubordination."

"That's not what he deserves."

"Maybe you should've thought of that before you took him up on his offer."

"Have you talked to him…" Roble thought back to the moment he completed his puzzle inside the Raptor *Super Kai*, "…talked to Sircor, since it happened?"

"I said *a* question." He pressed himself off the wall with his boot. "This ends my interrogation."

After that exchange, Roble looked forward to the infrequent ones with Ronin that followed.

When not being interrogated by anyone, like today, Roble sat in this cell, designing and redesigning the specifications to the idea he once carried on his scrap of paper. Each of its thousands of parts he remembered by specific reference in his mind.

He finished engraving a curve into the bedsheet and sat up, tilting his head in appraisal. *The longer it takes to get out of here, the better the design will become.*

The walls of the cell appeared as sky before his eyes. He watched a projectile roaring across it. *And if I never get out*—his wrists twisted, hands gripping the air as if controlling the projectile—*at least it will have existed in my mind.*

An actual jet rumbled over the prison, and that's how he knew they held him on Futenma Marine Base. The constant noise from VTOL F-35s, F/A-18Fs, and Chinook helicopters proved too easy for him to recognize.

"You're one step away from platoon commander or drill instructor," Danny's father wrote. "Both positions are almost equivalent to graduating from the CMI as a commissioned officer."

Pushing hard for either promotion, Danny performed his

duties more vigorously than any of his squad leader peers. Ignoring his distaste for ordering around his subordinates, he demanded more of them, even sacrificing his leave days and those of his men to show his dedication.

Time melted under his relentless drive, and each day that disappeared was one fewer he had to suffer through again. Whenever he unconsciously sketched something in a rare free moment, he wished to show Roble, before remembering and throwing it away.

Late one night he rolled sleepless in his bed. *What if I could make Father proud of my art as well as my efforts in the Marines? It would eliminate my conflicts and integrate my life into a single whole, just as Nishiko said I needed to do with my art.*

Sitting up, he pictured a Japanese version of Robin Hood, stylized after his dad's counseling business logo. *With my current skill level I could draw Father's hero better than he has ever seen.* He grinned. *An integrated whole…no conflicts.* He gripped his gut, not wanting to feel the sudden pain or consider where it came from.

For the next month, Danny worked on the storyboards, naming his new Robin Hood hero *Ritashugi*. The art combined every technique Nishiko had taught him, pouring with life across the artboards. Ritashugi embodied in beautiful artistic detail everything his father admired—honor, duty, selflessness, and respect from others.

On a rare visit to the Yuki Manga Shop, he showed Nishiko his Ritashugi storyboards, all complete except for the last undrawn scene.

Nishiko appraised each scene, taking her time. When finished, she said, "Other than your missing ending, you've created an exquisite spark extinguisher."

Danny scrunched his brows. "What?"

"Your character, Ritashugi, extinguishes sparks." She tapped her own forehead with a finger.

"I don't think you understand the story," he said. "Ritashugi takes from the rich and gives to the poor. He's not a fire fighter."

"A spark," she turned her finger to point at Danny's forehead, "comes from the mind. And sparks are transformed into reality using these." She opened her hand, wiggling her fingers. "To take away someone else's wealth, the results of what one creates, is to attempt to extinguish the spark."

"Uhmm…." He scratched his neck. "I mean…maybe the translation into Japanese culture doesn't translate as well as in the west. He is actually a hero because he helps the needy."

"Who someone deems a hero or villain depends on the shade of one's own soul. Many of my best art pieces were commissioned by those judged by others to be villains, some of them living in your own country."

"I didn't say I liked this story." Danny rubbed his forehead, feeling sick, and not wanting to think of where the story idea came from. "I was just trying out some new techniques."

"Superb techniques, Danny-san." She bowed.

That night, each time Danny tried to finish the final Ritashugi storyboard, his hand froze. *Maybe Nishiko doesn't understand what I'm trying to do, but it would simplify everything with Father—simplify my life. I have to finish it.*

Eyes wide with determination, he tried again, but still couldn't get his pencil to move. He dropped it, pushed away from the table, and sat on his bed with his laptop. *What if I just floated my story idea out there for Father to consider? Maybe I'll get the right response and have the motivation to finish it.*

He e-mailed him and confessed his art classes, and most importantly, the production of a story based on his father's hero. Donald responded within an hour, writing at length about his own successes in the Marines and how well his counseling business was going, but he didn't mention Danny's art idea.

Danny smiled and stood up, knowing his father's silence in this case meant acceptance. He breathed deep, standing at the cusp of everything he ever wanted, the impossible—his father proud of him while still allowing him to be an artist.

But the next morning, he still couldn't finish the storyboard; in fact, he couldn't draw anything. His desire to draw had vanished into thin air, just like Roble.

He pulled every sketch off of his wall that Roble had wanted to keep, plus his new horse rider drawing Roble never saw, and tore them up. With tears in his eyes, he rained the scraps into the trash. All that remained on the wall were the storyboards of Ritashugi, his father's unfinished hero.

Chapter 34

Alexandria Patra stood, hair pouring over her shoulders like liquid granite. Her onyx eyes focused on the snow-dusted, black robed judge. She spoke with reverence, repeating the oath of office on the capitol's steps in Carson City, Nevada.

Preton Moore smiled as the crowd applauded, but recoiled when he saw Alexandria's eyes.

"Frightened?" she asked.

"Of…of what?" He shivered, moving away from her. Descending the stairs, he shook hands with everyone in his path, sucking in the congratulatory words like a man starving for reassurance.

Alexandria approached a woman in a blue overcoat and said, "As your first assignment, please do not pay my salary or benefits during my term as lieutenant governor."

The state treasurer stared at her. "I'll need Governor Moore's permission to do that."

"No, you don't need his permission."

"Uhmm…" The treasurer scrunched her brows.

"I wish you success with your new job," Alexandria nodded at her, and turned away. Noting her parents in the crowd below, she strode down the steps past a group of eager reporters.

They peppered her with questions. "Ms. Patra, where were you during the campaign?" "Why did you resign from the CUH?" "Where have you been hiding?" "Where are you going now?"

Alexandria glanced again at her parents, continued away from the steps, and turned down a side street. Stepping into a secluded parking lot, she stopped, her back turned to the capitol building. Snowflakes gathered like feathers on her hair as she waited.

"Honey!" Her mother scurried up from behind. "Didn't you see us in the crowd?"

Alexandria faced her. "Thank you for following me here. I wanted to speak to you and Dad alone."

"We've been worried sick." Thema hugged her. "I know you told us you'd be 'out of sight for some time' but we didn't know what you meant—or that it included from us as well. It's been almost a year. Why didn't you return our calls? And we're so sorry to have missed your election night celebrations in November. Your father had an important dinner scheduled with the Secretary of the United Nations that day. It was for the children; you understand." She studied Alexandria's frame. "You look so thin. Have you been sick?"

"We're so proud of you for taking public office, sweetheart," Darius said, catching up with them, his dress shoes squishing into the slush. "But where have you been?"

"Mom, Dad," she touched their gloved hands, "I'm sorry if you worried about me. That was never my intent." Dropping her hands back to her sides, she added, "It means a lot to me that you attended my inauguration today. And don't feel bad about missing my election night celebrations because I didn't stay."

"I can't believe you sold your house and moved without telling us. Where are you living, princess? Do you have a new phone number?"

"I don't expect you to understand, and I mean no disrespect, but it's important to me not to say."

"But why not tell us?" Thema asked. "You'll be serving in a public office. Everyone will know."

"If you're not ill," Darius interjected, "why leave your inauguration so soon? Everyone is expecting you to explain all the things you plan to accomplish as Nevada's Lieutenant Governor."

"Now why don't you go back there and make a speech," Thema said, nodding in agreement. "This is a big day. We should savor this moment in front of the whole world. Then afterward," she adjusted her pearl necklace, "we can talk about where you've been."

Alexandria brushed snow off her coat sleeves and took a breath. "Mom, Dad, even though I'm now in public office, nobody, including you, will see *me* again for a long time."

"But," Thema gripped Alexandria's wrist, "'a long time?' Where will you be?"

"Please don't worry." Alexandria wiped a snow crystal off her mother's cheek. "Just know it's what I want."

"We're your parents. You can tell *us*," Darius said.

Alexandria formed a gentle smile. "I'm happy again. That's all I can tell you."

"Honey, you weren't happy before?" Thema asked.

Alexandria stepped back, her lashes lowering.

Thema shot Darius a worried look.

"Growing up…you wanted me to be happy?" Alexandria asked, her voice soft.

Darius shuffled on his feet. Thema's lips twitched.

Alexandria searched their eyes.

"Sweetheart, we raised you in a way that was best for everybody. See?" Darius pointed at the capitol building. "Look at how many people you'll help. This is what we've always talked about."

Alexandria's chin sank. Melting snow glistened atop her lashes

Thema fidgeted with her pearl necklace. "Why weren't you happy, princess?"

"Because I…" Alexandria lowered her voice, "I actually believed what you taught me."

Thema closed her eyes. Darius averted his gaze.

"But no matter what each of us now believes," Alexandria stepped close and hugged them together, "you will always be my parents, and I love you."

Thema and Darius held still for a long time. Then they wrapped their arms around Alexandria. Falling snow hushed away the rest of the world.

Danny stepped back, studying the unfinished Ritashugi story-boards pinned to his barracks' wall, the only surviving art he'd drawn in Okinawa.

His heart fluttered. *It's a technical masterpiece of manga. Father will like it if I can just finish it…he will…* He winced, his body hunching over in pain. *Why do I hate it so much?*

Turning away, he stared at his Marine uniform hanging over a chair and the new, brass drill instructor insignia. Two weeks ago he received the promotion. His father almost seemed proud in his e-mail response. For those next few days Danny didn't think of anything except the idea his dad might be proud of him.

Shaking his head, he faced the wall and touched Ritashugi, drawn stealthily scaling a building. A groan escaped his throat. *I should never have drawn this for Father.* He pulled the storyboards from the wall and dropped them to the floor.

He fell on his bed exhausted, one arm draped over his forehead. He despised his new drill instructor duties, hated chastising the younger Marines. Every time he put one in his place, he loathed himself but knew he did it for a higher calling, a calling his father would approve of—that of enforcing duty upon others. He felt sick all the time, which helped his face look menacing to the recruits. Yet he knew he wasn't convincing enough because his first trainees ranked in the bottom quartile of all drill instructor cohorts, putting his new promotion at risk.

I must become more forceful, like Father. He gripped his hands. *I must.* Both fists slammed into his gut to stop the ache.

Lifting his head, he listened to jets flying over Futenma, surprised that he missed working on them. *Roble.* He sat up, rubbing his eyes.

The Marines had wanted to transfer him to Europe a year ago, but he went out of his way to obtain permission to stay by networking with his superior officers and promising to perform extra duties. He shook his head. *Roble, are you ever coming back to Okinawa?*

He glanced at his wallet sitting atop the dresser, but forced himself to look away. It held a picture he hadn't looked at in months. Lunging off his bed, he grabbed the wallet and removed the photo. *Why did I ever leave her?* He felt like calling—no, not calling—going to her on the next plane out of Futenma.

Excitement surged through his body just like when she'd touched his hand as they passed each other between high school classes. Then he remembered everything and slumped into a chair. His forehead lowered to his knees, a weight pressing on his back.

A bugle sounded outside and he shot to his feet, sending Jenny's picture to the floor. He pulled on his uniform and marched from the room.

Ted Hollings slipped behind a red curtain at the rear of a circus ring and walked down a flight of stairs. He wound past dressing rooms, costume closets, and makeup counters—all teeming with a motley assortment of performers.

Descending another level, he emerged into a vaulted basement. A squat man with a wing-tipped moustache sat behind a cluttered table below a dusty chandelier. Behind him hung the glue-glittered words: *Manager of The Virtue.*

To his right, a silver star on a door read: *Sitra.*

Mr. Hollings had read *The Virtue's* only performance review when the show started without fanfare six months ago. The theater critic panned it as both "monstrous and immature—an embarrassment even for a third rate casino."

But within a month of its opening night, it became the most popular performance in Las Vegas. Each week, Mr. Hollings noted the show's ticket prices increasing until the price of its best seats had ballooned from eighteen dollars to one hundred and fifty dollars.

Removing the medieval cowl from his head, Mr. Hollings bowed to the man behind the table. "I am here to meet with Ms. Sitra."

The man jumped to his feet, his moustache twitching. "No one is allowed down here. Get out," he pointed up the stairs, "before I bounce you back up those stairs in your ridiculous tuxedo." His voice echoed with a Hungarian accent.

Slipping an identification card from his breast pocket, Mr. Hollings laid it on the table. "I have an appointment."

The man picked up the ID and glanced between it and Mr. Hollings. "Hmm…" He huffed while flicking the card a few times. "You are on her list." He waved at Sitra's door for him to enter.

Mr. Hollings waited for the return of his ID.

The man stuffed it into a box on the table. "You can have it once you leave."

Mr. Hollings bowed again before opening the door.

Sitra stood alone in the center of a large dressing room in front of an illuminated mirror. She wore skintight, grey chainmail, her red hair cascading down her back.

Clothes racks along the walls displayed colorful handcrafted circus costumes. A low-hung tightrope stretched across the space just beyond Sitra and her dresser.

"What brings you to the north end of the Strip, Mr. Hollings?" Sitra's gaze caught his in the mirror.

He closed the door and bent low, an arm crossing his waist. "Good evening, Ms. Patra." He straightened. "Forgive me for using your real name, but I most prefer it. And it is a great honor to have been entrusted with your secret."

She faced him, her silver irises shimmering in the mirror lights.

"You look immaculate, if you don't mind me saying." Mr. Hollings cleared his throat. "And I very much appreciated your show tonight."

"Thank you for attending." She smiled. "What did you want to meet about?"

"Now that your show is up and running successfully, I'm here to collect a debt."

"Yes, of course." She picked up an eyeliner pencil and a performance flyer from her dressing table. Holding the tip to the paper, she asked, "How much do I owe?"

"The price of each dose was one hundred thousand dollars."

Alexandria swallowed and wrote, "Pay Mr. Hollings $600,000 in cash," signed it as Sitra and handed him the flyer. "Give this to my manager outside and he will pay you. Is there anything else I can help you with?"

He slipped the flyer into his back pocket. "Yes, Madam. I'm also here to extend an offer."

"Oh?"

"*The Sin,* at my discretion, wishes to purchase the rights to host *The Virtue.*" Mr. Hollings watched her hands swaying happily by her sides. "What percent of the ticket revenue does this casino pay you, may I ask? Thirty-five?"

"Fifteen."

He glanced up. "Then this negotiation might be simple."

She pursed her black lips. "I would have taken even less from them. This was the *only* casino willing to take the risk of hosting an unproven show with an unknown performer...offered to take a risk on me more than once, in fact. So perhaps you shouldn't assume anything."

He bowed and continued with his offer. "Based on *The*

Virtue's current ticket prices and the *much* larger auditorium at *The Sin*," he adjusted his wrist cuffs, "a thirty-five percent cut of ticket sales to you would equate to an increase of almost twelve times your current pay."

"That," she breathed in, "sounds very lucrative for me." Placing her hands on her hips, she added, "However, I believe that would also be very profitable for *The Sin*, and I've heard it never earns a profit. Am I mistaken?"

"Quite right," Mr. Hollings nodded, "upon my employer's request, it never earns a profit."

"Do you always help your employer get what he wants, Mr. Hollings?"

"I always optimize the highest and best outcome for the owner of whatever hotel I manage, based on the constraints given me."

"Interesting. And offering me a thirty-five percent cut of ticket sales optimizes that outcome?"

He blinked. "No it does not."

"Well, Mr. Hollings, what is your optimal management solution to this *problem*?"

"Ms. Patra, if I didn't know better, I'd think you'd planned this negotiation in your mind for months."

"No," she smirked, "just a year."

"Then I will reveal the offer which optimizes the outcome for all parties involved." He rolled a hand down from his body. "Due to *The Sin's* initial capital expenditures to modify the theater for *The Virtue*, you will only receive eighty percent of the ticket sales the first year."

Alexandria's eyelashes fluttered.

"Each year after that," he continued, "you will receive eighty-five percent. *The Sin* should break even at those levels, if not take a small loss." He removed a contract from an inside suit pocket and handed it to her. "This deal would increase your income by almost thirty times."

She stared at the prefilled contract giving her eighty percent of the first year's ticket sales at *The Sin*. "Tell me this, Mr. Hollings, why would I move my show from my favorite casino for money, however much?"

"And thus we get to it," he grinned, "the *true* exchange of value."

"But whatever do you mean?" She returned his grin.

"You know Stock will never attend *The Virtue* here, or attend any show at any other casino, for that matter." He straightened his suit collar. "But I just *might* be able to convince him if it were at his own hotel."

"You *are* utterly presumptuous, Mr. Hollings," Alexandria winked, "and correct." She lifted three fingers. "We have a deal under three stipulations."

"I accept in advance."

Alexandria's fingers waltzed in the air. "If Stock doesn't attend *The Virtue* within the first year, the contract ends and my show returns here. My manager will come with me and will be my exclusive contact to the outside world. If anyone not in *The Virtue*, including Stock, approaches me backstage, the show leaves *The Sin*. I must keep my identity secret at all costs."

He held out his hand. "Your wishes will be upheld."

"You are a superlative manager, Mr. Hollings." She shook his hand, but didn't let go. "Perhaps someday you'll expand your services beyond hospitality and into the realm of government operations."

"As I said, I am proficient at running operations according to the constraints given me," he narrowed his eyes, "and thus I would *never* assist this, or any other regime, to become more proficient in imposing their beliefs on others."

She tilted her head. "Remind me to introduce you to a certain mathematician sometime. I imagine you two might get along."

He nodded. "As you recommend, Madam."

"Thank you very much for coming, Mr. Hollings." Releasing his hand, she turned back to her mirror. "*The Virtue* will relocate to *The Sin* as soon as my contract here expires in six months. Make sure your auditorium is ready."

Roble stood, staring at his cot.

Two fingernail-drawn diagrams filled the bedsheet. He moved his head from side to side, comparing both dual mode engine designs, envisioning the intricate details in his mind.

Scratching his forehead, he wondered if he needed to narrow the ramjet's combustion chamber to give it more pressure. His gaze shifted to the scramjet schematic. *Will it be able to ignite at Mach 5? And more importantly, will it stay lit as it accelerates?*

He placed his hands on his hips. After thinking for three hours without moving, his lips curved upward with satisfaction. *It will work.*

A clanking on his cell door caused him to smooth out the sheet and sit on the cot. It wasn't a scheduled meal time, which meant a special visitor, and those rarely happened anymore.

A tanned man with rolled sleeves and khaki cargo pants walked in. He closed the door and leaned against a wall. "Miss me?"

"Ronin." Roble nodded.

"I'll take that as a 'yes.'"

"How is Sircor?"

"With his military conviction and jail time, he's lucky to be a single prop tourist pilot now."

"He's too good for that."

"How about you? Have two years in detention been enough time to think up another smartass project others might consider extremist activity?" Ronin massaged his facial stubble.

"I wouldn't know what people might consider it, but yes, I'm working on it."

"Good. I enjoyed your first one."

"But I didn't realize it's been two years." Roble rubbed his nose. "Feels shorter."

Ronin narrowed his eyes, his lips pursed with amusement.

"I haven't had a visitor in months." Roble's hands ran circles on the sheet at his sides. "Thought maybe I was forgotten. Can't say I haven't liked the peace and quiet, though."

"Yeah, well, I got too many people to kill and secrets to steal to sit around in this little paradise." He pressed a boot heel against the wall. "But I need to talk to someone sane every once in a while. And maybe you don't realize it, but being forgotten is exactly what you need."

"What I need is to get out of here."

"That will happen just as soon as some bureaucrat dares make the correct, career-threatening decision."

"How long will that take?"

"How long you got?"

Roble stretched out on the cot, hands clasped behind his head.

"But just in case you've been locked in a dungeon somewhere…" Ronin coughed to hide his laugh, "…you might find it interesting to know that a certain deputy secretary of state resigned in disgrace over a year ago. And a certain general at Kadena retired five months ago. And it is very possible a certain joint chief retired yesterday. Those are three people you don't know, who no longer care about you." He coughed again, grinning. "As sad as that may sound."

Roble sat up. "What are you saying?"

"This concludes my interrogation." Ronin pushed off the wall.

"When will you be back?"

"The day one of us does something stupid."

Chapter 35

Svetlana Jevic blinked her sweat-drenched eyes, shoulders rolling forward as though she held a tennis racket made of lead. Her long hair stuck to her neck just as her feet appeared stuck to the court.

For three years, the Serbian's toothy smile plastered the covers of every sports magazine in the world. Now, her fans watched in disbelief. An hour into the Melbourne Open final and she had yet to win more than two games off a player few had heard of.

Cameras panned to the far court, to the bouncing golden spring of a girl, her blonde hair cascading past striking blue eyes: Nicolette Popov, two years after the World Amateur Junior Championship in Miami Beach.

Her right shoulder bore a vivid black tattoo, which hadn't been there during her semifinal match—a capital S with two lines drawn vertically through it.

Shushes doused the crowd's murmurs as Nicolette walked to the baseline to serve for championship point. Equations arced through her mind. She tossed the ball in the air. It hung as if gravity surrendered for one breathless moment. The racket whipped down, spinning the ball on a precise axis. A yellow streak grazed the top of the painted tee on the far side of the net.

Svetlana lunged for it, grunting with effort, and missed the ball by a foot.

"Woohoo!" Nicolette yelled.

Svetlana raised her racket, calling for an electronic review of the line shot.

A smile stretched across Nicolette's lips as she walked in short steps to the net. Everyone in the stadium except Nicolette watched the electronic replay on the screen.

The crowd cheered. It was over. Svetlana shuffled to the net.

Nicolette shook her hand, saying, "You have the best forehand in the game next to Jordon Taylor. I think it's the way you apply torque through your waist and in your shoulder joint. I'm such a big fan."

Coach Thatcher's sunglasses failed to hide his contentment. At Nicolette's age, he had helped crunch the equations to land a man on the moon; today he watched the successful launch of a human rocket. Nicolette's parents stood next to him, beaming.

Commentators repeated how easily the eighteen-year-old upstart won the Melbourne Open. "A game changer," one said, and added, "It didn't even look like she was playing the same sport."

Nicolette remained at the net, hearing no one, thinking of her years of preparation, all the calculations. Not one day had been a sacrifice, because there had been nothing else she'd wanted to do, and no other way she'd wanted to do it. Now she knew she was ready, ready to take on the world.

The sparsely populated stadium seats from the women's championship filled in anticipation of the men's final.

The world's number one seed, Jordon Taylor, strolled on to the court like a clothing model, dark hair pushed back except for a perfect wedge dangling over an eye. He sat in a chair and raised a water bottle to his lips as though sipping a cocktail on a croquet lawn. He was the spokesman for several high-profile, nonprofit organizations and called three heads of state by their first name. A deodorant label embroidered his shirtsleeve. Deodorant advertisers loved him because he never seemed to sweat, not even on the court.

During the championship match a newcomer—twenty-fifth seed Emilio Estrella—attacked the ball like a hungry animal. Fans cheered with delight at the prolonged rallies, pushing the match to five sets. But as expected, the composed Jordon Taylor held on to his title.

The players from both the men's and women's finals joined in the arena for the awards ceremony. A curly-haired announcer stopped next to Nicolette and in a jovial Australian accent asked, "How does it feel to come out of nowhere and win your first slam title?"

"I'm excited to earn my first paycheck," Nicolette said, in a southern American drawl, not the Russian accent most had expected.

He chuckled. "People have been talking about your tattoo. What does it mean?"

"Just what it looks like."

"The dollar sign?"

"Cha ching." She jabbed a finger as if hitting a cash register and laughed.

"Well, since the Melbourne Open loves to recognize new talent," he grinned, "here's a check for one million dollars. How's *that* for your first paycheck?"

"About thirty percent too much." She pulled out a folded personal check from an interior pocket and handed it to him. It was written out to Jordon Taylor for three hundred thousand dollars.

The announcer stared at the check, lowering the microphone. "What's this?"

She leaned down to the microphone. "It's your overpayment, but don't cash it before I deposit my winnings. I'd rather Jordon's fans' admission money go to whom they intended it. I counted close to thirty percent fewer spectators in the stands during my match than his, but you gave us both a million dollars." She pointed at the check. "Math problem solved."

"You what? Counted?" He lowered the microphone farther.

She bent closer to the microphone. "Thank y'all for paying me to do what I love." She stood on her toes and waved at the stands.

The other players shook their heads. The announcer groaned, scratched his face, and moved to Jordon Taylor.

Jordon smiled, swirled an arm in the air, and bowed to Nicolette acknowledging her humor, however inappropriate. Plucking the check from the announcer's hand, he ripped it to pieces, letting the scraps flutter to the court. Into the microphone he said, "I've long been an advocate of equal pay between men and women. Problem solved."

The crowd laughed and cheered. The announcer nodded with satisfaction. Nicolette yawned.

Emilio held out his hand for the microphone. In broken English he said, "I speak for all of Spain. We, too, believe in equal pay no matter what. I play tennis for the benefit of all of you, and would gladly give up my winnings if all players would do the same."

The crowd clapped. Emilio patted his heart. Jordon patted Emilio's back. Nicolette rubbed her neck, looking bored.

After the ceremony, Emilio ran after Nicolette. "Hey, want to get a drink and celebrate? We should catch up."

"You never called me back." She twitched her nose. "Ever."

"You don't understand the pressure I was under, Nicolette. My family, my coach…" he opened his arms, one hand holding a silver plate, "…my country. It wasn't my fault."

"Oh, I was hoping it was your fault. At least then I'd know who you were. Congrats on making it to a slam final." She pecked him on the cheek. "Bye, Emilio."

"But—"

Nicolette strode off, carrying her bag and trophy.

Two weeks after the Melbourne Open, Nicolette signed her first endorsement contract with Sydney-Osaka Sushi, a high-end restaurant chain. She didn't appear in their commercials or wear their trademark on her clothing, but agreed to have a chef deliver a logoed white cooler to her chair at the end of each match and practice session. Various wrapped sushi always filled it, and she shared them with fans.

After a hot afternoon practice session in Paris, preparing for the Paris Open, Nicolette removed her soaked shirt, leaving only a white sports bra and skirt covering her tanned body. She held a racket in one hand and sushi in the other and took a bite. The picture splashed across the internet.

Sydney-Osaka Sushi restaurant sales increased noticeably the next week. Some reporters and several politicians called the photo tasteless and her actions demeaning to women. A spokesman for Sydney-Osaka Sushi insisted they didn't approve of the photo.

After another practice session in Paris, a pepper-haired video blogger approached Nicolette as she handed out sushi. "Are you aware Sydney-Osaka suppliers kill dolphins every year while fishing?"

She autographed a sushi wrapper for a fan.

"Did you consider the impacts upon the earth before taking that endorsement money?" He inched closer, followed by his cameraman.

Nicolette picked up a bottle and sipped some water.

"How can you condone the killing of dolphins in the pursuit of profits?"

The cameraman zoomed in on Nicolette. She lifted the Sydney-Osaka Sushi cooler so the camera could see the logo.

"You don't have anything to say?"

"Oh, yes actually," she said, her face brightening. "Please come to my Paris Open matches. I'm working on a math problem and it will require more paying customers."

The blogger shook his head. "I gave you a chance."

In response to the blogger's critical post about Sydney-Osaka Sushi, which went viral on the internet, two international nonprofit organizations launched a publicity campaign to boycott Sydney-Osaka Sushi. Jordon Taylor spoke on behalf of one.

Sydney-Osaka Sushi promptly sent out a press release. It said in part:

Everyone at Sydney-Osaka cares about dolphins, and our suppliers have measures in place to minimize the catching of all untargeted species. We are not in business just to make profits, but to provide seafood at refined dining locations for all of society. We set the price of our high-quality menu to allow our hard-working employees to also feed their families. And a portion of our profits goes to the needy. If anyone felt offended by the recent news stories, we sincerely apologize.

When asked to respond to the Sydney-Osaka Sushi's press release, Nicolette said, "Spineless, just as I like 'em."

"How can you say that about your only corporate sponsor?"

"Because it's the lack of all those small bones that makes their sushi so edible."

A week into the lingering controversy, the Sydney-Osaka Sushi's board of directors called an emergency meeting. They voted eleven to one to end Nicolette's contract. In the sales update after the vote, their accountants revealed that sales had increased dramatically since Nicolette's video appearances. The chairman moved to delay the firing until further discussion.

The only board member who had voted against dismissing Nicolette said, "Why not go ahead and dump her since she increased the very profits we are embarrassed about? I propose we pay her more to solve that dilemma."

Nobody seconded the motion, but a motion to delay action against Nicolette was seconded and passed with a vote of eleven to one.

At the Paris Open, Nicolette struggled in her early matches. She won, but barely, because line judges called out most of her close line shots. Unlike the Melbourne Open, the tennis courts in Paris didn't use electronic line monitoring cameras, except on center court.

One TV sports channel unveiled a hastily put together documentary entitled, *One-Hit Wonders*, based on all the young tennis players in history who burned out after their first major tournament win. With a picture of Nicolette on the screen, a commentator said, "Obviously, looks can only take you so far."

Even with an error rate double that of her competitor because of the line calls, Nicolette still won the tiebreaker in the third set of her semifinal match.

As she walked onto center court for the championship match, she bore a new tattoo on her left shoulder—the design often referred to as the "peace sign," only drawn upside down.

During the match, Nicolette landed most of her shots on the white lines as though the red clay wasn't in play. She challenged every out-of-bounds line call and the monitoring cameras vindicated her every time but once. She enjoyed watching the replay videos; they gave her a chance to see how close her calculations matched the accuracy of a high-speed camera.

To placate the French crowd, who became agitated by Nicolette's frequent challenges, the umpire overruled the camera calls, giving the points to her opponent. When Nicolette walked across the court and circled each overruled shot impact, or lack thereof, in the clay, the umpire stopped interfering, and the crowd fell resentfully silent. Nicolette won the match, scoring 6-5, 6-1.

Emilio won his first major tournament on his preferred clay surface, beating Jordon in the final.

At the awards ceremony, the presenter doled out the shiny trophies. But, for some unexplained reason, he handed out no prize checks on the court this year.

Nicolette carried her silver trophy to the sideline and set it down. Picking up her equipment bag, she jumped into the spectator stands and climbed without pause. The crowd rumbled with excitement as her nimble body rose ever higher while tournament officials scurried about talking on radios.

In the uppermost section of the stadium, standing atop a railing, her skirt stirring in the breeze, Nicolette extracted fistfuls of loose paper currency from her bag and showered them in waves over the fans. The crowd swarmed below the rolling and twisting paper.

Nicolette met hugs and high-fives as she descended through the ecstatic mob. The master of ceremonies and the three other tennis players stood dumbfounded as she walked in short steps back on the court, smiling.

She strode toward Emilio. Her unabashed approach made him step partially behind Jordon, gripping his silver chalice like a teddy bear. Stopping before his heaving chest, she stuffed two large bricks of paper currency into his trophy. "I believe your fans wanted you to have this," she said. "Congratulation on the win, Emilio."

"My, fans?" he said, his voice cracking. "Wanted me to have…?" He peered into the chalice.

She turned, skipped to the sideline, retrieved her trophy, and exited the stadium.

"I think we may have just witnessed the birth of a new Robin Hood," a TV sports announcer said.

"Then why did she give money to the men's champion, Emilio?" his cohost asked. Both men shrugged.

The French media and fans outside the stadium accosted Nicolette as she marched across the grounds. She led the wave of followers to Renny's waiting car.

"Why did you throw money to the people?" a reporter shouted.

Nicolette stopped. "My match had twenty percent fewer paying spectators than Emilio's, yet I was paid the same. From my expected winnings I split the overpayment between the fans and their intended recipient, Emilio." She laughed. "It's just math."

"So you consider tennis to be a business transaction?" a woman with white braids and a long cigarette asked.

"Not tennis, the award money. And I'd like to get paid more, so please come to London." She pulled the elastic tie from her ponytail, shook out her hair, and opened the car door.

A paper cup smacked the closing door, splattering soda across her arm and reporters.

Still standing on the Paris Open center court with Jordon at his side, Emilio spoke to the cameras. "I'm donating Nicolette

Popov's money to a women's charity in her name. Call it a symbol of equality."

Jordon slid into the camera shot, his princely eyelids drooping. "I will match Emilio's donation, also in Nicolette's name, for the sake of the sport."

"The next player who attempts to throw money to the crowd will be slapped with a fine," a spokesman for the Paris tournament said afterward.

A month later while Nicolette trained for the London Open, a reporter asked her, "What do you think of the donations made by Emilio and Jordon to a charity in your name?"

"I hadn't."

Once the London Open began, Jordon and Emilio apologized frequently to the sports media for Nicolette's behavior and promised to do everything within their power to maintain the integrity of the game.

The stadium attendance for the women's championship final hit record levels.

Walking onto center court, Nicolette displayed a new tattoo in blue ink on the back of her left hand; it appeared to be a water fountain. Announcers began speculating about its meaning, but stopped as Nicolette won the first game before most spectators had adjusted to their seats. The match ended quickly with a score of 6-1, 6-3.

At the net, Nicolette said to her defeated rival, "I love your balls' RPMs. You averaged somewhere around twenty-four hundred, the quickest I faced in the tournament. On grass I can't stop and reverse as quickly as I'd like, so next time, try spinning the ball on an axis to the outside and aiming for each sideline one after another."

"What's an RPM?"

"Your coach doesn't measure your balls' rotations per minute?"

"I don't know any coaches who do that."

"Huh. Well, I've found I can make more distinct ball marks on the court if I spin it over four thousand."

At the awards ceremony, the tournament director presented the golden goblet to Nicolette. She clasped the handle and reached for the microphone. He withheld it and discoursed on the history of tennis. She waited, listening to every word.

After a few minutes, somebody in the stands yelled, "Let her speak." A chant rose from the bleachers crying, "Let—her—speak—let—her—speak…"

The director glanced to the sidelines for help. The crowd's mantra intensified. After a nod from a group of huddled officials, he tilted the microphone to Nicolette. The crowd roared.

Nicolette looked across the stadium. "Today, for the first time in London Open history, more fans attended the women's final than the men's."

The audience boomed with applause. Emilio and Jordon clapped politely.

"Thank you so much for attending my match. By my count, four percent more spectators paid to watch it than Jordon's. So why award us the same amount of the fans' admission money?" She handed back the microphone and bounced off the court carrying her trophy, waving to the crowd.

Booing and hissing from the stadium mixed with cheers. The audience quieted as Emilio and Jordon jointly took the microphone.

With eyes glistening, Emilio said, "Perhaps some players do not understand that money is not the object of tennis."

Jordon leaned in, shaking his head. "On behalf of all of Americans, I want to apologize for Nicolette's words."

The two men hugged under the shower of the crowd's applause.

"At least some players still care about something other than themselves," a sports announcer said.

As Nicolette arrived at the Atlanta airport from London, a young couple running a popular sports blog stopped her. "You may not realize it, but most of our site visitors are disgusted by what you said in London. Do you wish to take back your statements?"

Nicolette set down her bags. "Yes, I most certainly do. After reviewing the London Open's increase in TV viewership and online visits, I'm revising the estimate of my underpayment from four to seven percent."

The bloggers stared, flabbergasted. "How do you feel about Jordon and Emilio calling you the most selfish player in sports today?"

"One hundred percent of nothing."

The pair shook their heads and walked away. Their published blog story said in part, "It's too bad Nicolette Popov sets a poor example for the youth because she is obviously blessed with talent. We wish she understood that neither looks nor talent will ever justify bad behavior."

Sydney-Osaka Sushi dropped Nicolette's endorsement contract without comment. One board member resigned.

At the New York Open, the media derided Nicolette's view on award money as a national embarrassment. Charity events sprouted up around New York to raise funds to support the awareness of equal pay in sports. Nicolette received public advice from current and former US professional players stating a desire to help her become an acceptable player citizen.

As Nicolette walked onto center court for the championship match, she displayed a new tattoo on the back of her right hand—the United States' flag adopted in 1877.

"Is that a bribe to placate the negative publicity by her own country?" a sportscaster asked.

Nicolette danced across court during the match, her expression indecently happy. Her shots drew a rough approximation of her tattooed flag with yellow dust on the far court, balls sometimes ricocheting off the top of the net and dropping in difficult spots to complement the pattern.

Sports announcers appeared agitated seeing the court marks displayed by their digital cameras on screen, saying she needed to take the match seriously. The audience cheered in awe at her strangely artistic display under the pressure of a championship match.

When Nicolette won the match, scoring 6-4, 6-2, a sports commentator said, "Such showboating is disgraceful for the sport. It might be time for somebody to do something."

TV stations sold their most expensive ads of the year in the period between the championship match and the typically mundane awards ceremony. TV announcers asked, "What would Nicolette say or do this time?" "Should she even be allowed to speak?" "Is she bad for the sport and for the country?" They conducted audience polls.

A former multi-time New York Open men's champion, acting as host, held the women's championship trophy and approached Nicolette. Before handing it over, he said, "Having won all four grand slam tournaments, how do you feel about becoming an ambassador of tennis?"

"I'll let Jordon keep that title." She laughed. "He's so good at it."

The crowd turned their attention to the New York men's champion, Jordon Taylor. He forced a smile.

"Would you like to take this moment to correct any misunderstandings regarding your prior actions and statements?" the host asked her.

"No, but Emilio can apologize for being a professional tennis player if he wants. He's getting good at apologizing for things he does."

The host cringed. "Okay ladies and gentlemen, let us move on to the men's champion."

Nicolette reached out and took the microphone. She turned to the New York Open's organizers' box, her hair falling off one shoulder. "The women's match attracted three percent more paying spectators than the men's, but we were paid the same." She pointed her trophy at the stands. "These fans handed over their money to see who they wanted to see. I played my best to give them something to watch. The next time you want to see equality in sports, why not make the scores equal and see what's left."

The crowd rumbled a chaotic mix of cheers and boos. The host tried to jerk the microphone away but failed, his face blushing.

"Next year," Nicolette said, "I'll only enter tournaments that respect the integrity of proportionally earned prize money. It's just math."

The host yanked the microphone away. It hit his chest with a loud thud. A metallic screech echoed through the stadium.

Somebody from a lower spectator box threw a snow cone. It arched over the court, wobbling across the illuminated air, and pelted Nicolette across the back.

A hush rippled through the spectators.

"Greedy bitch!" a voice yelled.

All eyes watched as the blue slush dripped down her white tennis outfit. She lifted her trophy and waved, eyes gleaming in the lights. With short steps, she walked from the stadium.

In the stands, Nicolette's parents told a nearby sportscaster that their daughter didn't mean what she said and would be honored to play again in the New York Open. They went on to tell their story about how they left the former Soviet Union as young Olympic gymnasts to evade oppression and were grateful their daughter lived in a free country.

As Nicolette approached her parents' home in Atlanta, after returning from New York, a reporter in high heels confronted her. "Did you hear your parents' plea?"

Nicolette opened the front door, ignoring her.

"They implied that you're throwing away the freedoms they fought so hard to find by acting this way."

Nicolette whirled around and stared at her.

"Nicolette, listen to me. I'm here to help you. I don't think you realize what you're fighting for."

"I don't care to *play* equally to anyone, so why should I care to be *paid* equally?"

"But *we* have sacrificed a lot fighting for equal pay."

"No, *I* have not."

"You have a lot to learn about how this world really works, Nicolette. For your own good, as a favor to another woman, I won't publish what you just said."

"Publish whatever you want. My favor to you." Nicolette entered the house.

The reporter sighed and walked away.

At a joint press conference, the organizers of all four major tennis tournaments and several of the top players, including Jordon and Emilio, sat behind a long table in front of a chorus of bright lights, cameras and microphones.

A bald man with bushy brows and tan suit seated at the center, said, "As a representative of the World Open Tennis Federation, I regret to announce that in order to maintain the dignity of this great sport, Nicolette Popov is hereby suspended from playing in any of our tournaments for one year or until she apologizes for publicly opposing equal pay between our men and women players."

The media and tennis players in attendance applauded.

Stock Brant, standing in the penthouse of *The Sin* in Las Vegas, turned off his TV and laughed.

Chapter 36

Dangling bulbs flashed light across Stock's face as he walked along the tunnel. He swung open a door marking the boundary between his underground world and his private hangar at McCarran International Airport.

A plain-clothed guard stepped aside, allowing access to a massive object draped with a satin sheet.

Stock yanked the sheet by its edge, sending it fluttering in the air. It drifted to the floor, revealing a white-painted *Sovereign* aircraft. He glanced at the tail numbers designating its registration as a Libby II *Wyvern*, and climbed to the cockpit.

Up in the air, he peered at the horizon, thinking of where he headed, and for a moment forgot he hated the world.

At the Atlanta International Airport's private terminals he hailed a taxi. It delivered him to a gabled house, and he climbed out.

He stood on the sidewalk, watching children ride bicycles down the street, baseball cards clicking in their spokes. He couldn't remember the last time he visited a suburb. Inhaling, he noted ammonia in the air and glanced across the Bermuda grass. *Too much fertilizer.*

Walking to the home's front door, he glanced at his scuffed combat boots and hesitated. He shook his head and knocked.

A middle-aged blonde woman answered and quickly closed the door to a crack. "May I help you?" she asked in a Russian accent.

Stock removed his dark glasses, inclining his head. "I'd like to speak with Miss Nicolette Popov."

"What do you want?" She glanced behind her as if seeking help.

"I'm here to offer her an endorsement contract."

Nicolette bounced down the stairs near the entryway, hair swaying behind a snug t-shirt. Gliding past her mother, her eyes flicked to the profile beyond the door. She stopped, tennis shoes squeaking against hardwood. She pulled her mother by the arm, exchanging places.

Opening the door, Nicolette stood before Stock, arms hanging at her sides.

His chest heaved with shallow breaths.

"Do you know this man?" her mother's worried voice asked.

"It's fine, Mother." Nicolette stepped forward, pushing her body against Stock's and pulled the door closed.

He stepped back. "I want to—"

"Hire me for something? I know. I heard you tell Mother," she said in a southern drawl.

He waited.

"My answer is yes."

His eyes narrowed. "You don't even know who I am."

She leaned back, folded her arms, and scanned him up and down. Biting her lower lip, she said, "Don't I?"

He slid the shades back over his eyes.

"You're not the mysterious Stock Brant?" She scrunched her nose.

"How did you know?"

"The gossip columns always seem to put your picture right next to mine. They say the silliest things, those reporters. They claim you're a *bad* man." She looked him up and down again. "Although, I must admit you do kinda look like one. Are you, Mr. Stock Brant? A bad man?"

His jaw tensed. "Will you still sign my endorsement contract?"

"You don't listen very well," she said leaning in, "for having such cute ears."

"But you have no idea what you've just accepted to endorse."

"No, I haven't a clue," she stepped closer. "Please, tell me."

He took another step back. "I thought you were supposed to rip my head off and hand it back on a platter, like I've seen you do to others on TV."

"Is that what it looked like to you?" She smiled innocently.

He surveyed the tree-lined street and manicured lawns, then her attentive face. "Come with me."

Glancing at the empty street, she said, "Wait here," and entered the house.

He stood on the doorstep wondering if this was what it

would've felt like to have had a prom date. He sucked in the moist air, and for a split second almost grinned.

Nicolette burst from the house with a small designer handbag tucked under an arm. Wrapping her fingers around his leathered bicep, she said, "Let's go."

She asked no questions as they walked, his boots stomping along the concrete.

After a few blocks, they intersected a busy thoroughfare and Stock flagged down a taxi. "The airport, private terminals," he said.

The driver kept looking in the rearview mirror at Nicolette. When the car arrived at the airport, she winked at him.

"This one's on me, Ms. Popov," the driver said.

"Why, thank you." She pulled a couple of large currency bills from her handbag and dumped them over the seat. "And these are on me."

At a private hangar, Stock rolled open the large door.

"It's a white dragon," Nicolette gasped, running up to caress the *Sovereign's* nose like a child petting a horse.

"Get in," he said.

She climbed the boarding ladder, legs flexing against yellow tights. She slid into one of the side-by-side seats in the front row.

Stock remained below, gazing at the spot she had caressed.

After climbing up and sitting next to her, he pressed brushed-alloy buttons and flipped metallic switches, all outlined against a gunmetal console. Nudging the throttles forward, the massive engines roared into an ovation.

Nicolette grinned.

The jet rolled from the hangar and to the start of a runway. With a crackling growl, the *Sovereign* punched through the humid air, lifted off the tarmac, and pulled up and to the west. Atlanta fell away.

From the cockpit the transparent canopy allowed for panoramic views. Staring at Nicolette's face reflecting off the glass, Stock watched her eyes studying the curved lines of the aircraft.

"What kind of jet is this, Stock?"

He liked the way his name sounded coming from her lips. "It's the kind that's illegal to fly anywhere on earth."

"Is that why you like it?"

He looked at her, his mouth half open. Snapping his head forward, he punched the afterburner, shooting them like a streak of light over the Appalachian peaks. "Yes."

Her fingertips slid along the canopy, the sun warming her blue fountain tattoo. Glancing between a line of high-voltage transmission towers on the ground and the jet's nose, she counted under her breath. "Something close to seventeen hundred miles per hour, I think. Altitude…" she whispered, staring back and forth between the clouds and a radio tower on a hill, "a bit more than twenty thousand feet, or maybe just under." She craned her neck, peering at the jet's domineering haunches. "Who made this jet?"

Stock didn't answer. She relaxed against the seat.

Grain fields unfurled below like patterned quilts.

After a while, the jet slowed and dove toward the ground. They zoomed low over a patch of plowed dirt, a barn, and columns of maple trees.

Stock glimpsed his childhood home, giving him a twisted sense of comfort and torture, like a hay bale infused with barbed wire. *Why?*

He jerked back on the stick. *Because I said so!* They pulled up into the sky, engines rumbling, rebelling against the world and its gravity, hurtling them west.

Twenty minutes later, they glided between the parched walls of the Grand Canyon before shooting out over the glassy surface of Lake Mead.

Nicolette stared at the concave shield of the Hoover Dam and the great arched bridge to its south, beyond the profile of Stock's face.

Descending over the jagged, burnt ridges of the Sunrise Mountains, the cockpit provided a perfect view of the great mountain-rimmed basin. A tall crystal shard pierced it like the center of a transmitting dish, its white shaft reflecting sparks of flame up silver-edged planes.

"Las Vegas," she said, "I've never been here. It's so pretty."

Stock circled the Las Vegas Strip, tilting a wing downward. He pointed at his naked marquee and thought of Alexandria, knowing she'd been missing the three years since her inauguration. *She is almost an unreal dream now.* "That is what you will endorse. *The Sin.*" He added, "…my sin."

"Yes." Her voice rang with reverence.

"I've never advertised it before," he said, looking away. "I'll pay you whatever increase in gross profit your endorsement brings in."

"All the increase?"

"Yes."

"What's in it for you?"

"That's none of your concern."

"No, of course not, Mr. Brant."

Stock frowned, disappointed she hadn't used his first name this time.

Once he parked the jet in his private hangar, they entered the passageway to his underground world. He didn't consider what she might think of the desolate place and she said nothing.

When they reached *The Hole* and the graffiti-covered elevator door connecting it to the underbelly of *The Sin*, Stock said, "I want to take you out tonight, to celebrate our contract."

She watched rough-looking men wandering by in the grimy hallway. "Yes, I want to celebrate."

Inside the ornate elevator, Stock opened a mahogany panel, inserted a key and pressed the penthouse button, surprised that he wanted to take her there—a place he'd only hosted Alexandria. *Have I fallen so far that I'm willing to take someone to the penthouse as bad as me?*

Nicolette pressed the lobby button. "First, I'm buying some new clothes," she gripped her handbag. "Does *The Sin* have shops?"

When Nicolette emerged from one of Stock's extra bedrooms that evening, the sunset painted her long braid and naked shoulders a metallic bronze, highlighting her tattoos. She wore a fitted red dress, the elastic fabric clinging to her small breasts and fit torso, only relenting into waves at mid-thigh.

Stock sat, legs crossed, in the center of a clean-lined sofa, his spiked hair glowing like embers before the dying sun.

Searching his eyes, her taut brows furrowed. She turned, observing the clean design of the penthouse, the view of the white glass tower across the street, before returning to him. She appeared as if she wanted to laugh, but instead frowned.

Stock stood and walked to the elevator.

She wrapped both hands around his arm and followed. "Where are you taking me?"

He pressed the lobby button without answer. As the numbers counted down, he realized with surprise where he would take her.

At Ted Hollings' unrelenting insistence, Stock had attended *The Virtue* last year. And once Stock had looked upon the mysterious redhead with silver flaming eyes, he saw nothing else in the theater. *She's too good, too beautiful for anyone here.* When Ted inadvertently bumped Stock's arm during the first minutes of the show, Stock leapt to his feet and pushed past the seated guests. With his head lowered, he'd slunk from the auditorium.

That night, he sent an invitation to Sitra's dressing room summoning her to his penthouse. When his phone rang, he answered quickly.

"Ask to see Sitra again, or come within a hundred yards of her dressing room and she'll move the show," *The Virtue's* manager said in a Hungarian accent.

Stock lowered the phone, holding it over the receiver and let it go. He walked to his mini bar, and for some inexplicable reason, removed the still unfinished bottle of *Wayne Smoke* bourbon he saved from Alexandria's visit nearly five years earlier. He had poured it down his throat, eyes burning as he gazed across the blurry city lights.

Now, seated in the center of *The Virtue's* theater with Nicolette, Stock rubbed his hands on the plush chair and stared at the curtain. Once again, he felt surprised at his decision to bring her here. He glanced at Nicolette's serene face and reclined against the seat.

During the show, he felt wave after wave of unidentified guilt, mixed with some obscene mirage of hope. He gripped Nicolette's hand and squeezed every time he couldn't take it any longer. Her fingertips feathered his sweaty palm between squeezes.

Nicolette joined the crowd in the standing ovation. Stock remained seated. *None of these people deserve to be here. I will order Ted to cancel the show.*

Sitra stood at the tip of the stage, not bowing like her fellow performers, her gaze moving across the auditorium until it met Nicolette's.

Stock glanced at Nicolette and watched her tremble with what looked like pleasure. He looked at Sitra, but their eyes didn't meet. *No one is like that in real life. Sitra must be some kind of fraud, it's the only explanation.*

As Stock escorted Nicolette from the theater, she ran her hands up his arm and asked, "Will you take me to dinner at *The Spirit of Man?*"

He froze, thinking of Halvern's dedication speech, forcing the exiting crowd to detour around them. *I can't enter that building.*

"Please, Stock." Her fingers found his calloused hand.

His shoulders relaxed. "If you wish," he said, not looking at her.

On the one hundred and ninetieth floor of *The Spirit of Man* sat The Comstock Terrace, the finest restaurant in Las Vegas. An open kitchen in the center of the floating space shot fiery plumes into the air which reflected off the panoramic windows like dancing spirits above a molten city.

Nicolette stood at the threshold, dress aflame in the fire's light, her skin and hair glowing.

The maître d' bustled over. "This is an honor, Miss Popov." He escorted them to a secluded window table. "We have nothing available until March, but please, take this table."

Gazing upon *The Sin's* rooftop, Nicolette asked, "Do you know that performer, Sitra?"

Stock's pupils contracted into sharp points. Her question hit him deep inside, somewhere dark and fragile—the same spot pricked by *The Virtue*—because it contradicted his understanding of the universe, his very premise of good and evil. Then he remembered that Sitra had refused his invitation, and he breathed with relief. "No. We've never met."

"Thank you for taking me to see her. I hope you pay her what she's worth."

"I'm going to cancel the show."

She scrunched her brows. "Why would you do that?"

"It's unrealistic," he said, frowning.

She laughed. "Don't like happy outcomes?"

"It's giving false hope to naïve people."

She laughed again, only more amusedly.

Stock entrapped her hand with his. "You took a big risk coming out here with me."

Pulling herself toward him, using the strength of his hold, she tilted her head and breathed across his cheek. "This naïve girl took a very dangerous risk."

Chapter 37

Stock awoke and rubbed his face, feeling comforted by some forgotten memory. He lifted his head off the pillow, smelling lavender and Russian sage. *Nicolette.* Rising to his knees, he scanned the penthouse.

Shadowy letters stretched across the floor. He followed the shadows up to the red lipstick scribed across a panel of sun-soaked glass. *Stock, Checking into* The Spirit of Man. *Send over endorsement contract—Nicolette.*

Jumping out of bed, he moved to the balcony facing *The Spirit of Man.* He counted the floors until they dissolved into a solid beam of morning white. His chin remained lifted until he remembered his dream last night.

He sprinted to the elevator.

Flying into his underground drug lab, he passed the startled Kat, brushed a tabletop clean with a swipe of an arm, and picked up a marker. Atop the table he wrote formulas and diagrams to a biologic cure he'd been struggling with for years.

Last night he dreamt of Nicolette, Sitra, and the white tower. He couldn't remember the details but the sensations unleashed a subconscious flow of genetic code before his eyes. He hadn't felt so inspired in years.

"I figured out what I was missing. Throw everything away on the L557s and start over with this," Stock said.

Kat sighed and walked over to the table. As she studied the diagrams, her eyes widened. He tossed the marker to the floor and left.

Stock thumped his fingers against a stone counter in front of a smartly braided receptionist at *The Spirit of Man.*

"I'm sorry, sir, Ms. Popov's room didn't answer," she said.

"Where are the tennis courts?"

Approaching the courts, Stock heard Nicolette's staccato exertions, but spectators lining a fence blocked his view. Pushing a man aside, he gripped the fence and watched her bounce the ball before a serve. He surveyed her athletic legs up to her determined face. She didn't seem to notice anyone, not even her male opponent.

She darted across the court, again and again, whizzing balls over the net. He imagined her drawing a pattern on the court with the ball, a design resembling a double helix from a genetic strand of DNA. He thought of his formulas in the lab, piecing together another difficult issue he hadn't considered. Releasing the fence, he knew he must return to the lab, but his feet wouldn't move.

An hour later, Nicolette looked at him for the first time, eyes greeting his with a sensuous wink. He wanted to tear through the meshed steel and take her pulsing body right there. She turned away and served the ball, playing for two more hours. He waited.

Nicolette finally packed up her gear and walked in short steps to him. "Hi," she said.

"You practice hard for a banned player."

"You should know."

He waved his hand with impatience. "Nicolette, I want to show you something."

"I'll shower and meet you in the lobby."

Stock walked into *The Spirit of Man* lobby, hands in pockets, hating the idea of waiting there, like a gargoyle stuck in a holy temple. He leaned against a secluded corner. After a while, he lifted his gaze to the looming five story statues of a naked god-like man and woman, their heads held high.

He pushed himself off the wall with an elbow toward the male statue's base. He read the engraved quote. *The possible springs from the thinking man—to make it real is his exaltation. Mae Black.*

"I'm ready." Nicolette passed by him in her tight jeans and tennis shoes, hair hanging behind a yellow tee.

Stock caught up and led her across the Strip and through the secret entrance into *The Hole* before descending underground.

At the furthest extremity of the tunnel system, they entered a secured white door and walked in to the biologics lab. The concrete walls and the humming genetic sequencers greeted them coldly, impersonally.

Nicolette smiled at the energy of the rational computations.

She walked up and down the aisles, scanning the research papers, beakers, vials, computer screens, and climate-controlled cabinets. Turning around, she pointed, "What's behind that metal door?"

Stock stared at the stainless steel door imbedded in the far wall. His breathing deepened. "My sanctuary. What lies in there, I've taken from the world…because of what they've taken from me." His eyes moved back to hers.

"Huh."

Stock frowned at her response and opened the lab door to leave. When she walked past him with a bounce in her step, his stomach tightened wishing she would have begged him to stay.

Reaching a wide wooden door, Stock stopped, unlocked it, and pulled it open. Light flooded into the tunnel. Touching his arm, she breathed in the warm air, fluttered her eyelids, and entered like an angel through a secret entrance to heaven.

Kat glanced up from behind a row of wheat and met Nicolette's gaze, before lowering her head and clearing her throat.

Nicolette strolled through the cave, observing everything. Stock remained at her side.

Near the back of the cavern, he picked an orange from a leafy canopy and squeezed it until a citrus-drop splashed in the palm of his hand. Waving it under his nose, he inhaled. *It will reach peak ripeness in two, maybe three days.* He handed it to Nicolette.

She smelled its dimpled skin, eyelids lowering with pleasure.

"There is more," Stock said.

Nodding, she followed him to the exit.

As they passed Kat, Stock said, "Reduce the grove's water consumption by two percent."

Kat typed on a handheld device as Stock and Nicolette left the growing room.

They walked down a concrete corridor and climbed a winding flight of stairs. From an intersecting passage a smooth voice said, "Hello there. Who have you brought us, Stock?"

Nicolette turned, glaring at the smiling, boyish face.

"Not now, Jesus," Stock said.

She glanced at Stock, tilting her head, brows scrunched.

Jessy bowed, offering his hand. "Nicolette Popov, so flattered to meet you. We are most—"

"—Scurvy," she said, dropping Stock's orange into Jessy's palm.

Jessy frowned and glanced at Stock as though gauging something.

With a spurt of interest, almost sympathy, Stock said, "What did you want to speak with me about yesterday?"

"Oh that. To go over our...acquisition...of a certain group in the North Valley." Jessy smiled at Nicolette. "But, we've already taken care of it."

Stock said nothing and grabbed Nicolette's hand to leave. She resisted, still observing Jessy.

Jessy rubbed the orange against his cheek then tossed it in the air, catching it with a grin.

Stock pulled harder. She wrinkled her nose and let him lead her up to *The Hole*.

Their footsteps echoed against crumbling concrete as they entered its secluded parking garage. Stock climbed atop a curved black jet-bike sitting near a rough pillar and tossed a helmet to Nicolette.

"Have you canceled *The Virtue* yet?" she asked.

His thumb swiped the bike's ignition and its fiery anger roared from within, concussing the confined air.

She smiled, setting the helmet on the ground. "I'm glad you didn't." Stepping over the seat, she wrapped her arms around his waist and rested her chin on his shoulder.

Stock coaxed the rumbling beast onto the Strip, eyeing cars with distrust, and merged onto the freeway.

Exiting westward, they climbed into the cool air of the Spring Mountains. Bristlecone and spruce pines leaned over the narrowing road as it wound toward a gorge. Dust kicked into the air as the Hell Hound veered onto an unpaved trail. When they reached a chained gate, Stock dismounted and opened it.

Nicolette took the handlebars, her thighs squeezing the fuel tank, and throttled the bike across the threshold. Stock locked the gate behind them, reclaimed the motorcycle, and steadied it down the grooved path, traversing a steep forested ravine.

As they slowed to a stop, young pinyon pines rustled their branches like happy children, encircling them. Nicolette jumped from the seat and twirled around, golden streams of hair flowing behind. She skipped through the grove, sliding fingertips along rough bark.

She reached up and picked a football-sized pinecone with

both hands. Holding it under her nose, she drew in its pine scent. "I want to endorse your creations as well," she said, breathing easy, eyes happy.

Stock grimaced.

"Why not, Stock?"

"They're illegal," he said, his tone harsh. "Everything I do is…except for *The Sin*."

Her tennis shoes crunched along composted needles over to him. Gripping his jacket, she pulled her lips to his scruffy cheek. "I love all of it."

He turned away. She coaxed his chin back to her.

"I hate their laws, and everyone who supports them," he said.

"I see that."

"So you think I should obey them? Stop all this?" His eyes trembled.

"Stock…" She lowered her gaze to his chest. As the wind rustled through the pines above, she looked back to his eyes. "I know it's not my place to ask, but who was that man you called Jesus?"

Stock tensed. He wasn't sure why, but her question struck a buried fault line inside, and he knew just such a vibration could unleash a fatal quake. "You're right—it's none of your business."

She stared at him, her face calm.

"Jessy and I are the same! We live as outlaws from society because our dreams are illegal. And we will live as such until the day they dump us in the grave."

She laughed and covered her mouth. "The same?"

His eyes flared, his hands clutching her wrists. "The world banned you as a player. Sinners have no right to throw stones. You of all people should understand what it's like to be condemned."

She ripped her hands free, eyes compressing into sapphires. "Understand? I know I had no right to stick my nose in your business, but I won't apologize for what I see." She pointed at his pinyon pines. "And I see what your creations are, and I see who made them. What do you see?"

He looked at his genetic outcasts. "You don't understand, Nicolette."

She stepped into him, pressing her lips against his pulsing neck and sighed.

He froze, her revelation of sympathetic pain crackling ice

down his spine. *I knew I would hurt her. I shouldn't have invited her to Las Vegas.*

Her body melted into his, her scent mixing with his pines. His hands moved to push her away—but instead they wrapped around her unguarded frame. "Move in with me," he said, but his tone sounded more like, *Save me.*

"No, Stock."

"This is all wrong, Nicolette. I'm canceling your contract. I'm sending you home."

"Do it." The moist vibration of her lips sent tingles along his skin.

His lips dropped to hers. She clung to him as he guided her body to the soft pine needles. She looked up through the mess of her feathery hair, at his pinyons, and smiled.

Kat watched Stock working under the growing lamps as if he were Mother Nature's underworld son. He had yet to pause for a break in the fourteen hours she had been there. She hadn't seen him this motivated in years. Finally, forced by fatigue, she swept the hair from her eyes and left him to the solace of his subterranean world.

Shuffling along the dim passage, she climbed the concrete steps, wondering why Stock's renewed vigor hadn't left her with the long-sought relief she'd expected. Perhaps it was because Jessy made a visit to the growing cavern two days ago and dropped veiled hints about acquiring drug territories using armed force. Kat had expected Stock to rebuke him, or worse, for challenging Stock's only unbreakable rule—a single, uncompromising pillar in a career built on the premise of breaking all rules and pillars. But instead, he waved Jessy away without comment, seemingly without interest. Kat could still see Jessy's triumphant grin slathered on his face behind Stock's back.

As Kat passed the opening to Jessy's underground dominion, fear shot through her, and not just for her life, but for everything she valued in this world. She accelerated her ascent.

Entering her apartment in *The Hole*, she locked all four dead bolts, and leaned against the door.

Nicolette touched her nose to the window, watching the blushing mountains dissolve into the morning's silent birth. Its brilliant shockwave ripped across the sleeping basin, reflecting off the endless white skyscraper glass below her.

Looking to the west, she smirked, knowing the first day of the Melbourne Open had ended without her.

With tennis gear slung over a shoulder, she skipped from the elevator into *The Spirit of Man* lobby, heading to the courts.

The head concierge ran from behind his counter and placed an envelope on top her swinging bag, saying, "Special delivery."

She glanced at the golden lettering in the upper left-hand corner—*The Sin*. Without breaking stride, she ripped it open. A check and a note slipped into her hand. The note read:

Ms. Nicolette Popov, The Sin's room rates and occupancy have increased every week since your first ads ran. Enclosed is a check representing our increase in gross profit versus the prior month.

She knew that *The Sin's* ads had exploded into instant popularity and controversy. And one news reporter seemed to have summed up everyone's opinion, for or against the commercial endorsement, when he declared, "Nicolette and *The Sin* are a match made in hell."

But popular or not, seeing one more digit than she'd expected on the check, she blinked and stuffed it in her bag.

On a tennis court behind the glass tower, her practice partner hit the first ball across the net.

Nicolette sprung forward, feet lifting off the court, upper body torquing back in a wide, fluid motion. The racket ripped forward, arcing around her body. The ball disintegrated into vibration, reappearing as a yellow glint across a far baseline corner. Everyone on the other courts turned toward the stark detonation and gaped at the blonde nymph standing on one foot, gazing dreamily at the ground.

Under her breath, she laughed. "A sin."

When the sun moved overhead, Nicolette grabbed her gear and dashed off the court. Still sweat-soaked, she asked the concierge to send for a car. "Something not slow, if possible."

The man stared, momentarily paralyzed by her burst of color splashed across a monotone lobby. He picked up the phone.

A convertible supercar, its bright yellow body pressed low and wide to the ground, pulled around the valet circle. Its sharp angled air inlets in the hood and doors melted into curves; its curves melted into an aerodynamic flow like water over a torpedo. Its cylinders roared, begging to rip the asphalt off the road. A winged door lifted and a valet stepped out.

Nicolette jumped in. It rocketed away, blue flames pulsing from the center exhausts, leaving a throaty gurgling backfire as she braked for a turn.

Speeding along the western edge of Las Vegas, hair flying in the wind, she scanned the tops of the houses flashing by. Slamming on the brakes, she exited the motorway and rumbled to the entrance of a residential neighborhood.

She stopped at its guard gate. "Any homes for sale in there with multiple tennis courts?"

The guard's face beamed, first at the car, then at her. He fumbled off his hat and handed it to her. She signed it and revved the engine a few times, watching the corners of his mouth lift with each press of her toes. He directed her on a map to an estate perched on the edge of a ridge with views of the Strip.

Pulling in to its driveway, she leaned close to the windshield, studying the home's architecture. It possessed huge glass panes stretching high above double doors that connected to a slanted, single planed roof.

A white-haired man with a cigar between his teeth answered the door. He stared at Nicolette's disheveled hair.

"Good afternoon, sir. Is this house for sale?"

"What?"

"Same question."

"Who are you?" He munched on the cigar.

"How much do you want for it?"

"Six million dollars, but—"

"May I look around?" she interrupted.

He glanced at the supercar in the driveway then back at her unflinching face. "Don't you need a real estate agent, young lady?"

"No." She flanked around him and into the house.

He turned around, speechless. Two small dogs scurried across on the glossy tiles, spinning circles, whining nervously.

Nicolette paused in the vaulted entryway, studying the clean style, then marched to the backyard. Canary palms and island vegetation lined pathways leading around two dark-tiled pools and an open pavilion.

The five tennis courts beyond the pools pulled Nicolette to them like magnets. She traced the white lines on the courts with her tennis shoes, mouth moving silently.

"Now wait just a minute," the owner growled, catching up to her, his two whimpering dogs zigzagging around him.

She continued her calculations, ignoring him. He huffed, grinding his cigar.

Nicolette walked along a set of bleachers lining center court, then faced him. "I'll pay your asking price."

"What? Well…I don't know," he stammered. "Selling real estate doesn't just happen like this. How do I know—"

She walked around him toward the house in rapid steps. He blinked with surprise.

Waving his cigar, he ran after her. "Stop, young lady."

Nicolette whirled around.

"I'll sell it to you. I just thought this was going to be complicated with lots of agents, tons of paperwork and all that. You know how it is."

She extended a hand. "Six million dollars, wired to your account in five days and I'll take possession then. Whatever paperwork is involved, let them do it."

He stared at her open palm.

She tapped her toe.

He thrust out both hands and shook. "You got yourself a deal, Miss…"

"Nicolette Popov."

"Oh…oh, I knew you looked familiar." His faced brightened as if contemplating which of his buddies to call first.

She wrote her hotel room number on the back of an empty envelope and flicked it out to him with two fingers. "Have your agent call me at *The Spirit of Man* this afternoon."

"Yes, ma'am."

He stood in the doorway, watching her skip away and sink into the yellow supercar. Ashes fell from his cigar as the engine revved. Its tires growled a trail of untamed rubber out of the cul-de-sac.

Back at *The Spirit of Man*, the car purred around the valet circle. Nicolette leaped out, dropping its key in the palm of the man who had summoned it. "Good choice," she said.

"It was named after a bull that refused to die, even after twenty-four sword strikes."

"Bill it to my room."

"The...rental?"

"No, *my bull.*"

"Yes, of course," he said, dashing to open the lobby doors.

A dozen athletes sat on a bleacher watching a tennis match, while other matches popped and squeaked in the background.

Nicolette sat in the center of the stands, her mind calculating every movement on the court. Renny Thatcher stood on a sideline, arms crossed. A male player, ranked eighth in the world, lay on a beach chair with his head propped on an arm, the only spectator of an impromptu doubles game on a far court. A group of teenage girls in tennis outfits sat under an umbrella by a pool, eating walnut-sized pine nuts and sipping multicolored sports drinks. On a balcony overlooking the pools and courts, Stock sat alone at a table with papers and plants in pots scattered around him.

The informal tournaments had turned Nicolette's backyard into an oasis for many of the world's best players, and many more unknown but up-and-coming players. There were no uninvited guests, no announcers, no media, and no fans.

The players themselves umpired the matches and kept score. Sensitive line cameras adjudicated all challenged calls. A whiteboard under the outdoor pavilion highlighted the progression of the tournaments. Occasionally, side bets erupted among the players, rivaling the payouts at the top international tournaments.

Rumors of the private Las Vegas tournaments circulated around the sports world, but most commentators and nonattending tennis professionals dismissed them as irrelevant.

The players who competed in Nicolette's backyard privately adjusted their official rankings to reflect their inside knowledge of the tournaments. Some fans began to quote the unofficial rankings to the frustration of sanctioned ranking organizations, tournament directors, and the media.

Jordon Taylor laughed whenever questioned about Nicolette's Las Vegas tournaments, saying, "I don't think they're important or they would be publicly sanctioned." He pledged to never disgrace the game by playing in nonpublic tournaments. He was never invited.

Chapter 38

Kat's padded footsteps scuffed along a concrete tunnel while the world above slept. She stopped in front of the white lab door and peered behind her.

The remoteness of the lab and Stock's unquestioned authority used to give her a sense of safety, but now the place felt more like a prison—or worse—a guarded tomb. The type of men in the subterranean world and in *The Hole* above had changed recently. Shaking her head, she knew that wasn't right; they had changed long ago. She saw them watching Stock with their eyes filled with disdainful pity, and saw that Stock didn't seem to notice or care.

Kat stood in the dim silence, thankful to be alone, until she noticed the lab's door ajar. *No one should be in there.*

Swinging the door open, she jumped back at the sight of an intruder. She gripped the doorframe, heart thumping in her ears. Drawing a gun from her overcoat, she pointed it at the back of the man's head.

The trespasser stood by a workbench, a single lamp casting an eerie glow over his hands. The trigger dug into Kat's skin.

Wait.

She swiped the gun barrel across the light switch. The overhead fixtures blinked sporadically, then beamed down. *Stock!*

Stock remained motionless, as if nothing had happened. Everything in the lab appeared normal, too normal.

She holstered the gun, feeling helpless against Stock's increasingly erratic research habits and moods. She tried to slow her breathing, but it was no use. Shuffling over to Stock's workbench, she peered over his shoulder. Even after he'd gone missing for a week, he'd picked up the experiment where she'd left off the night before. It felt comforting somehow.

Kat smiled, wondering why she'd overreacted, and measured out reagents before mixing them together. But when she glanced behind her at the lab entrance, thinking of those above, she felt the imprint of fear. "Stock," she whispered.

He didn't respond.

"Can I speak with you?" she asked.

Stock's hands stopped working, but his eyes remained on the experiment.

Reproaching herself for feeling vulnerable, she rubbed the dark circles beneath her eyes, and continued mixing reagents.

"What?" he said, his tone carrying a veiled warning.

"It's nothing. I was just…curious how the *Sovereign* was flying."

"The *Sovereign*…" His face relaxed. "Nicolette, she—"

"Oh, good," Kat interrupted, her hand shaking a beaker.

"That's not what you wanted to ask."

She sighed. "You've been gone a lot lately. There are *others* who are always around."

Stock's eyes narrowed, daring her to continue.

Kat turned away, staring at a vial of their latest biologic prototype. "The first thing you ever taught me was that drug compounds require purity. You demonstrated by mixing a drop of pollutant into a vial of water. You asked—is that 99.9% pure? I answered—it was mostly contaminated. You said—it's 100% contaminated."

Shooting him a glance, she watched his bloodshot eyes darken. "But, it's not important," she said under her breath.

Stock straightened up and walked to the exit.

When she felt the door slam shut, she gripped her hair. *Damn.*

The Marine Review Board's deliberations droned on and on. Seven recruits from seven consecutive training cohorts testified that they'd received unnecessary bodily injury under the direction of Drill Instructor Danny Sands.

Danny sat in the humid, constricted room, horrified at the testimony. *I don't even remember doing it.*

Two years ago, after seeing his initial group's low training scores, he began channeling his father's sense of discipline on the recruits. He hadn't wanted to harm any of them, blocking out the images of his actions at the end of each day to survive. But the forceful measures had worked, and within a few months he'd increased his ratings to the top quartile of all drill instructors. His father flaunted the ratings at his former Marine buddies and highlighted the achievement to his youth counselling clients.

At the end of the Marine Review Board's proceeding, the court officer declared, "I find there has been sufficient evidence to construe a pattern of overzealous negligence but not willful injury. Please approach the bench, Sergeant Sands."

Danny rose and stepped forward, eyes on the floor.

"This isn't your father's Marine Corp, Sergeant. We are kinder and gentler now. I hereby remove you as Drill Instructor. I strongly recommend you take a voluntary discharge; if not, one more battery complaint will trigger a formal court-marshal. Do you understand?"

Danny almost tipped over, his head dizzy. He blinked to stay conscious. *What will I tell Father?*

"You will answer the board, Sergeant."

Danny lifted his chin. "I just tried to make everyone do their duty." A tear rolled down his cheek. "But I hated doing it…I…"

The court officer leaned back, shaking his head. "I'm making the decision for you. You're discharged. An attorney will facilitate your departure. Dismissed."

The gavel dropped, striking like the hammer-pin on a loaded revolver.

Danny's head slumped forward.

Sitting alone in his barracks, Danny confronted the unbearable thought—the whole world had united to destroy his father's respect for him. He'd given up so much for it, given everything.

His forearms constricted, producing two knotted fists at their ends. Rising to his feet, he punched the wall one fist after the other. The pain soothed his thoughts so he punched harder. Pops and cracks echoed inside his flushed ears. He gripped his right fist, realizing he had broken bones, and collapsed on his bunk, teeth grinding.

The door opened and a uniformed attorney walked in carrying a folder. Danny slid his broken and bloodied fist behind his hip and faced forward, cheeks twitching.

"To which city do you want to be discharged, Danny?"

"Please address me as Drill Instructor," he rasped. "Please, just address me as…" He wiped his eyes. "I didn't mean to hurt anyone."

The officer frowned. "Where does your family reside?"

Danny swallowed, closing his eyes.

"Do you want me to notify them for you?"

He thought of his father's face. "No…" His body wilted until his forehead touched his lap. "Don't tell him, please." His back heaved with soundless sobs. After a moment, he caressed his face against a knee.

"Is there anywhere else you could go other than to your parents? We need to deliver you somewhere."

Jet engines rumbled overhead, shaking the barracks. Danny clenched his broken fist, the purity of the pain somehow making him think of Roble. "Dump me in Las Vegas."

When the attorney departed, Danny gathered up the unfinished storyboards he'd made for his father, along with the folded piece of childhood art Roble had returned, and stuffed them into a bag.

Wincing from the pain in his hand, he typed a message to his father that said in part: *Drill instructor activities are going well. Duty and honor, Danny.*

General Yamatomo picked up the ringing phone. "Yamatomo."

"General, I have a caller who…" the woman's voice hesitated. "I apologize for bothering you with this; it's highly unusual. It may be a prank call, but…he sounds…"

Yamatomo remained stoic, the receiver pressed against a grey sideburn.

"I'm sorry, sir. I'll get rid of him."

"Did he give a name?"

"Just…Ronin."

General Yamatomo blinked. "Put him through, on a secure line."

"One moment, sir."

"General Yamatomo?" a sturdy voice asked.

"Hai, Ronin."

"Obsidian," Ronin said in Japanese, "when sharpened into

a point, may cut rope. But when lashed to a stout heart, will eventually pierce any unjust bond."

The general glanced at his desk lamp where an arrowhead necklace hung.

"Exactly one week from today," Ronin continued, "a passenger is scheduled to transfer from Futenma Marine base to Guantanamo Bay. The plane will land at Naha Airbase at exactly 0900 hours for an unexpected maintenance issue immediately after takeoff. If that passenger were to somehow disembark and accidentally get on a private flight to an undisclosed location... that would be a damn shame. Don't you agree?"

Yamatomo stood up, lifting the necklace. "Hai, Ronin."

The C-130 transport barked onto the Naha Airbase runway at 0900 hours.

Roble, in aviator sunglasses, a baseball cap, and a bomber jacket, walked down the cargo ramp to an awaiting car. The car's rear door opened and he slipped in. It sped away along the tarmac to the private terminals.

A bony hand pressed something into Roble's palm. He clutched his arrowhead for the first time in three years and looked into the steely eyes of the grey-haired man at his side.

As the car screeched to a stop, Yamatomo said, "Go, *Kaze u~ōkā.*"

Roble bowed, opened the door, and ran to the boarding ladder of a long-range private jet.

Its turbines hummed as he entered the refined, wood-trimmed cabin. A hand from the cockpit motioned for him to find a seat. The entrance door closed on its own.

He sat, noting no other passengers on board. Ten minutes ago, Ronin had unlocked his cuffs, removed his head covering, and handed him these clothes, saying, "Get lost, scoundrel."

As the jet lifted into the air, Roble gazed down at the hangar where he'd modified the *Skeleton Eagle*. He snapped a salute to its pilot.

He didn't know where he was flying to, yet he felt protected somehow. There was so much to think about, but exhaustion overtook him. Caressing the arrowhead with his thumbs, he fell asleep.

Cracking his eyes, he realized he wasn't in a jail cell, but on a leather seat inside a jet, soaring above a monotone sea of haze. The horizon beyond the window appeared limitless, like a blank sheet under his hand. He turned and stared at the cockpit door, recalling the hand that had pointed out when he entered the jet. He got up and opened it.

"Sugemi!"

Sugemi pushed buttons on the control panel and rose, facing him. He studied her perfect, unsmiling face, and stepped forward pulling her to him.

She pressed her chin against his shoulder and whispered, "I'm so happy you're free."

"I missed you." He held her, feeling her heart beating.

"Roble...I have to tell you something."

A strange tingle shot down his spine. He coaxed her back so he could see her eyes.

"Roble, it's been three years." She grimaced. "I'm in love with someone else."

"I don't care who you've been with, that doesn't change anything. All I care about is what you are."

"I know." She touched his chest. "But this is different. I'm going to start a family with him someday."

Roble felt numb. He forced himself to look at her, at the woman he was proud to have been conquered by. He saw only guiltless calm. Her expression said she understood everything he felt, yet regretted nothing.

"He's one lucky guy." He rubbed his nose. "But I want to kill him."

"He's the one who asked me to fly you to Seattle."

"Who?" he asked, unable to picture anyone good enough for her.

She gripped his hand. "Kazuki Takinato."

"Takinato," Roble repeated, rubbing his nose again.

She caressed his hand.

Breathing deep, he said, "You deserve each other. You always did."

"Yes."

"Seattle, huh?" He cleared his throat. "Takinato wants to dump me off in the rain and mud?"

"It's a long flight." She spun him around and pushed him into the pilot's seat. "And I know how you love jets more than me." Kneeling between his knees, she fastened each end of the seatbelt around his forearms until they pinched against the armrests, securing him to the seat.

"But you just said…?"

"I meant it. Now shut up or I'll gag you as well." She grinned.

Roble felt his hands vibrating as Sugemi removed his pants. "Oh…" He watched the clouds rolling by, until her lips found his skin and his eyes rolled back in his head.

When she finished, she untied him, sat in the co-pilot's seat, and let him take over flying the jet. He didn't wish to speak, just feel how he did at that moment.

"You will get off at a private landing strip near the coast," Sugemi said. "Keep a low profile. I'll report I had unexpected engine trouble and was forced to land temporarily. Then I'll fly on to Seattle to register my entry, with myself as sole occupant."

After they landed, Roble made for the exit, not wanting to say a final goodbye.

She caught him by the arm and slipped an envelope into his jacket pocket. "An American gave this to Takinato while you were in detention."

Roble removed it, looking inside. Along with about fifty one-hundred-dollar bills was an unsigned note in a woman's handwriting that read: *Not unity or sacrifice, but freedom and happiness. And for what you said—gratitude.* He furrowed his brows.

"When you create your next jet," Sugemi said, causing him to look up with surprise, "fly it to Japan and show it to us."

He pulled her close and kissed her. She didn't resist.

"Say hello to Takinato for me," he said, tucking away the envelope.

He descended the steps into the mist. Dripping wet pine trees lined the crumbling asphalt airstrip. As he walked away, he watched the jet carrying away the only woman he had ever loved.

Ronin rolled down his wrinkled sleeves while holding a file in one hand. He stood in the doorway of an office in front of a man in a black suit sitting at a desk. "He disappeared. That's all I have to report."

"How in the hell do you lose somebody over the Pacific Ocean?"

"Shall I mobilize resources to track down a stale person of interest who we claim we never possessed?"

"God *dammit*, Ronin. Give me the file."

Ronin tossed it to him and rubbed the back of his neck with a yawn.

The man flipped through the pages, cursing under his breath every few seconds. He couldn't seem to figure out who they should notify or who was supposed to care whether they found Roble Santos or not. Taking any action suddenly seemed more politically risky than doing nothing. He threw the file back at Ronin.

"That's what I thought, sir. Now if you'll excuse me, I have some actual bad guys to track down."

Chapter 39

As the bus crested the Apex Summit, Roble jumped from his seat and slid past sleeping passengers to the expansive front windshield. He looked down on the sea of lights under a dark red sky, marveling at the radiant city he hadn't seen in five and a half years.

He focused on the unexpected white blade piercing both sea and sky. After a moment, he looked left at the illuminated twin runways at Nellis Air Force Base, surrounded by a moat of darkness. *I'm home.*

When the bus stopped, he stepped down into a litter-strewn parking lot north of downtown. He walked the streets, hearing scattered blurts of sirens and occasional bottles breaking on concrete.

He approached a squalid, mustard-colored motel. It advertised rooms by the day or by the hour, and he knew that meant no names, no ID, no questions asked. He paid the man behind the bulletproof glass.

Sunlight bled through the dirty, frayed curtains, waking him the next morning. He dressed and jogged six blocks to the Road Runner Motorcycle Shop.

Scanning the used motorcycles from behind a chain-link fence, he selected one and entered the shop. He spotted the familiar owner in the back and avoided contact, considering his so-far undetected entrance back into the country. He paid cash to an abundantly tattooed and unfamiliar worker and rolled the motorcycle to the street.

Its engine burst to life and Roble flew down the wide boulevards with a sense of uninhibited motion. And with his first act of freedom, he performed a pilgrimage. Not to a dank shrine dedicated to suffering, but to a manufacturing temple used by a saint to send mankind into the heavens.

He swung the motorcycle in to an empty North Las Vegas

parking lot. Tumbleweeds edged the faded and cracked asphalt. The outline of a removed capital *L* with a dot above it marked the front door. He peered through a dusty pane. Crushed boxes and litter covered the floor of a dark reception area. *Where is everyone?*

He tore away from the abandoned building, front tire rearing in the air. Veering onto a freeway, his hair flattened with speed, eyes squinting. He turned on Charleston Boulevard heading west and weaved around vehicles until reaching the Calico Basin turnoff.

The Libby House sat perched high on a cliff. His bike accelerated toward it.

Entering a crowded parking lot, he recoiled at the sight of an exterior elevator bolted incongruously to the red cliff, and at the aluminum railings scarring the home's balconies like sutures over wounds.

A sign above the large sheet metal structure at the base of the cliff, read: *The Calico Center for the Preservation of Our Heritage.*

He parked on a sidewalk and looked around. Fencing blocked access to the stone switchbacks and hiking paths with signs reading: *Park Rangers Only.* Near the building's entrance, a patch of sand wedged between two concrete slabs held a signpost reading: *Please keep off for revegetation.*

He opened a glass door with the words *Public Lands in Public Hands* captioned across it. Inside, a woman with a ranger hat made announcements to a tour group. The floors were not natural stone as Roble had imagined, but a commercial blue carpet. Florescent lamps on the ceiling shellacked the interior with a pale sheen.

Approaching a smiling attendant at the information desk, Roble asked, "Isn't this Libby Dodge's house?"

Her smile vanished. "Ahem. Sir, this is The Calico Center for the Preservation of Our Heritage." She pointed to a stack of glossy brochures as evidence.

"Who owns it?"

"The upper floors are for public servants. You can buy a tour ticket to visit the museum or watch a short video presentation that starts in twenty-five minutes," she said, like a prerecorded message, then added, "Next."

Roble leaned against the counter, watching a tour group

follow a park ranger into an elevator. As the doors closed, the ranger said, "Remember, don't touch anything."

Where is Libby?

The information attendant stretched her neck to the side to speak to a tourist behind Roble. When Roble didn't move, both the tourist and the attendant rolled their eyes.

Roble staggered from the visitor center, bewildered. He plucked a parking ticket from his motorbike's handlebars and handed it to a man walking by in a Chinese tour group. *She doesn't live here anymore. Her manufacturing facility is closed. What the hell happened?*

On the way out of the Calico Basin, he focused on the distant white tower; he could think of nowhere else to go. The closer he came to it, the more it drew him in, until he found himself standing below it. He lay on a bench to see the top without falling over. *It's unreal. Who built this?*

As the clear sky darkened into dusk, his stomach rumbled, and he knew he was no closer to finding Libby.

In an outdoor plaza, he ordered a burrito and a bottle of water from a vendor. Sitting near some youths, he watched them browsing on handheld devices. After a few bites, he asked one if he wouldn't mind searching something on the internet. The young man agreed, and at Roble's request, searched for all property in Las Vegas belonging to Libby Dodge.

"Nothing came up," the teenager said.

"Can you find any information about Libby Industries?"

"Says here it filed for bankruptcy three years ago."

Roble slumped into his seat, losing his appetite. Then he remembered the private mailbox number he used to correspond with Libby from Okinawa. He bought a postcard and addressed it to her. He wrote down his motel address, requesting contact.

Four days later, his own postcard slid under his door with a stamp across it. *Recipient moved. No forwarding address.*

He sat on the bed and watched a cockroach scamper across the matted carpet. Falling back on the concaved mattress, he listened to screaming and banging from another room. He dipped a hand into his pocket and felt the shrinking roll of bills. *Where are you, Libby?*

The next day, he joined day laborers along a dirt lot, knowing he would have to work with undocumented workers to avoid giving out his real name. A truck picked him up and the driver paid him to haul away runoff debris from the renovation of an older casino on the North Strip.

As he pushed a debris cart, he noticed a worker two floors above installing mechanical hardware. Something about the guy's manner seemed familiar, but before he could get a better look, the man disappeared. Every time Roble returned to the casino worksite, he eyed the workers above in the steel frame, searching for that guy.

He repeated his morning routine for weeks, sometimes hauling away debris at the casino, sometimes doing other odd jobs, and sometimes waiting half the day before going back to his motel without work.

Every evening, and on days he found no work, he sat on his bed below a single bulb and drew his long-envisioned aircraft. Sketching the detailed renderings without destroying them at the end of each day felt satisfying. He pinned them over the stained walls. The last of the envelope money purchased a laptop so he could translate his sketches into computer-assisted design diagrams and automate the aerospace calculations.

Leaving the casino worksite one afternoon, he glanced up. Danny Sands walked in front of him toward a gravel lot. *I knew it!* Roble jogged after him, accelerating his pace, not wanting to lose him again. "Danny!"

Danny turned and stared, eyes wide, at Roble's dust-covered face. "Holy shit, I thought you were dead."

Roble shrugged. "Not yet."

"I mean…wow." Danny shook his head, arms lifting. "Have you been in Vegas this whole time? Where are you staying?"

"I got back from Japan a few weeks ago, and in a roach motel." He pointed downtown.

"What the hell happened to you in Japan?" He brushed dirt off Roble's shirt. "You're a mess. Come to my place and tell me everything. Where did you park?"

"I came by truckload." Roble rubbed his forehead and looked at his muddy hand.

"Come on," he slapped Roble's shoulder, and took them on his motorcycle to his apartment a few blocks from the construction site.

"Don't mind the place, I've been meaning to find something better," Danny said as they entered.

Roble glanced around at the newer tile floors and fresh paint.

"So, what happened to you? You just disappeared from Kadena, like—literally vanished."

"They dishonorably discharged me." Roble walked into the kitchen to wash his face. "Then they locked me up."

"In jail?" Danny blinked. "For what?"

"It doesn't really matter now."

Danny stared at him, mouth open. "Well, don't feel too bad. I saw a lot of guys trip up in the Marines. For me, I'd just had enough. That's why I left. I'd made it all the way to Drill Instructor, but the prestige didn't mean much to me. My father actually begged me to stay in the Marines, if you can picture that." He laughed, but choked a bit at the end. "I'm doing mechanical work full-time now, pays pretty well."

Roble dried his face with a paper towel. "I can't wait to see what else you've drawn."

"Jail?" Danny blurted. "Dishonorable discharge…man…."

Facing Danny, he said, "I witnessed more honor the day they discharged me than I'd seen in my life."

"Whose?"

"The officer who discharged me."

Danny's face flushed and he raised the back of a hand to his mouth.

"What's wrong?" Roble asked.

Danny took a breath and wiped his forehead. "Nothing. Nothing." Swallowing hard, he said, "Look, let me put in a good word with my boss and get you hired full-time. You don't want to do day labor for the rest of your life, do you?"

"I appreciate the offer, but I'm just doing this until I figure out a way to build my jet."

"What?" Danny lifted his hands. "Don't you think it's time to get serious about life? Build a jet? You? Here?" He laughed, but choked again.

"I've never been so excited about anything."

"God," Danny shook his head, "you never change, do you?"

"I should head home." Roble walked to the front door. "It was great finding you."

"Wait," Danny stepped after him, lowering his voice. "If your place is as bad as you say, live here and split the rent. I have a spare room."

Roble inhaled, not smelling any unidentifiable rot. He heard no screaming. "All right."

"It will be just like old times." Danny ran a hand through his hair, a smile below his worried eyes.

"Speaking of old times, you never answered me about your drawings. Your art under Nishiko was...mind-blowing."

"I stopped drawing," Danny winced. "I mean...I drew a little more before I got too busy with the Marines. But, I don't think I care about it anymore."

Roble tilted his head. "Can I see what else you drew?"

"It's not like the art you saw...really." Danny walked to his bedroom and brought back storyboards, guarding them against his chest. "This is more mature...and stuff. I think it shows—"

Roble pried the storyboards from Danny's hands and flipped through them.

Danny watched, studying his every breath. "You probably won't like it, but...what do you think?"

Roble looked up. "I think you shouldn't care what I think."

"I knew you wouldn't approve. It's for more traditional audiences, you know? At some point you have to balance your ideas with what others will accept. You can't stay a kid forever, right?"

"If you like it, that's all that matters."

Danny coughed. "Forget about art." He grabbed his storyboards and tossed them to the couch. "I just can't believe we're roommates again."

Roble shook his head. "My only concern is we won't have parental supervision this time."

Danny breathed in, shoulders dropping. "Just two little shits," he smiled.

Motorcycle engines wailed, shifting into progressively higher gears. Roble and Danny weaved in and out of Saturday traffic on a desert road, taking advantage of their day off.

Roble took the lead, pushing over a hundred miles per hour.

Ahead, a stocky figure riding a curvaceous motorcycle came

into view. An aircraft image flashed through Roble's mind as he overtook it. He gripped the brake and turned, mouth gaping at the blue-grey cycle next to him. *It's like a* Sovereign *but in motorcycle form.*

The jet-bike roared ahead. Above its exhaust sat an unusual Nevada license plate, pitch black with white lettering—*MAN.*

Roble pulled alongside it again, matching its speed. He pointed to the shoulder of the road, signaling the rider to pull over. The rider, wearing a matte-black helmet and dark visor, didn't acknowledge.

"Roble, what are you doing?" Danny yelled, moving close to him.

Speeding in front of the rider, Roble pointed again while gradually braking. The jet-bike kicked forward, thundering past Roble, barely missing his leg. *That was a bit close. This guy has balls.*

Danny pulled alongside Roble again. "He almost hit you—just let him go!"

"Move up to his left side. I have an idea," Roble yelled. He tore after the mystery bike, passed it, and blocked its path again.

Danny shook his head and moved up the man's left flank, cutting off his escape route. Roble slowed, and the rider pulled over and stopped.

The large man, wearing a black leather jacket, stepped off his bike, his metal tipped cowboy boots glinting in the sun.

Danny dismounted, turned to Roble and said under his breath, "What the hell are you doing?"

Ignoring Danny, Roble walked over to the jet-bike. A platinum capital *L* with a dot over it marked the gas tank. He studied the motorcycle's fuselage. *It must be made out of some kind of new superalloy.*

Danny fidgeted, eyeing the man in black.

Amazing. Roble touched the jet-bike. "What's—"

The man punched Roble in the chin, sending him twisting backward and skidding on his back in the gravel.

Roble's jeans and t-shirt lessened the abrasions but his elbows stung, caked with blood-mixed dirt. He sat up, rubbing his jaw.

"Nobody touches my property without my permission," the man said with a deep-chested voice coming from inside his helmet.

Danny stepped forward, hands curling into fists. The man

stood, unflinching. Roble scrambled across the gravel on hands and knees, reached out, and grabbed Danny's shin.

"If he wants a fight, I'll show him how a Marine hits back," Danny said, trying to free his leg from Roble's grip.

Roble climbed to his feet. "Danny, I *need* to talk to this guy. It was my fault he hit me."

"You're damn right it's your fault," Danny said. "Why did you make him stop?" He held his fists at the ready, glaring at the man.

Roble brushed himself off, his face and elbows pulsing with pain. "I'm sorry for touching your bike, sir. Thank you for pulling over. I need to ask you something."

The man removed his helmet, revealing a humorless, strong face, black skin, and grey sprinkled hair. "Ask," he growled.

Roble looked into his cold unmoving eyes. "Your motorcycle, I know who made it. I've worked with her."

"And?"

"I need to find her."

"Did you quit with those cowards at her North Las Vegas Facility after the raid, or were you one of the upright ones who were fired a week later?"

Roble lifted his hands. "Libby Dodge helped me modify some jets in Japan, but I've never actually met her."

The man raised an eyebrow. "What's your name, son?"

"Roble Santos."

He tilted his head and then extended a hand. "Halvern Black."

Roble grasped it. "Do you know where she is?"

"How much does it mean to you?"

"I'd do about anything." He looked down, brushing off his jacket.

Danny released his fists and stepped closer.

Halvern studied the pair for a moment. "I'll make a deal with you. If you and your sidekick get some work done for me this weekend, I'll take you to Libby."

"Don't trust this guy," Danny said. "What type of person has a license plate that says *MAN*?"

Halvern chuckled. "Never seen one before?"

Roble gripped Danny's arm. "What do you want us to do, Mr. Black?"

"I own a ranch in the Calico Basin. It needs work, starting now. You'd be done by tomorrow evening. That's my offer."

"Work for free?" Danny asked.

Turning to Danny, Roble said, "If you come, I'll give you my next week's pay."

Danny rubbed his forehead, watching a truck rumble by on the highway. "Roble, come on. This is crazy. We don't know who this guy is."

"Okay, two weeks of pay for only a day and a half of work," Roble said.

Danny looked Halvern up and down. "All right. But if he kills us, it's your fault."

"Done," Roble said.

Halvern led them to his ranch. The multi-acre plot stretched out below and to the north of the former Libby House.

He gave them a list of duties including mending fences, pruning nut trees, moving water troughs, and digging trenches. Ordering them to, "Stay away from the other horse stable and the water tank to the south," he rode away.

As they worked, Roble kept glancing at the water tank sitting on the grounds to the south. Its domed roof gleamed like crystal, burning in the sunlight, absorbing light into the water.

They worked hard all day, drinking from a water pump to survive the heat. The next morning when it was time to return to the ranch, Danny asked, "Are you sure this guy knows where Libby Dodge is?"

"No. But if this ends up being a waste of time, I'll also wash your clothes for a month to make you feel better."

Danny sighed and walked from their apartment out to his motorcycle.

As the sun eclipsed behind the former Libby House, Danny moved about Halvern's horse stable adding touch-up paint to old ranch equipment, making a few artistic embellishments. Roble finished up the construction of a corral fence.

A low whirl from a jet turbine made them look up. Halvern glided into the stable. He removed his helmet, picked up a white cowboy hat, and strolled out to the ranch.

"You worked hard," Halvern said, returning. "I figured you would."

Roble pointed at the cliff. "How did Ms. Dodge lose her house?"

Halvern scowled.

"When did it fall into public hands?" Danny asked.

Halvern held a large hand before Danny's face. "This is a hand, son. Have you ever seen a public one?"

Danny stared without answer. Roble rubbed his nose.

Pulling out a slip of paper, Halvern handed it to Roble. "This is where you'll find Ms. Dodge. Wait until tomorrow. Now get off my land." He mounted his bike and rode away.

Danny sidled up to read the address. "What? Are you kidding me?"

The listed address sat three blocks from their apartment. They passed by it every day. Roble laughed and patted Danny on the back.

"There is something seriously wrong with that guy." Danny jumped on his motorcycle. "We worked our asses off for *that*? You owe me, Roble."

It had grown late by the time they rode by the property matching the address. Roble stopped beyond its corrugated steel fence. *She's so close.* He rode home telling himself one more day wouldn't kill him. He lay awake all night.

Chapter 40

Roble stood, hand hovering over the toaster, head bobbing, trying to mentally accelerate the toasting.

Danny yawned and shuffled into the kitchen. "Are you really skipping work?"

Roble caught the toast in the air and took a bite.

"I think you owe me some money," Danny rubbed an eye, "if I remember correctly."

"You'll get paid." Roble searched the refrigerator for something to drink. "Maybe you'll see me later at the job site."

"Oh no, I'm not going to work while you screw off." He leaned into the fridge next to Roble, rolled a melon out of the way, and handed a protein shake to Roble. "Here. I'm calling in sick and coming with you. I want to see what this Libby person is all about."

Roble's motorcycle skidded to a stop outside Libby's metal fence. Danny pulled in behind.

The partially open gate revealed an asphalt driveway leading to a single-story house. A thumping noise and the haunting voice of a woman's singing came from somewhere inside.

Roble slid the gate open and entered. The large lot contained a grassy area and cottonwood trees to the left of the house, and two large metal buildings, a garage, and gravel pathways to the right.

As they walked up the drive, the singing became louder, flowing through octaves in rhythm with the thumping beat. The notes without lyrics evoked stressed gayety. Roble and Danny glanced at each other, raising their eyebrows.

A pine scent filled the air as they skirted the house to the right. Between the house and a metal building a woman chopped wood, her back turned. She wore an untucked explorer's shirt with rolled-up sleeves, hiking shorts and boots. Her axe swung with fluidity, splitting the cords in sync with the still unseen voice.

Libby Dodge? Roble lost his breath.

Without looking at them, the woman set down the axe. The voice in the background ceased. She pulled a device from a pocket, pressed its screen, and the front gate closed under its own power. She faced them, revealing strands of wet hair falling mid-cheek and brilliant green eyes.

Yes, of course. Roble bowed low.

Smiling, she approached in wide steps, and clasped Roble's hand. "Mr. Roble Santos, I presume?"

Roble tried to speak but only managed, "Mmhm."

She hugged him. "It's so good to finally meet you." Pulling away, still smiling, she said, "Welcome."

Roble nodded, still unable to pronounce words.

Turning to Danny, she extended a hand. "I'm Libby."

"Danny." He swallowed as if meeting a celebrity.

"Come, make yourselves at home." She directed them into the house.

The same singing voice as before hummed from somewhere in the back of the home.

Libby picked up a pile of grey chainmail off a couch in the sunken living room and deposited it under the coffee table. "Please sit down." She sat on the opposing couch across the table.

Roble took a seat and felt along his pockets, opening his mouth to speak.

"What's with that crotchety old man—Hazard?" Danny blurted, sitting down next to Roble.

"Halvern?" Libby smirked. "He's my architect."

Danny shook his head. "The guy who made that strange-looking center for heritage place?"

Libby raised an eyebrow.

"I don't think it was originally built like that," Roble said.

"I'm so glad Halvern found you, Roble," she said. "I've been worried ever since the F-22 crashed."

"What?" Danny eyed Roble. "You crashed a fighter jet?"

Roble shrugged.

"No fu…" He glanced at Libby before continuing at Roble, "…no freaking way. You never flew fighter jets."

"Well," Roble looked at Libby, "it's a long story."

"Did you hijack one or something?" Danny gripped the couch cushion. "Is *that* why they locked you up?"

"I mean…" He scratched his head.

"Roble, once I heard that you were still alive," Libby said, "I figured they had you locked up somewhere. Did they—"

"And wait," Danny interrupted, "Halvern knew you were looking for Roble? And he still had us work on his stinking hot ranch before giving us your address?"

Libby held still for a moment then shook with silent laughter. "You will have to excuse Halvern's unique sense of humor. I didn't know he'd found you until he called this morning." She leaned toward Roble. "Did they just release you?"

He coughed. "Sort of."

"Okay," Libby laughed. "I suspect you have something else you want to discuss first, but you better tell me the whole story sometime."

Roble ran his hands along his pockets again, his breathing pronounced.

Libby smiled and turned up her palms. "What do you want to exchange with me?"

Danny looked back and forth between them, his brows furrowed.

Roble pulled three folded sheets of paper from his pockets and laid them on the coffee table, smoothing out their wrinkles.

Libby picked up the side profile of Roble's design. The melodic humming continued in the background, giving a soundtrack to Libby's thoughts. After a while she picked up the front and rear profile drawing, fingers tracing it like a Victorian scientist observing an atom diagram for the first time. Last, she studied the technical overview of the parts and assemblies inside the aircraft. She spread the papers out, leaning over them, eyes moving back and forth.

Roble watched her, hand caressing his arrowhead.

The humming stopped, and a woman entered from the kitchen almost floating across the floor, a tray with three tall glasses balanced on her fingers. She glided down into the living room on bare feet, her red hair flowing like satin. Reaching out to offer the drinks, the scent of rosemary and desert rain wafted across the couch.

Danny's jaw dropped at her grey tee stretched over her curves, above a crystal-studded belt and tight white leggings.

Roble watched her silver eyes shift to him; they seemed both exotic and inexplicably familiar. He couldn't guess her age; she appeared physically young, yet held a glance too astute for youth.

Libby stood. "May I introduce, Sitra."

The pair shot to their feet and introduced themselves.

She nodded to each, but her gaze lingered on Roble. "Would you like iced tea?"

"Thank you." Libby took a glass and sat down.

Moving the tray to Danny, Sitra's hair grazed his shoulder.

Danny reached, grasping twice before gripping a glass. "Thank...pleasure's all...you...mine."

Roble took a glass. Sitra turned and glided back up the steps, disappearing into the kitchen. Both men remained standing.

Hearing the clinking of ice cubes in Libby's glass, they looked away from the kitchen and sat down.

"A geared step to SCRAM for escape velocity?" Libby tapped a diagram. "Using two separate dual-mode engines? And the way you shaped the wings and fuselage are...well, this is no mere aircraft, Roble."

"No," he said.

"What you've designed would require the most advanced alloys and carbons known to exist. It would push the limits of aerospace computer processing. Have you thought through all the components and their integration?"

"I have a few unresolved issues, mainly because I need more computing power to sharpen my estimates into aerospace precision. And I'll need avionics software. But I've worked through a solution on most everything else. I'm producing all the technical drawings right now. When I'm done, I'll bring them over."

Libby massaged her forehead.

"When do we start?" Roble asked.

Libby gazed across the house and through the dining room window. The leaves on the cottonwood tree quivered. She shook her head. "I know how to acquire and develop the materials; I can get the software; I can fashion the components; and I can assemble it...but I don't have the resources any longer to fund it."

"How much do we need?"

"A hundred million dollars," Libby said, "maybe more."

Danny gasped. "Our rent is fourteen hundred per month and we split it to save money."

Roble's gut sank as if falling from a shot down plane. He tried to grasp the amount of money mentioned, but it seemed unfathomable. "I'll find a way, somehow."

"Well, if you do, I'll require a twenty-five percent interest in all sales, patents, and technologies derived from it as my payment for constructing it. The other seventy-five percent you can split with financial backers. You can use my name to try to raise the funds if you wish. I'll give you a list of bankers and investors I've worked with in the past. But keep in mind, Libby Industries went bankrupt, so I'm not sure if it'll be much help."

"We have a deal." Roble reached out and shook Libby's hand.

Danny threw his hands up, rolling his eyes.

"With that done," Libby said, "would you two like to stay for lunch?"

Danny looked toward the kitchen. "Absolutely."

"I need to get to work," Roble said.

"Of course." Libby stood.

Roble reached for his designs but Libby spread her fingers above them. "Please leave these."

He nodded.

As they reached the front door, Sitra's voice cut across the room. "One heart way."

They all turned.

"Did you say…?" Danny almost choked.

"On your jacket, a patch of the Isshin-Ryu."

Danny looked at his arm. "I know an Isshin-Ryu Sensei in Naha, Okinawa. I met him while I was in the Marines."

Sitra's hair poured to her waist as she bowed. Her hands pressed together in the greeting gesture of an Isshin-Ryu master, one in a fist the other an open palm. "How very fortunate of you, Danny."

"Uhmm…yeah. Thank you." He bowed back. "I love Isshin-Ryu…and stuff."

"Farewell," she said.

Danny beamed at Roble. Libby opened the front door. Roble

pushed him outside. Danny's neck craned back to prolong his view of Sitra.

Roble sat on the apartment couch sketching an aircraft part.

"What do you think of Sitra?" Danny asked from the kitchen. The grease-stained microwave hummed as a bowl of noodles and chicken rotated inside.

Roble stopped and erased an errant mark.

"Do you think she and Libby are…?"

Roble looked up.

"I'm not saying I'm interested in Sitra or anything like that," Danny said. "I'm just curious, that's all. She's different, really—" The microwave beeped. "Unusual." He removed the noodles, walked to the coffee table, and set down a bottle of spicy teriyaki sauce. "Libby didn't sound too helpful with your jet. Asking for a hundred million dollars? That's like…nuts."

"I guess." Roble studied the curve of the teriyaki bottle. "I was hoping she had the money to fund it."

"Well, you used to work for Stock Brant, right?"

Roble's mouth opened.

"That criminal is loaded." Danny sat on the couch next to him. "Maybe you could find a way to pinch a hundred big ones off him."

Roble turned his head, locking eyes. "Let's *not* discuss Stock."

"Ever heard of Robin Hood? Take from the rich and give to the…" He waved his fork around the room, stopping when it pointed at Roble. Danny raised an eyebrow.

"I don't rob people."

"Just like you don't steal fighter jets?" He twirled noodles on the fork.

"The pilot let me fly it." Roble looked at the floor. "And an Air Force general decided to destroy it."

"Uhhh…military pilots don't own those jets, the taxpayers do. And if you didn't steal it, why did they lock you up?"

"I never had a trial so I can't know for sure why they locked me up." Roble shook his head. "And I've never understood who owns public property—whether it's the taxpayers, the government, or the person who uses it." He exhaled, tapping his eraser against his drawing. "But what I do understand is that Stock made his money, so it's his. I don't rob people."

"If you want to make excuses for your actions," Danny took a bite, "I won't stop you."

"I want to use reason."

"You *can* just accept the way things are. You don't have to try to re-figure out everything yourself." He poured teriyaki sauce into his bowl. "You know that, right?"

Roble glanced away from the teriyaki bottle and drew a curved engine part.

"Do you know how many people need that money more than Stock?" Danny ate chicken off the fork. "Need it even more than us? I think it's wrong for Stock to have it. Most people would agree."

"You mean your father agrees."

Danny winced. "Come on. I'm trying to help you."

Roble rubbed his forehead.

"Okay, just think of it this way." Danny held the bowl between his hands. "If Stock got his money through crime, wouldn't that mean it's not wrong to take it?"

Roble wadded up his sketch.

"I hear Stock's gang is killing rival members," Danny said, "some right here in this neighborhood. You'd be doing the world a favor if you liberated his loot. That's justice, right?"

Roble dropped the crumpled paper to the floor. He'd read the recent headlines and wondered if Stock and the street violence had some connection. It *had* been over a decade since he worked for him.

"But if you think more highly of a criminal than of the needs of society, or even of funding your dream, well then," Danny set the bowl on his knee, "that's your choice."

Roble gripped his own hair, exhaling. He needed money so desperately he almost wished Danny were right and he didn't care about Stock or how he got the money.

Danny twisted noodles on his fork.

"Maybe Halvern will fund it," Roble lifted his chin. "He must have money if he can afford a Libby jet-bike and a ranch."

"Uhmm…yeah, Roble, go for it. He made us work for free. And he hit you just for touching his motorbike, remember? Good luck getting a penny off that guy." He took a bite. "But promise you'll take me with you if you ask him. I want a front row seat to that show."

Roble opened his laptop and typed in a search. "Whoa... Halvern Black is the architect and builder of *The Spirit of Man*."

"What? He built that? Isn't it like a hundred stories tall?"

"Over two hundred, and from what this says, he lives at the top."

Danny spilled noodle broth on his lap.

"Halvern certainly has money, but you're right, he's no pushover. Before I beg him for a hundred million dollars," Roble kicked the wadded paper across the floor, "I need to do my homework."

The next morning after Danny went to work, Roble started calling Libby's prior investors. Of his forty-eight phone calls, half the recipients refused to speak with him. Of the half who did, half of those hung up at the mention of Libby Dodge. Of the twelve who didn't hang up, half of those refused to meet. The final six invited him to their offices—four in Los Angeles, one in Silicon Valley, and one in Las Vegas.

When Danny returned home, Roble looked up from his laptop and asked, "Can I borrow a few hundred bucks?"

"Don't you work anymore?"

"A few hundred dollars. I'll pay you back."

"I mean..." Danny threw his jacket on the coffee table. "How can you pay me back if you don't work?"

Roble glanced at his own stained t-shirt. "I need a suit and some gas money for these interviews."

"I want to help you," Danny lifted a hand, "but come on. I'm not exactly loaded myself."

"Look, if I don't pay you everything I owe by the end of the month," he scratched his head, "you can have my motorcycle."

Danny pulled out his wallet. "All right, but that's it."

Roble nodded, returning to the financial spreadsheet.

Roble carried his business plan and jet drawings into a tall building in downtown L.A. The lobby smelled of cut flowers and polished stone. Sitting in his cheap suit on a marble bench, he stared from behind hair falling to his eyes at all the people striding about in their fitted business attire and stylish hairdos.

Closing his eyes, he ran the proposal through his mind. Sell a forty-nine percent stake in his prototype, its related patents, and its future sales rights in return for one hundred and ten million dollars. That would leave him and Libby with a controlling interest and a bit of extra cash just in case. He would explain how a new era of jet travel would begin, and much of the profit would be reaped by the initial investors. He loosened his tie and swallowed.

"Libby Dodge?"

Roble jumped.

A woman in a trim suit stood over him. "I assumed Libby was a female name. But whatever, the investment committee will see you now."

"Ms. Dodge is my business partner."

"I didn't catch your name."

Roble scratched his neck.

"How should I introduce you?" She tapped her sharp-toed pump.

"As Rob," he stood up, "Rob Santo…Santa Cla…" he straightened his tie, "as Rob Santa, Ms. Dodge's aerospace designer."

She turned on her heels and walked off. He followed her to the boardroom.

After five days of grueling meetings and road trips around California and Nevada, Roble had obtained three investment proposals. His best came from an investment bank in Las Vegas on his last day; they were early investors in Libby Industries who sold out at a profit before the bankruptcy, and their president loved jets. They wanted a fifty-five percent stake in the venture for investing forty million dollars. Roble told them he'd think about it.

Still wearing his suit from the meeting, he rode to the street south of Nellis Air Force Base and parked below the runways. The investors had offered more money than he could ever imagine, but it wouldn't build the aircraft he designed. *Scale back the plans? I don't need to make my dream jet right out of the gate, do I? What's so wrong with a little compromise?*

An F-15 Strike Eagle came in low for a landing, growling over his head. With his hands vibrating, his mind drifted to Okinawa and the *Skeleton Eagle*. He grinned at the thought of Takinato taking him to his garage and discussing the modifications, modifications that seemed impossible at the time. He remembered his excitement at the Misawa Air Show, seeing Libby's jets for the first time. *Everything less advanced than my design has already been done. I can't compromise.*

Touching his arrowhead, he thought of Sugemi. *She of all people would want me to build it. She has money. And it would be a chance to speak with her again.* He sat motionless on the humming motorcycle. He reached for his phone, and stopped, kicking the ground. "No." *She risked her life to help me. I can't ask her for anything that might connect her to my escape.*

He sped off down the street and parked behind Lou's Gas & Lube. Jumping onto a trash dumpster, he climbed up to the gas station's flat roof. Lying on his back at the center, he pushed gravel into a moat around his suit, feeling fifteen again. *I missed this place.*

Thunder boomed down. An F-22 Raptor rocketed off the runway in full afterburner, its landing gear retracting. Roble reached into the air wanting to grab on. *I must hold on.* He sat up, watching it climb until all that remained in the sky was the sparkling tower on the other side of the valley.

An hour later, Roble entered their apartment, ripped off his dusty, sweat-stained suit, and turned to Danny. "It's time to see Halvern. If you want to see the show, let's go."

Chapter 41

Stock didn't move as the stands behind Nicolette's home erupted with applause.

Nicolette skipped to the net to shake her opponent's hand, her face beaming, even though she'd lost the tournament final to the seventh ranked man in the world. As the audience of tennis players dissipated and mingled, Nicolette remained on the court, her shoulders back, neck elongated.

Stock gripped the bleachers, wanting to run to her, press her glistening body to the ground, and take her right there. With his chest heaving, he enjoyed the pain of her not giving him a glance.

"Let's get out of here," Stock said a half hour later, after everyone else had their chance to speak with her.

Nicolette moved her lips close to his ear, almost biting. "I'm starving." She touched the sweat at the base of her neck. "Give me a minute to clean up."

Entering Stock's penthouse, Nicolette strolled over to the intimate table set up on the balcony with steaming shellfish. He pulled out a chair and slid it in behind her.

He filled flutes with champagne and sat down. Lifting a glass, he said, "To you, Nicolette."

She tapped her rim to his, its chime hanging like audible joy.

"Move in with me," Stock said.

She took a sip, her stare warming his stomach more than the champagne.

"I need you, Nicolette."

"Perhaps," she leaned in, "but you can't have me—at least not in the sense you mean."

"In what sense?" He swallowed.

"In the sense you think I can save you from yourself."

He sat motionless, heart thumping with unwanted panic, staring at her serene face.

Nicolette stood and moved behind him. She squeezed his broad shoulders and kissed his temple. "Stock—"

"I love you," he said, cutting her off.

She kissed him again.

He stood and faced her, his eyes pleading. "I need you. I can't explain it, but I love the way you are."

"What way am I?"

"You're…" he paused, struggling to release the word from his tightening throat, "good…for me. I don't know why."

"Did you say, 'good'?" Her voice twinkled with amusement.

Stock cringed at the sound of that word.

Nicolette pressed her forehead to his. "Not evil or misguided like most people say?"

"You're not…those."

"Then why support those who believe I am?"

"Support them?" He glanced out across the city, at all those who had made his dream evil. "I hate everything they believe."

"Then why believe in something you hate?" Running a hand through his hair, she added, "Stock, would you try to create a biologic cure out of a sense of rebellion…against nature?"

He shook his head, feeling his mind hit a contradiction like a concrete barrier. "You're confusing physical laws with morality."

"But of course."

"They're different."

"Are they?" She pressed her palm against his beating chest. "What's the first step in creating a biologic?"

Stock lowered his eyes.

"Tell me."

"I identify its nature," he said, not looking at her.

"And what is *mankind's* nature?"

He felt a surge of hate, hate for all of mankind…and then Nicolette's lashes feathering against his cheek, a sensation so subtle, yet more powerful and concrete than his unwanted view of morality.

She watched him, her eyes tranquil.

If only I could live inside those eyes, as pure as spring water. He winced. *But a spring must never be polluted.* "You are right not to move in with me, Nicolette. I'm no—"

"This," she grazed her lips against his, "is not an idea unconnected to reality, or done for or against anyone, not even you. She pressed her body against his. "This," she said, moving her hand down his back, "is real, and it is mine." She kissed him.

Kat breathed with relief as she heard Stock enter the lab and continued extracting a biologic sample. She'd hoped for his return, and not just because she'd been stuck for days on a difficult research problem.

She jumped when he touched her shoulder, liquid shooting from her syringe across an array of tubes. And that's when she realized his return had provided no relief to her fears.

"You wanted to ask me something the other day," Stock said.

Inhaling a breath of courage, she tossed the syringe to the table, and turned. "The genetic code obeys you, because you understand it." Her heart beat against her ribs. "Have you ever considered if you understand Jessy?"

Stock tensed, his teeth gritting together.

She pressed herself to her feet. "Look around—with the same eyes you use to cure diseases and make new life."

His fists tightened.

Ignoring her shaking knees, she said, "Jessy is doling out bribes to authorities behind your back. He's begun taking out competitors—and some of his men, *your* employees, are dying in the violence, including ex-foster kids. And it won't end there, because there is no compromise between what you wanted to be and what Jessy is." She smacked the table. "The vial is not 99.9% pure, Stock. It's 100% polluted!"

He stumbled back, pressing a knuckle to an eye, a sickening moan escaping his throat. "You're wrong." He kicked the table over, sending vials exploding across the floor. Turning, he staggered from the lab.

Kat gripped a table leg, lowering herself to her knees. Her gloved fist hit the floor, breaking glass. Blood seeped through the latex in widening blotches.

Stock followed the maze of passages upward, passing no one he recognized, and stopped in front of a reinforced door. He turned its handle. *Locked.* He pounded on the door, not knowing if he was trying to break in like a criminal or break out like a prisoner. Above his head, a camera zoomed in with an electronic whine. A lock clicked, and the door swung inward on its own.

Jessy sat behind an ivory inlay desk, illuminated like a Dark Age monarch beneath two gold-leaf sconces. His cherub face flickered in the light, making his smile seem obscene in its friendliness, like an executioner observing an infidel burning at the stake. Two of Jessy's men stood in front of an ancient mural.

"Come in, Stock," Jessy said, maintaining his grin. "To what do we owe the honor?" He nodded, and his men exited around Stock's stiff body.

"This is *my* empire, Jesus!"

"Please sit down." Jessy pointed to a baroque chair. "Whoever said otherwise?"

"Are you paying bribes behind my back? Have you started a street war?" Stock yelled, eyes cutting.

Jessy stood up and held Stock's gaze for the first time—held it with ease.

Stock looked away, not believing he'd just seen his most loyal assistant challenge him without a hint of trepidation. His elbow pressed against the doorframe for support. He felt like vomiting over the ornate tile floor.

"Don't look so glum, Stock. Everything is as you've always wanted. Go back to your lab or to your girlfriend's house, and do what you do best. And as usual, we'll call when we need your advice."

"You don't run this place." Stock stepped forward, fists clenched. "I started this operation so I could create what I wanted and sell it to anyone I wished. Your job is to serve and to protect me to that end. We don't force anyone to do anything—not customers, not employees, not competitors—no one!"

Jessy caressed the desk with his fingertips.

"Stock, that hurts." He opened his arms. "Have our roots not grown strong and wide to protect your home above and overflowing vaults below? Have we not kept the government from striking a decisive blow against you by donating to the right people and making the right political connections? You've said before—you hate all laws, nobody can tell you what to do, you are a criminal, and you are evil." He waved a hand in the air. "So *let us* be evil, let us be criminals, let no one tell us what to do, and let us break *every* law."

Stock glanced around the office as if he were in a dream, unable to absorb the sounds attacking his ears, because he had no answers to what he heard. He thought, stupidly, that he disliked this room because it looked like *The Sin's* lobby. And for the first time, he realized that he'd never liked Jessy's face. *It's his eyes.* But he didn't know why.

He heard muffled sounds, and realized Jessy still spoke, but the words passed through his body as if he had never existed. He wondered if this is what it felt like to disappear, like Alexandria had done, to give up and surrender to the world.

"Have we not served you selflessly," Jessy continued, "giving everything and compelling others to do the same for your dream? And now, here you are after all these years, the architect of everything you have wanted, resting upon our services for everything you hold dear. Tell me, Stock, as our master, is there anything else we may assist you with?"

Stock's shoulders sank, hands falling limp. Jessy sat down and leaned back in his chair, a smile across his lips. Stock stumbled from the office.

Opening a swollen eye, Stock stared at the cone of light spilling from the liquor cabinet, uncertain how and when he'd gotten to his penthouse. But his throbbing head reminded him he didn't wish to be conscious.

"Stop thinking, you bastard," he mumbled. His body rolled off the couch and hit the floor face down, a knuckle touching a half-drunk bottle.

Pulling himself up against the couch, he moaned, "It's all a crime anyway." He picked up the bottle and poured it between his lips, choking. "What choice did I have?"

I wanted to be good. His head slumped forward. He envisioned the genetic sequence of his new biologic hovering just above the floor, followed by a polished shoe stomping on it, smashing it to ooze. He smiled sickly, eyes half closing. "That's what I thought."

The bottle found his lips again, and he emptied it. "Because I said so!" he said. "Because I said so," he repeated in a drooling whisper.

He flung the bottle. It crashed against a wall, raining shards across the penthouse.

One's fate is always tied to others. There is no hope...

He drifted into the peaceful evasion of unconsciousness, but an unwanted spark, an image, interrupted his peace. He saw Nicolette on a tennis court slamming a ball up in the air. It soared, reflecting off white glass. As it passed the top of a skyscraper, its yellow fuzz ignited into flame, extending behind a sleek aircraft. It rocketed into a dark, stormy sky, claps of thunder and lightning all around. It shot past an illuminated marquee hanging above the entire world—but it was not the faceless silhouette he had made—instead a naked woman stood with no detail hidden from the sun's unfiltered beam. It was Sitra, and her eyes held a ferocious clarity, shining silver and guiltless.

He reached out, grasping, trying to understand that look in her eyes, to feel that glimmer of hope, but the image faded as his head hit the floor.

Chapter 42

S weat vaporized off Danny's temples as he tailed Roble's motorcycle down Las Vegas Boulevard, the white skyscraper rising ever higher before them. Danny blinked. *Oh God, Halvern must be loaded.*

They pulled to a stop below the tower and glanced at each other before entering.

"We're here to see Halvern Black," Roble said, at the front desk.

A receptionist with intricately braided hair and an understated black outfit studied the pair. "Who may I ask is calling?"

Danny looked at Roble's t-shirt and dust-covered suit pants and cringed.

"His ranch hands," Roble said.

She waited for more information. Receiving none, she typed a message on a keyboard. "Please take a seat while I await a response from Mr. Black."

Roble walked over to the massive statue of the woman and gazed at her proud pose.

Danny stood, watching the well-dressed hotel patrons and residents coming and going. *No way he lets us come up.* Whipping out his phone, he typed his weekly e-mail to his father stating that his new cohort of Marine recruits at Futenma progressed well and that he remained high in the drill instructor rankings. He ended the message with: *Tell Mother I love her. Duty and honor, Danny.*

Slipping the phone in his pocket, he rubbed the back of his neck. *I have to find a way to redeem myself before Father finds out.* He glanced at the two statues. *No matter what it takes, I have to become the hero he wants me to be.*

"Please follow me."

Danny jumped. Roble turned toward the receptionist.

She led them to an elevator and swiped a card over a panel.

The doors opened and she motioned for them to enter. Reaching in, she typed a code and pressed the second to last button—*221*.

Here goes nothing. Danny shook his head.

They shot upward, grasping the side rail for balance. "Whoa," Danny moaned, wobbling on his feet.

They reached the two hundred and twenty-first floor within seconds. "Must be maglev powered or something," Roble said.

The doors zipped open, revealing a curly-haired teenage girl and a slightly older boy with a sunburnt face. "They're here!" the girl yelled over her shoulder.

The boy clasped his forehead. "Excuse Samantha, she's kind of a spaz."

"Takes one to know one, Jack Attack."

Danny glanced at Roble. "Is this the right floor?"

Samantha laughed.

"Come in," Jack said, stepping aside.

The teens led them through the quartz and platinum accented entryway to an open dining area with floor-to-ceiling windows facing south over the Mojave Desert. A frosted glass table ran along the window with a jumble of children sitting around it, talking and eating. A mature, attractive Chinese woman sat at the far end.

Halvern walked in holding a tray of broiled fish. "Sit if you want dinner, gentlemen."

The pair stared at the chaotic gathering.

"At the end there," Halvern said, his voice booming.

Danny and Roble shuffled up to the table and sat down.

"This is the jet pilot-slash-mechanic, Roble Santos," Halvern gestured at him, "and his companion, Danny Sands."

A few impressed "ooohs" and "ahhhs" came from the younger boys at the table.

Halvern introduced each child, announcing their favorite interest with a single curt sentence, and then indicated the woman. "This is Mae Black, the sculptor."

"Do you have any sculptures here?" Roble asked, glancing around.

"No," Mae smiled, "they're too large to display in the penthouse."

Roble rubbed his chin.

"Nice to meet you Mrs. Black," Danny said.

"Oh, we're divorced," she said. "And Mae is fine."

Danny's face melted with embarrassment. "I'm sorry. I'm very sorry."

"Don't be," Mae said.

Danny's eyes shot to Halvern's at the realization they'd brought up their divorce in front of the children. "I'm—"

Halvern scowled yet somehow looked untroubled.

Danny slumped back in his chair, recalling his mother's muffled cries beyond the bedroom door threatening to divorce his father. He knew Donald was a tough man, so anything that scared him into obedience must certainly have been a disaster to avoid at all costs. He glanced across the children's faces, feeling pity because of how their lives would now turn out. He furrowed his brows seeing no uncertainty on their faces and wondered why only he understood their fate.

Halvern shuffled trays along the table, then walked over and kissed Mae on the lips. "You deserve the best this world has to offer. Maybe someday you'll find him." He caressed her shoulders. "But I sure as hell hope not."

Mae beamed. Samantha and another girl giggled. Two of the younger boys rolled their eyes.

Danny frowned and turned to a Persian-looking teen seated next to him. "So you're all adopted?"

He shook his head. "None of us are. We live here by invitation."

Danny shot a surprised glance at Halvern, then asked the teen, "What grade are you in?"

"I don't go to school. I learn what I want. I've written a novel but I think it sucks. The deeper I dig into my antagonist's characterization, the more he feels like a Pandora's Box. You know what I mean?"

"How old are you?"

"Fifteen," he said. "What do you do?"

Several children looked at Danny with interest. He straightened his posture. "I…uhmm…draw. I am…was a sergeant in the Marines." He saw approval sprouting from a Hispanic teen's face.

"Ever kill any bad guys?" the Hispanic teen asked.

"Well…" Danny said, as his young audience leaned in. He glanced at Mae Black and saw her brows rise. "No, of course not. I've just had to discipline some…" He paused, seeing Halvern out of the corner of his eye, "...guys way over in Japan, but I wouldn't recommend it."

The teen pouted, grabbed a water glass, and downed it as if sitting in a western saloon. "Do you at least draw bad guys getting what's coming to them?"

"I actually don't draw much anymore," Danny said.

"Art is a very delicate thing," Mae said, her sympathetic gaze embracing Danny.

He thought of his art he destroyed in Okinawa and rubbed his eyes.

"So, nobody here goes to school?" Roble asked. "Where was this setup when I was their age?"

"They are taught every topic they're interested in," Halvern said. "And they understand that everything they are taught must be proven."

Danny studied the children's faces and stabbed an asparagus with a fork. "Don't they need to go to school to learn social skills?"

"And what skills are those?" Halvern frowned.

"You know, how to share and be nice and stuff." The asparagus wobbled uncertainly over his plate, Danny having heard no one question the need for social skills before.

"Share what and with whom?" Halvern sliced a filet. "Be nice to whom and for what reason?"

All the children turned to Danny.

He wiped the sweat off his brow and glanced at Roble for help, but Roble kept eating. "Well you know, share and be nice to everyone to fit in and be a good person. Right?"

The children looked confused.

"What's the goddamn purpose—the goal—of politeness and sharing?" Halvern asked, taking a bite.

"Goal?" Danny bit off the end of the asparagus. "It's just the right thing to do. Isn't it?"

Halvern set down his knife, eyes narrowing. "Politeness is the attempt to influence another person's feelings. Sharing is the voluntary transfer of material from one person to another. Now," he exhaled, shaking his head, "what in the name of the Almighty makes those actions the *right* thing to do?"

"I mean..." Danny winced. "Do you actually believe you

shouldn't be nice to others if you don't want to?" He poked his steak with a fork.

"Perhaps when there is no value to be exchanged," Halvern picked up his knife, "no interaction is necessary."

All the children nodded and continued eating.

What's wrong with this guy? Danny folded his arms. *He's not going to give Roble a dime.*

The conversation at the dining table continued with no topic off limits. Mae held a book in one hand while nodding to a talkative young boy seated next to her.

Danny watched, feeling uncomfortable that these children hadn't learned proper manners and that Halvern hadn't legally adopted them, things his father would never approve of. His eyes moved back and forth between Halvern and Mae. *I wonder if they would have accepted my art if I'd grown up here?* Shaking his head, he stared out the window. *Would they have approved of Jenny?*

As the walls melted from light blue to a golden red from the setting sun, the children left the table one by one. Danny watched as nobody excused themselves.

Halvern stood, motioning for Roble and Danny to follow. They entered a different elevator and ascended one floor. Halvern walked toward a platinum-plated door, but stopped. To his right, thirty feet away near a window, stood two thin men, one with grey hair and one with black, leaning over a table under brilliant white lights.

"Excuse the interruption," Halvern said.

The men lifted their heads in acknowledgement and returned to their work. Roble and Danny stared, squinting to get a better look.

Halvern opened the door and motioned for the pair to proceed. They entered and climbed the steep stairwell.

"Who were those guys?" Danny asked.

"I've seen one before. Mr. Hollings is the manager of *The Sin*," Roble said, walking up the steps.

"Why is he here?" Danny looked back at Halvern.

"Mr. Hollings is a neighbor, and perhaps I'm just being social." Halvern chuckled. "The other was my substitute math teacher about forty years ago in Atlanta."

"Substitute teacher?" Danny asked.

"He's my guest here. We've stayed in touch through the years, probably because he taught me the only lesson worth a damn in high school."

"What lesson was that?" Roble asked, continuing the climb.

"After Dr. Thatcher left NASA, he took over my math class for a month. He taught us that mathematical formulas, like all abstractions, can be used to understand and organize concrete reality. Once you understand that, he told us, everything can be determined, and therefore acted upon for a desired outcome."

"What does he do now?" Danny asked.

"Like a typical substitute math teacher—he's a coach."

Roble snorted and stopped before the door at the top of the stairs.

"Just push," Halvern said.

Roble opened it, sending air rushing down the stairwell. Stepping outside, he inhaled the pinnacle of the world.

The deck encompassed half the skyscraper's roof, bracketed with a single thin rail along the edge. Nobody spoke as they walked to the brink. The evening sky seemed as far below as above. Lake Mead flashed like a distant glass sheet in the dying sun.

"Oh…" Roble said, losing his breath.

Halvern placed a hand on Roble's back. "What brings you to my home?"

"I've designed an aircraft…" He watched the contrails of a jet streaking like flame, ignited by the last rays of the sun. "Now I need to fund it."

"When it comes to investing, I only understand land and buildings, and I don't like partial ownerships. But since you made the effort to come here, you can pitch me your idea, if you don't mind getting rejected."

Roble swallowed, glanced at Danny and licked his lips. "Okay, well…it will be able to fly from here to Asia in just over two hours, revolutionizing travel almost as much as did the airplane itself. And that's just its commercial passenger use. It can do more," he said, waiting for Halvern to stop him.

Halvern stared, revealing nothing.

"Ms. Dodge estimates we'll need at least a hundred million dollars to develop it," he continued. "In exchange for the money, you would get a forty-nine percent financial interest in the prototype, its technology, and any future profits."

"I own a *Wyvern*. I love it." Halvern watched the last of Lake Mead's glassy sheen drain into night. "So why should I pay four times its cost just to own a piece of an experimental jet and its unproven technology when no market for it currently exist?"

"I'll admit that the market size for it is unknown, just like it was for the first airplane. Libby thinks we would break even after selling just four aircraft, and would achieve a thirty percent gross margin after producing ten. So you can imagine the profit potential if we sold more."

Halvern caressed his chin. Shaking his head, he said, "I'm not the right investor for you. But I wish you success."

Danny scrunched his forehead. "But you have the money."

"And?" Halvern scowled.

"Sometimes the little guys just need a chance," Danny said under his breath.

"I only bet on my judgment, regardless of the size of the guy," Halvern said.

Roble bowed. "Thank you for at least considering my proposal."

"If you can make it work someday," Halvern said, "fly it over here. Maybe I'll trade in my *Wyvern* for one."

"It must be nice just sitting up here above everyone else, with all that money," Danny said.

"Don't." Roble touched his arm. "It's okay."

"Perhaps," Halvern said to Danny, "you were too busy learning social skills in school to understand the law of cause and effect."

Danny's face flushed. "Well at least my parents never got divorced and failed at love."

Halvern stared at him for a moment. "Are marriage and love the same thing?"

Love…and marriage. Danny turned away and peered over the edge, wondering if Jenny walked down there somewhere, breathing this same air. His knees weakened, and he gripped the railing. *Why did I leave her?*

"Mr. Black," Roble said, "may I ask you something else, since you know Libby?"

Halvern waited.

"That red-haired woman, Sitra, who I met at Libby's house," he cleared his throat, "who is she?"

"Hmm…" Halvern narrowed his eyes.

Danny turned, staring at Halvern, also wanting to know.

"I guess you two have been out of the country for a while. She's the star of *The Virtue*." He pointed down at *The Sin*. "You can catch the show tonight if you wish. I'll call down and have the concierge dig up tickets. Consider it a consolation gift since we didn't come to investment terms."

They gazed down at the distant casino and its marquee.

As the penthouse elevator doors closed on Roble and Danny, Halvern said, "May you discriminate well, gentlemen."

Chapter 43

"We gotta go, we'll be late," Roble said.

Danny walked to Roble's room, buttoning up his dress shirt. "Then why aren't you ready?" He pointed at Roble's t-shirt, the one he wore all day. "You can't go like that. Sitra will be there." He rummaged through the closet and found a collared shirt. "Put this on." He grabbed a brimmed hat and dropped it on Roble's head. "There, *now* let's go."

The warm night air swept across their faces as they rode along the Las Vegas Strip. *The Sin's* marquee rose into view. Roble stared at it. *It's strange to be going back after all these years.*

He slipped on his hat and sunglasses as they parked. *It's probably best to keep a low profile considering who may still be working for Stock.*

As they entered the theater, an usher guided them to their center seats. Roble glanced from under his hat brim at the elaborate hall made to look ancient like a mausoleum, hoping no one would recognize him.

The curtain rose.

Colorfully dressed performers danced in silence onto the stage, forming choreographed patterns, their costumes swirling together.

Two harmonized high notes from two electric guitars pierced the theater, and the notes held. Goose bumps shot down Roble's arms.

The performers slowed their movements, listening. The reverberation altered notes and climbed in a rebellious, soaring advance, shredding the air like twirling axes. The notes came faster, louder, moving through octaves, reaching toward something unknown, something unobtainable.

And then it became clear that the music hadn't come from two guitars, but one accompanied by a woman's voice. A note sustained, resonating with such purity it felt as if time itself had been stretched by the very force of human breath.

A woman ran on stage, flowing red hair chasing her grey metallic costume. She leapt in the air, body rolling into a quadruple somersault over the flowing progression of dancers, and landed on her feet center stage. She faced the audience and silenced her long note as did the guitar.

Roble stared at Sitra's inescapable silver eyes. She appeared so close, her costume bending light, distorting perception. The other performers surrounded her, reached out to her, and covered her in a colorful swell until she was no more.

An explosion rocked the hall. Sitra shot into the air, body twisting, rolling, and diving upward into darkness. She stopped, suspended high above the stage, a hand gripping a dark ring, body stretched taut above the united conglomeration below.

Driving drumbeats began from off stage. Sitra dove off the ring, catching a black trapeze bar crossing her path. She flew through the air, released the bar, and bounced off a hidden platform before catching another disguised swing as if gravity no longer existed. She sang again with the unseen electric guitar in powerful melodic waves—waves crashing over the rocking drums.

The performers below restarted their colorful choreographed patterns, chanting in hollow progressing chords.

The audience stared, mesmerized by the contrasting scene of unexpected dark feats above and meandering monotonous color below. Then they gasped. Sitra missed a swing and spun into a falling somersault. Extending her arms at her sides to stop her rotations, she bounced feet first down a series of hidden platforms before tumbling to the stage, rolling, and lying flat.

The group picked her up and carried her until she jumped down and moved on her own. They reached out their hands and Sitra latched on, joining them. The audience cheered.

Sitra led them. They shifted together in peaceful, repetitive patterns. Sitra broke away, but returned to the group, and broke away again. The crowd's applause waxed and waned with the conflict inside her. The breakaways and the reunions continued, becoming more violent, the disparity between her grey costume and their colors becoming more obvious. Roble sat riveted.

Sitra shot into the air again. The pattern of performers

stopped and looked up. A woman in the audience behind Roble muttered, "Shouldn't somebody stop her? What if she gets hurt again?"

A few performers broke away from the pattern, trying to follow Sitra up the hidden platforms into darkness, but most were pulled back. Sitra reached down and lifted two above the reaches of the others.

The three flew above the stage, crossing paths on trapeze swings, tossing each other to ever higher swings and hidden platforms, each singing in alternating turns with the guitar and the beat of the drums. The group below moved again, together, chanting somberly, caringly, as if commanding those above to return.

Sitra's companions stopped and looked down. They descended, rejoining the pattern. The reunited group flowed in unison, eyes glancing upward.

The audience murmured as the same two acrobats climbed back to Sitra, encouraged by the group's chanting. She welcomed them with open arms. They gripped and held her wrists, then cast her to the stage.

The united conglomeration shouted in triumph, linked into a circular assembly and progressed in slow lazy steps around her. A smattering of *boos* and applause escaped from the audience.

A man sitting a few rows in front of Roble clapped above his head, saying, "Well it serves her right for going off on her own like that."

The pattern continued as the stage lights dimmed. Some in the audience strained to see Sitra lying somewhere under the moving feet, while others looked away, shifting in their seats. Roble's eyes remained open and forward.

A light beamed down on Sitra's body, creating a blinding vision of spilled red over metallic grey, surrounded by blackness. The theater hushed.

As the progression circled in the surrounding darkness, Sitra rose, head bowed, body wobbling on one leg, holding one arm under the other. When she reached full height, her chin lifted, pitching back her hair, eyes sparkling in the light. Roble felt a shockwave of courage pass through him.

The circular pattern broke into a line and spiraled inward toward Sitra. She stood, unflinching, aflame in light.

The performer at the tip of the spiral latched on to her arm. Sitra pushed him back. He fell into the woman behind him; that woman knocked down the performer behind her, and the impacts continued in synchronized succession. After the first few, the falling performers gripped and brought down the next in line not wanting anyone to be left out. The performer at the end of the spiral stepped away and remained standing. She looked at the others and dove to the ground, uniting herself with them.

Sitra stood alone.

She jumped in the air and soared above the stage. The audience held their breath as she increased the intensity of her acrobatics, attempting feats beyond what she'd done before, as if she wished this to be her life's final performance. But her movements were not rushed or desperate. They were joyous, like those of a young girl.

The spectators shrieked as her body arced down like a whirling blade from the highest point above the stage, her chainmail-clad hand gliding along a black rope to the floor. She landed, rolled, and came to a stop on bent knees at the tip of the stage.

The other performers scrambled to their feet and formed lines at her sides, grabbed hands, bowed, and remained lowered. The crowd roared; some even cried.

Sitra rose from her knees and stood in the manner of *The Sin's* marquee, scanning across the audience. Her gaze stopped on Roble.

He gasped.

The curtain dropped. "*The Virtue*" glistened in silver across the red fabric.

Danny mumbled something, but Roble heard nothing around him.

When they exited the theater, an usher pressed a note into Roble's hand. He slipped it into his pocket, lowering his hat brim. Danny continued gabbing about the impossible feats and about how he might start drawing again.

Riding home through the canyon of casino lights, Roble thought only of Sitra's gaze, his hand covering the pocket containing the mysterious note.

At their apartment, Roble shut himself in his bedroom and pulled out the note. *Meet in the Arizona hot springs below the Hoover Dam at 2 AM tonight. Don't park near the trailhead. Tell no one. K.L.*

He glanced at the clock: 11:35 PM, and changed into hiking shorts and boots.

"I have to go," he said to Danny on the way through the living room, and ran out to his motorcycle.

The freeway heading east from the city opened wide, nearly empty of traffic, allowing Roble to rip around rocky curves at high speed. He released the handlebars, motorbike arching into the air over the convex center of the Colorado River Bridge. The tires landed, his hands gripped the bars revving the engine, and he flew on.

A few miles later, he parked off the side of the road behind a cluster of large sage bushes and hiked south along a desolate canyon riverbed. He scrambled down rock formations and climbed through jagged gullies under the dull moonlight.

At the base of a tight crevasse, his boots sunk into wet gravel. Steaming water trickled from mineral-caked rocks along the walls. Water channeled from the gravel into a slick rock chute, pouring into a pool between sheer canyon walls.

Stripping to his underwear, he placed his clothes on a rock ledge. He slid down the chute into the uncomfortably hot water and waded to the far end dammed with sandbags. A missing bag along the top row allowed water to funnel into a lower pool.

Peering over the sandbags, he saw the shadowy face and thin bare shoulders of a woman sitting against the far side of the lower pool. Her chin lifted, revealing the bored, but confident face of Kat Lister—the only runaway Roble ever recruited for Stock. He met her on the streets just weeks before he left Stock to be on his own, and he hadn't seen her since leaving.

He climbed down and waded over. His arrowhead pierced the water as he sat, feet burrowing into smooth pebbles. "Kat…" Staring at her, he felt amazed at both the familiarity and the changes. "It's been a while."

"Only a decade."

"I didn't see you in the theater. How did you know I was there?"

"Someone I trust spotted you," Kat said. "Roble," she shook her head, "before tonight I honestly thought you were dead. The fact you aren't tells me you wised up to the ways of the world, or you're the luckiest bastard on earth."

"It's good to see you again too."

Taking a breath, Kat asked, "Why are you back?"

"Why did you ask to meet me here?"

Kat narrowed her eyes, frowning. "Before I tell you anything, I need to know where your loyalties lie."

"I'm back in Vegas to build a jet. But what's that to you?" Roble's head dipped under the water and he smoothed back his hair.

"I assume Stock doesn't know you're around?"

He shook his head.

"And Jessy?" she asked, lowering her voice.

"Of course not."

"Good." Kat looked behind her, over the ledge at the waterfall and canyon stream far below. "I used to hate you for leaving. But I don't blame you anymore. You couldn't have stopped it if you'd stayed."

"What do you mean?"

"Why were you at *The Virtue*?"

Roble wondered what *The Virtue* had to do with this. Then he remembered their conversation in this very hot spring. She'd invited him here right after she joined Stock. They discussed Alexandria Patra, both having met her before running away from foster care. They talked of their contempt for her authority over their lives, but admitted there had been something inexplicable about her, something inescapably powerful...and possibly, an understanding carefully hidden. The susurration of the water relaxed him and for a second he thought it sounded like a woman humming.

"Where is Alexa Patra?" Roble asked, startled by his own question.

Kat faced him, eyes widening. "Why did you ask that?"

"I...I've been out of the country."

Kat furrowed her brows. "If you know to ask that..."

"I've met that performer...Sitra. And as strange as it sounds, she reminds me of Alexa Patra."

Kat stood up, scanning the dark pools. "Ms. Patra disappeared after her inauguration as lieutenant governor three years ago." Sitting back down, she added, "Now, I'll tell you what I think you already suspect."

Roble's heart fluttered.

"Even though Mr. Hollings gave me a ticket to *The Virtue*, I avoided going, figuring it was a stupid tourist trap. But last week, after a terrible day in the lab I decided, what the hell, I need a distraction. I sat there, center stage, feeling helpless and furious at Stock, or maybe the entire world." She paused, hands rippling across the water's surface. "That's when I saw her. She peered into my eyes." Kat gasped as if she experienced it again. "And I *knew* she recognized me."

Roble swallowed.

"It might sound silly," she said, "but her show reminded me of what I'd wanted from life, as I had envisioned it when I was young. I'd once sought that inspiration from Stock, and it came close, but something was always wrong. Her show gave me courage."

Only the water flowing through the narrow canyon sounded for a long while.

"Did you talk to her," Roble asked, "after the show?"

"No, there is much to the story you don't know. And I'm sorry, Roble, just inviting you here has put your life at risk. I'll understand if you don't want to get involved. If you don't, for the sake of Ms. Patra's life, don't contact her or let anyone else know who she is now."

"Kat, tell me everything."

"I'm leaving Stock. Blood is being spilled and he can't understand what went wrong. It is not going to end well for him."

Roble inhaled as though punched in the gut.

"I know you didn't want to hear that."

He rubbed his nose. "And Alexa, what does she have to do with it?"

"After she disappeared, Governor Moore put her on permanent medical leave so he wouldn't have to deal with a lieutenant governor at all. But neither Moore nor anybody else had any idea where she was…or who she is now." Kat picked up a rock and tossed it across the steaming pond.

"I guess Moore's plan would've worked for him," she continued, "except a few weeks ago Jessy demanded, in private, to be named lieutenant governor in her stead—which Moore has the right to do if she is incapable of fulfilling her duties. But

Moore was scared Ms. Patra might reappear and reveal something damaging to his career if he attempted to replace her."

Kat picked up another stone, gripping it. "Unfortunately, his balls were so tightly in Jessy's fist he couldn't refuse outright. So he made a deal with Jessy that if Ms. Patra were to permanently and verifiably disappear, he would give Jessy what he wanted."

"Jessy wants to kill her?"

"This isn't just a hunch." She threw the stone into the water. "I still know an ex-foster kid on Jessy's side. And Jessy won't stop with Ms. Patra. If Jessy becomes lieutenant governor, Stock will be next and one of Jessy's thugs will be installed to run the underground."

"Why haven't you warned them?"

"I don't dare approach Sitra or leave her a note because Jessy is monitoring me too closely, which is why we're meeting in the middle of nowhere and at this time of night. And you must go soon."

Roble opened his mouth to speak.

Kat waved a hand over the water, interrupting him. "Since Jessy doesn't know you're back in Vegas, you have an opportunity to warn Ms. Patra and convince her to take cover until the dust settles."

"Dust from what?"

Kat lifted a fist, water trickling down her arm. "After I leave, I'm going to bring it all down, to save both Stock's and Ms. Patra's lives." Her fist smacked the water. "In a matter of days, I'll have the evidence ready to expose Stock and Jessy's illegal acts to the feds; they're the only ones not being bribed well enough. You won't be able to find me after tonight."

"Kat, I won't see Stock go to jail."

"If you warn him, he'll be dead. You know how he would react if you told him about Jessy or the feds' plans. At least in jail he'll have a chance for a trial and to get out some day."

Roble shook his head.

"I know this is a lot to dump on you. Please don't hate me. When I heard you were at *The Virtue* tonight, it gave me hope everything might work out." Kat wiped a wet hand across her face.

He closed his eyes.

"Roble?"

He remained silent for a long time, the cool air caressing his shoulders. The trickle of steaming water echoed effervescent up the canyon walls. "You were right to invite me here, Kat."

Her lower lip quivered. "Can I hug you?"

He leaned in and she gripped him tight.

"I know I'm supposed to be tough," she said against his shoulder, "but I'm so scared."

His arrowhead pressed against his heart.

She pulled away, hands lingering on his shoulders for a moment. "If you're making an aircraft in Vegas someday, talk to Libby Dodge and Sigmund Evert, if you can find them. I know what I'm talking about."

Roble raised an eyebrow.

"What?" Kat asked.

"I know her."

"Oh." The corners of her mouth tugged into a smile. "Figures, I guess."

He sighed. "It's just I'm short on capital to make it."

Kat ran a hand along the water, sending out a wake. "There is something else. Another reason I wanted to talk to you."

His eyes narrowed.

"When it all goes down, if the feds don't loot Stock's vaults fast enough during their raid, Jessy's thugs will. The thought of either group getting Stock's money kills me," she said. "However, there is a window of opportunity to rescue it before the raid. It's incredibly risky because there are many layers of security. And if Stock's vaults are cracked too early, it will alert both Jessy and Stock to the pending raid and that would be Stock's death sentence. I won't be sticking around to risk my life for money; I have a research job on the East Coast I can do. But if you're interested, the diamonds and gold are there. I'm not asking you to do it. I'm just letting you know."

Roble gazed up the cliff walls and focused on a blinking pinprick passing between two bright stars. He thought of his aircraft design sitting unfunded on Libby's coffee table.

"You know the layout of the underground; it hasn't changed. I have all the security and access codes, combinations, and keys necessary to get you into the vaults. Plus, there's somebody who might be able to help you bypass some of Jessy's men."

"I…I don't know, Kat."

"I'm glad you're hesitant." She touched his forearm. "You probably don't know this, but Stock never got over losing you. I think he flew jets just because they reminded him of you. I watched him almost achieve his dreams, and they were big as you know, but he threw them to swine." She squeezed his arm. "If you decide to take the money, use it to build your aircraft. Stock's money was always meant to fund a dream, and I kind of like the thought it still might."

Roble breathed deep.

She reached up to a ledge, lifted two keys, and held them before Roble.

He submerged his head in the hot water for over a minute. Coming up for breath, he said, "Give me everything."

"Don't write anything down in case you're caught." She dropped the keys in his hand. If you think you're being tracked, don't contact Ms. Patra, or she's dead."

She explained all the technical details. He memorized everything the same way he memorized parts on his aircraft.

"If you decide to do this and you run into Stock," she said, "don't reveal what's about to happen. And also, if you can…let him know I'm grateful for everything."

"Come here," Roble hugged her again. "I'm proud of you, Kat."

Hiking back, Roble thought of the underground and Jessy, flinching at every unexpected noise.

When he spotted his motorcycle and another car along the road, chirping birds signaled the approach of morning's first light.

As he passed the two young men in the car, they appeared more like the nightclub types than the hiking variety, and made too great an effort to avoid eye contact.

Roble quickened his pace, jumped on his motorcycle, and opened the throttle. He flew at speeds that pushed away the fear of being followed and replaced it with the fear of barreling off a cliff.

Entering Las Vegas, he rode through random neighborhoods, just in case. As the sun broke over the eastern ridges, he parked behind their apartment, hiding his motorbike under a canvas cover.

Chapter 44

Waking early, Danny leapt from his bed, got dressed, and smoothed back his hair. *The show last night was incredible.* Whistling from the bedroom, he stopped and scratched his head.

Roble sat on the couch staring at the wall.

"Where did you go last night?" Danny asked.

He didn't respond.

"At least tell me you're working today." Danny squinted at Roble's dust-caked boots and messy hair. "The rent is due and I don't have enough to pay your share."

Roble turned his head. "What was that?"

"You remember—work, pay bills, responsibility."

"I have something I need to do." Roble ripped off his shirt, walked to the bathroom, and turned on the shower.

Two minutes later, he exited in a wet towel.

Danny stood in his path. "You're going to see Sitra again, aren't you?"

Roble flanked him, entered his bedroom, and shut the door.

"I thought about her show all night," Danny said through the door.

Leaving his bedroom dressed, Roble headed for the apartment exit.

Danny followed along.

Roble whirled around. "Where I'm going doesn't concern you."

"Are you going to see Sitra or not?"

"You're not coming."

"Try to stop me." Danny slipped around him, opened the front door, and waited.

"Sit down." Roble pointed at the couch.

Danny shuffled to the couch.

"Look," Roble exhaled, "I'm involved in something I didn't

expect. I'm actually putting you in danger just by being here, so I'm moving out this afternoon."

"Moving out?"

"I'll send you your money as soon as I can." He turned to leave. "Please don't follow me."

"Roble..." The name poured to the ground like molten lead. Roble froze.

Danny rocked back and forth on the sofa, rubbing his arms. "I lied."

Roble turned around. "What do you mean?"

"I didn't quit the Marines." Danny groaned. "They kicked me out." He lowered his head. "My father doesn't know." He gripped his arms until they turned red. "I can't draw anymore and I don't know why." He glanced up, his eyes red. "And I ruined everything with Jenny. I miss her so much."

Roble rubbed the back of his neck, blinking his eyes.

"Don't move out," Danny said. "I just don't..."

Roble glanced at the door, then back at Danny.

"I don't have anyone else to turn to."

"Danny, I—"

"I'm sorry." He shook his head. "Don't listen to me. I'm just being stupid."

Roble sat down on the edge of the coffee table. "I want to talk to you about this, but I honestly don't have time right now." He rubbed along his pant legs. "I wish I could explain, but I can't."

"Why can't I go with you?"

Roble opened his mouth, but hesitated.

"Is there money involved or something?"

Roble winced. "I won't lie; there is, but it's not ours and I doubt it's worth risking your life."

"But it's worth risking yours?"

"Danny...." Roble hit his own legs.

"Just tell me what's going on. I won't tell anyone. I don't even have anyone I *could* tell." He leaned forward, eyes pleading.

Taking a breath, Roble said, "I'm going to rob Stock's vaults."

Danny threw his hands in the air. "That was *my* idea."

"It's not what you think," Roble sighed. "I'm going to do it, but I can't share it with you."

"You want it all for yourself. That's why you wouldn't tell me. That's why you're leaving."

"I can't explain it all right now."

"Oh, I see. You're stealing Stock's money, but you're doing it for some higher purpose? Like you're Robin Hood or something? Is that it? You told me you don't believe in higher purposes."

Roble flipped up his palms.

"Let me help you get that money," Danny said. "It could benefit so many people. We could be heroes. Real heroes, Roble."

Roble let his hands fall to his sides. "I knew I shouldn't have told you."

"Wait a minute." Danny's forehead scrunched. "You didn't deny you were going to see Sitra. Is she involved?"

Roble pressed a fist against his own nose.

"I *knew* you were going to see her this morning," Danny said. "I just knew it."

"If I tell you something will you swear not to tell *anyone*, or do *anything* about it unless I say so?"

"Of course." Danny stood up, looking around for his jacket.

Roble motioned for him to sit.

Danny dropped back on the couch, twitching. "I swear to God. I won't tell anyone and I'll do exactly as you say."

Roble rubbed his temples. "Sitra is in danger and I need to warn her."

"Danger?" He jumped to his feet. "I'll kill whoever lays a hand on her."

"Sit down."

Danny sat, face flushed. "What danger?"

"Listen, people within Stock's organization are planning to kill her. They're too powerful to stop directly, and something's already in motion to bring them down. We just need to keep Sitra hidden for a while."

"I'll kill that evil bastard. I will."

"Danny, stop it. You're wasting time." He stood up. "After I warn her, I need to detail a plan to get Stock's money. I only have a day to prepare."

"Tell me again where the money is going?"

Roble pointed at his own chest. "I have the information to pull this off. So *I* will decide what happens to the money." He picked up his motorcycle keys. "I'm not asking you to come. In fact, I wish you wouldn't."

"But…all right, fine. I'm coming."

Roble studied him, releasing a breath.

"I'm serious, Roble. I'm going to help you."

"I'll explain the details later." Roble walked to the door. "Whatever you do, don't talk about Stock's money to anyone. If *anyone* gets word of the heist, it's off. The element of surprise is our best advantage. Understand?"

Danny nodded.

A gust of sand whipped across Roble and Danny as they approached Libby's compound gate. Atop the fence, a camera panned the length of the street, stopping on their faces. The gate unlatched and rolled open.

Danny stepped in, but stopped, blocked by a chainmail-clad figure with platinum hair blowing like a candle's flame. His indigo eyes seemed to pierce the flying sand like laser beams.

"Please state your business, *Messieurs*," he said in a French accent.

"Where's Sitra?" Danny asked.

The man touched an oddly round pistol holstered on his hip. "State, your business."

"I'm Roble Santos." He stepped forward. "I know Ms. Dodge."

"Ah, *Monsieur* Santos." The man nodded. "And who might you be?" he asked Danny.

"This is my friend, Danny Sands," Roble said. "We need to speak with Sitra. It's important."

"And what makes you assume someone by that name is here?"

"You can ask Ms. Dodge. We've met Sitra here before," Roble said.

"Are you certain you weren't followed?" He waved the pair aside. Stepping out of the gate, the man scanned in both directions before reentering and slamming it shut.

"Followed by whom?" Danny asked.

The man lifted a gauntleted finger. "By anyone, *Monsieur* Danny. Are either of you armed?"

"No, we—"

The Frenchman whipped out a metallic object and waved it in front of them. When it passed their midsections, it beeped. He held out his armored hand. They emptied their pockets into his palm. Glancing at the keys, he tossed them back. "Follow me, if you will." He turned and walked to the house.

They scurried after him. Reaching the front door, Roble asked, "Who are you?"

He opened the door, bowed, and pointed inside. "Victor Lafayette. Welcome to my family's house."

Roble tilted his head sideways.

Sitra's humming flowed out from the doorway, followed by the waft of breakfast griddle aroma. Danny smiled at Roble.

As they entered, Sitra emerged from the kitchen wearing skintight grey chainmail with the same hexagonal pattern under its surface as Victor's. It covered her from collared neck to ankles. She carried a tray with steaming mugs to the dining table, red hair cascading in her wake. Returning to the kitchen, she asked, "Joining us for breakfast?"

"Mhmm," Danny mumbled.

Victor sat at the table, his posture as formal as an aristocrat's. Roble and Danny took seats on the other side. The humming resumed from the kitchen.

Roble scratched his forehead. "I thought this was Ms. Dodge's house?"

"Indeed." Victor leaned down, allowing coffee vapor to caress his thin nose.

Danny furrowed his brows.

"Is she here?" Roble asked.

"Why, yes." Victor lifted the mug with the tips of two fingers.

Roble glanced around but didn't see Libby.

"What's with the armor...and stuff?" Danny asked.

"Protection."

Danny lifted his hands. "From what?"

"Harm." Victor took a delicate sip. "Naturally."

"Oh, great. Thanks for clearing that up."

Roble studied the framed drawings on the wall. Some displayed his artistic jet renderings from Japan.

Sitra brought in a large tray covered with bowls of oatmeal, cups of blueberries, and sandwiches filled with eggs, bacon, and diced mushrooms, and placed it on the table. She sat across from Roble.

He stared at her silver eyes, recalling when those same eyes, only black, had looked at him from behind a soft veneer, demanding his obedience. Now, she appeared implacable, almost merciless, yet supremely respectful. He wanted to ask "how," but couldn't form a single word.

Danny angled his shoulder toward Sitra, highlighting his Isshin-Ryu decal. He opened his mouth to speak, but her eyes shot to his and he froze.

"Please, allow me the honor." Victor closed his eyes and placed his hands together like a praying Charlemagne Paladin.

Danny looked at everyone before folding his arms. Sitra bowed her head. Roble watched with interest.

"I offer my gratitude to *Madame* Sitra for preparing this food. And to *Madame* Dodge for acquiring it. May we each obtain exactly what we deserve in *this* life. I do solemnly pray."

Roble said "Amen" to a prayer for the first time in his life, and Danny skipped it for the first time in his.

Staring at Sitra, Roble raised a knowing brow.

"Yes," she whispered, her lips smiling.

"What was that?" Danny glanced between them.

"Can I trust everyone here?" she asked, holding Roble's gaze.

"What do you mean?" Danny asked.

Roble rubbed his nose and turned to Danny. "Can you keep another secret?"

Danny jabbed his oatmeal with a spoon. "Of course."

Sitra waited, her face somber, watching Roble.

Roble nodded at her.

Sitra touched her eyes, removing the contact lenses. "I am Alexa Patra." Her irises glinted obsidian.

"What?" Danny choked on oatmeal, wiping his mouth with a napkin. "What do you mean? You don't look like her. *You're* the missing lieutenant governor?"

"Yes."

"Well, what the…?" Danny looked around at everyone. "How is that even possible? You just magically turned into Sitra?"

Alexandria didn't answer.

"And if you're really the missing lieutenant governor," Danny continued, "why haven't you been doing something in office all this time?"

"Doing what, and to whom?" she asked.

"I don't know…something. What will people think once they find out? Shouldn't you at least appear like you're doing something in office?"

Alexandria smiled. "Would that make you feel better?"

"Well, yes…I think so."

"The day may come when I act in my office, but it won't be for appearances."

"Ms. Patra," Roble said, "we came to warn you."

Victor's face snapped toward Roble, then made its way to Alexandria.

"What is it?" she asked.

"Elements in Stock's underground are trying to find Alexa Patra and assassinate her—you."

She bit her lip. "Stock would *never* allow that."

"It's not Stock who ordered it."

She exhaled, touching her neck, as if remembering something.

"Stock is no longer in charge. Don't ask me how I know," Roble said.

"Tell me," Victor demanded, "have they discovered Sitra's true identity?"

"I don't think so, but you should act as if they have."

Victor pulled out a gleaming pistol and placed it on the table. He raised an eyebrow at Alexandria.

"I know," she said, "I haven't ignored you. I'm wearing your armor."

"Your heavy armor will be finished today. I'm dropping everything until it becomes so."

"Did you know about this, Victor?" she asked.

"I needed no one to tell me you were in danger. I have eyes, *Madame*. The gang wars in this district are spiraling out of control. And secret identities are risky by nature." He twirled the strange pistol on a finger. "If it would have been up to me, I would not have moved you and *Madame* Dodge back here after the government raids."

"I know. Thank you, Victor."

He nodded and set down the weapon.

After a sip of coffee, Alexandria rose. "Roble," she said, her tone saying, *Follow me.*

Roble stood.

She turned to Victor. "Danny is a former Marine. I'm certain he'd like to hear about your adventures in the Legion's special ops during the African wars."

Danny shot Roble and Alexandria pained looks and tossed his egg sandwich onto the plate.

Alexandria escorted Roble out the back of the house. They walked under a vine-covered archway and into a rose garden surrounded by tall lilac bushes. The latticed vegetation blocked the blowing sand creating a peaceful interior. Rock paths meandered through grass leading to benches and a koi pond at the center.

She pointed to a bench for him to sit.

He obeyed, then smiled at the memory of the last time she had asked him to sit.

She sat across from him, placing her hands in her lap and crossing her bare feet. "Roble, I've thought of you many times over the years." She paused, eyes watering. Her lashes shuttered and two crystalline tears fell, shattering on her armor. "I was wrong for demanding your submission. And I know I have no right to ask for your forgiveness. All I can say is—thank you for saying what you did to me that day in my office."

"I received your letter. I saw your show." He rubbed his scarred chin, nodding with a smile. "You've forgiven yourself, and I'm glad of it."

Alexandria bowed her head.

Roble waited.

She lifted her chin. "Now, please tell me why I'm in danger."

"In a few days the reason won't matter. You just need to stay out of sight until then. Cancel your performances. The threat is that serious."

"What about Stock?"

"How do you know him?"

"Just understand," Alexandria inhaled, "it would mean a lot to me if he were safe."

"No one is safe when the danger comes from within."

She exhaled and closed her eyes.

"But Stock still has a friend or two," he said. "If that makes you feel any better."

She touched her neck. Opening her eyes, she cleared her throat and asked, "Danny…you trust him with my secret?"

"I believe he would give his life before he betrayed your identity if he knew it could lead to your death." He swallowed. "And I'll remind him of the consequences."

She nodded. "Come," she stood up, "I'll take you to see Libby."

Sand whipped across them as she led him from the garden and across the compound.

Entering the largest outbuilding, Roble saw rows of robotic manufacturing stations surrounding a domed metallurgical forge. Suits of armor hung on machines and lay on workbenches to his left. A bank of computer servers purred and blinked against the wall to the right. The building looked newly modified, with burnished metal walls lifting the ceiling over twenty feet high. A spiral staircase stood in the center reaching up through the roof. Beyond the stairs lay an open gymnasium with mats, vaults, bars, trapeze towers, swings, and rings.

Walking past the forge, he found Libby hunched over, hair fallen over her face, studying an alloy shard with an eyepiece. Sketches, digital devices, strange parts, and raw materials lay scattered around her.

Scanning across her workbench, he saw the side profile drawing of his new aircraft taped to the surface with *ROBLE ARROW* scrawled across the top. "You named it."

Libby spun around, smiling. Alexandria touched her shoulder.

"I love your black eyes," Libby squeezed Alexandria's thigh. "I take it from your lack of contact lenses that he…?"

"Yes, he knows. Go ahead and talk shop."

"What are you working on?" Roble picked up unfamiliar objects from her workbench.

"I've been experimenting on ways to construct the *Roble Arrow's* fuselage. Derived from Victor's latest light armor, I've toyed with the idea of infusing my newest vanadium/titanium/molybdenum alloy into a reinforced carbon-carbon matrix for the leading edges."

Roble shook his head in wonder and glanced at Alexandria.

Her sober stare turned his thoughts back to the mission he was about to attempt.

"But you were right the other day," Libby added. "We are going to need a ridiculously good amount of computing power to pull off the math for this aircraft."

Victor entered the building with Danny. "Ahhh, there you are, and here is *Monsieur* Danny." He flicked his gauntlet in the air and strode away to his armor-crafting station.

Danny walked over and stood between Alexandria and Roble.

After Libby finished explaining a few more ideas, Roble said, "I've only received a commitment for forty million dollars. Does your original estimate still hold?"

Libby fumbled through a stack of papers and pulled out a sheet. She turned it upside down and placed a finger at the bottom. "Good news. My latest estimate is ninety-seven million. I came up with a few cost efficiencies."

Roble winced.

"That might not be a problem, right, Roble?" Danny said.

Roble placed a fist over his own mouth to hide his disbelief. Alexandria stared at him, scrunching her brows.

"You still have some promising investor prospects?" Libby turned away to finish her analysis.

Danny stared at Roble, tilting his head.

Roble cleared his throat. "No one else has promised anything."

Danny frowned. Alexandria crossed her arms, watching the pair.

"Well, keep trying," Libby said. "I'll endeavor to have a few more kinks worked out by the time you get it."

"We must be off to work." Roble glanced at Alexandria. "I'm glad your French friend will be close by for a few days. Thanks for breakfast."

"Farewell," Alexandria locked eyes with Roble, "and *good judgment*."

Danny bowed to Alexandria. Roble gripped his arm and pulled him to the exit.

Chapter 45

Roble unlocked the side door to Stock's private hangar and entered. Danny followed, swinging a toolbox under his arm. They headed toward a large, satin-covered object.

A guard at the rear of the hangar raised a hand against the rectangular burst of sunlight. When the door closed, he gripped his holster and ran across the floor. "Stop!" He leaned into his run, unholstering his pistol. "You're not supposed to be in here."

Roble changed course, veering into the man's path.

The guard stopped, his bulging eyes staring at Roble's face. He shifted his glance, noting Roble's beige work cap and overalls, the type Stock's Asia-based jet mechanics always wore. His gun wobbled. "How'd you unlock that door?"

"Stay out of our way," Roble said with a Japanese accent. "You know why we're here."

"Ain't nobody scheduled to be here this morning," the guard said.

"Today is July third, isn't it?"

The guard squinted. "I didn't see nothing about a maintenance visit."

"How far out of the loop are you?" Roble pointed at the covered jet. "Everyone knows the FAA is making document sweeps to find this *Sovereign*. This visit is off-record because Stock doesn't want any traceable documents. And I sure as hell didn't fly all the way over here to waste his money."

"I dunno…" He scratched his arm with the gun barrel. "This has never happened before."

"Call it in and verify." Roble pointed at the man's radio.

The guard shifted on his feet.

Roble whipped out his cell phone and dialed. "That's it. I'm calling Jessy Gorronza."

"Hold on." The guard's cheeks flushed. "No need to involve *him*. I just didn't hear about this is all."

Roble scoffed, turned, and strode to the satin-covered jet. He grunted commands in Japanese at Danny, who uncovered the aircraft. Danny responded in a poor attempt at Japanese. Roble motioned for Danny to lower his voice.

The guard watched for a moment before nodding and holstering his gun. "Go ahead. I'll be over here."

Roble examined the *Sovereign's* muscular body, still amazed at its beauty. "Libby's thoughts in material form," he said in Japanese. He walked under the rear haunches, hand sliding across the smooth skin. *To make something like this is to feel respect for the possible…and for one's self.*

Tapping Danny's shoulder, he nodded at the engines. Danny detached an access panel and removed parts from inside, just as they'd discussed. After lining them up on the floor, he replaced them, creating the illusion of work but changing nothing. He repeated the process behind different panels.

Fifteen minutes into the operation, the guard approached and peered at the complicated array of internal parts, listening to the sporadic blurts of a foreign language. He bobbed his head, reassured.

Roble climbed into the cockpit and flipped on the auxiliary power.

Danny waved the guard closer. As he neared, Danny said, "We need to test the engines. It will go smoother with three people, and the last thing we need is a problem. After the test, my boss," he pointed at the cockpit, "will leave to get any needed replacement parts. So you'll just see me working alone until he gets back."

The guard frowned and opened his mouth to speak just as Roble hit the ignition, whirling the turbines to life. The low octave deafened the ears, vibrating deep inside their lungs.

Danny reached out and led the guard to an exposed engine panel. He placed the man's hand on a wrench fastened to a large bolt. After a few seconds, the guard smirked boyishly as though controlling the powerful engine. Danny pointed to his own chest, then at the other engine and walked away.

A minute later, Danny climbed into the empty cockpit as the door leading from the hangar to the underground access tunnel closed. He disengaged the turbines, kicking Roble's uniform and cap under a passenger seat.

When he returned to the rear of the jet, the guard still held the wrench, as if letting go would destroy the craft. Danny pried the handle from the man's grip, cringing at the dampness left behind. "Thanks. You should be a jet mechanic."

The guard pulled a pleased-with-himself smile and strutted back to his post.

Roble marched along the airport access tunnel and down the first flight of steps into Stock's underground, his dress shoes scuffing against concrete. His hair was gelled back and his eyes focused behind black-rimmed glasses. A red tie contrasted with his freshly dry-cleaned black suit.

From up ahead he heard someone approaching. Being too far along the corridor to retreat without being seen, he walked on. Two men in leather jackets rounded a corner and slowed, staring at him. The darker, thinner one lifted an open palm.

"Excuse you, gentlemen." Roble knocked the man's hand from his path as he continued.

"Stop, right there," the heavier, lighter-skinned man said.

Roble didn't stop.

"Wrong decision, dumbass," one said, followed by two metallic clicks.

Roble stopped and turned, looking at the pair now holding handguns. "Come on guys. What would Jesus Gorronza think about using such ugly language? Next time, perhaps try saying something nice like, 'May I help you?' See? Now you try."

"Huh?"

"Don't tell me you don't know," Roble said. "I just flew in from Carson City to advise your boss, the next lieutenant governor. And so far, I'm thinking of recommending some personnel changes around here."

"Hold on. I thought that was only a rumor," the heavier man said.

"Wait." The dark one aimed his gun between Roble's eyes. "Who let you down here?"

Roble pulled out his cell phone. "I hate to pull rank, but you asked for it."

"Calling Jessy, are you?" The dark one scoffed.

"That's right."

"Go ahead." He laughed. "There's no cell service down here, suit."

"Hmm…" Roble scratched the phone against his cheek. "Well you can't blame me for not knowing, right?" He slipped the phone back into his pocket. "I don't usually get to leave my air-conditioned office."

"Let's take him in. See what Samuel has to say about this," the heavier one said, stepping closer.

"Bad idea, guys. If I were you, I'd radio in to verify before you make the biggest mistake of your lives."

The dark one lifted his radio, turned a dial, and pressed a button. "This is Ricky D. I need to verify a visitor in the underground. Over."

Roble swallowed. *Oh man, this had better work Kat.*

"This is central. Please proceed," an elegant voice said over the speaker.

Hearing the voice, Roble opened his mouth in thought.

"Says he's from Carson City," the man said into the radio, eyeing Roble. "What's your name?"

"Rob…" he coughed, "…bger."

"Did you just say Robber?"

"No," Roble shook his head, "Roger."

"Roger who?"

Roble massaged his chin. "Moore."

The man scoffed.

"I'm related to the Governor…third cousin." He glanced at his own hands, suppressing a wince. "From a Mexican maid. They don't like to talk about it."

The man rolled his eyes and raised the radio to his lips. "Says his name is…Roger Moore."

"Does he have dark hair and a scarred chin?"

"Uh, yeah."

"Let him continue. Jessy is expecting him," Ted Hollings said from the radio.

Well done Kat. I wondered who you were going to use to help me get in.

The dark one frowned and gestured his hand. "Get out of my sight."

Roble brushed down his suit sleeves. "You'll be working for

a lieutenant governor from now on, so mind your manners. And remember, every smile—a vote." He forced a smile.

Both men smiled stupidly. Roble walked away, wiping sweat from his temple.

The final descent to the lowest level of the underground brought with it an eerie silence, the density of the walls absorbing his footsteps. As he passed the door to the subterranean green house, he wondered what new plants grew in there after all these years. When he reached the lab door, he hesitated. *These better still work, Kat.* He inserted a key and turned the handle. *Click.*

He pushed open the door. The low hum of the machines inside exuded rational computations—as if he peered into the dark recess of a man's brain. *That smell, so familiar—a mixture of organics and electricity.* Flipping on the light switch, he gazed across tables covered with beakers, tubes, DNA sequencing machines, refrigerators, and computers.

He cut through the lab to the stainless steel door in the back wall and inserted a black carbon key. The keypad beeped musically as he punched in a code. A heavy clunk sounded and he swung open the thick door.

The void beyond sucked in light as if gasping for breath. He flipped off the lab's lights, leaving only the faintest pulsing of LEDs flickering behind him.

He stepped inside the sanctuary—the only place in the underground he had never been—and pulled the door shut, sealing himself in silent darkness.

Sliding his hand along the wall, he flipped on the light switch. A rectangular chamber illuminated and stretched out in both directions. To his left, a row of four box-edged pillars cut the room in half, forming two distinct spaces.

Behind the row of pillars sat an empty, brushed-aluminum desk. Glass shelves ran along the far wall holding double helix models, bottles containing grain seeds, and other oddly shaped artifacts of the early genetic engineering era.

To the right of the entrance, two metal vaults glistened in the far wall, and near them, a floor-to-ceiling fresco covered the wall opposite the entrance.

He approached the painting, astounded at how he felt before he comprehended the visual details. It depicted a whimsical, slender jet aircraft in vertical flight, its wings stretched out like the nimble arms of an acrobat.

Stepping back, overwhelmed by its sense of joyous unconstrained energy, he thought he should almost be able to hear its engines and smell its jet fumes. He knew with certainty who designed the aircraft, yet also that he'd never before seen or heard of it.

Pulling away from the fresco, he stepped in front of the safes, knowing that behind those fortified doors lay the concentrated residual of Stock's work. The lock combinations ran through his mind like aerospace formulas.

Beep, beep, chirp, beep…sounded from the entrance behind him.

His head snapped around, his heart beating louder than the codes being punched. He sprinted to the light switch and flipped it off.

The locking mechanism inside the door clanged like a hammer hitting his clenched stomach. He jumped behind the closest pillar, just as the sanctuary door swung open.

The lights flickered back on with a low hum. He pressed against the pillar, eyes blinking, adrenaline pumping through his body.

Footsteps behind him thumped toward the safes. He edged farther around the pillar but froze when he recognized that distinctive gait and stomp. *Stock.*

After him came the soft padding of someone else. A dial spun, the combination on a keypad beeped, a low buzz sounded, and a heavy metal door clanked open.

"It's beautiful, Stock. Show me your gold in the other one," a girl with a southern drawl said. Her voice wasn't giddy or patronizing, but certain, and also sexy. Roble concentrated his willpower on not glancing around the pillar.

"Why?" Stock asked in his raspy voice.

"I want to see it. Touch it." The girl's voice echoed low and husky through the room.

Who in the world is that?

"Do you love me for my money?" Stock asked.

"Do you think I love you? And yes, that is precisely why I do."

"And you had me believing you weren't evil, Nicolette."

Roble heard another dial spinning, more beeps, and a buzz preceding the opening of the second safe.

"There lies my greed."

"Yes." Her voice held admiration.

Somehow Roble knew they kissed. He sensed it more than he could hear it.

After a moment Stock said, "Why don't you despise my filthy lucre like everyone else?"

"Why would I?"

"People say greed is evil."

She laughed helplessly as if he were joking.

"Buy your diamonds from a jeweler next time," he said, his hard voice hitting into her soft laughter.

"I like yours, Stock," she said, her tone innocent. "Plus, I enjoy it when you bring me underground; it gives me a chance to collect more plants for my backyard."

Roble couldn't stand it any longer and peeked around the corner, just enough to see their hands.

Stock removed a velvet pouch from a safe. The girl held out the back of her right hand. He shook a few colored gems onto it and then held her hand with his. "What does this tattoo mean to you?"

She took the bag with her free hand. "You mean my pretty 1877 US flag lying naked under a sheet of your sacred lucre?"

Stock waited.

"It represents a time and a place when visionaries, unbridled, changed the world in the blink of an eye. And I believe that if they would not have considered their own creation of wealth as a vice—but instead a virtue—the industrial revolution would have continued on, like the continuous compounding of a mathematical equation."

"No one thinks that amassing all that wealth by just a few people is a virtue. I don't even believe it...and I'm a ruthless bastard."

"As *you* already know with genetics, and *I* know with math, concrete results exist independently of who believes them, bastard or no."

I've never heard anyone speak like that. Roble's face flushed.

"Don't you ever want others to consider you to be good?" Stock asked. "And don't you hate everyone for being hypocrites? How do you reconcile it all?"

"I don't reconcile anything with anyone."

Stock still held her spangle-covered hand as though forbidden to let go.

"Stock, do you actually believe that producing wealth is evil? This money in your vaults was paid to you because whoever gave it thought it was worth less than what you created. You gave them life and they gave only metal and rock in return. What are you guilty of? Maybe you enjoy pretending this world is hopeless and depraved and that others mystically understand what is right and wrong, but I can't. Money is the mathematical outcome of my actions, and my aim is the pursuit of my happiness. I can't live in any world but this one, because it exists, and I want to *live*."

Releasing her hand, Stock spun around and slammed the safes shut. "Don't ever ask to open my safes again."

Looking away, Roble rubbed his palms against the pillar.

Stock walked to the sanctuary door and opened it. "Choose your gems," he said his voice cold, and closed the door behind him.

Roble blinked with anticipation. As Nicolette walked to the desk, he skirted around the pillar in the opposite direction, but couldn't stop himself from spying on her from behind the corner.

She wore a short, white sundress. Her blonde mane swayed behind a bronzed body. With her left hand holding a pouch, she pulled out the desk chair and knelt on it. Her right hand remained level, with gems still covering it.

Red, blue, and clear diamonds splashed into a glittery pile as she emptied the pouch on the desk. The stones reflected off her large eyes, making them glow purple. Her left hand spread out the stones, her gaze upon them showing deadly intent. She balanced more gems across her tattoo.

Roble swallowed.

Opening the middle desk drawer, she placed her left hand inside, leaving it there while her eyes studied the diamonds. Her hand emerged holding a long-barreled revolver. Crossing it over her right arm, she pointed it at the sliver of Roble's exposed face, her eyes still focused on the gems.

He shuddered, but it wasn't from fear.

"Who are you?" she asked, still not looking at him.

Counting his breaths, he tried to stay calm.

"You are three and a half meters away at an angle of forty-four degrees. I'll hit you if I pull the trigger, provided there are bullets inside. Want me to check, or do you want to speak?"

He stepped out, hands at his sides. "I'm Roble Santos."

She raised her eyes and searched his face. Glancing at his cheap and poorly fitted suit, she said, "Did you get lost on the way to your own funeral?"

Roble looked at his clothes.

"I've never heard of you," she said. "Why are you here?"

"I'm here to rob Stock."

She laughed. "Oh my, an honest thief?" She set the gun on the desk, smiling. "Stock would almost appreciate that, I think." Leaning back in the chair, she placed her diamond-covered hand on the armrest. "You look like a criminal. But you're not...are you."

Roble's eyes widened at her appraisal.

"Do you work here?" she asked.

"No."

"So you don't work for Stock—and I know you don't work for Jessy." She scrunched her small nose. "You don't, do you?"

He watched her, rubbing his chin.

"No, you couldn't. Not someone who looks like you."

"Like what?"

Her gaze roamed his body before stopping on his eyes. Biting her lower lip, she asked, "Do you need money very badly, Roble Santos?"

"Desperately."

"Need it for a good cause?"

"A very selfish one."

"Well then, I'm baffled. Despite your preposterous outfit, I know what type of person you are just by your face. But your words don't match. Where am I wrong? Are you really here to rob Stock? Or are you what you appear to be?"

"What type of person am I?"

"The," her eyelids drooped before opening again, "dangerous kind."

"Am I?"

"That's what I mean. I don't think you're robbing Stock but I also don't think you've lied to me. Well, mystery man, explain it to me."

"I'd rather not."

"So you want me to tell Stock you're here?"

"That's up to you."

"You speak as if you know Stock but that doesn't make any sense. He couldn't ignore someone like you." She stood up, balancing the diamonds on her hand.

Roble stepped toward her.

She remained still.

"Not afraid of me?" he asked.

"I can see you're dangerous," she said, "but not to me."

Her eyes transformed from purple to dark blue as he moved closer.

"You're Nicolette. I heard Stock say it."

She smirked. "Never heard of or seen me before?"

"No."

Laughing, she said, "Your mother must've taught you to mind your own business. You don't watch or read news?"

Stepping closer, his body almost touched hers.

Her left hand flicked off his glasses, sending them to the ground, before her forefinger pressed against the center of his tie.

He felt a current run down his body.

Raising her right hand to his breast pocket, she poured in the diamonds. "If you're a robber, start with these."

He grabbed her right hand, forcing it palm up. With his other hand he fished the gems from his pocket and pressed them into her flesh. "I didn't come here to rob you."

She frowned. "What a shame."

Gripping her other hand, he lifted it to his chin. He studied its fountain tattoo then questioned her with his eyes.

Her right hand squeezed the diamonds until her face winced with pain. She squeezed harder, quickening her breath.

He pressed the fountainhead tattoo to his lips.

She sighed. "You need something very badly, don't you?"

His legs pressed against hers. "Yes."

Her mouth moved close to his.

"I need to fund my jet."

Her eyelids winked sensuously. "More than life itself, I bet."

His mind buzzed as though drugged, as if her presence erased his reason for being here, replacing it only with the desire to not let her go.

Beep, beep, chirp, beep... The code sequence began on the other side of the sanctuary door.

"Too bad." She kissed him, biting his lip, her right hand slipping into his front pants pocket.

He gasped at the cocktail of fear and pleasure surging through his body. Swinging his head around, he scanned for a place to hide.

Leaning back, she placed a foot against his abdomen, and kicked the air from his lungs. The force of the thrust ripped his hand from hers, flinging his body back against the wall.

Stock entered the sanctuary.

Nicolette stood next to the desk, pointing the fifty-caliber revolver at a suited man slumped against the wall. "You have a visitor."

Stock glared at the intruder, taking a step closer.

Roble faced him.

My little mechanic. Stock blinked his eyes.

Roble held his breath.

"You're back..." Stock trembled. "Why?"

"To rob you."

Stock lunged forward and punched him in the face.

Nicolette lowered the gun, placing it on the desk. Stock struck him again, and this time Roble sank to the floor.

She slid the revolver across the desk toward Stock. "Do you want to shoot him? That's what I'd do if he were stealing my money."

Turning to her, Stock's face twisted with misery. Never in his life had he struck anyone without first being attacked. He examined his bloodied hand in disbelief. *What have I done? This isn't how I envisioned Roble's return...and oh, how many times I envisioned it.*

"I'm going home, Stock," Nicolette said, walking to the exit. "I took the diamonds I wanted. I'll give you the money out of my next endorsement check." She stopped. "If you're interested, I have a tennis final today at five." She glanced at Roble, whose eyes locked on hers. Rubbing her lips together, she left the room, closing the door.

"Why?" Stock whispered, still staring at his own hand. He

stammered back and sat on the edge of the desk. "Why would you rob me?"

Roble didn't answer.

Stock tried to focus his eyes, but they blurred. "You wanted revenge?"

"For what?" Roble asked, blood seeping from his forehead.

For my sin. Wiping his stinging eyes, he asked, "You need money?"

"Yes, I need money."

Stock slammed a fist on the desk; diamonds jumped in the air. "I offered you second in command. You would've been rich. You left without a word."

Roble swallowed.

"You left me!"

"Stock—"

"And now you come back for my *money*?"

With a hand on the wall for balance, Roble climbed to his feet.

"This is the respect I get for all I did for you?" Stock asked.

"Yes," Roble said, his tone calm, "this is exactly what you get."

Scooping up a handful of diamonds, Stock threw them at the shelves. A symphony of chimes ended with a bottle filled with the first genetically modified corn seeds breaking.

Watching the grains pour like time from an hourglass, Stock felt his heart sink as he pondered his life's inexplicable outcome. "Why...?" He stood frozen until the bottle emptied. "Why do you need money?"

"To create a jet."

"That's why you're stealing my money?"

Roble didn't answer.

"Is that why you left me?" Stock asked. "To build jets?"

"That's why I left."

"You've been building them all these years?" His eyes darted to the fresco.

"I haven't built one yet, but I plan to."

Stock scoffed with relief. "I overestimated you."

"I've only modified a couple of fighter jets so far."

"Modified? Where?"

"The F-22 is strewn across Mt. Fuji, but the F-15 is still flying."

Stock furrowed his brow. He'd followed the news of the F-22 crash in Japan three years ago. Something about it had always bothered him; the stories never made sense. "How did it crash?"

"The air-to-air missiles that shot up my tailpipe had something to do with it."

"You were the pilot?" He leaned against the desk for support.

Roble nodded.

"You could fly something like that? You could improve something like that? And now you're a thief?" He looked down, his face darkening into shadow.

Roble wiped away the blood seeping into his eye.

Stock picked up the revolver and aimed it at him. "Nicolette said she'd shoot you if it were her money. What do you think of that?"

"I'd rather not say."

"If you were wise enough to leave me," Stock steadied the gun, "you should've been smart enough never to come back. You want to make jets like *you* could envision? Want to make them superior to everything that exists? That's a fool's dream. No one will let you," he waved the gun, "even if you could get the money. Don't you understand? Even if, against all odds, you actually succeeded, they'd steal it and call you a criminal. And then, after you'd wasted the best years of your life, you'd realize you'd become the lowest form of creature on earth, with only thieves and murderers to call friends."

"Stock—"

"Don't try to convince me of anything! I know how the world is!"

A knock echoed from the sanctuary door. Stock stared at it, knowing no one ever knocked on that door. Another knock.

Narrowing his eyes, he walked over and opened it. "Samuel…"

A young man, almost a head taller than Stock, stood, towering at attention. "Sir, Jessy captured an intruder in your hangar. And he didn't come alone." He glanced inside the sanctuary.

Stock followed his gaze.

"Jessy wants all captives."

"This one stays here."

"I…I can't allow that, sir." Samuel lowered his eyes.

Stock couldn't believe the insubordination from a teenager he'd saved from the streets, one who possessed a promising scientific mind. Scratching his head, he wondered why he'd let Jessy train Samuel in distribution all these years. *I always meant to bring him down here, to tutor him in genetic research...*

"I'm sorry." Samuel brushed past Stock. Pulling out a plastic tie, he secured Roble's hands behind his back. He started lifting Roble to his feet, but froze at the click of a revolver cocking. He turned.

Stock aimed it at Samuel's chest. "He stays."

Samuel released him to the floor. "This is a mistake, sir." He backed away to the exit.

"More than you'll ever know," Stock said.

Shaking his head, Samuel left, pulling the door closed.

"Trade me to Jessy for his captive," Roble said, lying on his stomach.

Stock walked over and stood above him. "Tell me why you came to steal my money? You never answered me directly."

"The guy Jessy captured doesn't know anything. He couldn't tell you what you want to know even if his life depended on it, so make Jessy release him."

"If you won't talk," Stock said, "Jesus will find out the truth from him."

"Jessy will find out *the truth?*"

Stock's face contorted, as though slapped. A moan erupted from within his chest before he hit Roble's head with the revolver. As Roble's face hit the floor, Stock threw the gun. It struck the glass shelves, smashing the top panel, sending genetic collectibles crashing to the floor.

He stood in the after-silence. *Have you ever considered if you understand Jessy?* He shook his head at the memory of Kat's words.

Exhaling, he shuffled to the door and opened it. He held the light switch between two fingers, like holding the breaker to his own soul.

It flipped down, burying Roble in darkness.

Closing the sanctuary door, Stock moved through the lab, head lowered, his limp hands knocking over vials.

Chapter 46

Blood dripped from Danny's bangs, a swollen eye peeking through a gap. He hung from his wrists, naked, tied with electrical cords to a ceiling hook. The stone walls were streaked with stains, the air cold, the odor like a sop-pool at the bottom of a fridge.

How long have I been here? Days? Or has it been weeks?

Every time black-masked interrogators roused him from unconsciousness with a whip or an electrical shock, he regretted being alive, half because of the pain and half because he disliked hearing his own words.

After each question they forced him to answer, his words continued, flowing like a guilt-cleansing confessional. He squirmed below the hook, bewildered by his own admissions as they painted the incomprehensible mosaic of his life.

In the middle of a ramble about his regrets with Jenny, Danny inadvertently compared her to Alexandria, and the torture stopped.

Are they going to kill me now? The cords securing his wrists creaked as he swayed. *It doesn't sound so bad.* He gritted his teeth, turning his head, trying to see what instrument would end his life.

A black-haired man entered the chamber with a smile on his youthful face. He opened a water bottle and gave Danny a sip. Pulling on a pair of latex gloves, he caressed Danny's wounds, watching Danny with concerned eyes.

Am I rescued? A wave of relief washed over his stinging body.

"Good morning, Danny." The man slid a gentle hand from a whip-tear on Danny's shoulder to an electrical burn on his chest.

Who is this guy?

"Just look at what Roble Santos has done to you." Breathing in, the man shook his head. "Roble Santos…the one you thought a friend."

Danny blinked. *Roble did this?*

"Roble planned this little endeavor," the man pulled out and glanced at a portable electronic display, "you've admitted it…six times to be exact." He brushed dried blood and salt off Danny's neck with a fingertip.

Danny thought of wincing but knew moving would hurt more than the effort.

"Danny Sands…Danny Sands, you've confessed many things to the truth seekers these past thirty hours." He pointed at the masked men behind him. "They don't usually add salt to exposed cuts. And the electrical amps they used…?" He whistled. "You've endured more than most. But physical pain is so superficial, isn't it? It's obvious what hurts us more, and where that agony resides." He touched Danny's heaving chest.

Blood and saliva drooled down Danny's chin as he again glimpsed the indescribable pain he'd buried within his heart.

"And considering how well we both know Roble," the man continued, "who could blame you for hiding your pain so very deep inside."

How does he know Roble? Danny swallowed metallic-tasting phlegm.

"Still not convinced Roble caused all this hurt inside you?" His finger slid off Danny's chest. "Not convinced he did this to you with full intent?"

Danny pressed his raw lips together, listening.

Scrolling down the hand-held screen, the man asked, "Roble didn't ruin your chance to become a Marine officer like your father always dreamed? He didn't introduce you to a," he zoomed in the display screen, "a certain immodest girl named Jenny Beekam? Your mother didn't plead with you to date respectable girls while Roble just stood by watching the disaster unfold? Roble never encouraged you to draw unseemly animations and rebel against your father's will, when all your father wanted was your rightful success and esteem in front of others? Roble never scoffed at your legitimate desire to make your father proud of you?" He opened his arms, shaking his head. "Roble never did any of that?"

Danny moaned, gut contracting. *That's all true.*

"Traitors are so very fascinating," the man said. "They care for no one but themselves. But they do have idols, just like anarchic devil worshipers, and they will sacrifice anyone they push to the ground below that dark pedestal. Perhaps you've heard of one such person Roble worships, a certain Stock Brant?" He smiled. "Yes, the one idol Roble would sacrifice anyone for—and for whom he has sacrificed you."

That's not true…is it?

"You've been so expertly deceived by Roble," the man lowered his eyelids, "it's understandable why you feel lost. Nobody has ever told you that your father was right about everything, but someone must reveal the truth."

The man strummed through the digital notes. "You said Roble came here to rob Stock, yet Roble didn't reveal who would receive the loot. Would someone who really cared about you withhold the truth?"

Danny shook his head.

"But Roble wouldn't rob from his idol. So you've been misled by him once again."

Danny coughed blood, forcing an eye wider.

"You suspect Roble wanted to steal the money to make a jet. It's believable since Roble cares for things more than people, but that isn't why he came," the man ticked a finger back and forth, "at least it wasn't his driving purpose. Roble's purpose is the most selfish in the world. But let's not discuss it because you've already endured so much pain from him—no need to make you hear the reason why human nature is so completely hopeless."

"Why," Danny asked, more blood escaping his lips, "are you telling me all this?"

"Why help you to understand Roble?" He feathered Danny's wet hair. "Because unlike Roble, some of us, like your father, care about other people, as a rule, as a principle in fact. That is why we help them, whether they think they need it or not."

Danny's eyes closed at the soft touch against his hair.

"This is charming," the man said, reading the screen. "You came along with Roble because you actually thought you could play Robin Hood." His smile broadened. "Take from the *haves* and give to the *have nots*. Your father would approve of that, wouldn't he? …as he should. Noble, selfless, brave—all the traits of a good soldier, or should I say, Marine officer. You came here to make your father proud of you, to make up for every-thing you did for your own misguided desires. Your instincts for redemption are saintly." He brushed a strand of Danny's hair over his ripped ear. "We are very much alike, which is why Roble and his idol are our common enemies."

Danny exhaled, amazed at this stranger's insight into his soul. *He actually seems to care if Father is proud of me. Maybe Father was right about Roble, Stock…about everything.* Lifting his chin, ignoring the soreness in his neck, he waited for him to speak again.

"Now that you understand we're on the same side, we must address two more questions, one of which you neglected to answer for the truth seekers." He traced his finger along a purple welt on Danny's arm. "Why did Roble come back now? The timing is a bothersome conundrum, for it brings up several unpleasant possibilities, some of which require us to pack up and sail to safer harbors."

"I don't know why he decided to do it now, but I think someone asked him to do it. Someone gave him the information and keys."

"Who?"

"I don't know. But if he would have just taken me with him that night—"

Tossing the electronic video pad to a masked interrogator, the man picked up two electrical clamps connected to cables.

"I honestly don't know!" Danny screamed, tasting metal again.

"Are you aware you actually died, Danny?" He lifted the clamps higher. "They revived you from the grave twice during the interrogation. Twice is a record by the way. And since you've cheated death for the last time, you now have a final opportunity to repent and serve those who know best—just as you should have obeyed your father." He sparked the clamps together. "Who gave Roble the information, and why did he come back now?"

Danny shook his head. "I swear to God! I don't know! Please—"

The man smiled. "It's a joke, Danny. Just a little kidding among friends." The clamps fell to the floor. "We know you're telling the truth about that."

Danny exhaled, opening his mouth with relief.

"But now we must discuss the second question." The man's eyes enlarged with the upturn of his lips. "It relates to your association with Alexa Patra."

Nausea churned in Danny's gut, curling his spine. His eyes squeezed shut. "I don't know anything about her."

With a soft touch to Danny's shoulder, he said, "Come now, Danny...sharing is caring."

"I don't know her," he snapped.

"Oh, but you do. You admitted it..." He glanced at the masked men.

"Seventeen minutes ago," a man in a mask said.

"I made it up."

"Please tell us where she is hiding," the man said. "Holding back truth is so unkind."

"I don't know where she is."

He lifted Danny's cell phone in front of Danny's face. "But your GPS history knows, doesn't it? Her location must be on here. We've already plotted everywhere you've been this past week."

Danny swallowed, tasting iron.

"You've suffered enough protecting those who don't care about you," the man said. "For the sake of your life and to save us time, just tell us where she is."

Danny shook his head.

"Is she using...an alias?" The man raised an eyebrow.

Danny's heart pumped in powerful clutches, engorging his aching body as he pictured Sitra bowing to him the first day they met. *One heart way," she'd said. I can't let them hurt her.*

"Why reveal everything except this one little detail, Danny?" He waved the phone in the air. "Simply tell us the truth and you can walk out of here."

He will let me go if I betray Alexa to her death? Danny felt his body being electrocuted by his own soul. *I can't.*

"We will find her either way eventually, so this offer is one of mercy from one humble servant of truth," the man touched his own chest, "to a wayward son who could live to have another chance to make his father proud."

Oh God, don't make me choose between my father and...my own soul. Danny squirmed, body swaying.

"Ahhh...you look upset." The man stepped closer, his eyes sympathetic. "Let us make this decision easy, shall we? Tell us where Alexa is hiding," he leaned close to Danny's ear, "or Jenny will meet her same fate."

No! Danny writhed on the hook, shaking his head. *Just kill me!*

The man grinned. "And if you think dying a martyr in this room will save Jenny's life," he ticked his finger back and forth, "you are mistaken. If you die—she dies. And if you live—she lives. It's quite poetic. Don't you think?"

Danny heaved, tears streaming down his cheeks, stinging his open wounds.

"Last chance," he said, turning toward the doorway. "Jenny's life and your freedom—or nothing."

"Please," Danny moaned. "Don't hurt Jenny."

The man held still.

"Alexa…" Danny closed his eyes, his lungs hyperventilating, "…is hiding at Libby Dodge's downtown compound. Just don't hurt Jenny." His body fell limp.

"Very good." The man faced him. "See, sharing with others is so liberating, isn't it? And just so you don't feel responsible for Alexa's fate, remember," he touched Danny's chest, "Roble and his idol Stock caused all this. And if you wish to take revenge for everything that's been done to you—want to make your father proud—you know where to look."

Danny lifted his chin.

"We will release you as promised, right after our assassins return. And for as long as you keep your mouth shut about this little heart-to-heart chat, Jenny will live."

The man touched his own chin. "By the way, now that Alexa's fate is sealed, *did* she use an alias?"

Tears formed in Danny's eyes, remembering Sitra at *The Virtue* and how she gave him the courage to want to draw again. "I…I don't know."

"It would be strange if she hadn't," he said, "but no matter." Spinning on a heel, he tossed Danny's phone in the air. "Ms. Patra is going to have an explosive Fourth of July celebration tonight." Catching the phone, he skipped from the chamber. The torturers followed him out of the room.

Danny hung in the darkness, numb to the insufferable pain compressing into his heart.

Chapter 47

Stock awoke, lying face down on something hard and hot. Craning his neck, he focused on his hand hanging off a balcony. *Where am I?* His swollen fingers contrasted against the glass of the nearby casino.

Struggling to his feet, he glanced around with eyes half shut, head hurting. He saw smashed electronics, splintered furniture, punctured cabinets, and broken liquor bottles. Stumbling a few steps into the penthouse, he bumped against a couch turned on its side.

Blinking his eyes, he stared at the stranger reflecting off the TV screen. *What day is it?* He moved closer, looking at himself. *Stock Brant.* He grinned. *Why can't everyone be just like you?* He punched the screen; fault lines rippled out from his fist. He barely felt the pain.

He turned on the TV. Behind the splintered glass at the bottom of the screen rolled the words: *Happy Fourth of July.*

He rubbed his inflamed eyes. *I missed Nicolette's match yesterday.* Then, he froze, nausea stealing what little strength he still possessed. *Roble...* He fell to his knees. *He came back. Why?*

Crawling to the open liquor cabinet, he pulled out a bottle. He climbed to his feet, popped the cork, and poured the scorching liquid down his throat. *Jessy will find out from the other intruder.* He coughed and drank more.

Shuffling back to the balcony with the bottle in hand, he stared at the outlying suburbs *Nicolette...you don't understand. Jessy and I are the same.*

He turned his gaze to his marquee. *Alexandria...* The bottle found his lips again. *Your eyes...if only I could see them again as they were that night.* He wiped his face with the back of a bloodied knuckle. *If only you could have stayed and held onto your impossible darkness, maybe then...maybe then I would have discovered that opposite thing within me, some light to blind me to all that's true and that I hate.* He lowered his eyelids. *But it's a false hope, I know.*

Stumbling back, he landed on a deck chair. *You were right to abandon the world. But I wish…I wish on my life you were here right now.*

He watched the sky darken into blood as crowds gathered below. After a while, echoing detonations caressed his numbness. *Independence Day.* Streams of sparks sank down from above. *No one is independent of the truth—not Nicolette, not Roble, not even that fraud…Sitra.* A moment of silence passed between explosions. *I had no choice but to rebel against what I could not understand.*

Smoke wafted across the balcony like a citadel under attack. *This is where I belong, in a dark tower besieged by angels.* He shook his head. *If only it had been that easy, to recognize my enemy, so I could have fought back.* He dropped the bottle.

The fireworks erupted in a finale of flame and distorted space. The peace of surrender pulled him to sleep.

He didn't remember waking the next morning or entering the shower. The hot water sprayed over his head until it turned cold.

Ambling naked to the middle of the bathroom, he shivered and stared at the half-drunk bottle by the sink. He reached for it, but hesitated, remembering Roble. *I wanted you to come back.* The bottle shifted in his unsteady gaze. *But you should've known better.*

He glanced at the closet behind him, focusing on a suit hanging in a corner. Leaving the bottle, he dressed in the same suit he wore when he first beheld Alexandria across that ballroom. He looked into the cracked mirror with a fleeting sense of expectation, then turned and walked away.

The illuminated Roman numerals inside the elevator counted down above his head as he sunk toward the underground, toward Jessy's office.

Exiting into the bowels of *The Hole*, he saw three armed men huddled near a doorway. The youngest of the three, with shaggy hair and a dimpled chin, approached, his footsteps treading with caution.

Stock stared at his eyes. They sparked with life unlike most of those in *The Hole* these days. *His face reminds me of…*

"Sir," the youth whispered, leading Stock into an armory closet near the garage entrance. Shutting the door behind them, he glanced at the racks of guns and ammo. "Jessy has been waiting for you. He wants your prisoner from the sanctuary."

Roble... Stock's eyes glazed over. *The way you were back then... you would never rob me now.*

"Sir?"

Stock refocused his eyes.

"Jessy wants to interrogate your prisoner," the youth said. "You must take me to get him, or things will get bad."

"What did the other intruder reveal?"

"I'm under orders not to say."

"What's your name?"

He winced. "I'm just the messenger. Please—"

"Your name. You remind me of..." Stock rubbed his forehead. "...another time."

"Jimmy."

"Jimmy," Stock repeated, his voice detached. "I found you on the streets." He shook his head. "I should have remembered."

"Sir, I—"

"Have you ever stopped asking yourself something," Stock swallowed, "something so vital that your very soul depended upon it...stopped asking because you were afraid the answer might not exist?"

Jimmy shifted back and forth on his feet. "What...?"

"It's what I think Nicol...it's what I think someone once tried to explain to me." Stock's gaze moved along a row of assault rifles. "Do you ever wonder if moral truth is discoverable from within, instead of from others? Not from the heart," he touched his eyes, "but from *here*? It would simplify a seemingly impossible equation into rational eloquence, making all things knowable... genetics, good, evil...all knowable. It's such a strange thought."

Jimmy blinked his eyes, his mouth open.

"But the answer to that question is a cruel mirage," Stock sighed, "a shadow which can never be touched, Jimmy."

"I don't know what to say." Jimmy stretched his neck to the side, grimacing. "You haven't spoken to me in years."

Stock exhaled. "You must leave this place."

"What for?"

"You don't belong here. Promise me *you* will never come back."

"Sir," Jimmy turned and locked the door, "you wanted to know about the other intruder. He came to rob you. But that wasn't what Jessy was interested in."

Stock narrowed his eyes.

"Please don't tell him I said anything until I've left. You know what would happen."

"Go on."

"Well," he cleared his throat, "Jessy discovered something unexpected from the interrogation. I'd never seen him so excited. Yesterday morning he learned where Alexa Patra was hiding. You know, the missing lieutenant governor?"

Stock wobbled on his feet. "Where?" he breathed.

Jimmy's eyes slunk away. "I never wanted anyone to get hurt. I wanted to create things, like you. That's why I joined...but now that seems so—"

"Where is she?" Stock demanded.

"Last night, Jessy had her assassinated. Samuel's group did—" He stopped when Stock's chest expanded as if to explode. Glancing at Stock's eyes, he fumbled to unlock the door, and ran from the closet.

No!

Stock collapsed to his knees, eyes flashing unfocused colors. *It can't...* He imagined Alexandria standing on his penthouse balcony, white dress fluttering. But the image dissolved into a silhouette. He couldn't see her eyes.

No!

I killed her.

His chin sank to his chest. *I rebelled against what I couldn't comprehend...and I killed her.*

He felt the icy numbness of a life that should never have been lived. He stood up in a daze. Instead of heading to Jessy's office, he walked with leaden steps to *The Hole's* abandoned parking garage.

Two men followed behind. "Sir, you will come with us." One raised a compact assault rifle.

Stock mounted the Hell Hound and flared the afterburner, erasing the voice. The men jumped from his path as he roared ahead on the jet-bike, crashing through the rusty garage gate and into the alleyway. He rode through the city without aim, his suit blowing in the wind.

Nicolette lay by a pool in a two-piece bathing suit and sunglasses, like a picture in a vacation magazine. She sipped orange juice picked from a tree replanted from Stock's underground cave. Turning her head, she watched Stock's somber approach.

Sitting down next to her, his engorged eyes stared at a waterfall. "I think you've always known you were too good for me."

"Did you come here to insult me?" She set down the juice.

"I'm here to thank you," he said, his voice eerily gentle.

"For what, Stock?"

"For proving me wrong." He looked at her, his eyes defeated.

"Stock?" she said with a hint of panic.

"You gave me more than I ever imagined…taught me things." He wiped his cheek with a suit sleeve. "But there are some paths which can be too far traveled, and some mistakes which can never be undone."

"If you really believe that, then you deserve it." She sat up straight, her nose flaring.

"I wish I'd been able to glimpse the world through your eyes long ago."

"I wish I despised you so I could feel pity," her chest heaved, "but I can't."

"I think that's why I loved you."

"If you understand that," her hands trembled, "then you have no right to say it!"

"Please forgive me for upsetting you. I wish I hadn't had the strength to come and say goodbye."

"*Goodbye?* If you've given up on yourself," she leaned in, removing her sunglasses to reveal her watery eyes, "I can't stop you. But I'll always love what you are because I can't erase the things I saw you create."

He rose to his feet.

"Wait," she said.

He stopped, his eyes staring at his shoes.

"That thief in your sanctuary…"

Stock glanced up. After a moment he grinned but his eyes winced with pain. "You didn't want me to harm him."

The faint downturn of her lips exposed that truth within her.

"As perfect as you are," he said, "it's a shame you have a soft spot for criminals."

"Perhaps. Or perhaps you never understood the meaning of crime."

He nodded, straightened out his suit, and walked away.

"Don't…" she said.

Stock rumbled along the Las Vegas Strip, staring at his marquee, knowing he would never see it again.

Instead of parking in *The Hole's* hidden parking structure, he pulled in below *The Sin's* marquee for the first time.

"Whoa. What kind of bike is that?" the valet asked.

Stock dismounted and headed to the grand entrance.

"Sir, you didn't take a parking stub. Want it parked in valet?"

"It's yours," Stock mumbled, opening the ornate hotel door.

He moved through the lobby, not hating its decorations any longer—he felt nothing about them. Entering an elevator, he flipped open a hidden panel. Tourists almost joined him inside but glimpsed his eyes and veered away.

As the doors closed, a suited man slipped in.

"Get out." Stock hit the button, opening the doors.

"As you wish, Mr. Brant."

Stock glanced up at Ted Hollings, and let the doors close with them inside.

Ted inserted a key into the exposed panel. "Penthouse, Mr. Brant?"

"*The Hole*," he answered, as if a bottomless pit had sucked in his voice.

Mr. Hollings pressed a button and they descended.

"Rip down the marquee," Stock said. "It doesn't belong here."

"As you wish, Mr. Brant."

The elevator stopped, but the doors remained closed. Mr. Hollings drew in a breath. "May I just say, it has been an honor."

Stock froze.

"I will be resigning shortly from *The Sin*," Mr. Hollings said.

Stock blinked, not expecting that, but felt strangely relieved Mr. Hollings hadn't meant what Stock had thought he'd meant.

"I apologize for the inconvenience, Mr. Brant."

"You…you have a better offer?"

He nodded. "I am entering the protection business."

"What do you mean?" Stock frowned. "You're the best hotelier in Vegas."

"I mean that—people need protecting."

"You're not making any sense."

"I truly wish I wasn't." He crossed a suited arm over his waist and bowed. "The marquee will be removed, as you requested." With the press of a button, the elevator opened into *The Hole*. "Your destination, Mr. Brant."

Stock exhaled, wishing it wasn't. "It *was* an honor, Mr. Hollings," he said, exiting.

Staring into *The Hole*, Stock recalled watching Midwestern families in shorts and Hawaiian shirts pulling luggage through the once cowboy-themed lobby, the same lobby he walked into fourteen years ago upon arriving in Las Vegas. But instead of bright colors and smiling tourists, he saw bare walls, dim halls smelling of decay, and two rough-looking men leaning against a doorframe.

One of the men raised a radio, "He's here."

The other drew a pistol.

Stock passed them without acknowledgement. Footsteps followed.

"Tell Jesus," Stock turned to face them, "I'll bring the prisoner to him." He lifted a finger. "Follow me and you both die." His bloodshot eyes seared their faces.

Neither followed.

Stock descended to the nadir of the underground. Opening the greenhouse door, he noticed Kat's absence and thought it fitting that nobody would witness his last act here, as nobody had witnessed his first.

He walked through lush crops to the rear of the cave and swung onto a path leading to an orange grove, his first genetically modified trees. A plump orange sprayed citrus as he picked it, stinging his injured hand like the acidic bite of a green dragon.

Ducking below branches, he located a wall panel with electrical conduits sticking out from all sides. He opened it, gazing at the controls. As he gripped a large lever, his mind replayed the last day on his family's farm, the day he rebelled against the whole world. With a contraction of his wrist, the cavern disappeared into a murdering darkness.

It's so easy—to stop—to achieve what everyone celebrates as peace.

Carrying the orange, he made his way to the exit, relying only on memory as a guide. But with each touch against vegetation he recoiled knowing its fate, a fate long sought by those above, and now given to them as an unholy final offering.

He stopped near the exit and faced the black void. *If heaven existed, perhaps this is what it would be like, a final tomb for those who never belonged on earth.*

When he entered the pharmaceutical lab, the lights were on, the room ransacked. Blast marks scarred the sanctuary door, but it still held its integrity. He looked at his life's work scattered across the floor. *It wasn't the world that destroyed this…*

Entering the darkened sanctuary, he pressed its cold door closed. His thumb stroked back and forth across the orange.

A flash of brightness distorted his sight as he flipped on the lights, making the room seem unmolested, as if he'd gone back to his first day here. He breathed with relief until he noticed the broken shelves, the seeds and diamonds spread across the floor—and Roble lying by the wall.

He set the orange on the desk and continued to the shelves. The revolver pressed cold against his skin as he picked it off the floor. His other hand scooped up a long glass shard.

Moving to Roble, he crouched down, studying the gun and sharp glass in his hands. He cut the plastic cords binding Roble and threw the glass, shattering it against a wall.

Roble's eyes cracked open. Stock aimed the revolver between them. "I could kill you and nobody would ever know."

Roble pressed against the ground, but fell back down, only to try again until he sat up. Dried blood caked his forehead and chin. His mouth moved, but his words sounded like crackling paper. "One person would know."

Stock stroked the trigger.

Pressing his shoulders against the wall, Roble wheezed, arms dangling. He gazed at the orange on the desk and licked his dry lips.

Stock watched him for a moment. "If you could take my gun or my orange, which would you choose?"

Roble's eyes moved to him.

"One steals life, the other sustains it," Stock said.

Roble stared down the barrel.

"In the world above they are both called evil," Stock said. "They see no difference."

"I have nothing to offer you for either," Roble rasped.

"You won't beg me for a simple piece of fruit or steel?" He cocked the revolver. "But you would rob my vaults?"

"That's right."

Stock walked to the desk, picked up the orange, and threw it, hitting Roble in the chest. It bounced off and rolled a few feet away. Roble crawled to it, lifted it, and peeled it. Holding the dripping orange to his nose, he breathed in with euphoric desperation.

"So disappointing," Stock said.

Roble coughed dryly, his hands trembling. "Did you want something in return?"

"I want to know why you'd steal my money."

Roble attempted to throw it back, but it skipped across the floor and smacked the bottom of the desk.

Stock picked it up, pulled off a slice, and ate it. "Don't need it?"

Roble grimaced.

"Tell me why you're really here."

He held Stock's stare.

"Why do you refuse to answer me?"

Roble glanced at the fresco.

Stock's gaze followed his. "Think you can make a jet as good as that?"

Roble lowered his chin.

"The world doesn't deserve it, Roble."

"It's not for them."

"Why won't you believe me that no one can live without the consent of others, unless you wish to kill? It's what you were taught by everyone." Stock threw the peeled orange at him. "I give you consent. Eat."

Roble pressed it to his mouth, eating it, dribbling juice down his dusty suit. Regaining his breath, he whispered, "Thanks for the gift."

"I was insulting you by proving my point."

"You created that orange—a point that required nobody's consent."

Stock sat against the desk, tapping the gun against his leg. Freezing his motion, he remembered that Roble's accomplice had known of Alexandria's location, which meant Roble must have as well. He opened his mouth to speak, but it no longer mattered; he would never see her eyes again.

Turning away, Stock wiped his eyes with his suit sleeve and walked to the vaults. "Nicolette…" he said, not looking back, "what do you think of her?"

With difficulty, Roble climbed to his feet, his body hunched over with cramps.

Stock spun around, aiming the gun at him. "I asked what you thought of her."

Reaching into his front pants pocket, Roble felt the unexpected jumble of cut gems and glanced up.

"You fell for her," Stock said. "Didn't you."

Roble sifted the diamonds through his fingers.

Stock laughed, enjoying his own pain, the sound echoing through the sanctuary. Turning back to the safes, he entered the combinations. The first one buzzed and clicked open.

As the second vault buzzed, he said, "Nicolette saved your life." The heavy door swung open. "You might have had the combinations." He faced Roble. "But you would've been electro-cuted if you'd opened them. I added the security measure. Nobody, including Kat, knew about it."

Roble cringed.

"I realize now Kat must've helped you."

Stepping forward, he pointed at the open safes. "There. Steal it all, if that's what you desire."

Roble looked only at Stock's eyes.

"You don't seem interested in robbing me all of a sudden."

Stock got down on his knees, head tilting to the floor. Raising the revolver, he pointed its barrel at his own head, the butt of the gun presented to Roble. "I didn't understand something when you left me, and now when it is too late, I see just enough." Cocking the gun, he said, "Shoot me, and I'll gift it all to you. You'll be held blameless in my heart and won't become a thief."

Roble glanced at the open vaults.

Closing his eyes, Stock added, "If it makes you feel better, consider this final act of mine a trade—and I'm getting the better deal."

Part 3:
The Untethered

Chapter 48

The night sat motionless.

Victor and Libby stood atop a flat roof watching the sky. Fireworks detonated in a bright oval above a downtown casino, their red and blue sparks cascading in long strands.

"Ahh, your Fourth of July celebrations have begun," Victor said.

As the second glittery burst scattered across the horizon, Victor's body flew backward, feet lifting, left shoulder leading the involuntary retreat. His back slammed down against the asphalt shingles, and he rolled over his head landing on crouched knees, a hand on the roof for balance.

His mind raced, ignoring the pain shooting through his chest. He recalled a muzzle flash at eleven o'clock and the distinctive report of a high velocity 7.62×51mm NATO round diffused with a suppressor, timed exactly with the boom of the firework. His next thought was that the slug had hit his heart.

As the fiery sparkles disintegrated over the casinos, Victor touched his chest—the chainmail had stopped the round from penetrating.

His platinum hair hung down as he looked up. He lunged forward, arm chopping the back of Libby's knees, buckling her forward below the low railing. Another projectile whizzed over their heads.

"Someone is behaving poorly," Victor said. "Please stay down. I will see to *Madame* Sitra and return."

Libby crouched on hands and knees, her body shaking. "What the hell...?" She glanced behind, but Victor had left the roof. Her heart beat like the firecrackers all over the city. She cringed as more explosions erupted in the sky.

Pulling out her mobile device, she steadied her hand and searched the compound's security camera feeds—all displayed static. She dropped it and rolled onto her back, trying to breathe. "What's happening?"

Victor sprung back onto the roof from the spiral stairs, body encased in white plate armor. Fireworks gleamed off his helm's transparent green visor. One gauntleted fist held a smooth stainless steel gun, the other a black pistol with an extended ammo clip. He tossed the pistol to Libby and walked to the railing. Multiple rounds ricocheted off his armor.

Peering through the visor, he saw glowing outlines of bodies below. Six men with assault rifles had breached Libby's compound wall; another two perched behind the fence with sniper rifles, and an extremely tall man stood in the street beyond.

Victor aimed his weapon. An invisible beam seared through the metal fence, penetrating both snipers' chests in quick succession. Their bodies thumped to the ground. The tall man behind them ran.

Bullets slammed into Victor's armor from below. He spotted two men kicking the building's front door. Aiming with the barrel steadied on his forearm, he hit them, one after the other. Their curt screams absorbed into the celebrations in the sky. He moved along the edge, hunting the remaining four.

Libby sat holding the pistol, only discerning fireworks from gunshots when her hair vibrated. "Victor, what about Alexa?"

Victor turned. "I strongly advised she stay downstairs unless the door is breached. Unfortunately, she wears only light armor. The heavy armor is in the house." Bullets pelted the back of his helmet. He swiveled around and pulled the trigger, slicing an ultraviolet burst through a woodpile, and a man's face behind. Over his shoulder, he said, "Which is more than I can say for the *Madame*. You did not even trouble to wear my light armor. Please stay down."

"They're coming in," Alexandria's faint yell sounded from below.

Libby jumped to her feet.

Victor spun around, "Stay dow—"

Libby lurched forward, a bullet ripping through her left shoulder from behind, just below the collarbone. She tumbled to the roof, roiling in pain.

A high caliber sniper round ricocheted off one of Victor's back plates. Gritting his teeth, he faced the street and triangulated the shot's origin. The tall man lay in position atop an apartment building. Victor raised his weapon but hesitated, thinking of

Alexandria downstairs alone with the intruders. He glanced at the stairs. She hadn't come up.

Libby moaned, eyes half closed, a bloodstain expanding down her torso.

Victor's arm twitched and he heard a nauseating buzz in his head. "No, this is most inappropriate timing for a—" His body stiffened.

He tipped over backward. His armored calves caught the low railing and flipped his body head over feet off the roof. His body smacked the ground with a heavy metallic thud.

"Victor…" Grimacing in pain, Libby rolled onto her stomach, and dragged herself with one arm to the stairs.

Alexandria's face popped up from below. "Libby!" She slapped a hand against her own forehead. "What happened?" She tore off Libby's shirt and inspected the wound. "A clean exit. Oh thank…God," she said under her breath. She ripped the shirt into long strips and wrapped them around Libby's shoulder and torso. Laying her down, she pressed Libby's hand over the exit point. "Keep the pressure on and don't move." She glanced around. "Where's Victor?"

Libby rolled her head back and forth. "Fell…"

"No…" Alexandria rubbed her eyes. "I need to go down and help him."

Libby tried to sit up, but Alexandria held her down. "Don't move."

Lifting her head, Libby said, "The pistol. Take it."

Alexandria scrambled low across the roof, her chainmail as sleek as skin, and picked up the gun. On the way back she brushed lips with Libby and disappeared down the stairs.

Crouching near the top of the steps, Alexandria gazed at the dark maze of machinery and equipment below. Fireworks glinted in through the kicked-in front door. Sinister shadows danced across the walls, revealing three men spreading out.

She caressed the pistol. Victor had trained her to use it, but she never thought she actually would. Tears of anger, determination, and uncertainty filled her eyes. She concentrated on breathing, lowering her heart rate to control the flow of adrenaline through her body, an Isshin Ryu technique. Her eyes locked on the nearest intruder twenty yards away.

As another fiery explosion died into darkness, Alexandria

gripped the spiral railing and jumped over the edge. Her hand maintained a hold as she swirled down the banister. She hit the ground running on bare feet.

Jumping in the air, she cocked her left leg, body flying horizontal. The masked man whirled around. She released the kick to his chest. He tumbled, rifle firing in the air. She somersaulted behind him, tracking his fall.

When he stopped, she knelt over his dark form, her gun at his chest. She considered pulling the trigger, but asked, "Who are you? Why are you doing this?"

A volley of bullets from behind thumped her back, cracking pain through her like hits from a baseball bat. The man on the floor screamed, thrusting his elbow into her shoulder. She lunged between two manufacturing stations, rolled through a nearby desk, and slid to a stop near a rack of hanging metal ingots.

No matter how much she tried to breathe, she couldn't escape the pain across her back. She scanned for a route to the exit until she remembered Libby couldn't be left alone with these killers. Her eyes narrowed.

She sprang to her feet, running silently, weaving, sliding, and diving around obstacles until she stood atop a manufacturing station, concealed next to its robotic arm. Of the three men below, she could spot only two, and one was near. She leaped off the robotic arm, gripped a cable from a hydraulic lift, and swung feet first over the domed forge, kicking the man in the back of the head. He fell to the ground. She landed and knocked his assault rifle away with her forearm.

Pointing her pistol at his masked face, she knew she should pull the trigger, but hesitated again. "Don't move."

He rolled, attempting to escape. The deafening crack of the gunpowder, the recoil of the gun, and the man's head thumping against the floor made her ears ring and body numb. "Goddamn you," she hissed.

She heard footsteps running toward her. Tracking the noise through the darkness with her barrel, she fired several shots, creating cover. She sprinted in the opposite direction, cut through the gymnasium, and ran to the far side of the shed, hoping to outflank them. Within moments she moved atop machinery, stepping and leaping stealthily as she tracked them below.

When one moved in front of the other, she leaped off a rack

of armor, kicking both feet into the leading man's back, sending him flying into an anvil. Using his body as a springboard, she dove in the opposite direction, tucked, and landed in a crouched position next to the other man. Spinning her body, she swept his legs out from under him. She rose and kicked the rifle from his hands, then thrust a heel to his gut. Feeling body armor under her foot, she sent a knee into his masked face. She aimed her gun at his neck and turned toward the first man who had climbed back on his feet.

A pause in the fireworks outside created a silent wave of blackness. "Drop it or I'll shoot," she said.

The man fired his rifle, spraying lead into the darkness, hitting Alexandria's body armor three more times.

"Uhggg…" *The pain.* Forcing an inhale, she swung her barrel toward the shooter, firing several shots, hitting him.

He ran. She sprinted after him, weaving through the maze.

When he stopped to inspect his bulletproof vest, he screeched in horror, hearing Alexandria's breathing behind his neck.

Kicking the back of his knee, she grabbed his hair through the mask, and yanked down, punching his nose with her pistol. His body slammed the floor. Releasing his mask, she slapped his gun away, pointed her pistol at his head and fired.

He sprawled lifeless. Her pistol locked in the recoil position, out of ammo. She tossed it.

She glimpsed a towering shadow against the wall as another man entered the building. *No! Who* are *these guys?* She hated this fight, didn't want it, but knew she must end it. Something inside her seemed to snap, or rather reconnect, amplifying her fury into calmness.

Retracing her steps to the prone man she'd hastily left, she peeked around a row of manufacturing robots. The man ran toward the exit with his rifle.

"Stop!" she commanded, the tone powerful.

He stopped.

She moved behind him. "Hands on your head."

He raised the rifle above his head.

"Turn around."

He obeyed. A sustained flash from outside illuminated her. He gasped. "Sitra?" He dropped his gun, ignoring the fact she held no weapon.

The tall man stepped into view, blocking the exit, raising his rifle. Looking around, he approached. Another shimmering explosion flashed in through the doorway lighting Alexandria's face. He stuttered in his step. "Sitra?"

She pointed at his masked face. "You. Come here now." She indicated the floor in front of her.

He walked in careful steps toward her, lowering his rifle.

Sensing the danger diminishing, Alexandria's suppressed pain burst forth. She felt like screaming, curling into a ball and disappearing. Instead, she stepped toward the tall man in perfect form and balance. She ripped away his weapon, snap-kicked his groin, and shoved his shriveling body to the floor. "Remove your masks. Both of you."

The shorter man complied. The tall one, lying on his side, did not.

"Now."

He too pulled off his mask.

Alexandria studied the shorter man's face in the dimness. His pale, soft nose and cheeks contrasted against sharp golden eyes. *No, it can't be, not one of my lost foster kids.* He lowered his face from view.

She stuck the rifle barrel under his chin and lifted. "Gabriel?" She turned and studied the other. "Samuel..."

Both men focused on Alexandria through the flickering shadows. "But...you can't also be Sitra," Samuel said. "You're... It just can't be."

"What the fuck," crossed Gabriel's lips.

"Why are you doing this?" Alexandria aimed the rifle back and forth between them.

"We can't talk. We'll be killed," Gabriel said.

"You forfeited the right to your life the moment you tried to kill me." She fired a round over his head, dropping him to his knees. Resting the rifle butt on the ground, she leaned on it for support, head spinning. "But I'll give you a life-redeeming opportunity. Tell me everything and do as I ask, and I'll let you live long enough to turn yourselves in to the police."

The captives glanced at each other.

"And I hate to put a rush on such a weighty decision," she said, "but you have ten seconds to start talking."

Samuel lunged for Gabriel's abandoned assault rifle near

Alexandria's feet, lifted it, and aimed it at her face. She stared into glazed, empty eyes, so different from the ones she remembered in her foster care office years ago.

He fired, just as her arm flashed downward in a defensive arc, knocking away the barrel. Her hand followed the rifle, gripping and pulling it away as her elbow slammed against his nose. He hit the floor. She dropped one rifle and lifted the other by its barrel. With tears in her eyes, she raised it above her head and slammed the heavy butt into his skull.

Alexandria turned. "Five seconds, Gabriel."

"I'll talk!"

She wiped a tear from her cheek.

An armored white knight charged through the entrance with laser weapon in hand. Alexandria's relief melted into unstoppable, unsuppressed pain. Blood drained from her head, eyesight going blurry. She dropped to her knees and collapsed before Gabriel.

"Please do not move," Victor said, approaching, "or I will most certainly terminate you." He stretched Alexandria's body flat on the floor, elevating her feet. Removing his gauntlets and helm, he checked her pulse and breathing. Finding no holes in the armor, he pushed a hand through his sweaty hair with relief.

After tying up the captive, he ran up the spiral stairs. Libby lay at the top. Victor checked the bandages. "An excellent battle wound dress, this," he said, picking her up. "How do you feel, *Madame* Dodge?"

Libby moaned, but still managed a faint smile. "I'm so glad to see you, Victor. Next time, save the base jump for the cliffs, okay?"

He carried her downstairs, sitting her next to Alexandria.

Libby watched Alexandria lying on the floor. "Look after her," she rasped, "I'm fine."

Victor brought over some water, lifted Alexandria's shoulders, and poured water across her lips. More fireworks flashed in through the entrance, their light shimmering across her hair like red glowing alloy.

Alexandria lifted a hand and touched it across her chest and neck. Pain radiated between the wounds. She opened her eyes but saw only darkness—then indigo and white, like a South Pacific shoreline. "Victor," she whispered, "you were only sleeping?"

"Bad timing for a nap, indeed, *Madame*. I very much dislike missing fireworks."

Alexandria tried to laugh but it hurt too much. She heard someone else laugh and craned her neck to see happy emerald eyes peering back. "Libby."

"*Madame* Sitra, how many impacts did you take?" Victor asked.

Alexandria continued moving her hand over her body, feeling the tenderness of each bruise, almost enjoying them as badges of courage. She gripped Victor's arm and stood, legs wobbling.

"Please rest," Victor said, but he still helped her up.

"It's just a few bruises," Alexandria said, wincing. Placing her fists on her hips, she glared at Gabriel. "Is anyone else coming?"

"There were nine of us. No more will come until we report back."

"Four are accounted for in here," Alexandria said. "Where are the other five?"

"I eliminated them," Victor said. "However, since the security cameras were disabled I will search the compound to make sure this one," he pointed at Gabriel, "is not being deceitful." He rehelmed and walked outside.

"Gabriel, who sent you?" Alexandria asked.

"Jessy Gorronza."

"Who the hell is that?" Libby asked.

Alexandria stepped closer to Gabriel. "Did Stock know about this?"

"No." He shook his head.

Libby rose to her knees. "Why attack us?"

Gabriel stared at Alexandria. "Jessy wants you...gone for good," he coughed, looking away. "I don't know why. But I'm certain he doesn't know you are also Sitra." He shook his head. "*I* still can't believe it."

"How did you know I was here?"

"We captured a couple of guys. One of them told us."

Libby climbed to her feet, holding her arm, and gritted her teeth. "Who?"

"A guy named Danny. Jessy had him tortured...pretty fucking badly."

Scrunching her brows, Libby asked, "Please tell me the other guy wasn't...Roble."

Gabriel rubbed his hands. "Yeah, I think that's his name."

Libby's jaw dropped. "Did this Jessy bastard torture him too?"

He swallowed. "I don't know."

Alexandria leaned closer to Gabriel. "Why did Jessy capture them?"

"They entered the tunnel complex below *The Sin*, trying to rob Stock's vaults."

"They did what?" Libby shook her head. "I can't believe that."

Alexandria closed her eyes. *I knew something was up with those two. But is that really what they were doing?* She crouched by Gabriel. "Regardless of why they were there, are they alive?"

He shrugged, fidgeting. "I think so."

"Will they be killed?" Alexandria asked.

"If Jessy thinks they're of no more use."

Libby closed her eyes. "Oh my god."

"How are you expected to report back and when?" Alexandria asked.

"He'll expect a coded text from Samuel, and soon. After that he'll want us to lay low for twenty-four hours until we see what kind of heat we may have attracted."

"Do you know how to send the message from Sam's phone?"

He bobbed his head.

Victor reentered the shed, twirled his weapon and holstered it. "Only the five expired intruders were outside. I've piled them up by the wood." He removed his helm in one easy motion.

Alexandria nodded and turned to Libby. "We need to get Roble and Danny out of there."

"You're damn right we do, as far as Roble is concerned," Libby said. "Where's a phone? I'll call the police."

"No," Alexandria said. "Jessy and Stock have been paying bribes to the governor and other officials, possibly to some in the police force as well. I won't risk tipping off Jessy and getting Roble and Danny killed. We will have to get them out ourselves. I have a contact at *The Sin* who might be able to help us."

Libby sat down to stop herself from fainting. "I can't believe this is happening."

"May I suggest such a rescue attempt is too dangerous, *Madame*." Victor said, holding his helm under an arm.

Alexandria stood, shoulders back, chin elevated, eyes focused on the exit. "No one besides Gabriel need come."

"I can't believe you want to do this on your own." Libby caressed her injured shoulder, grimacing. "But if you go, I'm going with you."

"Would anyone here by chance know how to infiltrate an armed and fortified bunker and get back out again—alive?" Victor asked.

Everyone stared at Victor.

"Precisely what I thought." He flicked his fingers in the air. "What would you Americans say? 'Let's get down to business?'"

"Thank you, Victor." Alexandria touched the swollen bump on her collar. "At least we will have the luxury of being thought dead for twenty-four hours."

Libby glanced around. "What about all these dead bodies in my workshop? We can't call the police for those either?"

"Gabriel, did you bring a vehicle?" Alexandria asked.

"A delivery van, parked one block away."

"We will dump Jessy's trash on his doorstep when we go in to rescue Roble and Danny," Alexandria said. "I'll let Jessy fill out the police paperwork."

Libby raised an eyebrow. "Whatever you say, Lieutenant Governor," she smirked.

"Search him for a phone." Alexandria pointed at Samuel's body.

Victor found one and handed it to her.

She held it in front of Gabriel. "Type a message stating your assassination proved successful, only four of you survived, and that based on information you found at this compound, Roble and Danny should be kept alive until they've been interrogated further. But *don't* hit the send button."

Gabriel reached for the phone.

"Victor," Alexandria lifted a finger, "burn his eyes out if I give you the signal."

Victor yawned, drew his weapon, and pointed it at him. Gabriel squirmed and began typing. Alexandria watched.

"That's the message," Gabriel lifted the phone. "It'll go to Jessy if you push send."

Alexandria took it and studied the message and listed recipient. "I don't understand your codes." She quizzed him on the meaning of all the symbols, several times and in different contexts. "Now repeat the codes to me verbally," she said, looking at the phone.

He repeated everything without contradiction. "The message is exactly as you ordered."

"Your life depends on it, Gabriel." Alexandria looked at Libby and Victor. "You sure you want to come?"

"Push the damn button," Libby said. "You're not going alone."

Alexandria hit send. "Victor, have Gabriel draw you a detailed map of the tunnel complex below *The Sin*."

"Yes, *Madame*. I'll cross-reference it with the city flood canal blueprints. I have an idea." Victor grinned. "By tomorrow morning I'll have all the weapons and armor ready...among other things."

"I'm taking Libby to the house to work on her wound," Alexandria said, helping her up.

Victor saluted and marched to a workbench.

The brilliance from the fireworks' grand finale danced through the manufacturing shed, its metal walls rumbling from the sustained concussions.

In the house, Alexandria stood Libby under the flowing bathroom shower, then walked to the kitchen to sterilize makeshift surgical instruments. For the first time since college, she actually wanted to use her nursing skills.

She laid instruments out on a clean towel and handed Libby several pills. Libby sat on the shower bench, swallowing each one. As she bit down on a rolled washcloth, Alexandria sanitized both sides of her bloodied shoulder.

"Take long, deep breaths as best you can and don't stop," Alexandria said.

Libby winced, eyes watering, as Alexandria pierced and pulled the needle in and out of the skin on her back where the bullet entered. Turning Libby around and supporting her arm as she moved, Alexandria stitched up the larger exit wound.

Libby observed her confident movements, delirious with pain. Alexandria's hair draped across Libby's abdomen and legs, brushing against skin as she worked.

"You're so strong, so beautiful," Libby whispered, watching Alexandria's wet chainmail cling to her body.

"Just one more," Alexandria said, breathing in prolonged breaths to soothe her. She reached out and dropped the bloody bandages and surgical tools on the bathroom floor.

"Libby," Alexandria's eyelids trembled, "there's something you must know. It may change your mind about coming with me."

Libby waited, eyes blinking into focus.

"It's possible during the rescue tomorrow," Alexandria exhaled, "one of us may be forced to kill Stock Brant. And I want you to know I'll hold you blameless if you do."

Libby frowned. "I have no intention of killing anyone, but if I do, it will be to protect you."

Alexandria looked away to hide her eyes. "I know."

"What is it?"

"Remember I told you I was in love with someone else. I met him long ago, before you. I'm…" Alexandria faced her, "…I'm still in love with him."

"Stock Brant?"

Alexandria held her stare. "Perhaps now you have less of a reason to come, or perhaps an extra incentive, I don't know. But my feelings for you have always been sincere."

"You don't need to explain anything." Libby touched her hand. "You are so brave."

Alexandria glanced at her own hand as it shook. A faint sob escaped her lips.

Libby stopped Alexandria's trembling. Rising and grimacing with pain, she coaxed Alexandria to her feet and pressed her back under the steaming showerhead. "Don't think about tomorrow right now."

Alexandria closed her eyes, intoxicated by the flow of water and the control of Libby's hands.

Helping Alexandria remove her chainmail, Libby tossed it to the floor. She watched the water flowing over Alexandria's naked shoulders, spraying off erect nipples, and studied the purple and black bruises trailing from her neck to her hips.

Libby kissed the dark wound on her neck while her hand cupped Alexandria's bruised breast.

Alexandria gasped.

Wincing from her own soreness, Libby slid her hands down Alexandria's body and pulled her close. "It's going to be okay."

Chapter 49

Confident warm hands touched Danny's face and a reassuring voice caressed his ears. Blinking in a daze, he beheld glowing silver eyes above him and realized he was lying on the floor.

I must be dead. He smiled, for meeting Sitra in heaven felt even better than on earth.

So it seemed odd when pain coursed down his neck as she lifted his head. Her lips moved and male voices grumbled in the background.

"...and I need you to be strong," she said, bracing his neck with a rolled cloth. "No matter how much it hurts, you will have to walk." Salving and wrapping his wounds, she asked, "Where's Roble?"

Danny gazed at her crouching body, at her shins covered in gleaming metal plates. She wore a black jacket, the same variety as the men who had tortured him. Beyond her red hair lay the sprawled bodies of two masked men, but three others stood above him. Sucking in his breath, he tried to roll away, but she held him still.

"They're with me," she said.

His eyes returned to her. *Sitra...she is still alive!* Relief pumped through his veins. "They made me give them your—"

"Shhhhh," Alexandria soothed, touching his lips with her fingers. "They tortured it from you."

More pain poured down his body as she raised him to a sitting position. "But," Danny rasped, "I never revealed your secret identity, Sitra."

"I know. Drink this," she placed a flask to his lips. "Where's Roble?"

"He..." Danny drank it empty, gasping for breath, "...he said he went to rob Stock's vaults."

Gabriel lifted Danny to his feet and helped him into a dark set of clothes. "Lean on me while we move."

Alexandria donned her helm, pulled a mask over it, and tucked her hair into the jacket.

Handing a compact assault rifle to Danny, Victor said, "You might require this, my fellow *fantassin*."

Danny clasped the rifle, but it drooped in his weakened arms.

"Stock's vaults are on the bottom level. I'll show you," Gabriel said, slinging Danny's arm over his shoulder.

Danny cringed in pain from the movement, but a smile formed on his cracked lips. *If we rescue Stock's loot, maybe I can redeem myself before Father finds out about the Marines.*

"I shall take point, naturally," Victor said. "*Madame* Sitra, please protect the rear flank. *Madame* Dodge, take the middle with Gabriel and Danny so you may deflect any bullets against them off your armor. This might become unpleasant once *le Roi* of the underworld discovers we're not his returning hit squad."

Victor stepped into the passage just as three men exited from a doorway ahead, blocking access to the stairs. They stood, staring at him. He slipped a gauntlet in front of his shiny weapon.

One jumped back into the chamber. The other two drew guns. "Who are you?"

"A nightmare dressed as a daydream?" Victor tilted his head. "Or is that just a song I have stuck in my head?"

One of the men fired his gun, the flash blinding, the crack of gunpowder echoing. The bullet pinged off Victor's chest.

Victor returned the favor, firing his laser pistol from the hip, slicing both men across their midsections in one motion. They collapsed to the floor.

Whipping off his mask, exposing his white helm, he said, "Apparently it has become unpleasant, *Messieurs*."

"Go." Alexandria pressed on Gabriel's back.

Marching to the stairs, Victor seared a laser beam through the door where the third man had entered.

Alexandria checked their flank as they descended a sequence of stairways. Reaching the bottom, they heard raucous footsteps descending from above. "Faster," she said.

They moved along the deepest tunnel, Victor lengthening his lead on the group.

"The next door, the white one," Gabriel yelled as they passed a wide wooden door.

Victor holstered his laser pistol. From his belt, he removed a metal nozzle connected to a cord at the base of his backpack. The pack emitted a high-pitched whine as he toggled buttons on its side.

Shadows stirred behind them. Alexandria fired a burst from her gun at the stairwell. Bullets buzzed off the stone walls.

Plasma arced from the tip of Victor's gouger, vaporizing the door lock. He kicked the door in and entered. The others followed.

"There." Gabriel pointed at the blast-scarred stainless steel door on the far side of the lab.

Victor set his pack next to the sanctuary door and recharged its ultra-capacitors. "This one will not be defeated so easily."

Libby removed her mask and jacket, revealing bluish-grey plate armor covering her entire body. Alexandria did the same and bounced nimbly off armored toes. Footsteps and voices from the stairwell and hallway intensified.

"Ready?" Alexandria picked up her compact rifle.

"No," Libby double-checked her gun clip, "but here we are."

They jumped from the lab back in to the hallway, rifles raised. Muzzle flashes danced like camera bulbs in front of them, distorting the oncoming rush of bodies. Bullets riddled their armor like BBs bouncing off tin cans.

Returning fire into the chaos, Libby pressed her injured shoulder against the wall for support.

Alexandria stood still, studying the results of Libby's shots. Kneeling down, she fired at the legs of the approaching men. Attackers dropped to the floor one after the other, forcing the survivors to retreat up the stairwell.

Libby inspected her pockmarked armor. "Hah!" she said over her shoulder. "It works, Victor. Why'd you wait so long to make me some?"

Victor finished burning out the stainless door's supporting hinges and deadbolts. He and Gabriel gripped the door handle and pulled. The heavy slab tipped toward them. They jumped from its path, and it slapped the floor with a shocking concussion, revealing the lit sanctuary beyond. Victor restrapped on his backpack and entered first. The others followed.

Stock knelt on the floor by the vaults. Roble stood over him holding a large revolver.

"Shoot me," Stock rasped, pressing the back of his head into the barrel. "Please."

Roble lowered the gun. "Never."

Stock twisted around and ripped the revolver away.

"Don't, Victor!" Libby yelled as Victor quick-drew his laser pistol.

Alexandria flew like a metallic blur across the room, kicking away the gun Stock pointed at his own temple. It slid across the room. Stock fell to the floor. Roble staggered back.

Danny narrowed his eyes, staring at Roble's bloodied face. He turned to Stock, squeezing the butt of his assault rifle, but froze when he caught the inescapable gleam of gold beyond.

Alexandria stood above Stock like an armored goddess and tilted her helm downward.

Stock sat up, gazing at her. "Who are you?"

"Let's get the hell out of here," Libby said.

"Everyone who desires to remain living, please get in formation." Victor flicked his fingers in the air as he moved to the sanctuary exit. "The unarmored will stay in the center. I will be the fist, punching our way back up to the garage."

A dark, egg-shaped object skipped into the sanctuary from the lab. It bounced off a wall with a dull clink and spun to a stop near Stock.

"Grenade!" Victor yelled.

Alexandria dropped on top of it, her outstretched arm pressing Stock's chest to the floor.

The grenade detonated. The shockwave sent Roble flying off his feet. Alexandria bounced into the air, rotating and landing with a steel thud next to Stock. Those without helmets held their ears, registering an earsplitting silence.

Victor sprinted to Alexandria's side, rolling her over. Her curved chest plates appeared tarnished but intact. She reached up, gripping his forearm.

"Are you okay?" Libby rasped.

"The carbon-ceramics in your under-armor likely shattered absorbing the blast," Victor said. "Are any ribs broken?"

Alexandria stood, glanced at Stock, found her rifle, and moved to the sanctuary exit.

"Please do not take another point-blank detonation," Victor said.

Libby shook her head and helped Roble to his feet. "You look as awful as I feel." She handed him a canteen. "What in the hell were you thinking, coming here?"

Roble drank it, dribbling water down his dirty tie. "I'll explain later. I don't know how you did it, but thanks for rescuing Danny." He knelt down, inspecting Stock's torn suit for blood.

Alexandria fired a barrage of bullets from the sanctuary doorway at shapes moving near the lab's far entrance.

"Victor," Libby pointed at the lab, "how do we take unarmored men out of here if those bastards are lobbing grenades?"

"We don't, *Madame*." Victor removed a folded map from his pack, flicked it open in one motion, and knelt by Stock. "*Monsieur* Brant, where is the closest point to the city flood canals?" He indicated a spot on the map. "Is it here?"

A small object bounced into the lab from the hallway. Alexandria spun away from it. A bright flash accompanied an explosion. Fragments pinged off her armored back and legs. Glass and equipment shattered, plunging the lab into darkness. Red backup-lights flashed dimly along the walls.

"Let's get farther from the lab," Roble said, leading Stock closer to the sanctuary's vaults. "Danny, over here."

Gabriel helped Danny to the vaults and sat him next to Stock.

Stock pointed at the fresco without looking. "That wall is only four feet from a canal, but it's made of doubly reinforced concrete."

Libby glanced at the painting, then at Stock.

Danny stared at the fresco, eyes blinking. "Is that…a Nishiko?" He looked at Stock. "You son of a bitch, where did you get that painting?" Turning back to the art, he shivered at its beauty.

Victor walked to the fresco and folded up the map. Setting his backpack on the floor, he pressed buttons on its side. A whining sound built. He stripped off his black jacket, revealing white plates beneath.

"Do you have to destroy that painting, Victor?" Libby clasped a hand to her helm.

Victor nodded.

"What? No…" Danny moaned, attempting to stand.

Roble held him back. "It's probably our only way out."

Libby shook her head and ran to the lab, joining Alexandria.

Multiple grenades flew into the lab from the far exit, bouncing and clanking off equipment. One skipped off a table and flew toward the sanctuary entrance. Alexandria jumped in the air and kicked it across the room into a bank of computers. She crouched low. "Get down!" she yelled.

Libby dropped to her hands and knees.

Explosions flashed in a chain reaction across the lab, shaking walls, collapsing concrete chunks from the roof. The shockwaves slammed Alexandria and Libby to the floor.

Men poured into the lab from the hallway, rifle barrels blazing. Alexandria pushed herself up and scrambled along the littered floor, drawing fire. She cartwheeled over a crushed refrigerator and dove onto her stomach, facing the attackers.

Libby rose to her feet, guarding the sanctuary entrance, armor absorbing bullets while she fired at the intruders. Her rifle received a direct hit and flew from her hands. "Damn…"

Alexandria aimed low and fired at their legs, sending intruders to the floor. Screams and confusion swirled in the blinking dust-filled lab.

Libby pulled her rifle from the debris as bullets sparked off her armor, inserted a new clip, steadied herself against the doorway, and continued firing.

After several deafening seconds, the few invaders still standing retreated to the hallway. The others who couldn't lay sprawled across the lab, groaning.

The crushed ceramics in Alexandria's under-armor bunched up, pushing into her prior gunshot bruises. She coughed, pumping her fists for relief. Despite the pain, she steadied herself, elbows planted on the floor, rifle resting on her shoulder, aiming at the doorway through the dust.

Libby smacked her own head with a gauntlet, trying to stop the spinning from the prior grenade concussion. Wheezing from the dust, she lowered her arm, her shoulder shooting pain down the side of her body. "We can't keep this up." Glancing back at the sanctuary, she watched the fresco melting into lava before Victor.

When Libby turned back to the lab, Alexandria stood by her

side. A fire crackled across several workstations, bellowing smoke to the ceiling. The cries from the injured on the floor continued.

More grenades flew into the lab. "Seriously?" Alexandria hissed, swatting one away from the sanctuary entrance as she dropped to the floor next to Libby. The room quavered, debris raining on their armored backs. The screams of the fallen men ceased.

"Those mindless bastards!" Libby smacked an armored fist against the floor.

Alexandria jumped up. Dust cascaded from her armor as she sprinted to the far lab exit, hurdling burning debris and bodies.

As a man peeked into the lab, Alexandria jumped feet first, kicking his face. He flew back into the hallway.

Yelling and footsteps filled the tunnel beyond the lab. Alexandria pointed her rifle out the doorway. Incoming bullets sparked off her gauntlets and gun. She sprayed lead down both sides of the hall, hearing men scuffling for cover. After two recoilless clicks, she tossed the empty rifle.

Sprinting back through the lab to Libby, Alexandria coughed, saying, "That might slow them down a bit."

"I hope so. I can't take any more grenades." Libby gripped her own shoulder.

Alexandria bent over, hitting a fist against her armored chest. "I need to get this off...the pressure is killing me."

Pyrotechnics erupted from cabinets along a lab wall, the heat reflecting off their armor. Multicolored smoke mushroomed up, then pressed down, pouring out the doorways.

"That's not good," Libby said.

The lab's door to the exit tunnel slammed shut.

Squatting down, Alexandria tried to lift the sanctuary's fallen steel door. "Help me! We have to stop the smoke from entering the sanctuary."

Libby heaved with her at the edges, but it wouldn't budge. "Ten people couldn't lift this." Sticking her head into the sanctuary, she asked, "Victor, how long will that take? We've got a problem."

Victor didn't answer.

Stock watched the wall behind his former fresco slump away. Thick smoke from his lab churned above.

Roble held his nose, cleared his throat, and squinted at dust sifting down through cracks above. The sanctuary lights shorted out and red emergency lights blinked on.

Danny looked away from the eviscerated painting and stared trancelike at the gold bars. "So much wealth held by a criminal," he swallowed, "when so many others need it." He glared at Stock.

Victor's hissing plasma arced through the descending nebula-like smog. He bent over to draw breath, then stood to get the plasma high enough to open the improvised doorway. He wobbled on his feet, coughing.

Kneeling down, he toggled switches, and resumed. The plasma flashed brighter, and the flow of molten concrete and steel increased, as did the heat.

When the last of the reinforced concrete slag fell to the ground, so did Victor. He ripped off his helmet. Drenched white hair covered his face. He rolled his head back and forth, groaning. Then, his body sprawled limp.

"Alexa!" Libby yelled, scrambling to Victor.

Alexandria helped pull off Victor's sizzling chest armor. "He's burned. Find me some clean dry fabric."

"Get him into the canal first," Libby said. She stripped off her own armor and laid the plates over the melted rock, forming a cool bridge out the new exit. Taking a deep breath, she lifted Victor under his armpits with Alexandria's help. "Dammit, I didn't know I could feel this much pain."

"You've obviously never tried ballet," Alexandria said, helping Victor through the opening.

Libby laughed, almost dropping Victor.

Gabriel scurried out the hole, stopping on a canal ledge about two feet wide above a drop-off into stagnant water. Faint light beams penetrated the massive rectangular tunnel in sparse intervals from above. "I know how to get out from here. Follow me."

Libby watched smoke escaping into the flood canal from the sanctuary. "I'm going back to see what's taking everyone so long. We can't leave Victor's pack behind either; it contains a tritium battery."

"No, you and Gabriel wrap Victor's burns. I'll go." Alexandria ran back to the sanctuary.

She knelt below the smoke next to Victor's pack and stared at the three men still in the room.

Danny sat before the gold vault. Stock and Roble crouched to his right, further from Victor's exit. None moved to leave.

Lifting his rifle, Danny aimed it at Stock's head. Stock smiled, eyelids drooping. Roble scrambled in front of Stock and the rifle barrel.

"Move," Danny said.

Roble didn't flinch.

"You care about a criminal? His men tortured me. This is all his fault. He doesn't deserve to live."

"Put the gun down," Roble said.

"Move or I'll do it."

Alexandria caressed the floor with her armored fingertips.

"Danny—" Roble said.

"You were never going to steal his money, were you." He coughed, his gun shaking. "Why did you come here, Roble?"

"I am here to take it, Danny."

He pressed the barrel against Roble's forehead. "Then why are you protecting your unholy idol from me?" Tears welled up in his engorged eyes. "You never cared about me, never even cared if I jumped off a cliff."

"I'm only protecting one person right now. Who do you think it is?"

"Him!"

"He wants to end his life, and that's *his* choice," Roble said. "*You* want to murder him." He closed his eyes. "If I wasn't selfish, I'd step aside to make your unredeemable act easier—but I'm not moving. So do what you're going to do."

Tears ran down Danny's bloodied cheeks.

"The day you arrived at my house," Danny said, "you told my father, 'I don't care what you want of me. So do what you're going to do.'" He shook his head. "I can still hear your words in my mind. Why did you antagonize him like that?"

Roble breathed, his eyes still closed.

Danny glanced at the gold bars, his body trembling. He lowered the barrel to Roble's scarred chin. "He hit you in the entryway for saying it. You fell and cracked open your chin." The barrel traced across the scar.

Roble opened his eyes.

"He just wanted you to do your duty, Roble." His finger caressed the trigger. "But I wish he wouldn't have hit you."

"At least it made it clear what he actually wanted."

Danny shook his head. "I still don't get what you mean, but…" he dropped the rifle and wiped his face. "But I believe you now—that you came to take Stock's money. And I promised I would help you."

Turning to the vault, Danny reached in and hefted a gold bar, straining to hold it with both hands. "He doesn't deserve this. Let's be heroes." He limped, hunched over, to the punctured exit and fell through the opening, head first, feet still anchored inside the sanctuary. The gold bar bounced off the canal walkway and over the ledge, disappearing into the dark sludge below. His face lowered to the concrete.

Roble removed his suit coat and ripped a Velcro strip from his waist, releasing an empty folded backpack. He cleaned out the diamonds from the left safe, filling the pack. Securing it to his back, he faced Stock. "*This* is what you deserve."

Stock lowered his eyes.

Glancing at Alexandria, Roble moved to the opening in the wall. He pulled Danny through it and disappeared into the flood canal.

Stock fell back off his squatting legs, hands gripping his torn suit. He gazed at Danny's rifle, then at the armored woman still kneeling by the melted exit.

Staying low, she moved to the vaults. Stock picked up the rifle. She continued past the safes and knelt on one knee before him.

He studied her battle-scarred armor, wishing his life had been as valiant as this woman's living silhouette.

She spoke, her voice resonating from within her helm, "You once told me a story about a boy."

His eyes widened.

"You said he asked—'*Why?*'"

"Alexandria?" He gasped. "But I thought—"

"I finally asked."

"I don't…understand."

"We both made a similar mistake, Stock." Removing her helm, she shook out her red hair, silver eyes somehow glowing in the dimness.

"Sitra…" He swallowed. "How?"

She smiled, guiltless as a young girl.

"Your show…" Stock said.

"I wrote it for you, and all who dare to ask your question—to give them courage."

Stock looked away, lost in thought.

"You understand now...what I did for myself."

Stroking the rifle, he watched the swirling, red-illuminated smoke, the last remnants of his creations. "Why am I so afraid?"

"You will pay for your mistakes—as we all must—but never accept guilt for something you didn't do, or accept guilt for what others believe." She removed her contact lenses, letting him see her real eyes. "You're still that same young boy, Stock, that boy who actually wanted to understand morality with his own mind. It's not too late."

Tears filled his eyes.

She reached out her hand. "Come with me."

He gazed into her watery black eyes, but did not move.

"Please, Stock."

"Alexandria, if you believe what you just said," he drew in a breath, "you will leave me here...and let me do what I must."

She lowered her hand.

A tear rolled down to his chin. "No matter what the cost."

Wiping his cheek, she turned her head, and stared at the sanctuary entrance.

"Go," he rasped.

Turning back to him, she brushed the soot from his lapel, and kissed him on the lips. "Don't be afraid." Rolling back onto her feet, she rehelmed, moved below the smoke to the exit, and picked up Victor's backpack.

He watched the armored warrior, the ghost from the crypt, the goddess of *The Virtue*, his marquee of *The Sin*, his siren of death, his love...leave.

Stock sat alone.

Chapter 50

Shock grenades exploded across the sanctuary floor, pulling Stock from his thoughts. He noted with surprise the room no longer swirled with smoke.

Four men stormed the chamber, pointing guns. One aimed at Stock, kicking the rifle from his hands; one searched behind the desk and pillars; and two ran to the hole in the wall.

Jessy Gorronza strolled to the center of the room and spun on his heels. Approaching the vaults, he gazed inside. "That bitch is not only alive, she used my own assassins to sneak in here and steal all my diamonds."

Stock didn't look up.

"But don't look so dour on my behalf." Jessy smiled. "This is actually the best day of my life, and I thank you for dressing up for the occasion. Alexa's decision *not* to call the police on me only proves that she never intended to abandon her public seclusion. And becoming an illegal vigilante takes away her high ground if she ever *had* wanted to point a finger at Preton Moore for taking bribes." He pressed a hand to his lips. "As such, I think Preton can safely appoint me as lieutenant governor without any messy assassination headlines."

Waving a hand in the air, he added, "I can't wait to join the real game above us, Stock—that sweet, unlimited democratic system, allowing plunder at the drop of a vote. Power over others—in the name of a good cause—now that's the highest law of humanity. And I'm a people person, as you well know.

"Want to know the icing on the cake?" Jessy shivered with giddiness. "Your precious little mechanic? He really *is* a thief. That's stupendous for two reasons. One, he didn't come here to convince you to double-cross me, as I feared. And two, I honestly worried somebody called the feds, and he was part of the sting." He spun on his heels again, his gaze stopping on the empty diamond vault. "But I didn't see any law enforcement officials down here shooting things up, did you? No, just harmless, petty thieves. I told you Roble was a traitor. Oh, what an amazing day this is.

"And since you ignorantly ran *The Sin* at a loss just because others allowed it to operate, without these," Jessy lifted a gold bar from a safe, "it will be forced into bankruptcy, to be purchased by your ever-humble servant. Thanks for everything, Stock." Turning to a henchman, he said, "Take the gold up to my treasury, and collapse this place with detonation charges."

"Jesus," Stock whispered.

Jessy turned to him, his eyes attentive.

"Why didn't I ever understand what you were?" Stock asked.

"You don't know what made *me* possible?" Jessy raised the gleaming bar, smirking. "You won't understand my explanation, but I'll tell you anyway since I've been waiting for this moment for so very long."

Jessy reached out and tussled Stock's sooty hair. "Stock, *you* control mere things." Touching his own heart, he said, "*I* control men. Which is a greater skill?

"Do you think I could survive in a world where I actually had to produce something?" Jessy asked. "Not a chance in that place called 'Hell' you think you're going.

"Ever wonder why the price of corn is pennies per kilo and cocaine more than a thousand times that?" Jessy pointed across the sanctuary at the spilled corn kernels below the shattered shelves. "Do you still not appreciate how much skill and effort it takes to make a profit selling plants for pennies per kilo? How much intelligence it requires to grow enough just to break even? But what does it take to make a profit selling that same thing after a government declares it illegal. No skill at all, just violence to push out the other lowlifes, and the easy profits allow for an unlimited amount of arms. I love that drugs are illegal. I *love* it." Jessy stomped his foot with joy.

"You claim to hate those who make the laws," Jessy continued, "but the reality is you hate yourself because you think they are right and *you* are evil for breaking their rules. How could someone with your scientific mind be so stupid? Without your brains and these beautiful laws, I would be spit-shining shoes. But look at me. I win, and you and every producer of mere things will be willingly sucked dry, feeling guilty all the way to a premature grave." He laughed, and kissed the gold in his hand. "You never wondered if the laws were unjust, and everyone else wrong, never once. It's so fascinating."

"Strange," Stock said, "how I've never heard you say the word *I* before today."

"Oh, you finally noticed." Jessy beamed. "Most people understand that selling drugs like desomorphine is deadly because it controls people's lives—but *every* drug in the world pales in its ability to control lives next to selling the ideal of *selflessness* combined with *togetherness*. Convince everyone to surrender the selfish *I* and embrace the self-sacrificing *we* and the world suddenly belongs to its humble, caring leaders." He drooped his eyelids with a sly sneer. "It seems contradictory, of course, but that's because people like you rarely connect abstract ideals to their actual outcome in *this* world."

Jessy brushed his hands together and turned to leave. "Ahhh, *I* feel so much better now."

"Sir, want me to shoot him for you?" a flat-faced man asked.

Jessy spun around. "It's almost heartbreaking, isn't it? That we must kill one of the truly poor and miserable of this world— because we actually might have won his vote in the next election." He grinned. "But one cannot in good conscience overlook the sheer poetry of burying him alive with his failed creations." Whistling a children's rhyme, Jessy strode from the sanctuary.

Stock sat, watching men rolling out wires and securing plastic explosives on pillars. After a while, he straightened out his mangled suit and stood.

"Get back on the ground," the flat-faced man ordered as the others continued to work around the pillars.

Stock walked to the sanctuary entrance, his head held high.

"I guess we will bury you already dead," the man said, aiming his rifle.

A gunshot shocked the air within the sanctuary.

Stock fell forward, landing atop the prone sanctuary door just inside his charred lab.

A hooded figure, standing in the dimly lit lab near Stock, holstered his smoking pistol. The flat-faced man in the sanctuary collapsed to the ground.

"Pardon me for tripping you, Mr. Brant," Mr. Hollings said, removing his hood, before tossing a grenade into the sanctuary.

"But, now, please run!" Pulling Stock to his feet, Mr. Hollings rushed him to the far lab entrance.

The grenade exploded, detonating the plastic explosives attached to the pillars. The sanctuary collapsed, the shockwave knocking Stock and Mr. Hollings off their feet, tumbling them into the tunnel outside the lab. Dust bellowed out the exit.

Mr. Hollings coughed in the dirty haze, helping Stock up. "That proved more effective than I anticipated." He adjusted his dusty sleeves, blinking his eyes. "Are you all right, Mr. Brant?"

Hacking on the dust, Stock nodded. With Mr. Hollings' assistance, they moved along the tunnel, passing the former crop cavern. Climbing the stairs, Stock rasped, "You have always been," he cleared his throat, "my most loyal employee."

"I truly appreciate that, Mr. Brant. However, I am no longer in your employ."

He coughed again. "You resigned already?"

"And as promised, *The Sin's* marquee has been removed."

"Then why," Stock choked, gasping for a breath, "are you still here?"

Mr. Hollings paused their ascent. "I now work for someone who wishes to protect you from others."

Stock touched his lips.

"Come," Mr. Hollings said, continuing their climb.

Reaching a cross-tunnel atop a stairwell, Mr. Hollings pointed to the right. "Exit out through the airport hangar." He rehooded and presented his gun to Stock.

Stock gripped Mr. Hollings' shoulder, not taking the gun. "Thank you."

Mr. Hollings inclined his head and marched away toward *The Hole*.

Stock moved along the access tunnel to the airport.

A guard jerked around as Stock emerged into the private hangar. "Are you supposed…?"

Stock headed to the white jet.

"I mean, you shouldn't…" the guard said. "I have orders."

Stock climbed the *Sovereign's* boarding ladder.

"Sir, stop!" the guard yelled, drawing a gun.

As Stock dropped himself into the cockpit, the guard ran to the ladder and fired at the ceiling, the report cracking through the hollow building. "Don't make me do it, Mr. Brant."

The jet canopy lowered.

The guard shot at Stock's head, but the bullet bounced off the clear canopy. The engines ignited and throttled into a whirling thunder.

As the hangar door rose, the guard whipped out his radio. Unable to hear himself speak, he threw the radio, ran to the door control, and punched the stop button. The *Sovereign's* nose slipped beneath the stalled door and continued forward, the tailfins ripping off the bottom panel. The long metal strip teetered atop the aircraft before falling to the tarmac.

"Tower, this is *Wyvern* delta four-four-two, ready for takeoff on runway three," Stock said.

"Negative, delta four-four-two. Runway three is in use. Over."

Stock aimed the jet between runway two and three, and ignited the afterburners, launching it between long rows of lumbering airliners.

As it lifted into the air, the *Sovereign* reflected like a glimmer of hope across the glass of *The Spirit of Man*. It streaked west over the valley, detonating a sonic boom against the blue-domed sky.

Hurtling toward the Mount Charleston peaks, Stock scanned along the jet's wings. He looked behind at the shimmering vapor stream, like an elastic cord still tethering him to the beliefs of all those below.

He pushed the throttles to maximum, drawing back the stick, pulling the jet vertical, extracting whines from the engines. His body pressed against the seat. The world below flattened into a rusty plane, shrinking until it transformed into a bluish-white sphere.

As the turbines begged for air, the ramjets ignited, blasting him farther from earth. The tethered cord below him stretched thin like a thread.

Nearing the atmospheric edge, the salted blackness of the universe opened before him. Warning signals spread across displays. *"Engine stall danger. Auto recovery system engaging,"* a voice from a speaker said.

Stock toggled the manual override, disengaging the auto recovery system.

"Warning. Maximum altitude breached."

The ramjets lifted him still higher. The center console flashed chaotically from red to white.

Then, the fuselage shuddered.

Looking behind, Stock imagined the cord breaking, untethering him from the beliefs of others. He sucked in a breath of euphoric wonder, and gazed up into the crystal clear blackness, then at his own hands.

At the peak of the ascent, the *Sovereign* held a single point between space and time, a point at the center of one man's universe. The engines fell silent and he heard his heart beating.

"Ramjet stall," a speaker said.

Stock smiled when he felt the drop. The descent tickled at first, then crescendoed into an unstoppable plunge. The craft gyrated as it accelerated downward.

"Please fasten safety restraints."

His body thrashed around the cockpit. Warning signals chirped from the speakers and cautions flashed across all monitors.

The aircraft's nose pitched down, throwing Stock against the canopy, before the jet's erratic motions knocked him back to his seat. Racked with pain, he chuckled as if riding a carnival ride.

"Warning…warning. Engine stall unrecoverable. Backup auto eject sequence initiated. Error…Error. Please fasten safety restraints…please fasten safety restraints…please fasten—"

The aircraft flipped upside down and entered a flat spin, sucking Stock upward, keeping him in his seat. He watched the ground spinning toward him. His body felt damaged but he thought so clearly now, more clearly than he had ever imagined possible. He made connections in his mind he thought unconnectable, connections from moral abstracts to concrete reality and back again. Contradictions he once evaded, evaporated like clouds in the desert.

"Warning. Impact in fifteen seconds. Prepare to eject. Please fasten safety restraints. Fourteen. Warning. Warning. Impact in ten seconds—"

"Why," he whispered, not as an unknowable plea, but as an answer to all that still lay ahead. Reaching down, he brought the safety restraints together in the middle of his chest. The canopy exploded downward. His seat launched after it. Rockets under his seat vectored it to an upright position and propelled it into the sky.

The cold wind distorted his grin, eyelashes and hair fluttering. Gazing at the Las Vegas valley, he focused on its crystal skyscraper.

The ejection seat stalled, leaving him sitting alone above the world.

The *Sovereign* exploded in a fireball below, cascading down a wooded ravine, having kept its integrity until its end.

A parachute unraveled above Stock's seat yanking him upward. He drifted under the silky umbrella, relaxing with a sense of certainty he had never felt.

As the breeze carried him down the eastern mountain slopes, he scanned the pyramided pine branches beneath him, pondering their still untapped genetic possibilities.

When Stock's dress shoes neared the treetops, he spotted a familiar clearing.

Nicolette returned serve with a swift backhand and felt a sonic boom overhead. Dropping her racket, she ran from the court to the top of the bleachers.

A jet, in the shape of a white dragon, barreled west across the sky. *Stock.* It went vertical somewhere above the mountains, swallowed up by blue haze, leaving a contrail like a rope reaching to heaven.

Ignoring her interrupted match and everyone around her, Nicolette sat on the top row, elbows pressed to her knees, eyes searching the sky. When she saw a periodic glint falling toward the mountains, she dashed to the garage.

The yellow supercar scorched a trail of rubber down the driveway and onto the freeway as she shifted it into higher and higher gears. It hugged the corners as it ascended the winding road to Mount Charleston, roaring with fury out of every turn.

Higher up the mountain, she saw a trail of smoke reaching up to a diffused grey cloud. A helicopter thumped overhead and sirens blared from rescue trucks.

Her car skidded to a stop along a gravelly road, its door lifting in the air. Nicolette's tennis skirt fluttered as she ran down a path through pine trees, a tennis ball still bulging from her hip pocket, her white shoes stamping craters into rusty powder.

Bounding a locked gate, she quickened to a sprint along a rocky grooved track. Stomping breathless into the center of a young pinyon grove, her expectant eyes drew in the diffused light. *He's not here.*

She collapsed to the ground, back arching as she cried. She'd accepted he might take his own life, but now, sitting below his abandoned creations, it felt too real. Gripping fistfuls of dirt and pine needles, she wiped them across her white outfit. She brushed away tears, leaving clumps of mud on her cheeks.

"Nicolette," a faint voice said.

Looking up, she saw Stock limping down a hill toward her. She jumped up and ran to him, tackling him to the ground. He winced as they rolled to a stop at the base of a pine trunk, her hair covering his face. Pulling away, she peered into his eyes surrounded with bruises and scrapes but impossibly clear and alert. She rubbed her cheek against his, smudging mud along its prickly surface.

He grinned. She slapped his face, startling birds in the tree above. He held his grin, almost laughing.

"That's for being so damn stubborn." She squeezed her thighs against his hips.

"I tried to warn you about me."

She wiped away a tear. "You look hurt."

"Never felt better," he said, lifting his head.

She slapped him again, sending his head impacting into pine needles. "And that's for hitting Roble."

His tongue felt along his bloodied lip.

Touching his cheek in a mock slap, she added, "Hitting him twice." She pressed her body to his and kissed the blood off his lips. "I'm so glad you're alive."

"Nicolette," he said so easily she almost didn't recognize his voice.

She sat up, observing him with brows furrowed.

"I don't hate what others believe anymore," he touched her hand, "because I finally realized something."

"Are you in shock?"

"No," he inhaled, "I'm in love."

Narrowing her eyes, she said, "She's very beautiful."

He scrunched his forehead. "You know?"

"Of course, you took me to see her on our first date." She laughed.

"I saw her today," he said, his eyes losing focus.

"Oh?"

"She visited me where you met Roble."

"The sanctuary?"

"It's gone," he whispered. "I've lost everything, except these trees."

"I wanted to see you like this." She pressed a hand against his chest.

"All beat up and poor?"

"Happy. But beat up and poor also suits you. Does it bother you?"

"No."

"In that case, can I have this pinyon grove?"

He scoffed. "What do I look like?"

"A bad ass." Nicolette winked and jumped to her feet. "With your ripped suit and messy hair, I can see why Sitra snatched you up." Reaching out a hand, she helped him up.

He held an arm, keeping his weight on one foot. "I do think she liked my suit, but did I also mention she left me for dead in the sanctuary?"

"Is that why you love her?"

He shook his head, grinning. "Yes, that's exactly why I do."

She laughed. "I want to meet her."

Stock brushed his soiled dress shirt, but it only made it dirtier. "How's *your* new boyfriend treating you so far?"

"Who are you talking about? Roble? I was going to ask what you've done with him."

"He robbed me. Made out like a bandit."

Touching her finger to his nose, she said, "I warned you."

"You sure you want to fall for a thief?"

"No."

"Then you're uncertain about him?"

"Is now a good time to admit that I kissed him in your sanctuary? He is something. Something *smexy.*"

Stock shook his head and glanced up, hearing the thumping of helicopters nearby.

She draped his arm over her shoulder. "Let's get out of here."

At her house, she undressed him and laid him on a bed. From what she could determine, in addition to the bruises and cuts, he had a broken forearm, a sprained ankle, and a few cracked ribs. She suspected he also had a concussion, but he was thinking too clearly for that. After summoning her sports therapist, she canceled all scheduled tennis sessions at her house.

The next morning, Stock lay bandaged on a lounge chair by the pool, studying the vegetation along the walkways, chewing on a leaf.

Nicolette stepped from the pool, skin glazed like ice. Wrapping a towel around her waist, she sat next to him.

"I love it here," he said.

"You're not getting these plants back."

"I was referring to watching you play tennis."

She walked away and brought back a pinecone. "But I have one consumer complaint. My lone pinyon hasn't produced any pine nuts."

"It won't; elevation's too low."

"Will you sell me your grove then?"

"Stop it."

She leaned forward, wringing water from her hair. "Well then, will you create me a variety that produces nuts down here?"

He tried placing a hand on his chin, but winced and laid it back on the armrest. "That would cost you."

"How much?"

"How much you got?"

"Stock."

He laughed. "You'll have to wait. I'm taking time off to find a place I'll be free to create whatever I want without anyone, legally or otherwise, stopping me. If I find it, I'll take you up on your offer because I'm going to need all the money I can get."

Sliding a finger along the chair, she asked, "What if that place doesn't exist?"

"You once showed me a tattoo representing such a time and place."

"Would you risk your life for it?"

"If I can't be free, I'm dead already," he said.

"That's what my life coach once taught me."

"Who, Aristotle?"

"Renny Thatcher, silly."

"I thought he was your tennis coach."

"He is," she said. "Growing up, he was the only person who ever made sense to me, so I listened to him."

"You're lucky you had someone like that."

"This tattoo is for him." She pointed at her upside-down peace symbol.

"He hates peace?"

"No, loves conflict. He said when the price of peace with others is the surrender of one's highest values, conflict become one's greatest asset."

"Well, that explains a lot." Stock rolled his eyes.

The doorbell rang. Nicolette got up, pulled on an oversized t-shirt, and walked to the house.

Stock glanced at an open newspaper on the drink table. The headline in the top left corner read: *Governor Moore to announce new lieutenant governor today.* He chuckled. Below that story a headline said: *The Sin's bankruptcy imminent, manager resigns.* Scanning down the column, he read that an unfamiliar corporate entity had offered to purchase it in a prepackaged deal. Near the end of the article, legal experts speculated that any bankruptcy judge would most certainly cancel Nicolette's endorsement contract, calling it, "indecently extravagant."

Nicolette returned with a strange look on her face. "There's someone here to see you."

"Does he have a smile and a gun?"

"Come on." She reached out, helping him up.

Slinging his better arm over a crutch, he hobbled in to the house. Entering the foyer, he saw a silhouette in front of the glass doorway. He squinted, studying the person's confident stance.

"Hello, Mr. Brant," the man's deep voice said.

"I know you," Stock said.

"You should."

Halvern Black stepped forward, holding a backpack by its strap.

The two men stood like opposing mountains, long drifting toward each other atop the Earth's crust.

"Jack, Ramsey, Samantha, Gordon, Kavika, Malik, and several others wanted me to tell you hello," Halvern said.

"It was you..." Stock blinked. "You, who stole my best ex-foster kid workers all those years?"

"Sure."

Stock wobbled on his crutch.

"I never could convince Kat to leave you, though," Halvern said. "She's a tough one."

"I watched your building go up."

"Of course."

"I heard your speeches," Stock said.

"I was speaking to you, and those like you."

"What do you mean?"

Halvern touched his abdomen. "L523."

"You have pancreatic cancer?"

"Had."

Stock lowered his head, nodding a few times.

"I have something that belongs to you." He tossed the pack forward. It smacked the smooth tiles like a sack of gravel.

Stock stared at it.

"*This is what you deserve*—I think were Roble's words."

Stock opened his mouth to speak.

"Don't," Halvern interrupted, "it's not necessary."

Stock glanced behind him at Nicolette. She winked.

"I wished *I'd* been Roble's foster father," Halvern folded his arms. "But he had good enough taste to choose his own."

"Where is he?"

"That will cost you ten dollars."

"Ten...dollars? You want ten dollars?"

"No, I said it will cost you ten dollars."

Stock frowned.

"Want to see him or not?" Halvern groused.

"You have a deal." Nicolette stepped forward. "Want me to spot you, Stock, or are you going to stop at a jeweler on the way and break a diamond?"

"I'll be outside," Halvern said, walking away.

Stock hobbled out the front door carrying his backpack and circled behind a sports utility vehicle. He noticed its pitch-black license plate with white letters. *PROVE IT.*

Halvern sat inside, tapping the steering column. Stock climbed in the back seat.

Nicolette ran out from the house, the tip of her wet ponytail swaying behind a red t-shirt and above yellow leggings. She climbed in the SUV through a rear door and sat next to Stock.

Everyone remained quiet as Halvern drove. He took them

west to the Calico Basin. In the parking lot of The Calico Center for the Preservation of Our Heritage, he wedged the SUV on the sidewalk before the front doors. His right front tire mowed down a sign sticking up from a strip of sand in the walkway.

Halvern climbed out. The others followed.

Chapter 51

Halvern pressed against a glass door, flinging it inward. Stock followed, holding it open for Nicolette. He waited as a young girl leading a class field trip approached.

Stopping at the door, the girl stared at the stenciled words. *Public Lands in Public Hands.* She focused on Halvern's handprint atop the letters and gazed at her own small hand. She laid her palm on Halvern's print.

A teacher walked up from behind, brushed the girl aside, and said over her shoulder, "No touching anything. No talking. No leaving the group."

"Unless you really want to," Stock said.

The young girl stared at Stock in wide-eyed wonderment, before the entering class swallowed her up.

As Halvern and Nicolette waited to purchase museum tickets, Stock wandered into the gift shop. A television blared near the back of the shop with a group of tourists watching. The reporter on the screen said:

"Federal agents, with the assistance of state police, raided The Sin *early this morning in response to an anonymous informant's tip, detaining over fifty suspects including the alleged second-in-command, Jesus 'Jessy' Gorronza. One witness reported agents removing body bags and gold bars from a previously unknown parking garage on the property. Authorities have issued an arrest warrant and are searching for Stock Brant, the alleged kingpin of the underground drug circuit.*

"A copy of the whistleblower's accusations, obtained by Channel Four News, also points a finger at Governor Moore as a recipient of bribes from the cartel. His office has denied the allegations."

BREAKING NEWS… flashed across the screen. *"We are now joining the governor's live press conference…"*

Governor Moore, wearing eyeglasses, spoke at a podium flanked by two flags. *"I am saddened that individuals would commit such insidious crimes within our great community. It is unacceptable in our day and age for anyone to profit from banned substances. These are greedy and violent men who must be stopped."* He removed his glasses, leaning toward the camera. *"As your governor, as the one in charge of your safety, rest assured, I am doing something."*

Replacing his glasses, he turned to a different camera. *"Now let me address these careless rumors."* He pointed at the camera. *"Those pointing a finger at me care only about lining their own pockets. They are complicit in a conspiracy to destroy everything we've sacrificed so much to achieve together."*

"Governor Moore," a straight-haired woman from the press corps said, *"the informant cited specific evidence that you received bribes from this illicit group. Why would he lie about your involvement but give the correct information leading to this morning's raid?"*

"Shame on you for spreading irresponsible rumors. Shame on you."

The woman cringed and looked around at everyone staring at her.

The camera panned out, revealing a number of reporters raising their hands.

"Honorable Governor," a man in a sweater vest asked, *"will you still announce the lieutenant governor replacement today as planned?"*

"This is no time to talk politics."

A voice from off camera yelled, *"Have federal authorities indicated they will investigate your administration?"*

"I am," Moore said, his voice cracking, *"as much a victim of these crimes as anyone."* He walked in front of the podium, loosening his tie. *"Like that performer in* The Virtue, *I too am being wrongly singled out and maligned. And while I am just as strong as her, ordinary folks like you must never be made to feel alone, but made a part of something greater. It is my love for our society that…"* a tear streamed down a tanned cheek, *"…drives me in this calling. That is all I can say at this time."*

A reporter appeared back on screen. *"As is standard procedure in such matters, the US Department of Justice announced they will investigate the allegations against the governor."*

Pictures of Stock Brant splashed across the TV. *"The public is being asked to provide information leading to the arrest of Stock Brant, but be advised, he is considered armed and dangerous."*

Nicolette gripped Stock's crutch and pulled him from the gift shop, his heavy backpack rustling as he lumbered along. "Keep your face down," she whispered.

They met Halvern at the elevator. A mustached park ranger

reached for their tickets, glancing at their faces. Nicolette winked at him. He blushed and missed a couple times before hitting the button to summon the elevator. As the doors slid open, Nicolette pursed her lips, holding the ranger's attention as the other two entered the elevator. Halvern pressed the museum button and Nicolette slid inside just as the doors closed.

When the elevator opened at the museum floor, a matronly ranger stared at Stock. "Do you require a wheelchair, sir?"

He shook his head, not making eye contact.

"Who in god's name remodeled this place?" Halvern growled.

The ranger looked behind her. Fluorescent lights glared off white and brown vinyl floors. Clear plastic boxes on pedestals filled the cavern, half of them stuffed with paper money and labeled: *Please donate to save our heritage*. The other half contained artifacts from early settlers and Native Americans in the Calico Basin. Red signs dotted the museum like chickenpox blaring the words: *Please don't touch*. Rubber stoppers plugged the original waterspouts and troughs throughout the floor. A sign posted in one trough read: *This museum has initiated a water conservation program to save our heritage*.

Turning back to Halvern, the ranger said, "All relevant museum information can be found on listening devices rentable for eight dollars at the front desk." Glancing at Stock, she lifted her radio.

"I thought those headphones were only seven dollars," Halvern grumbled. "You're not charging me more because I'm *Black*, are you?"

"What? Because you're …?"

Nicolette led Stock from the elevator.

"Of course not, sir." She dropped the radio to her waist. "That would be against policy."

"What a relief." Halvern watched Nicolette and Stock disappear behind a cabinet displaying twine-covered sticks.

The ranger followed his gaze.

"You need to revegetate that patch of sand in the front sidewalk. It's a scar on the face of mother earth." Halvern's forehead scrunched with disgust.

"Uhh. Yes, sir," she snapped back to attention. "I'll report it to the grounds crew. And between you and me," she whispered as if to a fellow conspirator, "I've been hounding them to put up more protective barriers. People just trot around here like they own the place."

"You poor thing. Well," Halvern shook his head, "good luck corralling your feudal serfs."

She nodded with an appreciative sigh.

Halvern walked away rolling his eyes and found Stock and Nicolette in the interior of the museum behind an exhibit of beaded headdresses.

"What are we doing here?" Stock asked. "Am I supposed to find Roble stuffed in a display?"

Halvern frowned and led them down a rock hallway past some restrooms and rounded a corner to a dead end. Dry troughs ran along the walls at eye level. He glanced behind him and reached into a trough, pressing and twisting something inside. A faint clicking sounded and the dead end wall swung open. Beyond it lay five additional feet of passage. "Come on." He stepped forward.

They squeezed in behind.

"Pull it shut," Halvern said.

Recessed lighting illuminated the ceiling as the rock door closed. Halvern ran his hands along a raised border lining the walls. At one spot on each side, his finger sunk a small cube into the surface. He stood tall and nodded at the ceiling. Nicolette and Stock looked at each other.

A metal grinding sound came from the next dead end wall before it swung outward.

A woman with neck-length hair, wearing grey adventurer's clothing and an arm sling, approached from the revealed corridor.

Halvern walked forward, squeezed the woman's good shoulder, and continued on.

"Welcome." The woman bowed to Nicolette. "I'm Libby Dodge."

Nicolette curtsied, grinning. "Nicolette Popov." She extended a hand.

Libby took it and kissed it. "I'm honored."

"You're the inventor of the white dragon?" Nicolette asked.

Libby glanced at Stock.

"Oh, sorry," Nicolette said, "I don't know its real name. Only I love…loved that jet."

"Thank you." Libby swept a hand behind her. "Come in."

Nicolette walked away down the hall.

Stock set his crutch against the wall, squared his shoulders, and stood at attention.

"It's strange we've never formally met," Libby said, "considering you're one of my best customers." She picked up Stock's crutch. "I apologize for our uninvited visit to your workspace yesterday, but you know Roble; somehow trouble always finds him. I'd actually be worried about him if it were the other way around."

Stock remained at attention, thinking Libby Dodge appeared too casual and unburdened for everything she had created.

"Please, come in," she said.

"Your *Sovereign*..."

She smiled, emerald eyes twinkling. "Yes?"

"I...I can't explain. It took me...its integrity...I can't explain it."

"You have as interesting a taste for jets as you do for art." She handed him the crutch. "And I don't know about your other genetic experiments, but your pine nuts are ridiculously delicious."

He took the crutch, nodding his head, wondering why he'd waited so long to meet her.

They walked together up the corridor, passing an antique-framed portrait of a thin, blond officer wearing eighteenth century revolutionary war attire.

Beyond the painting steps curved upward, opening into a spacious, vaulted chamber. Cream-colored rock formed the ceiling. The walls were carved of red stone and the floors covered in patches of black and red. The air smelled like the mist of a waterfall below a natural spring. Two doors and another passage led off the chamber.

Three leather couches and a low redwood table sat in the center. The outer wall opened onto a balcony wedged within a deep crevasse, undetectable by the other floors or from the desert basin below. To the right of the balcony sat a high stone bar and a kitchen lined with stools. Water poured down the face of the bar into a recessed trough at its base.

Roble sat on a barstool, his back turned. Nicolette leaned against him.

Stock limped over to them.

Nicolette stepped away. Roble stood up and faced him.

"Your interpretation of Robin Hood is...interesting," Stock said.

Roble's eyes remained steady.

"Since you were too selfish to steal the diamonds to build your jet," Stock said, "I suppose you're also too conceited to expect a reward."

Roble's arms hung loose, relaxed.

"I'm curious though. If I'd died after you left, would you have kept the money?"

"It would have gone to the person you would have wished."

"Who?"

Roble rubbed his chin. "Alexa."

Alexandria. Stock's eyes widened, and he glanced around the room. *Where is she?*

"But it would've been a shame," Roble said, "because I rescued your diamonds only because I wanted to see what else you could create."

"That was the stupidest thing I've ever seen anyone do," he said, "stealing my money...for me." Reaching out his good arm, wobbling on the crutch, he hugged his little mechanic. "Thank you."

Roble held him. Nicolette smiled.

Letting go, Roble pointed at the sofas. "You should probably know," he walked over and sat down, "robbing you was entirely Kat's idea. And she wanted me to thank you for everything. So..."

"Is she all right?" Stock lowered himself to a sofa with his crutch.

"She'll probably start a genetic research lab someday based on what you taught her," Roble shrugged, "and bankrupt you."

Stock grinned. "More than probably." He rubbed his eyes, looking around. *Where is Alexandria?*

Nicolette strolled to the balcony and stood by Halvern. Libby made iced tea behind the bar.

"Ms. Dodge," Stock said, "how did you keep *this* floor from being confiscated by the government?"

Libby brought over five tall glasses and placed them on the coffee table, sitting down next to Roble. "Blame Halvern. He's the paranoid one who insisted I build a hidden level. But I foolishly leased it to a friend right after Halvern built it. Now I can't get the impertinent Frenchman to leave."

"He comes and goes through the museum?"

"Rarely," Libby said. "There's an entrance tunnel leading in from my…from Halvern's ranch in the valley, but it's a good mile hike in. Halvern must've had mercy on your injured leg. Plus, he seems to get a kick out of messing with the rangers." She glanced behind at Halvern. "He didn't park on the revegetation sandbox again did he?"

Stock chuckled and ran a hand along the backpack. Roble touched his arrowhead, his eyes following Stock's hand.

"You could still ask me to fund your jet," Stock said.

"I'm not going to," Roble said. "I've already told you why."

Stock rubbed his injured arm, shaking his head. "I hope to create again someday, but not here, not in a place with rules and laws like these. These diamonds will have to wait."

Roble looked away from the diamond pack. Libby sipped her iced tea.

Stock fidgeted and glanced around the room again.

"She's below in the water cavern attending to injuries," Libby said, her eyes searching Stock's.

Stock blinked, his heart racing. *Libby doesn't want me to see her.* Then he dissected her words. "Injuries…" He winced. "I think I owe some of you compensation for what my organization did. Please sell any part of these diamonds to that end."

He picked up a pencil off a notebook, leaned over a cocktail napkin, and wrote, *Gygax Diamonds* and an address in Newport Beach, California. "This is my diamond supplier. Sell them back to him. He knows their worth, will give you a fair price, and won't report it to the authorities."

"We'll take you up on that for injuries and damage we received at the downtown compound," Libby said. "However, Roble and Danny entered your property voluntarily and we rescued them at our own risk, so any losses tied to that excursion are our own fault. Everyone is responsible for their own decisions…" she looked away, "…no matter how personal the choice, or how much the results hurt."

Stock dropped the pencil and pushed himself to his feet with the crutch. "Please excuse me. I—"

"Take the elevator." Libby pointed at a hallway.

Stock looked down at his bandaged ankle, pressing his foot to the floor to test the pain level. "Are there stairs?"

Libby stared at his ankle and then his eyes. "The door after the elevator."

Chapter 52

Stock hobbled down the spiral steps, drilling himself into the sandstone cliff. After a while, the stone dampened and an occasional drip from above tapped his shoulders. When the stairs ended, he entered a rock tunnel.

On the other side, a grated, stainless steel bridge stretched across a rock shaft. Water drizzled into the widening hole below. He peered over the edge at the shimmering bottom, which cast liquid shadows up jagged walls. Flaring his nostrils, he inhaled the scent. *That's odd.*

Across the bridge, steel stairs corkscrewed down the shaft. He gripped the wet rail, feet searching for traction as he descended. At the bottom, he limped between lit pools spiked with stalagmites, his wet body shivering.

He stopped and tasted the water in a pool. *Algae.* His tongue moved across his teeth. *What allows it to live in the dark and in cold water? If I could replicate that in…* Shaking his head, he swallowed. *Not now.*

A narrow tunnel led him from the pools to an elevator. Beyond the elevator the passage transitioned from cut stone into transparent glass with curved edges, the walls somehow illuminated from within. It ended at a tall redwood door.

As Stock opened the door wind threw him back, the sound of rushing water sweeping over him. Steadying himself, he gazed through the entrance.

A water funnel beamed down from the center of a large cavern as if the sun had liquefied and poured into the earth. It pierced a dark pool in the center of the cave, swirling the water like luminescent dye, reflecting its imbedded light onto the glass walls.

And then, he saw her.

Alexandria stood in the crystalline mist by the rimmed pool, wearing jeans and a white sweater, hair fluttering. The churn of water seemed to fade, leaving only the hopeful melody of her voice.

"...*Somehow the trees are much greener; Desert buds bloom to adore you; Everything's brighter when you're around; The scent of the Pinyon is sweeter; Lilacs grow higher before you; Everything's brighter when you're around...*"

She turned, red hair whipping off a shoulder, silver eyes shimmering in the cascading light.

He moved to her, welcoming the pain in his ankle as a guarantee she was no mirage. Water vapor wafted across his body like surf breaking upon the bow of an approaching ship.

Her warmth pressed into him and she feathered the bruises and cuts on his face. "You're alive," she whispered. Droplets glistened upon her eyelashes. "I've waited so long for you to be with me."

"Alexandria..." He pressed his forehead against hers, losing all sense of speech, but wanting to say so much.

She kissed him, the softness of her lips drawing his eyelids closed.

"I..." he gasped against her mouth, but lost his words again.

"You don't need to explain anything to me. I understand what you've gone through." She kissed him again.

"Please..." He gripped her shoulders. "I have to tell you everything, Alexandria." He swallowed. "I must say it for it to be real."

She nodded, her eyes encouraging him.

"I was blind," he rasped. "I assumed morality was something that came from others, something mystical and untouchable. I believed them—and hated them so much for it." He gripped his injured hand into a fist, cringing in pain. "And that's why I didn't know how to live without rebelling," his fist pressed against his own heart, "while feeling both sinful and ashamed."

Alexandria took his fist into her hands, opened it, and caressed his palm.

"I had to witness with my own eyes, Alexandria, what was never taught to me—right and wrong in concrete form. I had to observe someone unattached to what everyone else proclaimed, acting according to her own code yet not consider herself evil." He lowered his voice, "I had to see it in living art—a breathing marquee.

"Your show reignited an extinguished spark inside me," he continued, "which made me want to ask *why* again. It gave me a hope I didn't think I deserved. And yet," he lowered his eyes, "I still didn't ask, because I was afraid the answer to my question was unknowable." He stopped, remembering the smoke from his creations swirling above his head. "Until I saw you, Alexandria," he gripped her hands, "in the sanctuary."

She raised his hands to her lips.

"And," he groaned at the pain in his arm and her gentleness against his skin, "if someone else hadn't tried to help me recognize my own blindness—I might not be here."

"The girl you brought to *The Virtue*."

"Yes." He raised his gaze back to hers. "At first I thought Nicolette was like me—evil...rebellious. But she wasn't, Alexandria...and she knew she was not. I wanted her to save me somehow, but—"

"No one can save anyone else from their own beliefs," she said.

He nodded, looking away. "I almost died before discerning what I wouldn't let myself see. And much, much worse than that," he winced, "I almost got you killed." A tear ran down his cheek. "I would never have seen you..." He trembled, unable to bear his own words.

She reached up and touched his cheek, her other hand comforting his calloused palm.

He exhaled at her soft strokes.

"Stock, if you hadn't been willing to die to comprehend for yourself," she turned his face back to hers, "we wouldn't be here together now." Her thumb wiped away his tear. "I'm glad that you realize you were never evil for doing what you loved."

"But I did commit a crime," his hand slid from hers, "and I must pay the price, as you said in the sanctuary."

She bowed her head. Each shallow breath she drew revealed the pain his last words inflicted on her. He reached up and ran his fingers through her long hair, and she sighed at his touch.

"Because I accepted their proclaimed morality as truth, regardless of my rebellion of it," Stock said, "my rational capability to discern right and wrong atrophied like an unused brain, and I could no longer judge those around me." His body trembled atop his wounded ankle. "And *that's* why I looked away as my men assaulted others. I looked *away*."

"Shhhh," she soothed, her voice mixing with the hum of flowing water. "Don't think of that now." She laid her head on his shoulder and breathed against his neck. "You have so much to live for."

Sliding his hands down her body, he drew her against him. "Last night I dreamt of a place where I could create again." He peered at the illuminated waterfall. "A place I wouldn't have to bribe my own government to let me live on my own terms. A land, Alexandria—where I wouldn't have to hide because of what others believed." He shook his head. "But...I don't know where it is."

"It doesn't exist, Stock."

"How can you say that?" He stepped back. "After everything you've done for yourself and for me. How can you say there is no place we can live free, according to our own consciences?"

"I'm telling you the truth, Stock." Her voice flowed with tenderness, her eyes sympathetic. "There is no sanctuary against those who impose their beliefs on others through laws, not one single strip of dry land on this Earth."

"Nicolette told me," he swallowed, "that there was a time and a place where people were truly free."

Alexandria exhaled. "Those people willingly gave up their freedoms long ago."

He closed his eyes. "Then if I was born into a world that won't allow me to live as I am," his shoulders slumped, "I don't wish to."

She pulled him close, lifting her chin, her eyes searching his. "You would leave me now?"

"Alexandria," he rubbed his hands against the back of her sweater, his eyes watering, "as long as I can touch you...I will sacrifice who I am to remain in this world without hope."

"Stock," she whispered, her lips grazing his ear, "come with me. I want to explain something."

A door slammed shut, and they turned toward the sound. Of the three doorways in the far cavern wall, Gabriel approached from the middle one. Stock squinted, recognizing his face but not his confident gait.

"I'm more hopeful after removing Victor's bandages," Gabriel said to Alexandria, "but you should take a look before I rewrap."

"Gabriel..." Stock said.

Gabriel looked at him, but Stock found no more words. He felt the same emotion as with Samuel and Jimmy—that helpless sense of remembering a long-forgotten son too late.

"I'll be with Victor," Gabriel said, and walked away.

"Gabriel," Stock said again, "I'd like to speak with you sometime...to understand how your world is treating you."

He paused, nodded, and continued away.

"Wait here," Alexandria said.

Stock gripped her hand. "Don't—"

She touched his chest, her eyes giving assurance. "I will be back."

He took a step after her, drawn in by her wake, but stopped and sat on the damp pool rim. He rubbed his throbbing ankle, watching her disappear into the center room. His gaze shifted to the open doorway to its left. Someone lay on a bed peering out.

He stood and limped to the doorway. *Danny.* "May I come in?"

Danny's lips drew tight, his pupils shifting.

"I'm sorry about your injuries." Stock looked at the bandages on Danny's face and body. "I don't blame you for wanting to shoot me, and now, I'm grateful you did not." He bowed. "You and Roble are honorable men to have done what you did."

"What are you talking about?" Danny sucked in a breath. "I'm glad we robbed you. Now that money can help people who deserve it."

Stock stared at his swollen eyes.

"You have no right to be here." Danny gritted his teeth. "Get out."

Stock lifted an open palm.

"And stay away from Sitra, you son of a bitch."

Only the cold rush of water sounded as Stock turned to leave.

Alexandria wrapped her arm around Stock's waist, stopping him. Looking in, she said, "How are you feeling, Danny?"

He lifted his head. But seeing Stock still there, his eyes trembled before his head hit the pillow. "Stay away from her," Danny mumbled.

"Get some rest," she said, closing the door.

Alexandria took Stock's hand and led him around the spiraling pond, her bare feet moving over the wet stone.

"Will he be all right?" Stock asked as he limped by her side. "Anything that would help his recovery, I'll pay for."

"Danny's injuries are healing well. But like you and me, he carries deeper scars," she squeezed Stock's hand, "which won't heal simply with time."

Stock shook his head.

On the eastern side of the pool, they entered a passage that exited into an even bigger cavern. Light glowed from within the cave's glass walls as though they encased a sun-drenched cloud.

Stock's eyes raked across rows of dormant manufacturing robots and production equipment. *Libby Dodge*. Trapeze swings hung down in the distance between glass columns. *Sitra*. "Why is all this here?"

"Come." She pulled him through the cave, along rows of machinery, until they reached stacks of black and blueish-grey fuselage parts. Beyond them lay an extensive gymnastics mat, uneven bars, vaults, and aerial platforms, all below a trapeze apparatus.

Alexandria stepped onto the mat, stretched her arms up and bent over backward, feet pointing to the ceiling, hands holding her below.

He stared at her statuesque poise.

Bending over again, she landed her feet on the floor and continued back-bending across the mat.

He watched the stretch of her jeans, the shift of her curves beneath the sweater, and the firmness of her core pulling her through each turn.

She stopped next to a springboard, facing him. "Stock, when the laws of your own country oppress you, instead of protect you, and you are made a criminal only because you wish to live according to your own terms, you—"

"You hide underground," he whispered, lowering his head. "That is what you wanted to explain. *This* is the hole where I can cower from the world once again."

The cave fell into blackness. "No, Stock."

Stock tried to see around him, his heart racing in the silence.

A beam of light bathed Alexandria as she stood. She backflipped, landing feet first on the springboard and shot up in the air. One foot reached an elevated platform and sprang off. The other foot found another platform and launched her higher. She dove upward toward the light as if reversing gravity.

Stock staggered back, amazed at her power and composure, his mind picturing a rocket blazing up to the sky.

Clasping a trapeze bar, she hung, body taut and toes pointed. Her eyes sparked in the spotlight as she looked upon him.

He rubbed his face, remembering his vision of Sitra hovering above the entire world. An unexpected hope filled his heart now like it had then. As with the gradual warming of a new dawn, the cave walls reilluminated.

Alexandria swung back and forth, lengthening the arc until she flew across the cavern almost touching the ceiling. She released the bar into a triple-back-layout.

His eyelashes fluttered, his heart pounding within his ears as she spun end-over-end across the cave until she caught the next swing.

Pulling herself above the swing bar, she let go and dove hands first toward the mat. Spreading her arms out wide, she touched platforms passing by her sides, reversing her body into an upright position as she descended. She landed on a spring-board and launched in the air toward Stock.

Hitting the mat rolling, she stopped in front of him, pressing up into a backward facing handstand.

His chest heaved at her nearness, feeling her heat on his damp skin.

"This cave is not a place for you to hide," Alexandria said.

"I don't understand."

"Imagine, Stock, what it would feel like to work in the open among everyone else, and yet never think of asking…" one of her feet lowered and touched his chest while the other stretched straight in the air, "'is this *allowed* or do I *have to*?'" Her toes slid down his shirt to his navel and hovered.

He touched her calf, wanting to feel her skin press against his.

"But instead asking only…" she held her leg in position, torturing him, "'is this *true*, is this *good*, or is this *possible*?'"

He pulled back his hand, trying to focus on her impossible words.

"Picture a land," she said, "where the government doesn't sacrifice you to everyone else's beliefs." Her foot continued down, close to his body without touching until it found the floor. Her other foot descended, grazing along his pants until it touched the ground.

She pushed her hands off the mat and stood facing him.

"But…" he swallowed, "you told me that place doesn't exist."

"It doesn't." She touched his sides. "But every dream, when based in reality, can be made real. *This* is what I wanted to explain to you."

Trembling at her touch, he stepped back onto a jet-black aileron. "It is a beautiful vision, Alexandria. You know it's what I want, but you can't change what the world is."

"The world?" She moved close. "No." Her nose grazed his chin. "Just one spot under an open sky, in all of existence, is all we need."

His lips brushed against her hair, inhaling a crimson sunrise beyond an endless horizon. "Where would it be?"

"A seed has already been planted," she ran her fingers through his hair, "below the feet of those who claim a right to control others." She turned her back to him, pressing the length of her body against his. "And it will sprout up into a desert made fertile." Lifting onto her toes, she rubbed up his front, contracting her muscles against him, and laid her head back on his shoulder.

His chest heaved, his hands wishing to touch her body, but he held still. "Who could create such a place?"

"You know some of them." She pulled his head down so their lips almost touched. "You have seen their works. You can imagine their capabilities as you can imagine your own." Her lips parted his. "And there are others who will recognize what is possible for a free mankind." Spinning around, she faced him.

He closed his eyes. "It still just seems…seems like a fairytale… to be truly free on this earth."

"Stock, it will take time, and it will meet resistance—but so does all life in its beginning." She stepped back and waited until he opened his eyes. "And even if I were alone in my vision," she held his gaze, "you will not sacrifice what you are…to anyone." Her hands pressed against his heart. "Because I will protect you."

"Alexandria," he stepped into her, "show me your eyes."

She held still, silver irises glistening. Raising a hand before her face, she flicked away her contact lenses.

Her eyes opened, penetrating him, wrapping around his

soul—defending him. He inhaled, pulling in her strength. A ravenous desire surged within, an inexorable need to live and to touch her.

Stock clasped her wrists, pain spiking up his injured arm. His mouth went to her neck and she moaned. Following her beating artery, his lips absorbed the salty pulsations of her life.

When his mouth found her ear, her body melted into his. With his head swirling with desire and her weight against him, his injured leg buckled. He fell, pulling her with him, his back hitting the floor, and she landed on his chest. He grimaced as her hair fell over his face.

Pushing herself up, she knelt on his forearms pinning them down.

He wished to roll her off and press her to the floor, to control her body with his hands and mouth—but her black eyes held him captive. He felt her breathing, like a lioness. She slid back, ripped open his shirt, and ran her fingertips down his chest.

He trembled, watching her curves press against her sweater as she moved. With agonizing slowness, she leaned down and kissed his skin, her breasts pressing against his abs.

Unable to stop himself any longer, he rolled her onto a detached aircraft wing. She gasped, hair spilling across her eyes. Lying sprawled against the metal, her palms caressed the wing like a lover.

He straddled her waist, relishing the pain shooting through his ankle. She purred, eyelids half open, hands moving at her sides. He watched her fingertips stroking Libby's hand-forged alloy. The thought of her touching such a sublime creation, touching Libby, drove him even madder with hunger.

With his hands against her breasts, he bent down, capturing her lips. Their tongues intertwined, and he understood her thoughts, obscene in their unrepentant need.

Thrusting his hands beneath her sweater, he kneaded her hot skin. The pain in his arm and the silkiness of her body intensified his ragged breathing. She groaned at the pressure on her bruised flesh, and arched her back, pushing harder against his hands.

His insistence on her jeans promised he would offer her no escape and no mercy from what he craved. Her fingernails scraped against the aircraft wing at her sides. He forced her hands flat against the metal until she looked him in the eyes.

"Stock," she breathed.

Sometime later, their bodies lay inside an upside down, transparent canopy of a Libby Jet. He watched her face as she slept.

"This time," he whispered, his fingertips grazing along her stomach and the smooth carbon below, "you didn't leave."

Chapter 53

Danny stepped out of the elevator and shaded his sullen eyes from the sunlight.

"You finally made it up here," Roble said. "You look a little better."

"Why is Stock here?" Danny shuffled to a couch, sat down, and stared at Roble across the coffee table.

Roble resumed working on his laptop without answering.

Danny's gaze shifted to the backpack by the table. He reached for it.

Roble glanced up.

Danny slid back against the seat cushion, folding his arms. "How much did we liberate from him?"

"Nothing."

Lunging for the bag, Danny ripped it open. "That's not nothing." It sparkled like a silo of crystalline grains. "After we pay for your jet, who are we going to give all this to?" He caressed the diamonds and cleared his throat. "My father knows some worthy charities."

"All the diamonds in that pack are Stock's. Everyone else's share of them, like mine, is exactly zero."

"What? After *everything* we did? You're going to let Stock get away with this?"

"What's he getting away with?"

"This was your grand plan?" Danny smacked the top of the diamonds. "What the fuck? Why do you idolize someone like that, while ignoring everyone else who needs this money, including you?"

Roble reached into his pocket and removed a handful of colorful diamonds. "Here," he held them over the coffee table. They dropped into Danny's open palm.

"What's this?" Danny stared at the thirty or so gems, then at the backpack with thousands. "I don't want any of Stock's blood money for myself."

"Those aren't from Stock. Now I've paid you back, with interest. Donate it to the poor if that's what you want."

"If not from Stock, where did you get these?" Danny stared at his gems.

"It doesn't matter."

"So wait, Stock already *knows* you're going to return all his money, and he didn't even offer you a reward?"

"I asked you not to come along. Why did you?"

Danny flushed and stuffed the handful of diamonds in his pocket. "Maybe I thought you were going to do the right thing for once in your life. You could have become a hero. *We* could have." He stared at the pack, envisioning what his father's face would look like seeing him as a real life Robin Hood.

Roble set his laptop on the coffee table. "You wanted to talk to me the other day before all this happened." He leaned forward. "I have time to listen now."

"You never cared if my father was proud of me." Danny shook his head. "Did you?"

"Why would anyone else's opinion of you matter more than what you think of yourself?"

"You'll never understand." Danny climbed to his feet. "You're incapable of caring how others feel." He pointed at Roble's laptop. "Where would the world be if everyone thought only about material things like you?" Shifting on his feet, he swallowed and added, "It would be a hopeless place, Roble. That's what the world would be...hopeless."

Roble rubbed his nose, picked up his laptop, and continued working.

Danny watched him, exhaling. *That guy who stopped them from torturing me was right about Roble.*

He walked to the balcony and wobbled at the edge until he sunk to his knees. *Father will find out about the Marines, and when he does...* Collapsing onto his back, he draped a forearm over his eyes. *I need to redeem myself before it's too late.* He lifted his arm, turned his head, and peeked at the pack of diamonds. *I won't get another chance.*

Stock stood in hiking gear, grilling a row of beef filets, a tuna steak, and wild mushrooms in the cliff house kitchen. In between grilling, he tossed a leafy salad spiked with nuts and berries.

Roble, Nicolette, Libby, Halvern, Victor, and Gabriel sat along the kitchen bar, watching.

Flipping over the sizzling mushrooms, Stock observed the griddle fumes swirling into a pattern. *There must be a way to modify mushrooms to give them as much protein as steak.* He narrowed his eyes and turned over a filet.

Halvern scowled. "Medium rare, for god's sake."

Stock pulled the lightly seared tuna steak off the grill and placed it on Nicolette's plate. He set the filets one at a time on the other plates. "Thank you all for being here. And you, Mr. Lafayette, for giving me shelter in your home these past few days."

Victor, his chest bandaged above his chainmail leggings, nodded.

"I know some of you don't like to be thanked." He stared at Halvern. "I've never known such people as you existed, or maybe I didn't let myself see it. In any case, I'm grateful." He looked at Nicolette and dished salad onto her plate. "*Very* grateful."

"Sitra is performing again as we speak," Stock continued as he dished out mushrooms to everyone. "For protecting her life, I am in debt to some of you." He nodded at Libby and Victor. "Sitra has shown me things in *The Virtue* and elsewhere I find— what Halvern would probably call—exalting of mankind."

Everyone sat without touching their food. Libby ran a hand through her hair, her eyes on Stock.

"I'm rambling." Stock waved the grilling tongs. "Please eat."

Victor placed his hands together. "Allow me."

Everyone but Stock bowed their head. The water cascading down the front of the kitchen bar hushed the air with reverence. The solemnity of these men and women bowing sent a shiver down Stock's spine.

"Just as we all must acquire knowledge and prepare in order to elevate our own lives," Victor said, "I thank *Monsieur* Brant for acquiring and preparing this food. May each of our journeys and destinations in this life be well-deserved. Amen."

"Amen," Stock said for the first time since childhood.

Roble squirmed as Nicolette tickled him under the bar.

"Where is Mr. Sands?" Stock asked.

Roble pointed at the balcony. "He took a Calico Center tour bus to the airport yesterday to retrieve his motorcycle. We left our rides outside your hangar."

Halvern frowned. "He's not back yet?"

Roble shook his head. "I think he needs some time to be alone."

"I wish he were here. According to Gabriel," Stock said, "if Mr. Sands had revealed Sitra's secret identity, Jessy may have attacked her backstage at her show. And it may not have ended in the same way."

Roble nodded at Victor and Libby. "Thank you again for rescuing Danny."

"Alexa made it happen," Libby said. "No one can stop her from protecting what or who she values."

"You couldn't convince Mr. Sands to come with me?" Stock pointed at three large hiking packs leaning against a leather sofa.

"No, he…" Roble paused, "he said he didn't want to go with you."

"I thought maybe he would have enjoyed it." Stock turned off the grill. "I'm looking forward to getting away and living off raw land for a while, with nothing between life and death but the Earth's flora and fauna. We live amid a genetic sequence of life that is beyond wonderful, its possibilities to be crafted for our own use, endless." He looked at Gabriel. "We will learn a lot, probably more so about ourselves than anything around us."

Victor nodded. "Truly."

"If Mr. Sands isn't coming," Stock eyed Roble, "I have an extra pack loaded and ready to go. We'll be gone for months but you could join us for as much time as you can spare."

"Take Prince Charming with you," Halvern gestured at Victor. "The French love being all natural, hairy, if not stinky."

"I would fancy that, *Monsieur* Black," Victor said. "However, seeing as you are of retirement age, I'll give you the opportunity to be one with the land before you must return to it."

Nicolette covered her mouth, eyes laughing. Halvern scowled.

"It sounds like an adventure," Roble said, "but I need to start fundraising again. A hundred million dollars doesn't just sit on hiking trails. Plus, I'm still working out some details on my aircraft."

"Speaking of aircraft," Stock leaned over the bar, looking at Libby, "I seem to have lost my jet."

Staring at his plate, Roble poked a mushroom with a fork.

"And I'd like a new one," Stock said.

Roble dropped his fork and looked up.

"With the amount of diamonds I have, I'd still have more than enough money to continue my genetic research someday. Libby, do you have any more *Sovereigns* left?"

Roble glanced at her.

"Uhmm…" Libby rubbed her chin. "Nope, I'm fresh out. Sorry."

"Know anyone with something as good?" Stock asked.

Roble's eyes widened.

"Sure don't." Libby plopped a mushroom in her mouth.

Roble squirmed. Nicolette smirked.

"That's a damn shame," Stock said.

"But," Libby lifted her fork, "if you're looking for something *better* than a *Sovereign,* maybe I could refer you to someone."

Roble looked back and forth between Stock and Libby, picked up a knife and sliced across his plate, missing the steak.

"Nah," Stock said, "I never operate on hearsay."

Roble leaned in, eyes bulging. Everyone looked at him and laughed. He wiped his nose, frowning.

"I've always wanted to fly the best jet in the world." Stock folded his arms. "So tell me Roble, how much and how long would it take to build me the greatest flying craft the world has ever seen?"

Roble dropped his knife. "Are you being serious?"

"I don't want to invest in a business, mind you," he said, "just own a jet."

"I—" Roble coughed, gripping his arrowhead, and glanced at Libby, "would need almost one hundred million dollars to make it. But if you only want the jet and not ownership in future sales and technology, it's way too high of a price for just a prototype."

"And conservatively, it would take about two years to complete," Libby added.

"Too high a price?" Stock raised his brows at Libby. "How much is your very first prototype worth?"

Libby pushed a hand through her hair.

Roble turned to Libby. "Wait, what *was* your first prototype?"

"The Libby I," Halvern said, rolling his eyes as though it were obvious.

"Why haven't I seen or heard anything about it?" Roble asked.

"Only a few people have seen it," Halvern grumbled. "She only made the one and keeps the damn thing on loan in some junk picker's barn in Kansas."

"I've seen it," Stock said.

Roble coughed.

"It's about a hundred miles from where I grew up," Stock said. "I spotted it in a field as I flew over years ago. I had to land and see what it was. It's the lewdest aircraft I've ever beheld. I actually offered to buy it, but the old farmer didn't speak English, just shotgun."

"The jet in the fresco," Roble whispered, picked up his fork, and slid a piece of steak in his mouth.

"So," Stock nodded at Roble, "I'm offering to buy *your* first prototype before you fall in love with it and sentence it to life in a godforsaken barn. But I don't think I have the luxury to wait years. I'd like it in six months."

"Whoa…" Roble choked on the steak.

Nicolette slapped his back.

Roble cleared his throat. "That's such a short period of time."

Nicolette slapped his back again, only harder.

"It's technically possible," Libby said, "but it would raise the cost by about half."

"What would it be called?" Stock asked. "The Roble I?"

Libby sipped her tea. "The *Roble Arrow*."

Stock picked up a pen and wrote on a napkin: *I, Stock Brant, will pay $150,000,000 for the first* Roble Arrow *to be delivered by Roble Santos and Libby Dodge to me within six months from today.* He signed and dated the napkin and slid it in front of Roble. "I need two more signatures."

Roble's chest heaved. Nicolette slapped his back again. He picked up the pen and signed across the napkin and slid it to Libby. Nicolette grinned.

"I don't know." Libby massaged her chin. "I kinda like having the best jet aircraft in the world."

Roble rubbed his nose.

Libby laughed, eyes twinkling. "But maybe I'll learn something from this and upstage you on the next one." She signed it.

"Where are my diamonds?" Stock asked.

"They're tucked away in my closet." Roble glanced behind him. "Want me to get them?"

"No, that won't be necessary. They should fetch between three and four hundred million dollars if you sell them to the dealer I wrote down for you. Raise the cash as needed."

"Roble, I think that leaves you with a seventy-five percent ownership in future sales and technology," Libby said. "Well done. This aircraft will be beyond astounding."

Roble smiled, his glossy eyes gazing at an unseen horizon.

"Libby," Nicolette stood and draped her arms around Roble's shoulders, "you never told us the Libby I's nickname?"

"The *Acrobat*," Halvern said, finishing his salad.

The Acrobat? Stock stared at Libby, his lips parting. *So that's who you designed it after.*

Libby pushed back her hair. "Despite what everyone thinks they know, the *Sovereign* isn't my greatest creation. Some inspiration just can't be replicated."

Roble brushed the dinnerware out of his way and strewed papers and a laptop across the bar.

Stock walked to a couch and picked up a camping pack. Gabriel jumped to his feet and joined him.

"We still have an extra pack going to waste," Stock said. "Nicolette, want to have some fun?"

Nicolette massaged Roble's shoulders. "I dunno. What do you think, Roble?"

Roble's eyes raked over his drawings.

She kissed him on the ear. "Are you going to be too busy making your jet to play with me?"

Roble flipped through diagrams, one hand typing on the laptop.

"I guess I'll go with you, Stock," she said.

"What?" Roble looked up. "Go where?"

"Stock wants to know if I will camp with him for months on end. Out there," she pointed at the balcony, "on cold desert nights in cozy sleeping bags under the stars."

Roble shot to his feet, pulled Nicolette to him and kissed her for so long she laughed against his mouth.

Stock shrugged, looking at Gabriel. "Let's go." They disappeared down the elevator with the packs.

Nicolette turned Roble around and sat him back down in front of his laptop and sketches.

Libby moved next to Roble at the bar. "Where is your latest side profile diagram?"

Roble dug through the papers.

Nicolette rested her chin on Roble's shoulder and gazed at his drawings. "Did *you* do the math on those plans?"

"Most of it." He handed a diagram to Libby.

Nicolette leaned back, folding her arms. "Those are some really interesting guesses you've made."

"You could do better?"

"With the math? Easily. But I'm too busy. My coach on the other hand would probably leave me high and dry if he knew somebody was working on a project like this."

"Your coach?" Roble asked.

"Would you like me to ask Renny to help you?"

"Renny…Thatcher?" Libby dropped the diagram.

Nicolette grinned.

Libby smoothed a hand through her hair. "*The* Renny Thatcher is your tennis coach?"

"Last I checked."

Roble glanced at Halvern and raised a brow.

"What, goddammit?" Halvern scoffed. "I told you he was a coach."

"I knew your coach's last name was Thatcher," Libby said, "but I didn't make the connection. Beyond what he did at NASA, his formulas revolutionized aerospace computing software. I thought he was dead." She scratched her scalp.

"Okay, I'll ask him tonight after practice," Nicolette said, and tilted Roble's head back until he stared into her eyes. She kissed him, sucking on his lips before releasing.

Roble hunched back over the aerospace diagrams. "Victor, in Stock's underground I saw you holding some kind of laser weapon. And the pack you carried must've had some ludicrous amount of battery storage for the plasma gouger. Any chance you could help me develop a laser-powered solar sail? That would be a huge leap beyond a liquid fueled rocket engine."

"Whoa…that's…an insane idea," Libby said.

"Propulsion by laser sail…" Victor withdrew his curved pistol and walked to the balcony, hair wafting in the breeze. "To sail upon the unimagined, to discover the unseen, to glide beyond the possible without fear." He twirled the weapon. "A chance, there is, *Monsieur* Roble."

"Roble, where do you come up with this stuff?" Libby asked.

"It's just kinda obvious, isn't it?"

Libby smirked. "Yeah, in a way it really is."

"Let's get started." Roble stacked drawings into a pile. "First I'll fly to L.A. and sell some diamonds." He looked at Halvern. "Mind if I borrow your *Wyvern?*"

Libby laughed at Halvern's expression.

"What?" Roble asked. "We only have six months to get this built. We can't waste time driving around."

Libby laughed again. "You're not just trying to pilot a *Wyvern?*"

"Well, of course I am. But no, not just. I also want to visit a pilot who flies single prop tourist gigs down in San Diego. He's the only test pilot I can think of who could take my aircraft beyond the edge. I'd test fly it myself, but I won't have time to train while I'm making it."

Halvern frowned. "Use your own goddamn jet."

"I'll remove the Mach regulator for free," Roble said.

"I bet he'll even wash it for you and top off the gas," Libby said, smiling at Halvern.

"He better," Halvern said, his lips cracking a grin.

"But Roble, a light aircraft tourist pilot? Really?" Libby rubbed her forehead. "We will need the best trained test pilot in the world."

"This is the guy we need. You'll just have to trust me on this."

"I always seem to for some reason," Libby said.

"All right, Roble Santos…" Nicolette ran her fingernails along the nape of his neck. "You're busy, so I guess I'll call you tomorrow?"

Roble jumped up from the table, lifted her in his arms, and carried her down a corridor.

"Woohoo!" Nicolette yelped, raising an arm in victory. They disappeared in to a bedroom.

Halvern shook his head.

"Want to come out of architectural retirement?" Libby leaned an elbow against the bar and sipped her iced tea. "We might need a control center, a hangar, and a runway built somewhere."

Halvern glared at the diagrams on the bar. "Goddamn it, Libby. Doesn't *anyone* around here ever grow up?"

"Oh, I'm going to be so sore tomorrow." Roble sprawled naked on his back. "How'd you get so fit?"

"I like sex the same way I like tennis." Nicolette traced a tennis court across his abs. "In contested sets with me winning each tiebreak."

"I can't move."

She kissed his belly button, which doubled as a tennis court's baseline. "Poor little Roble." She sat up. "Now I need to go play my other tennis. Don't sleep in too long; I hear you've got things to do. Dangerous things." She pinched his nipple and jumped off the bed.

"Ouch."

"I'm going to find out what you're really into, and then you'll be in big trouble," Nicolette said, getting dressed. "Any old girlfriends I could call?"

"Get out of here."

She tied her hair in a ponytail. "Bye!" She skipped from the cliff house bedroom.

He rolled over, his muscles not even having the decency to wait until tomorrow to be sore. *Damn, Nicolette.* He fondled his arrowhead. *These are going to be the most sleep-deprived six months of my life.* He drifted off to sleep.

Is it AM or PM? Roble squinted at the clock across the room. Widening his eyes, he rolled off the bed. *I gotta fly to California.*

Picking up a half-filled glass of water on the dresser, he drank it in one gulp. *Danny's been gone for two days now.* A shudder poured down his spine. *What's taking him so long?* He glanced at the closet, but turned away. *Don't be ridiculous.* He peeked at the closet again, not wanting to feel so desperate to look inside. He pulled on a pair of boxer shorts and stood, staring at the clock. When he gasped for breath, he realized he hadn't taken a breath for over a minute.

He strode to the closet and peered inside, his gaze locking on the backpack nestled in the corner. It appeared full and undisturbed. Stepping closer, he rummaged through shirts, telling himself he needed to find something to wear on his trip to L.A.

With a random shirt in hand, he walked back to the dresser. He reached for the water glass and realized he'd already drank it. Seeing which shirt he held, he frowned and marched back to the closet.

As he reached for another shirt, his toes pressed against the backpack. It felt heavy and correct. He held still, wishing to feel relieved, but instead dropped to his knees and ripped open the pack. A laugh poured from his lips as he saw diamonds.

When his fingers dipped into the gems, he heard himself groan. He punched deep under the surface, sucking the thin layer of diamonds into a sea of vomit-colored corn kernels.

Shooting to his feet, eyes wide, he held his nose, wavering—almost passing out. The backpack leaned to one side and tipped over, dumping seeds across his bare toes.

He staggered from the bedroom searching the other cliff house rooms and the caves below, all the while knowing that every second he spent was beyond futile.

Ambling to the cliff house balcony in a numb daze, he strained his neck to look south at the base of a cliff. Giant split boulders lay below it. With a shudder, he looked away. *Danny...*

Chapter 54

Libby and Roble stood near the closet, gazing at the spilled corn kernels.

Victor paced the corridor outside. He stopped at the bedroom entrance and lifted a hand, his chainmail gleaming in the overhead light. "This is less than ideal."

Libby looked up, brows raised. Roble rubbed his nose.

"We shall search for *Monsieur* Danny," Victor said. "Perhaps we can rectify the situation."

Libby massaged her neck. "The police and any remnants of Jessy's henchmen are likely searching for those same stones. If Danny unloaded any into the wrong hands, searching for him would be like walking into a trap."

"I'll go," Roble said. "I have a few ideas where he might have gone."

Victor withdrew his stainless steel pistol, spun it on a finger, and reholstered. "I am not wanted by your CIA, *Monsieur* Roble. I have tracking skills. And most importantly, I have no problem dealing with…*le traitre.*"

"He's not a…" Roble started to say. "He's just…" He winced. "Don't hurt him, Victor."

"But of course I will not," Victor tilted his head. "He has already done that to himself."

"Check our former apartment," Roble said, "Jenny Beekam's, and Danny's parents' home in Idaho. I shouldn't contact any of them since they know who I am." He gripped his arrowhead. "I'm taking Halvern's *Wyvern* to Los Angeles. Danny has the address to Stock's diamond supplier. If he is going to sell the diamonds, that's his best place to go."

"I still don't understand why Danny would rob us," Libby said.

Roble shook his head and opened his mouth, but nothing came out.

"Take heart." Victor placed a fist against his own chest and strode away.

"Libby," Roble said, "I'm—"

"Don't say it." She smiled, her eyes glazed. "And Victor is right; you're a wanted man, so keep a low profile and make your trip short. It won't do us any good if you get caught and returned to detention." She held his gaze. "Are you with me on this?"

Roble exhaled and nodded.

Libby walked from the room.

Roble collapsed to the floor, his gut churning. "Danny…" The name evaporated like the diamonds.

Roble walked along a flower-lined sidewalk to the front door of a small cottage in the San Diego valley. *What am I doing here?*

He felt helpless, remembering his conversation at Gygax Diamonds in Newport Beach a few hours ago. They wouldn't give him any information at first, but after some persistence and dropping Stock's name, they admitted that someone sold a backpack full of colored, flawless diamonds to them two days ago for cash.

Glancing at the cottage tile roof and windowsill flower boxes, Roble winced. *There is no point in coming here now, and I promised Libby I'd go straight back to Vegas.* He spun around, striding away from the house.

The front door opened behind him. "May I help you?" a woman asked.

Roble whirled around, staring at an attractive, middle-aged woman in the doorway wearing a sundress. "Oh, uhmm…"

She waited, smiling.

He coughed and took a few off-balance steps in her direction. "Hi. I'm a…looking for Lieutenant Colonel Sircor."

Her eyes narrowed. "Did you fly with him in the Air Force?" Two teenage girls with long hair peeked out from behind the woman.

Just walk away. Roble cleared his throat. "You could say that."

"What's your name? I'll go get him."

Roble swallowed.

She remained attentive.

"Rob…" He shook his head. "Roble Santos."

She frowned and stepped outside, closing the door behind her. The pain in her kind eyes made him look away.

"How dare you come here," she said, barely above a whisper. "Do you have any idea what you did to Gavin?"

Roble forced himself to look at her.

"He served time in the brig for you. You ruined his career as a fighter pilot. Do you understand how much he loved it?" She raised a finger. "Do you?"

Roble opened his mouth without answer.

"Didn't you realize he had a family relying on him? Do you have *any* idea how hard it was for our daughters when they court-martialed him?"

Roble pressed the back of a hand against his nose. "Sircor is—"

"Please go." She pointed at the street. "I will never tell him you came."

"…a hero to me," Roble said, his voice diminishing with each word.

She wiped her cheek, turned, and entered the house.

Roble lowered his chin and walked away.

The next day, back in the Calico Basin, Roble stood in the water cavern staring into Danny's former makeshift bedroom.

Libby approached from behind. "Victor is back. Come," she said, and walked to the elevator.

"Unless he has Danny with him," he said, following, "I'm not sure anything he has to say will matter. Did you tell Victor that Danny sold all the diamonds?"

"Yes, but that doesn't mean he didn't come back to Las Vegas with the money."

Roble pushed the elevator call button.

"You were in California longer than I expected," Libby said as they entered the elevator. "Did you meet with your test pilot?"

"Libby…who cares. The money is gone." He slapped a hand over his face. "I'm sorry. It's just," he exhaled, "been a really bad day."

Libby squeezed his shoulder. The elevator doors opened and they stepped into the cliff house.

Victor stood near the kitchen bar wearing a suit and sunglasses, his hair slicked-back. On his lapel gleamed a *United Nations Financial Regulator* badge.

"What in the hell are you wearing, Victor?" Libby grinned, pushing back her hair. "*United Nations Financial Regulator?* Is that even a thing?"

"As far as you know, *Madame*." Victor flicked his fingers in the air. "Never underestimate the need of a smaller geographic government official to feel obligated to obey a greater geopolitical entity. Hence," he polished the badge with his sleeve, "this five Swiss franc bauble gave me the authority to interview anyone I wished."

"You are something else." Libby shook her head. "I just wish this situation was funny, Victor."

"What did you find out?" Roble asked.

Victor paced the kitchen. "The feds know Stock's diamond signature: ultra-high quality, colored, and flawless. Since the government raid on his underground, a web of surveillance monitors all locations that purchase diamonds in Las Vegas and the surrounding states—the unregistered and unlisted Gygax Diamonds in Newport Beach being the obvious exception. Danny was clever to sell to them.

"Someone ransacked your former apartment," Victor continued, "probably *le Roi's* men while they held and tortured *Monsieur* Danny. I detected no evidence the police had been there, which means the authorities don't yet know *Monsieur* Danny is connected to the missing diamonds. From my inspection of footprints atop the debris, and from the recent residue in the microwave, he likely returned to the apartment before he left town. Perhaps he needed to appropriate something?" He raised an eyebrow.

Roble scratched his head. "I don't know...clothes? Or maybe the storyboards he brought from Japan?"

"I found this in the untidiness." Victor held out a folded paper.

Roble took it and unfolded it like a delicate artifact. He studied the art cell, with eyes hopeful that after all these years the determined boy on horseback would get away from his oppressors.

"*Monsieur* Danny hasn't contacted his family or *Mademoiselle* Beekam," Victor added. "Nor has he returned to Las Vegas after selling the diamonds as far as I can determine. We could attempt to pursue him to wherever he may have sojourned; however, I have no leads at this time."

Roble shook his head. "I never should have involved him. I just thought…"

"You could help him?" Libby asked.

"No…I mean…" Roble rubbed his nose, looking at the art cell. "I thought he'd make a different choice."

Victor removed his sunglasses and suit coat.

Roble bent over, placing both hands on his knees, and swallowed hard. "I made a deal with Stock. I took his money. I owe him."

"We both made a deal with Stock," Libby said.

"My condolences." Victor walked way.

"I have to find a way to raise more funds." Roble knelt on the floor and lowered his head until it touched the floor. "I have to find…"

Libby took a breath and left for the elevator.

Chapter 55

Father, I am…Robin Hood.

Holding a mobile device, Danny typed his weekly e-mail to his father. *Marine instructing is going well with top marks. But more importantly, I'm on the verge of achieving something greater. You will be proud. Once I've accomplished it, I'll visit you and Mother to explain. Duty and Honor, Danny.*

He peered out the dusty window at the motionless ponderosa pines, a faint smile on his lips. The cabin outside Flagstaff, Arizona, sat quiet. A cuckoo clock ticked behind him, marking each second as it disappeared from existence.

Pressing a pencil tip to an artboard, Danny drew a line, having drawn nothing since Okinawa. After a few hours, he leaned back in the pinewood chair and caressed the final, completed scene of his Ritashugi storyboards. *I am finally one with my art and what Father expects—an integrated whole.*

He studied Ritashugi in the finished scene and cringed. *Something's not right…* He scratched the pencil behind his ear. *His proportions are correct, his stance perfect.*

*It's…*he swallowed hard.*…his face.*

Erasing the lines from Ritashugi's face, Danny peered out the window again. *I have to get this right. Father must think my art is as noble as what I've become for him.* The pencil trembled in his hand. *I have to…*

He stared at the faceless Ritashugi, the character who'd fulfilled his mission gallantly, taking from the rich and giving to the poor. Ritashugi stood atop a Tokyo building, above the slums and distant figures of those he'd helped.

Bricks of one-hundred-dollar bills crunched together as Danny kicked a large duffle bag below his chair. *We are the same, Ritashugi, you and I. Father will see…and be proud…proud of both of us.*

The erased lines of Ritashugi's face radiated an empty anonymity. Danny shivered. He rubbed his own face, feeling the outline of its features, imagining what a hero's countenance should look like. He held his expression and redrew the lines of Ritashugi's face.

Lifting the pencil, he stared at what he'd drawn. *Ritashugi looked...* He ran to the bathroom mirror, a pallid bulb illuminating his facial scars and frozen expression. He tried to breathe. *How could* remorse *be the price for being noble? It doesn't make sense.*

He hobbled back across the creaky wood floor and studied the final scene again. *I can't let Father see Ritashugi looking like this.* Gripping the final storyboard, he ripped it to shreds and brushed away the pieces.

Gathering all the storyboards he'd drawn in Okinawa, he reread them up to the final missing scene. *I can't believe how well drawn these are.* He exhaled, reassured, and whipped out a blank artboard.

Ritashugi sacrificed everything to help others, so maybe...maybe it is those he helped I should highlight in the final scene, not Ritashugi. And I won't have to show my...his...expression. Danny tilted his head in thought.

He drew several vignettes on the final storyboard, one for each person and group who'd received money from Ritashugi. *That's it...maybe...*

Now, what do their expressions look like? He held the pencil tip to the first face and recalled back to Phoenix, the first city where he stopped after selling Stock's diamonds. He'd felt euphoria surging through his veins as he rolled into Phoenix, like Ritashugi would have after a big hit on his way to help the needy.

Danny had parked downtown, several body-sized duffle bags full of money in the trunk. Stepping from the car, he stuffed packs of one-hundred-dollar bills into his pockets, then strolled along the wide streets ready to make a difference. *It's time for my life to mimic my art, just as Nishiko said it should.*

In a cracked-stucco alleyway wedged between a pawnshop and a cash advance store, he noticed two homeless men sitting on cardboard. *They look like they could use new clothes and a shower.* He scanned the surroundings. *But this place looks scary.* Approaching with vigilance, Danny handed each man a one-hundred-dollar bill.

The first man, longhaired and older, gasped. The second one, middle-aged and balding, bulged his eyes. "Thank you, sir."

That was easy. Danny smiled, feeling triumphant. *So that's how Ritashugi felt.* "It's the least I could do."

The balding man stood up, sending a rat scurrying out from under a newspaper.

Danny stepped back, his heart thumping with unwanted caution. *What's wrong with me? I'm helping him.*

"If you have the means," the balding man said, pointing to the seated elderly man, "his heart is failing and he could use a little help with his meds. Don't worry about me. I'm on government disability and my aunt brings me food and things."

Danny exhaled, relieved at the sincerity in the man's voice. He peeled off ten more one-hundred-dollar bills, gave one to the balding man for being honest, and nine to the older man.

"This will help so much." The elderly man pumped the cash in his fist. "You don't even know. It's a miracle."

"I just want you to know that the world isn't hopeless," Danny said, and glanced down the alleyway, spotting two more homeless people. "Some of us actually put others before ourselves."

Walking to the other end of the alley, Danny found a woman in a tie-dyed dress with a three-legged dog on her lap. A legless young man with tattoos sat next to her. *These two could use some serious help.* He dug into his pocket, removed a brick of cash, and counted out two thousand dollars each.

"Whoa…" the young man grasped the money. "God bless you."

The woman stuffed her share down her dress and glanced at the two prior recipients who had followed Danny. He spun around, hands covering his pockets, hating the alarm permeating his bones on such a noble occasion.

"I don't mean to be rude," the balding man said, his voice courteous, while helping the elderly man limp closer. "But I think he needs just as much assistance as them." He nodded at the wad of cash in the legless man's hand.

"Oh," Danny uncovered his pockets, ashamed at his own defensiveness. "I didn't even think about keeping it equal." He peeled off one thousand dollars and handed it to the elderly man.

"Well," the woman touched her friend's shoulder, "Ethan is actually worse off than anyone here. So I think he could use extra. And it's not for me, but Duchess is a rescue dog. Aren't you,

Duchess?" She kissed the dog's nose. "She has a liver condition and the drugs are more costly than you would think."

The balding man reached down and petted Duchess. "Cutest little dog ever."

"I think what I gave each of you is a lot," Danny mumbled, thinking of how much money he lived on in Las Vegas. "How much more do you need? Ethan and the dog, I mean?" He counted out more bills, while eyeing the balding man with his peripheral vision.

"Oh, just anything you can spare, really." The woman watched Danny stop counting. "But," she added, batting her lashes, "another two thousand each would go a long way."

Seeing the balding man inch nearer, Danny twisted his body, holding the money away. "Please don't get too close. I'm here to help, but I don't know you."

The man stepped back, and coaxed his elderly companion closer. "He could probably get off the streets altogether for another, I dunno, five or six thousand dollars. I mean if you have that kind of money. If not, that's fine too."

Danny rubbed his forehead, looking at everyone around him, trying to calculate how much to give each. *Do I donate according to what I think they need?* He winced at the difficulty of the math. *Should I give to them equally? Or just hand them what they ask for?* He exhaled. *What would Ritashugi do?*

Another man approached from the main street. His tattered overalls hung loose over a stained t-shirt, but he possessed a taut posture and well-combed hair.

Danny studied him, trying to determine how much he needed as well. *This is getting complex.*

"I'm willing to work." The new arrival pointed at the money in Danny's sweaty hands. "What do you want me to do for you?"

Danny pursed his lips. "Uhm… I don't have any work. This is just me…giving back."

The man in overalls glanced back at the main street with its rows of parked cars. "If you have a car, I'll wash it for fifty bucks. Even clean out the inside too." He lifted a sullied hand. "I figure if I can wash two cars a day, I'll be able to save enough to get an apartment."

"I believe this is just for those who need it." The balding man glared at the new arrival. "This good man," he pointed at Danny, "is not looking to get something in return. So why don't you move along?"

The man in overalls looked at Danny, awaiting an answer.

"He's right, I don't want anything for myself," Danny said. "But I'll give you a hundred bucks if you need it." He held out a crisp bill.

"Of course I need it," the man said. "Was I talking Chinese or something?" Shaking his head, he walked away.

Then why didn't he take it? Unease swirled in Danny's gut as he replaced the bill atop the stack.

"I apologize for that jerk. Don't let him get to you," the balding man said. He lifted the elderly man's hand and opened it palm up before Danny.

"You can wait your turn," Ethan said. "She asked first."

Danny wiped the sweat off his brow, feeling everyone's eyes on him. *I know this is what Ritashugi would do, but why do I feel so uncomfortable?* He coughed and peeled off a few dozen one-hundred-dollar bills, stacking them on the elderly man's palm as the others watched. He handed the woman and Ethan two thousand dollars more each, and turned to leave, not feeling as heroic as he had hoped.

"When are you coming back?" the woman asked.

Danny walked faster until he heard the woman scream and her dog yelping. Glancing back, his heart thumping in his chest, he saw the balding man sprint away. *What happened?* With adrenaline surging, he ran back to the others.

"He stole all my money," the older man said, his hands shaking.

"Dammit!" Danny lunged after the man, but stopped and slapped a hand against his own forehead, wondering how it would look if he took money from the homeless. *What would Ritashugi do?*

"Thanks for chasing him off," Ethan said.

The woman calmed her dog with kisses.

"I thought he was my friend." The elderly man lowered himself to the ground.

Searching his pockets, Danny extracted his remaining bundle of one-hundred-dollar bills and placed it on the elderly man's lap. "Here, don't ever get near that guy again."

The woman and Ethan lifted their eyes, staring at him.

Danny patted his pockets. "That's all I have on me." He slunk away to the main street.

"When are you coming back?" the woman asked again.

A drop of Danny's sweat hit the storyboard in the cabin, blurring a faceless woman Ritashugi had helped. He moaned. *I can't draw those faces. This final scene needs to look noble…not helpless.* He glanced at the sweat rings below his armpits.

He pulled out receipts from the duffle bag and shuffled through them. Luckily, the homeless hadn't been his only beneficiaries. After he'd left downtown, he had driven to the Phoenix suburbs, figuring a novice hero needed practice—maybe with something more organized and less gritty.

He found masses of people walking through a park with banners hung between trees and along tables, some sort of walk to fight cancer. Approaching a table, he set down a ten-thousand-dollar cash brick.

The woman behind the table, with rosy hair and rosier cheeks, flashed a smile and filled out a form.

"I don't need a receipt," Danny said. "I'm just trying to be part of the solution."

"Oh," she smiled again, holding it longer this time. She gathered up the cash and placed it in a metal box.

Danny waited, brows raised.

"Thank you. Your donation is very much appreciated." Looking around Danny's shoulder, she added, "But would you mind moving just a bit so I can get everyone's donation before the walk starts?"

His brows sank. He went to his car and pulled out an armful of cash bricks. Returning to the table, he piled them into a pyramid.

"Wow." The woman's cheeks reddened a shade darker. "That is a lot."

He held back his grin, straightening his stance.

"This will be a great help with the research." She glanced around, eyes wide. "But wouldn't you rather write a check for so much?"

"I'm just glad to make a difference."

"I'm sure they'll want your name in the annual brochure for donating so generously."

"A name for the brochure…?" Danny leaned over the table.

"Yes, write a receipt out to Donald Sands and put him in the brochure for…" he glanced at the banner, "to fight breast cancer or whatever this is."

"The breast cancer walk is in the next park. This is for pancreatic cancer," she said, inhaling. "It's a terrible disease, with no approved cure. My father died of it last month. With your donation I'm hoping we'll be a step closer to finding a legal cure." She wiped a hand across her cheek and wrote out a receipt.

Danny held the receipt, staring at the woman, trying to envision how his father might react when he learns of this altruistic act. But the next donor pushing past him with impatience tarnished his appraisal. He returned to his car, extracted more cash and strode across the street to the other charity walk.

The man behind the table counted out the bills, slapping them into piles in quick succession. "I can't believe it. That's…one hundred thousand dollars. I've never seen such a large donation. Uhmm…do you need a receipt for taxes?"

"Make it out to Donald Sands," he said. "Are you here because you know someone with breast cancer?"

"Who doesn't, right? My family has been helping out with the cause for three generations. Almost forty years."

"Forty years? And they still haven't found a cure?"

Patting the stack of cash, the worker said, "They're working night and day on it, I'm sure."

Danny swallowed and nodded.

"Thanks for the donation." The man handed him a receipt. "Have a really nice day."

The clock in the cabin counted down behind Danny, his life evaporating in even increments. He stared at the faceless recipients on the storyboard. *I can't draw the charity workers either, their faces are not—I don't know…confident enough or…triumphant enough or something?* He tore up the final storyboard again and pressed his forehead against the scraps.

Touching the charity receipts by his hand, he sat up, flipping through them again. His eyes widened, reading his father's name.

Maybe Ritashugi had a father who never thought he would amount to anything. Maybe his father discovers how noble he became and stands before him, like a royal samurai knighting a hero ninja.

He gazed out the window. *Now that's an ending. It almost makes up for the rest of the story.* He rose and took a breath, before sitting back down, shifting in the seat to get comfortable. *Yes…this might accomplish everything.*

Laying out another blank artboard before him, his hand shook. *I need to finish this before Father discovers what happened in the Marines.* Gripping a pencil with a white knuckle, he drew Ritashugi's father as a samurai holding a sword. He sketched the son kneeling before the father, both solemn in their poses. He studied the scene, the hazy Tokyo skyline as a backdrop. *This is almost good…* His heart fluttered. *No, this is good.*

Now, to draw their faces. The pencil hovered over the father's blank oval. He envisioned Donald's face as he sat on the couch in Pocatello as Danny left for the Marines. The pencil fell to the board.

The clock ticked away like a time bomb.

Lurching back, he stood up, the chair tumbling to the floor. He hefted the duffel bag and thrust his hand into the cash bricks, shuffling through them. He exhaled. *It's okay. I can buy time until I get this scene right. I have time to make Father proud of me as a hero, and as an artist.*

He gathered up his storyboards and receipts, stuffed them in the bag, and left the cabin.

Chapter 56

Libby sat at a stone desk gazing out a narrow window. Water trickled along two floor troughs next to her feet. She lifted a phone, pressed a buzzard icon, and held it to her ear.

"Hello?" Frederick Compros mumbled over the line, his mouth full, fingers smacking in the background.

"I'm..." Libby said under her breath, her heart skipping a beat, "...willing to sell."

"Libby Dodge," labored breathing distorted the phone speaker, "so good to hear from you."

Pressing a hand against her heart, she asked, "How much will DCU pay for the rights to produce my jets?"

He cleared his throat, lowering his voice. "You're actually prepared to sell me the production rights...to make Libby Jets?"

"The payment must be an upfront lump-sum, not a royalty stream. What's your offer?" Libby asked, wincing at her own words.

"Well," Frederick said, trying to sound somber but was betrayed by the giddiness in his voice, "as you know these are difficult times in the industry. Nobody is expanding or making acquisitions. We're in cost-cutting mode. The price of our jets drops every year."

"That's because you're selling antiques."

"Don't..." He coughed. "When is the last time you sold a jet, Libby?"

She gripped her hair, knowing he knew she hadn't manufactured one in three years.

"How do you expect me to peddle the idea of buying the production rights from a nonproducing, bankrupted company to my board?" he asked.

"Frederick, just," Libby tried to catch her breath, "make me an offer."

He smacked the top of his mouth with his tongue a few times. "Maybe if I pulled a few strings I could squeeze out say… twenty million for you."

Libby shook her head.

"Reality's a bitch—didn't you say something like that once? You should have sold years ago."

"A foreign buyer will pay much more than twenty million."

"The US government," his fist slammed a desk on the other side of the line, "will never allow you to transfer advanced technologies to a foreign producer. You know that damn well."

"Do I?"

A palm squeaked across glass over the line. "All right, don't be hasty," he said. "You're selling the production rights to the *Wyvern*, the *Succubus, and* the *Sovereign*?"

The phone trembled in Libby's hand. "To those three. Yes."

"How much do you want?"

"More than you'll ever be worth." She squeezed her eyes shut. "Just give me two hundred million."

"Let me remind you, those designs are on the Department of Defense and FAA shit lists. Nobody is going to pay more than seventy-five for that gamble, not even foreigners, if they can even remember you made jets."

Libby pulled her hair until it hurt.

"But you know," he said, "I've always thought of you as a daughter and I want the best for you. Let me save you the trouble of shopping it around. One hundred million, cash."

I've already called everyone else who might've been interested in the rights. Libby exhaled. "I need more, Frederick."

"You wouldn't even sell me a used tire off a landing gear before today—not for all the money in the world." His grin leaked through the phone line. "Now you're begging me?"

She lowered her forehead to the desk, wishing she could hang up.

"So you want DCU to overpay for the rights to make toys for the rich when so many in the world are suffering?" Frederick asked. "What would people say if it cut into our charitable donations?"

"Frederick, I will not say this again." She gripped the phone. "Offer me one hundred and seventy-five million for the production rights…or *hang up*."

The sound of a suit flapping against resistance and excited breathing filled the phone line as though someone jumped in the air, feigning punches. "I had no idea today would turn out so well. Consider your jets…in my hands."

Libby tried to breathe. She coughed and forced out the words, "I'll send over the contract and funding instructions."

"You know, my grandfather always used to say—"

Libby tossed the phone.

The next day, Libby shuffled *Roble Arrow* diagrams across the kitchen bar in the cliff house. *This thing still blows my mind.*

Roble sat on a couch holding a laptop. "Libby, what are the odds of partnering with a foreign aerospace company or," he rubbed his nose, "or maybe DCU to manufacture the *Arrow*? We'd lose control of the design but at least it would get made."

"You're not giving anyone access to your idea." Libby pressed a wild-haired Einstein icon on her phone and lifted it to her ear. "Hold on one second, Roble, I need to make a call."

"Hello," a sedate voice answered, almost drowned out by a drilling noise in the background.

"Siggy." Libby's eyes brightened. "I have a job for you." She lifted a drawing of the *Roble Arrow*.

"I can't talk right now, Ms. Dodge. I'm in class."

Libby scrunched her brows. "Class?"

"I teach high school shop."

Libby dropped the schematic to the counter. "You turned down the head of hypersonic development at DCU to babysit outcasts with chains hanging from their belt loops?" She laughed. "Oh my gosh, I can almost picture it. Where?"

"Cedar City, Utah."

"I adore that little town." She smiled, looking at the balcony. "Listen, what would it take to steal you away from a high school?"

"Depends. What are you doing?"

"A new aircraft." She smoothed out a drawing.

Roble looked up, his eyes widening.

"You're not still banned by the Department of Defense?" Sigmund asked.

"I am, but—"

"The FAA doesn't still hate you?"

"Well yeah, I guess, but—"

"And the bankruptcy?"

"Jiminy P. Christmas, Sigmund P. Evert," Libby slapped the bar, "ignore those petty details for a moment and ask me what it is."

"The Libby V?" he droned, like it were obvious.

"No, not my design."

"Whose?"

She looked at Roble. "Roble Santos'."

Roble jumped to his feet, hands gripping his laptop.

"You mean the kid in Japan who got us into all the trouble?" Sigmund asked.

"Uh, well, yeah, but no not *all* of the trouble, and that's not the point." She walked to the secluded balcony, peering across the desert blotched with shadows from clouds.

Roble raised a hand as though requesting to ask a question in class.

"Where's the kid been all this time?" Sigmund asked.

"In jail, but don't worry—"

"Jail? Is that where you want to end up?"

"Well, no—"

"How are you funding it?"

"It's all lined up, Siggy. Don't worry about the funding."

Roble widened his eyes and set the laptop on the couch.

"What kind of aircraft is it?" Sigmund asked.

"Well let's see…" Libby gazed down to her former Libby House office balcony. "A top atmospheric speed of escape velocity using staged SCRAM, a—"

"What? SCRAM…for escape velocity?"

"Exciting, right?"

"And I suppose you have a decade to develop it?"

"Roble already figured it all out, well mostly figured it out. We should be done in six months." She looked up, scanning the distant Vegas skyline. "Hello? You still there, Siggy?"

Roble took a few steps toward Libby.

"This is suboptimal," Sigmund groaned.

Libby pressed the phone to her ear. "What? I can't hear you over that bell. Do you need to get back to class, or is that a fire alarm?"

"I'm being pulled over for exceeding the posted speed limit."

Libby almost dropped the phone off the balcony. "Did you ditch class right when I called, or did you at least wait until I mentioned jail?" She laughed. "Oh, man."

"I'm glad someone is enjoying this."

Wiping her eyes, Libby cleared her throat and said, "Now, once you get here, hire back all our best engineers, but only the ones we can trust to stay quiet. And make sure you get some quantum computing specialists. Oh, and I'm going to need the model rocket engine guys too, just in case Victor can't figure out the laser sail. Are you getting all this?"

"Hello officer," Sigmund said, his voice muffled.

"Tell him to lecture you for talking on the phone while driving," Libby said, "that's unsafe."

"Yes, officer, I realize there is a speed limit in Utah. Here…"

Libby turned to Roble and pointed at the phone with a smirk.

Roble returned an awkward smile, his brows furrowed.

"Ms. Dodge, he went back to his car to write the traffic violation," Sigmund said. "So, how do you expect me to rehire everyone? They've all moved on to other opportunities."

"Offer them *whatever* it takes. I'm paying cash, nothing on record."

"You can start by paying my speeding ticket."

"That's your fault for driving a car slower than the police." Libby winked a Roble.

"Let's just talk when I get there. Uhhh, no officer, I wasn't speaking to you…"

Libby hung up the phone and faced Roble.

"What are you talking about?" Roble flung his hands in the air. "What money?"

"I acquired some."

"From where?"

"All you need to understand is that Stock ordered your jet from us and he's going to get it. Are you still on board?"

Roble twirled his arrowhead between his fingers, shaking his head. "You're…amazing, Ms. Dodge. I don't know what more to say." Staggering back, he collapsed on a couch. "I've never been so relieved, and in need of a long nap, in my life."

"No napping. This is going to happen, so get back to your design." Libby pointed at his laptop. "Victor will set up the manufacturing cave to our specifications within a couple of weeks. That should give us just enough time to finalize the design plans and integrate the computing requirements."

"Wait," Roble scratched his head, "why won't you tell me where you got the money?"

She gazed at the desert basin, ignoring his question. "If we manufacture in triple shifts, I don't see why we can't have the parts done in three months. Still," she scratched her head, "we need a hangar for assembly and a runway for testing. The fact that you're some kind of fugitive, and I'm just plain banned from making jets, means we'll need some place…off the radar, but still close."

Roble studied the crystal formations in his arrowhead. "I know a place like that, but it might not have the best runway or even a hangar."

"All we need is some accessible, but unassuming land. Halvern can build any facilities we might require. Where are you thinking?"

"I'll tell you if my idea works." He sat up. "How much money do you have to spend on the hangar and runway?"

"Whatever seems reasonable. I have enough."

"Mind if I borrow the truck at the ranch stable?"

"Knock yourself out."

"I'll go tomorrow." Roble glanced at his laptop. "I need to finish this wing redesign and get it into computer wind-tunnel simulations." He slapped his cheeks with both hands and stared at Libby. "You found a way to fund it."

When Libby retired to her room that night, she discovered a handwritten document on her desk chair. The single sheet of paper, signed by Roble Santos, forfeited all design, technology, and ownership rights in the *Roble Arrow* over to Libby Dodge.

She sat down on the edge of her bed, the paper in one hand, and pushed through her hair with the other. *Our decisions define us, my friend.*

Chapter 57

Roble drove a dented truck along a tumbleweed-lined road, its tires crunching against gravel. Cranking the steering wheel, he pulled to a stop in front of the Paiute Tribal Smoke Shop.

Inside, shelves spread out below sun-bleached displays, the aroma of tobacco in the air. A round-faced man stood behind a cash register.

"Is there an airstrip around here?" Roble asked.

The man rolled tobacco in his lower lip without answering.

Roble raised his voice. "Does the tribe have an airport?"

"Who's asking?" The man wiped his mouth.

"Uhhh…" Roble glanced around the empty shop.

The man narrowed his eyes. "You Paiute?"

"From what I've been told."

He pointed at a wall stacked with beer cases. "You'll find him over there."

Roble twisted around. "Find who?"

"The airstrip. Look for the antenna." The man spit in a cup.

"Oh," Roble said, both relieved and confused, "thanks." He purchased a salted nut roll and left.

A golf course rolled along the sides of the road as he drove away from the shop. After passing the lush landscape, he swung onto a rutted street. Lines of tiny cinderblock homes with dirt yards created a maze before him.

He glanced back at the smoke shop and then in the direction the man had indicated. An antenna stretched to the sky below the Spring Mountains.

He traversed a sagebrush field on a bumpy path beyond the homes, tires whipping dust in the air. At the trail's end he found the antenna bolted to a dirty white shack. An old single prop airplane sat nearby on worn-out asphalt.

Parking in front of the shack's dilapidated screen door,

Roble leaned from the window, staring at a century-old Indian motorcycle.

He stepped down from the truck and circled the motorcycle, wanting to touch it. Instead, he scanned for its owner. Seeing no one, he caressed the faded red and gold gas tank, tracing its lettering. He lurched back when he spotted a rattlesnake intertwined in the frame, its head recoiled below the handlebars. After a few breaths, he realized the snake was carved of wood and patted its smooth head.

Sensing eyes on his back, he turned and faced the outline of a man behind the screen door. Roble saluted out from his chest in greeting. He'd neither made the gesture before nor remembered where he'd learned it. The man didn't respond.

"Hello, sir. I'd like to inquire about using this airstrip." Receiving no answer, he took a step closer. "Are you in charge of the airfield?"

The door creaked open, revealing a man with a wrinkled face, long black hair streaked with grey, and observant eyes. "Come in," he said, his voice deep and crackly.

The cinderblock shack held a desk cluttered with radio equipment, a frayed polyester chair, a few books, and many empty beer cans. A hole in the wall led to a closet with a narrow bed and a small TV sitting below it.

"You came only looking to use the airstrip?" The man motioned for him to sit.

Roble remained standing, staring at the man's face. "A hangar as well."

"We don't have a hangar." He glanced at Roble's necklace. "You a pilot?"

Roble nodded, touching his arrowhead.

"They call me Longbow," the man said.

Roble shuffled his feet, hesitant to give out his real name. "I'm Rob."

"May I see your arrowhead…Rob?"

Roble gripped it without answering, surprised at his own quick response.

Longbow stared for a moment, turned, and looked out the screen door. "Why do you wish to use the airstrip?"

"To assemble and launch a jet. No one outside of here must

know about it. My business associate can compensate you for the use, and for the confidentiality."

"The Chief won't support any activities deemed antagonistic to the US government," Longbow cleared his throat, "especially by non-Paiutes."

Roble exhaled, scratching his nose.

"However," Longbow said, "by treaty, this *is* sovereign land." He glanced again at Roble's necklace. "I'm being presumptuous, but if you were to register as a member of the tribe and live here, the Chief would be obligated to protect you and you could fly your jet. Does that interest you...Rob?"

He shook his head, caressing his arrowhead. "Joining a tribe does not interest me."

Longbow opened the screen door.

Roble rubbed along his pant legs, too desperate to leave.

"All right, man without a tribe," Longbow said, studying him, "what's your offer to use this airstrip? Maybe I'll speak with the Chief on your behalf."

"Please tell him that we need exclusive use of this airstrip for six months, his vow of secrecy, and his protection. In return, we offer to build a state-of-the art hangar, a new runway, and a paved access road."

"Hmmm..." Longbow flicked loose paint off the screen door. "Our annual tribal budget is two million dollars short this year."

"What if we offered a million cash, plus the improvements?"

"Come back in a few days." He pushed the screen open wider.

Roble nodded and walked out to the truck. Glancing back, he saw Longbow salute out from the chest.

Victor, clad in dark chainmail, hair pushed back over his ears, marched into the glass-walled manufacturing cavern from the waterfall cave.

Sigmund followed behind with a notebook, explaining in detail which aircraft parts needed to be made and in what order. Victor ran his hands along robots and machines, nodding and making suggestions about potential assembly positions. After a few hours, Sigmund finished a rough sketch of a manufacturing layout.

Walking onto the gymnastics mat, Victor climbed the uneven bars and sat, balancing on top. "The forge shall be set up over there." He pointed at the northern wall.

Sigmund made the addition to his layout sketch.

An open-top vehicle rolled down the ramp into the cave from the ranch stable. Libby and Halvern jumped from the back seat, Renny exited from the front, leaving Guardo to drive it back out.

"Roble just called," Libby yelled. "The Paiute Chief accepted the proposal. We have our assembly hangar and runway."

"Not yet we haven't," Halvern grumbled. "We have a barren piece of wasteland in the middle of nowhere." He kicked the scuffed glass floor. "Once I'm done with it, *then* we'll have a hangar and a runway."

Libby poked an imaginary dot in the air. "Indeed-a-roo."

"And get the hell down from there!" Halvern shouted at Victor. "What do you think this is, Cirque du Soleil?"

Sigmund walked off the mat and pushed his way between Libby and Halvern to grip Renny's hand. "Dr. Thatcher, it is a great honor."

"Oh, that is very kind of you." Renny shook his hand. "I've waited a long time to find another project like this."

"We'll have a full crew working down here in days, and three shifts within a week," Sigmund said, turning to Libby. "To conceal our activity, most will live in the caves and I've disguised a cattle truck to shuttle in the remainder."

"I'd like to keep Stock informed of the progress." Libby glanced around. "Is he still camping with Gabriel?"

"That he is," Victor said, approaching.

"How long were they going for?"

Victor flicked a wrist into the air. "One cannot rush a decent outing."

"Sounds French enough." Halvern rolled his eyes. "Next time, join 'em instead of tromping your stinky French feet around Alexa's mat."

"Perhaps you will bring a bottle of *Domaine Leroy Musigny* so we may enjoy our own outing together, my romantic friend," Victor said, keeping a straight face.

Halvern scowled.

"To each his own." Libby jumped on a manufacturing robot and climbed to its highest point. She gazed across the manufacturing cavern like a giddy ten-year-old girl, or a miser from the industrial revolution. "Gentlemen, let us begin."

Reflective shimmers washed over Roble as he jogged from the water cave into the glass manufacturing cave.

He sped past lines of robotic arms twisting and spinning in rhythmic motions, dodged unmanned carts delivering parts between machines and workers, and gave high-fives to men and women orchestrating the manufacturing process at computer terminals.

He came to a stop behind Libby who hammered an alloy billet on an anvil. Fire growled in the nearby forge as Victor compressed the bellows.

"Where's that extra metallurgical hammer?" Roble mumbled, searching through a rack of tools.

Libby's sweaty hair flew back as she glanced at him. "Done with the final design revisions?"

"Yes and I've run all the calculations by Dr. Thatcher." Roble rolled up his sleeves, inhaling the delicious forge fumes, his eardrums pulsing with mechanical cheers. "I can't believe we're actually making this thing." Locating a pair of tongs instead of a hammer, he gripped Libby's glowing alloy and turned it on its side. "Did you find a test pilot yet?"

She struck the ingot. "I've interviewed a few, but this flight is so unique I'm not sure we'll be able to find someone with all the skills we need. What about your guy in San Diego? You sure he can't do it?"

"I'm…" Roble winced and rolled the tongs, "pretty sure."

"Damn. Well, I'll keep looking." Sparks burst from the metal. "How are Longbow and Halvern working together?" she asked, between blows. "Any better?"

"You should've seen them arguing yesterday about the airstrip layout." Roble flipped over the smashed alloy. "Like a pair of geriatric mules speaking in two-word sentences. They should've just skipped to blows and saved time."

"*Monsieur* Black must really like *le Amerindien*." Victor stoked the forge. "I've rarely seen him so betrothed."

"I bet nobody has said '*le Amerindien*' and 'betrothed' in back-to-back sentences since 1796." Libby laughed.

Roble squinted as embers exploded off the billet. He rolled it over again with his tongs. "I've been on the design and assembly end of things most of my life, but this manufacturing stuff is fun."

"It's ridiculously fun." Libby smashed the alloy with an accelerated swing. "But they are behind in lathing the interior struts, spars, and ribs at station six. I've got this. Why don't you go put us back on track?"

Roble stepped away and hung the tongs on the rack. "All right, but I'm going to help pour the leading edges." Pointing at Libby, he said, "Don't let her do those without me, Victor." Rolling down his sleeves, he jogged to station six.

Two days later, Roble assisted Libby with the molten pour of a leading wing edge. Steam simmered up from the metallic ooze like a curtain between their bodies.

"Oh…" Roble shivered, trying to concentrate after feeling lips kiss the back of his neck. He finished the pour and turned. "You're tasty when wet," Nicolette said.

He wiped his dripping forehead. "You don't see me sneaking up and sucking on your neck when you're playing tennis do you?"

"I know," Nicolette pouted. "Why not?"

Roble coughed. "Come on." He grabbed her by the hand. "I can take a short break."

"Hello, Nicolette," Libby said as they walked away.

Nicolette lifted a hand in the air and called out, "Hello, Ms. Dodge."

"What brings you here?" Roble asked as they neared a quieter section of the glass manufacturing cave.

"Why didn't you tell me your 'friend' stole Stock's diamonds?"

"Uhhhh…" Roble winced.

She tapped her foot, frowning.

"There is nothing you could've done anyway."

"Stock's only means to fund his future creations are gone

He promised to make me a new variety of pine trees someday. It really upsets me."

Roble lowered his head and wiped his face.

"I'm not mad at you. I know he basically stole from you as well." She took his hands into hers. "I'm just tired of people thinking Stock owes them something."

Roble squeezed her hands and looked up.

"At least I heard you found a way to fund Stock's jet." She exhaled. "Where did you get the money?"

"Libby acquired the funds but she won't talk about it, which tells me she must've sold something she really cares about." He let go of one of Nicolette's hands and rubbed the back of his neck. "I just hope the *Arrow* is a success someday so she can recoup whatever she gave up."

Nicolette glanced across the cavern at Libby. "When does Stock get back from his camping trip?"

"Not for months, I guess…like he said. He didn't take a phone or anything."

She pecked him on the cheek. "Sorry for the distraction. Once Halvern told me the news about the diamonds, I just had to come and see you." Slapping him on the rear end, she added, "Get back to work."

He gripped her arm and pulled her against him. "You can't just kiss me when I'm making a jet, you know. Now I'm all hot and bothered."

"Hmm…interesting." She grinned. "From the jet? Or from my lips?"

Roble swallowed.

Reaching down, she picked up an alloy aerospace part with a rounded end and two holes drilled into it. "This looks like it might come in handy." She winked at him. "Wanna find out?"

He pulled her by the hand to the water cave.

"Woohoo," Nicolette whispered, raising the part above her head as they walked.

"Just promise you'll leave me with enough strength to work the rest of the day."

"Okay." She swung the metal part down as if serving a tennis ball. "We'll only play three sets like women. But that means I get to call the shots."

Chapter 58

Camera bulbs flashed across the Paris stadium as Jordon Taylor pressed the silver championship bowl to his lips. He lowered it, absorbing the prolific kindness of the lights and applause—until he spotted a white flag with writing on it waving in the upper stands. It fluttered in the section Nicolette had climbed to and thrown cash upon the crowd two years ago.

It read—*Who is #1?*

"How does it feel to finally win the Paris Open and complete your long-sought-after grand slam?" the tournament announcer asked Jordon.

Jordon's eyes remained on the flag.

"Ehm…." The announcer wobbled the microphone.

Without smiling, Jordon said, "These four major tournaments are the ones that count. Nobody can question that fact."

"Well of course not. Congratulations. You are the best in the world."

Jordon blinked. "No, it is my fans who are the best." Looking away from the flag, he forced a smile.

Tennis fans had expected Nicolette to return to the major public tournaments after her one-year ban, but she hadn't, already skipping both the Melbourne and Paris Opens.

Jordon felt relieved, but wished fans would stop talking about her. He laughed every time they asked, "Have you played Nicolette in Las Vegas?" the kind of laugh that skids at the end like raw skin across hard court.

When the number four seeded player, Emilio Estrella, played at Nicolette's Las Vegas house a month before the Paris open—and lost to Nicolette in three sets in a tournament final—even the Hollywood entertainment press descended on her front yard requesting access to the games. But Nicolette admitted no media, saying they could pay to watch the private matches on web cameras just like everyone else.

After a TV sports program announced that Nicolette had reached the unofficial number one woman's ranking in the world, Jordon's publicist, Rick, called the station and yelled, "Nicolette Popov didn't even *attend* the Paris Open! How could she be number one?"

The station manager insisted that they'd used journalistic restraint because the ranking calculation—which now included private tournament results due to fan requests—also placed Nicolette above all the men players.

Rick slammed the phone down.

On the way to his hotel from the Paris trophy ceremony, Jordon glared at chalk scrawled in French on the sidewalk. *Nicolette is #1. Chicken, Jordon?* He rubbed his foot across the chalk, smearing the words.

A young boy snickered at Jordon's flailing leg, yelling, "*Poule.*"

At his hotel room, Jordon called Rick and set up a press conference for the next day.

Jordon sat wearing a wide grin and white cardigan with his ten major tournament trophies spread along a table. A microphone and a row of cameras formed his audience.

"As a beneficiary of this great sport, I'm here today to give back, and to offer this same opportunity to another player, a player who up until now has shirked her social responsibilities. I will donate one million dollars to Nicolette Popov's favorite charity, assuming she has one, if she wins a match against me. In return, I challenge her to pledge the same amount should I win. I will play for the Children for Universal Hope. If she accepts, no matter who wins, the victory will be for tennis and for all of society."

Over the next several days, Jordon interviewed with international media outlets, accepting their praise for the challenge. Overnight, everyone trumpeted his status as the number one player instead of questioning it.

A longtime deodorant sponsor announced with fanfare that they would match Jordon's one million dollars to Nicolette's favorite charity, should she win. In private they told Rick: "Jordon is a genius. This is the best free publicity we will ever receive."

When Nicolette failed to respond to the challenge, the media circulated questions about whether professional players should be compelled to play for charities to uphold the dignity of their sport. TV stations and websites conducted audience polls.

After another week with no response, the questions about Nicolette's character morphed into wholesale rumors. The story that stuck—with the help of several dated magazine photos of Nicolette and Stock Brant sitting by a pool—claimed that she'd become a drug addict and lived on the lam with her fugitive boyfriend. One sports channel ran a special program showcasing all the washed-up athletes who became drug addicts.

At a Sydney Osaka Sushi restaurant in London, Jordon delivered an impromptu speech regarding the proposed charity tournament, signed autographs, and paid for all the guests' dinner tabs. The incident—filmed and posted to several social websites—spread like a wave of goodwill across the face of the earth.

Standing atop a London hotel balcony, Jordon waved at the fans below, having predicted Nicolette would reject his altruistic challenge. But what he hadn't anticipated was the political windfall of her ignoring his dare altogether. Her miscalculation ballooned into his wildest dream—him being loved as a humanitarian and her being abandoned on a deserted island of her own ego.

When his cell phone rang, he placed it to his ear, smiling at his fans beneath the balcony.

"Turn on the TV. Channel fifteen." Rick's tone suggested some type of unspeakable disaster.

Jordon ran into the room to the television.

On the screen, Nicolette stood under the former marquee of *The Sin* as it towered above a tennis court in her backyard. She wore ripped jeans over metal studded boots. Straight hair hung in front of a black t-shirt, her big eyes watching the jostling news cameras.

"I am extremely pleased to receive Jordon Taylor's offer to play tennis for charity." She glanced at the marquee. "However, I believe it falls well short in its potential to do good. If I am to play for those in need, I don't wish to pledge a million dollars or even two—but every dime I own, my entire net worth of forty-seven million dollars. I will give it all to The Children for Universal Hope if Jordon wins the match. If I win, I expect the same amount, paid in cash, to what I designate as a charity."

Stretching her arms wide, she added, "If giving is good, then giving everything down to one's last bread crumb must be divine."

The media lining her tennis courts fell silent.

"I propose we play the best of five sets like men," Nicolette continued, "since last I heard Jordon claims to be one. He can choose the venue. I want to play two weeks from tonight. Here is my proposed charity match contract. Please pass a copy along to Jordon." She pulled a folded paper from her back pocket and handed it to the closest reporter. "If he accepts, I hope everyone will support Jordon's great cause for humanity." She smiled, pushed through the crowd, and entered her house.

Jordon slumped into a chair. The TV reporters carried on, their voices pitched with excitement, repeating the amount of money Nicolette pledged if she lost. They interviewed Emilio Estrella, asking him if he thought Jordon was brave enough to accept the challenge and if so, who did he think would win the match? Jordon threw the remote at the TV.

His phone rang all evening, but Jordon didn't pick it up until the next day.

"Nicolette is just a publicity hound making an amateurish mistake out of desperation," Rick said over the phone. "No one will think of her again after you win."

Jordon nodded, his stomach rolling. *Why did she accept, and why on earth for all her money?* "She doesn't play for *charity*," he whined, "she's too goddamn selfish. And five sets? Why would she do that?"

"Everything is to our advantage, Jordon. You'll crush her on court...a court we get to choose."

"I want to play at her house," Jordon spat. "On *her* courts."

"What? Are you crazy?"

"I want to play there!" Jordon beat the phone receiver against the armchair. "Why should I be the only player not invited?" He sat fidgeting. "She won't expect it. She can't say no." He laughed, his voice squeaking at the end.

"She'll have the home court advantage."

"But we could question the fairness of the results if I—"

"If you *lost*? What the hell is wrong with you?"

Jordon curled up in the chair, holding his knees to his chest.

"She's an outcast...you're popular," Rick said. "Pull yourself together."

Jordon closed his eyes.

Roble peered through a lens, watching laser beams dance across black carbon.

Turning his head, he studied line graphs on a screen. *Perfect.* He pressed a button and a robotic arm lifted the carbon sheet and stacked it on a cart. A tag sticking out between layers read: *Starboard Heat Shields 14-28*.

As the cart drove away through the cavern, he listened to the whining of robots, the striking of metal, and the clicking of keyboards—the sounds of his thoughts taking material form.

Jogging after the heat shields, he ascended the ramp to the ranch stable. Humid air, smelling of damp sage and creosote bushes, wafted over his body.

He loaded the heat shields into a cattle truck and walked to the stable exit, peering out. Dark clouds churned along the western horizon, and he realized with surprise that summer had passed.

Jumping in the truck, he drove out of the Calico Basin. Lightning streaked across the sky, followed by the sustained claps of thunder. Twenty-five minutes later, as the rain began to pour, he pulled into Halvern's new hangar.

He stared at the long metallic frame of the *Roble Arrow* lying beneath the silver-blue dome like a prehistoric sea fossil submerged under a crystal clear bay.

Sigmund stood in front of the frame, directing workers and machines like a maestro. Libby sprawled atop its head, her body flat against alloy struts, her hands busy welding alloy joints. Longbow swept the floor below with a broom, face stern and proud. Renny stooped over a table at the side of the hangar, a flat-screen device and piles of paper scattered below his hands.

Roble stepped from the truck and folded his arms, soaking it all in, knowing he had no legal claim to a single gram of the *Roble Arrow's* structure, yet also that no one on earth owned it more completely. He scaled a hydraulic lift and straddled a beam next to Libby. Pulling out a piece of chalk and a handheld device, he started mapping out the path of the electrical system inside the frame.

"I still haven't found a suitable test pilot." Libby flipped up her welding visor. "If he's as good as you say, why not ask your San Diego guy again?"

Roble winced. "I think he's already paid too high a price for helping me once."

"Who is he?"

Holding on to an alloy rib for support, Roble exhaled and shook his head. "Libby, if I had all the specialized skills for the test runs, or had enough time to acquire them, I'd take her up myself." He stopped his chalk. "Why don't you be the test pilot? You've certified all *your* jets."

"I'd love to, but you know this isn't just a jet. More than that, Victor is now worried the test flight might be contested in the air, and his instincts are rarely wrong. I don't have any aerial combat evasion training." She flipped her visor down. "I'll make another search for the right pilot, but we're running out of time."

Roble glanced out the hangar exit and watched a lightning bolt flicker across the desert sky.

On a bright cloudless day, news trucks and police barriers lined the cul-de-sac in front of Nicolette's home.

The modest-sized bleachers on her center court filled with tennis players and celebrities. Cameras hung from lifts above the court. The former marquee of *The Sin* stood as backdrop to the spectacle.

Jordon Taylor, in a V-neck cardigan and yachting shoes, interviewed with the media on a sideline, accepting credit for the event. His charity co-sponsors took turns joining the interviews, including the local homebuilder Bill Jerrgin. Jordon volunteered fifteen million dollars of his own money. His corporate sponsors, and even some media outlets, made up the remaining thirty-two million to match Nicolette's offer.

Skipping all interviews, Nicolette strode onto the court in a white tennis outfit and a ponytail, appearing as calm as if she were alone. During warm-up, she lobbed shots over the net as though passing time. Jordon couldn't stop watching her, but glanced away whenever he thought she might look back—she never did.

Before the match started, Nicolette walked to the sideline and reached for a water bottle. Her shirt lifted off her lower back revealing a new tattoo—the outline of the state of Nevada.

Spectators hushed as the match began. The squeaks from tennis shoes echoed as though amplified by a speaker; the distinct pops from the ball blasting off racquets vibrated the audience's lungs and eyelashes.

After the first few volleys, Jordon grinned, not a drop of sweat on his forehead. Nicolette played as he had expected and practiced for, hitting most balls to the lines, except for a few odd shots placed mid-court. He stayed back and deep, returning her shots with ease. He won the first two sets 6-2, 6-1.

The news media remarked how wonderful this charity event had been for the sport, and how necessary for society to peel back the curtain on Nicolette's private matches.

One sportscaster said, his voice lighthearted, "Did anyone else think she drew some kind of fish or a dolphin on Jordon's side during the second set?"

Sitra, seated next to Renny in the front of the stands, turned to him, raising an eyebrow.

"She took my advice." Renny glanced at his watch. "She didn't think she had the strength to play five contested sets against Jordon."

Sitra scrunched her brows. "So what did you advise her to do?"

"I said she's right, she doesn't have the strength."

Sitra glanced at Nicolette.

"So I told her to only play the last three sets," Renny whispered.

Before the start of the third set, Nicolette changed out of her white outfit into black, her hair loosened from the ponytail. She strode back onto the court in measured steps, her forward momentum held back by flexing thighs. Stopping well inside the baseline to receive serve, she stared at Jordon, her eyes mere slits as if seeing binary digits.

When Jordon's serve left his racquet, Nicolette surged forward, hitting the ball early and hard. It launched, spun on a cross-axis following an acute angle, and skipped like a blur between Jordon's feet, like her swing had been an experiment to challenge the laws of physics.

After losing ten straight points, Jordon rubbed his magazine-cover hair with his racket. *Is this even tennis? Why can't I remember how to return the ball to the other side?* The third set ended in Nicolette's favor, 2-6.

As Jordon sat in his chair during the changeover, he stared from under a towel at his peers in the stands, feeling as he always did when he was a child—like he hated tennis. *I must not lose in front of everyone.*

When the fourth set began, Jordon felt a renewed focus and determination. *I'm winning the match—up two sets to one.* In the first game, he maneuvered across the court better than at any time in his life.

He lost the first game of the set in four quick volleys.

Standing behind the baseline, he wondered if getting injured would look better than losing by the score. Before he knew it, he blinked his eyes, shocked at the scoreboard. The fourth set score: 1-5. *I'm going to lose.*

During Nicolette's set point to tie the match, two sets to two, Jordon rolled to the ground while diving for a return. He lay, face pressed against the court.

Reaching for his knee, he smiled with relief, feeling some actual pain there. The crowd murmured with sympathy. He liked hearing it and drew in their pity like an intravenous transfusion from a collective vein. When Rick knelt at his side, Jordon whispered, "Don't make me get up."

"Come on," Rick said, his voice shaking, "get your head back in the game. You're not losing; the match is tied." He helped him to his feet.

The crowd cheered. Jordon jerked away from Rick and limped to the net. Nicolette stood at her baseline, ready to receive serve. Jordon motioned for her to approach.

Nicolette strolled over to him. "Hi, Jordon." She glanced at his legs. "I really need to find something that works better. Did you get that baby smoothness from those Rizzet razors you've been advertising, or is that natural?"

"What?" He glanced at the cameras while trying to reform the hair curl in front of his eye. "Look, we gave them a good exhibition. A tie for charity is good for publicity. We each donate half. Nobody loses."

Nicolette spun around and strode back to the baseline.

"Wait," he hissed.

"What's going on?" someone in the stands yelled.

Nicolette bounced off her toes, waiting for his serve. He motioned for her to approach again. She shrugged and walked up to the net.

"You're making me look bad," he whispered.

"Huh."

"This wasn't a competition." Jordon thumped his racket against the court. "This was for the children for God's sake."

"Oh," she said. "I agree. I haven't had this much fun since I was five."

"What does that have to do with anything?"

"Apparently nothing." She extended a hand.

The crowd gasped.

Jordon wiped the first drop of sweat from his brow. "I didn't concede."

"What will it be, one shake or one more set? Personally, I think the set would be more fun."

He looked to the spectators and media for help, but nobody seemed to appreciate his situation. Nicolette returned to her baseline. He stormed off the court, remembering to limp after a few steps.

"Woohoo!" Nicolette raised an arm, the dollar sign on her shoulder flexing as she waved.

"That's it," a sportscaster said, "she won!"

The crowd cheered. Renny jumped to his feet, beaming.

Nicolette's wild hair bounced against her shoulders as she skipped off the court to a makeshift podium by a pool. Two huge piles of bricked currency bills lay on a table in front of burly security guards and several news cameras. She plucked a microphone off its stand.

"For those who donated today in accordance to my contract," she began with a smile, "you should feel delighted. My designated charity sets the standard of need at the highest possible level. So high, in fact, only one recipient in the world qualifies. His need is to produce the greatest genetic creations in history without being molested by any of you."

Nicolette raised a money pack in the air. "And so, on behalf of Jordon Taylor and all the generous media and corporate donors, I present your forty-seven million dollar donation to Stock Brant."

The crowd inhaled a collective breath. Nicolette almost expected someone to yell: *Somebody should do something!*

"Thank you for making the world a better place." Winking at a camera, she ordered the security guards to take all the cash into her house.

She remained in the backyard, mingling with guests, signing autographs and congratulating reporters on their companies' donations.

After an hour, Emilio Estrella cornered her near a canary palm. "Any chance we could have dinner sometime?"

"A one hundred percent chance," she said. "Let's make it a double date. My boyfriend doesn't get out of the garage much so I bet he'll be excited. I've been dying to go back to this great little hole in the sky called the Comstock Terrace."

"El doble with…? Perhaps…ehm…" Emilio smiled, eyes squinting. "Perhaps another time."

"Okay, but don't keep me waiting so long this time."

Once the crowd dissipated, Nicolette entered her house. Alexandria stood on the curved stairway. Nicolette met her, and they ascended to a balcony overlooking the Las Vegas Strip.

"Impressive match," Alexandria said.

Nicolette tamed her hair with both hands and smoothed it over one shoulder. "Maybe not as dramatic as your show, but still…" She laughed.

"It didn't lack dramatics. But neither did your choice of charities."

"Will you take his money to him?"

"You've attracted the attention of certain government organizations by naming Stock as the beneficiary. If you don't mind," Alexandria exhaled, "I'd like to take *all* the cash with me for safe keeping, even your forty-seven million."

"All right." Nicolette turned to the railing and leaned over, her shirt lifting a bit. "Just as long as I get it back."

"When did you get the new tattoo?"

"The day after I met Nevada's Lieutenant Governor." Nicolette stared at the white shard piercing the sky.

"So you think you came to the right state?"

Nicolette turned, resting her elbows against the rail. "I think, Ms. Patra, she has potential."

Before sunrise the next morning, federal agents along with local SWAT members stormed Nicolette's house.

After searching every inch, the agent-in-charge, DaSilva, lit a cigarette and strolled to the backyard. Taking a puff, he heard tennis balls popping somewhere in the darkness.

He found Nicolette at the back of the lot, ripping balls against a concrete barrier. She didn't acknowledge him or the others as they trickled up behind.

"May we speak with you, Miss Popov?" Agent DaSilva tapped his cigarette.

"About what?" she asked, still playing.

"We have a search warrant."

"For?"

"Stock Brant and his assets."

"Oh, how exciting," she said, hitting the ball harder.

The agent coughed, wiping his mouth. "We didn't find anything."

"Oh, how disappointing." She hit a ball between her legs and pivoted to take a backhand stroke.

Stamping out the cigarette on a tree, he yelled, "All right everyone, pack it up. We're leaving."

Chapter 59

Danny sat, looking out his Key West apartment window at a kidney bean-shaped swimming pool beneath a row of palm trees.

This marked his tenth location and fourth month since leaving Las Vegas. He lifted a large duffle bag from below his chair onto his lap. Inside it, atop his storyboards, he found the final three remaining bricks of one-hundred-dollar bills.

I did it. He leaned back in the chair. *I gave it all to those in need.* He scooped out a thick pile of charity receipts with his father's name written as the donor and flipped through them. *It's time to let Father know the truth about the Marines. He will see that what I've done is greater than catching a football in the state championships, greater than being a top drill instructor, and even greater than graduating at the top of a CMI class to become a Marine officer.*

He pulled his storyboards from the duffle bag and shuffled through them until he found the final scene with the unfinished faces of the father and son. He swallowed. *Just finish it.* He reached for a pencil but stopped.

His fingertips caressed the storyboard. *What if I completed it in a way I didn't hate…a way that made it only mine instead of Father's? Is it possible for him to also be proud of what I want?* He reached for a pencil and froze again. *But if he didn't like it…* He rubbed his eyes.

He stared out the window again, at the pool surface rippling in the breeze.

One month later, Danny sat in the same Key West apartment, gazing out the window at the motionless water in the pool.

He glanced at his unfinished final scene sitting before him. *Why can't I finish it?* He gripped his hair, his bloodshot eyes wide. *I can't delay any longer.* The wristwatch by his ear marked off the seconds.

An e-mail notification beeped on his mobile device. He lifted the screen and read the only two words sent from his father. *We know.*

Danny swallowed and opened his mouth. His fingertips typed one character at a time. *What do you mean, Father?*

The Marines dishonorably discharged you six months ago, he read. *You failed, and you lied to us. Don't ever come home. THAT'S what I mean.*

No… Danny's stomach sank, his eyes glued to the message. *You don't understand.* He lifted the charity receipts, clenching them tight.

He glanced back to the storyboard with Ritashugi and his father and their undrawn faces. A ticking noise pounded against his brain. He slammed his wristwatch against his phone, smashing both to pieces atop the table. *I just needed a little more time to finish this story for you. Just…*

Grabbing a pencil, he held it above the storyboard, his mind numb. *There is nothing left to lose.*

Out of nowhere, he pictured Jenny's face when she first saw his animations and drew her expression on Ritashugi's father. He pictured Roble's face after he built his first rocket at Danny's childhood home and drew his expression on Ritashugi. Then he sketched the horse of his boy rider, inspired from the drawing Roble had stolen, behind the father and son as if Ritashugi had ridden it the entire story.

Sitting up, he stared without hope at the final scene. His heart pounded, eyes flashing in red pulses, head wobbling with dizziness. *I can't believe it. The son looks triumphant and his father— proud. That's it.* He threw the pencil across the room. *Father will understand this art, understand everything I've done for him.*

Packing up the duffle bag, he ran from the apartment and jumped on his motorcycle. He angled away the side view mirrors, not wanting to see his own face, only to think of his art—the expressions of the father and son, and what it would feel like to be made real. The tires screeched along asphalt as he sped away.

During the three days of riding, his mind pictured his father's face as it appeared in his art over and over again. He stopped only for gas and to sleep at rest stops until he crossed the Idaho state line.

At a classic car dealership outside of Pocatello, he purchased a split-window vintage sports coup, the year and make his father always talked about. It cost him his last three bricks of one-hundred-dollar bills and his motorcycle, with just enough left over to purchase a suit.

When he parked in front of the red brick house, the silence assaulted his mind like a shriek of terror. He stared at the home, eyelids twitching, yet he saw nothing disturbing. A sprinkler chopped in repetitive spurts above a neighbor's cut lawn.

He shuffled to the front door, carrying the duffle bag, body swaying as though aboard a ship at sea. A fingertip touched a crack in a brick, a crack he never noticed before. After a glance down at his new suit, he knocked.

His father answered, filling the doorframe like a monolith. Danny bowed his head, accepting some unidentified yet comfortable guilt. He blinked when he noticed Donald's droopy brown socks peeking out below green slacks, too short at the ankles. Donald's belly hung over his belt, pulling his shoulders forward. The arms Danny once thought indomitable cannons, appeared boney, covered with pasty skin and albino hairs.

Straightening up, Danny whispered, "I have something to show you."

Sunken eyes like those of a stranger stared back—no, not like a stranger—like those of someone who didn't want Danny to exist.

"I'm sorry I lied about the Marines," Danny said. "But I didn't want to show you what I've become until I'd succeeded."

Donald gazed at the vintage coup parked along the curb. "What are you talking about?"

"Can I come in?"

"After what you've done to your mother? You've disgraced her your entire life because you never had the fortitude to do what's right, to do your duty."

He heard his mother sniffling somewhere within the dark cavity of the living room. Lifting the car keys, he said, "It's the one you've always talked about."

Donald looked at the keys, then the car. "Think you can make it all better by showing me a car that will be repossessed in a week? This is why you came back?"

"No." He opened the duffle bag and removed the stack of

charity receipts. "I made these in your name. It's for millions of dollars, maybe hundreds of millions." He handed them to his father.

Donald sifted through the receipts, his brows furrowed. "How did you get these?"

"Here," Danny set the keys on top of the receipts. He reached into his pockets and fished out the colored diamonds Roble had given him at the cliff house.

Donald stared at the glitter, shaking his head. "Where did you get those?"

"Mother can pay off the house. You can expand your business."

"You expect me to believe any of this is real after what you've done?"

His mother emerged from the shadows and let Danny pour the diamonds into her apron. "See Donald? I prayed. I prayed for this."

Inhaling, Danny lifted the storyboards from the bag. His hands trembled as he presented them to his father.

Donald placed the car keys and receipts on a table behind him and took the boards. He skimmed through them one at time until he came to the final scene. Danny stepped back, peering at his father's lowered face, waiting for the final verdict upon his soul. Donald stared at the final scene for a long time.

"It's like your hero, Robin Hood." Danny swallowed. "All of it is like him. I am. You were always right."

His father set the art against the doorframe and lifted his eyes. Danny wanted to feel something resembling redemption or at least relief, but he felt nothing—no, worse than nothing—he felt emptied of all he ever had.

"You think drawing a hero makes you one?" Donald asked, his face expressionless as if the lines had been erased. "You think I'm just supposed to believe any of this is real after everything you've pulled? You probably got yourself kicked out of the Marines just to be with that Jenny girl."

"Come in and have some supper. I'll make your favorite soup," his mother said. "Everything will be okay."

Donald tossed the keys to Danny, shaking his head. "I told you not to come back."

Danny felt something ignite inside himself like the fuse of a

Marine's grenade. He stuffed the keys into his pocket, grabbed the storyboards, and tore them to pieces. "I sacrificed everything," he ground the scraps into the porch with his new shoes, "my whole life." He staggered back. "And for what?"

"Danny, don't leave," his mother cried.

With his body shaking, he asked, "Do you have Jenny's current address?"

His father folded his arms and looked at Mrs. Sands as if saying—*See what I told you?*

"Jenny?" his mother asked as though never hearing the name before.

"Yes, Mother…Jenny!"

Her shadow disappeared inside the house. Danny stared at Donald's face; Donald stared at the split-window coup. When his mother returned, her shaky hand held out a holiday card envelope.

Danny ripped it away, picked up the duffle bag, and ran to the garage. Lifting the garage door, he spotted his old German-built motorcycle. After a few attempts, he started the engine and pulled it next to the sports coup. He picked clothes off the passenger seat, stuffed them in his bag, and tightened it over his shoulders.

Glancing up at his father looking through the charity receipts, Danny pulled the car keys from his pocket, threw them at the house, and tore away on the motorbike.

The Paiute hangar echoed with mechanical dynamism. Workers swarmed around the *Roble Arrow*, its outer skin almost complete.

Roble secured hydraulic lines inside an open fuselage bay to a solar sail. As he tested an O-ring between his fingers, he noticed a shadow stretch across the sail. He glanced at the hangar entrance and dropped the O-ring.

The silhouette of a man stood at the opening, hands clasped together, boots spread apart—poised like a military officer.

It can't be. Roble caressed the edges of his arrowhead, his gut swarming with butterflies.

…Sircor.

Gavin Sircor walked in to the busy work zone, chin level, shoulders relaxed. Passing Roble without making eye contact, he paced around the *Roble Arrow*, inspecting it.

How did he even know I was making this? Roble watched him, opening his mouth a few times to speak, but failing. *How did he know the location of this hangar?*

After examining the engines, Sircor stopped in front of him, his stance resolute, greying temples adding a wise patina to his already forged titanium features. "So, Santos," he said, his voice low, "here we are again."

Roble swallowed, absorbing the image of Sircor standing once again next to his almost-completed creation.

Sircor gazed along the stretched line of the *Roble Arrow*. "It looks fast."

Roble kept his eyes squarely on Sircor. "I spoke with your wife at your home five months ago. She said…" He bowed his head unable to finish.

"If I could go back in time to Kadena, I'd do it all again."

Roble shook his head. "I never considered your family when I took you up on your offer to fly the Raptor *Super Kai*."

"That's because it was *my* job to consider them, not yours. And I don't blame Stephie for not telling me about your visit. She protects her family."

"Wait," Roble raised his chin, "if she didn't tell you I visited, how did you know I was back in the country?" Furrowing his brows, he added, "And how in the world did you know where to find me?"

"Listen, Santos," Sircor stepped closer, "a man told Stephie about this place and about your jet. After speaking with him, *Stephie* convinced me to come here."

"How did he do that?" Roble shook his head. "And hold on *who* convinced her?"

"I don't know the answer to either question. I thought maybe you did."

"No. I mean…I honestly don't have a clue." Roble looked around the hangar. "It doesn't make sense. I've never given anyone your name, let alone your address."

"I guess you have a secret admirer then, and a unique one at that."

Roble rubbed his chin, trying to think.

"So, are you glad I'm here or not?"

Roble blinked his eyes and cleared his throat. "I've wanted you to be the test pilot from the start, more than you'll ever know, but—"

"Good. When will it be completed?"

"In just over a month. But you have to consider this—it will be more dangerous than just a complex test flight. You will likely have company up there," he pointed up, "and not friendly company."

"Permission to train," Sircor clicked his heels together and saluted, "and take her beyond the edge when she's done."

Roble studied him, thinking of the morning Sircor gave him access to the completed Raptor *Super Kai*, and how that flight unlocked the final puzzle piece which enabled the *Roble Arrow* to exist. *I promised myself I wouldn't forget. And I never will.* He saluted. "Permission granted, with honor."

Chapter 60

anny crested the Apex summit on Interstate-15 and beheld the vertical casinos melting into the Las Vegas mirage. He rounded the city to the southeast, to the off-ramp leading to Jenny's address.

Winding through the residential streets, he couldn't believe he'd waited so many years to see her again. He stopped in front of an unfamiliar mansion on a rocky hill with a lush lawn and succulent plants lining a path to a front door. His motorcycle engine sputtered as he glanced around at the prestigious neighborhood.

Glancing at his suit, he shook his head. *This isn't me.* He sunk his hands into his pockets and felt the sharp points of a gem. He searched the inseam until he found one more.

A vintage sports coup rumbled by along the street. Danny turned and watched it, grimacing at the thought of his father. *Jenny must hate me.* He left the diamonds in his pocket, tapped the cycle's clutch, and tore away from the house.

Spotting a pawnshop near the freeway, he pulled over and entered. The two sparkling gems dropped from his hand and bounced across the glass counter. The store attendant studied one with an eyepiece and walked to the back.

While he waited, Danny counted his remaining cash. *Forty dollars.*

Upon returning, the attendant scanned the shop and slapped ten damp one-hundred-dollar bills on the counter. Danny stared at the filthy money but didn't reach for it.

The man counted out ten more. "Take it or leave it."

"I…" Danny grabbed the gems. "I'm sorry. I can't." He turned and rushed to the exit, bumping into one of two suited men wearing earpieces near the entrance on the way out.

Riding to downtown, he found the cheapest place to stay he could find. It wasn't a motel so much as a converted storage facility. The bed lay wedged between two metal walls, its mattress springs sticking out from soiled fabric. The ceiling was streaked with rust, and the carpet sprouted like a petri dish. Despite the room's condition, he liked the place; it seemed real, unlike the past five months—or had it been most of his life?

Each day he collected bottles and cans off nearby streets, selling them at a recycling center. He noticed two suited men who often sat in their car on the dirty streets, but they neither seemed interested in him nor did he care if they were.

Most of the time he made enough money to eat, and most of the time didn't care what he ate. The weeks he spent there held no purpose other than to draw. He sketched in cheap notebooks, filling up page after page of anime characters and scenes. His fingers ached and sometimes bled but he didn't stop.

One day when he found two abandoned shopping carts full of cans, he took the proceeds to an older shopping mall, the one he occasioned with Roble without his parents' knowledge as a teen. He wandered the music-filled halls, staring at the store displays with a sense of detached nostalgia.

Stepping inside The Gorge Clothing Company felt like crossing back in time to high school. He browsed the scented clothes and tried on an outfit in front of a dressing room mirror. Ignoring his belly, he thought the clothes looked youthful, defiant perhaps. He liked seeing his own smile until he noticed dark rings under his eyes and bloated cheeks like his father. Tearing off the clothes, he carried them to the counter and bought them.

He noticed suited men with earpieces standing partially concealed behind mannequins outside the store window. *This is getting weird.* They turned and walked away as he exited the store.

"Can I help you?" Danny strode after them.

They ignored him, continuing down the bright corridor.

"Whatever," he mumbled, shaking his head, letting them go.

On the way out of the mall, he passed a row of teddy bears hanging from a booth, like the one he gave Jenny when she turned fourteen. He bought one.

Donald Sands felt shocked to discover that Danny's diamonds proved authentic, and even more so to learn their incredible worth. He tried contacting Danny but he didn't respond to his previous phone number, e-mail address, or his social networking websites.

Mrs. Sands called Jenny, but Jenny claimed she hadn't seen Danny in years. The police visited Jenny's home on Mrs. Sands' urging, but they found no evidence of Danny.

"I told you our son would make good," Mrs. Sands said to Donald every time she left for Boise to sell diamonds to the highest quality jeweler in the state. He nodded without comment.

The Sands bought a bigger house on a hill overlooking Pocatello. They donated to their church and local community causes, earning engraved nameplates on bricks and benches.

Donald resurfaced the porcelain Robin Hood logo above his counseling business in gold leaf. He also gave photocopies of the donation receipts in his name from charities in cities stretching from Phoenix to Key West to a local newspaper. The headline in the paper read: *Pocatello philanthropist strikes the south.*

With his increased popularity, Donald ran for city councilman. His campaign consisted of driving his vintage sports coup, with his gold counseling logo painted on the door, down Main Street in a parade throwing candy to children and waving to those without vintage sports coups.

Whenever locals asked how they acquired their new wealth, Mrs. Sands answered with a casualness that implied the answer had been inevitable: their son, using his former Marine skills, followed in his father's footsteps to become a successful self-made man, just as she'd always hoped. And she said often in front of small gatherings of women, "If you teach your child correctly when he's young, no matter how far he may stray, he will eventually return to your principles."

Mrs. Sands made a ring with one of the flawless blue diamonds. Donald resented it at first, the stone being much larger and more expensive than her engagement diamond, but after a neighbor praised him for his good taste, he encouraged her to wear it more often.

During that remarkable month, a month Mrs. Sands referred to as "blessed," she told Donald she'd never felt so respected.

Danny's stomach growled as he sketched on a notepad, trying to ignore the fact his rent expired at noon.

Woozy from lack of food, he reached into his pocket and touched the two diamonds. Shaking his head, he gazed at the unworn mall outfit hanging from a rusty hook. He stared so long he thought maybe he sat before his childhood closet on a middle school morning.

The ride back to Jenny's house felt unreal, like watching an out-of-focus car scene in an old movie. Pulling to a stop in front of her lawn, he gazed at the mansion, recalling all the times she'd snuck out from her mother's old apartment window to meet him.

When he heard a car approaching from behind, he released the brake, rolling the tires forward. But they lurched to a stop as a silver luxury sedan swung onto the driveway. He gulped, expecting to see a baby seat or a husband in the window.

Jenny's hair funneled down behind a low cut dress as she stepped from the car, alone. Turning to him, her eyes glistened in the morning's soft glow. Her ankles seemed too delicate to support her as she approached, hips swaying.

The teddy bear fell from his hand and bounced off the blacktop.

"Danny?" She tilted her head.

He coughed to clear his throat.

"What are you doing here?" She glanced at the discarded stuffed animal.

He stared at her model-like body and home beyond. "Uhmm…"

She scrunched her brows.

He pushed a shaking hand through his hair.

"You have scars on your face," she said, her voice softening. "What happened? Is everything all right?"

"They're nothing, really." His lips tried to smile but his eyelids sagged. "I'm…fine."

She crossed her arms, her gaze moving to his shirt.

He glanced at the new shirt and sucked in his gut.

"I don't understand why you're here," she said.

He tapped the handlebars, trying to breathe. "I was just thinking…about the old days, I guess. I dunno." He coughed again. "Thinking about us, and maybe…"

She turned up her palms, narrowing her eyes.

"I know I never called you, and have no right to be here." He looked down. "It's just that…I missed you, Jenny…this whole time." He lifted his gaze. "Do you think…do you think you could ever forgive me for the way I…?"

Her eyes formed perfect ovals, the shape she always made when frowning. "Look, Danny," her lashes blinking once, "I can only thank you for what you did."

He rubbed his eyes, trying to stop the burning. "I hurt you something awful, didn't I?"

"Yes." She took a breath. "But I'm happy with the way things turned out for me."

He picked at the rubber on the handlebars. "I wish I could go back…go back to the way—"

"I don't wish to go back." She glanced at her house. "I don't mean to sound impolite but I have a photoshoot soon. Maybe we could visit another time?"

He stared at her, feeling betrayed, but knew it wasn't her who had ever betrayed him. "It was good…good to see you again. Take care, Jenny."

She wiped an eye and nodded.

He released the brake, jumping the bike forward a foot and stopped. His head drooped, unable to bear the thought of leaving.

"How are your parents?" she asked. "They're looking for you."

He trembled. His tears couldn't be held back as the overwhelming pain he'd trapped in his heart emptied through his eyes.

"Danny? I didn't mean to…" She stepped closer and reached for his shoulder—but pulled back.

He wiped his face several times, breathing in short gasps. "I didn't want you to see me like this."

"It's okay. It's…okay."

He felt so vulnerable as the tears poured, more exposed than if he sat there naked. "No, I don't think it is okay." Turning off his bike, he sniffed and rubbed his cheeks. "I've made huge mistakes, Jenny. Things I can't change."

"It's probably not as bad as you make it sound. Don't do anything you—"

"I'm pretty sure it's worse than it sounds." He wiped an arm across his face to try to stop the deluge. "What I did to you…or rather, what I wanted to do but didn't." He rubbed his nose on the back of a hand. "What I didn't do for myself. God, Jenny, I even robbed someone because I thought my father would think it noble." He exhaled. "I don't think I even comprehend everything I did wrong or what price I'll have to pay."

Catching her gaze, he added, "So, yeah, it's worse than it sounds. I am worse, Jenny."

She bent down, picked up the teddy bear, and held it in both hands.

He watched her, not believing how beautiful she'd remained after all these years.

"I have to go, but…" she paused. "Would you meet me for coffee in the morning?"

"Are you sure you want to see me again?" He coughed and scratched his neck. "After everything I just said?"

"No, not after everything you just said." She touched the stuffed animal against her cheek. "*Because* of what you just said. Meet me here at nine."

He started his engine, inhaled, and looked forward. "Tomorrow at nine."

As he walked into his dilapidated motel room, his stomach knotted from hunger. He removed the two gems from his pocket. "I have to give these to Stock."

Gathering up his art notebooks, he whispered, "I'll sleep in the park tonight or something, but it's okay." He looked around at the rusted walls. "Jenny said it will be okay."

Everything around him exploded in a bright flash followed by thick smoke. Armed men in jackets and helmets burst into the room. "Federal Agents! Get on the ground!"

Danny stood, unmoving in the chaos. *Jenny…*

Agents gripped his arms and pressed him to the bed.

Chapter 61

Renny Thatcher felt a buzz in his pocket as he entered calculations into a computer. Glancing at his mobile device's screen, he read a text from Nicolette. *Check out the news.*

"Hmm..." He slid a finger across the screen. Two Nevada headlines popped up. *Jessy Gorronza turns federal state's witness*, and, *Governor Moore resigns after federal indictment.*

"Excuse me," Renny said as Victor adjusted the magnetics in a power coil, "would you care to learn that the Nevada governor resigned?"

Victor spun a wrench on his finger like a pistol and slapped it down on a workbench. Narrowing his eyes, he strode across the Paiute hangar. Renny followed behind, a smile on his lips.

Stopping in front of Libby, Victor said, "*Madame* Dodge, where might we locate a television?"

"Are they rerunning your favorite French soap opera again?" Libby welded a seam on the scramjet combustion chamber.

Longbow swept a broom near their feet. "There is one in my house, if you don't mind a little static."

"Please accompany me, if you would." Victor shut off the welding gas line, and grabbed Libby's hand.

Renny, Libby, Victor, and Longbow marched out of the hangar, passing Roble and Sircor as they spoke near the *Roble Arrow.*

"*...as the Lieutenant Governor is unavailable to fill the office,*" a reporter said on Longbow's TV, "*the Nevada constitution states that the President Pro Tempore, Aaron Jenkins, will serve as governor until the term expires in January. The gubernatorial election this November is now an open race as Preton Moore was the undisputed front-runner—*

"Breaking news. We now go live to the governor's office where Mr. Jenkins is about to make a statement."

A stubby man with curly hair seated at a desk opened his mouth to speak. With a sharp flicker, the image disappeared from the screen, replaced with the view of a cascading silver fountain before white glass.

Alexandria Patra walked in front of the fountain, stopping near the TV camera, her onyx eyes steady.

"Uhhh…" a TV reporter mumbled. *"We have switched live to Las Vegas where the missing Lieutenant Governor is apparently going to give an address."*

The rushing of water hummed from the TV speaker. Alexandria leaned into the breeze, straight, black hair drifting behind her as if she stood on a mountain's peak. She gazed beyond the camera. "I am Alexandria Patra."

She stood without speaking for a moment as people trickled in to *The Spirit of Man* plaza. "For those Nevada residents who do not deserve what anyone else believes," she opened her arms, "today, you will finally get what you have always deserved."

The crowd continued growing.

"Since free individuals survive on this planet only by rational judgement, the greatest need is the liberty to act on one's own thoughts. Civilized people do not use government or any other authority to compel others to act, or not to act. They live of their own accord, exchanging value if and as they wish, and are held accountable if they harm anyone else."

"Therefore," Alexandria lifted her chin, "I will oversee a state that physically protects you from all who would impose their beliefs by force—a protection all thinking individuals require in order to seek their own happiness. And because you are *not* indentured servants of this state, it will be funded voluntarily—or not at all."

"In the remaining five months of this gubernatorial term, these are the principles under which I will operate. Now," she said, "I will answer any questions."

The crowd murmured but nobody raised a hand.

A young girl wearing a primary school uniform and standing near the camera rose onto her toes. "Ms. Patra, where were you?"

Alexandria pushed a strand of hair over her ear, her lips

curving into a smile. "Achieving my dream. I am the performer Sitra at *The Virtue*."

The girl gasped. "Really?"

"Now that you will be governor, will you quit the show?" a woman standing behind the girl asked.

"Oh no," Alexandria said, her voice soft. "Of course not."

A man in jeans lifted his hardhat.

Alexandria nodded at him.

"How do you feel about the federal bribery charges against former Governor Moore?" he asked.

"I feel that receiving bribes was one of Mr. Moore's least offensive actions while in office."

"What do you mean?"

Alexandria looked up the length of *The Spirit of Man*, her hand dancing in measured pirouettes at her side. "Many of those who allegedly gave bribes to Mr. Moore did so as their only recourse to avoid prosecution for breaking unjust laws—laws that would have stopped them from acting according to their own values."

"Are you saying," a man wearing eyeglasses and a tweed suit gestured his phone at her, "the state shouldn't regulate how people act? What about the greater good?"

"Making someone a criminal," Alexandria motioned a hand across the crowd, "only because he doesn't share your beliefs is what defined the Dark Ages." Stopping her hand, pointed in the man's direction, she added, "If *you* believe others should act, or refrain from acting, according to *your* ideals—*be* the example of those ideals and use rational persuasion. Do not expect this state to impose them, even if you label them 'good'."

"Young lady," an elderly man pushed into the open space before Alexandria, his shoulders hunched forward, a finger raised, "what if no one donates to this state? What money would you use to protect anyone, or to do anything?"

"If no one supports the only Free State on Earth, it will fail. And we will all deserve it."

He pressed out his gaunt chest "I didn't say I wouldn't pitch in, young lady." Glancing around at the other people, he added, "I've just never been given a choice before." He scrunched his grey brows and inclined his head. "Thank you."

Alexandria smiled.

"Ms. Patra," a woman with short hair raised her hand,

"the gubernatorial election is in three months. Will you seek reelection?"

"If by November you long for the days you were ruled by a government claiming your life is subordinate to any cause or group, or if you miss participating in the forced sacrifice of other residents to you and you to them," Alexandria narrowed her eyes, "as is happening everywhere else in the world today—vote against me. I will not waste my time or yours campaigning, but I will be on the Nevada ballot."

Ted Hollings, wearing a streamlined black suit, escorted Stock Brant from the crowd up to Alexandria's side.

"I'd like to introduce my first cabinet member, my Chief of Staff, Ted Hollings," she said. "I'm contributing the funds for his salary." She winked at him. "So I expect him to work hard."

"Why is Stock Brant with you?" a man yelled from the multitude.

Touching Stock's hand, Alexandria said, "Mr. Brant has been charged by this state with murder, accomplice to murder, drug trafficking, illegal substance production, gun trafficking, money laundering, and bribery."

Stock lowered his head.

Alexandria peered across the street at *The Sin*, then at those in the assembly before her. "The production and exchange of goods and services among adults is as necessary for survival as drawing breath. And money belongs to anyone who makes it, no matter how laundered it becomes, or how it is used. On those last five charges against Stock, or against anyone else in this state, my prosecutors will suspend charges. If the Nevada legislature does not change the laws, I will pardon every resident convicted of such a charge until I leave office."

She squeezed Stock's hand, and he looked up. "I now place Mr. Brant under arrest to face murder and accomplice to murder charges. He will have his day in court as all accused of an actual crime will."

Facing the camera, her voice somehow carrying across the reaches of *The Spirit of Man* plaza, she concluded, "For however long this newly Free State lasts—be it only months or longer—may you each act according to your own values and pursue your greatest dreams."

Alexandria pulled Stock close and kissed him on the lips.

Without another word, she and Mr. Hollings walked through the crowd and disappeared into *The Spirit of Man*.

Stock stood before the silent throng, the shadow of the white tower slicing behind him like an approaching guillotine blade. Yet the sun blazed upon his hair like a torch, his tranquil eyes sparkling.

Two Nevada police officers approached. Stock offered his wrists, and they cuffed him. Gabriel stepped from the crowd and offered his wrists as well. The police led them both away.

Libby turned off the TV and faced those in Longbow's tiny home. The others stood at attention, watching her.

"What's everyone standing around for?" Libby pushed back her hair. "Our customer wants the *Roble Arrow* completed in a week. Let's make it happen."

Chapter 62

Danny sat catatonic at a table; a mirror and a steel door outlined against pale walls.

Three men entered the room, two in suits and one in a wool sweater and khakis. The two in suits, who Danny recognized from the pawnshop and the mall, introduced themselves as Agents Wilson and DaSilva. The other referred to himself only as Mike.

"We are not the enemy, Danny. We're the only ones who can help you," Mike said, gesturing at the agents. He sat down on a corner of the table. "How did you get those diamonds?"

"A friend gave them to me to repay a debt."

"Who?"

"None of your business."

"We know the diamonds came from Stock Brant." Agent Wilson folded his arms. "Their quality signature is unmistakable."

"Those two diamonds on me were from a friend, but I also stole all of Stock's diamonds and gave the money away."

Mike tilted his head. "Why?"

"To be fucking Robin Hood."

Agent DaSilva rubbed his forehead. "Oh Lord. That's why you gave the money to charity?" He glanced at a paper in his hand. "We didn't think to look at charities for the diamond proceeds until we read your father's news story."

"We know you and Roble were foster brothers," Mike said, "and have been in contact since he reentered the country. We also know of Roble's association with Stock Brant, making Stock a potential source of Roble's funding. Did stealing Stock's diamonds take away Roble's ability to fund his next extremist event?"

"Extremist event?" Danny scoffed. "All he wants to do is build a jet."

"Uh-huh, right." Mike rolled his eyes. "Just a jet." He leaned forward. "Does Roble have other sources of funding?"

"I doubt it, but if anyone can figure out a way, it's Roble."

"Is he in contact with Libby Dodge?" Mike asked.

Danny dropped his forehead onto his arms.

"We know somebody is acquiring top grade alloys and carbon fiber with cash," Mike said. "A source at a supplier suspects their material was shipped to somewhere in the Calico Basin. Do you know anything about a hidden facility?"

Danny didn't move.

"Because of your association with an international extremist fugitive," Mike said, "you could be detained indefinitely without a trial. So, I will ask you again." He gripped the back of Danny's hair, sitting him up in the chair. "Is Roble in contact with Libby Dodge? And what's he plotting?"

Danny shook his head free and brushed a hand through his hair. "You can't force me to talk. I've been roughed up better than this, so do your worst."

Mike smacked the table. "Where is Roble?"

Danny stared at the wall.

Agent Wilson paced behind Danny. "Even though you might think you did the right thing by taking those diamonds and donating the money, you're in big trouble with federal laws—possessing illegal drug proceeds and money laundering. You're looking at years in prison."

"Look," Mike said, "just set up a meeting with Roble. Have him talk about his plot." He rapped his knuckle against the table. "In exchange we'll give you a deal that avoids terrorist detention and reduces your jail time for your crimes."

"Lock me up forever," Danny mumbled. "I won't help you set up Roble."

"Your parents will be arrested for taking those diamonds if you don't help us," DaSilva said. "Is that what you want? All the charity receipts are in your father's name."

Danny closed his eyes.

"What if I promised that your parents wouldn't be prosecuted if you helped us?" Mike asked. "I'll put it in writing right now."

"Leave them out of this. They didn't know where the diamonds came from."

"Not only will your parents go to jail, but perhaps we need to detain Jenny Beekam. She must know something."

Danny shoved off against the table and stood. "If you lay a hand on her, I'll kill myself before I tell you anything."

"All right," Mike massaged his chin, "just tell us what you want for your cooperation. The ball is in your court."

"Nothing you can give me."

Mike rubbed his eyes.

"Oh dear," Mrs. Sands said, opening her front door.

"This is federal agent Wilson and DaSilva," a man wearing a sweater and sunglasses said. "Please call me Mike. We need to talk about your son."

She backed away, brushed off an already spotless couch for them to sit, and ran to the garage. Returning with Donald, she pushed him into the living room and left for the kitchen.

Donald sat in a recliner across from the men, his shoulders pinched forward. "What did Danny do?"

Agent Wilson pulled a transparent bag from his breast pocket. Two clear gems glowed in the bottom corner. "Do you know the origin of these?"

Donald shook his head. Mrs. Sands returned with a plate of cookies and a forced smile.

"Your son robbed Stock Brant," Agent Wilson said, "the head of a drug cartel in Las Vegas."

Mrs. Sands gasped. Donald leaned back in his seat, eyes narrowing.

"If this were merely a case of possessing illegal drug proceeds or money laundering," Mike said, "I'd let these fine agents just confiscate everything you own and arrest you." He squished a cookie between two fingers, dropping the deformed pieces to the plate. "But this is far more serious."

Mrs. Sands pressed a hand over her mouth.

"When these agents identified your son a few weeks ago as the seller of Stock's diamonds…" Mike glanced at his greasy fingers, and Mrs. Sands handed him a napkin, "…your son's background search led to something unexpected. Actually, it led to the rediscovery of *someone*. You were Roble Santos' foster parents, correct?"

"He was a child from Hell," Mrs. Sands cried, wiping a frilly sleeve across her forehead. "Danny is impressionable. Roble must have tricked him. We told Danny to stay away from him."

"Indeed, Mrs. Sands," Mike cleaned his fingers on the napkin, "Roble Santos is very cunning. He is also an international fugitive. We suspect he is funding his next extremist event, perhaps from the same source of diamonds that purchased this very house."

Mrs. Sands vacillated in her seat, about to pass out.

"You are both well-respected in the community. Respect is quite a valuable asset, but like all stolen effects," Mike nodded at the mutilated cookie, "so very vulnerable."

Donald blinked.

"We monitored Danny's movements," Mike adjusted his sunglasses, "hoping he would lead us to Roble, but we had to accelerate things for fear Roble might act. The problem is, your son refuses to cooperate. So here I am," he opened his arms, "and I'm offering you a deal of a lifetime. In exchange for your help in achieving Danny's complete and immediate cooperation, you can keep everything he gave you, and your little secret will remain with us."

Donald adjusted his pant legs, further exposing his socks. "So," he coughed to clear his throat, "my son actually took that money from a criminal and gave it to the poor? Stole from that notorious bastard, Stock Brant?" Looking out the window at the vintage sports coup, he said, "And if taking that money slowed Roble from doing…whatever you said he's trying to do," he shook his head, "isn't Danny a hero?"

"Oh, yes, your son is a real Robin Hood, Mr. Sands," DaSilva said. "And everyone who doesn't cooperate in apprehending Roble Santos will be written into children's stories too—right *after* they rot penniless in a federal maximum security prison."

Mrs. Sands' body lurched forward with a dry heave.

"If my son cooperates," Donald inched forward, stroking his arm hair, "you won't press charges against any of the family? Nobody will know where we got the money? And," he glanced out the window again, "we keep everything? I can even deduct the charity receipts on my taxes?"

Mike picked up another cookie and took a bite. "Absolutely

delicious, Mrs. Sands. I'm sure you're looking forward to your son's return."

Danny sat in an illuminated cell that somehow felt dark.

The door rolled open. His father, wearing a tailored suit, filled the doorway with a storyboard in his hand.

The door clanged shut and Danny hunched forward, expecting the silent treatment or a beating, and feeling indifferent between the two.

"Son," he said, sitting next to Danny. He lifted the taped-together final scene with Ritashugi and his samurai father and placed it on Danny's lap.

Danny stared at his repaired storyboard, eyes wide, then at his father. The contrast between Donald's compassionate expression and the sight of his own tainted art somehow felt more awful than the honesty of a good beating. Danny turned away.

Donald hugged Danny's rigid shoulders. The pressure felt unnatural but Danny didn't wish it to stop. He tried to recall the last time his father had hugged him, but couldn't remember.

"We all make mistakes, Son. They're what define us as human. And I'm here because *I* made a mistake—not you."

He couldn't believe his father's words, words he'd wished to hear his whole life. They felt better than he ever imagined, yet he knew they couldn't be trusted.

"Your mother and I have only wanted what's best for you. I want you to know that."

Danny listened, feeling an unwanted desire for hope, a hope he felt terrified he might actually receive. He almost nodded.

"Son, what you did with that money is honorable. You took from the undeserving and gave to worthy causes. You helped many people and are still helping some of them because of your selfless actions. It took courage." He touched the storyboard on Danny's lap. "Your cartoon shows this same sense of morality. I didn't believe the good you had done when you came to the house, and I'm sorry for that." He caressed the ripped anime father. "So what I want to say to you now, which I should have said then is this—*I'm proud of you, Son.*"

Danny felt it deep inside before he comprehended the words.

What a sensation—both euphoric and soothing—like crossing the finish line of an impossible race, or entering heaven. If he could have felt his fingertips or any part of his numb body, he might have tried to pinch himself.

"These are the values we taught you," Donald said, staring at the storyboard. "Sacrificing for others *is* duty and honor."

Danny glanced at his art, the proud father and triumphant son, and wondered if his father had always wanted to be proud of him, and if he'd ignored it out of selfishness.

"Roble is an evil person," Donald said, "a person who cares only for himself. You're not like him. I'm proud you are not. And you can help bring him to justice."

Danny's gut wrenched, but he pushed away the pain and grasped on to his father's words, trying to hold on to the seedlings of Donald's pride in him.

"Do you understand what I'm saying?"

His eyelids drooped. "Yes, Father."

"Good. I'm proud of you." Donald sat up, straightening out his suit. "Now, listen to what I'm about to say."

Danny nodded, but felt an unwanted hesitation inside. He nodded again, trying to shake the feeling.

"Do exactly as Mike says. If you do, they will let you come home. We want you home, Son."

Danny's eyes watered. His hands ran across the storyboard over Ritashugi. "Yes, Father."

Donald hugged him again. "When this is all over, I'll put you through any school you wish. We can work together as youth counselors—Sands and Son. How does that sound?"

Danny wanted to like the sound of those words, but his body compressed under the pressure of his father's arms, and the weight built along his spine. Sweat formed along the top of his lip. *Why does this conversation feel so familiar?*

"Your mother met a beautiful young lady at church a few weeks ago," Donald continued. "She'll introduce you when you get home."

Why does this feel like torture? His gaze moved to the horse in his drawing, wishing he could somehow mount it and escape.

"But don't think about that now, Son."

The weight kept pressing down, expelling the air from Danny's lungs, suffocating him. "Don't squeeze so tight…" he gasped, turning his head, only to realize his father no longer hugged him.

Exhaling, Danny straightened up, balancing an invisible mass on his shoulders. He wiped the sweat from his lip, and looked at attention, hands open at his sides, just as he did before every football game. But the pressure squeezed out a tear. It rolled down a cheek and fell, absorbing into his prison uniform like a man melting into something greater than himself.

Donald rose to leave. "I'm proud of you, Son. Don't forget."

Chapter 63

Roble lay exhausted, watching LEDs twinkle in the darkness like stars within his own personal universe. At the end of each workday stretching into the night during this past month, he had collapsed on this mat inside the *Roble Arrow's* fuselage. And each night, he had slept without stirring until he inhaled the next day, recognizing each scent within the aircraft, knowing where a single line of new wiring ran between struts, a new assembly with lubricated ball bearings fastened to the floor, or a silicone computer panel sat freshly installed between a rib.

The next morning, the whiff of coffee from the arriving workers erased his mind's view of the jet, awakening him to see it with his eyes.

He sat up, observing the elaborate guts of his dream. His hands caressed the wire-filled creation, thinking of all the decisions he'd made and lessons learned—everything he'd done to make this real. He touched his arrowhead.

Climbing to his feet, he walked to an open hatch and gazed out into the silver-blue dome. The sun's early light breached the hangar doors, sparkling across the hangar's womb and his nascent aircraft. He inhaled his creation and smiled.

Danny stood barefoot on his prison bed, staring down at his taped-together storyboard, at the sword in the Samurai father's hand. He swallowed, pressing against the sheet tied around his neck and the ceiling fire sprinkler. He looked up and thought of Nishiko touching his forehead. *A spark extinguisher.*

He glanced at his sleeve, at the number 884892 stamped across orange fabric. *Just a meaningless number, melting into a sequence of all others.* He leaned forward, feeling the pressure tighten around his windpipe. Blotches danced before his eyes coalescing into a scene…

Under a row of leafless crabapple trees, in a snow-covered cemetery, he envisioned a gathering in black standing around a casket suspended above a dirt hole. A preacher stood before them. Most of the downturned faces expressed guilty comfort in the inexplicable, yet inevitable tragedy of life.

"Of everyone I've spoken with about Brother Danny Sands," the preacher said, "it's clear that one quality saves him a place in heaven." He gazed across the bowed heads. "He thought of others before himself in everything he did. He was a selfless hero, and a loyal son. Amen."

As the image faded to darkness, Danny rasped, "I'm dead." He liked the way the words sounded in his constricted throat, so final and disconnected.

He extended a leg off the bed and held it there. He realized he wasn't breathing and didn't care. Reaching up, he gripped the sheet with both hands, and extended his other leg off the bed until he hung suspended in air. His core muscles contracted beyond any pain level he'd ever felt, yet he held still. *I, Danny Sands, am leaving everyone's expectations behind.*

Feeling faint and his body lightening, a scene reformed in front of his eyes…

Roble and Jenny stood next to each other, wearing black, their heads lowered. But they were not in the cemetery; they stood atop the Calico Basin Cliffs.

Jenny held Danny's anime drawing of a young man escaping on a horse with an arrow imbedded in his shoulder. The breeze fluttered the paper's edges and Jenny's long hair. She handed the art to Roble. He knelt down and folded it many times on a rock.

Rising to his feet, Roble lifted the paper plane and gazed across the horizon. The plane launched off the cliff, piercing through the air. The wind caught it, sending it up into the sky. It rose, untouched by everyone below, until it disappeared…as did the vision.

Danny tried to breathe, blinking his watery eyes, and glanced down at the storyboard on the prison mattress. With one hand now holding the sheet and all his body weight, he used the other to remove the noose. He landed feet first on the bed and smashed his storyboard with his heel.

Guards burst into the cell and tackled him to the bed.

Mike entered and glanced up as guards untied the sheet from the fire extinguisher. Tilting his head, he asked, "Couldn't go through with it?"

"No," Danny made eye contact, "I actually think I did."

Mike shook his head, scrunching his brows. "Your father promised you would cooperate. We have a deal." He waved the guards away.

Danny felt along his throat. "My parents deserve many things, but going to jail because of what I did isn't one of them."

"Smart decision, Danny."

Danny sat up. "I want to speak with Sitra in private. After that, I'll meet with Roble like you want."

"Who the hell is Sitra?"

"Governor Alexa Patra."

"Governor Patra?" Mike scoffed. "That's out of the question."

Danny stared at him without blinking.

"Not going to happen," Mike said.

Lying back down, Danny dropped an arm over his face.

Mike exhaled, pulled out his phone, and swiped an icon. "Get me Governor Patra."

Danny lowered his arm, watching him.

Holding the phone to his ear, he glared at Danny. "Governor Patra? We have a Mr. Danny Sands who would like to meet with you—"

Danny narrowed his eyes.

"You will? It must be done here in a federal prison cell and be supervised," Mike said. "Your office…with only Danny?" He swore under his breath. "Right now?" He rolled his eyes, shaking his head. "We'll be there shortly."

Mike rubbed his face. "Tell me this can't get any more bizarre."

A message headline popped up on Roble's laptop as he ran a diagnostic of the *Roble Arrow's* engines. *Meet at 8 PM in front of RR, Danny.*

Roble had to stand up. He gazed around the hangar, eyes stopping on the *Roble Arrow*. He looked back to the screen. "Danny Sands," he whispered, picturing the floppy-haired kid he first met so long ago. He pulled a wrinkled art cell from his pocket and stared at it.

Hearing Libby's faint laugh, he looked up. Libby leaned from the *Roble Arrow's* cockpit talking to Sigmund below. Sigmund glanced at Roble, raising a hand. Shaking his head, Roble minimized the message and resumed the test of the scramjet.

He studied the results—*flawless*. Raising a thumb, he whistled.

Libby gave a thumbs-up in response.

The whine of the *Roble Arrow's* auxiliary system shot anticipation down Roble's spine. Two monstrous turbines whirled to life making the air within the hangar shimmer like liquid. The jet's sleek body yawed forward as if stretching, not rolling, out of the silvery dome. It didn't stop until it reached the center of the virgin white tarmac.

Workers ran around securing its landing gear with anchors bolted into concrete. Roble moved next to its tailfins, standing closer to the craft than anyone. Hunching over, hands on his knees, he scrutinized every nuance of the idling engines.

Sigmund lowered a hand and the engines ejected long purple streaks. Their roaring pitch dropped into progressively lower octaves until it shook the ground.

Roble gasped, having never heard anything so exhilarating.

The left side exhaust cone dilated, bellowing an amber flame. The right exhaust melted into a colorless translucent blur stretching without end. Straining forward, the *Roble Arrow* begged for release.

The sides of Roble's mouth hooked up into a grin. He raised a fist and both engines fell dark, their final roll of thunder echoing off the Spring Mountains. A cheer erupted from the workers.

Jogging over to Sigmund, Roble asked, "When is the earliest we can complete the preflight testing?"

"A couple of days," Sigmund said. "We're on schedule."

"What if," Roble glanced at the hangar, "we needed it to launch…today?"

Sigmund frowned.

"I'm ready," a voice said from behind.

They turned.

Sircor stood in flight gear, his eyes fearless and alert. "I feel like I've prepared for this my whole life."

"We could have everything tested and ready to go by 8 PM." Roble turned to Sigmund. "Right, Mr. Evert?"

Sigmund sighed, shaking his head. "Does Libby know about this?"

"Well," Roble swallowed, "not yet."

"And to think I could've been peacefully teaching kids how to make ice scrapers." Sigmund brushed down his lab coat and walked away.

Sircor chuckled. "I see you haven't changed."

"I'm glad you're up for an early launch. But," he squinted at the *Roble Arrow*. "I won't be here for it. I have something else I must do."

"Well, I take it back then," Sircor rolled his eyes. "You? Missing a maiden voyage? Now that's a change."

Roble exhaled and touched his arrowhead. "Sir, make it soar."

"Like it's my last day on earth."

Roble nodded. "Will you please excuse me, I need to—"

"Giddy up," Sircor grinned. "Time's a ticking."

Roble ran in to the hangar and picked up his laptop. Maximizing the message on the screen, his heart beating within his ears, he typed: *See you at 8 PM. Roble.*

When the aircraft rolled back inside the hangar, its shadow stretched under Roble's feet.

Libby descended the boarding ladder and approached with a phone to her ear.

Roble closed the laptop, making eye contact with her.

She lowered the phone.

"Danny is back," he said.

Libby exhaled. "I know. Alexa just called and said Danny is going to trap you in a sting operation."

"Governor Patra knows about Danny wanting to meet with me?" He scrunched his brows.

"It doesn't mean she can protect you if you go." She slipped the phone into her pocket. "And that's not all she told me. Nevada police, working with the feds, discovered the location of our manufacturing cavern through an informant at one of our suppliers. Agents have the ranch stable surrounded and they've closed off the cliff house to the public in anticipation of the raid."

"Damn, that's what I was worried about. But I'm glad it wasn't Danny who gave them that information."

"Regardless of how they know, as soon as they raid the cavern," Libby said, "they'll find information leading to this airstrip. We might only have a few hours before they arrive here. We can't get the *Roble Arrow* flight ready that quickly."

"I don't think they'll raid the cavern before I've met with Danny for fear of scaring me off. That gives us ten hours until 8 PM. That's enough time to rush through the pre-flight tests. Sircor is ready."

She pursed her lips. "If Governor Patra hadn't just given Victor a special assignment today, I'd have him try to sneak in to the cavern and destroy our location information."

"If you think it's possible, I'll go."

"No," she shook her head. "Without Victor's expertise it's too dangerous. And if we want a real chance to launch tonight, I'll need you here to help accelerate the tests. Look," she said, "agree to meet with Danny; just *don't* show up. That will still give us until 8 PM to launch."

"Let's say we *do* get the *Arrow* off the ground tonight." He exhaled. "You know it's really the second, critical flight that's at risk. They will find this airstrip after the first flight no matter what."

"You just focus on getting the first flight ready. I'll see what our governor can do to delay them until we can achieve both launches." Libby touched his shoulder. "If we can get Sircor in the air a second time, we will pull this off." She tilted her head and cleared her throat. "You're *not* going to meet with Danny, right?"

Roble swallowed.

Libby searched his face, still holding his shoulder. "You and Danny were friends. I know it must hurt."

"Friends," Roble lowered his eyes. "Why do people say friends should love each other unconditionally—like unpaid whores exchanging favors, valuing nothing and accepting everything?" He inhaled, shaking his head. "I wish you'd met Danny when I did, saw what he could create." Gripping his arrowhead, he added, "I am going to meet with him, but not for his sake, Libby."

"Well," she pushed a hand through her hair, "for whatever

reason you're doing it," she exhaled, "good luck." She released his shoulder and glanced up. "I'll leave you two alone."

Roble turned. Nicolette stood behind him.

"You never told me how attractive Paiutes are." Nicolette winked.

Roble stared, surprised to see her in the hangar. *She belongs here...* He studied the contrast between her hair and the domed ceiling. *...like a golden goddess in a silver temple.*

"You'll be a handsome old Indian someday." She stepped into him, combing through his hair. "Just like Longbow."

"Longbow is attractive?"

"Very." She kissed his scarred chin. "*Smexy* eyes like you."

He wrapped his arms around her hips.

She glanced at the *Roble Arrow* and slid a hand between their chests, seizing his arrowhead. "It's you, Roble. That magnificent metal creature is *you*. You're giving the world a gift." She kissed him.

He kissed her back, drawing her against him. When they pulled apart, he said, "I have a favor to ask."

"Like a favor-exchanging-whore, kind of favor?" She narrowed her eyes, smirking.

Roble coughed. "You heard me say that?"

"I'll only let you ask it, if you let me be your unpaid whore." Her small nose twitched.

"Nicolette—"

She trailed her hands down his sides.

Roble breathed a few times, trying to regain his thought. "I'm going someplace this could get taken away from me again. Will you keep it safe?" He removed his necklace and pressed it into her hand.

"Will *you* be safe?"

Roble flexed his jaw without answering.

She held the necklace, her brows bent with concentration. "I know where to keep it."

"Thank you."

She took his hands. "What are friends for?" Her lips found his again.

Danny sat atop a motorcycle with its spark plugs removed. Across the street, the Road Runner Motorcycle Shop buzzed with activity.

He felt across his shirt, over the microphones taped to his body. He scratched at the speaker in his ear, his gut churning at the thought Roble might actually come. Yet he knew, as he always had, that Roble would always meet him here.

The punchy sputter of an engine pulled Danny's attention to a motorcycle stopping next to him. Glancing up, he saw grey eyes peering out from below flowing black hair. *Roble.*

"I'm glad you asked me to come." Roble revved the throttle, appearing ready to ride as he always did.

Danny grinned, wanting to ride away, ride with him anywhere. *"Keep him talking. Lead him into a conversation that will reveal his plot,"* a voice in his ear said. He glanced at the undercover agents in cars in front of and behind him, his spine tightening. He coughed, trying to catch his breath. "How are you?"

Roble turned off his engine. "Okay, Danny. You?"

Danny exhaled, looking at him.

"What information do they want from me?" Roble asked.

Danny picked at the handlebar grips. "You didn't need to come. I know you know that." Voices chastised him over his earpiece. "But I'm glad you did."

"I came because I wanted to say something to you." Roble felt along his pants pocket.

"Good, keep him talking," Danny heard over his earpiece. He swallowed hard, staring at Roble. *Don't tell them anything.*

"When—"

"Wait," Danny interrupted. "Let me ask you something first."

Roble nodded.

"Do you think death," Danny coughed, "is the only escape from what everyone else expects?" He held Roble's stare. "Is that why you've never tried to stop me?"

Roble's eyes gleamed like polished steel. "I never tried to stop you," his hand reached to his chest but grasped only air, "because choosing your own death is almost as selfish as choosing how to live."

He breathed a few times and nodded. "Roble, I think I finally understand."

"When I left the attic," Roble said, "I took two scraps of

paper with me, my idea and this—" He reached into his pocket and removed the crumpled drawing of the ragged young man escaping on a horse, and handed it to him.

Holding the drawing, Danny thought back to why he drew it.

"Here is what I came to say, something I tried to tell you back in Okinawa." Roble pointed at the art cell. "Your art reveals someone who chooses his own destiny. There is no way I can thank you enough for what you drew."

Danny lowered his head, closing his eyes. "Despite what I drew," his hands gripped the art cell, "I didn't choose my own course when it really mattered. I let others decide for me and I ended up at the only place I could have—somewhere I didn't recognize, somewhere inexplicable—and exactly where I was headed."

Breathing deep as if the air were pure oxygen, Danny opened his eyes. "But today, even though it's probably too late," he touched his own heart, "I have decided what I am going to be."

He gazed at the darkening sky; it appeared so expansive and open, like anything was possible. "Roble, don't tell them anything." Frantic voices pierced his ear, yelling, *"What are you doing? He's ready to talk!"* Ignoring them, he added, "You were always a friend to me, even when I wasn't to myself. And I'm sorry if I stopped your dream by stealing those diamonds."

"You didn't stop it. My dream, born on *my* scrap of paper, is…" Roble pointed at a glint in the sky.

Panicked voices in Danny's earpiece screamed, *"What did he say? What's he pointing at?"* Danny ripped the speaker from his head, tossing it to the ground.

Cars screeched up next to them, doors flew open, and agents jumped out with weapons drawn. "On the ground! Hands behind your head!"

Neither Roble nor Danny moved as they watched the *Roble Arrow* piercing the fading night sky, grinning like young boys watching a homemade rocket. Officers grappled them to the ground.

As men cuffed their hands behind their backs, Danny raised his head and looked again at his drawing. It lay on the curb face up, ripped in half by an officer's boot. He focused first on the arrow embedded in the boy's shoulder, then at the boy's dauntless eyes. He glanced through the spokes of the motorcycle wheels and saw those same eyes staring back.

Chapter 64

"Nellis Air Control," a radar specialist sitting deep under Cheyenne Mountain at NORAD Command Center said into a headset, "we are tracking an unidentified object one hundred nautical miles north of Las Vegas at sixty-five angels, heading: one-seven-five, moving hypersonic at twenty-six hundred knots. We need a visual. Scramble intercept."

"This is Smash Hammer at Nellis Air Control, copy that NORAD Command. We have birds in the air."

"Nellis Air Control," the radar specialist said, "we've lost satellite and radar contact with unidentified object. Last known location—fourteen nautical miles west, northwest of Nellis Air Force Base. Do you have a Judy on the bogey?"

"Smash Hammer, this is Royal Flush," Captain Wilks said, flying an F-22 Raptor one thousand feet above the desert, "no bogeys in the sky at coordinates. I have a visual on a remote airfield with no aircraft on the deck."

"Copy that, Royal Flush," Smash Hammer at Nellis Air Control said. *"Which airfield did you identify?"*

"Ah…it looks like a newly paved runway, possibly on tribal lands. There is a hangar and something written down the center of the tarmac."

"An Indian reservation?"

"Possibly," Royal Flush said, circling his Raptor. "Contact AWACS for confirmation."

"What is written on the runway?" Smash Hammer asked.

"It's in a foreign language, Spanish or Italian, possibly." Captain Wilkes dove the F-22 lower, vectoring its thrust for a slow flyby. "Ahhh…says, *Malo periculosam libertatem quam quietum servitium.* Not sure what that means."

"AWACS 277, can we affirm the jurisdiction of the airfield below Royal Flush?" Smash Hammer asked over the radio.

"Smash Hammer, this is Lieutenant Agassi aboard AWACS 277. The runway is located within the Las Vegas Paiute Tribal Lands."

"Copy that, AWACS 277."

"Nellis Air Control, this is NORAD Command. We are requesting you keep birds in the air. Central Intelligence indicates the landing strip is a potential terrorist operating base. All aircraft from that field are to be considered a national security threat."

"Copy that," Smash Hammer said, and swiveled in his chair to the lead air controller at Nellis Air Force Base. "Sir, we have a priority one."

The lead air controller widened his eyes, picked up the phone, and stared out the tower window. "Get me General Cassing."

"Fort Irvin, this is General Cassing, US Air Force, Nellis Commander. We have a priority one national defense emergency. Requesting ground troop presence on a landing strip at the following coordinates: ... Please advise corresponding Nevada National Guard back-up units. This is not a drill."

Six Nevada police officers led Roble and Danny toward the downtown Las Vegas police station. Ten federal officers followed along, glancing around in confusion.

"Hold up!" Federal Agent Wilson yelled, running after the Nevada officers. "Those prisoners are to be held at the federal facility." He pointed at a building behind him.

The Nevada officers halted. One, a sturdy-bodied, pock-faced man turned and swaggered over to Wilson. In a gritty voice he said, "My orders are to hold Roble Santos and Danny Sands in Nevada custody."

"Orders?" Wilson lifted his hands. "We're in charge of this operation. And where the hell is Captain Ames?"

"The Governor fired Captain Ames." He nodded at the other five Nevada officers, and they continued away with Roble and Danny. "I'm Captain Mendoza."

"This is outrageous. We have jurisdiction in this matter."

Mendoza cleared his sinuses with a sniff.

"I'm ordering you to bring back those prisoners." Wilson signaled the other federal officers and yelled, "Stop those men!"

The five Nevada officers escorting Danny and Roble drew their weapons. The three in the rear turned and walked backward as they continued to the police station.

The federal officers scrambled for cover, drawing weapons and aiming at the Nevada officers escorting Roble and Danny away.

"All transfers of Nevada residents to other jurisdictions," Captain Mendoza said to Agent Wilson, "must be approved by a state judge and the governor. So I suggest you order your men to stand down."

"Bullshit." Wilson's eyes locked on the escaping prisoners. "You were never to take custody."

As the Nevada officers reached the police station, one of the federal officers aiming at them yelled, "What are our orders?"

Agent Wilson rubbed his forehead.

"As a fellow law enforcer," Captain Mendoza said, "I'll do you a favor. File an enforceable criminal charge against Mr. Santos and Mr. Sands and prove jurisdiction and I'll petition the governor on your behalf for their transfer." He smiled, his deep facial scars twisting.

The Nevada officers led Danny and Roble into the building. Two guards, wearing grey metallic body armor and holding assault rifles, stepped outside, blocking the doorway.

The federal officers lowered their weapons and marched back to Agent Wilson.

Mike, wearing a turtleneck sweater, approached from the federal building and slipped in front of Agent Wilson, squaring his shoulders with the shorter Mendoza. "Evening, Captain. Apparently I need to clear something up. This is a *national security* operation. So, I supersede you, your governor, and even God himself." He touched Mendoza's shoulder. "If you want to keep your job, bring back those prisoners."

Mendoza folded his arms and spit near Mike's feet. "I suggest you take that threat and stuff it back down your trap." He spread his boots and lowered his hands to the nickel-plated revolvers on his hips.

Mike smirked. "What spot of the O.K. Corral did they dig you out of?"

The armed federal officers fanned out behind Mike and Agent Wilson.

Mendoza stared at Mike, his hands turned inward at his sides.

"All right, El Capitan." Mike chuckled. "You've had your little wild west show. Now, come back to reality. I'll even make you a deal. You hold onto Mr. Sands, and we'll take Mr. Santos. We'll share custody like practical law enforcement."

"You haven't charged Roble Santos with a crime," Mendoza said, "which is why we are protecting him from you. Danny Sands is charged with theft within this state by a Nevada prosecutor."

"Listen, el niño," Mike hissed, leaning in. "We have a federal plea deal signed with Danny Sands. And Roble Santos, the terrorist fugitive you just took away from me, almost started a world war outside of your jurisdiction. And I want him in my custody right…fucking…now."

Mendoza yawned.

Mike lifted his arms. "Well?"

"Well," Mendoza said, "if you signed an agreement with Mr. Sands, hold to it. As for Mr. Santos, have you charged him with 'not starting a war?'"

"*Almost* starting a war." Mike pulled at his turtleneck, face reddening. "He's too dangerous to try in court. And if you don't let me interrogate him, his terror cell could slaughter thousands of innocent Nevada residents. That will be on *your* head. Comprende?"

"Go ahead and show us your evidence and press charges. If you can't, he'll be freed. That's how a justice system works. Or do I need to explain it in Spanish?"

"What are you? Some kind of extremist wacko?"

"Here's your chance to find out." Mendoza clenched and released both fists next to his revolvers.

Mike rolled his eyes, lifted a radio, and said, "Deploy assets to extract Roble Santos from the downtown police station."

Two unmanned aerial vehicles launched off the ground near the federal building. Federal officers ran to a van and fitted themselves with body armor, then formed into a line holding a battering ram, facing the police station.

"If we go in," Mike said, "you'll be responsible for the

consequences." Pointing his radio at Mendoza, he added, "Do the right thing, Captain, and make the call."

Mendoza's elbows cocked back as the UAVs buzzed in the air.

"I don't think you understand," Mike pointed at the sky, "those UAVs are armed with Hellfire missiles. Tell your guards to step aside. Now."

Mendoza cleared his throat. "Not even going to give me a count to three?"

"You ignorant fucker." Mike shook his head and pressed the radio to his lips. "Begin extraction on the count of three. One... two—"

Both UAVs exploded in blinding fireballs, one after the other, their detonations shaking officers and buildings. Car alarms blared. Sparking electronic UAV guts cascaded into the parking lot. Everyone crouched low, looking around, hands protecting their heads.

The clopping of horse hooves cut through the aftermath. A plate-armored white knight, holding a shiny metallic rifle and sitting atop a black chainmail-covered Percheron, pranced up to Mike. "...*trois.*"

The cavalier flipped up his glowing green visor, revealing indigo eyes. "Ah...what a beautiful evening for fireworks. Would you not agree, *Messieurs*?"

"What the hell?" Mike asked, still covering his head with his hands.

"Nevada General, Victor Lafayette." He bowed low, sweeping out a hand. "Retreat your hostile forces and we will spare your lives...and likely spare myself an impromptu nap."

Agent Wilson blinked.

Mike lowered his hands, his eyes wide. "Am I going insane?"

"I would elucidate how you would most certainly lose this battle," Victor flipped down his visor, "but my forces have already demonstrated in a tangible illustration to save us time." He waved his rifle at the burning UAV carcasses.

"I didn't think this case could get any more bizarre," Mike mumbled. "What is wrong with you people in Nevada?"

"Stick around and find out," Mendoza said.

Mike glanced at the smoldering UAVs then back at the knight. "No one messes with the US government and gets away with it," he said. "You just wait; you're going to pay for this."

Shaking out his wrists, he snapped his body around. "Form a perimeter around the police station. Nobody gets out without my permission."

All the federal agents and officers in the parking lot dispersed into position as Mike strode away.

"Nevada General, huh?" Mendoza sneered up at Victor. "Don't generals usually employ an army?"

"I am without volunteers at the moment." Victor flicked his gauntleted fingers in the air and turned his steed around. "Carry on, my good Captain." Raising his weapon he said, "*Liberté and justice,*" and pranced away.

Alexandria walked past two federal agents and entered the downtown Las Vegas police station.

Captain Mendoza met her in the lobby and escorted her to an elevator. "The feds came at us pretty hard for taking Roble Santos into custody."

"It's going to get worse."

Mendoza raised an eyebrow and pressed the button to the third floor detention area.

"I've been ordered by the Joint Chiefs of Staff to hand him over," Alexandria said. "They claim he's an enemy combatant."

"What, the US military? They can't do that. How did you respond?"

"I said...no."

"Oh, Lord." Mendoza shook his head. "A few federal agents are one thing. What do we do if the military tries to extract him?"

"If *anyone* initiates force against you," she exited the elevator, "defend yourself. The chain armor your SWAT teams received from General Lafayette will hold up in a confrontation as long as the other side doesn't use heavy weapons. Equipping with plate armor will take more time and donations."

"Oh, yeah, I was going to ask you about...that *general*. With all due respect, Governor, what the hell?"

"He will be busy on an assignment tomorrow morning, so you will have to manage any defense here by yourself. But I don' think the feds will try anything stupid against you again, at leas not yet."

"Is it too late to turn down this promotion?"

"Yes."

Mendoza laughed. "Good."

They walked through a guarded entryway and security buzzed them through a steel door leading to a prison hallway. Mendoza stopped in front of a cell.

"Don't allow federal access to this facility until further notice," Alexandria said.

"Yes, Governor Patra." He unlocked and slid open the cell door.

Alexandria entered. He closed the door behind her.

Roble stood near a narrow window peering out at the moon.

"I thought you hated being locked up?" Alexandria paced the tiny cell. "Why turn yourself in?"

He turned around, rubbing his scarred chin. "Maybe I missed being in your custody."

"In that case," she stopped before him, "you can stay here where I can protect you."

"Oh yeah," Roble smirked, "now I remember why I hated it."

She moved closer, their eyes aligning. "Once we find you a safe route out of here, you can go. Until then, the feds could file enforceable charges against you and request your transfer. But when I say enforceable, I mean for an actual crime."

"Well," he said, "this will be the most exciting wait of my life."

"I see you've never outgrown your sarcasm."

"Sarcasm? I was being literal."

Alexandria tapped her foot. "I heard the buzz from the Air National Guard regarding an unidentified aircraft tonight north of the city. By their excited tones, I'm guessing *it* was a success."

"Since you know Libby, you already knew it would be. But that flight was just my former fighter squadron commander screwing around." He tried to hold back a grin. "The training wheels come off tomorrow morning."

"As I told Libby, I don't have the means to defend your aircraft against any belligerence in Nevada airspace. Maybe someday I will."

"If it can get off the ground again, it won't need protection— just an open sky and an untouched horizon."

"You never did grow up." She touched the scar on his chin with her fingertip. "And I'm so happy for you."

"Never grew up?" He rubbed where she had touched. "Speak for yourself...Sitra."

She smiled and cleared her throat. "Libby told me you didn't have to show up for the sting operation to get your aircraft off the ground tonight. So why did you risk meeting with Danny?"

Roble shrugged, tilting his head.

"All right, we all have our reasons." She turned and walked to the cell door. "For my part, I'm holding Danny in Nevada custody to ensure him due process for his theft charges. If the feds made a deal with him, I'll remind them to keep it."

Roble touched his heart and nodded at her.

"You don't have to wait in here," she said, turning back to him. "You're free to hang out in the officers' lounge."

"I kinda like this cell, brings back good memories." He glanced at the bedsheet. "And I'm still not being sarcastic."

She smiled. "I'll leave the door open."

"Good day, Honorable Governor Patra."

"Roble Santos." She nodded.

Terrorist Hideout? the news headlines asked.

Video of federal officials storming a ranch stable near The Calico Center for the Preservation of Our Heritage streamed from news cameras. A picture of the scowling ranch owner Halvern Black, filled the screen with the words: *Disgraced architect and person of interest.*

After federal agents had secured the area, they escorted TV reporters down a hidden ramp inside a horse stable leading to a glass-shrouded cavern. News videos displayed alien-looking robots, strange alloy parts, and banks of computers hinting at the creation of something secret and sinister within the subterranean lair.

"Based on what I've been told from top sources," Chris Wright of the Federal Aviation Administration said, standing in the glass cave next to an unattached *Succubus* wing, "I fear for the safety of those who might be exposed to whatever unapproved aircraft

Ms. Dodge devised here. We will be forming a commission to determine how this was allowed to happen."

"This is not the first time Ms. Dodge is suspected of providing material support to extremists," a reporter added.

As reporters moved from the manufacturing cave to the water cave, they whistled, eyes wide at the illuminated waterfall.

Another reporter, who had gained access to the hidden upper cliff house's floor, stood in front of the portrait of Gilbert du Motier Lafayette, the revolutionary war general who served under George Washington. "It is unclear why this shadowy group possessed a priceless piece of American art history," she said to a camera.

Throughout the day, federal bureaucrats in The Calico Center for the Preservation of Our Heritage interviewed with reporters while standing on balconies looking down on the raided ranch. All the Nevada State Park Service employees housed on the fourth level were conspicuously absent from the interviews, their offices abandoned.

The museum director, her hair tied in a chic chignon, said to a reporter, "I'm shocked and saddened to discover that a rogue passage connected in to this museum. We fear the worst and have initiated a review to determine if anyone stole public property."

"Not only did these people senselessly violate our under-ground environment," Diane Hughes of the Environmental Protection Agency said, "but they cheated taxpayers by withholding public access to the hidden floor of this center. This is just one more example of how reckless greed is ruining the American landscape."

"Libby Dodge and Halvern Black conspired to use public land for personal use," Dr. Hughbner of the Bureau of Land Management said, rubbing the aluminum balcony railing in his office, "to the detriment of society's sacred trust. A Department of the Interior investigation will be launched against both individuals." He stared at the sweat-smear his hand had left on the rail. "For now, the newly liberated floor and caves will be preserved under the direction of the Bureau."

Morning's first light painted the pyramidal ridges of the

Spring Mountains a blushing pink. News helicopters hovered at a distance above a convoy of Nevada National Guard trucks parked at the entrance to the Las Vegas Paiute Tribal Lands. A line of Army vehicles idled behind the Nevada National Guard trucks.

A local radio station called the Las Vegas Paiute chief on the phone, broadcasting the conversation.

"Is your tribe harboring extremists?"

"No," the chief said.

"Will you let the Army verify your claim?"

"No."

"That won't fly," a legal expert with a trim goatee said on TV, referring to another guest's remark that tribal lands are sovereign territory. "They can't just allow anyone to do as they please on land they claim is theirs. The safety of society comes before all other considerations, morally speaking."

Danny cracked his eyes enough to see a hand holding a document above his face. He sat up on the prison mattress, focusing on Mr. Greenly, his father's bearded lawyer.

"Please sign where I've indicated." Mr. Greenly held out a pen.

Danny wiped his eyes.

"It's the agreement with the feds." He tossed the document to the bed. "I advise you to sign it before they change their minds. I've never seen a deal this favorable to a guilty defendant, or even a not guilty defendant for that matter."

"I shouldn't have done what they wanted."

"But you did." The lawyer shook his head. "Sign it."

"On two conditions."

Mr. Greenly whipped out a phone and pressed a button. "Mr Sands, I think you need to talk to your son." He handed the phone to Danny.

Danny held it to his ear.

"Son?"

"Father."

"Things are absolutely chaotic around the house," Donald

said. "Your mother started decorating for a campaign function of mine. Maybe when you get here, you can manage this stuff. She uses too much pink…although I guess it shows my softer side to women voters. Did you get the deal signed yet?"

"No."

"Uhhhh…what's going on down there? Put Greenly back on the phone. We can't afford to lose this deal. Do you understand me?"

"'What's going on?' is a question I should have figured out long ago."

"Son, listen to me very carefully. Nobody knows what you did or where the money came from. A judge sealed the indictment due to national security concerns. If you don't sign that deal and you go to trial, your behavior will become public. No matter how noble your intentions, that's multiple felony charges." He lowered his voice. "Do you know how that will look? Your life would be ruined. No youth counseling…nothing."

"Those consequences all seem fair."

"Fair? Do you know how it will make your mother and I look?"

"I don't want to hurt you or Mother."

"Oh…well, good. I'm proud of you, Son, remember? Don't forget. Sign the deal, and we'll discuss everything when you get here."

"I have two conditions for me to sign."

Silence.

"Give all the money you have left from the diamonds to Stock Brant. I owe him every penny written on those charity receipts and this will be a start."

"You want me to give money to that drug dealing bastard, *Stock Brant*?"

"No, you're *going* to give that money to Stock Brant. And the second condition: apologize to Roble for hitting him while he lived with us. And since Roble won't want to meet with you, you're going to write him a letter. Deliver the money and letter to Governor Patra's Las Vegas office. Once you've done that, I'll sign the deal."

"Son…" Donald breathed over the line. "We are going to have a long talk once you get home."

"No, I don't think so. I'm crossing out my end of the federal plea deal. The State of Nevada can prosecute me for what I did. Not that I'm too concerned, because I've decided to opt out."

"Opt out? Of what?"

"Everything…everything everyone expects of me. I'm done."

After a moment of silence, Donald's voice exploded, "Don't you dare make threats like *that!* Do you know how many people rely on you? Do you have any idea how many people would be hurt if you…did that? Do you want to go straight to Hell? Suicide is the most selfish and cowardly act anyone could ever do. Do you hear me, Son? There is nothing more selfish." He cleared his throat. "And what about Jenny? Would you really hurt her too?"

"Second most selfish thing I could do. But I wasn't talking about suicide. I'm choosing an even more selfish option than that."

"What?"

"Bye, Dad. Say hello to Mother for me. Governor Patra will contact me once you've given her what I asked for." He took the pen from Mr. Greenley and tossed back the phone.

"Wait," the phone speaker yelped. "Remember that I'm proud of you, Son? Don't—"

"Get out of my cell, please," Danny said to the lawyer.

Chapter 65

The *Roble Arrow* poured from the hangar, its long, gloss-grey tube led by two delta winglets forming an arrowhead at its nose. Its matte-black canopy on top matched its light-absorbing heat shields underneath. Its tail formed three long fins, one vertical, two angling down. Twin engines behind the fins pulsed searing crimson circles. It looked like a metallic arrow, one that could pierce the very heart of existence.

Painted on the vertical tailfin—a youth riding a horse with arrows flying by his body. The whizzing arrows, the galloping horse, and the boy's spirited stance failed to catch the eye as much as the boy's expression of inexorable determination.

Two sharp-edged wings slid out from inside of the *Roble Arrow's* fuselage like blades from a two-sided pocketknife. The aircraft rolled to the end of the runway and aimed south toward the awakening city. A roar erupted from its engines, a violence detached from the jet's elegant lines.

US Army Major Everett, inside an armored personnel carrier near the Paiute reservation, picked up a radio and said, "We are a go. All units advance."

Diesel smoke bellowed into the air as camouflaged trucks lurched forward. But the charge ground to a halt before it began. The National Guard trucks at the lead hadn't moved.

"Advance," Everett ordered.

"Major Everett," Captain Kerr, the commander of the Nevada National Guard Platoon said over the radio, "I have orders from Governor Patra to hold position."

"I am giving you a direct order from the goddamn Commander-in-Chief. Advance!"

"We will not leave Nevada territory, sir."

"Son of a bitch-slapping governor." Major Everett lifted

the radio. "Flank the National Guard vehicles. We're taking the airfield."

Fourteen Army trucks reversed away from the National Guard vehicles. They formed a line and plowed a path through the desert and into the reservation, veering onto the main entrance road.

Longbow stood in the Army's path. The silver wings of an Air Force pilot gleamed on a necklace around his neck.

The convoy stopped. Major Everett jumped down from the lead vehicle. "Out of the way." He drew a pistol.

From the east, thumping hooves and a cloud of dust stole the Major's attention. Two dozen Paiute warriors, wearing full war regalia over chainmail, rode out on a hill next to the road. The lead rider wore white plate armor, a silver weapon crossed over his chest.

Soldiers scrambled from trucks, aiming assault rifles. Fifty caliber machine guns stationed atop the vehicles swiveled into position.

Longbow walked toward Major Everett, hands in the air. "This is not your land. You must leave."

"Tell those goddamn Indians to stand down. We are authorized to use force," the major said.

Longbow lowered his hands, planting his feet. The Paiute warriors on the hill jostled atop their steeds. Army soldiers shifted, awaiting orders.

"Very well then," Everett said, climbing back in the vehicle. He signaled the driver to proceed. The truck rolled forward. It stopped only when its bumper touched Longbow's thighs.

Longbow stepped back, pulled a revolver from a holster, and pointed it at the driver. "This is where we find out what we each believe."

"Shoot him," the Army driver said, ducking.

The armored knight twirled his rifle in one hand and pressed its butt to his shoulder plate, taking aim at the lead vehicle. Following suit, the Paiute warriors raised their rifles.

Army troops crouched lower, fingers on triggers.

"Hold fire!" Major Everett yelled, appraising the situation. "This wasn't supposed to happen," he mumbled under his breath and reached for the radio.

Libby sunk her climbing shoes into a patch of sand labeled, *Closed for revegetation*, on her way in to the reopened lobby of The Calico Center for the Preservation of Our Heritage.

With a twinkle in her eye and a leather pack over her shoulders, she passed everyone in the reception area—including the park rangers who stood around two TV screens watching video of the drama unfolding at the Paiute reservation.

"Why don't they just bomb 'em?" one ranger said.

At the rear of the lobby, Libby knelt by a secluded metal door and opened her pack. The whirling bit from her portable drill sliced through the door's locking mechanism. She slipped inside the emergency stairwell. Bounding up the steps, she slapped her hands against the rock to a rhythmic beat.

Reaching the third level of her former house, she strode into the Bureau of Land Management offices.

Most workers sat staring at their computer screens, watching the news. A few stood in front of windows looking north at the far-off helicopters and fighter jets buzzing over the desert.

Libby walked past an assistant sitting near Libby's former home office. "Please hold my calls," she said, entering the office. The door closed before the assistant could respond.

Removing a collapsible pick from her pack, Libby pegged it into a rubber stopper, dislodging it from a wall fountain. Water gushed into a dust-filled trough in the floor. Following the muddy flow to the balcony, she watched it pour over the edge into an empty pool now holding an air conditioning unit.

Brushing documents off a redwood table, she set down her pack, removed a hacksaw, cut the balcony's aluminum railing off at its base, and kicked it over the edge.

She pulled a canteen from her pack, opened it, and took a sip of iced tea. With arms stretched above her head, she inhaled, the sun caressing her face. "Ahhh…" she breathed, listening to the cascading water silence the air conditioning fan below. "There really is no place like home."

Roble stood in his cell, chin lifted, a sliver of sunlight from the window touching his closed eyes. His arms rested at his sides, palms open and facing forward. He awaited the greatest moment of his life.

Danny stood in his cell using Mr. Greenly's pen to draw a horse on his cell wall. Atop the horse rode a young man wearing a ripped prison uniform, gazing into the unknown.

Two F-22 Raptors flashed low to the ground over the *Roble Arrow* as it sat on the Paiute runway, a slap of thunder shaking the adjacent hangar.

A deep rumble echoed off the mountains as purple cones of fire extended out behind the *Roble Arrow*. For a moment the aircraft held motionless, then it launched, accelerating. Its exhausts melted into white, crackling like a bellowing forge.

"Smash Hammer, this is Iron Ace One," the lead F-22 pilot said to Nellis Air Control. "We have a takeoff underway at the Paiute airfield."

"Copy that, Iron Ace One. Force it to stay on the ground."

"Unidentified aircraft, this is Major Parker of the US Air Force," Iron Ace One said. "You are ordered to cut your engines. You will be shot down if you lift off."

The *Roble Arrow* lifted off the tarmac, its underbelly streaking just feet above the sage and Joshua trees.

"Smash Hammer, bogey is in the air. He's bulls-eye, heading: one-eight-six, on the deck, traveling at three hundred knots and accelerating."

"Roger, Iron Ace One. Do you have missile lock?"

Iron Ace One checked his tracking monitor. "Negative, can't paint bogey, too low to deck. I'm going to circle around and switch to guns."

Longbow turned and watched the *Roble Arrow* shooting across the desert. He lowered his pistol, saluted the Army soldiers, and stepped out of their way. The Paiute warriors on the hill scattered, horse hooves flinging dust in the air. The knight remained, watching the *Roble Arrow* barreling toward Las Vegas.

"Move out! Secure the airstrip," Major Everett said.

"Smash Hammer," Iron Ace One said, seeing residential rooftops flash by, "bogey is heading over civilian structures." His finger held near the gun trigger.

"Hold fire, Iron Ace One. I'm contacting civilian air control."

"Tally-ho, multiple civilian aircraft. I'm breaking high," Iron Ace Two said, pulling his F-22 Raptor up into the sky, following Iron Ace One.

"Civilian airspace is being cleared," Smash Hammer said. *"Pursue the bogey. Shoot it down only if you can avoid collateral damage."*

"Copy that, Smash Hammer," Iron Ace One said, his F-22 engines kicking on their afterburners as he dove, tracking behind the fleeing *Roble Arrow.* "Padlocked and fangs out. Waiting for a clean shot."

Libby stood on the cliff balcony, observing a grey blur jetting south over her former North Las Vegas facility, two fighters in tail. She lifted her iced tea in a toast.

The *Roble Arrow* zoomed between downtown casinos and followed the hotel-lined Strip southward. Tourists watching outdoor video displays of the news ducked their heads as the jets roared overhead, shaking windows.

Roble followed the growl of the engines, his eyes still closed, a fist clenched to his heart. He breathed in, visualizing his dream shooting by.

Danny felt his cell vibrate and took a step back, observing his rider galloping across an imaginary desert.

The *Roble Arrow* thundered toward the base of *The Spirit of Man.*

"Smash Hammer," Iron Ace One said, his voice rising, "bogey is on a collision course with a skyscraper. Request permission to kill with high probability of civilian casualties. I have missile lock."

"Please confirm threat, Iron Ace One."

"Affirm! Affirm!"

"Permission granted," Smash Hammer said, then whispered, *"Oh my God."*

Iron Ace One caressed the missile release, contracting his finger.

His finger pulled back as he saw the bogey's wing flaps, elevators, and engine vectors shift, creating lift.

The *Roble Arrow* snapped vertical, launching upward, its black belly reflecting off white windows as though two arrows raced into the sky, a flash of fire shooting downward.

The F-22s roared past *The Spirit of Man* and pulled up into the sky. "Holding fire," Iron Ace One said. "Bogey missed the structure. Blowers on; in pursuit."

The *Roble Arrow's* wings retracted inward as it ripped past the top of the glass, mere feet from Halvern Black who stood at the edge. Turbulence bent his frame backward but his feet held steady. His gaze followed the *Roble Arrow*, watching its engines release condensed ice crystals, forming its own ethereal skyscraper.

Army vehicles rumbled to a stop in front of the Paiute hangar. Soldiers leapt from trucks and scrambled about looking for resistance. Only one person could be seen, standing at the far end of the runway near a yellow car. A platoon ran in combat formation to the target.

As they neared, they slowed, lowering their weapons. A woman walked toward them in short steps, hair blowing in the wind, her nose tilted up.

The platoon stopped.

The woman took several steps closer and planted her yellow shoes on the runway, hands on her black tennis outfit. "I can't believe y'all missed it," she said in a southern drawl. "It was something *smexy*."

The platoon leader touched his helmet. "Nicolette Popov! What are you doing here?"

A young private stepped forward and rolled up her sleeves revealing two replicas of Nicolette's tattoos.

"Just propose to her already!" another soldier yelled.

Nicolette approached the private. "Why do you have those?"

The private glanced behind at the others. "I watched all o

your major tournaments online before they banned you. I've always wanted to know what your tattoos meant."

"What's your name?" Nicolette asked.

The other soldiers shuffled closer.

"Not too close." The platoon leader moved next to the private. "Give Ms. Popov some space."

"Tyrisha Benzo," the private said.

Nicolette gripped the bottom of her shirt and pulled it over her head, revealing a red bra strapped over a tanned body. The soldiers jostled with one another for a better view.

Looking at Private Benzo, Nicolette asked, "Which tattoo are you the most curious about?"

Her eyes shot to Nicolette's left hand with the blue fountain.

Nicolette glanced across the soldiers' faces. They leaned in.

"A fountainhead is a source of water—a source of life." She pointed to her own temple. "I am the source of my own purpose—*my* source for living."

The young faces stared at Nicolette. She turned, hair hanging behind her back, and walked in short steps to the yellow supercar parked behind her, swinging her shirt in a hand. The shape of Nevada glowed on the skin above her swaying hips.

She jumped in the driver seat and the winged door enclosed her inside the bull. Its engine burst forth like a chorus of fire devils. Liquid and fumes spit from the convulsing tail pipes. Two smoking trails painted the white tarmac black as the supercar tore onto the connecting street.

"Whisky Tango Foxtrot," Iron Ace One said under his breath, as a circular cloud detonated out across the sky. At its epicenter, the *Roble Arrow* hurtled up to the heavens, its wings retracted in against the fuselage forming a slender, delta-shaped projectile.

Roble felt the triple sonic booms penetrate his body. "Oh…" He slowed his breathing, eyes still closed, lips cracking a smile.

Feeling the sonic concussions, Danny looked up at the ceiling. "Go Roble. Rip the universe a new one."

The sonic thuds tickled Libby's eardrums as she watched the *Roble Arrow* piercing its own sonic wake, recalling how she felt sitting on her kitchen floor seeing Roble's first sketch from Japan.

Stock set down his pencil at the sound of the concussions, staring at a sketch of a mushroom's modified DNA chain. He rolled onto his back atop his prison cell bed and closed his eyes. "You're right, Roble. It's not for them," he whispered, "or against them."

"Iron Ace One, this is Smash Hammer. We are tracking bogey breaking above sixty angels. Do you have a clear shot?"

"Two miles in tail and falling behind." Iron Ace One watched the view of the *Roble Arrow* shrinking in his canopy.

"You are cleared to fire."

"Smash Hammer," Iron Ace One feathered the missile release, "what is the threat again? Over."

After a moment of silence, Smash Hammer said, *"Take the shot Iron Ace One."*

The *Roble Arrow* barrel-rolled, its engine exhausts flaring a blinding white pulse, separating itself farther from the F-22s.

"I've lost missile lock," Iron Ace One said, glancing at his tracking monitor that still displayed a weak missile lock.

"Iron Ace Two, this is Smash Hammer. Bogey is breaching maximum angels. You are ordered to fire."

"I've lost missile lock," Iron Ace Two said.

"What's going on up there?"

"You should have seen it..." Iron Ace Two said, his voice distant.

"Say again?"

"It was absolutely beautiful," Iron Ace One said. "If an enemy made that, we might want to reconsider who we call friend. Bogey is out of range. Disengaging."

"Houston Control, this is NORAD Command. We are tracking a unidentified aircraft at one hundred and fifty angels and climbing, traveling at Mach 4.3 and accelerating. Can you confirm?"

"NORAD Command, this is Houston Control," a tracking specialist said, sipping coffee as he sat in the almost empty

Houston Control Center. He peered at a screen, covered his microphone and called across the floor. "We need long-range optics." Uncovering his microphone, he added, "NORAD Command, we have it on radar. Moving extended range optics into position now. Please hold."

"Copy that, Houston Control. Can you contact the aircraft on long-range radio?"

"We will request radio contact on all channels." The tracking specialist signaled a communication specialist. Covering his mic again he yelled, "See if you can find out who's in that thing."

"Unidentified aircraft, this is Houston Control," the communication specialist hunched over his station, "please respond."

"Good morning," a voice echoed through Houston Control Center's open speaker.

The staff members at the Houston Control Center glanced at each other.

"With whom are we speaking? Over," the communications specialist asked.

Sircor glanced at the brushed-alloy cockpit controls below a clear horizon, his hands vibrating as the turbines pushed to their maximum velocity. "This is Gavin Sircor, aboard the *Roble Arrow.*"

"Uh, Gavin Sircor aboard the Roble Arrow, *please advise on your mission. Over."*

Sircor touched a video display and read: *Turbines A and B shut down.* Both dual mode turbines spun to a stop, silencing the engines, leaving only forward motion and wind resistance as though he sat inside an arrow loosed from the bow of a god.

"I repeat, please advise on your mission. Do you copy?"

Sircor's video screen blinked: *Ramjet A ignition.* The left engine's ramjet sucked in air and blasted it out the exhaust, pressing Sircor against his seat, propelling the craft like it had been standing still.

Opening the mic, Sircor said, "This is a private aircraft on a joy ride." He watched the needle on his Machmeter climbing. *Mach 5.0...Mach 5.5* "My God..." *Mach 6.*

At Mach 6.5 a screen blinked: *Ramjet A shutdown—Scramjet B ignition.* The right exhaust released a blurry streak of transparent heat into the upper stratosphere, accelerating the *Roble Arrow* as the left ramjet exhaust fell dark.

"NORAD Command, this is Houston," a NASA radar technician said, "We've made contact with the aircraft."

"Copy that Houston. Who is it, and what are its intentions?"

"Uhmm…a…joy… The pilot described it as a *joy ride*."

"Say again, Houston. A joy ride?"

"Affirmative." The Houston Control technician glanced up at a large screen above rows of workstations. "Our long-range optics are in position and we have a visual. The aircraft's left engine is shut down. It could indicate a malfunction."

"Is it falling?"

"Negative, it's accelerating. Tracking at over Mach 9 and its engine signature is not from a rocket. We don't know what to make of it."

The Houston Control Director, standing behind the radar technician, picked up a phone. "Get me a full mission crew down here *now*. We have an event."

Under the Cheyenne Mountain at NORAD Command Center, a threat monitoring specialist turned to a general. "Sir, we have a request from the Russians to explain an unannounced launch of a cruise missile into the lower mesosphere."

"Dammit. Tell the Russians it's a…it's a NASA engine test or something." The general moved behind a row of ballistic experts. "Could this be some kind of manned missile? Give me all possible targets based on its trajectory."

Internet bloggers in Russia, using unauthorized Russian military radar tracking information, posted updates on the speed and location of the unidentified aircraft. A Nordic TV station broadcast the leaked flight information.

Requests from around the world trickled into NASA seeking confirmation on the existence of an unannounced hypersonic aircraft in the upper mesosphere.

When Russian bloggers reported that the craft reached a speed of Mach 25, escape velocity, the story broke across the world's mainstream media. NASA confirmed the information and set up a media feed to give updates.

"Houston, this is the *Roble Arrow*. I have informed *my* ground control I've achieved lower Earth orbit," Sircor said, navigating past a telecom satellite.

"Roble Arrow, we never detected a rocket signature. How did you get there?"

"As a boy did you ever ride a bicycle at night below the stars?" Sircor grinned. "Getting here was like pedaling and shifting gears…only slightly faster and with a bit more thrust."

The *Roble Arrow* glided along an orbital arc. Sircor toggled a switch, unraveling a solar sail around the center of the craft. Three openings in the hull released laser turrets which aimed at the sail. The lasers fired, blasting the sail, propelling the craft away from earth.

Roble felt the sun's warmth upon his eyelids, his mind's eye watching his dream blazing a path across the blackness of space.

"He's heading out to space!" a NASA engineer shouted.

Activity surged across the Houston Control Center floor as though someone had pulled the fire alarm.

"What?" The Houston Director ran up behind the engineer. He pressed a headset over his ear and wiped the sweat above his lip. *"Roble Arrow, where are you going?"*

Sircor glanced behind at the bright azure orb falling away and then watched the *Roble Arrow's* nose piercing the dark void. "To see what's out there."

Chapter 66

Aerospace engineers and mathematicians at Houston Control Center huddled around computers making assumptions and entering calculations. The large screen facing rows of workstations displayed the *Roble Arrow's* speed: 41,075 MPH. And it was accelerating.

"Its ETA to pass the moon is four hours?" the director asked. "Didn't the Apollo missions take over three days to reach it?"

"That's correct," a nearby engineer said. "A Pluto mission set the record at a little over eight hours using rockets. This thing is using some kind of laser-powered sail. We thought it was just theoretical."

Dr. Hughbner shuffled out of the third floor elevator holding a large soda mug and strolled toward his office at The Calico Center for the Preservation of Our Heritage.

Federal employees across the floor watched their computer screens, listening to the crackling NASA broadcast of a man leaving the bounds of Earth's orbit. "Is he allowed to just do that? Without a permit or anything?" a woman asked from a cubicle.

Dr. Hughbner bounced off his office door, spilling fizzy brown liquid down his dress shirt. "Oh, dangit," he said, looking at the laminate-covered floor. "I hope this doesn't leak through to the rock." He turned to his assistant. "Why is my office locked?"

The assistant glanced up from her computer screen. "Uhmm, a woman went in there about twenty minutes ago. The way she spoke, I thought you were expecting her."

"Who?" He rubbed his wet belly and then tested to see if his fingers stuck together.

"She didn't give a name." The assistant scrunched her brows.

"She had neck-length russet hair, green eyes, and wore climbing gear of some sort."

Dr. Hughbner dropped his mug, splashing the soda across the floor and his assistant. He knocked on the door, his chest heaving. "I want my door opened, now."

The assistant dabbed a napkin against her drenched pants and picked up the phone.

A few minutes later, a security team and a locksmith arrived, jangling keys and weapons.

"I want Libby Dodge removed in cuffs this time," Dr. Hughbner said, kneeling on the floor inspecting a seam in the sticky linoleum. "We can't allow this sort of intrusion."

The locksmith swung open the door. The security team rushed in.

Dr. Hughbner waddled after them, cringing at the water pouring down a floor trough. Looking up, he saw everyone standing at the balcony's edge. Pressing his belly over the cut railing, he gazed at a rope dangling off the cliff, and shook his head. "This is against code."

A horse galloped away across the desert basin below, a trail of dust following behind.

"Oh dear. That's a revegetation area," Dr. Hughbner mumbled.

It's so stunning. Sircor's jaw dropped as he gazed at the moon's shadowy craters and bright plains as he flew by. *Look at it—a huge white rock just floating out here.* Peering beyond the moon, the universe begged for him to come and touch it.

"We're back at the moon," an excited voice at Houston Control said. "Beyond it, actually."

The Houston Director stared at the large screen, touching the mouthpiece of his headset. "*Roble Arrow*, do you copy?"

"Yes, Houston?" Sircor looked behind him at the three celestial spheres lined up in a row. One dark grey, one brilliant blue, one blinding gold.

"You should know," the director said, *"no human has ever been th* *far from Earth."*

Sircor beheld the solar system, breathing in the silence.

Alexandria sat in her Las Vegas office, a thin speaker restir on her desk like a sailboat on a reflective lake. Her hand hung of the armrest holding a document with the word *Directive* writte above the emblem of the US Department of Justice.

She thought of a blue file folder with red *Delinquency* stamp emblazoned on it in the shape of a launching rocket, and of scrawny boy with motorcycle and skateboard patches sewn o his greasy jacket.

"To Roble Santos," Sircor broadcast to the world and throug Alexandria's radio, *"the inventor of this spacecraft, the mechanic w never asked for permission to act on his dream, I wish to say—thank you*

Alexandria released the document, dropping it in th wastebasket.

Everyone at Houston Control stared at the screen displayir the *Roble Arrow* accelerating past seventy-one thousand miles pe hour.

"Now, if you'll pardon me, Houston," Sircor said over the radi *"I'd like to fly in peace and quiet for a few hours. Just soak it all in."*

Captain Mendoza led Roble down a corridor and pushe open a door to an alleyway. "The feds are distracted. We hop you enjoyed your stay. Have a nice day."

Roble nodded and exited out past trash dumpsters, walking t the gritty northern end of Las Vegas Boulevard. Turning soutl he glanced up at the towering casinos, almost expecting a B bomber to roar overhead like when he was fifteen years old.

A date scrolled along the bottom of a huge casino vide screen. "Hmm," he said, just then realizing he turned twenty-fiv today.

News stories of the *Roble Arrow's* flight flashed across giar screens as he slipped through the crowds. One woman watchin said, "Nobody told me we had a rocket ship like that."

"Can I fly past the moon too, Mom?" a boy asked.

When Roble reached a pirate-themed casino, he stood in front of its manmade sea and gripped the rope railing.

A man in khaki pants and rolled-up shirtsleeves leaned against the rope nearby, face hidden below a downturned baseball cap. Roble turned and studied his arrogant posture.

"Obsidian," the man said in Japanese, "when lashed to a wooden shaft, may shoot hundreds of yards." He lifted his chin, revealing a cold, hard face. "But when lashed to the desire to think, will fly true—piercing any limit."

"Ronin…" he gasped.

"Miss me?"

Roble reached for his chest, grasping air.

"I see you're pulling off your next stunt." Ronin glanced across the street at a video display. "That didn't take too long."

"What are you doing here?"

"I'm here to detain and interrogate you," Ronin said. "Apparently some idiot let you escape from Japan." He pointed downtown. "And, my fellow operative, Mike and I, were assigned to track you down a month ago."

Roble shook his head. "And you finally found me."

"I found you on my second day here." He rolled his eyes and turned toward the captain's quarters of *HMS Dauntless*. "Tracking you down is like searching for a drunk elephant on a cruise ship."

Roble scrunched his brows, staring at the ship. "How did you know I once lived there?"

"It's my job to know what I want to know, when I want to know it."

"Weren't you supposed to detain me a month ago then?"

"Supposed to?" Ronin scoffed. "Since when have I done what I'm *supposed* to?"

"But if you found me a month ago, why haven't I seen you?"

"You don't see anyone, Roble. It's a unique quality. And even though you figured out how to create that…" he pointed at a casino video screen, "you still couldn't convince the wife of one of the best pilots in the world he should fly it."

Roble tilted his head. "Wait…that was *you*?"

"You told me Sircor deserved better. I just happened to agree."

"What did you say to convince her?"

"I just didn't introduce myself as Roble Santos." Ronin

chuckled. "Nice woman—Stephie. Great daughters as well. One even argues like you."

"Wow." Roble rubbed his forehead. "You actually knew about the Paiute hangar and everything this whole time?"

"Stop asking the obvious. It's boring." He glanced again at the video screen.

Roble exhaled, lifting his hands.

"Congratulations, I liked it." He pushed himself off the rope, slapped Roble on the back, and said, "This ends my detention and interrogation."

After a few steps, he stopped. "Oh, one more thing." He turned and removed an arrowhead necklace from his pocket and tossed it to Roble. "For a geek outcast, you have surprisingly good taste in girlfriends. See you around, scoundrel."

Roble held his arrowhead in both hands, watching Ronin disappear into the tourist crowds. Shaking his head, he whispered, "Later, Ronin."

Libby jumped off her Arabian horse and caressed its nose. "Good girl."

Leaving her horse in a clearing, she crunched her hiking shoes through a pinyon grove and approached a slender wood cabin sitting at the base of a forested hill. Pine trees grew through the cabin's three vertical decks, and a camouflaged radar antenna poked up from its roof.

She read the wood plaque next to the front door. *Mankind's Nature. S.B.*

Swinging open the door, she ran up the stairs and barged onto the top floor. Sigmund and Renny paced in front of her monitoring screens and equipment.

"Roger that, Sircor," Sigmund said into a headset.

Libby patted Siggy on the back and pulled on a headset. "Hey Mr. Tourist Pilot, nice flying."

"Thank you, Ms. Dodge," Sircor said.

Sircor toggled the control stick, turning the *Roble Arrow* one hundred and eighty degrees. The lasers firing into the sail slowed the craft's velocity away from Earth. When it stopped, he shut them off.

His heart thumped in the vacuum of space like a sonic beacon to the universe. He pressed the switch opening communication with both Stock's cabin and Houston Control. "This is as far as I will go from Earth this day."

"Roble Arrow, this is Houston. What do you see out there?"

People around the world listening to the NASA broadcast waited for the answer.

Sircor peered at the countless celestial objects, including what looked like a tumbling asteroid adjacent to his view of Mars. Of all the things he beheld, his eyes drew back to the glossy grey fuselage enclosing him. *"I see the spirit of a man."*

A reverent static hummed over the two-way radio signal.

Sircor closed off the radio channel to Houston Control. "Mr. Evert, would you patch me through to Stephie's phone?"

"Certainly, Colonel."

Sircor waited in the silent void, thinking of the day he earned his wings in the Air Force, the day after he met Stephie.

"Hello?" Stephie said.

"Hello." Sircor's eyes hazed over, lips curving into a smile. "I love you."

She sniffed, taking a moment. *"I love you too, Gavin."*

Sircor wiped his eyes and gazed at the distant blue planet. The lasers fired into the solar sail and the *Roble Arrow* blasted toward Earth. "I'm coming home."

By the time the *Roble Arrow's* belly pressed into the thermospheric flames, the Earth had almost rotated back to the position at which Sircor left it. Once through the fiery barrier, the craft careened down like a missile.

"Tracking incoming bogey. Current trajectory is Las Vegas," NORAD Command said to Nellis Air Control.

"Copy that NORAD, scrambling interceptors."

The *Roble Arrow's* wings slid out of its fuselage into a sweptback position, lifting the craft into horizontal flight. It flew west.

Interceptors scrambled at Vandenberg California, followed by Pearl Harbor as the *Roble Arrow* glided around the globe.

Above Midway Islands in the Pacific Ocean, the *Roble Arrow's* twin turbines whirled back to life.

"Roble Arrow, this is Houston Control, relaying communication from US Pacific Command. You are ordered to land at Andersen Air Force Base in Guam."

"Houston," Sircor gazed at an endless ocean below, "tell them I appreciate the offer, but respectfully decline."

"Where do you intend to land?"

"Precisely where I want to."

The *Roble Arrow* sliced through the sky fifty thousand feet above Okinawa, turning southwest.

Four F-22 Raptors scrambled from Kadena Air Base.

"Cyclone, this is Kadena Air Controller, Giant Samurai."

"Go ahead, Giant Samurai," F-22 intercept leader Cyclone said, chasing the bogey between Taiwan and the Philippines.

"Cyclone, you have traffic at heading: two-seven-two, seventy nautical miles out, traveling at six hundred knots. Multiple bogeys descending at three-five angels."

"Say again? Multiple bogeys?"

"Affirmative."

"Copy that, Giant Samurai." Cyclone checked his radar. "Multiple radar contact tally-ho." He toggled the targeting computer and opened up the throttles.

Sircor looked to his side and saw a tailfin rising up like a shark. It displayed an eagle's skeleton crossed with missiles.

Aligning cockpits, the pilot of the F-15DJ faced Sircor, whipping a hand down in salute. *"Ivanhoe, this is Reaper,"* Takinato said in a Japanese accent, as another F-15DJ pulled in close to the *Skeleton Eagle's* wingtip, *"requesting permission to escort the* Roble Arrow *to its desired destination."*

"Permission granted, Reaper." Sircor saluted back, hidden behind his matte-black canopy.

The *Skeleton Eagle* peeled off, roaring higher into the sky trailed by the other Japanese F-15DJ. Three Japanese F-35Js fanned out behind Sircor.

"Giant Samurai," Cyclone said into his helmet mic, "bogeys are bulls-eye, three miles in tail. I have a visual on two Eagles and three Lightning IIs. Who are these guys? Over."

"Cyclone, say again. Eagles and Lightning IIs?"

"Affirmative."

"We have no scheduled friendlies in the area. Over."

"This is Major Barnes of the United States Air Force," Cyclone said. "Fighter aircraft please identify."

"This is Lieutenant Colonel Takinato, 204th Hyakuri Squadron, Japanese Air Self-Defense Force. I am escorting a private Japanese aircraft through international airspace with its permission. Over."

"The Japanese?" Cyclone whispered, scanning his targeting computer. "I have orders from Pacific Command to escort the aircraft to Guam, Colonel. Do you copy?"

"Negative Major, you are advised to break off intercept. Reaper out."

"Engage, but do not fire unless fired upon," Cyclone ordered. His F-22 rolled in behind a Japanese F-35J.

The Japanese fighter jets burst out in all directions like a swarm of flaming wasps. The Americans pursued, jostling with the Japanese for attack position.

"Giant Samurai, we're in a furball with the Japanese," Cyclone said.

Fighter jets slashed the sky, cracking thunder in their wakes. The turbulence from the maneuvers rocked the *Roble Arrow*.

Within minutes, the American F-22s had one Japanese F-15DJ and all three Japanese F-35Js missile-locked—all the Japanese fighters except one. "Giant Samurai, area is hot," Cyclone said.

Reaper's faceplate reflected two burning ovals as his *Skeleton Eagle* pressed in behind Cyclone's F-22.

A missile lock signal alarm sounded in Cyclone's cockpit. "Jink," Cyclone said under his breath as he snapped his Raptor vertical. Counter measures shot out from below his fuselage in an arcing trail. The Raptor back-flipped over itself in mid-air, as did the *Skeleton Eagle*. The *Skeleton Eagle* retained tail position and missile lock on Cyclone.

"Disengage before something bad happens, Major Barnes," Takinato said.

"Colonel Sircor," Cyclone pulled his F-22 close to the *Roble Arrow's* cockpit, trailed by the *Skeleton Eagle*, "advise your escort to stand down or most of them are going to crash and burn. have my orders."

"Duty and excellence, Major Barnes," Sircor said.

"Yes, sir. I mean…"

The *Roble Arrow's* wings swung out farther until almo perpendicular to the fuselage as the aircraft descended.

"Giant Samurai, this is Cyclone. The bogey is not respondin We will take casualties on both sides if we escalate. Fuel is bing to Andersen. What are my orders?"

"Cyclone, this is General Wadsworth—disengage. The bogey is reg tered in Japan as, Kaze u~ōkā, *a private aircraft under the control General Yamatomo. The Japanese have jurisdiction."*

"Disengage," Cyclone ordered.

All F-22 missile locks fell silent as did the *Skeleton Eagle's*.

Cyclone looked over at Sircor's black canopy. "What's you destination, sir?"

"It's dead ahead."

"Colonel Sircor," Cyclone said, "the entire 302nd listened you out there…in space. We're proud of you. Duty and exce lence, sir."

"It's good to see you again, Major Barnes," Sircor said.

The *Skeleton Eagle* pulled along the other side of the *Rob Arrow*.

"Giant Samurai, this is Cyclone. Guam is out of rang requesting permission to escort the bogey to Singapore."

"That's an affirmative, Cyclone."

The Japanese fighter jets fell into formation behind Reaper *Skeleton Eagle*. Three F-22 Raptors fell in behind Cyclone's. Th *Roble Arrow* led the armada's descent.

"Changi Tower, this is the Roble Arrow *zero-zero-one with esco requesting pattern for landing."*

"Roble Arrow zero-zero-one, all lanes are clear for arrival. Land will. And…welcome back to Earth."

The *Roble Arrow's* landing gear lowered. Reaper's *Skelet Eagle* and Cyclone's F-22 flew at the *Roble Arrow's* wingtips, the landing gears dropping.

The other fighter jets remained in level flight passing over th runway. From the other side of the airport, two black *Succub* flew over the oncoming fighter jets, and pulled vertical into th sky. Two *Sovereigns* followed behind the *Succubae,* releasing strean of colored powder behind them, ceremoniously showering the runway.

The *Roble Arrow* touched down.

Roble Santos turned away from the landing on a casino video screen and faced the *HMS Dauntless* sailing on a manmade sea. A jet roared by overhead, vibrating his calloused hands which he rested atop the railing.

His gaze followed a line from the sailing ship's quarters, to its helm, and up into the endless sky. *The density times the material derivative is equal to…*

Epilogue

Six months later.

Nicolette watched Roble shift the yellow bull into seventh gear. Her hair streamed behind in the wind, her eyes narrow, lips smiling.

The throaty whine of a black convertible hyper-car echoed off canyon walls as it careened around a bend, chasing Roble and Nicolette toward the Hoover Dam Bridge.

When the cars aligned, the other driver, Takinato, glanced at Roble, shifted into eighth gear, and sank the pedal to the floor. Next to Takinato, Sugemi's dark-lined eyes held the road.

Nicolette scanned the side of the highway, estimating the blur between orange reflectors. *A smidge over two hundred miles per hour, if I had to guess.*

At the bridge's convex center, eight wheels lifted into the air, both engines wailing like buzz saws. All four passengers peered over the railing as they soared. The Colorado River deep within the canyon's bosom flashed by. The bull touched down last and exited the bridge first.

"Woohoo!" Nicolette raised her hands in the air.

Fifteen minutes later, they parked at Willow Bay along the river and climbed out.

"You are going down on the way back," Takinato said.

"What I just did to you," Roble grinned, "tell Libby *that's* what to expect for Libby Aerospace. Once I hire away Sircor to be my lead test pilot, I intend to win away her best customers as well."

"Bold words from a penniless orphan. Perhaps you did not hear; Libby signed a deal with Nevada for fifty weaponized air-superiority *Acrobats* and twenty *Roble Arrows*. But she is making the *Roble Arrows* with a few changes to adjust for your mistakes."

Roble frowned. "Well I guess if the *Arrow* is to be converted into a bomber or used for high altitude surveillance, it should be shorter, if not also flatter." He rubbed his chin. "Come to think of it, those laser-sail turret bays could be converted into landing pods for hypersonic UAVs...all controlled from the cockpit." His eyes glazed over in thought. "Or...or maybe make the bay underneath the fuselage some kind of vertical takeoff assist engine." He blinked, focusing on Takinato's smirk. "Hey, you better not give her those ideas."

"Of course I am going to," Takinato said. "You think I hang out with you for your personality?"

Roble rubbed his nose. "It doesn't matter. Libby isn't going to sell seventy aircraft to Nevada anyway. Nevada has no money."

"Then I guess you need to talk to your foster mommy, Governor Patra." Takinato searched his pockets in vain for a cigarette. "Most of those jets are being purchased by private residents and loaned to Nevada."

Sugemi ran a finger up Takinato's arm. "Those bringing their dreams to Nevada have a lot to lose if it fails. They will protect it." Her finger continued up along the nape of his neck. "This is the only place on earth it makes sense for me to hold my businesses in my own name without forming a corporation. I'm freer and more protected than anyone in any country in the world." She removed an e-cigarette hiding in her bra and placed it between Takinato's lips. "And of those twenty *Roble Arrows* Nevada will receive—one is mine."

"Why in the world is everyone all of a sudden in such a rush to buy jets?" Roble asked. "My new design won't be ready for another year. Maybe I should just buy DCU's production rights to the *Sovereign* or *Succubus* and sell modified versions of those before Libby knows what hit her. I kinda like the idea of beating her with her own jets."

Takinato grunted, laughing the best he could while vaping. "You mean like what she is doing to you with the *Roble Arrow*?"

"Oh right..." Roble scrunched his nose.

"DCU will not sell their Libby Jet production rights to you anyway." Takinato walked close to the river and gazed up the cliff on the far side. "Libby already tried buying them back."

"Is DCU actually going to make Libby's jets?" Roble shook his head. "I can't picture it."

"They plastered a *Succubus* on the cover of their annual stockholders' report," Sugemi said. "I have a beautiful copy on my desk. But having met the illustrious Mr. Compros, I think that's as close to making one as he will ever get."

"Why bother putting it on the cover then?" Roble moved next to Takinato, watching water swirling at the river's edge.

"I don't know, but their stock price went up ten percent the day they published the report. At least they have that going for them," Sugemi said with a straight face, "which is nice."

Nicolette covered her mouth, eyes smiling.

"By the way," Takinato looked at Roble, "I did not know you obtained funding for your company. And if you have, why are you not stealing *me* away from Libby Aerospace to be your lead test pilot?"

Roble laughed long and hard, almost indecently.

"What?" Takinato asked.

"Oh…" Roble glanced at Sugemi, before facing Takinato. "Well, I guess I shouldn't laugh since you'll be the one benefiting. Your girlfriend now owns forty-nine percent of Santos Industries."

Takinato turned to Sugemi, releasing a cloud of vapor over his narrowing eyes.

"It was a good business plan." Sugemi leaned in to take a drag on Takinato's e-cigarette. "Plus you should see Roble in a business suit begging for an investment." She winked, illuminating the end of the vape with an indrawn breath.

Nicolette gripped Roble's waist and laid her chin on his shoulder. "Yes, like a *smexy* bullet covered in cheap wool… searching for a posh gun chamber."

"Great," Takinato sulked, "my girlfriend just funded the only competitor who can put my new boss out of business."

"Stop pretending you're worried," Roble said. "After I steal that military order away from Libby, she'll still have a shot at selling to that start-up airline in Vegas, which I happen to know is thinking of ordering sixty modified *Arrows* to fly to Asia."

Takinato raised an eyebrow.

"I know," Roble continued, "because they called me thinking I owned the production rights. Of course I explained how the *Arrow* is not the right choice for the job and that a superior jet will be coming out from Santos Industries soon. But apparently they only believe what they can touch."

"Well, if *our* aerospace venture ever fails," Sugemi winked at

Roble, "and you feel the need to borrow another Air Force jet, you have permission to borrow my *Roble Arrow* and trick it out. I won't mind. Just don't let anyone shoot it down this time."

"Takinato, your girlfriend is being a bad influence on me."

"Sweetheart," Takinato took back the e-cigarette, "do not tease the destitute orphan."

"Yes," Nicolette kissed the back of Roble's neck, "that's my job." She shoved him headlong into the river.

He popped up, splashing and gasping. "Holy ball sack it's cold."

Takinato bent over laughing. Sugemi and Nicolette grabbed his arms and threw him in as well.

"Watashi wa samui desu!" Takinato yelled, between short breaths, standing waist deep in the water.

"Go in head first, you wimp. Then you'll know what cold is." Roble pulled him under.

Sugemi sighed. "You gotta love boys."

"Speaking of," Nicolette said, "remind me to ask you some questions about Roble's *interests*."

"Gladly." Sugemi grinned at Nicolette.

"Hey…" Roble wiped his face. "What was that?"

"I said, I think we will be the ones driving on the way back." Nicolette took Sugemi's hand. "Not because we own the cars, or that you'll be too cold to concentrate—it's just that you're both too slow."

Danny held a drawing against the Plexiglas window. He imagined the unseen smile, then lowered the art paper and saw it on her lips.

"Can I have it?" Jenny asked, holding the visitor phone to her ear.

He looked at his sketch of a pigtailed girl piloting a vintage biplane in an epic battle. "The sketch is of you anyway." Glancing down at Jenny's flat tummy, he whispered, "Or…someone who would've looked like you, had we not lost her."

She smiled and wiped her cheek.

He turned away and pressed a hand to his eyes.

When he turned back to her, Jenny asked, "When are you eligible for parole?"

"In about a year, if I promise to pay back Stock Brant with every paycheck for the rest of my life. Which I would have done anyway." Tilting his head, he added, "I'll need to become very successful as an artist or live about fifty lifetimes to earn enough." He inhaled. "Come to think of it, both options sound fine to me."

"I like you like this." She batted her wet lashes.

"Like what?" He scratched his buzzed head. "A convict and hopelessly in debt?"

"Optimistic," she leaned close to the Plexiglas, "like the Danny Sands I first met. Only with less hair."

He knelt down on the floor, looking up at her, holding the phone to his ear. "Jenny, will you let me take you on a date when I get out?"

"Hmmm. Will you take me someplace we've gone before?"

"Anywhere."

"Well, I'm not an actual princess, but I still love Princess Fun Zones, so…"

Stock knelt, his biker boots planted in soft soil. He brushed the snow off his first new seedling.

Alexandria lay on the ground nearby, black hair spilled like paint on white canvas. "What's different about that one, Stock?"

He looked up. "It grows pine nuts at lower elevations."

"How did you think to invent that?"

"Your girlfriend's idea."

Alexandria laughed. "Which one?" Her arms stretched into the snow above her head and plowed down along her sides making a snow angel.

He caressed the seedling, watching her.

"What time do you report for your sentence on Tuesday?" she asked.

He looked away. "Nine AM," he said, his voice somber.

"Libby told me that Colonel Sircor snuck your *Roble Arrow* back to Las Vegas. Are you going to fly it before you go? You could take me up with you."

Stock sighed. "I thought I would want to; that's why I had them rush its completion. But I'd like to work here for as long as I can. Tell her to keep it in a barn for me until I get out."

"And all of this…" she blinked her eyes at the pinyons above, "…what will happen to it while you're away?"

"Kat is going to have two and half years to show me how it's really done."

"I thought you said she'd never come back."

He stood up, studying the surrounding trees. "She likes the governor of Nevada or something." Walking to one of his more mature pinyons, he withdrew a sword from his belt. "And maybe the fact I'll be in jail."

"*I* will miss you," she piled snow atop her jacket, "but I knew you'd be acquitted of murder."

"Oh? How did you know that?" He thrust the concave blade into the trunk and twisted. "Pull some gubernatorial strings?"

"Don't be ridiculous." She threw a handful of white powder in his direction. "You never murdered anyone."

He withdrew the tree sample and ran it under his nose, inhaling. "You make it sound so simple."

Alexandria raised her head, hearing the bellowing grunt of diesel exhaust. About sixty feet away, next to Stock's cabin, a large backhoe chiseled into frozen ground. "I hope you realize," she rolled onto an arm, "you don't have to hide underground anymore, even after you get out."

"The last I read," he pegged the sword in the snow, "ever since your reelection, there's been a national clamor to have the feds forcibly remove you from office," he ripped a pine needle from a white-dusted branch, "if not throw you in jail for presidential insubordination." Bending the needle in half, he tasted it

She smiled at him. "I like watching you work."

He spit out the needle and faced her.

"I love you, Stock."

Slipping his hands into his coat pockets, he trekked over to her. She rolled flat onto her back, her gaze swallowing his.

"I'm going to miss you, Alexandria."

She swiped snow across her cheek to hide a tear, her black eyes drawing him down to his knees.

Libby sat at a redwood table overlooking the Calico Basin, an iced tea in one hand, water trickling down a trough below her feet.

Victor's platinum hair wisped in the breeze as he stood at the balcony's edge, body clad in black plate armor. "Receiving back the fourth floor from the State of Nevada is a first step, *Madame*. Nevertheless, the federal government has not indicated they will return anything to you, including my rented floor or the manufacturing cave."

"Well," Libby took a sip, "if it's any consolation, Halvern jackhammered above the good Dr. Hughbner's office for two weeks restoring this floor to its original state. And the job didn't even require a jackhammer." She paused, thinking about it, a smile on her lips.

"Mr. Black is most proficient in using a portable pneumatic drill," Victor glanced at the floor, "but I find it to be no great consolation."

"Well, it consoled me a bit." She laughed. "But seriously, Victor, with me living here full-time you have tons of room in my downtown compound to do—whatever eccentric French guys do." She sipped more tea. "By the way, thanks for selling it and the North Las Vegas facility back to me. But I still think three dollars was too cheap a price."

"The Swiss trust made a forty-one percent annualized return on their one dollar, so they're content." Victor crossed his arms, peering at the far-off city bustling with construction cranes. "There is a hum of activity—an energy in Nevada—which is intoxicating."

"Amen." She raised her glass. "Libby Aerospace is running overtime shifts."

"However… " Victor breathed in, narrowing his eyes.

"However what?"

"This city—this state," Victor said, "is surrounded by something a bit too…quiet." A distant shriek of an eagle echoed off the canyon walls. "I've felt this before."

Libby set down her glass, watching him.

"I don't wish for the storm to come, *Madame*."

Libby stood up.

Victor held still.

"A French general once told me," Libby stepped next to him,

"the days of the knights in shining armor might return." Placing a hand on his shoulder, she looked across the basin. "So take heart, my friend."

"General..." Victor closed his eyes. "We are but few."

"But, we are free."

Excavators dug a giant hole into the shadow of *The Spirit of Man*. Halvern stood nearby, scuffing a boot against parched earth.

Stepping back, he peered through a handheld laser scope, measuring the dimensions of the crater. "Dammit all to hell," he mumbled, and flagged down a bulldozer. Ordering the worker out, Halvern climbed in.

In the plaza that would someday connect both the present and future tower, a crane lifted a massive statue of a woman and a man into place. They stood shoulder to shoulder atop a quartz pedestal, their eyes gazing upon the world. At its base was a poem by Mae Black.

> *Keep ye power mongers, from our land.*
> *Give us your thinkers, who will not obey you,*
> *your landless, who wish to own this earth,*
> *your creators, who wish to produce,*
> *your poor, who desire wealth,*
> *your rich, who long for justice,*
> *and your compelled, who wish to live free.*
> *Send us these, the living, from your oppressed lands,*
> *that they may seek exaltation upon this earth.*

The End

CPSIA information can be obtained
at www.ICGtesting.com
Printed in the USA
LVHW050041230520
656338LV00001B/12